I0602180

Armored Mage

THE FORGOTTEN SISTER: VOLUME THREE

Dalila Caryn

With illustrations by

Yenthe Joline

© 2021 Dalila Caryn
All rights reserved.

ISBN 13: 978-1-7338845-2-5
E-book ISBN 13: 978-1-7338845-3-2
Library of Congress Control Number: 2021908029
Evil Goddess Press
Riverside, California

Lake Noomah
Diddlyon
Ulm
Liadan River
Fairy Rea
Fairy Cache
Ever Spill
Turrlough
Turrlough Castle
Creelan Ruins
Creelan

GREAT ISLAND
Anwyn Palace
Anwyn
N
W   E
S
Enchanted Forest
Liadan River
Fairy Circle
Dragon's Breath
Stonedragon
Stonedragon Castle

For the Eberts who carried me with them into a wider world!

—Dalila Caryn

*To my dearest grandmother, Joaline, who shares my creative passion
and to whom I can always go for a hug.*

—Yenthe Joline

Day Breaker

393 days until Roisin returns

*T*hat was the bad time.

Yseult's hooves pounded against the soft ground, damp with near morning dew. Rowan leaned low over her neck. The wind tugged her braid out behind her and the cool of the evening raced like icy fingers across her cheeks. She pushed the horse as fast as she would ride, trying to outrun the voices and fears chasing after her.

Petal was helping Sorcha. Not just to trick her either, she took her side. Keagan's small frightened voice chased after Rowan.

They couldn't be headed to the bad time. Rowan wouldn't let them. So she raced forward not seeing her path, she just followed the hum of the whistle. But their pace did not take away Rowan's anxiety.

You are disinherited. —Father's voice pounded behind her.

We cannot train. You offer us this hope and then you just rip it away. —Peg cried out.

I am sorry, Rowan. —Petal whispered as she stole away with Rowan's heart.

Rowan pushed Yseult harder, trying to shake off Petal's heartbroken voice; her mind was screaming in fear and rage. She felt *so much* rage. With her father, with Colum, and Ardal—with herself. That nightmare she'd woken from tortured her, pounding through her mind like Yseult's hooves, insisting it was real.

"How can you be so cruel?" Gwyneth cried. *"They are your family. Don't you love them at all?"*

"Apparently not," Rowan said with a wicked laugh. *"I always thought I did....Thought I would sacrifice anything and anyone. But I was wrong."*

Rowan heard her own voice, the callous slice of it racing down her spine, making her shiver. She could feel Yseult noticing, but it didn't slow her pace. Yseult knew as well as Rowan that she had to leave the palace. Every day Rowan spent inside those walls allowing her father to control her, or Colum and Ardal to set her down, every day she spent ignoring the jeers of her father's soldiers, every day the women she'd conscripted went without training, *every day* Rowan felt smaller and grew more resentful. She grew every day closer to the vengeful woman of her nightmare.

But she might not have truly understood that, had not Petal stood before Rowan as she woke from the dream. Petal bathed in moonlight and as broken to look on as Rowan had felt inside. As much as her own callous attitude towards Father and Roisin in the dream bothered Rowan, that feeling that she had been willing to sacrifice *anyone* to save Roisin bothered Rowan more on waking. She'd already done the worst of her nightmare self; she'd sacrificed Petal's happiness and safety for Roisin's. Rowan couldn't keep doing it.

That was the bad time.—Keagan whispered.

Could you let her die?—Eachann asked. *Or will you choose family loyalty over loyalty to friends and followers?*

Rowan wanted to scream. She wanted to rip the world apart with nothing but her anguish and wake up. She wanted this all to be a terrible dream—but it wasn't. She couldn't wake up. And she couldn't see how either letting Roisin die, or destroying Petal were acceptable solutions. Something drastic had to change.

The way Rowan went about saving her sister had to change. She had to be better than she was in those walls. Within the walls of her home, Rowan was too desperate to prove herself to everyone, to prove herself willing to do *anything* for Roisin. So sure that if she proved how much she loved Roisin everyone would love her. They'd have to, wouldn't they? If she saved Roisin. If she never wanted for anything but Roisin's safety. If she was the hero.

Rowan had to be the hero. And a hero had to sacrifice, or die in the act of saving. It could never be easy. To be worthy of love, Rowan had to stand between Sorcha and her sister and bear the brunt of any suffering.

At least that's how she felt at home. But Rowan wanted—*needed* to be so much better than that. She needed to be someone who could love herself. She needed to be wiser, and kinder. She needed to defeat Sorcha's revenge, not just her curse.

Rowan needed to defeat that angry, resentful, lonely feeling that lived inside of her. Every word her father had thrown at her, and every look Colum had given her as he lectured, all of it had made that feeling grow. It was so large it was eating her alive, eating her common sense, her calm, eating her hope!

That was the bad time.

Rowan couldn't let the worst of herself, or anyone else, be their future.

So maybe it was cowardly, but Rowan the Eternal was running away.

Running from the question that wanted to destroy her.

"Its simple really: whom do you love more?"

The Fairy queen leaned against Gavin's desk toying with the well of infinity poison. It was odd that only now, when he was likely about to die, did that desk truly feel like his own. He'd wasted so much time thinking of it as his father's place, thinking of himself as only a steward of his father's legacy. He hadn't embraced his role as he should. If he had, things might be different. But it was too late to worry about what had past. All he could deal with was now and what was to come. Sorcha ran the quill around the rim of the inkwell and a sort of smoky luminescence haloed her form. Gavin forced his eyes away as the power of it danced beneath his skin, urging him to look on her face.

"This wasn't meant to be a poison, you know?" Sorcha said conversationally as they waited for her fairy to return with his family, and Petal. To return from disposing of two bodies, the one that Gavin had killed while trying to kill Sorcha —no, two. Gavin's hands might not have taken Molten's life, but his cause had. He could not shy away from that responsibility or he would be no better than the woman before him.

He should never have involved Molten. He should have listened to the man when he warned Gavin against seeking the infinity poison. *The poison has remained hidden to the benefit of all for centuries.*

Molten was right.

They had been together just before the Fairy queen came. Molten, his family, and Gavin. Molten's daughter had been trying to speak to Gavin since she arrived home with the other kidnapped girls, but she couldn't manage it. Then Molten came in with his whole family behind him.

"Finnola knows something. Something truly important, for the Fairy queen has put a curse on her soul. She has stolen her voice," Molten said.

"Can she write?" Gavin asked, looking at the sobbing girl before him.

"You do not understand," Molten replied tersely. "The Fairy queen stole her tongue's ability to speak, her hand's ability to write, even her mind's ability to formulate thoughts one might read. She stole her voice entirely."

Gavin had sunken, inside and out. His hand stretched out for the girl, and she took it, sobbing all the while.

"I am so sorry," Gavin whispered. "Have hope, we will find a way to heal you. I know it. For now...trust to fate, when it is time for you to share your message, the way will present itself."

Molten gasped and wrapped an arm around his daughter, pulling her against his chest. His son and wife joined the embrace, but Finnola, Molten's daughter, did not release Gavin's hand. Gavin squeezed it back, and felt his heart expanding. The plan was falling apart. The Fairy queen would arrive any moment, and there were still so many worries dragging at his heart. But he watched that embrace and he imagined his own brother coming home to find his daughters returned. They were home!

Gavin would not be himself if he did not take this chance to celebrate that. Whatever else had gone wrong, he had brought home the girls of his nation.

That was when Sorcha arrived, in a crackling show of light and with four fairy surrounding her, she appeared in this very room, before the family ceased embracing.

Gavin released Finnola's hand and wiped out his poisoned quill, swinging for the Fairy queen, without ever allowing his eyes to touch her face. But one of her guards dove between them, and was scratched with poison in Sorcha's place. She let out an agonized cry of pain and fell to the ground as chaos broke out.

Gavin tried to dive for the Fairy queen a second time, but another woman blocked him, drawing a weapon rather than throwing her body like a shield before her queen. Molten must have dove into the fray as well, but before he could reach the poison, Sorcha raised a hand and it took off into the air seemingly of its own volition.

Everyone froze.

"You must be Molten," Sorcha said coldly. "A traitor to you kind if ever I met one, helping a human acquire a poison like this." The Fairy queen's gentle sort of anger sent a chill through the blood. The poison circled through the air above Molten, and the well began to tip forward. One of Sorcha's guards without order or hesitation, reached out and snapped Molten's neck.

His daughter cried out, high pitched and shrill like and angry nightingale, her scream shook the windows, drowning out every other sound. When the last of the sound was rung from her throat she fell to the ground beside her father in silent tears.

"I gave you no order to kill, Dervla," Sorcha snapped. The poison settled back on the table as though it had never moved.

"My apologies, My queen." The fairy bowed her tone neutral. "I sensed he was trying to kill you."

"Trying and failing." Sorcha rolled her eyes and glanced at the rest of Molten's family. She opened her mouth, perhaps to order them all killed and Gavin dove between them.

"Molten and his family have lived in my nation for the entirety of their children's lives. They are no longer subjects of the Fairy. They are my citizens. And I demand you treat them accordingly."

Sorcha chuckled. The fairy Gavin had scratched, writhed and let out a moan, catching her queen's attention. Sorcha paused and the air grew angry with electricity a moment, biting at everyone's skin.

Gavin felt that sizzle again and heard Molten's voice in his head.

What fairy will die of it will be eternities business to determine.

Molten's death was on Gavin's hands. Gavin ought to feel it all.

Sorcha and Gavin were alone now, she'd had the bodies removed and the murderess fairy was sent to fetch Petal. Gavin was anxious and guilty, but Sorcha was at ease stirring circles in the inkwell. Gavin wasn't looking at her, he looked at a wall across the room, but he could see her —actually see Sorcha —as through the wall were a mirror, as though Sorcha had forced the image into his mind, because he refused to look on her with his eyes.

"At the time when this was made, fairy lived quite peaceably with humans. This island belonged to us and the dragons alone, but humans from the north, east, and west paid us visits occasionally. The magicians who made this wanted to be as Fairy. To force eternity into their beings though they were unprepared for its expanse." Sorcha sounded awed by the ambition. "They seem even to have succeeded—to a point. And in the process they did such terrible things that they might never be worthy of eternity."

"Surely you can relate?" Gavin asked, quietly enraged. "You are clearly losing touch with it yourself."

Sorcha pulled the feather quill from the pot. She lay it on the table leaning back on both her hands; a rather girlish pose. "Oh I have nothing on them. In pursuit of eternity, those magicians kidnapped and experimented on no less than a hundred fairy, most of them children. Experimented on several human children from their own nation, all of them dying terrible painful deaths as their beings were ripped apart and dragged through all time. The magicians all went quite mad in the process of creating a poison that decimated the population of sprites. I read their records once, it was a very interesting study in that old adage of being careful what one desires. I think you would enjoy examining it. You've clearly an eclectically inspired mind."

As she spoke, various books from around the room took off in the air and swirled around them. They flew in dipping weaving circles like a flock of vultures surveying a corpse, then one at a time dipped before the Fairy queen, until she found one to her liking. She took it in her hands and the rest flew back to their old homes, beating their pages like wings.

Gavin's stomach began to churn and his mouth grew biliously full, as his dread built. He knew she loved the sound of her own voice. He knew she loved a show. But he began to suspect that whatever she had planned for him would be very bad indeed, but not, he feared, for himself alone.

It is your mother and brothers and especially Rowan who will be sorry.

He wished he'd listened to Asia.

The fight led you to poison and plots and secrecy. All of which will now be used against you!

Sorcha was quiet a moment, the only sound to be heard was the slow swish of turning pages and Gavin's breath growing heavy as he tried to think of a way, any way to stop what Sorcha had planned.

Stop resisting the destiny you fear. Believe *in the one you desire.*

Gavin pulled in a breath and held it, forcing it out in slow measured flow. He repeated the process.

Sorcha chuckled and slammed the book shut.

"Ooh, she is an interesting one, that *Lady Asia* you courted," Sorcha said, clearly having been delving in his thoughts again. "Where has she gotten to?"

"Far away from you," Gavin said slowly, breathing out again. *Believe in the future you desire,* he told himself as he breathed out. Sorcha might know his thoughts, she might have his letters, she might appear to be winning, but that didn't mean she would. He just had to believe.

"I think we will meet eventually, two such interesting women should, don't you think?" Sorcha chuckled. She was quiet for a moment, then having gained no response she switched topics. She lifted the poisoned quill once more, playing with the fine hairs of the feather. "It has a will of its own now, this poison you acquired. It is a fantastical representation of eternity. For each being it takes on a new form, always trying to do the same thing—force all of eternity into one being, in one instant—but each being reacts differently. Dragons are nearly immune to it, if anything it makes them stronger. It created the razorback breed that first so frightened Tyrone that he set humans about destroying all dragons. Fairy, as you know, are killed—though first they are dragged through every moment of their own existence, and every moment of every being who was ever connected with them, future or past. It is a long, agonizing death, that shows one wonders as it feeds on them and drives them thoroughly mad."

Sorcha began to swing her feet through the air, back and forth like a child playfully. It sent a chill through Gavin's entire being.

"For humans of *no* magic it rips you fully apart, your every sinew flying in a different direction seeking to know all of eternity. Some believe that perhaps you get a glimpse of eternity before you are utterly destroyed. This is only a theory, of course, as no human whose been infected has ever been able to communicate before they burst apart. Are you curious?"

Gavin swallowed, but did not respond. *Believe in the future you desire.*

"No?" she asked with a bright laugh. "Just as well, because that wouldn't happen to you. You are touched by magic, not quite human, but not quite as blessed as fairy. For you it will do something *very* different. It wasn't the original creators that discovered this though. They were so disturbed by their creation that they attempted to destroy it. But—once found, this murky bit of eternity could not be extinguished. So they hid it away, dying without properly achieving their goal. It remained safely hidden until the unnamed king offered their descendants the nation of Ulm in exchange for its use. These new magicians having seen none of its horrors and covetous of a world all their own gave it over. Not one having ever tested it on themselves. Only one human was ever brave, or...*covetous* enough to try it of their own will. He wanted so badly to know what fairy know, to see and touch eternity, to be worthy of our world. Poor Devon. It took only a— single— drop." Sorcha lifted the quill from the inkwell and shook it out carefully. She crossed to where Gavin sat, and settled herself lightly against his knees.

Gavin flinched, he didn't dare move for fear she would scratch him with the poison. Slowly, Sorcha stretched the quill forward and carefully lifted the collar of his tunic, using it to clean the tip of the quill. His heart pounded against the air between them, desperate to shove her off his lap.

"Devon, you see, had been saved by fairy magic far too many times to be merely human any longer." Sorcha spoke with a conversational lightness that belied the tension between them. "So as the poison rushed through his blood altering him in ways his form was not prepared for, the fairy magic in his blood fought to preserve him."

Try though he did to look elsewhere, Gavin's eyes were drawn to the dainty cleaning process. She cleaned nearly every bit of ink from the tip with the outside of his tunic then let the dampened fabric fall against Gavin's chest. He flinched, anxious to get away from this ugly creation that he'd unleashed. But nothing happened when the dampness touched his skin. He felt it, cool and wet, and electric for all the fear she'd built around it, but nothing happened. Gavin couldn't help staring at the tiny bit of black inky poison that lingered on the quill tip.

"They are doing battle still, inside of him, never allowing him to die, but ripping him apart and leaving an entirely new animal in his place." Sorcha pulled up the collar, running her nail around the edges of the stain. "He is transformed into a beast of pain and power, cursed with enough eternity to continue living long past his life's natural end. But so hideous to look on, and so mad beyond controlling when the poison takes over that he hides himself away from the world." Sorcha paused, smiling broadly at Gavin's averted face. He could feel the power of her zeal.

"It is truly inspiring the perversions eternity devises for those who try to go against it."

"As you will shortly discover," Gavin bit out, and found his fight and his belief enough to shove her from his lap. Let her scratch him if she would, let her try to kill him. He wasn't done yet. He knew it in his blood. He just had to keep believing.

Sorcha tumbled to the ground with a little laugh. "Do you know," she said brightly as she regained her feet, with the quill still clasped in her fingers and the tip still wet with poison. "I was about to say the same to *you*."

"Family needn't be the people you were born to," Sorcha cooed softly from just behind Petal's ear. "Family wants whats best for you, they protect you, and treasure you. But these *people—*"

Sorcha stepped up alongside Petal, almost in front of her, but not far enough to block her brothers held in place by vines of trumpeter flowers grown up around their legs and holding their arms to their sides.

Keagan looked down at himself. This was the dream, he knew it, but there was something different about it. It was more powerful. He wasn't just seeing, he could *feel* Petal. Her anguish, and her struggle.

"They sent you into what they thought was danger. Now, they come after you with weapons and anger. They will never forgive what you did." Sorcha tsked her tongue and stepped behind Petal again. "They would have you believe I want to turn you against them, but the truth is they do that themselves."

Petal was breathing hard, her hands were clenched at her sides, and she was shaking. She didn't want to do what Sorcha wanted, but her eyes kept straying to the weapons in her brothers' hands and she was ripped apart inside, believing Sorcha as much as she doubted her.

Keagan couldn't understand why he couldn't make himself speak. He glanced aside and found Ferdy struggling to speak as well. Sorcha was stopping them. Every second that passed with them silent, Petal's heart broke further. He could feel her crying inside because they couldn't forgive her. He just didn't know what they were meant to forgive her for. This wasn't as far in the future as Keagan usually dreamt, he could tell Rowan was still alive, he and Ferdy were unharmed. What could Petal have possibly done to make her fear they would doubt their love? How could she believe that Ferdy and Keagan didn't care about her enough to keep her safe?

They'd never wanted Petal to go. She was the one so certain it was destiny. What had the separation done to her?

"They are the ones who bring violence into your life," Sorcha said in a voice soft in tone, but enormous in power. She was *so—full—*of *power*. Were any of them truly a match for her?

"Have I ever asked violence of you?"

"No," Petal whispered. She shook her head and tears sprayed the ground. "You do not want me to hurt them?" Petal asked, tilting her head back to look up at the Fairy queen.

"Oh, my dear girl, I only want you to be safe, and at peace, however you choose to be so."

Petal didn't move for a moment—not even to breathe. Slowly her hand rose to the talisman around her neck, she lifted it carefully over her head, gently disentangling her hair as it tried to catch the chain, fighting to keep the talisman near. Finally Petal looked at her brothers, straight in their eyes. She threw the necklace at their feet.

"This is your last warning. I'm not one of your thirds anymore. I am more powerful than either of you. I will be Fairy queen."

Keagan jerked awake, panting.

It felt so real. It still did. More than that it felt present. Like there was something breaking, like—

"Petal!" Keagan leapt from his bunk. Petal was near. He leaned in beside Ferdy's bed to wake him, but Ferdy wasn't there. He would have woken Keagan if he sensed Petal, so he must be up to trouble. They'd agreed not to do anything to the king until they saw if Mama's speaking to him fixed things, but Keagan should have known Ferdy wouldn't leave it at that. No one crossed Rowan without Ferdy exacting at least a bit of retribution.

It didn't matter. Keagan would find Petal, and once they were together Ferdy would feel them and come on his own.

Keagan vanished from the barracks and went to the place he felt Petal most strongly, appearing in the rose garden. He could feel her heartbreak, and guilt and her *need* for her brothers. But he couldn't see her.

"Petal," Keagan whispered. "Petal, are you here? We love you, Petal. We miss you so much. Are you here?"

He ran around the garden, shaking bushes and swinging his arms wide in case she was there but invisible. But he couldn't find her. She wasn't here. He didn't know if she'd heard his words at all, or had been gone for hours. All he knew was that her heart was broken, and she didn't have her brothers there to heal it. She was all alone.

He heard a shifting noise behind him, and looked around expecting Ferdy, but there was no one. The sun was just beginning to rise, and in the pale light Keagan saw what had made the noise. The roses lining the palace wall were growing before his eyes, faster than made any sense they climbed the palace wall. A bright orange, yellow and pink rose ahead of the rest.

Keagan's heart stopped as he felt the other change in the air—Rowan was gone. He spun around and around. Entirely lost for what to do. Petal had been here, broken hearted, but she was gone. And Rowan was gone as well.

It could not be a coincidence.

Now they come after you with weapons and anger.

Kermit met Petal at the door from Stonedragon. She did not meet his eyes, just held out the letters.

We love you, Petal. We miss you so much.

Her gut churned; she wished she could curl up and sob. Wished she'd dared to stay. Wished she'd dared to face Keagan, or Mama, or anyone. She wished she'd never wanted to be a spy.

"Come along," Kermit said in a tired, gruff voice. "I will lead you to the Fairy queen."

Petal put up no protests, just followed behind him. Her eyes stayed on the floor as she fought to shove her heart far away from her body, where it could not betray her.

Do not lie to the Fairy queen—about anything within your heart to reveal, Dervla had said.

Petal's heart could tell Sorcha so much tonight. How little she wanted to be here any longer. How much it ached being Rowan's betrayer, even if in service of her cause. She'd stolen Rowan's treasures, things Rowan had bound together and called *her heart.* Now Petal was to deliver Rowan's heart to a woman who hated her. It felt so ugly. Tonight Petal's heart hated Sorcha. It hated...everything. Absolutely everything in the world.

She'd never felt rage and disgust and agony like the anger that was inside her now. Her life used to be so blissful. But she wasn't Petal the Powerful anymore. She wasn't even an ordinary Petal. She was—

"Why are we here?" Petal shouted, backing away as they stopped at the door with the knotted barley stalk. The door to Turrlough.

"The Fairy queen wished you to meet her at Turrlough Palace."

Petal shook her head over and over, backing further down the hall. Kermit did not try to stop her, but Petal could feel that she would not be allowed to leave. She should have stayed in Stonedragon. That was what Rowan had said when she woke.

"Stay, please," Rowan begged, reaching out for Petal. "We will find another way."

Petal hadn't listened. She hadn't believe her, hadn't even believed Rowan meant it. What would have been the point in hiding in Stonedragon? The damage was already done.

Petal looked at the letters in her hand. Sorcha didn't need these. Petal wasn't even sure she wanted them. She'd just wanted Petal to go, wanted Petal to betray Rowan, wanted Rowan to see her do so. And now...the only reason she could want Petal to bring them to Turrlough was to do the same with Gavin and the girls Petal had rescued. Sorcha wanted everyone to know that Petal was hers.

"No," Petal wailed, aware that she sounded small and broken and childish, but not caring a bit. She was so alone. Why must she be alone with so much?

"She will not harm you," Kermit said softly.

"Do I look unharmed to you?" Petal demanded in tearful rage. As soon as the words were spent the rage deserted her and all that was left was the fear.

This was all so much easier before she went home. Before she went home she knew who she was, she knew her power, she knew her purpose. Now all she knew was heartache.

Kermit knelt before Petal, looking up and down the halls for spies. "Remember what you saw on the mountain?" he asked, but did not await a reply.

"Remember what you said? It lives inside me now, that bit of heart that you shared with me. Now I shall share some with you. This is your home. All fairy will feed you with the heart you need to remember that." He lay his hand over Petal's and she heard her own voice in her head.

"She didn't want to send me...She knew it was bigger than just the task she spoke of, knew I would be all alone with the responsibility...she sent me...to let you know, even though she could not be here that she loves the fairy and she means to care for you."

Petal looked into Kermit's eyes, her temples pounding and her eyes aching and her heart breaking, but for just a moment she wasn't alone. She might even be safe.

"What do I do?" Petal asked. "The Fairy queen will know how much I hated it."

He nodded. "Do not hide it. She expected it to hurt. That you did it anyway is all that will matter to her."

Petal's arm fell to her side and a shudder like ice slipped down her back. But she cried no more. She didn't want to see what Sorcha would do in Turrlough, she didn't even want to know it, but she had to go on anyway. She had a job to do here.

"Peg!" Astrid shoved open the door to Peg's quarters without even knocking.

"What is it?" Peg threw herself out of the bed. She hadn't slept, her mind was too busy, caught between righteous indignation and maybe a bit of guilt. Clearly it had not been Princess Rowan's best day, she could have been more patient with the girl. For all her weapons and bravado, Princess Rowan was a bit naive.

"She's gone," Astrid shouted. "I was out at the tower post keeping Mac company and we saw her ride away."

"He managed to see something with you keeping him company?" Peg asked with snide humor. Not really listening. They couldn't train! How was it, Princess Rowan, who claimed to have been fighting for this all her life did not understand?

It was...it was as if they'd emerged from a dank cave and seen the sun for the very first time, and now they were being shoved back into darkness. How could she just let that stand?

It cannot all be on me.

Astrid shrugged. "It weren't that sort of company. I was showing him what I've been learning."

"It'll work better if he doesn't know what you can do to him the next time his mood turns."

"Mac isn't like that," Astrid defended.

"They're all like that," Peg snarled, though she knew it wasn't true. But everything inside her was screaming, calling her a fool for ever trusting that she would be allowed to live in the sunshine.

Rage came and went across Astrid's face. She turned to leave, but just remained between Peg and the door to her sliver of a room. Peg's space. Hers. In the palace others controlled her, on the grounds she was liable to be victim to any drunkard who crossed her path, and in her home she was someone else's property. But in this tiny room—one cot, one candle that she could light for an hour a night, one chest of her clothes—in here she was all her own. So why was she even letting Astrid stay?

"I didn't come about Mac. Did you even hear me? The princess is gone."

"What?" Peg managed to speak the word—barely. The air felt too thin.

"She was galloping away from the palace, in full armor. And she wasn't following the roads either."

"She...she likes a gallop when she's troubled. She hasn't learned of better distractions," Peg tried levity though her heart felt heavy in her chest. Rowan couldn't have left them.

"There were packs on the horse. She just...ran away. She's letting them win! Once they know they can defeat her, they'll know they can defeat any of us. I can't believe she ran away," Astrid whispered, heartbroken.

"Maybe she didn't run away." Peg looked around her bare slice of self. There was a kitchen knife hidden under her pillow, had been for years. But now, because

Rowan had seen her practice and told Sir Colum that Peg might do better with a long dagger, there was also a blade resting against her chest of clothing.

Sir Colum said Rowan had selected the blade herself, but asked him to give it to Peg, because she was unsure if Peg would welcome the gift from her. A princess, afraid a servant would shun her gifts.

"I saw her myself." Astrid swung around with tears on her face.

"That isn't what I meant." Peg stood. "My family thought I was running away when I came here. But I was running *towards* this. My own place, however small and rat filled. It's mine."

"She's a princess, Peg. She has a suite of rooms and a whole wing of the palace she refuses to let anyone else use. And her garden. She has her own places."

"So maybe she's running towards something different." Peg shrugged. "But it won't stop us."

"How can it do anything else? They'll know—"

"It isn't about what the men know."

Neither king nor queen perceived you as having wills of your own. Were they right? Rowan's voice demanded.

"Princess Rowan chose *us*. Five women to stand like her shield before the women of her nation, and thats what we're going to do."

Peg watched the words bolster Astrid's spirits, and felt revived herself. Maybe both she and Rowan were right: Rowan should have fought for them, but they should also fight for themselves. Peg had run here of her own will, felt so confident that she was living of her own will after she arrived. But part of her still felt trapped, still felt a need to be protected from the world. It was time she rid herself of that voice and faced the world on her own terms.

Heart Ripped Wide

393 days until Roisin Returns

Rowan reached the five hills of Dragon's Spiral before mid day. At a distance they seemed grand and unreachable. But when she was within a mile of them she could see they were nothing more than ordinary hills. It was lowering. She had never ridden for five hours straight before. Never been this far from home. Never been this uncomfortable in a saddle. And she wasn't even fifty miles from her home. She had yet to achieve *anything*.

Leaving home at exactly that moment had seemed so essential in the middle of the night, when Petal had left with her letters and Rowan felt a failure in more ways than she could count. But here she was hours later, barely any closer to her goal.

She couldn't just march into the Fairy realm alone and bring Petal home without risking everyone more— especially Petal. Nor could she ride with shining armor into Turrlough and presume to take on the Fairy queen for Gavin's people.

Rowan was not their champion, nor their leader. They were a sovereign nation and Gavin was their regent. For the time being his rule was law, and he had chosen to collude with Rowan to overthrow the Fairy queen. That Sorcha had discovered the plot was a risk he had been willing to take. However guilty Rowan felt about that, however much she longed to fix it, it wasn't her place. Gavin would protect his nation. He was nothing if not a devoted ruler, his every letter showed it. It was *his place*.

Rowan's place was—

She groaned aloud trying to shove thoughts of her father from her mind. So he disinherited her, her sore hands tightened around the reins involuntarily.

Father's choice didn't signify. It contributed to her departure, but it was not the reason she left. She left to do what she'd been certain she needed to for months. She left to take the steps others were keeping her from. She left to find dragons.

Rowan needed a way to save the ones she loved, and defeat Sorcha without being completely torn apart in the process. She had put off love, and adventure, and... *want* in service to her mission. Now she could put aside her duty to Stonedragon as well. Honestly, Father's choice had freed her to focus on what was truly important. Stopping Sorcha and bringing her sisters home.

Petal's eyes flashed through Rowan's mind. Her heartbroken, burning eyes. She'd looked so different, nothing like the intrepid girl who winked, smiled slyly and bent the world to her will. She was...broken.

You poison everything you touch.

Rowan lay forward against Yseult's neck. Everything felt jittery and fatigued again. As if she was just waking from the nightmare with her heart beating too fast for her to breathe or think. She needed to act. She needed to make sure that Petal knew Rowan loved her. She needed...not to have poisoned this one, beautiful soul.

So she had to find the dragons. Once she had their aid, Rowan could walk into the Fairy Realm and live with the consequences for herself, as long as the ones she loved would be safe after. She had to stick to her plan, however frustrating and unfulfilling it felt at the moment.

None of that stopped her from finding a glen in the shadow of the hills, with a tiny pond and a few trees and flinging herself off Yseult's back. The horse seemed quite relieved. They had been avoiding the main roads, or any homes they'd seen from a distance, trying to stay away from anyone who might see her and report back to Father. He would look for her eventually. She couldn't let him send soldiers to bring her home, or to help her. No one else had been pulled to the dragons, or trusted that plan. Something was speaking to Rowan alone.

"This won't be solved in a week, will it?" Rowan asked Yseult. She walked away from the horse, exercising her legs and rubbing her sore rump. She'd been so...angry and determined and certain. She'd just rode away in the middle of the night, without really thinking it through. "I expected it to be like magic," Rowan continued aloud. "Like finding Roisin when I was fifteen. I would set out to find dragons, and they would just present themselves to me." Rowan laughed bitterly.

When had she become so foolishly hopeful? The Rowan of her childhood would never have believed something so impossible. She would have known it wouldn't be that way. No, this would be like training to be a knight. This would take work, and pain, and being ground down, but fighting on. The dragons meant to test her.

The whistle hanging off Yseult's bridle let out a low smooth note. Rowan jerked around. Yseult had her head down, lapping up water from the pond, her bridle shook with her movements, but that note was too smooth and too specific to be coincidental. It was answering her thoughts.

Rowan paced angrily away. The dragons were testing her, just like Fairy secrets remained out of her reach, and father had taken her birthright from her. Rage bubbled up within and Rowan tried to pound it down with her stomping feet.

She tried to calm her racing heart and mind, but she couldn't find her way past a fear of failure. Last year, belief and peace had helped her move past her fears. She needed some of that belief back.

Rowan stopped pacing. She breathed out, forcing everything from air, to anxiety, to anger out of her being. She needed to find Petal. Rowan began to spin, setting the bells ringing.

There was no feeling of peace to follow this time. What she felt was chaotic, and heartbroken, and *oh so familiar* from herself, but Rowan thought she felt Petal and she followed that feeling.

"You want me to believe that you acted alone in this treachery?" Rowan's heart caught as she recognized her Grandmother's tittering amused voice. What was she accusing Petal of?

"I imagine you would relate to trusting none but yourself," a man replied.

Gavin?

Why couldn't Rowan see anything? She could usually see when she cast her mind.

Her chest hurt from her heart being pummeled by an avalanche of fears.

"Oh," Sorcha said with a playfully pouty voice. "I give my trust. Don't I, Petal?" Sorcha asked.

The question tore into Rowan like a lance. She flew through the air, landing hard on her back gasping for breath. She opened her eyes. Every breath felt like it would crack apart her lungs and release the last of her life force into the world. She remembered holding tiny Petal in her arms, after she pretended to faint. Remembered that devious smile and innocent heart. Rowan had destroyed all of that.

How had she ever thought it acceptable to expose Petal to the influence of someone so evil? Rowan needed to go back. Now she needed to see more and to find a way to reach out as the boys had to let Petal know she was with her. But casting her mind had been so different this time—incomplete and disheartening. Rowan wasn't certain if the difference was in herself, in Petal, or in the pair of them.

Maybe she should seek out Gavin instead. He was there too if she was right. Yseult walked nearer and stood over Rowan, watching her closely. As if she could read Rowan's mind the horse nodded, promising to wake Rowan if she was gone too long.

Rowan lifted her right leg and shook the bells, reaching out to Gavin. It should be hope she felt, and peace, that was how she usually traveled, but there was too much anxiety in her to travel gently. She felt what she thought was his heartbeat and rushed towards it. She slammed into it in her haste to see—to connect.

A fog began to clear before her eyes, and she saw—hundreds of dagger like feathers flying at her—and Petal's horrified face. Petal might be screaming, but no sound reached Rowan's ears. She only saw. Then a searing pain thrust her back into her own body, slamming her against the ground again though she was laying down.

She sobbed as she felt her heart being clawed apart by vicious talons. Rowan fisted a hand over her chest, trying to hold her heart together. Something was terribly terribly wrong. The bells had stopped tinkling and Rowan felt their loss as acutely as the talons tearing into her heart. He couldn't be gone.

She lay so—hanging onto that shredded heartbeat for dear life—until the pain dimmed, growing further and further away. Rowan began to feel the shuddering weakness and chill in her own body. She hadn't felt this helpless since Sorcha first cursed Roisin. Her muscles quaked.

You poison everything you touch.

Tears raced down Rowan's cheeks, but she managed to force the sob back down her throat. He wasn't dead. She wouldn't let him be.

But he was in danger. And Petal was in danger. And Rowan's entire world was in shambles and she couldn't even blame all of it on Sorcha. But she could blame enough on her. And she *would* stop her.

Rowan leaned up on her elbows and closed her fingers around the crystal hanging from Yseult's bridle.

"I'm going to find you," Rowan vowed hoarsely. "And you are going to help me, because there is nothing left to take from me that isn't already under threat. Right now, I am a very dangerous creature."

Yseult tilted her head sideways, doubtfully, pulling the dragon pendant from Rowan's grasp.

Rowan fell back on the lumpy earth, achy and exhausted. "Maybe not at this exact moment," she admitted and shut her eyes around the remains of her tears.

Petal stared out the open window of Prince Gavin's office in Turrlough Palace, watching a bird disappear into the distance. Well, this had been Gavin's office. As it had been his father's office, and would have likely been Owen's office. Petal doubted it belonged to anyone now.

She stared after the black spot that used to be a bird, standing in this room that used to belong to people, because she couldn't face all the accusing eyes behind her. She didn't want to be here. A wolf's howl sang across the air and Petal's heart leapt.

"Aren't wolves nocturnal?" Petal wondered quietly, searching the distance for the wolf, for a pair of burning yellow eyes like she'd seen with Mama when she first set out on this mission; more than a year ago.

When she'd been hopeful and bright and full of belief.

Why had no one told her this mission would last forever? That she could never go home again?

"Most are, dear," Sorcha said sweetly, her hand settling on Petal's shoulder and giving her a gentle squeeze.

Petal's hand rose and covered Sorcha's. She needed so dearly to be held. Everything inside her was splitting apart.

"Why is this one special?" Petal looked up. Sorcha's face was right at her shoulder. Behind them, Prince Gavin's family were in silent tears or breathless horror. Petal couldn't face them. They all must hate her now. It was all her fault. All her fault.

But...he knew.

Gavin had asked her to do it. It wasn't Petal's fault. She knew it wasn't, but she knew it was too. She could have found another way. She could have let the girls stay with Sorcha, she could have lied and said she didn't know of anyone but herself who'd plotted with Rowan. There were so many things she could have done, other than delivering Rowan's heart to the Fairy queen and giving her a reason to kill the man Rowan loved.

Petal couldn't face them. But if she must be here, she could face Sorcha. She could ask foolish questions that served no real purpose, but nonetheless wanted to be answered.

Sorcha smiled. "I don't know, dear. Why, do you think?"

Petal shook her head. A month ago she might have playfully asked if it used to be human. A week ago even. But now she didn't dare anger Sorcha. Now everything felt dangerous. She hadn't really thought Sorcha would hurt Prince Gavin. She'd thought...Petal didn't know anymore. Why would Sorcha falter at hurting a prince who meant nothing to her, when she'd cursed her own son, and her granddaughter? But Petal had convinced herself she would do nothing but perhaps trap him in a crystal, or put him to sleep like she meant to do to Rowan's sister.

Petal looked at her feet. She couldn't face Sorcha either. She didn't know how to go on, even Kermit's words weren't giving her strength at the moment. For all she knew, he'd lied and only used those words to make her move, perhaps he didn't believe in Rowan anymore today than he had the day Petal arrived.

"I don't know," Petal whispered. The Fairy queen always wanted her questions answered.

"Perhaps it is looking for its cub, or is a young pup who got separated from its pack," Sorcha suggested, and turned away. "Separation is always painful— in the beginning. But come, girls, you will admit, despite being separated from your *family* there were times when my hospitality was better than anything you'd ever known here?" Sorcha asked Prince Gavin's nieces.

Elish and Shay were standing before their adoptive grandmother. Queen Aya had a hand on each girl's shoulder, and the pair were gripping one another's hands tightly. Shay with uncontrollable sobs, but Elish was in her element. She'd been forged in conflict. Her shoulders were back, her eyes were hard, she was holding herself together, might hold them all together. Her eyes bit into Petal so her skin burned without even facing Elish.

"It was lovely, thank you, Your Majesty," Elish said without an ounce of sincerity.

Sorcha actually laughed. "Do not fret, dear. You're quite safe, thanks to Petal. She is not your traitor, she did exactly what Prince Gavin asked of her. She freed you. He even had several hours to bask in his successful plan, before he was punished for breaking our bargain. He made his choices. Let his punishment be a warning to all of you, my lenience with the unending conspiracies against me from this nation is at an end."

Sorcha bent down and lifted a long black feather quill from Prince Gavin's boot, all that was left of him after the spell. She carried the feather with her, playing with its fine hairs as she walked.

Petal flinched; she saw it again, one moment he'd been sitting there a man as big as Pa, then Sorcha threw the quill. It split apart in a purple light, splitting apart into dozens and he cried out as they struck. Screams rent the air as the prince was devoured. When the light was gone so was he. Just—gone. Destroyed. So quickly that no one could do a thing.

"Any further aggression from you will be punished swiftly, and mercilessly." Petal jumped as the queen's words pulled her back into the present. Sorcha perched on the edge of Prince Gavin's desk and dipped the quill into a little well of ink. She stirred it around like a ladle. There was something off about that ink. The queen kept toying with it, and a maliciousness usually reserved for her rages stole over her features.

Perhaps doing evil once wasn't enough to make one an evil being. But if one did evil over and over, at every turn, it must turn your soul. That was how Sorcha looked when she stirred that inkwell, like the evil in her was growing. Petal shouldn't be near her. Already she'd helped this woman do too much evil. Soon she would be as twisted, maybe more. Because betrayal was an evil choice and Petal still intended to betray this woman.

"Now, Petal dear, come. These women wish to show you their gratitude."

Petal shuddered, but approached as instructed, her shoulders sinking inward as she sought to make herself smaller. She couldn't look up. She couldn't meet their eyes. They would never forgive her, and Sorcha would—

Petal nearly jumped when Queen Aya's hands reached out and pulled her close. She pulled Petal flush against her, and hugged her tightly. One hand slipped forward to raise Petal's chin, and she stared straight into her eyes. Queen Aya's eyes burned with rage and pain, but also with worry, for Petal. She dipped down and kissed Petal fiercely on the forehead.

"You are not to blame," she whispered in a heartbroken sob. "Thank you, for bringing my girls home."

She set Petal away from her, just when Petal would have clung on. Stepping back, Queen Aya nodded for the girls to do the same, her eyes biting into Sorcha as if to say she was not scared, though anyone could see that woman wasn't fool enough not to fear.

Shay forced the words of thanks past her lips with sobs, but could not be brought to hug Petal. Elish on the other hand stepped forward; never much of a hugger, she slung one arm around Petal's shoulder and squeezed tightly. "We are grateful for all you've done for us." Elish spoke careful of every word, investing them with meaning. "And for all you've helped us to believe."

A little pocket of fear unwound in Petal's chest. They might or might not blame her for the loss of Prince Gavin. But they still knew Petal had saved them. And Elish was assuring Petal she remembered the magic she'd learned.

All was not lost. Petal closed her eyes. In the distance she heard the wolf howl again, but this time its cry was a resonant comfort, reminding Petal of the girl she used to be. The girl who knew the power of her belief alone.

Maureen appeared with a tray of food on the landing of the third floor, and felt the riotous anxiety filling the air. That poor girl. When everyone woke up to discover Rowan gone they suddenly became so anxious that they forgot little things like the child who'd shut away her own personality to survive. The girl Rowan wanted to save—Colleen.

Maureen shoved away her annoyance at the various men around the palace. Even her boys were too caught up in worry to think straight. It would pass. Maureen shoved away her aches and exhaustion, she was feeling better, but not completely so. Today however she had what she had not had in the past several months: hope.

Rowan might be gone, but her power was growing. Maureen felt it wrapping around the palace, doing what it could to keep them safe. Rowan would want this girl cared for, so Maureen would do it.

It helped that she'd sent a gust of damp wind racing down the halls after the king. Balder was avoiding her, ducking around corners when he saw her, as if that would save him from her wrath. It wouldn't. The only thing that saved him was that Maureen knew, as angry as she was, Rowan continued to love her father. Maureen wouldn't hurt him, for Rowan's sake. But it was pleasing having the king fear her.

It was a Fairy feeling. The kind she hadn't had in years, mischievous, and *powerful.*

She'd needed to feel this for so long that she hadn't even known what she'd been missing. She was so used to pushing down parts of herself. Even before she ever came to Stonedragon. So used to it that it was second nature to her, to have a hole inside and no idea what filled it. This filled it. *Self* filled it.

Now she felt Colleen's familiar struggle in the air, the child's every thread of essence was fighting against her. She was coming back to herself, but...unlike Maureen, she hadn't known what she was doing when she shut away the pieces of herself. It was a far more chaotic rebirth.

This could not happen to Petal. Never to Petal.

Maureen took a step backwards onto the stairs. Two steps. She couldn't bring such fears with her. Last night when she'd dreamt of Petal, it had filled her with such hope. Petal had been close, but she'd left without seeing her mother. Which could mean only one thing, she'd been here to do something for Sorcha.

Maureen remembered that. She remembered being sent on a task, a small task that would hurt no one but Maureen, but was a test of loyalty. Had Sorcha been so forever?

Maureen had forgotten that over the years. But she remembered now. The feelings of sneaking invisibly into her family home to steal Orla's favorite things, like an ice charm Orla had made, years before she should have learned such a skill.

Sorcha hadn't asked Maureen to steal it. She never *asked*. She let you offer, let you know she needed some sign you loved no one above her, and you went out and proved your love, and she returned it with such overwhelming...power.

Maureen had thought it was love at the time. But it was just power, wasn't it? She gave you what you needed to continue showing her the love she wanted. She made you love her, but...she never loved you.

Now she was doing the same to Petal, warping her feelings until she wouldn't know how to do anything, but shut away any bits of self that let Sorcha believe Petal could possibly love anyone else.

More than anything, Maureen hoped Petal was stronger than her mother. That she knew her heart well enough to mask it from Sorcha, and still be herself, despite all that was asked of her.

There was something moving out the long thin windows along the stairwell. Maureen glanced over, roses were climbing up the outside of the palace, moving before her very eyes. It was as though Sinead was there beside her.

"Thank you," she whispered towards the roses. "I am sorry I never saw your strength until you were gone."

Sinead had been so strong. It was because of her entreaty that Maureen ever found the strength to leave Sorcha's side. And she had needed it so badly. Sinead had seen it all, Maureen was sure now.

"My word, your daughter is such a testament to you. A beautiful soul, and a strong one. I will honor her strength."

Maureen pulled in a deep breath. Rather than shutting away her feelings, she wrapped her empathy around each one. There were few here who knew as well as Maureen what this girl must be feeling, she would use that to serve her.

The girl's mother opened the door, with red rimmed eyes and a weighty air about her. Maureen lay a hand on the woman's shoulder, soothing some of her exhaustion with magic.

"Why don't you and your husband take this into the next room and eat. I will keep your daughter company a while." She looked over the woman's shoulder. "If you are comfortable with that?" Maureen asked Colleen.

The girl knit her hands together, and rocked a bit in her seat, but made no attempt to answer.

Her parents exchanged worried glances. They needed to block their worry for her, they knew it, but knowing and doing were different things.

Maureen gently walked forward, Colleen's mother backed into the room.

"I shall sit with you a while, and we shall try it out. If you become uncomfortable I shall leave and your parents will return," Maureen informed them calmly. She handed the tray to Colleen's father and nudged them gently from the room.

It was the sitting room of the king's old suite. A richly appointed room still, with comfortable lounging chairs and a bright crackling fire, and wide windows allowing gentle afternoon light into the palace.

Maureen took a seat across from the girl. She supposed she should have held back some of the food for her, but if Maureen's guess was right, this girl didn't yet trust her feelings enough even to know when she was hungry. Two nights ago after they'd settled the family in the suite, Rowan and Maureen had told her a bit of what had happened to her, and Maureen could tell her family had told her more. How hollow and alienating it was not trusting oneself. Maureen understood that.

"Long ago, shortly after Princess Rowan was born. I woke up one morning, in this strange place, where no one was like me, and nothing felt...anything but foreign," Maureen said shaking her head, as she puzzled through what she wanted to share with this child. "I didn't even know myself. Every feeling inside of me was frightening. I didn't know where they came from. I couldn't control them from moment to moment. I wasn't even sure they were mine, because I hadn't felt a thing like them in years. I was *so afraid*. Terrified that I would never feel anything but chaos if I stayed here."

Colleen looked up, her eyes locking on Maureen's for the first time. She searched her gaze, hungrily, but Maureen didn't feel her developing any sudden clarity within so she didn't think Colleen was siphoning off Maureen's inner needs.

"That morning..." Maureen took a deep breath, forced herself to calm her heart so that she could both feel the terror and shrinking she'd felt then, and feel her desire for this girl to know she was not just safe, but understood. "I was never *smaller* than that morning. The fear overshadowed me a hundred times. I felt shriveled and useless and I wanted more than anything to return to the place I had been before. The place where I didn't feel anything."

Maureen let her words breathe a moment, watched Colleen take them into herself, and recognize them like they had come out of her own soul.

"Were others to ask, others who do not understand, I would invent a reason why I stayed, a bird or a tree, or Rowan's smile, something that told me I was in the right place. But it isn't true."

"Then why?" the girl whispered in a breathy sob.

Maureen shook her head. "There is no why. I sat in a room, feeling small and afraid and wanting to go anywhere else. I sat. I did not go out. I did not speak to anyone. I do not even think I ate. And though it was the longest day of my life when it was over I was still here, and the next day the fear was a bit smaller. No one can tell you how to stay out of the other place, Colleen. Nor can anyone tell you it was a bad place."

"But..." Colleen gasped. "I...I...people say my name and I know it's mine, but it feels wrong. My parents hug me and tell me stories and I remember them, but I don't know if I'm remembering them, or if they are. I—" She shook out her arms before her. "I don't recall getting to be this big! I don't know what I did for years. How can that be anything but bad?"

"Because," Maureen spoke slowly, "you were all alone and unprotected, but you found a way to survive."

"But I didn't keep myself! I don't even know who myself is." Colleen cried.

"And here, you will be given the space to find that answer. I do not have the answers for you, all I can tell you, as one who has felt that chaotic, dwarfing fear inside, is that if you find a way to stay out of that other place, every day the fear will get smaller. And some days you will not feel it at all."

Colleen gasped, covering her eyes to cry. Maureen was fairly certain the girl was not ready to be held but she moved to the lounge beside her and lent Colleen her presence as she cried.

Rage with Fathers

"*Y*our Majesty, we've searched the north road and the western pass without any sign that the princess went either way. Perhaps the night watch were wrong," the guard informed King Balder.

"Or perhaps she simply left towards the north and changed directions when she was out of sight," King Balder muttered. "My daughter knows where the guard towers are."

The king didn't look especially comfortable, and he would be even less so soon. Ferdy leaned invisibly against the wall of the king's office, swinging his *half-brother's* crown around on his wrist. Ferdy hadn't decided yet how extreme his revenge should be. But it didn't matter that Mama had talked to him, or that Ferdy had overheard Rowan's confrontation with him in the middle of the night, or that he knew King Balder had tried—rather pitifully— to apologize. There would still be revenge. Maybe he should enchant the crown to bite the king's head. Or to talk! It could shout out Rowan's name, that would be fun! Of course that would only do something at formal functions, he didn't walk around with it on his head all day, or he would already have missed it.

But vengeance didn't need to be huge and constant to be effective, it needed to be pointed. Perverting the crown would grind home the point that Balder should never have threatened his daughter's heritage.

"Would you like us to continue the search, sir?" the guard asked. As if the king should just give up on finding his daughter. The guard seemed skeptical of their being any need to bring Rowan home at all.

"You see," Ferdy shouted, he'd spelled himself for silence so no one would hear him. But it was occasionally satisfying to shout at people who couldn't hear him. He moved off the wall to stand between the king and the guard. "You gave them permission to treat Rowan as worthless, and they don't even hesitate! She's your daughter! Whats wrong with you?"

The king's eyes clouded over, he looked out over the man's shoulder as if he could not see the room before him. Ferdy felt his muscles and magic coiling to launch at the man and rip him to shreds. He didn't deserve to have Rowan for a daughter, didn't deserve the protection she'd given him, by telling Mama she wasn't leaving because of him. He didn't deserve any of the love she gave him again and again.

Ferdy walked forward and flicked him on the side of the neck, a tiny prick of pain, nothing near what he would do later, but he couldn't resist.

King Balder slapped the spot on his neck as one would a bug bite. "What was your question?" He demanded of the man before him.

"Do you want us to continue searching for your daughter, Your Majesty?"

"Of course," King Balder snapped. "And you should not assume you can catch her riding at regular paces. Rowan rides wildly."

The soldier bowed and backed from the room.

For a moment when he'd spoken of Rowan riding there had been a look of love on King Balder's face, fondness. But as soon as the words faded he looked heavy and frightened. This was not a man who knew how to face fear. He was a coward. Ferdy could see it in his eyes, he was letting himself slip into the cursed place. Looking anywhere but around him.

Rowan might think he could be a better king without her, but Ferdy wasn't so sure. What good was a cowardly king in a battle for his nation. And there was definitely a battle coming.

Ferdy released his spell of silence. "You don't deserve her," he said as he vanished from the room.

Ferdy followed the guard out to the squadron at the stables. Balder was a far too casual ruler. One couldn't just give an order and expect it to be obeyed when everyone knew your weakness.

"We're to continue searching. He thinks she may be further ahead of us than we expect."

"On that pony she rides?" one man asked with a laugh.

"You five take the north road, you the west pass, and you five ride out to the village she's been to. The rest of you with men, we'll ride to Seaguard. We'll bring her back, and put an end to this tantrum."

The men laughed and grunted and all mounted, preparing to follow their instructions. There were knights near by, and servants, all eves-dropping and either agreeing or not caring about what the men said of their princess. Something needed to be done about them. Things had been going better for Rowan with her people this last year, but it could all be undone.

The men were walking their horses around the stables towards the wall of the palace courtyard when a few of the children Rowan had been training began raining clods of dirt on the soldiers.

"You can't stop Princess Rowan!" the littlest girl among them shouted, brandishing her slingshot like a sword.

Ferdy laughed as a clod of dirt hit the leader right in the shin and he spurred his horse forward accidentally. He bet the man would hop off his horse to give the girl a good beating, and she looked too foolhardy to run. So Ferdy did the group a favor and nudged along all of the soldiers horses.

Maybe these kids were just what he needed. Malleable, enthusiastic admirers of Rowan. Yes. They would do nicely. Nothing like devotees of your challenger to drive a man mad.

Rowan pulled her packs one at a time off Yseult's back, laying them out in the thicket she'd chosen to make camp in.

Fairy shouldn't sleep always in doors. You need to be a part of nature to understand it. Maureen's soft voice floated through her mind.

Maybe the journey could be good for that at least. Yseult wandered away; with the weight of Rowan and the packs relieved she seemed much better, though still overworked.

Rowan had no right to feel tired in comparison to the horse, but she felt tired. From her soul. The silence out here encroached on her mind and brought up thoughts that she would rather avoid. Worry for Petal and Gavin. Guilt for those she'd carelessly abandoned like poor Colleen who she'd been trying to save, or the women she'd conscripted who would have to fight alone now. Her mind was full of recriminations for how she'd handled the boys, they should never have been punished, they should have been heard and helped. Rowan was more worried than ever over what would become of Braden once he returned to the Fairy queen because of all their trouble on this last visit, and that vision he was still clinging to of a lovely future with *the princess of Stonedragon*. But strangely her darkest thoughts came when her mind turned to Father.

They think they are following a queen, but you are not one and may never be. You are disinherited.

More and more as she crossed her father's nation, her thoughts turned to him. He couldn't be kept out. She didn't know these lands, didn't recognize a single landmark. She hadn't known there were villages near the palace as bustling as Seaguard. She'd thought of most of her villages as small gatherings of people who lived near one another for convenience, but not all of them were. She had spotted a town from one of the hills of Dragon Spiral that took her half the day to get around. From a distance, she could tell that some of the buildings showed more artistic design than the castle. But she didn't know what the buildings were or what the town was named. She didn't know her lands. King Balder's lands. All her life she'd known that one day this nation would be hers to rule, but she didn't know it any better than she knew the rest of the world.

The more she thought of it, the more a sight intrigued her, or she felt hungry for some new understanding, the more her thoughts turned to her father and she ached with rage—and sorrow.

"It's so quiet out here," Rowan said aloud, though it was by no means a quiet evening. The sun was setting in the distance and in the trees, birds and squirrels or other animals could be heard scampering around, preparing for the night, she supposed. But there were no voices, no clatter of pans or horse hooves, or armor. None of the sounds of life that Rowan was familiar with.

Yseult, who had been walking around again and again in a tight circle, softening the area she'd chosen for a bed, stopped and looked at Rowan dubiously.

"There is no one but you to talk to," Rowan defended herself from the horse's censure.

Yseult dipped her head and whinnied in a way that clearly meant "obviously." Then waited for Rowan to speak.

Rowan had rarely been moved to speak like this even when there were people around her. But something of the quiet out here and the turmoil within... wouldn't rest until it was spoken.

"Its as though he found the *first thing* that I ever truly planned for that had a future. The first thing I prepared for that I could be proud of and call my own. He had pressed it on me again, and again, then—once he knew I wanted it—he took it away. And with such relish. Was I so awful a child that he should *want* me to suffer?" Rowan kicked her nearest pack and sent it slamming into a near by tree. But that wasn't enough motion, so she stomped towards the horse, and Yseult, her patient opposite just waited for her. "It wasn't just that I would rule. These past few months when we rode to the village together, and when he joined my court, even when he left me in charge, he seemed proud of me. We were *sharing* things again, like we hadn't since I was a child. I had such hopes for us. I wanted to *ride the roads* with him. I wanted to learn from him.

"Then he does this and I am back to only one goal." Rowan's hands fisted involuntarily as she spoke. "One course. Death."

Rowan's heart plummeted and with it her temper dissipated. Her hand uncurled and fell through the air to settle over Yseult's mane. She unstrapped the saddle and slowly she ran her fingers through the hair like she would a comb any other day after a wild ride. Untangling the knots, and smoothing down Yseult's neck as gently as she was able.

At home she might have talked this over with Maureen or Ardal. Except that Ardal agreed with Father, and it would only have angered and hurt Maureen. No. At home Rowan would have pounded these thoughts silent with a sword.

If Petal hadn't come.

But she had come, and Rowan had been so caught up with that dream, and her father's betrayal, and her own fears, that when Petal vanished with the letters Rowan had truly wondered if Petal might betray them. Rowan should not doubt Petal that way. Petal had always been the best of them. There was no destroying that goodness. Rowan used to know that. When she hadn't believed in herself she'd always believed in Petal.

But Rowan saw betrayal everywhere, saw her future stretching empty and aching, entirely spent in pain. All spent trying to find the magic to defeat her grandmother and prove herself worthy of leading the Fairy nation, that like Stonedragon, would not want Rowan for a leader.

Why would they? She'd never set foot on their lands. She had feared fairy most of her life. Even Rowan was shocked when she performed magic properly. But Petal...

Petal was good. Petal was loving and lovable. And Petal was powerful.

The Fairy would choose Petal for a queen.

That wouldn't have bothered her in the past, but it seemed to be bothering her now. The Fairy would want Petal. Stonedragon would want any ruler but Rowan. All Rowan would ever be was the murderer of her grandmother if she succeeded, or of her sister if she failed.

Rowan couldn't think like that for another three-hundred-and ninety-three days. Not if she was going to find a way to keep from living that terrible future Keagan had seen. She'd told Maureen that leaving wasn't about Father, or Colum, but it was. Because every time she did something even a little wrong they shoved her backwards until she begged and clawed her way back into their approval. She couldn't go backwards anymore.

Rowan patted Yseult three times, the same as she did at the end of a brush down each day, and wandered absently away. Her packs were scattered around the little thicket. She knelt down and dug into one pack, pulling out the blanket. It was a bit of good luck she'd thought to take a blanket, because there were a fair number of other essential provisions she'd forgotten to pack. Food chief among them. But she wouldn't even go back for that. She couldn't go back anymore.

Because even though her thoughts were tortured with worry for Petal, even though she kept reliving those heartbroken feelings that she'd felt when she tried to visit her in her mind, out here Rowan understood Petal's choice. Petal was as trapped as Rowan had ever felt. Petal the Powerful could not escape the Fairy. She would stand out like a peacock among hens, like Roisin would stand out in Stonedragon when she returned. Petal was beloved, but every eye must follow her. Despite all that, Petal was trying to help Rowan, trying to free her uncle as Rowan had asked.

So Rowan needed to find a way to help. A way to free Petal. A way to bring her home if Rowan could stop Sorcha, or to hide her if she could not.

From her heart Rowan felt a sharp piercing, like something digging into the muscle and trying to rend it apart. Rowan shut her eyes and fisted her hand over the spot. She rubbed hard against her armor with the heel of her hand, though she'd no hope of truly feeling the pressure that way.

It was like something was trying to rip out a part of her, trying to sever a bond. Rowan held on with every bit of power she could spare. Held them together.

Yours, Gavin.

He isn't dead, she assured herself in her mind. She didn't dare say the words aloud, they would emerge as a plea. For so long she'd fought against letting herself have this connection, against acknowledging that she loved him. And now that she had—something was trying to pull him away.

I will take from you what you love most.

She fought off the urge to cry. Rowan shouldn't allow herself to think of it more. It was like that dark vision Keagan had shared with her; if she thought of it, it felt more real, more possible. She couldn't let this fear be real. But nor could she let it shake her from her plan as it seemed to want. The searing in her chest pulling her every moment from the hum of the whistle and towards the heartbeat she'd felt within her own. She couldn't let that happen. She couldn't give up on Petal to save Gavin.

If she found the dragons she could save them all. She could stop Sorcha, she could bring Petal home, she could even save Gavin. She could do it all.

At home Rowan would have thought and behaved like the errant child her father wanted to treat her as. She would have ached and begged and chaffed, but out here she could work towards her goal.

Rowan arranged her pack of clothes at one end of the blanket for a pillow, and saw from the corner of her eye that Yseult had already settled on the ground. Rowan's stomach rumbled, but she had nothing to feed it. Tomorrow they would venture nearer a town and steal some food, or she could take to eating the same grasses and bushes Yseult did and hope the horse knew better than her what was safe. But for now she should sleep.

Every time her stomach rumbled, or a noise disturbed her, or Rowan felt cold or the ground felt too rocky, Rowan told herself she was working towards her goal. She just needed to find the dragons. If she found the dragons she could save everyone.

It was supposed to sound hopeful as it rolled through her mind, it was supposed to feel comforting. Instead it felt desperate. But she didn't stop reassuring herself until she drifted into sleep: I can save them all. I can save them all. I can save them—

392 days until Roisin returns

Braden should be gone already. He had been in Stonedragon two weeks as of yesterday. It was perhaps not his longest visit, but he could hardly justify staying longer to the Fairy queen, if Rowan was not here to woo. But despite that fact, and despite the fact that he had spent the last day and now half of this one being interrogated about every word that had passed between himself and Rowan before she left, and despite somehow feeling a bit worse about his fate in the world today, Braden wasn't rushing home. Wherever that was.

Braden saw like a flash that cottage, heard her humming and felt drawn to her. He knew it was Rowan. Sorcha had said as much and it felt so real. But just when he was about to reach her, to see her face. To know the truth for himself. The vision left him.

He had no home.

Braden had no real desire to leave, at least here he was safe. Rowan had asked him to lie to her family about where she'd gone, but had not mentioned what, if anything, he ought to say to Sorcha. He could hardly hide that Rowan had left. But nor could he tell Sorcha what he was telling Rowan's family, that she'd run away to be with the man she loved. Sorcha would put up with many things from him, but he doubted his failing to stop Rowan from seeing Gavin was one of those things. He had always felt so, but he felt so even more after that painfully uncomfortable sharing session four days ago.

He'd told Rowan—told her of his love and of the future they could have together. The peace and happiness they could share. He'd told her and in typical Rowan fashion she just dismissed him. Her hum filled his mind, and for every note his resentment grew.

She would never have put you in Rowan's path if you were her true love.

Rowan wasn't for him. That future wasn't for him. And apparently even Sorcha knew it. Everyone believed that Rowan and Gavin were meant for some earth shaking, magic breaking sort of love. And Braden's only purpose was to foil that love. If he returned to Sorcha and admitted to failing, Sorcha was capable of anything.

So as aggravating as it was to sit before Rowan's father as he paced in his study, Braden considered it the lesser of two evils. He tried to put the hum from his mind and banish the resentment. It wasn't Rowan's fault. Sorcha had manipulated him. The trouble was even that made Braden angrier with Rowan. So he tried to focus on thinking of something better to tell Sorcha. Could he tell her the truth?

It would tip her off to Rowan's plans. But she seemed to be privy to a great deal without Braden's help. Perhaps she already knew. In which case his telling could only make him seem more committed to Sorcha. It couldn't really do Rowan any more harm than Sorcha must have in store for her. But how to explain why Rowan left how she did?

The truth again? Braden looked up as the king slammed his fist down on the rough stone window frame. This castle had nothing on Anwyn's for beauty. All its windows were small. The walls were made of a rough stone that had never been refined, and showed no effort at artistry. The wall surrounding Anwyn's guard towers was more attractive. Barely any natural light ever made it into this palace. It was a glum place.

"They need to reach her before she makes it to Turrlough." The king rubbed his knuckles. No doubt he'd bruised, perhaps even cut them on these walls. "Are you certain she gave you no indication of which road she would take?"

"Your Majesty," Braden said carefully. "I really think all of you are overreacting to Rowan's departure. I am sure she is quite safe."

"Her physical safety is not my current concern." Balder spun around and for once showed the bearing of a king, his eyes boring Braden into place the way his own father's gaze often did. "Though you and the rest of her knights have given her a false sense of her own abilities as well, so thank you, I shall consider that presently."

Braden looked away to roll his eyes. This man had never faced his daughter with a sword. Until recently, Braden might have agreed with him. But two days ago Rowan had nearly killed Braden and two other knights of considerable skill, and she'd barely broken a sweat. She had been holding back all these years, but her father's betrayal had ended that.

"She is riding to a man she thinks loves her who has been courting another woman for months," the king explained his concerns. "A woman who resides in his palace."

"Oh." Braden leaned back shaking his head. "I had not considered her."

He should have told Rowan about Lady Asia. Of course Rowan wasn't headed to Turrlough, but there was nothing preventing her from going there once she'd found the dragons, or if she failed to. Not that Rowan had ever failed at anything.

Braden shook himself, was he now feeling jealous of Rowan? *Rowan?* He needed to get hold of himself. He'd felt better after all the confessions were made, after he and Rowan spoke. But there was something about this place. Rowan had been gone one day and the castle seemed darker, moods were less stable for those who knew and loved Rowan, but for the others, servants and soldiers and nobles who saw her daily but had never come to know her, their moods were suddenly... comfortable. Too comfortable. They did not notice the turmoil that gripped the others around them. The whole mood of the palace was getting to him. He should leave.

Today.

"Such a betrayal could break Rowan," her father said darkly.

Braden barely refrained from asking why that betrayal should be worse than Balder's own. But perhaps that betrayal would be harder on her. Rowan, like Braden, was quite used to disappointment from her father.

"I wouldn't worry, Your Majesty, you heard Maureen: Gavin is Rowan's *true love*. Surely he will send Lady Asia home as soon as he and Rowan meet."

The king moved very purposefully to his seat and slowly sunk into it, facing Braden all the while, as if to illustrate that this was a calm thought, and not the desperate grasping of a man who knew his guilt.

"For the entirety of my first marriage I was told by my wife that I was her true love. Over and over again until the words nearly drove me mad. Every time I heard of her love," his voice dropped low, "I hated her a bit more, because I didn't feel the same. I hated her for making me say it, for making me the villain of her story. I wanted her to accept that ours was a marriage forced on us, that love was no part of it. But she couldn't, and I...punished her for it. I became the villain of her story, and hardly the hero of my own, because I did not feel love like she did. I felt cheated. I set out to destroy her love, since I was denied similar feelings."

Braden couldn't speak. The dry scratchy feeling of his throat told him his mouth was open, but he couldn't seem to close it. He'd never observed this level of intensity from King Balder, in fact he was quite surprised he had it in him. It was all so...crushing. Braden felt the weight of the king's words, pressing him into the ground.

Balder had tried to destroy love he could not requite, and cost Rowan a mother. And Braden, not four days ago was ready to try and destroy Rowan for not sharing his love, and nearly cost her a friend. And all of them deserved love. They were not wrong to want it. Could none of them love someone who loved them back?

Could Rowan?

As if he'd only waited for Braden's thoughts to work their way around to his side the king spoke again. "Just because Gavin is Rowan's true love, does not mean she is his. I will not have such a life for my daughter."

It was the most profoundly paternal thing Braden had ever heard this man say about Rowan, and she had to run away from home for him to say it. Braden felt a burning seething rage growing inside him, for his own father, for Rowan's, for all the children who had to beg and dig and nearly die to understand what their parents were feeling.

"This is a story you should have shared with Rowan. As much as Rowan treasures her mother's memory, you are the parent she had before her. She would have forgiven you the mistakes of your youth, but you..." Braden paused unsure if he should speak. So much of his life was built on *not* speaking. On hiding who he was and what he felt and keeping all the powerful beings around him comfortable. But King Balder was the least of them. And Braden had seen how much shedding secrets, any secrets, helped him feel more himself.

"I warned her not to trust Prince Gavin, but she would not listen," Balder snapped.

"Did you tell her why you worried?" Braden demanded. "Of course not. Why share with her when she should just fall in line and follow your orders? Rowan is not one of your *subjects*! She is your daughter. She needed to hear that you were concerned for *her*, that you didn't want pain for her. Tell me truly, would you prefer she married me?" Now Braden waited, now his intensity bore the man into his seat and set the room on edge.

"You would love her," King Balder said flatly. "I think you love her now."

Braden stood and paced away shaking his head. He did love her. But not in a way that filled him up and that gave him joy. He didn't love her in the way she wanted or even the way he wanted. But he was hardly the point.

"Rowan wouldn't love me," Braden said flatly. He turned slowly back to face the man. "You would prefer that Rowan be you in your story, rather than her mother?"

"I...she cares for you. It would take time but eventually she would love you." King Balder didn't quite seem convinced of his own words.

"Are you sure? Because I think it would be far more likely to destroy Rowan to be the cause of my heartbreak than to have her own heart broken. She has suffered heartbreak before at the hands of those who should love her."

The words struck the man still and Braden spun to leave without the king giving him leave to do so. He didn't care for any formalities now.

"You will remain in my kingdom until my soldiers return from Turrlough with Rowan," King Balder informed Braden when he had reached the door. The king's voice was rough, but not lacking in any certainty. He was a king, and Braden would wait on his pleasure.

Braden angled his head around and executed an abbreviated bow, but couldn't help a parting rebuke. "You should realize, even if they find her, your knights are unlikely to bring Rowan back. You've disinherited her. What reason does she have to return?"

Brave New World

Sorcha should not have punished Gavin in front of Petal. And certainly not Owen as well. Petal didn't trust her as much now; she was sullen and grief stricken. She'd literally told Sorcha she didn't dare try again to free Desmond.

"My hands are tainted with betrayal. I cannot let them touch him until I have been cleansed, or he may wake with the betrayal on him," she'd said.

It was utter nonsense. "Petal, there can be no betrayal of Prince Gavin. You served your Fairy queen, as you should. He was the traitor, traitor to our deal."

"But I knew nothing of your deal when I agreed to spy for him. I made my promises freely. How can it be anything but betrayal to break that word?"

"Because you can owe no duty to such a man," Sorcha argued, growing frustrated. "His very essence was to betray. You served him because you thought you were serving that...*deficient* usurper through him. But even that is not true. His deal with me was to court her only to betray her."

The moment the words left her lips Sorcha saw her mistake. Petal may serve only Sorcha, but her love for that other family was not quite dead. Her eyes had widened and her sullen attitude only increased. The trouble was the girl saw herself as a traitor, when Sorcha needed her to see herself as betrayed. Having been betrayed by Prince Gavin was not profound enough. She needed her family to turn their backs on her.

A few months with no more of those obnoxious visits would do her attitude good. But she couldn't just be left to her own devices for that long. She couldn't be left feeling angry with Sorcha, and defiant, she might just build up a rebellion.

Already Sorcha's subjects were too fond of Petal. Sorcha knew better now than to fully trust fate, or to try to control it. It could be bent, and manipulated and molded, but it could never be fully controlled. She was certain it would be Petal to release Desmond, but the only way to guarantee that Sorcha was there when it happened was to tie Petal to her irrevocably.

The betrayal of her bond with that...*Knight of the Rose* was a first step. Now she needed to be betrayed by her family as well. And she needed to turn to Sorcha for her comfort, not some other fairy.

"Whisper," Sorcha cooed softly. At once the woman vanished from Petal's side and reappeared at a bow before her queen.

"Yes, Your Majesty?"

"Now that the humans are gone I have a new task for you," Sorcha said casually and saw Petal clench her teeth, well aware why the woman was being reassigned. Petal would chaff a bit from the changes at first, but she would come to love Sorcha again. There would be no one else for her to love. "Too long this forest has been without children. They needn't be hidden from the human contaminant any longer. Bring those who lived here back to the forest and set about teaching our youngest to harness their gifts. Petal has excelled under your tutelage."

"It has been my honor, Your Majesty. As will be this new task," Whisper bowed again. And without even the need for such an instruction, vanished without so much as a glance in Petal's direction.

Petal saw the woman vanish and walked forward, coming to sit before Sorcha, obedient to the silent command. She sat on an old mossy log to the left of Sorcha and looked away towards the hollowed tree that had served as her home up to now. She would sleep in the palace tonight and they both knew it.

"My brother's have never lived anywhere but at home. But I have traveled the island. Found friends to love in other lands. Slept in many beds." Her eyes came to rest at last on Sorcha, giving her the attention she needed. "I have had adventure, while they only get to play at it. And perhaps playing is more pleasant, but...if I do what you want, what you truly want: free Desmond, and become your heir, I shall have no more adventures. I will just be this." She nodded thoughtfully Sorcha's way. And Sorcha knew she was nodding to the throne, but it felt like she was nodding at her. It felt like a rebuke of all Sorcha was and all she did. Felt like Petal didn't see its worth.

Sorcha tried to remember what it was about *this* that she loved. She'd gotten nearly everything she ever wanted, but none of it was worthwhile.

In the distance a wolf howled. Sorcha startled, but Petal did not. She smiled softly. It was impossible. There was no way the wolf could have followed them, not onto Fairy land. They had never been able before, and Sorcha knew they'd tried. Why now?

Sorcha's eyes returned slowly to Petal, so composed and so defiant. Were they called to her, Sorcha's creations? Pulled to Petal as the fairy were?

It was dangerous to let one with such natural power draw in creatures with reason to see Sorcha harmed.

"What are you doing?" Keagan demanded of his brother with an intensity Ferdy would expect for theft, or at least minor mayhem.

Ferdy lifted the tray of food, shrugging at the same time. "What's it look like?"

"Rowan is missing. Pa's off on a fool's mission to fetch her back from Turrlough—"

"How do you know it's a fool's mission?" Ferdy asked as casually as he could. Ferdy had not told his brother what he knew from sneaking around the night Rowan left. And he knew Braden hadn't told the secret. So how could Keagan know? Maybe he felt Rowan, but if so why not just tell Pa he was off in the wrong direction?

"Braden's lying. I can tell."

"You've removed the veil in his head without my help?" Ferdy asked like it was a joke and walked around his brother, because he lied to Keagan better in motion. He'd intended to just vanish with the food but Keagan would follow and argue with him around Colleen, or go nutty over her again.

Honestly, Ferdy was a bit worried by the fact that Keagan hadn't tried to see the girl once since it was revealed what she was. He hoped Keagan wasn't still blaming himself for the wedge that had grown between them because of the insecurities Colleen had pulled out of him.

"Of course not. Why aren't you more worried? Why don't you want to find her?"

"If Rowan thought she was in danger she would have taken us along," Ferdy lied happily. It was odd how much more easily he was lying these days. Apparently holding everyone's secrets had made him a bit more comfortable with hidden things.

He'd had no trouble at all waving Pa off to Turrlough knowing Rowan wasn't there. It served him right for speaking to Rowan the way he had. He had a feeling, from watching Mama that she felt the same way. She barely spoke to Pa, her rage with him still palpable around her.

"No! Rowan wouldn't," Keagan argued. "Not if she was doing something bad."

Ferdy turned halfway around to face his brother in disbelief. "Rowan doesn't do bad things."

"She sent Petal." Keagan snapped. "And not for the reasons she told us at the time. She admitted it herself."

Ferdy stared at his brother, honestly baffled. How could Keagan talk that way about Rowan? He knew what she had been put through. They'd both helped Rowan train Petal to go. They were as much at fault—

"You had the vision again," Ferdy said, and the oddest thing happened: he felt the weight of the tray in his hands. He never felt the weight of things he carried.

Keagan's foot scuffed the floor. "Not the exact one. It was different, nearer to now, and not as deadly, but almost more...terrible."

"What happened?" Ferdy asked.

"Ferdy, I had it the night Rowan ran away. The Fairy queen was convincing Petal that we'd come to hurt her. You and I. She said we came after her with weapons. That we couldn't forgive her. And Petal believed her!"

Keagan was standing on the outside edges of his feet, as he always did when he was nervous, when he was trying to puzzle through too many thoughts at once.

"Alright, well, now we're forewarned." Ferdy tried to reassure them both. "If we meet Petal and the Fairy queen tries to convince her we're bad, we'll be prepared and convince her otherwise."

"She'd done something to us so we couldn't speak."

"Magic?" Ferdy asked.

Keagan nodded.

"So look in stupid Devon's stupider book. Figure out what spell Sorcha was using so we can make sure she doesn't."

"What makes you think I even can?" Keagan asked.

"You're smarter than her."

Keagan laughed like he didn't believe his brother. Not the praise, Keagan could believe himself that smart without effort. No, Keagan thought Ferdy was just funning him, that Ferdy didn't really believe it. Keagan was still insecure.

How could he honestly believe that Ferdy, of everyone, didn't respect his mind?

"Don't act so shocked," Ferdy said sharply. "You know you're smarter than her. No one is as smart as you."

"Not even you?" Keagan goaded.

"Obviously." Ferdy laughed. "I'm more handsome than you, more fun, a bit more confident. I have better hair. I'm faster, and better with a blade—"

"Did you have a point?" Keagan snapped, but there was a growing smile on his face.

"Yeah, Kee. We have our own strengths. But no one is as clever as you. This may be an after effect of Ma swapping our powers. You're getting too caught up in the emotions, and not thinking it through logically."

"What would happen if I did?" Keagan asked.

Ferdy shrugged, and again, for no reason he could explain the tray in his hands felt heavier. He might need to put it down in a minute. "You'd realize that the Fairy queen might just be manipulating you. Trying to make you so afraid that you did the wrong thing, and went after Petal with a weapon, and played right into her trap. Trust Petal, like I trust you. And Rowan. And even Pa, once he gets his head back on straight."

Keagan rolled his eyes at the mention of Pa. It seemed everyone was upset with him.

"What if...what if Petal did something bad? And Rowan went after her?" Keagan asked softly.

"If Petal did something bad, and Rowan went after her..." Ferdy shook his head not even wanting to think such things. "Then she went to bring Petal home before Sorcha makes her do something else bad. Rowan doesn't hurt people she loves."

"We all do."

"Ugh!" Ferdy rolled his eyes. "Not like that! Don't believe me if you don't want to. But you'll see, Petal won't turn against us. Rowan won't turn against her. And the Fairy queen *will not win*." As though a vehement belief was all that was required the weight of the tray vanished from Ferdy's arms. He looked down having to be sure it was still there. And it was. He just had to keep believing. Belief gave him strength.

"Are..." Keagan began to speak but couldn't seem to finish. Ferdy looked over, shaking his head for Keagan to finish. "Are you taking that to Colleen?"

"Yeah. I promised Rowan I would keep serving her and her family."

"May I come along?"

"Sure." Ferdy turned away, smiling. "If you think you can leave those big baby feelings here."

Keagan jumped at his brother's back, knocking him forward. But Ferdy didn't drop the tray, didn't spill a single thing. Now Keagan was feeling better, Ferdy didn't have a thing to worry about.

391 days until Roisin returns

Astrid was headed out to the guard tower to meet Mac when she was yanked hard by her braid. She cried out in shock and her hand reached out to wrap around her hair, but her assailant was too fast. Her body slammed into the wall of the palace.

Her entire body ached at the impact, but it was just startling and frightening enough to remind her that she knew how to fight.

She allowed herself to lay against the wall until her attacker moved closer, then she kicked backwards like a bucking horse and caught her attacker in the gut. She heard the grunt but didn't stop there, she spun around and charged with all her weight aimed low. Her head slammed into someone's stomach and the pair went tumbling to the ground.

They rolled around, grappling for power. It was so dark she couldn't see her attacker, but she could feel that he was small, but strong. Well, she was strong too. She shoved her body upwards as the man settled atop her, tried to shove him up over her head so she could roll away. But he dug a knee into her side and knotted a hand in her hair.

That was a mistake. Astrid let the pain drive her adrenaline higher, let it tie her attacker to her so she knew just where to strike, and she twisted her elbow up, slamming it into her attacker's jaw so hard she heard teeth clink together. He released her hair, rolling away.

"Curse you, Astrid," Megan wailed.

"Megan?" Astrid demanded.

A laugh sounded from the shadows next to them. Peg walked into the moonlight, clapping. "Marvelous Astrid, I think you broke her teeth."

"How is that marvelous?" Megan asked, angrily rubbing her jaw, and sounding distinctly like she was crying.

"Because she thought you were a man and she fought with everything she'd been taught. After a moment. You need to respond faster. You could have saved yourself some pain if you hadn't let her slam you into the wall."

Astrid pushed herself up onto her palms and glared at Peg. "This was what you meant about continuing to learn? That we should hurt one another so we're weaker when men attack us?"

Megan wailed, joining the revolt. "And ugly toothless hags."

"Quit griping," Peg ordered, annoyed with them. Did they want to train or not? Didn't they realize it was better to be prepared than to be comfortable?

Didn't they realize it was better to be hurt slightly by one another than to be taken apart by the men who taunted them daily about their reversal of fortune.

Those men were toying with them. They wanted to break them with words first, but the physical pain would come soon. This was for everyone's good.

Astrid rolled to her knees then to her feet and marched right up to Peg. "What we need isn't to be attacked, but to be better trained. To know how to use weapons. To have weapons. And to give them to other women."

"We'll get there," Peg promised. Though she'd yet to work out how. "But for now, we need to be prepared. And...none of us travels alone."

Now Megan shoved to her feet and walked over. She was wearing a man's tunic and thick stockings or the ruse wouldn't have worked. Peg was jealous of the ease it gave her friend's movements. Perhaps they should all dress so. They were already defying the king in one way, what was one more? Although, it wasn't only the king who would take exception to women walking about garbed like men.

Once Megan was right before her Peg realized the woman was likely in a great deal of pain. Her chin looked to be turning purple. She'd heard her teeth clink but if she didn't miss a guess, that sound might have covered a bone cracking. Peg almost wanted to dance around cheering for Astrid over the power behind such a strike, but was slightly appalled at herself for truly not caring that Megan was injured, as long as it was by a woman.

"What do you know?" Megan asked, cringed, and then shuddered as if both things caused her terrible pain.

"She knows that the people who want to hurt you aren't going to stop until you're hurt much worse than that." A little boy's voice came from behind the trio.

Peg spun around kicking up the sweep end of her broom and holding it before her like a quarterstaff.

Maureen's sons stood behind her with a group of children huddled around them holding all manner of devious things. Ferdy wore a superior smirk at Peg's defensive posture. But Keagan, who had spoken, looked mildly impressed. The littlest girl in the bunch, holding a bucket of manure with a slingshot hung from her arm had a wide eyed expression.

"Do that again," she ordered excitably.

"That's nothing," Ferdy bragged. "Rowan could fight with two staves, break a staff in half and use the halves as batons, or…"

"One doesn't have to be Rowan to be impressive," his brother interrupted. "Peg has only trained a few months."

"What are you doing here?" Peg demanded in her toughest voice.

"What are you doing here?" Ferdy countered.

There was an older girl towards the back of the group, the one from Turrlough, the longer they all spoke the further into the shadows she sunk.

Keagan, ever the more reasonable of the two boys looked not at Peg, but at the two women flanking her. "She's right. I didn't think so in the past. I thought it was better to let my enemies have small victories so they would get comfortable." He glanced back at his brother. Ferdy rolled his eyes. Peg almost let slip her militant stance, they were cute together. Was this why people wanted children?

"But anger like theirs doesn't go away until you are destroyed. You should travel in groups and always carry…" he smirked like his brother. "Innocuous looking weapons."

"What's inocctious?" Astrid whispered.

"Kee's just trying to show off for our new *gargoyle*," Ferdy said playfully. At once his brother reddened, his eyes darting backwards. "Just means normal stuff, like brooms, and ladles and—" he smiled with evil glee, "boiling water and such."

"Yeah," the littlest girl nodded up at Ferdy, evilly impressed. "Hot waters a *great* weapon. My uncle cried and cried when he burned his hand, couldn't do a thing for weeks."

"I don't want to be here," a tiny whisper came from Colleen, all but vanished in the shadows behind them.

"Then go," Ferdy said casually. "You know the way."

Keagan turned a vicious glare on his brother. "We're supposed to be making her feel safe," he hissed.

"What's safer than having her own choices?" Ferdy argued.

"I'll take you back to your parents, Colleen." Keagan rushed back solicitously. Peg actually agreed with Ferdy. From everything she'd heard, the girl's problem was all the choices that had been taken from her. Freedom might just be the most powerful thing she could be given.

"What about the statue and the banners?" Ferdy demanded of his brother.

"You and the others can do that," Keagan replied.

"Do what, exactly?" Peg asked, inching towards that bucket of manure. She didn't much want to touch it, but it was servants like her who would have to clean it up whatever mess they made, and she wouldn't get a proper bath for another week. She began to think the children might need minding.

"No," Colleen jumped forward, and the broom dropped from Peg's hands like it suddenly weighed a thousand pounds.

All eyes shot to the girl quivering and panting behind them. Ferdy was the first to regain his composure, he sighed, put upon, and walked between his brother and Colleen, giving his brother a sharp annoyed look. "Big baby," he muttered. Keagan's eyes widened and he took several careful steps away from the girl.

"Colleen," Ferdy said calm and even, but not gently. It put Peg to mind of his mother, perfectly able to soothe and comfort, but more inclined to force one to rely on their own strength. "What do you want to do tonight? I am personally after mischief. Peg and Rowan's other girls want—"

"Shield maidens," Peg interrupted, with a smile. "We're the future queen's shield maidens. Her guard for the women of this nation."

Ferdy glanced over his shoulder and gave Peg an approving nod. It didn't make any sense, but she felt just a bit taller, all from the approval of an eleven-year-old boy. These were strange times.

"The *shield maidens* are after a fight. And Keagan just loves to cosset you. What do you want?"

The girl took a deep, pained looking breath, and clenched her fists before her. "I don't know. But...I've never played a trick. I don't remember fun. I don't remember me. Maybe I'm fun."

Ferdy snorted. "Not likely, but you should have a chance to try. Mischief it is then." He spun around and pointed ahead. "Onward to the fountain of the babe!" The children started off again, laughing and making such a ruckus Peg had no idea how she'd missed them before. "If you're done training you should have Mama heal you. She'll like that you're Rowan's shield." Ferdy smirked.

Ferdy took up the front of the group, with Keagan taking up a heavy tail. Once they started across the courtyard the whole group literally vanished before them, as did their noise. Peg chuckled.

"Neat trick. Why do you suppose it's cute when they do magic, but was frightening when Princess Rowan did?" Astrid asked.

I find it difficult to love those who have looked on me as a murderer since I was seven when I became cursed as well.

"Because someone wanted it to be," Peg answered heavily. "Come on, the boys are right, let's get you healed, so you can stop whining."

"Easy for you to say." Megan wept. "It isn't your jaw."

"Oh it will be." Astrid put her arm around Megan's shoulders and led her towards Maureen's cottage.

Peg smiled at the backs of them. There was plenty of evil here, plenty to fear. But there was good as well. Peg would make sure the good was stronger when Princess Rowan returned.

390 days until Roisin returns

Braden left with a set of knights following reports of a Rowan sighting by the sea. He'd agreed to remain in the kingdom until Colum returned from Turrlough, but he would not stay a day longer. Still, that could take a week yet. Braden couldn't stay in the palace all day every day, being watched and interrogated and scrambling to think of ways to appease Sorcha once he was home.

So he'd seized the opportunity to leave the palace and in so doing the solutions to his other problems had fallen into place. Rowan always said she thought better in motion. Perhaps he did as well. He needn't tell Sorcha a thing of where Rowan had gone, after all, he *knew* nothing. Staying to participate in the search could only be seen as serving his queen. He would send a letter home by messenger tomorrow informing his family, and through them Sorcha, that Rowan had run away and he was staying to search for her.

He would prefer to give Rowan more time to get away, but if he waited forever Sorcha would know he'd done so intentionally. He would simply send the message by means of his slowest rider, and hope that Sorcha was not in residence when it arrived.

Stonedragon's palace and the kingdom both had more to recommend them from a saddle than indoors. It was quite lovely with the way the rose garden had overtaken the eastern wall of the palace. Braden wanted to paint it so, a sun rise itself as the light slid up the palace, awaking the blooms. The rolling hills behind it would give it a simplistic beauty that Anwyn's palace lacked.

It was an unexpected gift, riding out on what he knew was an utterly pointless task. He was sure he should be worried for Rowan. But out here, away from his problems he felt a lightening inside and was certain that was what Rowan must feel. It would do her some good.

There had been Rowan sightings pouring in from so far and wide across the kingdom everyone knew they couldn't all be accurate. Braden began to suspect that several of them were intentionally misleading. They were few and they were mostly quiet, but there was a new defiant faction running around Stonedragon, and not just the children who were defacing statues and paintings of the Rose Princess, and who had replaced the banners counting down the days until Roisin's return with a banner reading : *Four days without the Blade of Stonedragon.*

Braden got a good laugh out of that. And so, oddly enough, had Queen Gwyneth. She was in fact the first person even to spot it. The old banner was such a part of life now almost none of them marked it. But she had seen the new one on her "morning constitutional" and roared with laughter. The king had not reacted so nonchalantly, he'd ordered it taken down, and demanded to know where the old banner was. Which only made him look all the more pathetic when the banner could not be removed, and the old one was found in the fireplace of his own office.

But the children were not the defiant faction Braden had noticed. It was the women. Servants, Queen Gwyneth, and all these reports, every one was from a woman. Every one. He didn't think that was accidental. Rowan had an odd effect, he wouldn't have called her inspiring when he first met her, nor even when he joined her cause. But she was inspiring. Willing to fight though it cost her friends and safety and peace.

Braden had always preferred peace. But he never would have thought to find it by riding across the hills with a contingent of soldiers searching for a missing princess. And he had. And again he felt like Rowan was the cause.

Braden and the soldiers crested a small hill, and saw a much smaller group of soldiers riding straight up towards them. Sean, Andrew, and their squires. The lieutenant in command of Braden's search party called for a stop and waited for Rowan's knights at the top of the hill.

Braden could tell even at a distance that the knights knew trouble was brewing. Braden hadn't seen him at it before, nor even wondered, but as he watched Sean riding, controlling his giant mount with only the one arm, he found himself impressed, and feeling...small. Braden always held his reins in both hands as he'd been taught, always sat erect, always cantered, never galloped. But Sean held the reins in his only hand and lowered his body over the horse neck, urging it on quickly, and though it must be an additional strain, never looked anything but intent.

Was it just because he had to, because there was no other choice? Or were their men like Sean and Ardal who were just stronger than other men?

Not that Ardal was seeming especially strong in the past few days. Since Rowan left Stonedragon he had not left his home once. Would rarely accept visitors. Braden felt like he should be doing more to draw him out, felt like Rowan would want it. But he didn't know how. Ardal was feeling guilty for Rowan's departure, and to Braden's mind he should feel it. But perhaps not as badly as he clearly was.

"What's going on?" Sean called out as he was casually pulling up on the reins and bringing his horse to a sudden, complete stop. Andrew pulled up alongside him, with the rest of their party trailing a bit behind.

"His Majesty disp—"

"I was speaking to the prince." Sean interrupted the soldier, his eyes trained on Braden, and at once the other man silenced himself.

There it was again, that casual confidence other men had. That control over the rest of the world. His father had such confidence, and his brother. But Braden had always thought it a royal thing until he entered Rowan's world and found all these common men with such uncommon strength. He didn't understand it.

"Rowan has vanished. She made off in the middle of the night, four nights ago. We are heading to a town near the sea where there was a report of a sighting," Braden explained, choosing his words with care. All true, but very...unfinished.

Sean eyed Braden for a silent moment. No one would find anything strange about it, Sean was frequently silent, but Braden felt a studied difference.

Sean glanced side long at the lieutenant and nodded over his shoulder.

"Proceed, the prince will follow presently."

They waited until the soldiers were out of hearing, then Sean raised a brow and Andrew leaned in eagerly.

"Rowan and the king had a falling out after some private things about his past were revealed."

"She left because of the affair?" Andrew nodded. "I did think we should have told her."

"No." Braden shook his head. "*Rowan* revealed things the king did not know about his own past," Braden felt like he ought to protect the man's privacy, but he'd driven his daughter from the safety of her home for this secret. It would only serve him right to have it spread far and wide. "It seems King Flint was not his father. Colum is."

Andrew gasped, but Sean in usual fashion displayed not even a little shock.

"When he found out, he disinherited Rowan," Braden went on.

"What!" Sean shouted so loudly he unsettled his mount, and had it dancing sideways. It should have relieved or amused Braden seeing the man lose a bit of control. But it made him sad instead. This was the reaction that would have kept Rowan at home. Utter shock and anger in her defense. Her knights truly were her family.

"At first she was putting up with it," Braden said as Sean regained control of his mount. "She did nothing though the king disbanded her court, and put an end to the training of women soldiers that she had begun. But it was building up on her and she left."

Braden opened his mouth, to say more, but stopped. He should not tell them the truth Rowan had asked him to keep from the others. But he was saved speaking at all by Sean.

"But we weren't home, and Ardal cannot travel. Who did she take with her?"

"No one," Braden replied quietly.

"And you did not stop her?" Andrew shouted, vehemently.

"No one could have," Braden defended himself. "She was determined. There are search parties all over the kingdom responding to different reports, but I doubt any of them will find her."

"Of course they won't. She knows better than to go near roads and towns if she is trying to get away undetected," Sean snapped as if offended by the very idea. "What do Colum and Ardal say about all of this?"

Braden ground his teeth and forced himself to pull up his head and only speak the truth. "Colum and Ardal were...deferential to the king's orders. To the point where Rowan felt they were taking his side."

"They...but..." Andrew tried repeatedly to find his words at such an event.

"I did not want her to train when she was fifteen," Sean said so softly you would think another man were speaking. "I didn't like the idea of such a little bit plopped down among us brutes."

Braden grinned to hear Rowan described as a *little bit*. He supposed it was a matter of perspective, Sean was a large man in everything from height to muscle, beside him quite a few people were little bits. But usually quiet Sean was suddenly poetically moved.

"But when she fought she twinkled like a girl with a posey. And when she won she *blazed*— a fire of passion and energy. Woke the whole world, she did. I didn't want her to train—until the moment her father tried to take it from her, and I saw her fire dampened. How could they let him steal more from her? That was the oath we took, not to protect her, but to protect her fire."

Andrew seemed as stunned to silence as Braden felt. It was so true and so... shocking. Who knew Sean had such depth of feeling in him.

Sean pulled up on his reins as if to make his way around Braden but he paused. "You know she is not where you are searching?"

Braden nodded carefully.

Sean nodded again and again, looking into his lap. "Good man. Keep her secrets. Protect her fire." His knees squeezed the horse and he took off around Braden. Andrew and their squires followed behind.

Braden sat on the crest of the hill a moment more. His eyes caught on the palace, with the bright colorful array of roses growing up its eastern face.

Woke the world, she did.

What part of it would she wake next?

Other Worlds

Rowan woke to the sound of a struggle. She had been sleeping in the cover of a dense thicket of shrubbery about a mile from a small village. She'd ventured into the village when it was dark and stolen vegetables from an obliging field. She felt bad, stealing from her own citizens, but she would repay them when she returned. Once she'd stolen the food, she and Yseult had found a marginally comfortable place to bed down for the night, where no one would see them. Rowan liked being near the village.

The dragons were clearly leading her different places with a purpose. A positive purpose, she thought. And she'd wound up here, though she'd been avoiding roads and structures that could be seen at a distance. This village had snuck up on her, when she and Yseult emerged from a wood, there it was before them.

It was different from Stones Throw and Seaguard the only villages in her nation Rowan had properly visited. It had several homes spread about and a few with farms at its outer edges, one or two with a great deal of livestock. But in the center of the circle the village made was an open area, with wooden stalls around its perimeter that must be a market in the daylight. There were a few homes near the center of town, but most were further out, and even the ones that could not be called farms had little gardens. There were fires burning in most of the homes, and candles lighting the windows.

Rowan lay a long while looking towards those lights and trying to imagine the lives of the people inside. Every place she passed was so different, and she'd never even wondered about them. She couldn't help but wonder now. There was so much to her nation. She didn't know her roads.

Rowan fought the tears building in her eyes. It hurt to think of her father, in good moments or in bad. Every time she thought of him she would see again his pleasure as he ripped into her heart and tore her apart. How pleased he was when he convinced Colum and Ardal to turn on her as well.

How hard had it truly been to convince them? She knew they loved her. They believed in her abilities as a knight. Maybe even as a leader, but her court had always deferred to father when he was in the room. Why had she never considered what that meant? They saw him as the ultimate leader. Despite years of encouraging her, and taking her orders, and supporting her as she went behind her father's back to fight Sorcha. Despite all of that, when it came to a choice between Rowan and her father they chose their king. Rowan was a...usurper.

They think they are following a queen and you are not one and may never be.

The words made Rowan's teeth ache from clenching so hard, her entire body coiled tight. Knowing that she would one day be queen had at times scared her... dwarfed her, even inspired her. And he wanted to take it away as soon as she had truly wanted it. Well...it wasn't just a desire now. When she'd run away in the night she'd thought that she had accepted his disownment. Felt certain she could be easier without that responsibility. But the more Rowan saw of her roads, and *her* nation, the more certain she became that being queen of Stonedragon was now an eventuality.

She would be queen, because the more she saw the more Rowan wanted to know her nation, the more she wanted to meet her citizens and understand their lives. She wanted to work a farm, or learn to fish, or work in a smithy. She wanted to understand them. Not just ride the roads and see they were in good condition, but know what her people needed of her, and *be* it.

She wanted to be the queen they deserved.

Even in the days when she had expected to die of this battle, some part of her had known she would be queen. Almost as if the sacrifice of her life would be what made her their queen, she wouldn't rule, but she would be of such a service to her nation that she would be remembered as their queen. But it was all different now.

It was on that thought that Rowan had rolled over, determined to sleep. And she was awakened by clear sounds of a fight. She heard a strangled cry and the strike of flesh on flesh and rolled awake. It was fortunate that she had chosen to forgo armor every night in order to sleep, it would have made far too much noise for her to sneak over. It was dark enough that no one would be able to take a proper description of her back to her father, so Rowan left behind her sword, the carved rose on the hilt made it immediately recognizable. She slid the staff her packs were looped around free and tip-toed nearer to see what was happening.

"I don't know anything. I swear!"

"You wouldn't lie to me, would you, *love*." A man in a dark heavy cloak was restraining a struggling woman. He had her held up against him with an arm locked around her waist and pressed a knife to her throat.

Rowan's heart jumped for a terrifying moment. How was she to get the woman free before she fought the man? She'd never thought of such scenarios, only fighting an enemy directly or fighting several enemies, but never fighting with would-be victims near to be harmed.

Were the knife held on Rowan so, at her throat but not against it, she would jab up her arm between them at the same time as she was kicking back. Protecting her throat while she was attacking. But this woman wouldn't know to do that. If Rowan attacked from behind he might slit her throat accidentally. But what if she waited too long, and he intended to do that anyway?

"You wanting the bounty for yourself?" the man asked menacingly.

"I didn't even know there was a bounty. I swear I've never seen the princess!"

Rowan lay the staff against the side of the tree and stepped out of the shadows trying to appear casual. She had to get the woman away from the knife, that was the first aim.

"Good evening, fellow travelers," Rowan said lightly as Cassidy or Liam might and walked fully into the path through the wood lit only by moonlight.

"Who are you? What are you doing out so late, alone?" the man growled.

"What's this reward you mentioned?" Rowan countered.

She was slowly edging forward, but the man, though clearly confident in his power, was not a fool, he took regular steps away from her.

"Not a reward, a bounty," the thug snarled. "All of you women have been puffed up by that princess. You think you can talk back, and wander the roads alone. And fight." He spat. "You are going to learn your proper place again. The crowned princess ran away from her father. But she will be found, and you will all watch as the king shows her her *proper* place. Then you'll remember yours."

"Will they?" Rowan asked in a low, forbidding tone.

She vanished behind the man, unconcerned now that he might know who she was. She reappeared behind the man, and yanked his knife wielding arm high as she kicked him in the back of the knee. The woman he'd held went tumbling away. The man jerked around with an enraged growl, swinging his fist for Rowan's gut. But she was too fast, she leapt backwards and rolled away. Grabbing up the staff, she swung it for the man's head.

He was a thug of the lowest order, but he was a better fighter than Rowan had guessed. He caught the staff as she swung it for him, and yanked on it trying to pull her near. Rowan released the staff and his own force sent him stumbling back a few steps, but he had her staff now, and swung out for her knees.

Rowan actually laughed as she leapt over it. Balance was no longer a struggle for her and for every swing he missed he tired himself out and woke Rowan's powerful competitive spirit. He was growing enraged, swinging more and more wildly, advancing on Rowan the more she danced away. Rowan hadn't felt this alive since running away from home. This was what she needed. Someone to fight. Someone to defeat!

Brazenly confident, Rowan stopped moving. She stood right before the man and held still as he swung the staff over his head and down to beat in her skull. She waited until the very last second and vanished from his path. He tumbled to the ground. The staff struck first and bounced up to strike him in the face. Rowan reappeared behind him, and slammed his head against a tree trunk. He fell unconscious.

Once he was laying in a ditch near the thicket of trees Rowan had been sleeping in, she bent forward and pulled the staff out from under him.

She stood grinning and swung to face the woman she'd rescued. Her citizen. The woman stood several feet away holding the knife between both of her hands with her shoulders hunched around it.

"It will work better if you stand tall. And don't just swing with your arms, when you strike, use your hips and back, that's where the power is." Rowan instructed, moving her body to show the proper motion. It was exciting to be able to pass on her knowledge if only to this one woman and in passing.

Rowan ought to wake Yseult and press on despite the hour.

"You like those you fight to be a challenge?" the woman croaked.

Rowan rolled her tongue across her teeth, as the question sapped away bits of Rowan's excitement.

"I do." Rowan nodded. "Which is why I suppose I'll let you go."

The woman startled, she looked down at the knife in her hands and back up at Rowan. She shook her head and a smile grew on her lips. "I didn't mean that." She lowered the knife. "You are Princess Rowan, aren't you? The women who've seen you fight say you are powerful, and strong as a man. But they never said...you like it. You like it when they are a challenge and you win anyway."

"Oh." Rowan's stomach dropped a bit in embarrassment. "Yes. Every time I beat someone challenging, I feel more powerful, and more prepared."

"I'd prefer a fight I know I can win, if I must have one," the woman remarked, staring down at the man in the ditch. "Have you any rope? I can tie him and hide him for a few days, while you make good your escape."

"You want me to escape?" Rowan asked. The man's words running through her mind, with Peg's mixed in *A few days will be too late. Our right to safety will be seen as a kindness women are allowed when men are in a giving mood.*

She should have fought Father harder. There should have been more than five women training. As soon as she knew things like this happened she should have dispatched knights to all her villages, just to defend her women. But how was she to know which men were good and which were not? How was she to defend her sisters and her nation, and prepare for Sorcha, and be the kind of daughter her father could love?

She needed to leave, but part of her looked at the woman so uneasy with the weapon in her hands, so at risk on the roads of her own home and she wanted to stay. Rowan wanted to slay the beasts that roamed the land looking harmless. She could ride the roads of her kingdom and beat the brutes out of her people. That, Rowan could do with ease.

She glanced down at the unconscious man on the road.

"Do you know, at first I think I wanted it to be easy as well," Rowan admitted. "I liked winning when others thought I wouldn't, but I wanted it to be easy. I wanted to simply be more powerful than all of them. But I learned that it is more satisfying when I overcome the struggle."

The woman slid the knife into the belt of her girdle and smiled. "I do not know why you are leaving," the woman said. "There are only rumors. But when one of us escapes, all of us see it is possible."

"You *all* want to escape Stonedragon?" Rowan asked, appalled that she had not realized it was so bad.

The woman laughed. "Just our own oppressors, like him. Sometimes one needs to see it is possible."

Rowan took the words into herself and let them drift through her as she helped the woman truss up her attacker. They threw him over Yseult's back and walked down the path towards the village. When they had nearly reached the nearest home Rowan poked her head up above the unconscious man and looked at her companion.

"If you are unsafe, look to the women I have trained, or the Knights of the Rose. They will help you."

The woman regarded Rowan quietly. "Do you ever mean to come back?" she asked, her voice trembling a bit, betraying her discomfort with asking such a thing.

"Of course," Rowan replied. "I simply...cannot do all that I must to protect my sisters and my kingdom from within that palace. I need to be different from the women our world is comfortable seeing. And my father does not understand. Yet." It was the best excuse Rowan could make for him and even that felt too kind.

After a quiet stretch the woman smiled softly. "Have heart, Your Majesty," the woman said. "I have faith you can overcome this struggle as well."

389 days until Roisin returns

Colum didn't like the state of the nation he was crossing. It was too quiet. He hadn't traveled with a company of knights in many years, but the world could not have changed so much. When these villagers, farmers, and soldiers saw the knights approaching they averted their eyes, hid in their homes. It wasn't natural.

Even if they lived in fear of an attack, small children always darted into the path of approaching knights. Men stood tall and glared down their invaders. Something was very wrong. Colum had known it the moment he entered Turrlough, even the animals seemed quieter. He also knew the closer they grew to the palace that he would not find Rowan here.

Something was quite wrong, and if Rowan had passed this way she would have been about setting it right. He could not believe he had been so careless with her, could not believe his chastisement was the last thing she heard from him before fleeing. She couldn't truly believe he thought she should be disinherited. That wasn't what he'd been trying to say. He'd just wanted...he didn't know. He'd wanted her to be more circumspect in front of knights that were not her own. She'd worked so hard over the years to make more men see her value. The Knights of the Rose were fifteen now though they'd begun as only four. He hadn't wanted her to lose that in one day. And he wanted her to have more control over her temper, her tongue, and herself.

He'd been asking of her what he could not of her father. He'd wanted her to be better than the king, better than every man Colum had ever trained—better than himself.

He held Rowan to impossible standards. When had that happened? When she trained as a girl he wanted every man to see her value without her having to prove it. He wanted them bowing to her as their queen. But somehow he'd come to a place of waiting for her to prove her value.

It could not have only been those last few days. It was not only because of what he learned of the king. That only shoved it into the open.

It had more to do with Petal. Things between he and Rowan had changed the moment Colum saw his *little flower petal* knighted. Until then Rowan was his other girl, the daughter of his heart. He'd seen her worth a hundred times more highly than those around her, and he wanted everyone else to see it too. But when she asked for Petal, when his daughter was taken away, there were days when Colum—who had loved Rowan before he knew her—had doubted her. He had wondered if the curse might not make her murder her sister as it was intended to do. He'd doubted her.

Though he did not realize it, even when they became close again, Colum was trying to force Rowan to prove herself worthy of the faith he'd put in her. He wanted her to prove she was strong enough to win, good enough to protect his Petal. He'd needed to know that Rowan and the cause she called them to were worthy of the sacrifice Petal had already made.

He'd been pushing Rowan more than even he knew, and she fought to give him every assurance he sought. She threw herself into work when that was all he would give her, or offered her love again and again, tried to connect them all to Petal, fought to protect his sons and keep them bound with love. And what did he do, when she needed him to simply take her part? He told her to bend again.

Now she was gone. And nowhere in Turrlough. Were he being honest with himself when he rode away from Stonedragon he would have admitted he never thought to find her here. Based on what Ardal had said, Rowan had been doubting Prince Gavin as recently as a month ago. And every other man she trusted had betrayed her. Rowan would go back to trusting the only person she ever really had, herself. Maureen was right to have yelled at him, right to have refused to speak with him before he left.

It had broken Colum's heart to hear of Rowan doubting her beau when Ardal told him, but Colum had done nothing to reassure her. Because the thoughts roused doubts in him as well. He should have reassured her. He should have remembered how it was for Maureen in the beginning, when she had become doubtful and...angry when Colum voiced his love for the first time. How every show of love must be doubted, because she did not see her worth. He hadn't thought Rowan was that similar to Maureen. They had worked hard to show Rowan their love, hadn't they? But she still doubted her worth. She still doubted any love was forever. And she had all the more reasons now.

Turrlough Palace was the smallest castle on the island, it did not even boast a wall around it for defense. It was little wonder this nation of farmers had either been occupied by, or joined forces with every conquering force on this island at one time or another. A soldier wouldn't flourish in such a nation. But Rowan's beau...his letters made him out to be more poet than soldier. Colum knew he was a decent fighter, and his collusion with Rowan said at least he would not give in to the world around him. But if the state of his citizens were any sign, the prince, whether poet or fighter, was not flourishing here.

Colum dismounted outside the palace, leaving his horse in the hold of one of his men and climbed the three steps that led to the double doors of the palace. Before his hand could raise to knock he saw the first promising signs of life from this kingdom: a squadron of soldiers ran out from alcoves along the palace walls and formed a semi-circle around his knights with weapons drawn. One soldier moved through the line to the foot of the steps facing Colum.

"State your business," he ordered.

"We are knights in the service of King Balder of Stonedragon seeking an audience with crown prince Gavin of Turrlough."

"No member of the royal family can be seen, this is a nation of mourning," the soldier said sharply, and turned to leave, offering no more information.

Colum moved after the man. "Has King Thaddeus died?" Colum demanded. "Our deepest regrets, but—"

"The king lives," the soldier spun around to snarl. "It is his son and heir who has died. Your business—"

"Prince Gavin is dead?" A shocked murmur moved amongst the knights, and Colum's heart plummeted. "How? What has happened?"

"This is not your kingdom! None of our suffering would have happened if we stayed out of the business of other nations. Leave, or we will see you as a threat and act accordingly."

"Wait, please," Colum stopped the man with a hand at his shoulder. "We will leave, but my king dispatched me to find his daughter and I cannot return to him with such a lack of knowledge. How did this terrible tragedy occur?"

The soldier looked Colum over with contempt. "His daughter is one girl. We lost scores and what did Stonedragon do but offer us more tragedy? Tell your king no citizen of Stonedragon is welcome here. We no longer make friends with those whom the Fairy queen makes enemies."

He turned his back then and walked out motioning the soldiers to fall back and allow Colum and his men to depart. Colum stared after the soldiers at a loss. Gavin was dead.

He recalled the first time he'd ever caught Rowan reading one of the boy's letters, and blushing. Recalled her demanding a minstrel teach her the song of Branduff, because it was the prince's favorite. She'd sung it terribly through her exercises for a month. She still would when she was in a good mood, though the song was a terrible tragedy, and her voice was a strangled mess. And she wore those bells he'd given her everywhere, to practice, to balls, likely to sleep. Prince Gavin had been so much a part of Rowan's life for years now that everyone expected he would be Rowan's husband. But he was gone. One more thing ripped away from Rowan and at the very same time. And she was alone. What if she was alone when she learned this? What would become of her hope?

Slowly, Colum descended the steps and mounted his horse. From the corner of his eye he saw a face in a window high above him, Colum looked up absently, his mind full of other things. A little girl was shaking her head wildly, seeming to beg them to stay. Before he could do much more than see her, a woman came forward and yanked her away, throwing a heavy black curtain over the window. A mourning shroud over the entire palace.

He needed to get home. Maureen needed to know, so they could find Rowan together. Rowan had never lost a love like this before, it could destroy her.

Queen Aya yanked Elish away from the window, turning her into her chest and silencing Elish's voice by pressing her face firmly into her shoulder.

"What's going on in here?"

Elish stopped fighting at the sound of the fairy's voice behind her. She shouldn't have been so loud trying to get the attention of the soldiers below. Now she would be punished, like Prince Owen had been. Or her voice stolen like Finnola's or—or she could be killed like...

She should have kept quiet. But she needed to help. She'd promised Petal she would help.

"It's nothing," Queen Aya said softly, vaguely as if she had no fear, but Elish with her head shoved against the queen's heart could feel it pounding anxiously. "My granddaughter simply had a nightmare."

"It's not yet evening," the fairy observed disbelievingly.

"She'd fallen asleep at her studies," Queen Aya lied easily. "Come, dear."

Queen Aya pushed Elish away, now that she was quiet and not fighting back. "Visit your grandfather with me. I shall tell you both a story."

Queen Aya moved forward with regal ease, pulling Elish along with her silently. Elish went though her feet longed to race back to the window and her voice longed to call out. She had promised to help.

But she glanced over her shoulder as she passed him and saw the suspicious eyes of the fairy watching her. He didn't believe them, but he was letting them be.

And why not. The soldiers were already riding away, and Queen Aya, despite defending Elish would do nothing to fight the fairy guards, lest she risk Prince Owen's life further.

There was nothing Elish could do and the fairy knew it. She wasn't free just because she'd left the Fairy Realm. She and all the other girls had simply traded one prison for another.

Rowan dismounted and forced herself to walk, letting Yseult have her space. They were beginning to rub one another wrong—literally. But Rowan trusted

Yseult not to run off. They were stopped alongside a dry, rocky hill. It had a bundle of willow trees near its base and a little pool of water that appeared to come from nowhere.

It was for the water they had stopped. That and for a brief respite from riding. Days in a saddle was a distinctly unpleasant experience. Every day it grew harder for Yseult to keep up such a relentless, meandering pace. The dragons were leading her all over her kingdom, but she doubted it was much closer to them.

They led her to the edge of a hill overlooking a wide open field. Out beneath the clear sky was a young girl tending a flock of sheep. Rowan watched her for a long while, wondering what her life was like. She looked content alone among her sheep, without much of anything to defend her. Was her world just safe? Or was she resigned to the fact that her fate was not her own to decide? Rowan had never been one to resign to fate. She'd watched the way the girl was headed home and raced ahead of her to leave a dagger in her path.

In truth, if she were taught anything with it, the crook she used to lead the sheep would afford her better protection than the dagger. Distance was an advantage when one was smaller. But Rowan couldn't stay to guard her, or to teach her.

Yseult drew away from the water now and whinnied, shaking her head in distaste. After a moment she simply sunk her face back into the water to lap up as much as she could. As a rule, Rowan had been putting a bit of space between herself and the horse when not riding. Every once in a while Yseult would nip at Rowan to punish her for the discomfort. Rowan approached her now to see what about the water the horse disliked.

Rowan dipped her hand into the water to scoop some up and at once a tingle raced down her spine making her whole being roll with a sensation somewhere between excitement and soothing. She felt the power in it before she even noticed the warmth. Rowan shook the water from her hand and looked around more carefully. She drew her sword but allowed it to hang at her side in her right hand. She didn't exactly feel threatened, but at the same time there was something about this place that didn't feel...safe.

It was quieter here than anywhere she'd been. There were birds in the trees, and animals in the bushes and trees and everything moved, but so quietly. The air had a sizzle to it, as if it was licking at your skin to get a better sense of you. It felt powerful. *Magical.* Rowan lay her left hand on Yseult's flank, and patted twice.

"Stay here," Rowan whispered and edged quietly into the cluster of willow trees. The air began to thicken, heat, and dampen, as though she was walking into the mouth of a living creature. She heard the trickle of running water ahead. When she pushed aside the last fluttering curtain of willow branches she stopped and stared in wonder.

The ground before her was a rocky layered growth. Tiered pools of steaming water rose up towards the widest pool beneath the falls. Even the falls had tilted pools of water. There were scattered willows and plants popping up from between the pools. The largest tier looked wide enough for at least ten people to fit in comfortably. It held a deep pool of steaming water constantly running over its edges, dripping down on, or into, the uneven staircase the other layers of rock formed. Some of the pools were deep, others were like tiny bowls of water not even wide enough for an adult's foot. All of it overflowed with water, even down to ground level where Rowan stood. There were a few middling sized pools of warm water, each with its own kaleidoscopic misty light shifting around it.

This was Dragon's Breath! The hot spring.

Rowan had seen it on a map. She knew the villages closest to it warned travelers away, swearing that magical spirits lived there. But she'd never imagined it would be so lovely. It appeared entirely deserted, reminding Rowan of her rose garden, a magic place she could go into and shut out the world. But...it didn't feel empty. It felt crowded.

A head butted hard into Rowan's shoulder, shoving her forward. Apparently Yseult was not in a listening mood. Rowan took a few steps closer on her own, her boots squishing against the wet ground, and the magical feeling only grew larger. It was immense, slightly overpowering.

Was it the dragons?

Dragons would like a hot spring, wouldn't they? But she'd been so sure the dragons weren't in Stonedragon.

"This is a magic place," Rowan whispered. "But..." She shook her head, leaning into that sizzling feeling. It felt almost like that tingle that raced through Rowan's blood when evil was near. Almost like, yet completely different. Like it was both dangerous and incredibly safe at once. She felt the power pulling at her, calling her to stay, and discover all it had to offer. She could all but hear it. In the trees and bushes all around the animals stilled, waiting to see what she would do.

Rowan's heart fell over and over like a heavy stone, every beat telling her that this was a place where she could find all the answers she'd been seeking about her power. A place where she could grow in magic and knowledge. But this—was a staying place.

This was a place where a curse could fall, and a hundred years could pass, and no one would know. A world inside a world.

That was why she felt it biting at her skin, but couldn't see what she knew was all around her. It wasn't a place of dragons. It was a fairy place. And it was calling out to the fairy part of Rowan. It must be the sacred hot spring.

A memory of Maureen floated before Rowan's eyes in a pocket of colorful mist.

"There are five sacred sources of water around Great Island," Maureen said, her voice full of wonder. It was one of Rowan's magic lessons, but the triplets were sitting in, excited for any tale of magic and fairy. "Each water is a source of power, both known and unknown for magic is unknowable in all its wonder. But each has a specific power that fairy can tap into. Lake Noomah holds the power of travel, if a fairy dips into its waters, it can travel through it to any water in the entire world. The river Liadan holds the power of healing; it cannot stop death, but if one has life left in them the river will preserve it as long as they remain immersed. Ever Spill has the power of cleansing, that is why each new queen walks beneath its waters at her coronation, to cleanse away her fears and be only Fairy queen. The ocean holds the key to long life, fairy and beast alike that live inside it live three ages longer than those who dwell on land. And the sacred hot spring holds the power of seeing. It can show one far and wide on land, or answer the deepest question of their soul, but the answers shift like mist when one steps away. For life begs ever new questions."

It had seemed so...distant and magical when she was younger. She'd never even thought to ask where the hot spring was, because part of her was still terrified of fairy things. She'd wanted to know, but she'd been afraid of any desire but saving her sister. Other desires made her weaker, less worthy.

The mist sunk over Rowan's skin now, waking a new hunger. A hunger to know. She leaned towards the water as though it were a rich banquet.

Rowan's free hand moved back and found the whistle hanging from Yseult's bridle without looking. She felt it pulsing against her skin, neither burning nor soothing, just waiting like her heavy heartbeat, like the animals in the trees, waiting for Rowan to make up her mind.

"There are so many parts of this world I never knew existed. So much power and beauty." Rowan's fingers loosened one by one from around the whistle and she bent towards the closest pool. In the back of her mind she heard a voice telling her she would know all, see all the secrets this place had to offer if she just drank from that hot spring.

"So much, and I just stayed in my tower," Rowan whispered. "Why are you showing me this, when you know I cannot stay?"

A breeze swirled around her, gently stirring the untamable strands of her hair that were escaping her braid. "Can't you?" the breeze seemed to ask, not in a voice so much as in the manner in which it tugged at those wilder bits of Rowan. It asked in the stirring she felt across her skin. It promised wonder and answers, and *power*. Rowan had never thought she longed for power, but more and more she saw the urge in herself.

The rainbow lights of the pool before her shifted vibrant and bright, beckoning her nearer. Offering her its power, if she drank.

When Rowan had cursed Braden she'd relished the power. When her father disinherited her she'd felt such urges to unleash the full potential of her magic, and show him he could not stop her. Even when she'd used her magic to fight that man in the road, when she was entirely in control and more powerful, she'd felt charged from that too. If she stayed here she was sure to find power like she hadn't felt before.

Rowan could be wild. Connect with more of her Fairy heritage. She could rival Sorcha. Wouldn't that service her cause?

Rowan bent towards the water. She wanted to taste it. She wanted to know what it could show her. But the closer to the water she grew the more the water faded from her sight and a pair of eyes haunted her. Petal's. Every day that Rowan delayed cost Petal more of her beautiful intrepid spirit. This was a place Petal should see, with her brothers on either side of her, and laughter filling the air, and Maureen walking slowly behind watching them all with her warm smile.

Rowan almost thought she saw just that in the shifting misty light of the highest pool. It could be her imagination, her hunger to stay, that showed it to her. Or it could be the magic that permeated everything from ground to water, to air in this place.

Rowan released the whistle entirely and knelt on the ground with her sword trapped beneath her hand. She dipped her fingers into the warm water again and felt it soothing her aches, perhaps even some of her worries. Oh, this place had far more magic than just showing far and wide.

Rowan lifted her palm, cupped with a bit of water pooled inside. Could it show her her mother?

Rowan shut her eyes and tilted her head back. She ached so much. She ached from all the places inside her, pockets like the tiny hot springs surrounding her, only her pockets weren't overflowing, they were empty, longing for the loves she'd been denied.

"Your mother made me promise I would love you."

Rowan dashed the water back into the spring.

"He does love me," Rowan shouted as if someone else had brought the thought to mind.

She knew her father loved her. But she wanted to stomp back home and grab him by the shoulders and shake and shake and shake him until he swore it. Until he shouted it from the highest parapet of the palace. Until he promised nothing could ever take his love away. And she wanted to sob, because she didn't want to have to force the words from him. She wanted to lay down on the ground and shut her eyes and imagine a contented life like that shepherdess. But whenever she tried to picture such a life she didn't fit there. She didn't even fit in a world of her own imagining. What made her think she could possibly fit here? Fairy

Rowan shoved to her feet with more energy than she felt. This place might hold all the answers, but just now, she wasn't sure she wanted any of them. Fairy secrets always hid from her.

"Come along." Rowan tugged lightly at Yseult's bridle with one hand, sheathing her sword with the other. "We're wasting daylight."

Rowan tugged the reins toward the pommel to mount, but the horse pulled back sharply. Rowan braced for another bite, but Yseult surprised her, lifting her head, she licked away the tears Rowan hadn't realized she was crying. Rowan sighed and lay her head against Yseult's.

"Thank you."

After a moment, Yseult allowed Rowan to mount. As she swung her leg over the saddle she thought she saw figures standing in the pool, whole groups of fairy watching her. But when she was seated the figures were gone.

One day she would be back and force these fairy to acknowledge her, but for today she had dragons to find, and sisters to save. She couldn't afford to stay here seeking the deepest answers her soul sought. Like everything else, her soul would just have to wait.

Stronger Forces

388 days until Roisin returns

Rowan was fairly certain she was in the Enchanted Forest proper now, not just the bit of it that started on Stonedragon's land. The trees moved around when she slept. It made her smile to see it this morning. She'd gone to sleep under a tree that looked like a woman with her long hair blowing in the breeze, all its branches had been leaning one way, and its trunk leaned away from the branches and had a large protrusion, that looked exactly like a nose. But when she woke in the morning she was under an entirely different tree, its branches growing out like a tent, almost as though it were mocking her for not having brought anything to construct a protective structure. That or it was protecting her since she'd failed to do so herself.

There were several things Rowan had forgotten to bring, and their absence forced her to see things she'd taken for granted: a comfortable bed, a roof over her head, someone preparing all her food. That one was especially missed, both because she had no idea how to prepare food, and because she hadn't thought to bring any. For the last few days she'd been living on the food she'd stolen from farms. But she had no idea how to prepare it so it had been eaten entirely raw, and that was a very different business. Some vegetables seemed tastier that way, but most were bitter or had an entirely different texture she found unsettling, but she forced herself to eat it all. She hadn't had any meat, nor bread, or anything resembling a proper meal, and all she drank was water.

She should have begged food off the girl she rescued. She should have thought ahead and packed food. And she certainly should have been more grateful for the food and the shelter and the *baths.* Oh, she missed a proper *warm* bath—and soap! Her hair was getting to be an awful mess. There was plenty she had taken for granted. If she had run away simply because she was angry with her father, Rowan would have headed home on the third day of her adventure.

It was pleasing in an odd way, to be without so many things, it reaffirmed the necessity of her course. She would go on, without her comforts, knowing she could have them all at home, even if she had to bend to get them. She could be safe, and clean and fed, and she could even go on preparing to face Sorcha, the same way she always had. All of that waited for her at home. But out here there was something she needed and it drove her despite the discomfort of riding a horse all day, every day, and the discomfort of rocky ground, and a near empty belly. And the loneliness that had stolen over her since she passed by Dragon's Breath.

She was walking beside Yseult through the forest now. It was good for both of them. Yseult was tiring from working so hard, and Rowan needed to exercise her legs. She should likely exercise a bit with her sword as well. She didn't want her muscles to grow fatigued from lack of use. But now she just walked along through the forest, smelled the air and watched the trees waiting to see if they would get up and move before her eyes.

"Roisin lives here somewhere," Rowan whispered. She liked talking to Yseult, the horse never responded with words, but Rowan was certain she understood. She'd helped Rowan puzzle through many things already. "I imagine we aren't headed that way, but this is her home. Where the trees move in the night, and the air is almost silent. It's never silent at home. I wonder if she'll like it, when I bring her home."

Rowan wanted to correct herself the moment the words were out. Her tongue began to curl in preparing to say "if". But she forced herself to leave the words as she'd spoken them. *When.* She would save Roisin, she would save Petal, she would defeat Sorcha. It was only a matter of time, and of effort. So she walked on.

When she was riding the bells at her ankle would take on a jaunty rhythm with the pounding of Yseult's hooves, almost a song. But just now as she stepped they all plopped against her ankle together, seeming to say a single word, over and over: look.

It was hard to ignore in this quiet. All of the animals had been driven off. Rowan hadn't really thought about how such a thing might affect even the air. But it was quieter, colder...hungrier. This air wanted something to happen. It wanted activity. It wanted Rowan to look.

There was an odd feel to the forest. Like the hot spring but not quite the same. It was a magical place, and fairy lived here but it didn't feel like a Fairy place. It felt like this forest owned a magic all its own. And it wanted Rowan to look. To travel in her mind as she had not since the first day of her journey.

She'd been wary of looking. She didn't know exactly what she'd seen, but it wasn't good. She'd felt it like a lance through her heart. She couldn't be sure if something of how she traveled was what made the difference.

What if traveling with betrayal and worry coursing through her was what brought pain into the lives of those she loved?

"It doesn't make practical sense. It's not as though Sorcha felt me travel and decided to hurt people as a result. She curses and destroys and manipulates, I don't make her do it." Rowan stopped moving, couldn't bear for the bells to make another noise, but nor could she take them off, even to hide them in one of her packs.

To take them off would feel like giving in, like her heart believed Gavin was gone. She couldn't allow herself to do that.

"Yseult, when I traveled, every other time the things I saw would fill me up with hope. But I went with seeds of it already in my heart. And the day I left I didn't feel any hope. I don't make her do it. But, I felt so *devastated* as though everyone I had ever loved was turning against me and I—"

Rowan jerked away and the bells jangled—*look.*

"There were so few people on my side, but *Maureen* was." Rowan rubbed the palm of her right hand where her thorn scars used to be. "Maureen is always on my side, so I...hid what Petal had done. Because it was my fault. Any pain Petal is feeling, any betrayal she has to perpetrate to stay safe, all of it is my fault. She was the brightest, happiest, sweetest child in the world and I put her in the path of evil for my own ends.

"Maureen is *always* on my side. But for how long? How long can she continue forgiving me? What will become of me when it's too much? What will I be when there is no one left on my side?" Rowan asked and her drowning eyes began to spill into the world. "That is what Sorcha wants. No matter what I try to do, I help her get it. That is how I traveled, frightened and angry and lonely. And I felt all the same things from Petal."

Rowan shuddered and the bells let out an anxious little tinkle.

"And Gavin..." Rowan shook her head. "I don't know what happened to him, but it was terrible." Rowan ground the heel of her hand against her chest, against her heart. "I can't look again until I have hope to take with me. I can't. I might hurt them more. She is always inside of me. Always weaving her way between the chinks in my armor to pierce through me. *You poison everything you touch.*

"I wanted so badly to be rid of those words, but I am not. I may never be. And I can't—I just can't go when they are so loud in my mind."

Rowan stared at Yseult, waiting for the horse, to do something supportive, or to nudge her into doing what she wasn't ready for. Anything. The whole forest was silent, waiting on the horse. But Yseult just stared at Rowan, with huge sympathetic eyes. The wind picked up around them. It blew through the chambers of the dragon pendant hanging from Yseult's neck, the hum urging Rowan on.

Rowan nodded. She wiped the tears from her face and allowed herself to trust a stronger force than her own right now. She followed the sound.

"I think it might be best to have Maureen's children join us for dinner, so—"

"Why?" Balder demanded of his wife with a snap.

Gwyneth pulled in a slow deep breath and pretended her pulse hadn't jumped with his raised voice. He hadn't frightened her in the past. He used to be the safest man she'd ever met.

Something terrible was happening to his personality without Rowan here. No, Gwyneth admitted to herself it wasn't Rowan's absence alone that had effected this change. It was that secret. That secret she'd wanted him to know so badly. She could not believe Rowan had been right to hide it. It was why he was so quick to anger now. He thought she was trying to make him befriend his half siblings.

"They are defacing Roisin's statues, and changing the banners largely to get your attention, Balder. They think you've forgotten Rowan. They want to be her champions. But if they speak to you, if they know you want her home they will be easier."

"Who says I want her home?" Balder said without much heat, moving to the large high table in the middle of the room where he'd begun the plans for Roisin's party again. It had been over a year since Gwyneth had seen those plans. She desperately wanted to walk over, and lay her hands against those pages; they had always given her such hope. But she dared not take even a single step.

Balder lifted a page and a certain calm came over him that he did not display anywhere but at this table. An absence of worry. Gwyneth watched and wondered if that beautiful feeling she recalled was indeed hope at all. Or if it was only her mind hiding her from any real emotion.

"I know you want her home," Gwyneth said gently. "Balder, darling, I promise she is only...hurt. When one is young every pain is more intense. Every desire more urgent, but time will temper that. She loves you."

Balder looked up, his eyes found hers across the distance and seemed for a moment to question what she was speaking of at all. Then he shook his head and looked away.

"Rowan is fine. She is all powerful, apparently. She knows what she is doing. She is worthy of the dragon pendant. She is followed by *my* subjects." He lay down one page and lifted another, shifting the scraps around the table. "I think it's the Fairy blood. Sorcha warned me she would destroy all I held dear."

Gwyneth gasped, but Balder seemed not to hear her. He was not himself.

"But not Roisin," he said with resonant certainty. Gwyneth sighed, at least he still trusted Rowan with their daughter. It was so strange worrying about that. She used to be the one who wanted Rowan kept away from their daughter. She used to be the one who thought Rowan dangerous and headstrong. Now she saw Rowan as...a lone tower of strength and devotion.

"Roisin will be different," Balder said. "She will be sweet and biddable and *ours*. No one will take her love from us."

"Balder, no one took Rowan's—"

"It won't be much longer now." Balder's eyes shot up and captured Gwyneth's with their frantic intensity. "Roisin will come home and we will be a family again."

Gwyneth nodded. Couldn't seem to do anything more than that. He looked so different, at once wildly intense with need and steeped in an otherworldly calm. It seemed such a lovely escape, those plans. A pleasant dream to wander through, where their daughter was home and they were family again and all was peaceful.

Gwyneth had never imagined Rowan there. Not once.

All those years when Gwyneth planned Roisin's return with Balder. When she had tried to shame Rowan by asking her to help knowing she would not. In all that time she'd never once pictured Rowan as part of that beautiful existence. It had never occurred to her to wonder if it was the same for Balder. Looking at him now Gwyneth was sure it was so.

All those years when he'd planned with her, he would be wholly hers. Then Rowan would come in and part of him left her. Part of him rejoined Rowan, in reality. But Rowan wasn't here, and the longer he went without her to pull him from that void, the further he grew from Rowan. From Gwyneth. From anyone.

That party was such a lovelier place than reality. *Who I am, is the person who tucked him into bed like a child after he told me I should die so he could see Roisin once more...*Gwyneth heard Rowan's voice in her head as she watched her husband immerse himself in a fantasy where he could forget all the pain he'd caused. *I am the one who pulled him out from under Sorcha's spell.*

Gwyneth walked slowly forward. Through all those thousands of days as everyone else counted down awaiting Roisin's return, Rowan had kept the curse at bay—for all of them. Rowan had worked to bring her sister home, and fought with all her might to keep this kingdom free from the Fairy queen's grasp. It seemed rather unlikely that Rowan would be coming home to do so any time soon. So Gwyneth would have to do something for Rowan for a change, and protect the family she knew her step-daughter still loved.

Gwyneth lay a hand gingerly over her husband's, lowering the page, and drawing his gaze. "It is dinner time. Come along. The party can wait until tomorrow."

Balder nodded, but his fingers would not release the page. Gwyneth's hands shook as she reached out to take it. What if touching it was all it took? What if the curse captured her so easily?

She closed two fingers around the page and gave a soft tug. It slipped free of Balder's hands and at once Gwyneth opened her fingers, afraid to touch it even one second more than was necessary. She could actually feel the page calling out to her, promising everything would be alright.

Balder moved heavily around the table, his worry and anxiety weighing him down more with each step he took from those plans. He held out the crook of his arm, and Gwyneth silently slipped her arm into it. As they walked from the room Gwyneth's eyes strayed back to that table, and her voice emerged in a whisper.

"I do not think we should go near that table for a while." She could feel Balder beside her understanding why, but he did not respond. "It is so tempting to dream— But I think *both* your daughters need you to stay awake."

Balder squeezed her arm in silent agreement and they walked away from their fantasy.

"There must be something to do about him," Sean snapped.

He was with Maureen, Andrew, Tom and Liam, the latter two had returned only this morning and all were as appalled as Sean had been to learn of Rowan's departure and the events that led to it. Sean expected to be easier about it by now. Rowan was strong, if she'd left with a purpose she would achieve it. But more and more he saw people either pleased with her absence, or seeming not to mark it at all. And his anger grew. The curse was falling again.

Worse, it was falling on those who had never been affected. Ardal was sunken into a deep depression. He refused to leave his cottage, kept saying he wanted to die. But when the subject of Rowan was raised he seemed not to know who she was. He wallowed in his misery over the loss of his legs, over his uselessness. And the longer he complained the more true his words became.

"One of you stab him and have done with it," Maureen suggested. Sean knew she didn't mean it, but among soldiers her words were taken very much to heart, and as angry as they all were over Ardal's role in Rowan's departure there were those among them who might do it.

"I would," Tom said first, oddly. He still had not spoken of what had passed between him and Ardal when they were trapped, but he tended towards trying to protect Ardal. "But I think Rowan might object. Do you know...I would swear, somedays in that cave the waves didn't splash, they called out in her voice. 'Come back to me, Ardal.'" Tom laughed. He looked around sheepishly. "I know she loves us all, but I do not fool myself that it is equal."

"Oh, do not complain," Maureen grumbled. "I've had quite my fill of whining men. Rowan would stave off death for any of you."

"I am not complaining. Truly. I only meant...she will forgive him." Tom shrugged. "So we may want to find a way that doesn't cost his life. Satisfying as that would be for a time."

"Ardal wasn't much keen on living when he came back, how did Rowan help him then?" Liam asked.

Maureen shrugged. Despite what anyone might expect of her, in Rowan's absence Maureen had become their leader, and not a sweet resigning one either. She was sharp and demanding as any general. Colum did have a way of finding all the interesting women in the world.

"She gave him a purpose," Maureen said with a bitter snarl. "Asked him to keep all her secrets and advise her."

Sean nodded. "Well, he failed. His new purpose should be simpler."

Maureen chuckled evilly and winked at Sean. "Aye, that it should be."

"Are you saying that having a purpose can pull one from under the spell? Or are we only trying to keep him out of the grave?" Andrew inquired.

"To be pulled from under the spell requires a few things," Maureen replied. "He needs to remember Rowan, remember his love for her. And now that he's failed her, he will have to fight off the curse without her aid, and prove his love. A purpose might help him remember her, but the rest he shall have to do for himself."

"Perhaps not," Liam said, shaking his head. "What we need is a purpose that serves Rowan's ends. We need to reassemble her court, no matter the danger from the king."

Sean nodded. Then his eyes fell heavily on Maureen. "When Colum left," he spoke carefully. "He went after Rowan, to fix what he had done?"

"So he said." Maureen averted her gaze angrily. "To my back."

Sean chuckled. Interesting and difficult women Colum found. Perhaps only the difficult ones were interesting.

"Do you think he will find her?" Sean asked.

"No." Maureen raised an almost threatening brow at Sean. "He is looking in the wrong place."

Every one of the men chuckled now.

"Well, at least it means he's working towards fixing what he did with Rowan. We wouldn't want him falling under the spell," Liam said, getting at the point of Sean's question.

"It isn't about the curse knowing you're working to help Rowan," Maureen said with more worry than she'd expressed before. "The curse is...an illusion of peace. It doesn't *take* you, *you* surrender to it. And Colum," she sighed, "he knows he's done wrong. He's lost both his girls, and he ran away from this new reality he does not know how to handle. He is a strong man, he can fight the curse, but it will have to be a choice."

Everyone was quiet for a long, heavy moment.

"It needs to be treason," Sean said and drew every shocked eye. "Ardal's task. He bent to the king's will, and injured Rowan with the betrayal. To feel he is doing right by her it will need to be a risk that could cost his life."

Maureen bobbed her head from side to side. "I'm not certain I have anything that quite fits such requirements."

"I'll bet Ferdy does," Liam teased.

"And I'll thank you not to ask him for ideas. This week alone he's defaced seven statues, held choruses of chanting Rowan's name and 'long live the queen' outside the king's office. If he does much worse I may have to curse him to sleep for the next year." Everyone laughed, except Maureen. She was more worried than her fierceness was letting on. She sighed after a moment, bobbing her head sideways. "The king is still refusing to let Rowan's shield maidens train. They train in secret now, and come to me for healing when they're done." Maureen rolled her shoulders and Sean would swear he saw a strand of her hair turn grey before his eyes. "Ardal could flout that edict. I doubt it would lead to death but—"

"That'll do," Sean said. "But first we may need to beat a little memory into the man."

Ardal lay in his bed, all but cowering as the returned Knights of the Rose crowded around him. Sean, Tom, Declan, Michael, Andrew, and Liam, along with Maureen and Braden were crammed into the room, making the walls feel close and the air heavy. Ardal felt so...small.

Not just his size, not just his height, or his broken body. He was small in every way. He'd forgotten Rowan. Forgotten Rowan. The little girl he'd treasured like one of his own children for years. How could he possibly have done that? The curse had never taken him before.

Maureen and Sean stood above him, having reminded him of Rowan, they now extolled his faults, but he barely heard them. He just saw her, again and again, with her eyes all but swimming with tears, and her entire being so tense that she looked like she might split apart in a moment. He'd seen that. Before the curse had taken him, before he'd said the words she took as betrayal, he'd seen how badly she needed comfort. He just hadn't known how or what to give her. Because even then he'd been small. Less than he'd been when he left on the quest that cost him his legs. He'd thought he was getting better when he started working with the squires, when he became Rowan's secret keeper. He thought he'd found himself again, but he hadn't, had he? Because when he'd had his legs, if he'd seen Rowan standing there lost, and hurt, and angry, he would have gone to her and held on like he would with any of his children.

But instead he'd let her believe that he found her pain and her needs less important than those of her father.

"I should have died in that cave," Ardal whispered, interrupting the lecture above him. "I...ever since I came back all I've done—"

"You are being self pitying," Braden interrupted coolly. He didn't look comfortable being here. Few of them did. Tom and Liam were clinging to the sides of the room as if in fear that Ardal's failings might infect them. Maureen looked even more militant than she had when she threw lightning at him and Colum in her rage over Rowan. But Braden looked all sorts of uncomfortable; his muscles were tensed, his eyes were frantic, and he was sweating a bit. Ardal supposed he was worrying over how to conceal this moment from Sorcha. Ardal used to have answers to such questions. He used to have all the answers. But he knew now that he—knew nothing. He was useless.

"You were the one who told me I had no right to put one more thing on her; then you turned around and did just that. But that doesn't mean you haven't helped her at all," Braden shouted. "Stop wallowing in your mistakes and find a way to help her now."

Ardal sank lower on the bed and shut his eyes. How was he possibly to help her? He couldn't go to her. He had no magic to send her way. No knowledge to help with her quest. No—

"The point is, what will you do now?" Tom asked. "Ardal if you let yourself lay here you will have failed her, but if you move, if you work to help her cause she will forgive you."

"If she comes back!" Ardal shouted. His chest cracked with the awful power of the words. If she came back. She was gone, and what she'd heard from him in their parting was that he wouldn't take her side. "She wasn't ready and—"

"You saw her fight me," Braden scoffed. "And two other men. She will be fine."

"There is not a soldier in the world who cannot meet his match." Ardal said and the weight of the words dragged him even lower, as if it were possible. "She is out there all alone. We all know she didn't leave here seeking shelter in another nation. It isn't in her. She went after Sorcha and we do not know yet if she is a match for her. She might never come back."

"She will come back," Maureen growled, leaning down over the bed. "First you want to help her father stifle her and now you doubt her? I..." Maureen fumbled. "When Rowan was a girl I allowed myself to doubt her powers, because the alternative was more frightening. I couldn't bear the thought of that beautiful girl I had welcomed into the world being possessed of enough magic to rival the Fairy queen. It terrified me for her, because Sorcha does not allow such challenges to pass. But Rowan has it in her. And when it is time, she will find it. Do not dare doubt her."

"Maureen," Ardal said, pushing himself up slowly. He shook with his breaking heart. "It isn't her power or her rightness, or her that I am doubting. None of you was her secret keeper. She was so full of doubts, and this could only make it so much worse. How will she know all she can do if anger and doubt are all she is feeling? How can she face the world thinking that I would ever, now or even when she was a child, think her father was right to take her birthright from her. I never thought that. But...he is my king, I—"

"No. He isn't." Sean slammed his fist against Ardal's wall, shaking the room with the force. "He has not been from the moment she was born. All he is is the steward watching over *her heritage* until she is ready to rule. He isn't your king. She is. You swore your oath to her. You offered your service *to her*. We all did." Sean looked around the room, nearly burning, so intense was he. "The only ruler we serve is our queen. Call it treason if it makes it clearer to you, but we have no king. None of us can doubt it any longer."

That is where you are wrong. Where you have always *been wrong. He is your king; he is meant to serve you. If you think he is wrong you speak to it. Or you are just one more coward.* Rowan's words thundered through Ardal's ears as he looked around the room, took in her army. All the people she had inspired. She led the way she wanted her father to. Ardal had always seen it, Rowan was a true leader, willing—no, determined to stand beside the men she would send out to fight in her name. If they were injured, if they died she wanted to be beside them because she was one of them, even as she led.

He would honor that, and hope with every fiber of his being that she came home so he could tell her how wrong he'd been, and just how much he...*needed* her.

"Treason it is then." Ardal nodded. "When do we begin?"

"I will tell the women to expect you before dawn," Maureen said coldly, looking less than impressed. "They haven't the time for languishing, training must be snuck between their duties."

"And these women, are they comfortable with treason?" Michael asked.

"They were committing it already. And without all this dithering. Now they will simply do so openly. And you," Maureen pointed around the room at all of the knights. "Will see to it that they remain safe doing so."

Ardal nodded, pushing himself higher in the bed. He would protect these women, even if it cost his life to do it. He would not fail Rowan again. He would defend the world she was creating. What's more, he would send for more women for her cause. There should be shield maidens in every village. He would give Rowan an army. He owed her that much, as she had surely saved him again today. His queen.

Gathering Fuel

387 days until Roisin returns

Rowan and Yseult reached the Liadan a few hours before dark. It was only then Rowan realized she'd been an idiot. Of course she was still in Stonedragon, the river was the border. She should have brought a map. She should know these things. She should stop complaining to herself and find a place to cross.

It was quite wide where she and Yseult met up with it, by no means the river's widest point, but since she couldn't tell how deep it was in the fading light she thought it best not to try and cross tonight. So she and Yseult made camp and bedded down before night had even fallen.

She munched on a carrot she'd stolen and stared at the river, listening to it flow. There were places along the Liadan where it was wide enough for several boats to travel along it side by side. Slow smooth places, where old kings of Creelan had held massive floating processionals to display their wealth. Rowan had always wanted to see the river.

She stared at it now and across the slowly darkening waters. It was foreign, but it was...disheartening. Or she was.

A breeze shook the trees wildly. Rowan shivered wrapped in her blanket and huddled nearer Yseult. From her smallest pack Gavin's last letter began shuddering slowly upward, the breeze grabbing at to carry it away. Her last letter.

Rowan's hand shot out and yanked the letter to her, gripping it tight. No one could take this from her. Slowly her fingers slid between the fold, looking for words to comfort her.

Who are you and what have you done with my eternally correct friend? Others are wrong but never she. Excepting the rare instances when she doubts herself.

Rowan felt her lips curving at the words, but her eyes welling with tears as well. They were not rare at all, and he knew it. He'd always known it.

Rowan ran her fingers over the words again and again until the light had faded enough around her that she could no longer make them out. She lay her back against Yseult, curled up behind her but didn't shut her eyes. She continued to run her fingers over the words as if somehow she could bring back light enough to read by, just from her longing.

Her heart began pounding harder and harder, and a voice floated to her. A figure of shadow seemed to take form beside her, settling on the ground between her and the river. Rowan wasn't frightened, she didn't even stir. She knew who it was: Gavin. He settled there, and though she could not see his face, she knew he must be smiling at her, a patient amused smile, seeming to ask her if she would ever find her way out of the doldrums she was born with, but without minding that she had not.

"Do not let her words become so much a part of you. You are at the center of a very deadly battle, but being at the center does not make you its cause," he spoke the words of an old letter.

Rowan smiled sadly at the shadow of him, and spoke to this Gavin her memories and imagination had brought forth. "I thought you said that letter was the last time you would say that to me."

"I am your friend," he replied. "And friends do not ask each other to break their own hearts."

Rowan gasped and tears raced down her cheeks. She never cried so much at home. Why was she now?

"I am truly sorry. More than I can ever say," Gavin kept speaking words that broke her heart. Petal had told him to write that. Petal had gone to him confident and bright and happy. But she wasn't so now. And it was their fault.

"I used to think you were so lovely," Rowan snarled at her imaginary visitor. "So much better than me, composed of finer things. But...*you* asked for her. You broke my heart. I shouldn't be worrying about you. It shouldn't pull me apart. Petal is the only worry I should hold. But I question everything. I tell myself to find the dragons, and save Petal, then I—" Rowan fisted her hand around the letter, and ground the heel of her hand over her heart. "I feel this awful ripping inside, and I think it's you," she whispered. "And I want to go to you instead of her. But...she needs me. She's my sister. She needs to know that I don't choose Roisin over her. She needs to *feel* how much I love her. I can't...I cannot poison one more person I love. But it feels like I'm being forced to choose. Like I must poison one of you to save the other."

"You are not poison," he said gently. "If you do not know within yourself how wonderful you are, then the Fairy queen has already beaten you."

It was an odd sort of companionship, this, her mind was calling forth her old escape, promising her that Sorcha having the letters could not change their comfort, could not truly take them from her. Everything this shadow man said was from one of Gavin's letters. She knew the words, they lived inside her.

"There are *no* limits set on who or what you can become. It is up to you to set your limits."

Rowan snuggled deeper into her blanket, looking away from the shadow Gavin to the river. No limits?

There weren't, were there? There was no one to tell her no, or urge caution, or...put her in her place. It was up to her to set her limits. Up to her to decide her will and answer to it. It wasn't even up to anyone else to comfort her, or chase away Sorcha's voice, Rowan needed to do all of that for herself. And Gavin—

Wasn't here. This was *her own mind* calling forth his words. *Rowan* was telling herself she could do it all. She could save them all.

She had *no* limits.

"At home, whenever someone was angry with me, or seemed disappointed, even when I argued with them, some part of me would back down," Rowan said aloud. "I gave them room to control me and make me smaller, and the magic shrunk with me. I was trying so hard to be the perfect princess. To be what Father wanted, or what I thought my mother had been. Or anything but what Sorcha said I would be. I would back down and hide from all of the parts of myself that felt bigger than—" Rowan couldn't find a word big enough to explain how large her power felt sometimes, the power she hid from, trying to be ordinary. Or good. Or just loved.

Her eyes took in the river. She rubbed her head back and forth on Yseult's flank. At its widest point the Liadan was five miles across and her magic felt far bigger than that. The river wasn't anywhere near that wide here, only a quarter of a mile at most. It wouldn't take very long to cross if it was not too deep.

If either she or Yseult had felt anything but exhausted she might have waded in to get a better sense of it. But they were both exhausted and achy. Every day the aches got a little deeper and the exhaustion a little heavier, she knew she should be pressing on, that she should be racing forward. Every second counted. But the longer she was away from the comforts she'd been used to the harder every step became. At home such aches would have been eased away, Maureen would come to Rowan when she was exhausted or achy, and just lay a hand on her shoulder, or kiss her head, and the aches eased, the exhaustion departed and she was herself again.

"There are no limits set on who or what you can become," the Gavin shadow said again. Rowan didn't look his way. It wasn't the real him, just his memory keeping that old promise.

You will not be alone.

Rowan turned her head against Yseult, and kissed the horse, infusing the touch with all her gratitude and power. The horse whinnied wildly and leapt to her feet, knocking Rowan forward. Rowan fell sideways into the dust and laughed. She'd healed Yseult. Rowan shut her eyes and let her magic rush through herself as if Maureen were here with a hand on her cheek, *dearest.*

It raced tingling over her skin, a feeling like coming awake and floating and utter certainty. Rowan was laughing as she stood. She patted Yseult on the neck, grinning.

"Want to try something wild and foolish and just a bit dangerous?"

Yseult jerked her head up enthusiastically, they always had been well matched in daring. Rowan took a moment to strap the packs back onto Yseult then walked the horse back a ways from the river; she glanced over her shoulder and saw the

Gavin shadow absorbed back into the growing darkness. Rowan tucked the letter into her girdle, making sure it was tightly strapped to her and mounted the horse. There was no one to tell her no. Nothing to hold her back but herself. It was time she did away with her oldest and strongest constraint. Her self-doubt.

"Don't be scared," Rowan said as much to herself as the horse. "Out here...I have no limits." She spurred the horse forward.

They raced toward the river as fast as the clearing would allow. Just as they reached the banks of the river Rowan jerked up on the reins. Yseult leapt out over the water, they soared further and further from the land, further across the water, but there was no way they could make it to the other side. They were going to land in the river. With a wild laugh Rowan threw out her magic around the pair of them and they vanished from over the river and reappeared at the edge of the other bank.

Yseult's hooves hit the ground with a gentle plop. Rowan chuckled wildly, and Yseult yanked up and down on her reins in a way Rowan interpreted as "Wohoo!" Rowan threw herself against the horse's neck and wrapped her arms around her in a tight hug.

"I never would have been a perfect princess anyway," Rowan said, breathless from her laughter. She gasped for more air. Rowan grinned into the one of Yseult's eyes she could see. She stretched out a hand to wrap around the dragon pendant hanging from the bridle.

Yseult shook her head, in a fond, "you're ridiculous" sort of shake.

"Maybe my power can be as big as I let it. Maybe all that held me back were me and those walls trapping my imagination. I can save them all, Yseult. We can do this."

Rowan shut her eyes, this was what hope felt like, out here in the world, hope was a different creature than it was at home. Not so quiet, nor subtle, it was wild and excitable. It was immense. So large it was all Rowan could do just to grip onto its edges. But she had to keep trying.

The bells at her ankle tinkled. *Look.*

Rowan slipped off Yseult's back and nodded to no one. She was ready now .

She walked a few feet from Yseult and started spinning, not just her body, but her mind. She hadn't really thought about who she wanted to look in on, just cast out her mind and around and around it went in all directions—after her loves.

Petal sat a table across from the Fairy queen. It was late in the evening, and the room, though within the castle, was filling slowly with more and more stars, the full moon rose behind the Fairy queen, bathing her in a gentle glow. The room opened onto a cliff overlooking a dense forest. Petal had asked when they entered what nation they were in, but she shouldn't have felt the need. They were in the Fairy realm, the air caressed Petal's face and tickled the grasses on the cliff into dancing.

When they'd entered the table had not been here, they'd sat a while together in silence watching the day retreat and the night emerge. It was lovely. It was peaceful and it was new. Petal kept making herself see the lovely things in this world. She had to, because the alternative was to sink into sadness. Regrets were for after the task was done. She had to keep telling herself that.

There was so much beauty to see, she was part of nature here as she never had been before. She was exposed to so many more of its wonders than she could be at home.

When it was full night a group of fairy laid out a dinner of wild vegetables, bread and cheese before departing silently.

Sometimes, like now when she was sitting here quietly with Sorcha, Petal could pretend this had always been her life. She could pretend it was only peaceful and that she wasn't in any danger, that her choices had no consequences, that she had nothing to worry over. Sometimes she could imagine being everything Sorcha wanted of her and the world being a better place for it.

A howl sounded in the distance, Petal looked up from her meal, in the direction of the sound. Down the cliff of Mount Kieran into the forest at its feet. She was so far from home; Petal wasn't sure that even Papa had been this far from home before. But just at that moment she was startled by the sound of the wolf.

"Can they travel so far in one day?" Petal asked Sorcha. "I am sure he was in the Whispering Wood this morning."

"He?" Sorcha inquired in a tone that might fool some with its blandness, but Petal felt the woman startle. She did not like how drawn the wolves were to Petal.

"Malachy," Petal replied innocently. "He was the youngest prince, I think. His sister likes to keep all three of them near, but Malachy is the more wild of the bunch. He only remembers he was human when he is near me."

Sorcha raised a brow and made a sound of nearly sweet interest, but Petal could see the anger she hid as her teeth closed around her fork. No, Sorcha didn't like this connection at all.

Petal took a bite of sweet bread and leaned her face into the wind to let Malachy find her scent. She'd been seeing him and his siblings off and on since she carried the letters to Sorcha in Turrlough. She knew they'd followed her back to the Fairy nation, but Malachy was the only one of the quartet that ever ventured near enough for Petal to sense his past through him.

She had a feeling their father was dead, perhaps long dead, because Malachy seemed not to remember him.

An odd thought occurred to Petal as she chewed: there was no reason for Sorcha to be disturbed that Petal knew these wolves were once human. She'd displayed her power only to prove a point with Petal right beside her. Ripped Prince Gavin from his family, and punished his brother Owen, shrinking him to the size of a snail and leaving him in the hold of a fairy guard. She had left that family in tatters. So why did this disturb Sorcha? Merely because the animals were drawn to Petal? She didn't think so.

Her eyes drifted to the scepter leaning against the table beside Sorcha. Desmond slept within. He looked peaceful, Petal doubted he knew what went on around him, not truly knew. But every once in a while Petal would feel his magic stretching beyond the crystal, offering her comfort, so he must have some awareness. Did he know now that Petal was refusing to free him?

Petal glanced from the crystal to Sorcha and back again, the woman looked so bland, but Petal could feel her plotting, trying to find the proper way to twist Petal back into doing her bidding as she had not truly done since Turrlough.

Sorcha wanted Petal to break one of her spells. What if Petal was powerful enough to—break them *all?*

Malachy howled again, as if he felt Petal's thoughts and agreed with her. Petal slowly smiled around a bite of food. That was worth exploring.

Darling Girl sat on the floor beside Aunt B's chair and lay her head against her aunts legs, she was reading a story to everyone. Aunt C sat at her easel next to the fire, working on a secret project that none of them was allowed to see. And Aunt A sat in a round seat next to the open window, petting the owl on a tree limb just outside. Darling's friend had sent her the bird, Mother, a few months ago because Darling was lonely with all the other animals gone. Mother was a wonderful companion, quiet when Darling needed it, or encouraging, and always ready to dance under the evening moon. Everyone loved him.

Darling smirked, she liked that the bird was a boy but had been named Mother, it seemed so much more...silly than her friend usually behaved. Darling felt a presence and looked around, slowly so as not to alert her aunts. Aunt B might stop telling the story then, and Darling didn't want that. It was sad, but she needed to know the end. Aunt B was sharing a true history, she'd been doing this more and more since Darling's vision of Friend dying. All her aunts were teaching her things they never had before, about magic and hidden things, and eternity, and about Darling's true home. They were preparing her.

Darling spotted Friend in the center of a soft blue glow beneath the arch into the kitchen, she stood back and watched quietly. But her smile touched on Darling, full of warmth and love, making Darling feel just a little more alive than she had a moment before.

"You see, before this land was ever populated by humans," Aunt B was saying, "it was a land of dragons, and fairy and even a few giants, though they prefer the mountain ranges of Ether to anything so flat as Great Island, the only Mountains we have to boast of are Mount Kieran and Mount Anwyn, but Ether has seventeen large enough to cast the sort of shade a giant likes to sleep in."

Darling giggled as Aunt B played with the hair on her neck and continued the story. "But all the creatures of Great Island shared the space without much contact. We lived in peace, because we never came together, each of us understanding our own part in the world and tending to it. Then came the humans."

"And we brought the badness?" Darling tilted up her head to ask Aunt B, hoping she was wrong. But more and more when she heard a history humans seemed the cause of strife. Darling might know Fairy magic, but she knew she was not a fairy, it seemed wrong to be a part of such a disruptive species.

But Aunt B shook her head and leaned down. "There are many a fairy who will tell you yes. But it just isn't so. The first age was a peaceful age, then all species began to spread from their corners and more of the world was known. Humans have the shortest lifespan of all us creatures save for giants; the shortest lifespans but the most *curiosity*." Darling loved the way Aunt B said it. As though curiosity was a magic all its own. A magic humans had in great supply.

"As they spread they wanted to know *everything*. Every culture, every land, every hidden gem of the universe. And like any other group, among the humans there were those who sought out answers in terrible ways, and there were those who were frightened of any power beyond their own and sought to destroy it, but there were many who sought out only to know. Or to take part in the other ways of life."

Darling saw her friend smiling at Aunt B's reassurance as well.

"And one such man was the very first king of your true home. I cannot tell you his name yet, but we shall call him King the First in our studies. King the First washed up on this land with a few survivors of a terrible winter passing from the southern frozen lands. And when he washed ashore though he was little more than your age now, and had been nothing but a servant on the wrecked ship, he set about building shelter and protecting the few who had survived with him. And once that was done, his curious mind must explore the rest of the island."

Rowan stumbled forward after her second trip, and Yseult's large frame steadied her so she did not fall face first into the dirt. She'd made two trips in the span of a few minutes. Stayed with each of her sisters longer than she should be able to after such a long day. But she didn't feel finished. She felt a bit fatigued, weight settling over her, but she knew there was more to see. And out here, there was no one to tell her no.

She leaned against Yseult a moment, grinning. "King the First," Rowan said with a snort. "We are taught his story a bit differently in Stonedragon. A conquering hero who proved his royal blood with feats no other man could perform. I think I like B's version better. I wonder which is true."

Yseult snorted as if to say "does it matter to you?" And indeed, it didn't. Rowan would believe Bride's story now, wherever the truth lay. Rowan forced herself to straighten and stretched her legs a bit, walking towards the banks of the Liadan.

Petal had been on nearly the other side of the island, and she had seemed so... absent at first. Not terribly sad, nor frightened, just not herself. But trust Petal to be the one to find the lost Creelan royalty, even if they were only wolves when she found them. That had shown a bit of her old, natural confidence again. Rowan wondered what she was thinking when she closed her smile around that bread that made Rowan's stomach rumble. That smile made Rowan think of her letter from so long ago:

I saw a wolf! I think I should like one as a pet.

She'd been so full of spirit when she first left, but it wasn't all gone yet. Rowan was going to find a way to bring her home, and when she did, all the spirit would come back with her. It was in her, she just needed to find it.

Rowan dipped her hands into the cold water of the rushing river and pulled out a deep scoop. She drank from the river, and felt an internal shiver as the water chased away the few aches that followed her from her most recent trip.

She laughed. No, she wasn't quite finished looking yet, wise or no.

Rowan began spinning again.

Keagan jerked awake, panting and sweating and gripped onto his ankles. He bent over his legs and tried to breath as silently as he was able. Not that Ferdy had noticed this much lately. No one had.

Keagan kept having the vision, and it kept getting worse. This time Petal had a pack of wolves around her. They ran out doing her bidding—ripping her family apart. He couldn't understand it. He couldn't think of a single thing that would make Petal turn on them that way. She wasn't a vicious person. She didn't want anyone hurt. Petal was likely struggling with the plan she was taking part in now because it would see Sorcha hurt. So how could she be turned against them?

What was Rowan going to do to cause this? Keagan needed to stop her. He needed to know where she'd gone, or find magic enough to reach her without knowing where she was. Devon's book on the Fairy said it could be done. Like vanishing, if one had a strong enough bond, they could use the same magic they did finding a place to go to a person. But Keagan didn't feel Rowan the way he did Ferdy, and Petal, when Petal was outside of the Fairy Realm. Rowan wasn't in his veins the way they were. But he was sure he could find her if he had enough power.

He wasn't needed here at the moment. Ferdy had things well in hand. Keagan had not been terribly impressed by the army Ferdy was forming, at first, nor had he seen its point. They defaced images of the Rose Princess, and replaced her banner with paintings of Rowan's sword but it didn't really change anything. But that was only how he felt at first. By the fifth day of Rowan's absence things were becoming troubled. Almost half of the palace staff, seeing the banner in the courtyard each morning, would ask, again and again, as if the answer had not been given, "Whose blade is the blade of Stonedragon?" And most of the other staff, or soldiers or villagers who passed under the sign seemed not to notice it at all. It was seven days now and Keagan felt like they should do something bigger, but he could leave that in his brother's hands. Ferdy hadn't kept many of the mastermind traits, but at sabotage he was a different sort of mastermind. And now he had the following to destroy just about anything.

Ferdy had at first only had the littlest children following him. Then Brigid's cousin joined, and with him a few other children nearer Ferdy and Keagan's age. Then a few squires from Keagan's group joined. And eventually even a few of the older ones, though Keagan suspected they joined "Rowan's Sword" as Ferdy was calling them, more to be near Colleen than anything else.

Ferdy didn't mind that. He said the more people who remembered Rowan the better, whatever their reason. Keagan heard the words in his mind and agreed with them, but as he watched the boys trying to get Colleen's attention he wanted to fight them all, shove them away and keep her to himself. Not that she wanted to be around him.

He was letting his big baby feelings get to him still. Twice now it had been Keagan who caused her to latch onto someone else's magic. But it *was* different from before. When she used someone else's power now she knew it, and it made her nervous. She would back to the fringes of the group, or leave entirely. Most times she was just there, at the edges staring at everyone, venturing no opinions, barely taking part, just watching. She responded best to Ferdy. And why not, all of the sudden Ferdy was leading everyone. Ferdy was confident and calm, Ferdy was...stronger than he'd ever been before, and Keagan was getting weaker.

Every time he had the vision when he woke he told himself Sorcha was trying to manipulate him, but the more he said it the less sense it made. How would Sorcha even know about him? And even if she did, why was she concerned with him?

"So," Ferdy said, startling Keagan so badly he nearly fell from his bunk. How had he not realized Ferdy was up? "Did it change? Or was it just the same old dream?" Ferdy asked at last.

His voice was resigned, but heavier than Keagan would have expected. Keagan leaned out over the edge of his bunk and looked down at his brother, sitting there wide awake, as though he hadn't been to sleep at all. Maybe he hadn't, sabotage tended to be best done at night.

Keagan shrugged. "It was worse."

Ferdy nodded, looking away. "How?"

Keagan shuddered and rolled back onto the bed, looking up at the ceiling. He felt like he shouldn't share this with his brother. He still hadn't told Ferdy that he'd felt Petal here the night Rowan left. But he found himself speaking, needing that particular brand of confidence that belonged to no one but Ferdy.

"It was the night the Rose Princess returns. Petal came in with Sorcha, and fighting broke out, Rowan attacked and the knights and...just about everyone. Petal just stayed back and watched, and Sorcha was taking everyone on alone, but still nothing was stopping her. Pa wasn't there, I don't know how I knew, but I knew he was dead. Somehow we started to turn the tide, and Sorcha was looking weaker, and...Petal released a pack of wolves. They tore through us, bigger than humans and vicious; they attacked everyone, even us."

"Did I die again?" Ferdy asked nonchalantly.

"Everyone died, Ferdy! Do you think this is funny?"

"Not really," Ferdy said on a sigh and caught Keagan up short.

He bit back the angry words on the tip of his tongue and rolled back over to lean down and look at Ferdy. "You don't?"

"Course not! *Petal isn't here.* We can't help her and you keep seeing visions of her killing us. What's funny about that?" Ferdy shook his head. "Sometimes I do brazenly bad things, just to see if I can get the king to behead us before Petal comes back. At least that way it won't be her."

Keagan laughed. "I thought you were just trying to force him to admit he's our brother."

"Oh, he isn't our brother." Ferdy shook his head. "It takes people reminding him three times a day for him to know Rowan is his daughter. And it's not like he ever acknowledged Pa. No...look, Keagan, *we're better together.* So I don't know how, but we'll find a way to help Petal—together."

"I think we need to go after Rowan," Keagan said cautiously.

"Again with this. Kee, Rowan won't do anything to turn Petal against us. She didn't leave to hurt her."

"I know," Keagan said, but he didn't even sound convinced to his own ears. "But in every dream all of Petal's rage centers around Rowan. Around hurting Rowan for something. And the dreams got worse after Rowan left."

"It's Sorcha manipulating you."

"If you're sure of that then why are you trying to stop it happening? All I'm saying is we find Rowan, make sure she doesn't do anything to drive Petal away."

"No," Ferdy said flatly.

"What do you mean, no? I follow your lead all the time."

"Oh please, it's only been for the last few days. I've followed yours my whole life."

"If that were true you never would have been in trouble."

Ferdy chuckled. "Alright, I follow you when we're doing things together. But I do my own thing when you want to be a wet blanket. Keagan, you are so focused on the dream and on all the things that are going wrong that you aren't *doing* anything. You come along to play tricks then you just stand there like a look out. I convinced Colleen to join by saying you wanted her to, but you avoid her like—"

"You told her I like her?" Keagan demanded.

"No. She's a cipher, she can feel that." Ferdy snorted. "I just told her you wanted her to take part in Rowan's Sword. And you're missing the point...she said yes. She wants to do things that make you happy. And you're the only one she ever reacts to enough to steal magic."

"That isn't a good thing," Keagan said morosely. "For all you know she joined because you wanted it and she was siphoning off you. We're supposed to be helping her get better."

"We're supposed to be giving her the space to remember who she is," Ferdy argued. "Her power is awesome! She doesn't need to get better, just to get control. And she's getting there. Trust me, she doesn't do anything because *I* want it. People can't spend all their time tamping down their emotions for her. She's going to have to get used to feeling them and not following them."

"It's only been eight days since she was told what was going on."

"And tomorrow it will be nine, then ten, then eleven. How many more before you stop acting like she's sick?"

"How ever many it takes to get her well."

Ferdy rolled his eyes. "You're literally the only person who feels that way. Everyone else wants to get back to worrying about their own feelings and ignore her. And you want to run away and leave her alone."

Keagan felt sick, everyone just abandoned Colleen and he was going to do it too. He—

"Are you trying to manipulate me?" Keagan demanded incredulously as he noticed how quiet Ferdy had gotten.

"Is it working?" Ferdy grinned.

Keagan rolled to his back and stared at the ceiling, a little embarrassed because, yeah, it really was.

"Rowan?" Ferdy whispered.

Keagan sat up and searched the room.

"What is it?" Keagan demanded.

"I think...I think she's here," Ferdy said with a look halfway between a headache and a smile. "Like the way we visited Petal. I can feel her. I think."

"Rowan," Keagan searched the room. "Petal needs to know we love her." He entreated the empty air.

"Bring her home," Ferdy whispered.

Rowan fell to the ground, returning to her body. That last visit took quite a lot out of her. She sat on the bank of the river, panting, her lungs pinching.

She'd been relieved seeing that boost of confidence the wolves had given Petal, and maybe they were still a good thing for her, but that didn't mean they would be forever. Rowan might have no magical limits out here, but she certainly wasn't free of concerns.

"Come on, Yseult. Let's get some sleep. We have a lot of ground to cover tomorrow."

Unlimited

386 days until Roisin returns

Rowan woke to the sound of armor clanking. She lay still pretending to sleep. She shouldn't have camped so near the river. Everyone liked to be near a water source, it was such an obvious mistake but just now all she could do was listen.

Most people avoided the Enchanted Forest for fear of being lost within it, but perhaps they thought so near the river they would be able to find their way out. Otherwise, why have crossed the river?

Rowan opened her eyes a slit and found her answer. They hadn't crossed it. She had. Somehow in the night the trees had moved her back to her father's side of the forest. Yseult was on the other side with Rowan's packs, staring right at her. If it weren't for needing the soldiers to think she was asleep Rowan would have leapt to her feet and yelled at her namesake. Rowan trees really were the most frustrating plant in all creation! The trees rustled, laughing at her annoyance.

"It's her, I recognize her mare," one of the men hissed at his companions.

"A stallion could have gotten her further," another commented.

Rowan rolled her tongue over the inside of her teeth wondering what it was about this situation that made them think they needed to belittle her choices. She was asleep on the ground, apparently fleeing her father's decrees, how much lower did she need to be brought before they were satisfied?

She heard at least four pairs of boots moving towards her, flanking her. Unfortunately, her armor was piled neatly across the river with Yseult. But if it were just four...

A sword poked at her back roughly, rough enough to cut into her gown. That did it! She'd only brought two changes of clothes.

Rowan rolled over towards the sword, kicking up her leg to knock the blade aside. The soldier stumbled back, but kept his hold on the sword. Rowan crouched on one knee and looked between the men.

"If you're needing directions you find me out of humor, and without a map." She shrugged.

One of the men actually laughed at Rowan's dry remark.

"Your king, Balder of Stonedragon demands your presence."

Rowan shook her head. "I will not be returning with you."

Her sword was laying in the pile with her armor across the river, curse these trees. She usually slept with it in her hand, but she'd been feeling over confident. Of course, she did have the dagger in her boot. Slowly, as if only rolling her shoulders, Rowan slipped a hand through the slit in her long skirt and darted a hand into her boot.

"Feel free to tell him I am safe, if it matters," she said bitterly.

It takes people reminding him three times a day for him to know Rowan is his daughter.

A man's hand fell on Rowan's shoulder.

She hadn't realized there was a soldier behind her. His hand closed around her shoulder blade, he must be a big man, Rowan had muscular shoulders from years of knightly training. He tightened his hold, as if to pull her up—fighting it would be, then.

Rowan gripped her dagger tight in her left hand, and threw up her right hand to close around the man's wrist, she gave his arm a great tug forward, as she rolled back. The man was shocked enough by the move to tumble forward over her body, but he jumped to his feet almost as quickly as Rowan took hers.

Rowan transferred the dagger to her right hand and took a defensive stance. Five men, she'd never fought so many at once!

"You cannot take us all on, *princess,*" a soldier taunted.

Rowan didn't answer the taunt, she didn't when she was on the practice fields, she wouldn't here. But her heart sped up and she felt her mind emptying.

The man she'd thrown charged straight for her, but for the moment the others only watched. He was big, muscular, and young, he could likely take a beating and keep coming. Rowan stood her ground until he was nearly upon her then angled back on her right leg, so he moved right by her, she followed the motion through with her whole body, slicing his shoulder with her dagger, and kicking into his right hip with her left foot. He tumbled to the ground, by no means incapacitated but injured and surprised. The other men took that as a cue.

Rowan spun away from her attacker on the ground as the other men lunged at her. Rowan dove into a roll as the blade wielding soldier swung out for her. She came up between two others and rammed her elbow into the opening where one's armor was joined with straps, so she could dive between them.

She nearly made it, but a soldier caught onto the tail of her braid and yanked back with all his might.

Rowan howled angrily as her body was slammed backwards. One of them cheered and the other's closed in around Rowan. Rage and pain woke a different fighter entirely. Rowan saw an opening and threw her dagger with all her might at the closest man in front of her. It lodged into the underside of his shoulder, where his armor opened to allow him to move. He howled in pain, gripping onto his arm and the dagger he didn't dare move.

Rowan twisted around on her back, kicking out at the man who held her braid. She caught him in the gut, but it was well protected by armor and a layer of padding beneath. He did not appear even to mark the strike. He twisted his arm around under Rowan's braid and yanked her towards him with it. The man Rowan had injured first had rejoined the group and kicked at Rowan's side as the other man pulled her forward.

Rowan gritted her teeth and tried to dig her heels into the dirt, catching onto the base of her own braid as the pain grew and she heard twisting pulling sounds like her hair would be ripped right out of her head. The man kicked out again. Rowan didn't think. Didn't count her attackers and catalog the best ways to hurt them. Didn't worry about hurting them, or herself. She just acted.

She vanished, taking the man who gripped her hair with her. She reappeared, slipping between the branches of a tree. Rowan landed on one knee at the base of the tree, her free hand braced against the ground. But the man who held her hair got caught up in the tree. He released Rowan's hair, howling in pain as the branches attacked him.

Rowan couldn't even say what she did next, just rushed at the other soldiers. Using magic and fists and knees. Every weapon at her disposal, even the trees. When Rowan kicked one man away the branches of a rowan tree caught him and attacked scraping up every naked piece of flesh it could. And when Rowan was fighting with two more men, Yseult came charging over the river, carried by tree branches. She leapt free of the tree branches and kicked a third soldier away.

When all five men were incapacitated and she stood in the center of the clearing panting and aching from injuries she had yet to catalogue Rowan stared around her. The ache in her head left her in a woozy place between laughing and crying.

It takes people reminding him three times a day for him to know Rowan is his daughter.

This was so different than any fight she'd ever had. Her eyes took in the injured men, some bleeding, or struggling against tree limbs and she wanted to smile. She couldn't say that she'd ever really wanted to hurt the people she'd fought before. But she'd wanted to hurt these men. She wanted to hurt them more. She wanted to rip away every sense of power or pride they had and grind them into the dirt.

In the past she would have wanted their respect, even their approval. *Her* people. But not so now.

Look what she could do. The trees of a magical forest were answering to her will. Yseult nudged Rowan gently in the shoulder, checking her injuries but Rowan barely registered it. Five men. She'd fought five of her father's men and won. They were a perfect message to her father that she was done being controlled.

And of exactly which way she'd gone.

Rowan sighed. The boys wanted to come after her. If these men went back, like beacons to Rowan's path the boys would come and she would be putting more of Maureen's children in danger. She couldn't do that.

"I should have just used my magic from the first," Rowan muttered. The trouble was all her life she'd resisted using it. It was only this past year that she'd begun to think of it as an offensive tool, and even then she'd only used it when training with the boys, because they had magic. It felt wrong to use it against men without it. A sword in her hand was second nature to Rowan, but magic still took thought or desperate impulse. That was something she needed to get past. Men like these were happy to use any superior strength against weaker foes. She must be prepared to meet that challenge.

She couldn't let them go. But she couldn't just tie them up and abandon them in a magic forest that might just lose them inside, much as the thought held an appeal. And she most certainly wouldn't be going back with them.

"Your father will find you, princess," one of the men shouted, struggling against the limbs that bound him.

"I am no princess. Haven't you heard? I've been disowned and my court disbanded. I belong to no one." Rowan broke off. It was a heavy thought, but also...freeing. She alone had triumphed over five men. By blending her magic and her knightly skills, she could triumph over even more. Her search for dragons, her fight with Sorcha, she could triumph over even her own fears.

"I belong to no one now," Rowan said again. "I am simply—" she shook her head, "—an armored mage. There is no nation, nor any will but my own that might hold me back. You should be afraid of me, but...you won't remember any of this." Rowan smiled as an idea formed in her head.

She wouldn't waste her own magic healing men who'd injured her. The river would take care of them well enough, so Rowan walked around them through the trees and found their horses tied up not far away. She searched their packs until she found an empty flagon, and was about to turn away with it when another thought occurred. She went from one horse to the next stealing any supplies she might be able to use. Food, water, a map and an extra pair of blankets, even a small bag of gold. Weighted down slightly with her prizes, Rowan came back to the clearing where the men were bound. She dropped the packs and went to the river to fill up the flagon.

Armored mage, wandering thief. She might just like this new self better than the old versions.

"You cannot escape!" a man shouted.

"I already have," Rowan replied and held out the water. "Drink, it will heal your wounds, enough."

He eyed her dubiously. Rowan splashed the water across him. He was the man she'd sliced in the shoulder. At once his arm stopped bleeding and began to grow closed. Rowan watched with wonder. She'd seen many wounds healed by magic before but never just with a splash of water. It was incredible. His wound remained quite red, and there was a little pucker around the skin, but it was well healed. The man stared at his wound in wonder. Rowan went from man to man and splashed them and the worst of their wounds healed.

"How long ago were you sent?" Rowan asked. Her head pounded and the world was slightly uneven before her, but she wanted to know *why* her father sent them. Did he want her back? Or did he just want everyone to see his might? Rowan had been both too angry with him, and too scared of seeing he'd forgotten her already to try visiting her father in her mind. Now she only felt angrier with him, but anger, it seemed, didn't do away entirely with longing. "What were your orders exactly?"

"He sent us eight days ago. To find you and bring you home."

"He said nothing else?" Rowan asked, and hated herself just a bit. What did she expect, that he'd said to his men that he couldn't do without her, that he loved her, that he was worried for her? Even were any of those things true he wouldn't have told his soldiers.

A few of them exchanged discomforted looks, but no one spoke. Rowan felt herself smile in a slightly loopy way, she'd yet to heal herself and her head was pulsing from having been jerked around so much. "Don't worry, if you're lucky when you get home you can forget me all together."

She shut her eyes, and tried to find her way into all of their minds at once. When she felt them all she spoke aloud. "You didn't find me. You looked to the very edge of his kingdom, but I left no trace."

Rowan released their minds and opened her eyes, she nearly fell, the sudden light made her head pound a hundred times harder. The lance of it roused her anger and Rowan wanted to march forward and kick the dazed looking men. But another thought crawled around her mind.

If she could make them forget they'd found her, with her standing right before them, what else could she make them do with magic? She'd cursed Braden to kill his own father. She could *change* these men. She could make them do her bidding.

A tingle of power slid through her, speeding up her heart like the anticipation before she and Yseult jumped the river. She could fix things.

She could make these *thugs* into the sort of men she would like to lead. She could make them heroic, honorable she could make them respect her power. She could make them turn on her father. She could mold them into...

Rowan felt a sharp stab in her right hand and looked down. Like a mirage in this tilting world she saw the burnt rose she'd brought with her, pressed into her palm like it had been when she was six, with her skin growing shut around it. But there was nothing there when she tried to close her fingers. Her hand pulsed with a tingling cold like the warnings her blood gave her when evil was near.

She took a step back. "Sleep," she ordered. The man slumped within the hold of the trees and Rowan took another step away.

The trees released the men slowly so they lay quietly beneath their shade. The ache in her head wasn't gone, but Rowan had stopped feeling it as she imagined her power growing.

Those men might be so much better under her command— But she wouldn't be.

She liked the power too much. She liked the *control*. She liked knowing she could take power from others. As she'd liked the feeling of defeating Sorcha when she cursed Braden.

Rowan yanked her stolen goods into her arms. She threw the packs over Yseult's back but didn't bother strapping them down. She turned the horse with an arm around her neck and walked into the river.

It was a shuddering cold shock the deeper she went. She needed to feel it, because part of her still wanted to go back and change things to her liking. Maybe there should be limits to her power. The water was high, and though it was healing her smaller wounds Rowan's head still felt fuzzy. There should be a limit to her power. The river was at her waist before she gave in and vanished with Yseult.

On the other side of the river she was shivering, but most of her wounds were healed. Probably all of them, but not the piercing pain in her palm. That remained, reminding her of why she'd feared her own power in the first place.

There is something inherently bad in fairies, and in humans. But there is something inherently good as well. You must make the good stronger. Maureen's voice tried to soothe her.

Rowan strapped her packs and the stolen goods onto Yseult, taking out dry clothes. She stripped off the wet clothes, donning the others without really drying her body. She put on her armor over her damp clothes dazedly. She'd been so... happy, freed by the idea of having no limits. But it seemed she needed some very definite ones.

It was tempting, to just go home where she had people to tell her right from wrong. Maybe it was Rowan who had been wrong. Maybe she should be punished and disinherited. Colum agreed with Father. They never agreed. That said something, didn't it? Maybe she was more dangerous than she'd let herself believe. Keagan was afraid of something she might do.

But now that she had felt more freely the reach of her magic, she doubted there would be any holding it back in a rage. She might just be worse at home.

"It is up to you to set your limits," Gavin's voice commented, sounding far more pleased with the prospect than Rowan was right now.

Rowan spun around searching for him, and her head screamed at the motion, not healed completely. She thought she might vomit, but she did not try to heal herself. Nor did she return to the river for more water.

Gavin wasn't behind her. Of course not. She had not even tried to visit him last night, despite every hopeful feeling she'd had, before her last trip. She couldn't risk having her hope stolen completely.

She wanted to visit him now, wanted to see Gavin with her eyes, to know he was well, to take comfort in that. But just the thought had her stomach turning.

Rowan reached into the pack of stolen food and yanked out a chunk of bread. She *loved bread.* She couldn't recall ever really thinking about it before, but she loved it now. Without another thought, Rowan mounted Yseult and urged her forward; she needed to move, needed to stop herself from being just the sort of evil who might turn Petal against them all.

She needed to get to Petal, soon. Perhaps they needed each other.

386 days until Roisin returns

"I sent word to the fairy in Turrlough as soon as the message arrived, Your Majesty. We should hear from them shortly, if she goes that way."

"Well, that solves everything, doesn't it?" Sorcha snarled.

"No...Your Majesty. I only thought they would be on higher guard if warned that your—that the Knight of the Rose was headed their way." Mavis bowed, shuddering at her near slip.

Sorcha crumpled King Alistair's letter in her left hand. Rowan had left Stonedragon, and Braden, utterly useless Braden, was "staying to search for her." The liar. He'd probably helped that poisonous canker pack. Now he was hiding there as long as he was able to avoid Sorcha's wrath.

Sorcha scowled at the woman's arrested attempt to call that girl her granddaughter. They knew, all fairy knew that that intended usurper was no family of hers.

It was Petal's influence making them forget their place. Sorcha was annoyed with Petal for influencing them so. But Petal was the least of her concerns.

Braden, the useless fool, had lost the princess. Prince Gavin had forced Sorcha into dire action in front of Petal. The fairy were doubting their queen, again. And her sisters were proving harder to find than Sorcha would ever have guessed. And now that girl, that changeling who killed her daughter was out in the world away from all the tortures Sorcha had planned for her.

How dare she escape? She was meant to suffer. Every day meant to feel how others were loved more than her. Every day see how ugly she was. How dare she escape that? It wasn't to be borne.

"Utterly useless boy. The whole lot, useless." Sorcha threw out her hand and curved it around the staff of her scepter. She'd spent so much time shaping Braden into just the perfect foil to that girl's confidence. Wasted such energy convincing Prince Gavin to do her bidding and for what? With both of them that maddening *curse*-of-a-girl found some way to thwart Sorcha's plans.

But she wouldn't win. Sorcha would see to it. If she had to kill every friend the girl had before her eyes she would crush her. It all came back to her sister. Once the girl was found and the curse completed, *Rowan the Eternal* would crumble away like a clump of dirt and Sorcha could grind her down to nothing.

"Fine," Sorcha hissed, not to the fairy in front of her, but to the rushed plan forming in her mind. She didn't like straying from her original plan, but she would find a way to torture that girl even outside of Stonedragon. No part of the world would ever welcome her. She would be made to feel it.

"Fine, this accelerates the plan, but it needn't alter it completely."

"Your Majesty?" Mavis asked hesitantly.

Sorcha's gaze narrowed in to focus on the fairy before her and the woman took a half a step back, trembling slightly.

A long absent laugh rumbled through the back of Sorcha's mind.

"My word, Sorcha, when you get angry it is a terrifying sight," Nessa's old criticism pierced through Sorcha.

She remembered a time when those words had served their purpose well and Sorcha had tempered her rage to make servants more comfortable. But now all the words did was remind Sorcha that she had never been allowed to embrace her full self. Never.

Well, she could embrace it now. If others needed to tremble in her presence so be it. She was their queen, they should fear displeasing her.

"Bring me Sir Donovan, and send word to the fairy in Turrlough that none are to directly interfere with *that girl*. Let her reach the palace. Let her learn the fate of her love, and," Sorcha chuckled darkly, "let the palace be lit with warm, soothing lights to welcome her."

Sorcha bobbed her head from side to side, and began smiling. "That ought to do for the time being. Let the girl face all the foils I will lay before her. She'll be sliced to shuddering ribbons before the month is out, and begging to return home."

Sorcha laughed slightly as she waved her servant away. She would show that girl just how little the world beyond her cage had to offer her. Then watch her run back to it and bar the door herself. For all the good it would do her, Sorcha had an unlimited well of tortures yet to drown that girl within.

Two-thousand Seven-Hundred and Ninety-One Possibilities

383 days until Roisin returns

Colum rode into the courtyard of the palace, and climbed from his horse as fast as his aging body would allow. In his youth he had leapt from his steed, even after weeks in the saddle. Not so now. This was a young man's work, but Colum had been the one to drive Rowan from her home, so it should be he who brought her back. And he'd failed.

He should go to the king right away. For so many reasons: he was his king, he was his...son. A son Colum had failed for years. Again and again he'd left him to himself, knowing what a lonely child he was. He had tried for a time when he was little to befriend him, but not nearly as hard as a father should. And here were the results. This kingdom was falling apart, and as certain as Colum was that he would tell one of his own men such burdens couldn't rest all on them...right now it felt like his fault.

Rowan and her father should be closer. Balder could have been more loving, more understanding, more confident if he'd known just one person loved him unconditionally. That was Colum's responsibility, whether he'd known their relationship or not.

But Colum's feet didn't fall in with the rest of his men as they made their way into the palace. He couldn't face his own son. He didn't know how. He didn't know how to face him as his knight to inform him he'd failed to find Rowan, or as his father to apologize for all the ways he'd failed him.

He needed Maureen. He'd been without her too long.

His steps were heavy as he made his way towards home, weighted with all his guilt and worry. She would be enraged with him still, with every right, but he knew they would find their way back from this. They had to.

Colum heard a violent boom of thunder. The air and ground shook and from nowhere dark clouds built in the distance.

Despite aches, and fears and exhaustion Colum broke into a run. That was Maureen.

When Colum was near enough to see the earth beneath those clouds his eyes took in the sight with shock. Maureen stood in the middle of the training area near Ardal's house, with a group of no less than twenty armed women, and several of Rowan's knights, facing off against the king and his soldiers.

Colum wasn't near enough to hear, but the king shouted something and lightning popped at his feet. Colum watched his son jump away from his wife's magic and his heart twisted. His whole world was coming apart. He knew from the depths of his heart that a few weeks ago he would surely have been on Maureen's side in whatever squabble was going on. But now...

That was his son. Rowan had admonished him over failing to love him in the past. How could he fail to do so now? Colum rushed nearer.

"I have been giving the matter consideration as Rowan asked, but you have no right to go against my orders," Balder bellowed at the gathering.

Some of Rowan's knights took notice of Colum, but Maureen and Balder saw only each other. Or more likely, saw only their grievances.

"It is your duty to see these women safe," Maureen bit out. "And I do not recognize your authority to counterman one of *Rowan's* orders."

"Don't you?" Balder shouted, advancing though anyone could see the way he shook.

There was nothing to be done here. Both of them loved Rowan too well to hurt the other. And neither could back down. Was all the world so tattered, with such a little piece of knowledge?

My granddaughter.

Colum remembered the way his heart had burned when he said it, how right it had felt. It had given a bit of destined rightness to the feelings he had always held for her. It had only made those feelings stronger. But where Balder was concerned—

Colum had gone after him that day, spoken with him alone, but Balder would hear nothing on the subject. Nearly threw him from the palace until Colum gave in.

"Your Majesty, whether your mother's words were her desires alone, or absolute truth cannot alter what has been between us," Colum had admitted heavily. "I have never been your father. However before ever I knew of this, I had begun to regret that I was never a friend to you. I would not presume to know your feelings, but I desire to become your friend now, if you will allow it."

Balder had stared for the longest time before bending his head in an impatient acceptance of Colum's offer. But such a cautious acceptance that Colum felt its tenuous nature and worried about it. The knowledge changed everything. Perhaps eventually it would be for the better, but it wasn't now.

I will give him time to settle. I am sorry I spoiled things. He could see Rowan before him, standing on the sides of her feet the way she did when she was nervous, and her shoulders sinking. He'd seen that, he knew what it meant, what worry was cascading through her mind. And he'd held her, reassured her. But somehow he'd forgotten the need to help her the very next day.

No, the knowledge that Balder was his son had not been good for Colum. Nor it seemed, for his son. For any one of his sons. Ferdy wouldn't look his way as Colum approached, though it was clear he could see him, and Keagan was glaring dangerously.

"Rowan isn't here to protect you," Balder threatened. "She isn't your queen. If you were so important to her, then why didn't she stay?"

"She left to save your daughter," Sean shouted.

"Rowan may not be present," Maureen said in a powerful rumble of a voice that filled the air around them. "But her power remains, and so will the things she was building. Or have you forgotten our conversation so quickly?"

Lightning attacked the clouds above them, until even the sky beyond them seemed to shiver in fear.

Colum saw the king clenching up his muscles in preparation for some battle none of them should be fighting. Colum dove between the love of his life, and the child he'd never known was his.

"Your Majesty." Colum bowed to the king, putting his back to his wife. A wet wind swept over Colum's neck, slapping at him until he jerked straight, without the king's leave. "I have returned with news from Turrlough."

All around silence fell.

"Princess Rowan was not there," Colum said flatly. "Nor did I see any sign that she intended to be. But it seems Crown Prince Gavin ...has died."

A devastated pall fell over the gathering, even breath was too loud a noise to make at such a time.

"No," Ardal was the first to speak, alerting Colum to his presence. He had not seen him as he approached, but he looked back now and saw him in the middle of the group of women, sitting in his cart. The women looked equally shocked, muttering among themselves and clenching their weapons tighter. Before Colum's eyes could reach Maureen he saw his boys exchange dark looks and disappear from the field.

"How?" the king demanded.

Colum jerked his gaze forward again. "I do not know. The soldiers of Turrlough would not allow us to speak to the royal family, nor even to rest. We were told they would no longer associate with enemies of the Fairy queen. They blame us for his death."

"So we are to believe the Fairy queen killed him," Sean asked. "Do you think she would?"

Colum turned around to answer but cut himself off as Maureen answered, and indeed it appeared the question had been directed to her.

"She has used others to try before," Maureen said, but her eyes were glazed over and with a far off look. "But something, well, someone has always stopped her."

"Rowan?" a young woman beside Ardal asked, Colum thought it might be Ardal's granddaughter Nora, everyone was ignoring the presence of their king.

Colum didn't know that he would ever have been able to do the same, even when he knew nothing of who they were to one another. But he could not ignore his son now. More than that, he felt an itchy need to redirect the conversation so that Balder led it. He didn't scratch the itch, but it grew greater and greater the longer he resisted.

"No," Maureen laughed. "At first she knew nothing of him, she might have lent him some of her protection in recent years, but no. The messenger, who brings Rowan the prince's letters. His name is Eachann and he was at one time a member of the Fairy Court. He has been protecting the prince."

"He delivered Rowan a message the day she left," King Balder whispered, but garnered everyone's attention. "*I put an ally in danger*, that's what she said to me. That she needed to repair the damage."

"But that would mean going there," Tom said anxiously. "And Colum says she is not there."

"She has never traveled from home, we cannot know that she did not simply get lost along the way." Braden remarked from the edges of the group. "It might be prudent to send more soldiers, just in case she arrives later."

"You did not see the prince's body?" The question came from Liam. Colum glanced to his friend. Liam did not look precisely friendly now, but Colum merely shook his head.

"You don't think he's dead?" Braden demanded with an almost bitter laugh. "Him being protected is one thing, but he is no match for the Fairy queen. I do not understand why everyone persists in viewing him as some..." But words failed him and a few of the knights around him sniggered.

"I did not believe the prince is a match for the Fairy queen herself, though I have seen him fight, and he could hold his own against an ordinary fairy." Liam shook his head. "But during the war, when our forces fought for the Fairy queen, she sent down the order that Tyrone must be beheaded and his head carried out before his forces. She addressed us all herself, with tears in her eyes."

Sean and Ardal nodded. And Colum felt himself recalling the moment. At the time he'd thought how degrading a thing it was for a woman to lead, to be put into such a violent position.

"She said—" Colum began, but it was Maureen who repeated Sorcha's words. And her eyes met Colum's for the first time since he'd walked onto the field.

"Please understand this is not a show of power. I would forgo such a heinous act if I could. But I am known to be a fairy of many illusions, as is Tyrone. All Fairy must know the deed is done. They must see without question who they serve." Maureen looked away when she came to the end of the speech.

And Colum was stuck inside his own mind, reliving the moment, searching the crowd of fairies around Sorcha for Maureen. How had he never considered that she had been to Stonedragon long before she came with Sinead? They hadn't crossed paths. He was a young man, a soldier going out of his mind with worry for the woman he'd had an affair with who was wasting away in the palace dungeons. He hadn't even wanted to leave. He and Maureen had not crossed paths then, but Colum desperately wondered what Maureen had looked like. How brightly her fires had burned? Because when her eyes met his, Colum saw light around her like he had not in years, and he didn't know when it had dimmed. How he had failed to notice such a profound loss in the woman he loved?

"So..." Balder interrupted so hesitantly, it shocked Colum out of his contemplations and he looked at his son, a man, but saw the boy beneath. The hesitant, lonely child he should have outgrown. "You do not think the prince is dead?" Balder asked Maureen, with such a mixture of hope and anger Colum was sure he didn't know how he was feeling.

Maureen shrugged, and the field held silent awaiting her answer. "There are more ways to destroy a man than with death. Sorcha knows them all. If he...loved Rowan, and offered her his heart freely, I do believe the sacrifice Sinead made for her daughter will protect him from death. But if he is alive and Sorcha has found a hold over him, that may be a far worse fate."

Balder nodded. The rest of the gathering sunk under the truth of the words.

"Keep fighting if you choose," Balder said to Maureen with a bitter tone. "For all the good it will do any of you. Sir Colum, I shall expect a full report, presently." So saying the king swept away, taking his soldiers with him. Colum watched him go a moment, then turned back to his wife, wanting to heal their breach, or at least begin to do so.

But she had her back to him, and the men who had followed his lead for years all crowded around her seeking leadership.

"So, how do we help? How do we find out if the prince is alive or not?" Liam asked.

Maureen shook her head. "Rowan left to take care of her allies. We will protect her legacy."

Colum felt his feet moving. They stepped backwards. One step at a time, towards the palace, following his son. From the back of the crowd he saw Ardal's eyes following his retreat, but neither man said a word.

"Rowan would not go after Petal for revenge," Ferdy said the moment he and his brother appeared in the locked and overgrown rose garden. "Even if Gavin *is* dead."

Colleen felt her breath leave her body, but no sound did. She was sitting on the bench beneath the tree. She often sat here when she wasn't with the boys. She couldn't explain what it was about them that made her feel more comfortable, it wasn't only that they watched their feelings around her, many people did that. But Ferdy kept pushing her to do more and more on her own, while Keagan watched over her like she was a treasure. Something about the love they had for each other, and the fear she could feel in both of them, that they overcame again and again...she couldn't explain it. There was a soothing sort of balance to standing between them. Even though she knew standing between them had caused a lot of the fears they had now.

But they knew that too, and it didn't stop them trying to help her.

They walked right to the bench and Colleen who was sinking into herself trying not to interrupt realized she was invisible. She must have stolen the power from one of them. It made her shiver a bit. Made her wonder if she was about to lose herself. Every time she stole someone's power without meaning to, she had to shut her eyes and focus on the feel of her fingers locked together, or pull her hair before her face and remember that she had never cut it, nor even trimmed it, this hair had been with her since she was born. But she was invisible, and she couldn't even make herself feel her hands.

I am Colleen. I am from Turrlough. My father is a fisherman, and my mother a seamstress. I am Colleen. I was born beside a spraying sea, with fields of barley behind me, and the sun above me. I am Colleen.

She told herself to be sure she knew who she was. But the invisibility did not go away. The boys continued to fight, oblivious to her, and the more seconds passed the more Colleen realized the power might have come from them, but the impulse didn't. She wanted to be invisible.

She sat up, breathing a bit easier, and listened.

"I felt her visit us, she came because she cares. She loves us, and she loves Petal too," Ferdy shouted.

He was usually so nonchalant. So easy with every word or thought. That he wasn't now made Colleen wonder if he believed his words quite as much as he wanted to.

"I'm not saying she doesn't. But what if...what if she saw it? What if she saw the prince killed, and Petal was a part of it?" Keagan asked.

Prince Gavin was dead. Colleen felt the shock of tears and...grief. She remembered him. *I remember him. I remember...* but there her mind failed her. She could see in her mind's eye the prince walking through the doors of his palace to defend her, but she couldn't tell for certain if it was a memory, or an invention of some part of her who wanted to be protected. Because she could feel bits of herself shying away towards the quiet pit inside where she didn't have to know he was dead, where she didn't have to see her comforters falling into chaos. So much of her wanted to run away from the feelings.

"So now you're doubting them both?" Ferdy demanded. "Whose side will you take?"

"I'm not doubting either of them!" Keagan shouted. "I'm saying Rowan needs our help. If not to keep her safe, then to keep her...*her*. Once she knows he's dead."

"She's never even met him," Ferdy snapped.

"They've been writing letters since she was fifteen. She sent him *Petal*. She doesn't need to meet him. He's already changed her."

Ferdy paced away, kicking a rose bush so great was his frustration growing. He pulled back his leg, hissing in pain and stared down at some injury. Then as if it would change anything he kicked the bush again and again and again.

Watching him, more of Colleen crawled towards the empty. She was crying, but if all of her could get into the empty she would never have to cry again. She could be free of pain—forever. She wanted that back so much some days.

Maybe she would never know her name. Maybe she wouldn't know what memories were hers in truth, but she would never be torn and broken and destroyed. Like these boys were.

Keagan, for the first time that Colleen could recall looked utterly shocked. Bereft. He started forward, just one step, his hand outstretched, but he just paused there. Ferdy threw himself to the ground in front of the beaten rose bush, with its limbs hanging limply and petals and leaves strewn all about its base. Ferdy stared at the bush and took a long heavy breath. He lay that way for a moment, then his head tilted to the side, he took in his brother's shocked expression and something approaching a smile grew on his face.

"How many of your visions was Prince Gavin even a part of?"

"What?" Keagan squeaked.

"You've seen the end of this battle a million ways, a million confrontations. Sorcha winning. Petal killing us. Rowan winning. Rowan dying. Rowan turning evil."

Keagan startled. "I never told you about that one."

"You didn't have to," Ferdy replied. "It was there in the ways you would try to direct Rowan, like you knew better than her. I always knew. But you've never told me about Prince Gavin. How many of the confrontations was he part of?"

Keagan moved his head back and forth with his eyes on his feet. He was counting. With every tiny twist of his head Colleen felt *safer*. He could see it all. Good, bad, awful. He saw it every day. If this child could withstand all of that, and try to help make Colleen better, surely she could withstand a little pain. Especially knowing he wanted her to be well.

Oh, his desire for her to be safe and whole and herself— somedays it was so much stronger than her own want. Some days it was his want that kept her out of the empty. She could stay out, if he wanted it.

She just wasn't entirely sure that was a good thing.

That sounded quite a bit like what ciphers did. Gave everyone else what they wanted. Maybe she should fight it, but she leaned forward, waiting for him to finish counting. Waiting to know just how bad this was.

"Maybe fifty."

"Out of millions," Ferdy laughed.

"Not millions. I've only seen it two-thousand, seven-hundred and ninety-one ways," Keagan corrected.

"And the prince was only a part of fifty of them?" Ferdy smirked and leaned back on his hands. "How many of those were outcomes when we won?"

"Most," Keagan shrugged. "But there are a higher number of winning scenarios where he isn't there."

Ferdy waved a triumphant arm, as if to say the prince's death meant they would win. Anyone else might take it for callus, but Colleen felt his fear and his sadness. He just couldn't go on without a smile. He had to find the bright side. The bits of Colleen that had lingered, unsure if she should follow Keagan or not crawled away from the empty to bask in that light. When Ferdy shone like that Colleen felt stronger, more capable. When that light touched her, she felt like maybe the light could banish the empty forever.

"I don't think his not being a part of the scenarios necessarily means he was dead," Keagan argued, but his eyes were looking inward again. "There are a number where you can tell Rowan has suffered great loss to get there. And…I mean Mama and Pa aren't in all of them either, are we now assuming anyone who isn't in the vision is dead?" Keagan demanded.

"Of course not," Ferdy leapt to his feet. "I'm just pointing out that his death doesn't mean we lose either. Maybe Rowan will find a fairy to love, or marry no one. Or a million things. A million possibilities, Keagan. I know there are. You just haven't seen them all yet. So…get busy seeing them so we can be prepared. And I'll find a way for us to send Rowan a message."

Keagan perked up. "Do you think you can?"

"Of course," Ferdy shrugged. "I'll even read your stupid book."

"You know," Keagan said hesitantly. "If you can send her a message, then we can find where she is, and if we can do that we can…"

"One step at a time, Kee," Ferdy sighed.

"I just think we shouldn't rule out the possibility," Keagan said in a conciliatory manner.

"And we won't. But there is still a lot to be done here. We don't even know if we can go. Depending on how far away she is, we may not even have the power to get to her in one jump. We could faint like she did, and fall off a cliff to our deaths."

"I know," Keagan said in that busy mind way he spoke sometimes. He and Ferdy moved by the bench together, as if they would leave by the gate, but Colleen knew they wouldn't. The roses had grown over it, barring the way more securely than a raised drawbridge blocked a moat. "The more days that have passed the more I've thought of it. What we need is a way to get more power than belongs to us, replenishing itself so we don't fall ill from overuse like Rowan did."

Ferdy was nodding along, would probably reply, but Colleen wouldn't know what he said as they vanished from the garden.

She sat forward on the bench, and stared down, waiting for her hands to appear again. Their voices had long since faded away when she stood. This was getting boring. Colleen vanished from the garden.

Power of Grief

Balder sat behind his desk and stared at the empty page before him. He should offer his condolences to the king and queen of Turrlough. Their son was gone. Likely because of something Rowan had done to bring Roisin home.

Those women who are training to defend themselves...they just want to be safe.

Balder heard his daughter's voice and wanted to rage against it. Wanted her here so he could drive home his point. His stopping those women from training *was* protecting them. If they were all that could stand between Sorcha and her vengeance they should hide. He should bury them in the darkest corner of his domain to keep them protected. Like Roisin was protected. Like Rowan never had been.

He'd never protected Rowan. Never. Now she was out in a world she did not understand, alone. She could starve, or freeze, or be devoured by predators. There were so many more worries in the world than Sorcha, and Rowan was alone to face them. As his mother had been. As her mother had been.

Denying these women weapons wasn't fear of them rising up against him, or a changed world. It was absolute certainty that the longer they held those weapons the more danger they were in. He wanted his wife and his daughters and his citizens safe, he just should have fought harder for that with Rowan.

Now she was alone, and so confident she was bound to be broken down by reality. And the man she believed to be her destiny was gone.

A knock sounded on the door and Balder called out for Colum to enter. He knew it was Colum, he recognized the heaviness of his hand on the wood. Balder's body and mind tensed. One more person who thought they knew better than him. One more person to judge him unworthy. One more parent to do so. As if the two Balder had disappointed already were not enough.

Colum bowed, waiting until Balder waved him to a seat before sitting. Waiting for leave before he spoke. Respectful of his place. Just not of Balder himself.

"Well," Balder waved an impatient hand. "What have you to report?"

"There is little else to say, Your Majesty. I found the state of Turrlough disturbing before ever we reached the palace. Something has most certainly occurred there, of a powerful and frightening nature, but I cannot say what."

Balder stared down at the empty page.

"When Roisin was first cursed." Balder brushed the feather end of his quill back and forth across the page, seeing the past more than anything else. "The word spread out like ripples on a lake. The further it went the more sympathy was strewn at my feet. More and more, gifts and letters, and roses—I despise roses. The scent of them speaks of death to me. I thought I would drown in them. I needed the sympathy to stop. My daughter was still here! There was no reason for sympathy if there was still something to be done. So I rode to Fellstone to confront my citizens, and demand they work to find a solution, not mourn Roisin. When I arrived I was met by the most profound madness. My citizens weren't mourning, they were fighting one another. Trying to steal baby girls to send to Sorcha in Roisin's place— I was horrified."

Balder looked up, he had to look on this man's face, maybe he could find that comfort Rowan always had. Not that he expected that. He went looking, but he knew for him it would be derision, or disappointment. But Colum's face was a shock, quiet. Intent and open. He wanted to hear what Balder had to say and more words came pouring out in response.

"I was horrified, but for a moment I wondered if it might work. If I could trade some unknown citizen for my daughter. But," Balder laughed sadly. "Fellstone is where my mother was born. I looked around and saw her friends and neighbors fighting amongst themselves trying to help me, because they had loved her. For perhaps the first time in my life, I wanted to help my people, not because it was my duty, or to make my father proud...” His words fell away for a moment. *His father*. Things were so much simpler, when he had only one father to disappoint, one father to resent. So Balder spoke on, pretending the thought had never occurred to him.

“I wanted to protect my people for my mother. It was the first time I realized, they were her people too. So I told them what I’d said to Rowan already: that we would not trade one life for another. That we would not descend to Sorcha’s level of evil. I watched them calm and I was comforted by that more than I had ever been by the offers of sympathy. I meant the words when I said them. I meant them when I said them to Rowan.”

Balder allowed the words to stretch across the air, could not think what words more to say, but there was more inside of him. He’d meant the words.

“Your Majesty, you did not trade Prince Gavin’s life for your daughter’s. He chose to work with Rowan of his own volition and Rowan did not trade his life either. She would not. You raised her not to.”

Balder felt a burning rush up through his chest towards his head. Felt it pounding to escape his eyes but he fought it back with held breath and clenched fists. Men did not show such weakness.

“Well, I am sure Rowan knows what she is about. I dare say she’ll have everything set to rights in a week. With her fairy blood, and her knightly training, there is nothing she cannot do,” Balder said bitterly, reminding himself that despite whatever words of comfort this man offered, he was the man who took Rowan’s love and made her willful and overconfident. Colum was willing to trade her safety for—

But Balder couldn’t think why Colum had been so willing to risk Rowan. He had no more love for Roisin than he had for Balder. So why had he been willing to risk Rowan? Balder couldn’t understand it any more than he could understand his own choices, everyone leading right to Rowan alone, against a world much bigger and more powerful than she. Everyone of them, willing to risk exchanging her life for Roisin. Gwyneth might have been the only one of them to say it, but all of them had been willing in the end.

"She has failings like anyone." Colum looked aside. "Is there anything else, Your Majesty?"

"Yes," Balder snapped. "You trained her, so I am putting you in charge of the search to find her. You will report to me daily, and coordinate the search from my palace, so I may oversee the progress."

Colum bowed in his seat. "Of course, Your Majesty, it will be my honor."

Colum rose to leave, rightly interpreting Balder's silence for an end of their meeting. But his eyes rose to the portrait of Roisin that hung behind Balder's desk.

"The people of Fellstone were certainly your mother's friends, but there was equal madness taking place across your kingdom when the princess was cursed. I do not think you can credit your mother for all of it. Your people love you, and your daughters." He bowed again and quit the room with slow measured steps.

Balder waited until he was gone, and pulled open a drawer from his desk to remove the portrait of Roisin Rowan had given him. He ran a finger over it.

I will not be fighting for your love any longer.

His fingers traced Roisin's beloved face, the face he'd been without for so long. He'd wanted her home for *so* long. Somewhere over the years he'd wanted it so much that he'd forgotten to see the daughter he had right in front of him. Now she was gone. And he couldn't escape the sinking feeling that she was never coming home. He'd done it after all, traded one love for another.

What if neither of them ever came home?

Ferdy slipped into the family cottage to ransack Mama's room invisibly. She was changing things. Ferdy nearly laughed to see it, Pa was due for quite the shock. The window casements were all gone, and Mama's garden was growing in from outside. Clovers and moss carpeted the floor, there was even a tiny blueberry bush growing next to one window. It looked like a living cave, some of the moss was even growing up over the walls towards the ceiling.

Ferdy loved it! He thought Pa, however, might be a bit uncomfortable about the implications of such a change. Mama was embracing the fairy within. Not that she had ever hidden from it, or hidden her magic, or even her love for who she was. But she hadn't shared it with the world so openly. She wore human clothes, cooked as humans did, walked more places than she ever went to magically. All she really did with magic was teach Rowan and heal those who needed it.

But if their home was any indication, that wouldn't be the case anylon—

Mama appeared in her room with Ferdy mid search. She was breathing heavily, and her eyes were bright and growing red. She walked to the window frame and leaned her hands against it, wrapped her fingers around it like they could hold back her rage. At least that's what it looked like at first.

Then she gasped and leaned against the window with sobs shaking her body. Ferdy stepped forward, reaching towards his mother, but her legs gave out and she curled up there on the floor burying her face in her hands to sob, and Ferdy didn't know what to do. He knew she wouldn't have wanted him to see this. Mama hid her pain from all of them. But he didn't want to leave her there alone. Someone should hold her. Someone should help her. Pa should. He should see this. For surely his stupidity had hurt Mama and caused this.

Ferdy was shaking, his magic calling out to someone, anyone who could help her. He sat on the bed near her, not touching, just watching, sending out his magic to comfort her. Before his eyes, the clovers grew longer, thicker, crawling around Mama's shoulders, like a blanket. She lay a hand atop it and squeezed like it was someone's hand on her shoulder.

"I'm so tired, Sinead," she whispered, unaware that it was Ferdy's magic holding her tight just now. "So tired. I am trying to be strong, but I don't know anymore if it will be enough. The world just gets more troubled."

She stopped speaking then, and curled up in the embrace of clovers. She cried a bit longer, quiet, sapping tears that slid down her cheeks and watered the room. Ferdy watched it growing, glowing— spreading.

He'd taken the overgrowth for a powerful, joyous statement. But what if he was wrong. What if she'd grown this jungle with her sorrows alone? And it just kept growing, taking her magic with it.

It was the first time it truly struck Ferdy that Prince Gavin was dead. The man Rowan loved was dead. She could survive it. She didn't need a man to help her. But if it hurt Mama like this, what would it do to Rowan? It was no wonder Mama felt tired, she spent so much of her love and her power protecting them all, guarding their hearts and their bodies. And no one did the same for her.

When Mama was asleep Ferdy took a blanket from the bed and lay it over her. He crouched beside her, and shifted his fingers through all the life overtaking their house. In every bit he felt her life-force.

She needed this bower of lovely, growing nature in her home. But she was spending so much of herself to make it grow that she was tired and fading as a result.

Ferdy let his magic nudge the plants. It had never been his skill, but Mama needed it, so Ferdy offered the plants as much of his power as they needed, asking them to show his love. And watched as more and more plants grew in through the window. Until the walls and ceiling and floor all were alive. Until flowers drooped from the ceiling, and berries grew in plump clusters by the head of her bed, and everywhere was something to remind her there was hope.

Ferdy walked slowly from her room, watching her until the very last second. He tripped as he turned the corner, the moss catching his foot to stop him. He landed with a muffled thud and Devon's book on the Fairy slid his way on mossy fingers.

Ferdy lifted it with a hearty sigh. He wasn't sure he wanted it right now. When he touched this book he felt smaller. Felt as small and insignificant as this book called tricksters. No where near big enough to help or even to know how to help without someone else's direction. But this book might have magic that could help, and he had to help them all, not just Mama, and Keagan, but Rowan, and Pa, and Petal. Everyone. They were coming apart. He couldn't leave behind any means to help.

"Thank you," he whispered and vanished from the house.

Rowan had four very uneventful days. She and Yseult were not making good time, not that they knew where they were going. In the last day or so, Rowan was lucky to get even half speed out of the horse. She didn't blame Yseult, avoiding roads meant they frequently came up against obstructions, or difficult terrain, and Yseult was carrying Rowan and her packs, and her armor. The poor horse deserved a reward. Or a rest. Yseult would probably prefer the rest.

Rowan was worn out too. Just in different ways. They'd left the Liadan behind when they made it out of the enchanted forest. And Rowan at first used her power to soothe the horse, but the more she did so, the more she heard the word *limitless* whispered inside her mind. But it wasn't Gavin, extolling the virtues of setting her own limits anymore. It was Sorcha's voice: *enticing*.

Gavin's voice had gone slowly silent. Even Rowan had gone silent. She only really spoke to Yseult about difficulties they encountered with the terrain, or about the slowly dwindling supply of food.

So the ride had grown slower, and the reward seemed further and further away no matter how far they rode. What if the dragons weren't leading her to them? They'd led her to such odd places, perhaps they were merely having fun at her expense. What if they just liked tricking fools into wandering around half starving.

Rowan had officially run out of dried meat this morning. The soldiers hadn't had much of it with them, nor many vegetables or fruits. She still had a bit of bread, and maybe a bite's worth of cheese. Soon she would need to find more food. Now that they were on Anwyn's land Rowan had a feeling it would take a great deal of luck to stumble across another farm. They were in the forest near Mount Anwyn on the inland side, the nation did almost all its farming on their seaward edges. There were a few tiny villages, and Rowan imagined a few lone citizens living in the wood who were bound to have their own gardens, but she hadn't a clue where to look and she really shouldn't risk going near the villages.

She still didn't want word of where she was getting to her father, or to anyone. If word of where she was got out the first pair of ears likely to hear it were Sorcha's.

So it would need to be hunting and foraging. Rowan had never hunted before, but she supposed it should not be too different from hitting a target in practice. She could use the practice with a bow anyway. She hadn't much used it in the past year, much less the past week. But the bow and Rowan were old familiars.

Why was magic so much harder? She could hear one of the aunts in the back of her mind, admonishing her to think of magic like a limb. Just another extension of her being. But it never—

A force yanked at Rowan as if from within. It grabbed her by the gut, sucking her backwards, cutting off her air, driving her entirely out of her body. It was like...like when she traveled in her mind, but outside her control. Something was dragging her away from her body.

She fought the feeling, fought to stay with Yseult, to stay in the here and now, but she couldn't stop it. She had no power as she was dragged breathlessly, formlessly fighting for life.

With a plop like a stone had been dropped into her stomach, Rowan found herself dropped into a room. It took a moment to gain her bearings, everything inside still sloshed around. The room was unfamiliar. She thought perhaps she was in the Fairy court, because despite the very human look of the structure, nature had overtaken it, growing over walls and floor, and—

"Maureen!" Rowan dropped to her knees, and reached out for Maureen, lying on the floor, covered in a blanket and a patch of clovers. Rowan's hand passed through her, confirming what she'd already felt, that this was a travel in her mind. She just could not explain how.

Nothing had ever pulled her beyond her command before. Even when the travels first started it was her reaching out to her sisters. But this...

Maureen lay against the wall beneath a window, as if she had collapsed there, but Rowan didn't think she had been cursed. She couldn't sense any evil, nor remnants of a spell. The room was certainly flooded with magic, but it seemed mostly to be Maureen's. Rowan looked around the room. Maureen had said fairy shouldn't remain shut away from nature before Rowan left, apparently she meant to be sure she never was again.

It looked so different. Rowan wanted to get up and search the rest of the house, but she didn't move. Something had pulled her to Maureen, something or someone wanted to be sure she knew Maureen needed her.

Rowan let herself settle on the floor beside Maureen. She needed to reach her.

No limits. Rowan heard the words from far away, and ignored them.

"Maureen," Rowan said quietly, leaning nearer. "I love you so much. It won't be much longer," Rowan spoke, knowing it was unlikely that Maureen would hear her, but needing to reassure her, and perhaps reassure herself in the process. "Everything will be alright. I'm going to bring Petal home. We'll all be together and everything will be beautiful. I promise. Mama," she whispered the words hesitantly just as she had before she left. She wished she could reach forward and wrap Maureen in her arms. Wished they could feel each other's love.

No limits. The whisper sounded again, but Rowan pushed the voice aside.

"You told me, you felt my joy when I told you what our future would be. It's going to be beautiful, we just have to get there."

Maureen made a little noise, really just a hitch of her breathing, and a few tears fell from her closed eyes.

"Maureen," Rowan shuddered, she couldn't bear to see her this way.

There are no *limits set on who or what you can become!* Gavin's voice insisted. Rowan felt her heart pounding.

She stretched her hand through the space between her and Maureen. It shouldn't work. It never had before. But she *needed* to comfort Maureen more than she'd needed anything since she was a child. Maureen was the mother of her heart, her comforter, her friend, the person who loved her no matter what. She needed to return that love. For all the years that Maureen had sat beside Rowan when she was ill, or guarded her from a frightening world, or calmed her in a rage. Maureen had cared for Rowan at her best and worst, she *needed* to care for her now.

Her heartbeats burned. Each pulsation radiated fire in Rowan's chest. She could do this, she could reach her. She had to.

Rowan's hand slid forward right up to Maureen and her finger caught a tear from Maureen's cheek. She felt the wetness. Her pulse raced with excitement, she was doing it, she was touching her though she wasn't really there. But stealing a tear wasn't what Rowan was after. She bent over Maureen and lay her lips on Maureen's head infusing the kiss with her love, and her power.

"I love you," Rowan whispered, though already she felt her spirit being pulled away again, back to Anwyn, back to Yseult, and her body.

Yseult must have sensed her journey, because she was stopped, just waiting beside a tree. Rowan shuddered back into her body shaking from head to toe, but not from exhaustion. A bit was sadness, for what Maureen was suffering, but mostly her body shook from the power that seemed only to be building within her.

She'd touched Maureen, though she hadn't been in the room, though nothing in Devon's book implied such a thing was possible, though no one had told her it was possible. She'd reached her.

Rowan lifted her left hand before her, a tear sat at the edge of her pointer finger. Maureen's tear. Rowan rubbed the tear between her fingers, allowing her skin to soak in its dampness, then she ran her damp fingers through Yseult's mane and sent out her magic with the touch, healing the horses exhaustion, as well as she could.

Everything would be well. Rowan just had to, for once in her life, be her own source of belief. Maybe she could even be more than that, maybe she could be a source of belief for those she loved.

"We will all be well," she whispered, and kissed the horse's sweaty neck.

Strange Comforters

381 days until Roisin returns

Petal was feeling much better since she'd had her epiphany about Sorcha's curses. She had a new plan, it wasn't strictly speaking what Rowan had asked, but she didn't think Rowan would mind if Petal simply found a way to break Sorcha's curse. There must be a way. So, Petal the Powerful graciously gave over to each of the Fairy queen's lessons, learning what she could so that she might better understand her curses. If she understood them, the way she did Sorcha's scepter, then she could break them all. Just like she could certainly free the prince if she wanted to.

If she could save Rowan's sister that would make up for everything. Rowan would have to forgive her for Gavin then. Surely?

Petal felt certain the wolves were her key, so it was beneficial that Malachy was following her. He never ventured near enough for Petal to properly see, but she could feel him. Feel them. The princess, by far the best tracker of the pack, had found her littlest brother, and all four wolves traveled together now. Petal liked to feel them together. It made her think of a time when she was with her brothers. It made her feel at home. She almost wanted to join them, and be one more wolf wandering the world. It would be easier. But Petal the Powerful was not doomed to an easy life. She would have adventure and would work at unraveling the magic of the most powerful being on the island.

The closer the wolves grew the more impatient Sorcha became. She'd asked Petal three more times to free Desmond. And Petal was refusing now only to thwart Sorcha. Petal knew the sooner she got her hands on that crystal the sooner she got home, and she even thought the prince deserved freeing. And it was her mission.

But Petal didn't want to do anything Sorcha wanted.

As much as Petal wanted to see home again. She wasn't ready yet. She needed to *know* she had power enough to undo the curse on the Rose Princess. So everyone would forgive her.

What if they never forgave her?

The thought shuddered under Petal's skin most days, but she shoved it away with positive energy and a plan. Her plan. So she lied and said she wasn't good enough to touch his crystal. She pretended illness or exhaustion, and she felt for the wolves, who seemed to find her, no matter what door she went through in the palace.

So far she had only gone through doors that entered parts of the Fairy nation. But it was vast, and the wolves always found her. Last night she'd been on the inland side of Mount Kieran and they'd followed her. Today Dervla and Kermit were guarding Petal to see the very edge of the island's northern side, in the thick forest at the edge of the Blazing Sea, and the wolves were here again. She felt them a ways behind her. She had no idea how they traveled so far so fast, but she knew it was they, and not four other wolves. It must be some after effect of the curse Sorcha put on them. That or they had some magic all their own.

They were venturing closer and closer. As though they were stalking her. Petal smiled at the bit of fancy, imagining herself stalked through this dark forest by a pack of wolves intent on devouring her. But she knew that wasn't what these wolves were after. They wanted her help, the closer they grew the more she felt their desires. Most strongly their sister. She was worried for her brothers, worried that she was losing all of them. She hoped Petal could restore them.

Sorcha would never approve, Petal grinned. In truth she wasn't certain she should do it. The pack, as much as Petal loved them, were nearly lost to humanity, holding onto only two tiny bits of their old selves: their love for one another and their rage for Sorcha. Petal wasn't sure which emotion was the strongest.

If it were rage, and they were returned to human form, there was no telling what they might do. Or how Sorcha might react. Petal didn't want to restore them to themselves only to watch them be destroyed.

Petal's stomach sloshed violently. She didn't want to see that ever again.

"Were you there when the Fairy queen, in her infinite wisdom and massive power," Petal embellished her question with praise for Sorcha, lest the trees be listening, "cursed the royal family of Creelan?"

Dervla, as was frequently her way, disguised all expression in a shadow and made no response. Kermit, however, sighed and answered.

"I was."

"How was such a thing achieved?" Petal inquired as though awed. "I cannot fathom it."

"When the Fairy queen, in her infinite wisdom," Kermit said, with a small sideways smile, "determines it is time for you to know, you will learn the way."

"I do not mean to learn the spell," Petal lied, playfully. "I only wondered... how great a power it must take to do such a thing to an entire nation?"

"Who said the entire nation was transformed?" Dervla asked with a bit more bite than her face displayed.

"Were they not?" Petal asked innocently.

"I was not present," Dervla replied.

"The spell took different forms for different crimes," Kermit answered. "It could not destroy an entire people for nothing more than following their rulers. But nor could it allow them to go unpunished if they had not opposed him. So all were touched by the magic, but the royal family were the only curse wolves."

"And the rest made prisoners, with fairy guards?" Petal asked between her teeth, unable to keep the snarl out of her mouth when she thought of the fate that befell so many of Turrlough's citizens. The fate that befell the girls she'd *freed*.

"No," Kermit said with a question in his voice. "Why do you ask that?"

"It was done in Turrlough. Three male children from each village were...left in the guard of soldiers from my battalion who remain acting as stewards of the Fairy queen's will." Dervla answered, looking around for listening trees.

Kermit gave Petal a warning look that made it clear he would speak no more on the topic. And Dervla vanished entirely.

A very useful skill—for spies and assassins.

Petal shuddered and her heart caught in her chest. Had Dervla left to kill someone? Someone who had overheard Petal's questions and might put her in danger? Had Petal just cost someone their life, from nothing but speaking?

Her heart pounded so hard so fast, that she couldn't breathe from the rampage of beats. What was she doing? Trying to best Sorcha with trickery? Sorcha was happy to watch princes die, happy to rip families apart. How could Petal ever hope to out trick someone so ruthless? Already sweat was breaking out on her forehead from just the thought of what might happen because of her.

She didn't know what to do with Dervla and Kermit in her mind. Sometimes they were the closest beings to her, almost friends. Then Sorcha would see their closeness and do something to ruin it. Petal knew both of these fairy loved her, and wanted her safe. But neither would disobey the Fairy queen, and neither of them was on Rowan's side in this struggle. At least not entirely.

She wondered sometimes: what would happen if Sorcha decided Petal was not so special after all? What would they do if Sorcha ordered them to kill Petal?

Dervla reappeared, and her expression gave nothing away. But Petal could feel her understanding the direction of Petal's thoughts, and being injured by them. Petal wanted to take that pain inside herself and let it mark Dervla as trustworthy, but something wouldn't let her.

She hid too much. She was too good a soldier.

"Just ahead now, a midday meal is laid for you, and *the Fairy queen,*" Dervla said with special emphasis.

Petal swallowed, and pulled forth her smile, banishing her doubts into the back of her mind as one might flick away a gnat. She was growing skilled at that. As long as there was light on her face, and Sorcha near, Petal could pretend to be anyone. As long as there was light on her face.

They walked into a crescent of open space, with a jagged cliff for an outer perimeter and a sloshing wild ocean beyond it. Petal caught her breath, before she'd even taken in the Fairy queen. Petal could smell the sea! It smelled like life, and adventure and…something burning. It was glorious!

"What is that smell?" Petal demanded, excitedly innocent. Sorcha liked that, she wouldn't mind that Petal hadn't greeted her first, because she was so caught up in the beauty. And indeed when her gaze found Sorcha's face, she was smiling her genuine grin of pleasure.

"Ash." She took to her feet, leaving their table of driftwood, smooth to the touch and salty to smell, and walking around to show Petal where to look. "I thought you might like to see. Look there, in the distance, where grey is twirling into the sky, that is the nearest of the Blazing Sea's volcanos, and today it shall erupt."

"Truly?" Petal demanded, excitement filling her up. She leaned further towards the edge. "Ferdy and Keagan will be so jealous! Is it dangerous?"

"Not as far away as we are. There is a special form of fairy that are born from volcanic eruptions." Sorcha spoke in a friendly informative fashion. "Fire imps. They take a form like the ash clouds of the volcanoes, and they can throw fire and smoke, and turn their bodies into volcanic rock if need be."

Petal spun around with a bright smile on her face and looked up at Sorcha. "Will we see any?"

"We just might, but we shall have to look very close. They do not come to this island. For many long years all the forms of Fairy have kept to themselves. But fairy are everywhere, in numerous form." She was sharing with poetic, but practiced enthusiasm. Probably even a practiced speech. All at once her eyes grew distant as they did sometimes. The ash cloud grew higher; she stared into it instead of at Petal. "My sister Bride loved eruption days. She wanted our mother to bring all the forms of fairy together. She said it was because she wanted us all to live in harmony and create a fuller eternity. But in truth I think she just wanted to meet all the different varieties. She loved to learn new things."

Petal giggled, pretending not to have noticed that Sorcha was speaking on a subject that was generally deemed off limits, or that she was speaking of it in a nearly gentle, missing voice. "Who wouldn't want to meet them all? Think of all the new and wonderful kinds of magic you could learn," Petal said brightly.

"Yes." Sorcha nodded. She shut her hand, and opened it, and a tiny spy glass appeared in it. She held it silently to Petal. "The magic was never what interested Bride. She found every different being in the world an exciting new puzzle. Perhaps she has had a grand adventure in her banishment."

Once Petal took the spyglass, Sorcha walked away, settling back at their meal, she ate quietly, allowing Petal to look into the distance, searching for another world she knew next to nothing about.

It was a trick, Petal knew it was a trick. But the longer the silence stretched, even though Petal searched the distance for the fairy, her heart went out to Sorcha. She was such a lonely soul.

"You could do it," Petal said softly.

"Do what?" the Fairy queen asked.

Petal turned around, lowering the spyglass to her side. A bit beyond Sorcha she saw Dervla and Kermit standing guard, watching Petal and Sorcha, and the growing bond between them. "You could do what your sister wanted your mother to do. You could unite all Fairy."

Sorcha laughed. "Petal, my love, you are the only fairy who thinks so," she said. A very uncharacteristic thing to say, so full of doubt and self-awareness. It reminded Petal of before; before she'd watched her destroy Prince Gavin, before she'd admitted to being a spy. When Sorcha seemed to be crying out for someone to save her, to befriend her.

Petal took a step towards her. "You can. You could even bring back your sisters if you wanted. You are the Fairy queen. You know the beauty in all Fairy. You can unite us. Wouldn't that be such a lovely world for Desmond to wake to?"

Sorcha gasped, and looked up at Petal desperately, a single tear poised at the edge of her eye.

"He would love such a world, he was such a gentle heart," Sorcha said, the words on a lovely heartbroken sob. How could one sound so lovely when they were crying? Petal knew she sounded, and looked quite a fright when she cried, but not the Fairy queen. Sorcha was *glorified* by her grief.

Petal stepped forward, laying the spyglass on the table, she reached out for the scepter. "I will try again, if you like," Petal offered.

Sorcha, with tears in her eyes and trickling down her face, raised a hand and lay it against Petal's cheek. "Are you certain? You have been so angry with me." Sorcha's breath hitched as she said the words, and more tears fell. "You must know, my dear, I never wanted to harm Prince Gavin. I had given him *many* opportunities to mind his own affairs. I—" she gasped.

Petal felt her muscles knotting. She wanted to rage, and sob, and hide. Wanted never to have to think of him again. But she fought the feelings. She had a mission, and it wouldn't be helped by mourning or guilt. She had not killed him. Petal had not destroyed his family. Even his own mother said as much. But Petal felt it all on her whenever his name was spoken. She felt the letters she'd stolen in her hands again, felt the loss of the secret petals, as if they were the loss of her family's love. She felt broken and angry.

If she let herself feel.

Why was Sorcha making her feel so again, when she'd been working so hard to make Petal come back to her?

"I am so sorry. I loved the prince. Were I only Sorcha, I would have spared him. But there are things one must do as queen, terrible things, to see my nation safe."

Sorcha was awaiting some response, and Petal knew she should thrust out the words the woman was after. Should offer forgiveness and understanding. But she couldn't.

"Is that why you made me watch?" Petal demanded without meaning to. The words dove from her lips and she hiccuped, the feeling like an eruption pulling forth her own tears. Where a moment before she had been elated she shuddered and sobbed, but had to keep speaking. "Did you want me to feel the terrible burden you want for my future?"

"No. Never!" Sorcha shook her head. Her hand slid from Petal's face to her shoulder, drawing her nearer. There was barely any space between them now, and were it not for the scepter lying against the table there would be nothing between them. Petal's eyes wanted to desert Sorcha and hide in that crystal. She wanted to look on the fairy prince and take comfort in knowing she had the power to defeat one of Sorcha's spells. She wanted to feel powerful. But Sorcha would not allow Petal's gaze free.

"I had to have you there for the girls you freed," Sorcha said fiercely. "And for his family. They needed to know that you were not trapped with me, that nothing was forced upon you."

Petal sobbed all the harder with every word. That was so much worse. Why was that worse? She quivered beneath her cold, traitorous skin, every shake releasing a spray of tears. Any moment now she would crumble apart completely.

"I never want you to see such things. I do not want them for you when you are queen. That is why I do this. I am making way for you. For a better queen. I have seen the Fairy who unites us all and it isn't me, Petal. It's you."

Petal sputtered on tears rushing into her nose and mouth as she tried to breathe. She couldn't breathe, her heart hurt, her head was splitting apart in yawning caverns. It was too much. Too big. Too weighty. She wasn't good enough.

"Together you and Desmond will usher in an era of peace, not just for the Fairy, but for everyone. But that can only happen if I stop those who want to tear this nation apart. I am sorry. Please, tell me you can forgive me," she begged.

Petal was shaking her head, the tears were so numerous before her eyes that the whole world looked smudged and undefined. The only thing she knew was that she needed to be held. She wanted Mama. She wanted her brothers. She wanted Pa. But all she had was Sorcha, and Sorcha loved Petal like she loved no one else. Not even her son, really.

Petal needed love so— even though her mind knew Sorcha was the cause of all her suffering. Even though her mind knew there was a trick in every word this woman spoke. Even though her heart knew this love was not the love she wanted. Petal threw herself into the arms of the Fairy queen and held tight as the emotions overpowered her. She shuddered and shook and sobbed and Sorcha just held her near, and ran and hand gently down her spine. And for the first time since she'd watched Prince Gavin die, Petal truly began to feel safe.

Rowan thought she might vomit. Her eyes were watering, her stomach turned every time she chewed. But she forced herself to keep chewing. She never wanted to eat rabbit again.

It was the most disgusting thing she'd ever experienced. The hunting process had been so frustrating and fruitless for the last day and a half that when she'd finally managed to shoot a rabbit she'd danced. But...she hadn't really thought about having to prepare it. Having to skin it, having to see its eyes, having to drain its blood and see its flesh. Every second wishing that she'd never left home.

She wished she could call back the arrow that had killed it. It had been alive, and she killed it, and honestly if she hadn't had to prepare it herself that might never have struck her, but as she was skinning it she heard bushes shaking and thought of was Roisin with her forest friends gathered around her. Telling Rowan about the poor baby foxes whose mother had died. She wondered if this rabbit had been one of Roisin's friends before it was banished from the Enchanted Forest. She couldn't stop herself thinking about its children and family and wondering if animals thought humans were monsters.

But she forced herself to eat. Even though she knew nothing about how to prepare meat, and it tasted nothing like the rabbit she'd been served at home. She needed food, and the animal was already dead, but...she didn't think she'd ever eat meat again once she got home.

Rowan finished all she could stomach, each bite threatening to come back up. Then she shoved herself as far away from the spit that held the rest of the rabbit and looked up through the trees. She could see the tiniest bit of sky from here. A few stars winking through at her. She stared up at them, listening to Yseult's deep breaths.

Yseult had fallen asleep as soon as Rowan made camp. Every day the horse grew a bit more tired. Rowan wanted to keep reassuring her, *It's just a bit further now, just a few days more.* She had no idea how far they were traveling, or how long it would take. She had no idea if she was even heading towards the dragons.

She wanted to believe she was. She needed to believe it. She did. But she didn't *know*. She couldn't feed Yseult on vague hopes. She didn't mean to do it, but Rowan felt some power catch hold of her voice and pull song from her lips:

> *But Doben was no more content,*
> *Within her hidden bower,*
> *Her mighty form could not remain,*
> *Alone for one more hour.*
> *She crept out late that moonless night,*
> *And with light steps shook the hill.*
> *She followed her beloved's trail,*
> *To the world that he concealed.*
> *With each new sight Doben rejoiced,*
> *Twas so colorful and wide.*
> *She danced across valley and dale,*
> *Filled with joy she could not hide.*
> *Her wild steps trampled across*
> *The labors of the village.*
> *Laid waste to crops and toppled homes,*
> *A frantic pirate's pillage.*
> *The valley shook with cries of fear,*
> *Angry torch flames lit the night,*
> *As armies formed to kill the beast,*
> *Who dared to seek the light.*

Rowan stopped singing, and lay her head back against the tree, shutting her eyes as one of her own old letters to Gavin shifted again through her mind.

> *I cannot understand why you love this song so well. It is mournful. The only creature to be loved is the one who dies. She never meant any harm, if she had been raised with people she would have known better. But Branduff hides her, and keeps her*

hidden with promises he never means to fulfill. He promised this creature a world that would love it, but only ever meant to keep her in a cave, alone. —

It had bothered her so much. She could not make the song fit the happy man from her letters. It had actually made her angry with the character he loved. Branduff was a liar, a weaver of fantasies. He would tell the creature about color and wide expanses, and friends and paint the world as a beautiful place, but then he left, and Doben was alone again. No one should call such a man a hero. He created the monster he killed to save his neighbors.

Oddly though, it was only tonight that Rowan realized what angered her was the feeling that she related better to Doben than anyone else in the tale. She lived on promises—always a day more.

Or three-hundred and eighty-one days more.

It didn't matter how many days she counted down the end always felt just as far away as it had the day before. And now Rowan had gone and made Doben's mistake, escaping into a world that wasn't going to want her.

Rowan laughed. She wasn't out here seeking someone to love her. She was seeking help. Seeking power enough to bring her sisters home. But it still felt like she'd made Doben's mistake. She still felt like the beast the world would want to slaughter.

—I don't see the story so.

The Gavin of her memory replied. Rowan opened her eyes, and the shadow of him sat before the camp fire, speaking the words of his old letter.

Didn't you feel the love between them?
Branduff doesn't know what to do when he finds Doben. He knows the world will not love her, but he does.
So he offers her fantasies. Allows her live in his stories knowing, I think from the beginning, that one day the world

will find her and kill her. But for years before it happens he lets this monster feel loved, and experience wonder and fun. Yes, he kills her. But he does it as much for Doben as he does for his neighbors. He doesn't see himself as a hero, just as the one who made sure Doben's life and death were as peaceful as they could be. He protects her.

"He should have told her," Rowan answered the memory aloud. "He should have said you can never leave this place. She deserved to know that it would always be one day more, until the day she died. He should have told her she didn't belong in his world."

Gavin had no answer for that. He looked towards the fire and his voice in song floated to her deep and soothing:

> *Come now my lovely lonely friend*
> *And listen to my story.*
> *And I shall build a world for thee,*
> *The equal to your glory.*
> *A world as wide as oceans stretch,*
> *Vibrant as dancing flowers.*
> *A world in which your beauty's known*
> *And you're loved—for your power.*
> *Come now— be at peace in this place,*
> *There will be many great hours for grieving tomorrow.*
> *Let my voice be your talisman;*
> *The balm for regrets and banisher of all sorrow.*
> *I'll sing to thee of raging seas,*
> *Or of the quiet moonlight.*
> *I'll sing of valleys soft and wide,*
> *Or the mountain's towering height.*
> *I'll sing to thee of birds to fly,*
> *With thy spirit far away.*

I'll sing until thee drift to sleep
And ever dreaming shall we stay.

Rowan smiled at this man she'd created out of letters and one brief flash of a vision. He was trying to comfort her with a death song, with the words Branduff sang to Doben as he poisoned her. It was a ridiculous song to find comfort in, but she did. She even found humor in it. Or in her mind for calling it up.

"One day more then," Rowan whispered, pulling her knees against her chest and settling against the tree more comfortably. She shut her eyes and slept.

Waiting in the Future

380 days until Roisin returns

Braden didn't think he could put off returning home any longer. Sorcha must know by now that he had stayed to search for Rowan, but he needed to leave before soldiers searched half the island and Braden knew all the places Rowan had *not* gone to list for Sorcha.

He'd already sent his servant to gather his escort, and take his packs and was just slipping out the back stairs of the palace. He didn't want to be confronted by one more person. He'd left a message for the king, and one for Rowan's knights. Now he needed to—

Braden jumped and stumbled backwards onto the dark staircase, falling onto his behind. Keagan stood before him wearing a militant expression.

"Leaving so soon?" Keagan asked nonchalantly.

"It isn't precisely soon." Braden stood, dusting himself off and effected an air of calm disinterest. "This is the longest I have ever stayed, we cannot afford to make the Fairy queen suspicious."

"What about making other people suspicious. I know you're lying. Everyone knows it now. Rowan never went to Turrlough."

"As I said, that's what she told me she was doing. Perhaps she got lost, or perhaps she lied to me. But I cannot tell you where she's gone if I do not know."

"She needs me," Keagan insisted.

"Do you know," Braden said thoughtfully. "I don't think she does. I honestly think she is stronger alone."

"Then you're wrong," Keagan insisted. "None of us are. Alone Sorcha can prey on us, together we are strong. You should stay, Braden."

Braden shook his head, walking around Keagan. He'd like to think Keagan, his friend, was worried about his safety and trying to protect him, but he knew better. Keagan just wanted at what was inside Braden's head.

"I can't stand this place," Braden muttered, descending the stairs. "I don't know how anyone can. Rowan had the right idea leaving, maybe the rest of you should too. Just leave, let Sorcha divide her forces searching the island for all of you. Some of you might escape her entirely."

"Why are you lying? Is it for Rowan? Or for Sorcha?" Keagan demanded of Braden's back.

Braden spun around and stared at Keagan in shock. It was true that he and Keagan had not been as close on this visit as they had in the past. But he'd thought that ended when they realized Colleen was a cipher. But the look on Keagan's face was one of absolute distrust.

"How can you even ask that?" Braden demanded.

Keagan looked him dead in the eye and shrugged. "I see the future, many futures. I've been adding them up, deciphering the possibilities all the ways we win, all the ways we lose. And you...you betray us in half of them."

Everything inside of Braden clumped together and fell like led from his body, leaving him a vacant shell of a thing.

"Which half?" he asked breathlessly.

Keagan shook his head. "You don't understand. You betray us, in good outcomes and bad. You betray us in half of the futures that you are a part of."

Braden didn't realize it was possible to trip when he was standing still, but he fell backwards from nothing but the words. He stumbled into the wall and that alone held him up.

"I know you're lying," Keagan said making no move towards Braden, just watching him. "But what I need to know is for whom?"

Braden shook his head again and again. Didn't really hear Keagan. In his head he kept hearing *you betray us*. It couldn't be true. He wasn't a traitor.

But his mind taunted him with all the promises he'd broken, to Sorcha, to his parents. To everyone who'd ever meant anything to him. He was a traitor. Maybe it was all he was.

"I need to leave," Braden whispered.

"I need your answer."

Braden shook his head. Keagan had been his first friend here. The shy little boy who'd helped him overcome his fears by sending Rowan to save him. The quiet child who no one else could draw out. He used to be so...gentle of spirit. Now he was older than his age, and hard. Now he was changed. As Braden was. This battle was making monsters of them all.

"I hate this place," Braden repeated and raced down the stairs. He couldn't stay a moment longer. "I wish I'd never come."

Ferdy leaned invisibly against the wall of the palace as Braden ran past. Braden likely wouldn't have noticed Ferdy even if he were visible, he was that upset. Keagan walked slowly out the south entrance of the palace, watching Braden go and didn't notice his brother either.

Ferdy didn't like this one bit. He hadn't heard exactly what was passing between his brother and Braden, but it was clearly a fight. Ferdy never liked that friendship, mostly because it took Keagan away from playing with Ferdy and Petal. But he liked even less seeing the friendship coming to an end. Everyone was headed down a bad path.

Ferdy stiffened as his brother moved, not wanting to be caught spying, even invisible Keagan could usually sense him. But Keagan just vanished.

This felt wrong. Ferdy didn't like spying on his brother, he didn't like that he'd been lying to everyone. But to be fair to himself no one had asked what Ferdy saw of the future when he had Keagan's power. Not Mama, or Rowan, or even Keagan.

Of all of them it was strangest from Keagan. Rowan rarely tried to see the future, and Mama never pressed her children for things they weren't ready to share. But Ferdy wondered if Keagan hadn't asked because part of him doubted Ferdy was smart enough to use his power.

Ferdy groaned aloud. He was letting that bo—

"Ugh." Ferdy bent forward as a clod of dirt struck his gut and sputtered apart.

"I did it! I did it! I got you when you were invisible!" Brigid slid out of a tree to Ferdy's right and began dancing around despite the long scrape of skin she'd peeled off sliding down the tree.

Ferdy made himself visible. He was annoyed, but not thoroughly enough injured to be truly angry.

"Why are you always following me? Don't you have someone else to pester?" he said without much heat. Still a bit distracted by the distance growing into his family. And...honestly, he was very impressed.

No one but Pa and Ardal had ever caught Ferdy while he was invisible. Not even Rowan. Brigid was by far the most annoying saboteur Ferdy had. She was pushy, loud, rude, and over confident. But she was also one of the best. If Rowan had stayed this girl would most certainly have become one of her squires and eventually a shield maiden.

"I'm the best squire!" she shouted, ignoring Ferdy's insulting question.

"Not likely," Ferdy said dismissively though he'd been thinking along the same lines. "I groaned and gave away my position. Anyone could have hit me ."

Brigid fell still with her eyes narrowed, her energy wasn't gone, it was just converted into rage.

He didn't know why he was being mean to her. He just...she wanted so much to be Ferdy's best friend. To be the new Petal. He saw her trying to slip into his family like she could take Petal's place. Well she couldn't. She was nothing like Petal. And Petal wasn't dead. Ferdy wasn't going to waste all of his time looking out for her just because she was too brave for her own good.

"I'm better than all of them, and you know it. When the Blade of Stonedragon returns I will be her *only* squire!" Brigid declared, and spun around to march away. "You are just jealous that I beat you."

"What if she doesn't return?" Ferdy said morosely, and very quietly. Brigid really shouldn't have heard him, but she stopped.

Ferdy had been fighting his brother's urge to go after Rowan, because it felt like the wrong thing to do. But every day the world felt worse, and it occurred to him that Rowan might have been what held them all together. He began to worry that she would never come home again. Every day it was harder to shake off that vision of the future that he'd seen. His belief was faltering.

Brigid looked over her shoulder at Ferdy, with derision that slowly melted into pity. "Don't be an idiot. She's coming back. She loves you." The words, clearly meant to bolster Ferdy, seemed to depress Brigid and she walked away with her head down.

Ferdy ought to follow her and cheer her up. They could slice all the squire's hoes, she would like that. But he didn't move, that felt too much like something he would do for Petal, or Keagan, or Rowan if they were depressed. And that same dark vision was replaying in his mind, so powerfully it crawled over the now and seemed to be happening.

The Rose Princess was home, well and happy. She danced through the night laughing and smiling. Even Petal was home, because Sorcha was defeated!

But everything else was wrong.

Mama and Pa wouldn't speak. Keagan sat alone in a corner sketching deaths. And Petal was scarred and enraged. She hated the Rose Princess, and Braden. She barely spoke to her family, only enough to announce that she was leaving to rule over the Fairy.

None of them was happy.

None but the Rose Princess, Braden, and King Balder. Even Gwyneth was oddly morose. She hadn't wanted the ball—since Rowan was dead.

Ferdy hadn't known where he was at first, not until he'd paid more attention to what Keagan was drawing.

Ardal, bleeding out with an arrow in his chest.

Cassidy and Liam burned to death.

Peg and half of the shield maidens cut down.

Rowan, with her arms locked around Sorcha, falling into the yawning mouth of a dragon.

And Ferdy—at last he'd seen himself—drawn dead on the ballroom floor, with an arrow in his eye, and Brigid's dead body on the ground beside him, riddled with arrows.

So many dead.

But the death wasn't the worst of it. It was the distance. None of them loved each other anymore. The battle had destroyed them all.

Every day that Pa and Mama went without speaking, or that Keagan isolated himself more. Every day that future seemed more likely. Ferdy couldn't let it happen. They loved each other. They needed to keep on loving each other. Ferdy just didn't know how to do it but to hold on as tightly as he could to what he had.

Rowan made her way up Mount Anwyn slowly. When she reached a little outcropping part way up the mountain pass she pulled Yseult to a stop and hopped off. The mountain stretched up a good ways further, and it wasn't quite dusk yet, but this was a nice place to bed down for the night. The higher into the mountains they got, the colder it was, and there was a nice...not quite cave, but outcropping that would provide shelter if it rained.

She walked to the edge and looked away from the mountain. There were trees scattered up the side of it and a proper forest at its feet. But Rowan looked beyond all of that into the distance. Seeing the things she'd passed by or missed all together. A wide valley spotted with trees and sprinkled with clusters of flowers lay just beyond the forest. As Rowan watched a family of deer wandered through it, stopping to nibble on barks and bushes. There were four of them, a mother and three children. Two of the children stayed right at their mother's side, eating what she ate first, but one pranced away leaping through the flowers. She would stop to eat things that caught her attention but mostly she just ran around. Rowan watched in amusement as the mother tried to rein in her wayward child. They all froze for a moment, sensing something. The mother moved very slowly, searching for whatever had spooked her, but the children remained frozen. After a moment, the mother with more focused purpose rounded up her children to leave the open space. That one wild child, though, kept looking back, longing to stay.

All her life Rowan had been treated as though she were willful, but it wasn't until she was out in the world actually making every decision for herself and having to live with the consequences that she realized she wasn't terribly willful.

She had fought against rules she found ridiculous when she trained with knights. And yes, she did very frequently ignore things her father wanted if they weren't direct commands. And it was certainly true that she did not bend to the wills of men as other women must. But she wasn't *willful*.

She ate what was put in front of her without complaint. She dressed in the clothes provided, with a few minor adjustments. She sat dutifully through court functions. And slept when she was told, danced at balls when asked. Treated her father's advisors with polite respect—usually. She did many things she didn't care for. Did many things she would not have if left to her own devices. She wasn't willful. She was very nearly dutiful. Excepting only the things she did to prepare to save Roisin.

But...as much as she'd hated skinning and eating a rabbit, and as much as she struggled to sleep on hard rocky ground, and as much as she *truly hated* life without baths, Rowan didn't think when she went home that she would ever be dutiful again. She liked setting her own course. She liked stumbling through a forest she didn't know. She liked moments like this, when she looked out over the expanse of forest and sky and world spread before her, when she felt alive and her blood hummed and she realized she was further away from home than she had ever been. Every day she was a bit further from home, and somehow the further she got the less the anger carried her. Out here, there was so much to see, so much to feel. So much to be. She was limitless, not just in power but in awe and experience and room to be.

Out here, in moments like this, staring across the expanse of the world, she was more sure than ever that what she'd told her father, and Colum and Ardal was right. There were too many limits set on the women of her nation. When she was queen all of that would change. Possibly even before she was queen. Maybe she would take those women and form a new nation. All of them should be limitless. None of them should be...forced to wed a man of someone else's choosing. None of them should be forced to forgo their needs for someone else's desires.

Out here, responsible for no one but herself, Rowan understood better than ever before how truly responsible she was for her nation, and just how beautiful a thing that could be.

Rowan sat with her feet dangling off the edge of a cliff and stared into the distance, imagining how she might share these feelings with the people of her nation. Both her nations.

The ground was rocky and uneven beneath her, she shifted around, not wanting to move yet. Her gaze slid towards the western side of the island. Towards the Fairy nation. Towards the peaks of the tallest trees Rowan had ever seen. They seemed from here so densely clustered that it would be impossible to pass through them. But there was a river winding along through, bisecting the forest almost like a canyon between mountain ranges.

Rowan had a better sense of distance now that she'd been out in the world, so she knew she wasn't seeing the Fairy nation, but just looking that way made her feel closer to them. Her nation. That still felt shaky, and unlikely—frightening. But she knew it was true.

Rowan heard something rolling across the ground from behind her, and glanced back. A tiny ball rolled towards her with the last lights of the day bouncing off it. Rowan caught it just before it would slip past her and off the cliff. It was the shamrock that Petal had given her for her fifteenth birthday.

Keep it close. It will bring you luck.

Rowan felt her pulse quicken as she envisioned Petal's face, as it had been then. Rowan rolled the ball around in her palm wondering if Petal had felt Rowan near and sent the talisman rolling to her, to remind Rowan that she loved her. To remind Rowan that she had always been as much fairy as she was human. Rowan smiled

Beneath her the ground softened as she sent her magic into it and woke a fluffy patch of clovers to grow beneath her. Rowan allowed herself to fall back onto the pillow of clover and watched the slowly changing color of the sky.

One day, she would share this feeling with *both* her nations. One day.

The Air in Stonedragon

379 days until Roisin returns

Braden was putting the castle behind him faster than he'd intended. Keagan's voice wouldn't leave him. *You betray us half the times.* Good or bad. Whether they all died, or all succeeded, Braden was their traitor half the times. It couldn't be. But the words ate at him, and he could almost see it.

It was so much easier to just go along with Sorcha, so much safer and more comfortable. It was never a good feeling, never honorable or noble, but it was safe.

When he'd first started spying for Rowan he'd felt good and brave and almost powerful. But nothing ever changed. He went to Sorcha to report on Rowan, and went to Rowan to report on Sorcha. And with both of them it seemed almost as though his words were already known to them. As though he were just a toy used to taunt the other woman. He wasn't making a difference. He never discovered anything important.

Even Petal was of more use and power than he. *Petal.*

Petal was a real spy. Infiltrating the Fairy queen's own court. Winning her favor to the point where she wanted that child to be her successor. *Petal*—who blushed and stammered when she saw him and trailed him around like he was a god. She was all alone and spying on their enemy. Petal was trusted and necessary both to Rowan and to Sorcha.

No one would doubt Petal's loyalty. No one would allow Petal to suffer and die. Petal was just loved. And...

And Braden was somehow, unreasonably, idiotically jealous of an eleven-year-old girl trapped and spying in a world of enemies, far from the home and family she loved.

"I hate this kingdom," Braden said aloud. Some of his escorts grunted in agreement. Not one had made any protest when he insisted on riding through the night. They were more than halfway to the north road. If they rode through the night tonight as well they could be off Stonedragon land before dawn tomorrow. And he wanted to press on, but at the same time he wanted to go as slowly as possible.

He wanted to run away from home. He wanted to run away from the island. Just run and run and never stop. He wasn't important enough to anyone's plans for them to hunt him down. Now that Rowan was out of Stonedragon, Sorcha couldn't possibly have use for him. And he'd lied for Rowan, not that anyone believed it, but he'd bought her the time she wanted. Duty done. He could run away. It would be safer. Happier.

She was willful and independent...she intended to run away. His mother's voice caught Braden off guard. He so rarely thought of her when not in her presence.

Braden might not be needed here for anyone's plans. But he would be missed by his mother if he ran away. Although she would certainly forgive him. She only wanted him to be happy.

"Your Majesty?" The commander of Braden's escort Klein pulled up his horse and angled around in his saddle to glance back. "Should we help?" He nodded off to his left.

Braden followed the nod, in the distance a woman alone in a cart was under attack from several ruffians.

"Of course." Braden spurred his horse forward. Why was that even a question? A woman alone deserved to be guarded, she would need—

But the thought was cut off by the sight in front of him. There were three men, two had yanked the woman off her cart and were dragging her away, and the third had hopped into the cart to examine what lay under a canvas in the back. The woman shouted, but it wasn't a cry for help or a scream of fear. No, the moment her feet touched the ground she cried out in rage and launched herself bodily at her attackers, driving one back with her head slammed hard into his gut, while she kicked the second.

She was...saving herself. What was wrong with the women of Stonedragon?

Braden had slowed down at the sight, but his escort rushed on, leaping off their horses to attack the men. The attackers were restrained in a matter of moments, and Braden rode up alongside the little party in time to hear the woman's lackluster praise.

"I had the matter well in hand, but of course my thanks for the assistance."

"Only in Stonedragon do women thank their rescuers by saying they weren't needed," Braden said under his breath, to the nearest of his men.

The woman spun around with a brow in the air and Braden gasped in shock. "Was I rescued?" Lady Asia inquired, her tone repudiating any such thing. "I thought I had done the work of rebuffing my attackers quite well when your men swooped in for the glory. And you hung back to be—*entertained,* I suppose."

He knew she was Lady Asia, that face...she was startlingly beautiful. Her eyes were so large and her skin so smooth and unblemished, and Braden didn't know what, it was almost as though her skin glistened. She was Lady Asia. He would recognize her anywhere. But her attitude was so different from the woman he'd met in Ulm.

Braden slid off his horse and bowed before her in shock. "My lady, I beg your forgiveness. I should of course have rushed to your aid, but as you say, you did appear to have things in hand."

She eyed him oddly, as though she didn't know what he was talking about and glanced from her attackers, to Braden and his escort, her eyes darting around as if for some way to escape.

"Sir..." She laughed prettily and batted her eyes. "I do apologize, but your name quite escapes me."

"Oh, of course, we met only once." Braden bowed once more. "Prince Braden of Anwyn."

"Ah, Prince Pip, of course!" she exclaimed with a bright, broad smile.

The guards snickered at the old taunting nickname. *Prince Pipsqueak* other knights had called him in his younger days.

Braden bit back annoyed words. "My lady, I am surprised to find you here, in Stonedragon, and without escort. Was there some trouble with your fiancé?"

She chuckled. "I haven't any fiancee, that could be a bit of a problem with him. But if you mean to inquire of Prince Gavin... there were rather a large number of problems. And the fairy coming was one problem too many. A girl will go a long way for a crown, but it really didn't seem worth it in the end."

"Gavin sent you away without escort?"

Asia examined Braden from head to toe, with a bright smile. Then she turned aside, took the reins for her cart from the guard who held them and began to climb up.

"You two don't like one another a bit, do you?" she asked with her back to him. "No, he didn't send me away. I left. And I am not *Lady* Asia. I am not a great heiress from Reethurn. I am just..." She bobbed her head sideways, with a playful, intelligent smirk, something like Braden might have envisioned an all grown up Petal wearing. "A woman who knows what she is after, and how to get it. I wasn't getting it there, so I left to find what I want."

"A crown?" Braden asked, hesitantly. He was pleased to see his men fanning out in a way that would trap her should she try to make an escape. He needed to talk more with this woman.

"Umm." She nodded. "And the power that comes with it."

Braden felt his chest rise and fall slowly, felt the calm easing out from his mind through the rest of his being. But not at her words. It was another something, something odd floating through him. She was lying, and he knew it. He didn't know why, he wasn't sure exactly what she was lying about, but he knew she was lying and he felt oddly more at home in his skin from the knowledge.

"You aren't behaving a bit like yourself," Braden remarked.

"Ah, but you don't know myself." She leaned forward and winked. "I was playing a part in Ulm."

"I don't know. By all accounts you passed the princess trials, they are meant to test for avarice and malice and unworthiness."

She chuckled. "They test for biddability, delicacy, and a fragile back. And..." she leaned down and lowered her voice to a whisper. "The trick to passing them can be found in the kingdom's old logs."

Braden laughed with her. "Did Gavin know you cheated them?"

"Of course not." She blinked rapidly, tilting her head to the side, with a coy innocent expression painting her features to appear years younger.

Braden grinned. Gavin would trust that shy innocent routine. He would gobble it up, a woman leaning on him for help and behaving like everything perfect and biddable. Served him right to be tricked.

"Very well then, may we offer you an escort to wherever you are off to next?" Braden offered kindly. "Stonedragon has no crown to offer you."

Lady Asia smiled smugly. Looking just like Rowan before a fight. "Aren't you sweet? But I think no. I've gotten along well enough alone thus far. I think I'll be alone a while longer."

"But—"

She didn't wait for him to say more, just snapped the reins and had her little horse darting forward so fast his men jumped out of the way to keep from being trampled.

Honestly, it was the most ridiculous thing! Was there something in the air here that made women willfully stupid?

Braden raced to his horse, mounting as fast as he was able and set out after her. She was up to something. He had no idea what, or even if it had to do with Sorcha and Rowan and the battle, but he needed to find out.

Braden caught up with Lady Asia when the wheel of her cart broke and she was thrown cresting a hill. He saw her go tumbling down towards them. When he was within feet of her he threw himself off his horse and rushed over.

She was laughing. Actually laughing as she tumbled towards him. Braden bent down to stop her. She looked up and only laughed harder.

"Oh, you are going to be such a smug rescuer now, aren't you?" she said and fell forward, laughing and cradling her arm.

Braden sat on the grass beside her and started laughing. It was the oddest thing, she put him wholly at ease. Shouldn't he have preferred to have a woman to protect as he's always thought women should be. The Asia he'd met in Ulm was just such a woman, delicate like his mother, sweet and shy, exactly what women were meant to be. But the Asia he was meeting today was none of those things, she was rude, playful, and too dauntless ever to be viewed as delicate. Yet with her he felt lighter than he had since before he'd last seen Sorcha.

She looked up at him with her head tilted to the side and a coy smile on her face, waiting for him to claim some superior knowledge or strength because he'd kept his seat and she'd been thrown from hers.

"I am just glad I caught up to you," Braden remarked.

"In time to save me," she threw a hand to her heart and fluttered her lashes, and Braden was mesmerized. She was so enthralling. Gavin must have loved having such a woman in his home for months, on his arm, staring up at him with those big brown eyes.

"No," Braden said in an unintentionally soft voice. "I wanted to ask you more about what you were saying, about fairy coming to Turrlough."

"Ah," Asia leaned back, still cradling the arm and smiled up at him. "And for whom are you asking? The Knight of the Rose, or the Fairy queen?"

"I wouldn't imagine the Fairy queen needs me to bring her reports of her own movements."

"But I didn't say the Fairy queen came, only that fairy came." She smiled slyly.

Braden examined the woman before him like he would a portrait subject. "Who are you? Truly?"

"Liars do tend to recognize one another, don't we." She nodded and looked towards Braden's men.

"I shall tell you this," Asia said, lying on her back with her eyes closed. "I am not after a crown. And I am not working for, or with, the queen of the Fairy nation."

"Is Prince Gavin dead?" Braden demanded, surprised to feel his heart stop at the thought. He didn't know that he believed in true loves the way Maureen seemed to, and if he didn't miss his guess the way Rowan *wanted* to. But Braden knew whether Gavin was Rowan's true love, or simply a friend, his death would hurt Rowan.

Asia opened her eyes and stared at him with an oddly piercing gaze for a long fraught moment.

"I am not sure. I do not believe so. But...if he is alive he is in her hold somehow."

"Everyone seems certain he can resist her," Braden said, rolling away from the itchy, angry feeling crawling across his skin. "So I'm sure he will be fine."

"Do you not resist her?" Asia asked coyly. "Why should you be jealous if he can do the same?"

"I thought I did, but this last year...I was so sure I resisted her, but I let her manipulate me into fighting with Rowan."

Asia released her right arm, and using only her left pushed herself to her feet.

Belatedly Braden realized what all her favoring of the other side implied and reached out to help her.

"I am so sorry, are you injured, my lady? May I help you?"

"Don't go back to being the overly protective prince again. I'm fine. It's nothing but a dancing elbow bone."

Braden laughed. "Do you like to fight? Did you spar with Gavin?"

At this Asia threw back her head and laughed riotously. "Oh, both of you poor jealous boys. No, I didn't spar with Gavin. I find men in general mistrust meeting with a woman who is exactly what they want. Were I to have gone to him playing at being his Rowan he would have been endlessly suspicious of me. As you would have easily dismissed and forgotten a sweet biddable woman in need of rescue. I have to give you something to fight against to get you where I want you."

"And you want me here?" Braden asked, his hand falling to the hilt of his sword.

"Yes," she replied calmly. "So that I can see for myself what happens to one who is in the service of the Fairy queen and in her presence. So that I can feel for myself the effects of her magic. And know..." She tilted her head aside, and from nothing but a look in her eye Braden was certain that she was going to lie to him. "Just how far I need to run to be safe from her."

Braden thought over everything she'd said and what he knew of this woman and he was sure she was not going to run. Perhaps she wanted to know how to help Gavin if he was indeed alive.

"What..." Braden hesitated. She was very careful of her words. Perhaps she feared Sorcha was listening. But there were also his men to worry about. "What did you want from Gavin if not his crown?"

She shook her head. "It doesn't matter. He didn't have it. Perhaps no one does." She looked away with a heavy sigh. "I've been where you are, wanting to run away from home. I even did it." She looked back at him and shook her head. "But the fear lives inside us no matter where we go. I would never tell you not to run, I understand too well. But...don't expect it to change who you are."

Braden opened his mouth to tell her he'd no intention of running, but she held up a hand. "Please, I am far too tired to argue with you. I said my piece, do not worry, I know men never listen. Now, good sir, since my cart is disabled, perhaps you will escort me on my way to a hot spring nearby."

"A hot spring?" Braden asked incredulous.

"Oh yes, it will do wonders for my elbow before I flee."

Braden didn't believe her excuse for a moment, but nor could he deny a lady's request of escort and well she knew it. Her advice slipped right out of his ears as he helped her into his saddle. His mind was far too full with other puzzles than running away.

Crossroads

378 days until Roisin returns

Rowan had reached a pass between Mount Anwyn and Mount Kieran, it was steep and far too narrow for Yseult to pass along, but it seemed to be where the dragons were leading. It seemed strange that the dragons would be hiding on what was technically Fairy land. But she knew fairy had not been able to settle the whole mountain. So perhaps dragons lived near the peek. Or perhaps like the other places they'd led her the dragons wanted Rowan to see more of the Fairy Realm. Whatever the case, Rowan stood at the edge looking down to the drop below and across the long pass. There must be some way around it to reach Mount Kieran. She'd come so far, she couldn't just stop. And more than ever before she *felt close* to the dragons. Before she'd been sure they were leading her, and hopeful that they were leading her to them. But today she felt close to that heavy, oppressive power she'd felt when she tried to cast her mind to the dragons using the pendant.

She had to go forward. Excitement was building under her skin, imagining what help she might ask. She could ask for a group to fly to Turrlough and protect that nation and another to bolster Rowan's forces in Stonedragon, and take a few with her to march into the Fairy Realm and rescue Petal. She felt her pulse racing at the thought that this could all be over soon, all the years of waiting and fearing and planning. She could challenge Sorcha and defeat her and have both her sisters home before the week was out.

It could all of it be over, and with a year yet to spare before the curse was supposed to have fallen.

Rowan walked to the thin ledge that connected the two mountains and, just to see if she could, scooted out along it. It was so narrow she had to stand flush against the mountain. Her pulse was racing and she bit her lip as she scooted. Her eyes faced towards that long—endless drop. She was so high.

Her stomach fell out of her, slipping down that drop, leaving Rowan with a churning empty feeling.

She giggled and glanced back at Yseult on the path. The horse appeared to be glaring at Rowan.

"Oh, don't be such a worrier," Rowan said to the horse, and started back towards the path. "I'm perfectly—Aaaa!" Rowan cried out as the little bit of outcropping began to crumble under her feet.

Before it fell away completely she vanished from the ledge back to the path next to Yseult.

Rowan leaned against the horse, gasping for breath, but Yseult wasn't concerned with Rowan's comfort. She head butted her in the stomach, pushing her even further from the ledge and began nipping at her shoulder angrily.

"Alright, alright," Rowan gasped around her laughter, shoving the horse away. "I'm sorry. Quit it. Yseult! Stop." Rowan grappled for the reins as the horse continued to bite at her.

At her shout the horse stilled and stared at Rowan militantly.

"Fine, that wasn't the way." Rowan waved her arm broadly.

Yseult made a noise that could only be described as a growl, and were she any other horse it would seem funny, but Rowan knew Yseult's fierceness. Rowan nodded her head, holding out a hand in a half conciliatory, half protective manner.

"I'll be more careful, I swear."

Yseult grunted in apparent disbelief but jerked her head away and walked slowly back towards the trail they'd made through the growth of bushes and nettles.

Rowan looked at the packs strapped to Yseult's flanks. There was no way Yseult could make it across the outcropping, and Rowan needed her packs, but she certainly couldn't cross that tiny ledge carrying them.

"Maybe I can vanish us across." Rowan spun back to look at the distance. It wasn't too far. Not for someone limitless. But even on the other side of the pass the mountain looked much steeper than Mount Anwyn was. It had been such slow going these past few days. Half the time Rowan walked ahead of the horse, clearing the way for them. The only real benefit of having Yseult with her was company, and that she did not have to carry her own packs. That and she used the horse as a guide for what she could eat. Ever since she'd woken to find that some animal had made off with the remains of the one rabbit she'd shot and realized she wasn't at all sorry to see it go.

She supposed that was how it was, predators killed other animals, and there was nothing wrong or ugly about it. But when she'd been eating it with each bite she'd heard, *you poison everything you touch.* She just couldn't stand to be the monster that killed someone's mother or sister, or friend, even if that someone was just an animal. So now if Yseult ate something Rowan ate it, even if it tasted like dirt or hurt her teeth to chew. She just felt better that way.

But she was familiar with enough safe bushes and plants and tree barks that she could survive even without Yseult. And she could carry her own packs. But she couldn't just leave Yseult to wander around alone. And what would Rowan do without her company? She couldn't go on without her—

But a breeze blew up from that drop and sang through the whistle, calling out to Rowan. This was the way.

Rowan walked around in front of the horse and laid her forehead against her nose. "I remember the first time I ever saw you," Rowan whispered. "The trainers had bought you from Anwyn to breed more war horses, and you..." Rowan chuckled. "You were fighting them off like a warrior. You kicked the door to the pin so hard you broke it. You were this bright shining beacon of power and beauty. I wasn't a bit afraid when I walked up to you...you were as exciting as that drop over there."

Yseult played at trying to take a nip of Rowan's scraggly braid, but Rowan just laughed.

"Yseult, my warrior queen. I think I have to go on without you." Rowan kissed the horse's nose.

Yseult turned her head aside and rubbed it along Rowan's cheek gently. She understood. She'd always understood Rowan.

Even that first day. The trainers had been shouting, trying to get to a man who'd been kicked and Rowan had just walked through the mess of them straight to the horse, holding out her hand. She'd seen her there, trying so hard to be heard, Rowan had understood that so deeply. So she held out a hand. And Yseult had looked into Rowan's eyes for the longest time, then she dipped her head and rubbed it up against Rowan's palm. They understood each other. They loved each other.

"I have to go on without you. But I cannot just leave you alone."

The horse snorted and shook her head as if to tell Rowan not to worry about that. But Rowan couldn't dismiss such concerns. Yseult was as much family as anyone else in Rowan's life. Rowan needed to be sure she would be safe, and loved.

Rowan smiled crookedly as she removed the whistle from Yseult's neck, putting it around her own. "I know where you'll be safe."

Rowan set about rearranging her packs so she could carry them herself. She tied a blanket around Yseult to help keep her warm as she traveled without Rowan's fires or body for warmth. When everything was arranged Rowan leaned her head next to Yseult's ear and began to hum the way Roisin did. She let the hum build up in Yseult until she was sure the horse could feel it inside, and feel Roisin calling out to her. Then she stepped back, expecting the horse to run towards the sound. But Yseult surprised her. Nipping onto the end of Rowan's long braid, she tugged her forward and slipped her nose down under Rowan's hand as she had that first day they met.

"I love you too. Always," Rowan promised.

Yseult released her braid and turned down the trail, making her way between the trees. Rowan watched until she was out of sight, and until she could no longer hear the rustling of tree branches and bushes as she made her way through. Then she lifted the packs onto her back and turned to the pass.

Rowan's excitement and fear married into an utterly jittery feeling beneath her skin. She smiled. "Just a little bit longer now. We'll all be together soon." Rowan sent the promise into the wind and vanished from Mount Anwyn.

Sorcha and Petal lay on a blanket of marigolds snacking on fruit between lessons. Petal was slowly returning to her more curious self. It was a bit annoying that the majority of her curiosity now had to do with the war for Sorcha's throne between Tyrone and herself. But Petal should know her history. And she should know how to guard her throne.

"Why wolves?" Petal asked as a berry popped into her mouth. She giggled slightly, still encouraging the Marigolds to juggle the berries and compete to see which one could get the fruit into her mouth.

Sorcha smiled at the innocent display of power, even as she was annoyed with the question. But she did not feign misunderstanding.

"The nation of Creelan, of all human nations was the least in touch with nature. They built giant cities and paved endless roads, blocking the earth from the air, and the sun, and the rain. The land where they built their capital city was once the home of four different wolf species, but the leaders of the nation hunted them until there was only one pack of wolves left. The king kept in his throne room a wall hanging that stretched thirty feet made from the pelts of one wolf pack that had been hunted into extinction." Sorcha snarled it all, seeing the room before her again.

"When I went to Reagan to negotiate a peace treaty between us, and protect his people. He was more concerned with protecting his wealth, and the legacy of the city he had built up. He saw himself as the greatest king in history because he had tamed the wild earth and conquered it. So..." Sorcha shrugged, looking out of her mind's eye and down on the child before her.

The flowers had stopped juggling and Petal looked as confused and enraged as Sorcha had felt in that moment.

"I did not go intending to curse him. Or punish his nation," Sorcha felt the words of self defense slipping out without any intention of saying them. She knew what she had done was right, that was all there was to it. But she wanted this little girl to understand. "It was Tyrone who had tricked them all into thinking me evil. I understood that. But nor could I allow this senseless war, that had cost the lives of scores of my people, and his own, to go without recompense. My price was fair. He would forswear any acts of aggression against the Fairy forever. And force the hunters of his nation to turn preserves instead, guarding what animals his nation had yet to destroy and leaving any unsettled land as sanctuary to nature.

"But he could not countenance such strictures. He had plans. His nation would be a beacon of human power and superiority. He could not bend, even to defend his people. So I turned him into the very creature his family hung on their walls to display their power. I did not, however, transform his nation as a whole. Nor even his entire family. His bite transformed his children. As for the nation, they were given choices. They could stay, and live as I had offered the king, or they could leave, but if they stayed, and continued trying to tame the world, they would lose their humanity as did their king."

"Most left," Sorcha said casually. Lifting a piece of bread and chewing delicately. "A few still live there, more connected to the earth, and defended by my fairy from the rest of the world because they made this choice. And the ones who could not bend, nor sacrifice any of their comforts...became true wolves, not like the royal family who held onto bits of their humanity so they might feel the weight of their crimes." Sorcha finished chewing her bread. She waited for the censure, always she had been censured for this choice, but Sorcha knew the rightness of it, she would make it again and again were eternity to give her the choice.

Petal sat up straighter, her hand playing among the berries. "The ones who stayed and were transformed, did they become the wolves that their people had destroyed?"

"Yes," Sorcha said flatly.

"If they were given a choice and stayed all the same, then transformation was nothing they did not deserve. But...what did you mean, about the king's bite transforming his family?"

"Well...that was unforeseen and unfortunate. I'd no intention of destroying the entire family." Sorcha didn't feel the truth of these words as she said them. But they were true. She knew they were.

She'd cursed only Reagan. He'd refused her offer. Told her she had no power over him. Told her Tyrone was only the first and that other fairy would challenge her, and other humans. He swore someone would win. He would not back down. Sorcha had seen that hideous pelt on the wall, felt the cries of the wolves that had been destroyed to make it. Felt such pain for those lost creatures, and before she even meant to do it the pelt had flown off the wall, devouring Reagan as he struggled against it.

A growl came from under the pelt and it began to rise and fall like it was one creature, breathing. Then he leapt out from under the pelts, transformed, and the pelt shrunk, taking the skins of no less than five wolves to cover him.

He was wild. Feral. Attacking his wife and children as they shouted and fought and tried to force Sorcha to change him back. With each bite he took out of his family, another wolf was born. But still he wasn't to be calmed. The transformation releasing that voraciously greedy side. He attacked and attacked, killing his own wife with his teeth locked around her throat, shaking her with all his might. He would have done the same to his daughter had not his youngest son jumped on his back, tumbling him away from her. His children ran then, all together and Reagan howled over the corpse of his wife, whose elf blood kept her from transforming.

Sorcha hadn't meant for all of that to happen. But...She had wanted to take from him what he loved most, as he'd forced her to do to herself.

"He turned a bit wild, attacked them all. And they were transformed with his bite," Sorcha said without detail.

"What...became of him?" Petal asked hesitantly. "Did he remember who he was? Did he attack you?"

"He remembers. But he did not attack. The magic tied us together. He could no more attack me than he could reclaim his throne. He stayed in the palace for a great long while, mourning his loss. But do not be fooled into feeling sorry for him. The loss he grieved was not his family, but his power. He deserved to be punished."

"Yes," Petal agreed, nodding again and again. "All traitors should be punished." She looked heavily away.

Braden's company had to backtrack to reach the hot spring. It was tucked away in a shadowed glen with springs all around and one high rocky waterfall with steam rising off of it. Braden walked his own horse into the glen with Asia. He stopped his horse where the ground became rocky, a bit before the springs.

"I had no idea this was here," Braden remarked, dismounting and holding out his arms to help Asia from the saddle she'd shared with him. She slid down without aid and walked forward intently.

"No, I wouldn't have thought so," she said absently.

There was something off about this place. Braden couldn't shake the feeling that there was someone behind him, maybe many someones. He felt eyes. He felt power brushing against him. There was a stream running between a few of the pools of warm water, and he felt his feet moving towards it, though he could not explain why.

"No." Asia's hand fell on his shoulder.

"What?" he asked, shaking off her hand. But he couldn't seem to move away from her.

"You want to drink the water. And you must not. The seeing waters should not be taken in by those without magic, it changes them forever."

Braden looked at the woman before him, and then all around at the pools upon pools of water around them. "There are others here, aren't there?"

Asia nodded. Her eyes crawled over Braden carefully and a slow, small smile settled on her lips. "This is where we part ways, I think."

"Why?"

"The others will not come out if you are here. And I need to consult them."

"Are you one of them? Are you witches? Fairy? Some other beasts?"

She just smiled at the ground a moment, and Braden thought sure she would not answer. But she began to speak, and her eyes remained fixed on her feet with such intense focus he would usually say such a look meant one was looking into their mind, but he rather thought she was in fact looking right where her eyes were pointed.

"I cannot tell you what they are, that is for them to say. But as for me...I am not one of them. I am a being without nation." She laughed. "A bit of chattel that has thrown off its yolk for a time."

Braden heard breaking in her voice and thought she might cry, but when she looked up her eyes were dry and fierce. It was a look one might expect on Rowan's face, but somehow...harder. Wasn't that odd? Even when she was fighting him Braden would have described this woman as far softer than Rowan, but she wasn't, not inside. She was just...always in flux, changing her personality so fluidly that from one moment to the next one couldn't tell which was the real her. And Rowan was too solid to change so easily, her hardness and her softness all were in her constantly.

Asia smirked. "Do you know why you can resist her better than other men?" Asia asked. She did not need to say Sorcha's name for them both to know exactly of whom she spoke.

Braden shook his head. Afraid to hear the answer.

"You are a mirror spirit. You see into a being's deeper nature. But like all mirrors, the thing you cannot see is yourself."

Braden startled, as the words stabbed at him. Was he truly a traitor, as Keagan said?

"It is beneficial, because as long as you cannot see yourself, she cannot see the true you either. But it is also a detriment, because it makes you afraid of your own shadow." She lay a hand gently on his shoulder. "Mirror spirit, stop trying to *see* yourself. Trust in what you *feel* inside. And there ends my mothering advice," she said the last playfully and shoved at his shoulder.

"I...I cannot leave you alone," Braden said, fighting against the urge even now to dip his hands into the water and take a sip. He felt sure if he did he would be able to see with his own eyes all the people he felt around him. He was sure if he could only sip the water, he could, as she'd advised against: see himself.

"Oh, you can, and you will." Asia lifted a brow and stared him down not unlike a general. "I have the power to make you, but having been chattel myself I do not like to use it. Please, do not force my hand. Go now, Prince Pip, run along."

"Don't you mean run away?"

She shook her head, her eyes far too serious and old for such a lovely young woman. "No, I do not think so."

Braden looked around the clearing once more, walking away from her. Asia did not try to stop him this time as he walked forward. He stood over a misty pool of water, just wide enough to hold both his feet at once. He looked down expecting some magical power to clear away the mist and show his face in some murky, watery mirror. All he saw was mist. He felt like there was someone standing in the pool. Someone who would neither stop him from drinking nor encourage him to do so. Someone who'd stood by listening as this woman yanked out a piece of his soul and laid it bare.

Mirror spirit. What did that even mean? *Why* did it mean so much inside of him? When it was nothing more than words. But he felt the words inside him. When he sketched, when he looked into a subject, he could see the deeper truths about them, their hidden selves. And hadn't he known for a long while now that he could not sketch himself because he didn't know what was in his deepest heart.

This water might know. *Seeing waters.* He wanted so badly to know. But what good could come of it? If he saw his deepest self then Sorcha could as well. And Keagan saw so many futures they couldn't all be true, but Braden felt with sinking heart, as his feet stepped backwards, that he would surely be betraying them if Sorcha could see into his heart.

When Braden was feet from the pool he spun around, marching past Asia, before his curiosity could stop him.

"If you need help Rowan's knights will assist you," he said over his shoulder as he walked.

"Thank you," Asia called after him. "It's been charming getting to know you better."

Braden barely listened. He ran out of the clearing, and mounted his horse, trotting it out to join the rest of his party. He needed to get home. No more delaying. He wasn't going to be a traitor.

Asia waited, facing away from the hot spring until she could no longer see or hear Prince Braden's departing party. She felt the beings behind her slowly taking shape, pulling her into their pocket of reality, so that she could fully comprehend their world. She turned to face them.

All around behind her were bodies, young and old, some with all the appearance of youth, but with such weight about them they must be ancient, while there were yet others towards the back and peeking between the legs of the elders who were clearly small children. It was an entire village of beings huddled together in the steaming pools of water to face her.

"I would say you are a mirror spirit as well, mermaid," a woman in the body of a child said watching Asia with deep piercing eyes. "Your mother is looking for you."

"Not my father? Nor my husband?" Asia asked sharply.

It didn't bother her that the water sprites knew what she was, after all, these were the seeing waters. If they could not see even that much their power would be no use to Asia. But she felt wrong in her skin at the mention of her mother.

She wanted to ask if Mother was safe. She wanted to ask what Father had done to her. She wanted to ask if her reckless choice would destroy her mother entirely, just as her every breath had caused her pain. But she couldn't ask any of that, and for such selfish reasons.

If she knew her mother was suffering, she would want to go home, she would want to help her however she could. Even if it meant submitting herself to the sort of miserable existence her mother had lived, and still lived. She would *want* to return to the sea, in the hopes of freeing her mother from whatever torture Father had devised. But she wouldn't return. And not because she'd failed to find the power to overthrow her father and the husband he'd forced on her.

No, she wouldn't return because there were people here she loved. She wanted to help them at least as much as she wanted to help her mother. And here she was fairly certain she could help.

"Your husband seeks you, yes. Your father..." The fairy shrugged. "Your father is quite enjoying your escape. He uses it to manipulate your husband further, to mock him among his peers until he turns to your father for counsel."

Asia ground her teeth. She hated pleasing her father in any way. Almost as much as she once longed to please him. She hated him. With every fiber of her being. Except those few that hated herself.

"But you are not here for news of the sea, I think."

"No." Asia nodded at the largest of the springs, bubbling and steaming behind them. "I need to use the seeing waters, if I may. I have a friend in grave danger and I need to see more so I can know the best course."

"One cannot know the best course until the deed is done. But you know that."

"Madam, I have a great respect for the work you go to preserving these waters. But they do not belong to you, they belong to the world. I will use them."

"Once a princess, always a princess, eh?" A sharp voice sliced Asia's way but she couldn't quite make out the misty woman.

Among the other observers angry murmurs went up, several among them took on defensive stances. The real children vanished, off to safer places.

"I have no intention of fighting any of you, nor do I want to offend. But...I can help here. And I need to do so. I do not ask you to take part as I know you will not, bu—"

"Oh, you know, do you?" the leader asked. "If you are so certain, what need have you with these waters?"

"I know because as you say, I am a mirror spirit. And right now I see surrender to the evil in the world from you. You will hide from it. You will care for your own. But you will not fight her."

"The Fairy queen is hardly the only blight in this world. As your father is constant proof. What do you do about him, mirror spirit, but hide or surrender?" the woman-child countered.

"I can do nothing about my father."

"Not from here, no. But you are ten times as powerful as he, yet you cower from the one choice that can make your world better."

"I am not cowering from killing him. I simply do not have the means," Asia argued.

Among those haunched in preparation for a fight a bit of laughter sounded. And their poses relaxed.

"Killing your father would not make your seas better," the little old woman-child said. "It would only be cutting off the blight, not healing the sickness it came from. That is the power you have ten times greater than he. Healing. There are in you such masses of healing, such ways that they cannot even be contained in one being, but perhaps in six."

Asia startled. Not from the odd words themselves, but from the memory they woke.

Queen Aya had played her father's flute as Owen and Asia danced, laughing wildly. Everything was different with Owen near. Everything. He had such light in him. Despite the horrors in his world.

One moment she would be focused, searching for any sign of the power she was after. Any clue to where the rest of his wanderer relatives were so she could go seeking the power among them. Then Owen would come in all flirtation and teasing, and even though Asia knew she was thirty years older than the boy, married (albeit against her will) and not from his world, when he looked at her that way she giggled and her mind went blank.

"You've too heavy a heart for one of such a large heart," Owen had whispered in her ear, so seriously, then just spun her away wildly.

And she'd laughed and pretended not to hear, but she couldn't escape what she felt from him. He had such depths within. And just then all his depths had been churning with understanding for her. He reminded her of the sea. Wasn't that odd? When she'd fled it, seeking the power to destroy her father, she hadn't thought to miss the sea. She hadn't thought she wanted anything from it. She only wanted to free her mother from the torture that was her existence ever since her father had forced her to be his queen.

She'd left the sea so certain that anywhere above it must be better. But she danced with Owen and she recalled the way the sea embraced her, holding her up when she could not do so herself. Joining her in a wild race when she needed to break free, crashing across rocks, and freezing until it was near impassable, full of all the strength and wonder and delights she'd ever loved. Owen looked into her eyes and Asia recalled the silent depths she'd sung into, and the calm caves she'd hidden in, and the friends she'd made. She sat with Owen and she missed the sea like the home she'd never thought it was.

"Everywhere you go, lives improve, people improve just from your presence. Don't be heavy hearted, you make a better world," he'd whispered again, his lips brushing her ear with a gentle, tingling kiss.

Asia shook off the memory and stared at the woman in front of her. "I can feel him still, but so much less. Do you know how the Fairy queen has cursed him?"

The woman nodded. "Shrunk him. And left him in the hands of an assassin she left guarding that kingdom."

Asia's heart stopped, but the woman kept right on speaking.

"These very waters were used once to tell the Fairy queen that her daughter would unite the human realms under her own rule. Now...the Fairy queen means to make it so."

Asia barely heard her. Her mind was rushing away thinking of all the horrors that might befall Owen, and his mother, and Gavin. They were one of the loveliest families she'd ever known, she could not let the world destroy them. They deserved so much better.

Rival Magic

377 days until Roisin returns

Rowan was making slow progress up Mount Kieran. The further up she went the colder it got. The highest point of the mountain remained all year covered in clouds and was never visible to the eye. Just below that there was a near constant layer of snow. Rowan wondered if fairy disliked the cold as she'd yet to see any. Nor anything about the land in particular to mark it as theirs. Rowan wasn't quite at the constant snow level but she was reaching points where snow regularly fell. Stonedragon hadn't had more than an afternoon of snow flurries in over a hundred years, so none of her clothing was warm enough. Yesterday, she took to layering both her stockings and her dresses and wore leather padding and a cloak atop it, and carrying her armor in one of her packs, but she was still chilled through the night. She hadn't bathed since she left Mount Anwyn and none of her clothes had been properly cleaned in weeks. It was disgusting.

She'd never much minded dirt or being dirty in the past, but this was different. This wasn't a choice. She swore to herself when she got home to find every scullery maid and kitchen attendant, even if they hated her, and fall on her knees in gratitude for all they'd done for her to make her life easy. She could enjoy dirt, because someone had always cleaned up after her. She could train to all hours of the night, because someone cooked her meals, and prepared her bed, and drew her bath. It wasn't so bad that they didn't like her. She still owed them her gratitude.

She wondered if some of the women who had not volunteered for defensive training, or who had looked on the whole affair with a negative eye might not have been...*certain* that they could not have such luxuries. They must believe they had too much work to even find time to defend themselves. Rowan had only thought about the smallest part of the trouble: her father, and starting the initiative. She hadn't considered the massive world of other difficulties that went into it.

She needed to know her people better.

It was different traveling without Yseult. For one thing, every bit of weight was on her back. For another she had no one to talk to. And she had to pay more attention to where she walked as the whistle didn't hang off a bridle leading her on, it pulsed at her neck. But mostly it was the loneliness that was different. Dark thoughts ate away at her mind more.

And the urgency built its way back into her bones.

She'd tried to cast her mind but had been so cold that she couldn't make it work. And in truth she was a bit frustrated with the process. Four times now she'd tried and failed to cast her mind to Gavin, and she felt such a vacancy in her chest, his heart no longer beating in hers. She had to fight to keep from wondering if his heart beat at all. And what she'd seen the last time she visited Petal wasn't much more positive. She looked lonely and heartsore, and was turning to Sorcha for her comfort. Rowan needed to find the dragons now, or preferably yesterday, but the dragons weren't cooperating.

Rowan had woken today with a bit of a cough and all her muscles sore. It was so windy that she couldn't tell which way the hum of the whistle was leading so she'd taken to just searching every cave she passed.

If she didn't find the dragons soon this would be a wasted exercise. It would be back to being all on her, and however big her magic felt out here, when she tried to imagine challenging Sorcha with it she felt insignificant. Her mind would call up that tiny woman with her cool smile, and a room full of kings and soldiers jumping back from her as if burned.

Sorcha was *so* powerful. How was Rowan ever to rival someone like that? Were it not for needing to defeat her Rowan wouldn't even want to rival her.

Rowan wanted to be loved. By her family, yes, but also by the world. And she didn't know if that was a bad thing to want or not, but it was in her. And she knew, without any doubt, that if she was powerful enough to rival Sorcha, the rest of the world would only ever fear her.

Sorcha walked down the long palace halls. As she passed fairy stopped their business to sink into bows and curtsies. She saw them but her mind barely marked their passing. Her mind was far too busy devising a plan to find that Knight of the Rose. She had not gone to Turrlough, nor had any of Sorcha's spies spotted her.

When she was a younger girl and watched her mother make her way through a palace ignoring the staff, Sorcha had thought if she had been destined to be queen, she would have done things differently. She'd loved her mother, thought she was a wonderful queen, but too distant, too fond of her place. Sorcha knew differently now. Her mother hadn't been distant, she'd been consumed. Every moment consumed with concerns, for her nation, and her legacy. There simply wasn't time to return every bow, hear every compliment or complaint.

Nothing was ever done right unless she oversaw every aspect of a task. Sorcha paused outside the aviary door. Intersecting leafless branches grew together in a spindly pattern not unlike a cage. Between the branches a forest could be seen, with trees of thin white trunks and high held branches and leaves that danced letting out fluttering music. It was a lovely room. Once her very favorite in the palace.

The door had been different then: two crossed arms of aspens had met at the top, and nothing but the open space between their trunks made up the bottom of the door. It was the first room of Sorcha's design that mother ever allowed to be added to the public halls of Fairy Cache.

"Sorcha, this is lovely! You are developing quite the artistic talent. If you continue to develop it so, your artistry will be an excellent service to offer your sister's court."

Sorcha had beamed up at her mother. "Thank you, Your Majesty. I designed it as a home for my friends, so we can all gather in one place."

Mother smiled crookedly. "The fowl are not your friends, Sorcha. They love you of course, as they should. But they are yours to control, and one does not control friends. They are your servants." Mother ran a hand down Sorcha's cheek and under her chin, tilting it a bit to the side so she could take in all of her daughter's face.

"You are a...beautiful, talented young woman, Sorcha. But you have it within you to be even more. You can be shrewd, and strong and unmatched in power."

Sorcha had startled, surely her mother would not suggest that Sorcha should try to take her sister's place as queen. "Nessa is incredibly powerful."

Mother laughed. "Yes, she is. And when she becomes queen she will be even more so. I did not mean you should rival your sister, Sorcha. I meant that you should be an asset to her. A queen needs one with a mind like yours standing at her side and lightening her load by seeing so far ahead she is prepared for every threat. Nessa calls all together to serve a higher purpose. But you, my love, can be her greatest general. You can see to it that your sister's reign stretches longer than any queen or king before her. It is a noble calling."

Sorcha had never before or since felt as proud. She had worked every day to earn the praise. Honing her skills for deciphering the future, quashing threats before they could arise. And never, ever letting go of any leverage that might be used to her advantage. Not one piece.

The more shrewd she became, the better she understood her mother's lessons. And the more the door changed. The branches shed their leaves and grew down, twining together so that none of Sorcha's servants could escape.

Sorcha slid her hand over the smooth bark, and pulled the door towards her. Stepping in, she pulled the door shut behind her and walked out into the little wood. At once, birds of every kind swooped out of the trees to trail her through the wood like a fluttering, flapping train. She walked until she came to a half moon shaped clearing with a low smooth stone that dipped in the center like a comfy seat.

Sorcha settled there and the birds circled around her, over and over, looping until Sorcha stretched out her scepter and pointed to a falcon. Black and white with a split tail, the falcon broke away from the group and flew to the stone beside Sorcha.

"Now, Bran, my love, how are you fairing?" Sorcha ran a hand down the birds head. He was by far one of her favorite pets among those she'd changed over the years. She found the pets she made tended to be much more fun than the pets she collected among those born fowl. It hadn't always been so, but once she had enemies it was thoroughly satisfying to take her enemies' favorites and make them into pets.

The bird screeched loud and shrill. A love cry.

"My darling." She lay aside her scepter and lifted the bird with both hands, rubbing her face along his. "I've missed you too."

Sorcha heard the quiet brush of wood against stone and glanced aside. A woodpecker sat on the edge of her stone seat, having just knocked the scepter to the ground. And between Sorcha and the scepter, three ducks beat their wings as a shield for the raven on the ground poking at the crystal.

Sorcha laughed, and lay Bran on the stone beside her.

"Had I known you wanted to try your hand at freeing Desmond I would have given you a chance, love," Sorcha spoke to the bird, leaning back, unconcerned with the rebellion. So many were the birds who had thought to hang onto bits of themselves when they first came to her. But all were defeated in the end.

Bran settled comfortably on the arm of the chair, rubbing his head along Sorcha's arm.

After a moment the raven ceased pecking at the crystal and looked back towards Sorcha between the beating wings of the ducks, his eyes taking in only her legs. He always had been afraid to see her face.

"What now?" Sorcha asked playfully.

The raven spun around, closing his talons around the scepter and trying to take to the air. But the weight of the crystal and staff combined held him close to the ground, he screeched and from among Sorcha's flock another three birds broke away heading to the raven's aid.

Sorcha narrowed her eyes sharply. They couldn't get away. That wasn't what disturbed her as the four birds locked talons around the staff and rose into the air. It was the insubordination. It was the rabble rouser among them trying and it seemed at least somewhat succeeding in turning her flock.

The birds rose and with them the staff. Sorcha didn't even need to give an order. Bran sensed her anger and leapt from his perch, calling out and other falcons took off after him. They charged at the thieves and attacked them with tiny pecks and swipes with their talons, until one after another all the birds but the raven let go. He fell through the air with the scepter, but Bran wasn't done with him. He dove straight for the raven, catching onto the back of his neck and digging his talons in deep. But the raven was a fighter, he let his weight drop with the scepter, dragging Bran down, and leaned his head back to nip at Bran's legs.

Bran let go of the raven only long enough to swoop up from underneath and grab onto its throat beneath his head, and dig his talon into one of the raven's talons until it let go of the scepter. The two birds grappled with one another. Yanking out feathers and drawing blood until Bran at last stood victorious on the chest of his rival. The falcon locked both talons deep into the raven's flesh and lifted him into the air, carrying him to deposit him beside Sorcha's hand on the stone.

"Thank you, my love," Sorcha cooed to the falcon. He left his rival at her hand and swooped down with the other falcon's to set Sorcha's scepter to rights.

Sorcha grinned at the raven beside her, bleeding out. She ran a hand through his feathers soothingly. "Do you know the trouble I've found with most people, even most fairy? They are short sighted. They do not see that failure in the moment doesn't mean ultimate failure. If I'd given up when first I turned my falcon flock I wouldn't have half the servants I do today. I failed a hundred times to turn them, I could control them with focused spells, or train them like human pets tricked with food, but to get a soldier like Bran—"

Sorcha flung out an arm at the falcon struggling still to repair the scepter to its home. He vanished in a flash of bright purple light. A lanky man of about thirty appeared standing before Sorcha. At once the man took a knee, bowing low before the Fairy queen, and lifted the scepter between his hands, holding it out to

her.

"My queen," he said in a voice laden with desire. "How may I serve you?"

Sorcha took the scepter from his hands, depositing a soft kiss on his cheek. "You serve me constantly as an example for your fellow men. Would you like to leave me?" Sorcha asked sweetly, watching the raven out of the corner of her eye to be sure he was paying attention.

"I desire only to be at your side, My queen. But if you have a task for me I shall fulfill it with all haste."

"Thank you, my love. I do have a task for you. I need you to trail a wayward prince, can you do that?"

"I can do anything my queen desires."

He moved as if to stand but a light flashed again and he was a bird once more, flapping rapidly towards the door to the palace. At his approach the branches unwound to make a small hole for the bird to slip through, growing immediately shut behind him.

Sorcha made a light laughing noise, not quite a laugh, more like a hum with her nose and returned her attention to the raven. She lifted the scepter and lay it against him. A bright purple balm of light slid through the bird, healing all his wounds.

"To make a servant like that, one must be patient," Sorcha whispered softly, running a finger along the raven's head. "No one believes me capable of patience. They used to be right. But I have had to learn it. You see, the thing you failed to understand about eternity is that it isn't a long endless stretch that one is dragged through. No." Sorcha gazed off into the distance, her finger continuing to pet the bird in slow rhythmic strokes and her heart laid itself bare with her servants as she could not anywhere else.

"That would be so much easier. A fairy does not live *forever,* but she can exist in every moment of time if she is skilled enough. I am skilled enough. I saw him taken from me, my son, saw it before he was born, and in the moment of his birth. I committed my every moment to stopping it, committed my every moment to loving him so deeply and protecting him so well that none could touch him. But over and over I lived that loss. Until the moment that I...at a loss from fear and anger and helplessness to save him—trapped him with my own hand."

Sorcha lifted her hand away from the bird and stared into her palm, seeing nothing of the world before her. She lived it again. Arguing with Desmond, her sweet boy. Her gentle boy, so devoted to his sister, he could not stand the idea of her being married to honor a contract.

"I cannot break my word, Desmond. Do not worry. You can see her whenever you like and…"

"You never should have made such a promise."

"It was not ideal," Sorcha agreed, reaching out for her son's face, as she tried to explain what he could not possibly understand. How could he? His life had been sheltered from fear, and threats. He'd never seen any turmoil the likes of that war. He'd never experienced a loss like Sorcha had when her sister died, her lover turned on her, and she had visions of losing her unborn son, all in the matter of a month. He couldn't possibly understand.

He jerked his head away before she could touch him. "Ideal, Mother? It wasn't even acceptable! You dealt with humans, like a human. We do not exchange lives for favors as though they are ours to give. Fairy are better than that."

"Desmond, when you are faced with war and betrayal and out of options I shall take this sort of criticism, but…"

"You banished your other options," he shouted.

Sorcha's heart stopped. Always it came back to that for him. His father, and his aunts. He'd never met one of them, but he was so certain they were all better than her. How did he fail to see? Over and over Desmond failed to see that there was no one in the world who loved him like she did. Over and over, he failed to see that everything she did was for him. Banishing his father, and his aunts was all to keep him here! Did he think she would have given up her other sisters—who she loved—for anything short of him?

It was all, always for him. And he…

"If you weren't so threatened by greater power you would have had the best of the fairy here to help you," Desmond accused coldly.

The best of the fairy! *How dare he? How dare he think of her as so...small and petty? He was just like the rest of them.*

"Your sisters would never have made such a deal with humans," he pressed, impassioned. *"They wouldn't have needed to."*

"Needed to!" Sorcha laughed as her heart broke. *They were her family first, or didn't he remember that? His father, his uncle, his aunts. Everyone Sorcha had ever loved, none of them saw her. None of them loved her, or respected what she was forced to do.* "You may not agree with my choices, Desmond, and you may not think me the best of the Fairy." *She felt the power building in her and did not even know what she was doing, a purple haze filling the air like mist.* "But you will learn to respect me and what I will do for this nation. What I did for you!"

It just exploded from her hands, her power. Leapt from her and wrapped her son up so tight that no one could touch him. Even her.

Sorcha reached out for the scepter now but couldn't bring herself to lift it. She looked back at the bird beside her and expelled a tiny breath of pained laughter. "For so long my only goal had been to see him safe that I didn't worry for Sinead. I knew she would be with me always, I had seen it so. I had seen her returning to me, and ruling beside me for centuries. I had seen it. I knew it. But that *disease* perverted all of eternity. And now I must live Sinead's loss as well. *Again* and again. I live in all the moments when she would smile at me, and ask for my attention but I put her off for later, because I had her brother to save. I live it daily. So I learned a patience I was never possessed of. I learned the value of keeping seemingly threatening creatures, and waiting to make use of them."

Sorcha waved a hand around her flock of birds. "They are not all known to her. But those that are..." Sorcha laughed. "She has mourned them once already, and I shall make her mourn them again and again. She is not skilled enough a fairy to know eternity as I do. But I will teach her *all* its tortures. And you will help me." She kissed the raven on the head. "You don't think so yet. I know that, and I do not mind. Because I have learned the way to change you, body, mind and soul. I will be patient and loving, and allow you enough freedom to see that at my hand, is the only place you desire to be. To that end, I've decided to give you a little more...freedom."

The raven flapped into the air, his head darted back and forth between the wood, and the hole forming in the door of his prison. All at once, as if bitten, he shot forward, flying out the hole.

Sorcha chuckled as she watched him fly away. She stood and lifted her scepter without laying her eyes on it. Slowly she walked from her aviary, with a train of birds behind her until the moment her feet touched the halls of Fairy Cache.

Risk Takers

376 days until Roisin returns

Rowan was officially off the map. No one had charted this high on Mount Kieran. It was written that the mountain went up another two miles, but no one knew for sure.

Rowan had reached the level of constant snow, it grew steadily harder to breathe. Rowan was barely moving her breaths were so heavy. Yesterday she'd had to cut off a limb of a tree to make herself a walking stick. Every few minutes she would stop and just lean against it. But as achy and tired and as anxious as Rowan was to find the dragons, a bit of her was just...excited.

"I'm out of my tower now!" Rowan grinned and watched the words stutter into the air before her in the steam of her breath. They hovered there a moment, and Rowan felt a loopy urge to try and scoop her breath back up. She laughed at the thought and looked to her right. For sometime now she'd felt someone traveling with her. When Yseult was here she'd dismissed the feeling as just her magic feeling Yseult more strongly than she had at home. But she didn't think so any longer.

She thought it was Gavin. His spirit was with her somehow. Her mind conjured the shadow of him to walk along beside her, and answer her in the words of his old letters.

"I've told you you should be an adventurer."

Rowan grinned. "I'm the first person to set foot this high on the mountain."

"Awfully proud of yourself, aren't you?"

Rowan nodded. "Every day I am further from home. Further from anything I've ever known or understood. And I miss it, sometimes. But..." Rowan spun around, even though that little exertion left her winded. She looked into the snowy, heavily fogged wood around her, too dense to see more than a few feet before her. She grinned.

"I am seeing the world. I'm alone. And I'm dirty. And sometimes I'm so lonely. And truth be told I'm a bit hungry, and not even entirely certain now that the dragons aren't leading me towards a frozen death in a cave." Rowan stopped speaking and leaned forward, dropping her stick and bracing herself against her knees for a panting laugh. She dropped her packs into the snow as well. She wasn't as cold today, breathing was harder, and thinking straight was just out of the question. But at least she wasn't cold. She used to like feeling cold. But this cold ate away her will. It wouldn't abate. This cold wasn't a wakeful feeling on the skin, it was a solid state of being transforming her into a human icicle.

"I could die," Rowan forced the words out, still panting. She looked up at the shadow Gavin, imagining that brief flash of a face she'd seen when she visited him in her mind. "I always knew I could die to save her. But now...I will have seen something other than my tower. Now I will have seen something no one else in the world has seen. Now it won't be a tragedy." Rowan gasped and felt tears go crawling down her face as slow as glaciers.

The snow crunched as the Gavin shadow crouched. Odd, he'd never made a sound outside of talking before. She felt his hands settle on her shoulders.

"Rowan, I will not let you die. Do you understand me?" he said, but his voice was not his own, not the voice Rowan had imagined from nothing more than the few words she'd heard him speak. It wasn't his voice, but it was familiar. And the oddity of it was enough to wake her up a bit. Perhaps she'd traveled too high. "You need to get up. Stop looking with your eyes and ears. Feel what you are seeking with your power."

Rowan stood straight and blinked at the empty space before her. There didn't appear to be anyone there, but she felt someone.

"Gavin?" she whispered. But she shook her head almost as soon as she said it. It wasn't Gavin. She'd known it from the first. She just...she couldn't let him go, and the void in her heart pounded a reminder every second that she did not feel him any longer. He was gone and she'd never even properly met him.

This wasn't Gavin. But it also wasn't an enemy. Perhaps it was the dragons. Or one of the boys casting their senses as Rowan could.

Whoever it was, Rowan lifted her packs back onto her shoulders and used the walking staff to help her back up. She forced herself to do nothing but stand here breathing. *Stop using your eyes and ears.* Rowan shut her eyes, one hand held her up with the staff, and the other wrapped around the dragon pendant at her throat. It was so warm. With her fingers wrapped around it she felt the warmth drenching the bones in her hand until it felt almost hot despite the snow she stood in and the dusting of it falling around her.

Dragons were warm. Why would they hide in all this snow? Could they even survive in snow this thick?

Rowan's mind began to wander away to the old journals Ardal had given her about dragons and their powers, but as soon as her mind went to him teeth of rage sunk into her heart. He hadn't taken her side. He hadn't believed in her.

The warmth started to recede, and her fingers loosened around the pendant. She began to feel the cold again as she saw Ardal before her eyes. Before her fingers could loosen entirely, Rowan noticed his eyes, when he'd shaken his head, and said Father was his king, that he could not speak against him. His eyes were...sunken and small and frightened, as they'd been when he first came home. When he'd thought he would lay in his bed forever and die there. When he felt useless.

Rowan thought over all the things she'd been coming to realize about the women of her nation. All the things she'd failed to consider that stood in their way, making their path to knighthood, or even to recognizing their own wills much more difficult than her own. She'd forgotten to consider some of those things with Ardal too. Father was his king. He *served* at the pleasure of his king. How was he to know a way to challenge such a man? He'd felt useless, not because he doubted Rowan, and thought her father was right, but because he hadn't known how to help her this time.

She hadn't seen. Maybe she never could have seen at home. But she was as much to blame for the anger in their parting as he was. If she was to be a queen she needed to lead, not just expect everyone to know what she wanted and needed and do it without ever being shown the way.

She would go back and show them the way. But first, she needed to finish what she'd started.

Rowan released the pendant and let the icy wall of cold slam into her body. She sent her magic out into this frozen world around her to find the hidden fires within and marched towards that heat with her eyes shut.

"Do you know, I feel odd saying this," Ferdy said with a distinctly disgusted look on his face. "But this may be taking trick playing a bit too far."

Keagan snorted, taking a moment to laugh at his brother, though in truth there was nothing either funny or playful about this trick. It was a trick on the king so that Ferdy would go along, but its true intent was to see if Ferdy and Keagan could perform massive amounts of magic they weren't accustomed to.

Ferdy and Keagan were going to use magic to send their army into five different places at once to steal portraits of Princess Roisin. Three children would be sent to the king's bedroom. Three into his study. Two into Queen Gwyneth's room. Four into the Great hall. And the last three into the dining hall.

Both Ferdy and Keagan could vanish into any room they wanted, and maybe take a person or two along with them. But neither Ferdy nor Keagan were going. They would wait in the squires' barracks, across the courtyard and past the soldiers barracks, far from the palace. They weren't going to be near enough to hear with their ears if something went wrong, or if it went right, when the others called out for extraction. And they were both going to be sending multiple children at once to more than one location. With Keagan keeping a magical lookout for them and Ferdy spelling all the rooms at once for silence.

There would be a massive amount of magic spent between them. It was bound to be exhausting, and very dangerous. But if they could do this then they had enough power between them to find Rowan. This had to work.

Keagan was more concerned every day. He'd been trying to see the end more ways like Ferdy suggested, and he had. But all he was seeing was more bad. Even in the ends where Rowan defeated Sorcha, so much bad was a part of it. Half the new times he'd seen Rowan and Sorcha die together. And Ferdy kept dying. In nearly every vision Ferdy was dead. And if Ferdy wasn't, Pa was, or Mama. Keagan needed to leave. He just had to. The world was getting worse and worse.

"How is this too far?" Keagan asked nonchalantly, consciously lying to his brother, and not feeling bad about it. "You were aiming at changing or stealing all of the portraits eventually. Now we're doing it more efficiently."

Ferdy raised a brow. "Don't you think we should leave them a few?"

"Oh, there's one in the portrait gallery and the king has one in his desk that I didn't make anyone steal."

"I already changed the one in his desk," Ferdy said. "Every time he picks it up her face changes into Rowan's."

Keagan laughed, surprised and oddly happy from the thought. Ferdy did have a way about him. "That's terrific!"

"I know." Ferdy smirked. "Look, it's not so much the trick...but you're making it unnecessarily difficult. Why send them all at once? Why be so far away?" Ferdy lowered his voice. "One of the kids could get hurt, some of them are really little."

"And less afraid than you." Brigid slipped out of the corner to shout at Ferdy, sticking out her tongue.

That girl nosed in on everything. Keagan rolled his eyes, as Ferdy sniped with her. She was a bit of a help honestly. She egged Ferdy on more than any other child, she just might distract him from the danger.

"I'm not afraid. I'm trying to keep you from having your neck rung by the guards. I'm going to be perfectly safe." Ferdy stuck his tongue out in return.

"Is that what bothers you?" Brigid taunted.

"Just shut up, Brigid. I need to talk to Keagan." Ferdy yanked his brother aside and opened his mind to his brother, sharing his deeper concerns that way. *Why are you doing this? It isn't like you.*

If all we're going to do is play tricks, they need to be big ones. Keagan replied with his mind. *We need to be frightening them with our power. They need to wonder how many of us there are, and not think we're children either. I can't just go around defacing fountains and changing banners. It doesn't change anything.*

Ferdy wore a look like he wasn't fooled, but he nodded.

"Everyone in position. In each group it will work better if you are all touching, both when we send you and when you call out for extraction." Ferdy marched between the fifteen children they'd acquired for their army other than Colleen.

By and large, Colleen preferred not to take part in the more dangerous schemes, anything overly stressful and she lost a bit of control. She was more than happy to take part in the planning stages, but she couldn't take part in an event like tonight. It was too much of a risk. They hadn't even told her about this plan.

Ferdy thought Keagan was babying her. He said they might actually be more powerful if they let her take part. But Keagan felt too responsible for her. It felt wrong now— how much he still loved her, how much he wanted to be with her all the time. Wrong because she was bound to give him what he wanted if he didn't tamp down the desire. She was still a cipher, she just had more control of it. He wasn't sure she would ever know if what she wanted was what she wanted and not what someone else did. And he wanted her so much.

So it was wrong. It was best to put some space between them.

"Be sure you know what you're after and head right for it the moment you enter a room," Ferdy instructed. He'd make a decent commander. Every eye, even Brigid who seemed very much to dislike him, looked on Ferdy with respect. "Is everyone ready?"

There were nods from all around the room.

"Well, then," Ferdy said with bright, but false enthusiasm. "Lets go change the world."

Ferdy walked over to stand next to his brother and clasped a hand onto his shoulder. He braced himself, and Keagan did as well.

Then Keagan shut out his brother so he could focus only on the three groups of children he needed to move with his magic. He stared at them so hard his head hurt and tried to see the different places they needed to go like he could different futures, layered over one another, seeing them all at once.

Altogether, Keagan's eight children vanished. He could see them in his mind, taking their places in the layered rooms. He nearly did a dance. Then he realized that while four of Ferdy's children had disappeared, the last three had no—

The last three vanished.

Alright, not at once, but they had all gone where they were meant to. So that was a small mistake, but nothing worrying.

"We're doing it!" Keagan said aloud, allowing his mind to watch them all.

Keagan felt, more than saw, his brother nod. It was a heavy feeling, he seemed nearly to be leaning on Keagan's shoulder.

"We need to get them back," Ferdy said.

"They're nearly done. Let's wait and make sure we can hear them whe—"

"No Kee, now! Its..." Ferdy drifted off, slipping backwards to sit on the bottom bunk of the bed behind him.

"You okay?" Keagan spun around to look at his brother, all of his focus rushing back to this room. The children pillaging the palace forgotten.

"I can't...they're too loud. I can't keep so many places silent at once," Ferdy said heavily, his temples visibly pounding and he was even sweating.

"Okay, okay, hold on," Keagan said sharply. He was worried for Ferdy, but part of Keagan, the mastermind part, wanted to ask him to hold on a few minutes more. The mastermind part of him wanted to complain that Ferdy was just being lazy. Keagan was doing as much work as him, and he didn't even feel tired.

The mastermind part of him, the part that was less brother, less son, less person every day, that part wanted to push Ferdy to the brink, so he could know for certain what sort of weapon he had in him. But part of him was still more brother than mastermind. And neither part of him could let the plan fail completely. If Ferdy was tired enough to let go of the magic they might fail. So Keagan began layering the rooms over one another in his mind. Checking to see how far along everyone was. And even as he did he started hearing children calling out for extraction from the great room, and the king's study.

Keagan pulled both groups out, even as he was looking in on the others. But one eye kept darting to Ferdy, and despite their being two less groups to worry about Ferdy almost looked worse.

"Hurry," Ferdy's garbled whisper fell on Keagan's ears just as he was realizing part of the trouble. The last room fell atop the other's in Keagan's mind and he saw Brigid, Aiden and Molly, shouting in the dining hall. Brigid must have tried to reach a portrait by standing on a bench atop a table. She had fallen and the bench lay atop her.

At once, Keagan yanked back every other group. He intended to vanish himself into the dining hall and check on them, but Ferdy yanked the last group into the barracks with his magic, bench and all.

All of the children started screaming in shock, dropping their various portraits and rushing towards Brigid. But before they could get to her the bench flew up into the air above their heads and slammed into the wall across the room. Everyone froze with fear. Ferdy leaned forward from his place on the bed, and stared at Brigid, with sweaty face and wild eyes.

"Are you alright?" he bit out.

"I'm fine," she said with a pained squeak, trying to push herself up on her hands, but she couldn't manage it, and her eyes were filled with tears.

"This is what I was talking about!" Ferdy shouted at her, not at Keagan, when anyone could tell it was Keagan who should be yelled at. Why had Keagan been fine with risking children this way?

"Stay where you are," Keagan knelt by Brigid. "I'll take you to my mother to heal you. You too, Fer—"

"No," Ferdy snapped. "Take her. I'm fine. We need to hide things. That was quite the ruckus we just made."

Keagan didn't know what to say. He rather thought Ferdy needed healing too. But he suddenly wasn't confident enough to argue. He touched Brigid's arm, vanishing from the room. But he couldn't get his heart to stop pounding, louder and louder in his ears every second. What if he lost Ferdy before Sorcha ever came for them? What would he do without his brother?

Magical Discovery

owan startled awake in the middle of the night. Her tiny fire had died, and the blankets she'd piled atop herself before going to sleep were gone. Well, not gone.

They were folded neatly on the other side of the doused fire. Rowan sat up, shivering. She ran her hands up and down the upper halves of her arms, hugging herself to hold onto as much of the warmth as she could. Sent her power out seeking the intruder in her camp.

"In a trickster mood?" Rowan asked her invisible stalker. It was almost certainly a fairy.

Rowan was searching the camp with her eyes and her magic. It was really nothing but a few tightly grown bushes beneath a trio of trees. The trees had reminded Rowan of the triplets, and the bushes of them being bundled up on the floor of their cottage, so she'd chosen that spot to rest in. One of the times she'd felt the presence she thought maybe it was Ferdy. But she didn't think so now. It didn't feel warm and friendly, but nor did it feel malevolent. It felt...curious. And it felt familiar. It was challenging her. Rowan shivered. She just wasn't up to figuring it out. Couldn't they just let her sleep?

Rowan wondered if it wasn't just some strange fairy who had followed her from the lower part of the mountain, the part that belonged to the Fairy nation. Maybe it trailed her of its own volition, to see whether Rowan was truly fairy or not. Or maybe it followed her for Sorcha, and was stealing Rowan's warmth so she would fall ill and die before she could find a way to help her family.

As she thought it, Rowan realized something. She was cold, inside and out, but the longer she sat searching the distance and ignoring the chill that had woken her, the more the chill faded to the back of her mind and the physical sensation of it left her body. She was cold, but she didn't feel stiff, or shaky, or breathless as she had the last few days of marching through the snow.

You must be a part of nature to understand it.

Maureen's words from the night Rowan departed swayed through her mind. Rowan let her arms fall to her sides and stood. Her feet were bare but for the two layers of stockings she wore to bed now.

Rowan walked across the pine needles, twigs, grass, and tiny piles of snow, letting all the sensations touch her feet in different ways, allowing her body to become more familiar with them. Little sensations might sting her feet for a moment, or press into her almost painfully, but nothing truly hurt. Even when she let the snow soak through her two layers of stockings and felt the cold nip at the surface of her skin, nothing harmed her. She wasn't freezing, or cut or ill. She could breathe fine.

Just to see if she could Rowan leapt into the air and kicked out with her right leg. She punched at nothing and swung around for a low sweeping kick. Her heart pounded a bit faster as it always did with exercise, but nothing was stiff or strained or exhausted.

Rowan laughed and threw herself back on the ground by her bed.

"Alright, companion," Rowan said with a smile. "Point made. Now let me get some sleep." Smiling Rowan lay back down with no fire, and no blanket, but she didn't feel chilled at all as her body adjusted to the world around her.

375 days until Roisin returns

Keagan appeared at the fringes of the field where Ardal and several Knights of the Rose were training a group of women. Colleen was at the fringes of the group as well, but because she'd wanted to watch, and maybe learn, but not to have anyone touch her, or talk to her, or want anything from or for her, she was invisible. She watched Keagan scuff his foot in the dust, his eyes watching Ardal as if he wanted the man to turn around from the feeling alone, but couldn't bring himself to go and speak with him.

Keagan was never that hesitant. He always knew what was right. At least it seemed so to Colleen. He wasn't confident, or arrogant, he was just right.

She could feel such desire coming off him, such fear. He wanted to move, he wanted to fix the world. Colleen didn't have big desires. She might desire food. Or desire to hide. Or desire to learn, but only to learn the bits that interested her. She might desire to sit and read. All small, quiet desires. Nothing in her was that large, except the empty. And she hadn't wanted to go back there in a few days.

She liked the smallness of her insides, the simplicity of her desires. She could handle tiny, achievable ends. But she also liked that Keagan wasn't like her. His desires were three times as large as his body. Half of them seemed entirely impossible to bring about, and that he knew it too, but he didn't make an empty inside himself.

Sometimes she liked inching closer and closer to him, feeling his desires crawl into her empty and shout out that she could bring them about for him, knowing she could give him *anything* he wanted—but saying no.

Lord, but she loved the word no.

But just now, a wave of such utter fear exploded off of Keagan that it knocked Colleen's tiny desires away. She felt the magic she'd stolen from someone sliding away from her, and she appeared right next to him.

Keagan jumped. He was so shocked that his eyes widened. She felt him taking in that she was there, that she was using magic and that he was feeling large feelings, the kind big enough to make her forget herself. The moment it hit him, he jumped away and began to stammer.

"I'm s..so..sorry. I...Are you alright, Colleen?"

She nodded. But the truth was she couldn't tell. She didn't know if she nodded because she felt his worry and wanted to sooth him, or because she was actually alright. She backed up a step as well, fear starting to coat her cells. Who was she?

"I'm sorry. I'll leave," Keagan blurted out. She felt him trying to bundle up his emotions and coat them in his sympathy for her and she was so sick of that feeling.

"Just tell me what is wrong!" she shouted rudely.

Keagan startled. "Colleen, do you—"

"Yes, I know who I am!" she snapped, garnering attention from the soldiers behind them. Everyone spun to look. Colleen grabbed onto Keagan's hand and dragged him further from the group.

"I'm not trying to give you everything you want," she said as she walked. *I don't think,* her mind added. "But I can tell you are upset. What is the matter?"

"I don't know what to do. I've been trying to do something, and I very nearly killed Ferdy in the process."

"Because of me?" Colleen asked. Remembering what she knew of how she'd caused the brothers to fight when she was only a cipher, not a...*conscious* cipher.

"No," Keagan shook his head. "Because of me. Because I'm pushing too hard, and I'm doing all the wrong things."

"You don't do the wrong things. You never do," Colleen interrupted.

Keagan stilled, even his emotions froze at her words. She felt his desperate desire for her to love him, for her to kiss him.

Colleen took a step back and looked away from him. She could feel his one and only desire in the moment crawling around in her telling her that she wanted it too, but she didn't know. It didn't make any sense that she would, he was a child. But...she didn't exactly feel like anything but a child most days. None of it made sense. And she needed to know what feelings were hers and what were his, but she needed to help him too.

"I think you just see too much. You see it all, all of the bad, all of the good. All of the future and all of the past. I don't see any of that. I still can't really see my past."

"I think you will one day," Keagan said reassuringly. "You're getting better every day. One day you'll be able to see it all."

"I don't think so." Colleen shook her head. "I don't even know if I want to. The bad must have been very bad for me to hide from it so much that I cannot remember a thing. Why would I want to know it?"

Keagan was silent for a very long time. "Because it is yours. But…it won't be bad enough to hurt you now, because you have us. We will protect you, even from the past."

Colleen stared at him derisively, he was just a child, eleven years old and she was seventeen, but he was promising to protect her and she felt…safer.

"Aren't you ever scared of all the bad you see?" Colleen asked.

"All the time," Keagan admitted with a shrug. "That's why I'm trying to fix it."

Colleen laughed. "But with everything you do to fix it, do you ever see the badness actually going away? Or just shifting?" she asked, feeling these words actually come from her. "That's why I don't even want to know the past, because the badness never goes away. It's always going to be here. And as I am, I'm free. I think you should stop trying to fix it. I think you should do what I'm doing. You should enjoy right now."

Colleen felt her words create a storm of confusion in Keagan. The empty inside her wanted to reach out and fix it, but she just walked around him. Then she ran. Because with every step she took away from him the empty cried out for her to give him something. Anything.

She ran as fast as she could.

Asia sunk beneath the waters of the largest seeing pool. She pushed all the air from her lungs until she sunk to the very bottom. She stretched out along the uneven rocky floor and looked up through the shifting water. Delaney, the leader of the water sprites had been teaching Asia how to use the seeing waters. Asia's mother had tried to do it for years, but Asia had not wanted to see the future. Not since she was twelve; the first time she'd truly understood her mother's power and seen such evil things as a result.

"She wanted to teach you the art so you could focus," Delaney's voice filled the water. It almost was the water. "So you wouldn't have to see only the evil."

There was a vast difference between the magic of water sprites and the magic of mermaids. Water sprites could literally become water, could change their form to mist or liquid or ice. It was magnificent. But there was something at once confining and expansive about being a water sprite. When they became water they were all one creature, but with so many minds. Asia didn't understand it, and she was certain she didn't want to be it, but the sprites were helping her to understand what it was to be a mermaid. Something she hadn't truly understood until she shucked that form for a human body.

Mermaids were tied to the sea, it was in their makeup. When they died they united with the waters. But while they lived they were just another animal that the water gave life to. Mermaids trapped these seeing waters in shells and performed spells like the witches and wizards of the human world. But few and far between were the mer with actual magic in their own beings. Rather unfortunately for her sake, Asia was one of those few. Her father had aimed at creating such a child as his heir. He'd captured her mother and forced her to be his queen with just such a purpose. He just hadn't counted on his heir being female. He wanted his image but power such as he had never possessed. And Asia wasn't that.

When she was twelve, in a lesson with her mother on seeing the future, Asia, or Symphony as she had been then, saw her father raping her mother again and again trying to get his son. That was the last time she had ever tried to see the future. Until now.

Asia felt her heart racing and she opened her mouth in desperation for air but caught a mouth full of water instead. She flailed about wildly. Forgetting that all she need do was stand to be out of the water and back into the air that had begun to feel like home in this year she'd lived as a human.

The water around Asia took on solid shape and a pair of arms shoved her, sputtering, above the pool's surface.

A pair of sprites sitting on the pool's edge laughed. "You take to the water poorly for a mermaid," one taunted, her brow lifted in a superior smirk.

"I am a human now," Asia snapped.

"No. You aren't." The jagged voice came from behind them. So hard and angry, Asia half expected to turn and see a woman made of ice, but she was in fact composed of mist. She looked soft but looks were deceptive. "You are a spoiled princess, trying to have the best of all worlds. Sometimes, princess, you have to make a choice." The woman evaporated before Asia had even formed a response.

The girl who'd first laughed at Asia shook her head. "Ignore her, Orla was born with an angry heart."

Asia shook her head, quietly thoughtful. "Angry hearts are made."

"Indeed?" Delaney sat on the edge of the pool, the bits of her legs that remained in the water had no shape but the rest of her was in the body of a small girl. She watched Asia thoughtfully for a moment. "And Orla has a point, angry though she is. In order to learn to use magic this way you would have to choose. You still cling to your mer gift, and that is not for seeing the future but for using the powers of others. And our powers are not for seeing the future, that is a function of the pools."

"*Oh,*" Asia said in shock and felt that shiver beneath her skin again. That was the trouble. She was feeling their powers and her fear of that group being was what pulled her out of her focus.

Asia sucked in a deep breath, the force of the air bending her spine. She felt her arched back begin to dissolve into mist.

Terrified that she might never come together again, Asia held onto her breath and her every bit of being in a desperate hold, and became a solid thing once more.

Delaney laughed. Giggled really, as though she truly was the small girl her body showed. "It seems you need a seer. Or simply to trust in our answers."

Asia nodded, knitting her fingers together. She needed to stay together. Water sprite magic was *terrifying*.

"Are not all the powers you encounter terrifying until you come to know them?" Delaney asked, reading Asia's mind.

"Some more than others." Asia shook her head. "I am not trying to have both worlds. I am not trying to have any world. Or I wasn't when I came here." She spoke, a bit lost, but wandering through what it was that made her cling so tight to this body. "All my life I wanted him to see my value. I did everything he ever asked. I backed away from my mother when our closeness angered him. I learned everything he asked of me. I bent down to his rages and his edicts. I was everything I could be for him, except the one thing he wanted. I wanted to be queen, to carry on his legacy and make him proud. Even when I hated him I wanted that, so much that it made me hate myself. But he never could love me, he must have hated me as much as I did, because..." Asia laughed and felt tears slip down her cheek. She raised a hand to catch them, trying to shove them back inside. Mermaids could not cry. Their tears were bound into them, so that when they died they became the sea.

Asia stared down at the wetness on her hand. She'd not cried once since taking the potion to become human. Not once. But she stared at the tears now and was as frightened of losing more as she was of joining the water and the collective of the water sprites.

"Maybe I am trying to be everything. I don't know. I just wanted a way to... destroy him, as he did us. But I cannot find my way and he is likely torturing my mother to punish me, and I am as bad as him, because I know it but I cannot go back. I cannot save her with the sacrifice of myself, even though I know I should. He gave away his kingdom, *my* kingdom, to a man as unfeeling as he is." The words began desperate and soft, but the more she spoke the tighter into fists her hands curled and her tone turned as jagged as that woman who judged her. "He handed me to him to be tortured as my mother was to create some other man's legacy. Well...I won't go back. I won't let one more man build his legacy in me and break me into smaller and smaller bits until I am nothing that is mine. I won't let someone turn my children into weapons against me, into ugly memories that I cannot escape. I won't go back. But...I am not ready to be human either. I should be, shouldn't I? If I drink the potion, and speak the spell that keeps me here, I can forget it all. I can forget him. I can forget what I saw— forget the pain. Why don't I do it?"

"Only you can answer that," Delaney said softly. She stretched out a hand and lay it over Asia's. "But we can help you answer your other question."

"Which is that?" Asia asked with a watery laugh.

"How to help your love."

Asia jerked straight and shook her head. "I have no love to help. Just friends. Gavin and—"

The girl at the edge of the pool laughed uproariously, interrupting Asia. "You came to help Owen. You asked after Owen. Your heart calls out to Owen."

"He...is a friend. I asked after Gavin."

"Did you?" Delaney asked with a smirk. "Because we answered about Owen."

Asia swallowed uncomfortably. She'd known, hadn't she? Some part of her had known all along that they were speaking of Owen. She didn't even feel surprised. But she felt worried, because as much as she cared for Owen, Gavin was her friend as well. And if Owen's fate was dire, Gavin's must be so much worse.

Asia breathed out slowly. "What did she do to Gavin?"

Eternal

374 days until Roisin returns

This was the fourth cave today, and the fourteenth total that Rowan had searched. Every time she entered one she felt closer to that pulsing fiery power. But not one of them housed a dragon that she could find. Most weren't even very deep. But a few went on for what felt like miles into the darkness, only for Rowan to come up against solid stone with nary a dragon in sight.

She walked into every cave, with a little less hope than the one before, and with her father's voice growing louder and louder in her mind.

You don't know what you're doing.

You are meant to be led by me, not the other way around.

They think they are following a queen. But you are not one, and may never be.

His words ate at her the further she went without any success. They taunted her. Whispering that he was right and she didn't know what she was doing. Perhaps she was simply spoiled and—

"Thinking too much," Rowan said aloud to shut off her brain. It had been harder to be alone than she expected. Not that she was alone. The presence she felt with her had yet to show itself.

But the longer she went unable to travel in her mind, the harder it was to feel confident in her plan. And time kept passing with Petal stuck in Sorcha's hold and Gavin in terrible danger— if he was alive at all.

She'd wanted to set out and just be successful. She'd wanted to prove her father wrong and be able to shove her greatness in his face all the while saving her friends. She'd been gone nineteen days and all she'd achieved was leaving home and climbing up a mountain.

"Well, that's not entirely true," Rowan said aloud and heard her voice bouncing off the rocky walls around her. This was a deeper cave, she'd been exploring it for a quarter of an hour and it just got deeper and higher and the light from outside of the cave had long since vanished. She led herself through with a torch she'd made from a tree branch and an old stocking.

"There were moments when I felt more connected to my fairy powers," Rowan told herself as she walked. "And I got to see more of my kingdom, and my people. And I realized that I have something to offer them. And that I can be my own comfort, and..." Rowan searched her mind for more to recommend what at the moment felt like a miserable failure of an adventure. "I've been further up this mountain than any human before me, maybe even any fairy."

"Do you always talk to caves?" A deep voice rumbled through the darkness around her.

Rowan spun around, shining her torch in every direction. But she saw no one. Maybe it was just the presence that had been following her in the forest. But she didn't think so. This voice filled the cave.

"Only when they answer back," Rowan said cautiously.

The voice snorted. "You are wrong by the way. Both fairy and humans have been this high on the mountain. Sorry."

Rowan laughed. She didn't care if she wasn't the first being to explore this high, because she had found the dragons. At least she thought so.

"Where are you?" Rowan asked. "What are you?"

"Well, I am no cave. Keep coming, little adventurer, you'll find me."

Little? No one called her little. No one but Eachann.

Rowan thought of him, her grandfather, and she'd been pushing him away. What happened to him when he returned to Turrlough? Sorcha wasn't likely to tolerate his helping Rowan. He might be dead. Gavin might be dead.

Rowan's heart ached, racing ahead of her. She rushed deeper into the cave. She'd found dragons at last. There was no time left to waste. She needed to get to

Petal, and Gavin, and Eachann. She needed to make sure everyone she loved was safe.

Rowan came into a wide open cave and looked around, catching her breath. Here, deep inside a mountain, there was a waterfall and a rushing river, and all around it lush plants were growing. Berry bushes, what looked like squash, crawling across the ground and even a few trees. Trees! Inside a mountain. It was miraculous. And the cavern itself was so tall and wide it could fit hoards of humans. Pockets of misty light covered the cave walls, beckoning Rowan to look closer. Off at two sides there were tall wide tunnels that went even deeper into the mountain. It was incredible.

Rowan's mind began rumbling with thoughts of how many dragons there might be in here, and how she could best use them to her advantage. She knew they could travel great distances, that took humans on horses weeks to cross in only one day. Rowan might be able to reach Fairy Cache before dawn.

"My, but you are small." The voice broke into Rowan's calculations. "In my day, a woman was a huge figure, intimidating all around her. Maybe you take after your fairy ancestors. Tiny figures."

Rowan spun around, searching for the dragon. She couldn't believe her mind had been so caught on the sheer volume of the—

"My word," Rowan whispered as she caught sight of it. And it was surely a dragon. *She* was a dragon. She was massively tall, reaching almost to the top of the cave, she was a good ten times bigger than Rowan. Rowan laughed breathlessly. She *was* small. For the first time in her life Rowan felt what it was to be truly towered over.

Her blood raced with tingling skittishness through her veins and her ears seemed to whistle with a vibrant exhilaration. The dragon was magnificent. Rowan had never seen a thing like her.

"Like what you see?" the dragon asked and she lowered her head near Rowan, with its frilled, well Rowan didn't know what to call it exactly, it was some part of its body behind the ears and across the head. If Rowan didn't know it was part of the animal's body she might call it a crown. It was breathtakingly marvelous. Then Rowan looked into her eyes, her deep green eyes that seemed to roll like hills in

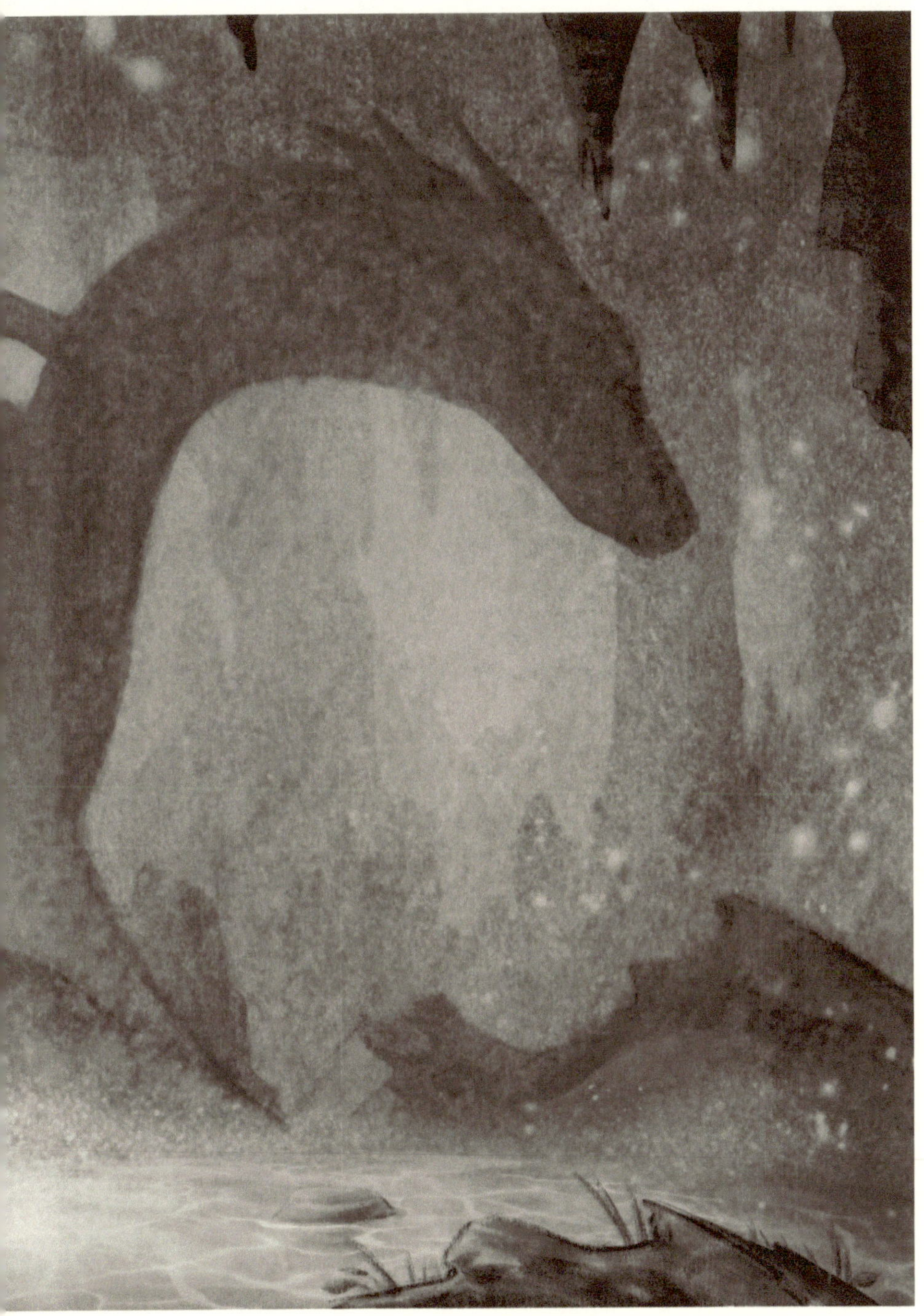

the distance and sway like leaves on a shuddering tree, and Rowan felt the answering call of nature in her heart.

"You are eternal too!" Rowan breathed, awed.

"Certainly we are," the dragon said with an offended tone. "Who do you think taught the first of your fairy ancestors the nature of eternity? Do they teach you nothing?"

"Apparently not." Rowan smiled sideways and shook her head. "Are you Tanith?" Rowan asked, thinking of what Colum had said about who the pendant called.

"Ha!" The dragon shook her head, backing away. "If it's young dragons you're after you have wasted the trip."

Rowan glanced over her shoulder searching the cave as her heart began to grow weighted in her chest. "But...there are other dragons than you here, aren't there?" Rowan asked, her hand dropping to the hilt of her sword and closing around the rose for comfort. "I need help. I need dragons."

The dragon turned away dismissively, lumbering towards the tiny waterfall.

"Fairy or human, it's always the same, not one manner to split between you. Nor very much sense."

Desperate

The closer to home Braden grew the more Keagan's words and Asia's warred within him. He did not want to be a traitor, but he couldn't say that he much wanted to be a mirror either. All he wanted was peace. Another world to vanish into where love conquered all and evil was defeated simply by the existence of goodness.

Braden's mount stiffened, growing skittish, and edging towards the wood to Braden's right. Focusing on the moment at hand, Braden nudged his horse away from the Enchanted Forest it was leaning towards.

They were but a three day's ride from his father's palace now. On his father's lands, on the south road that cut between Anwyn and the Enchanted Forest.

"Your Majesty," Klein, the leader of Braden's guard called out. He pulled his horse up and rode back between the two men ahead of Braden, reining in his mount beside Braden. At once the rest of the soldiers closed ranks around Braden.

Braden stiffened, and glanced around himself in concern. He was not close with his men. He doubted they even respected him. But he was royalty and it was their duty to protect him and he could see their steadfast commitment to do so rising up in their eyes.

"What is it?" Braden asked in an urgent whisper.

"Perhaps nothing, these woods can cause all manner of skittishness. But," the man broke off, staring into the forest at the parties left. Anwyn forest. "I believe, sir, that we are being followed."

"And your suggestion?"

Klein returned his gaze to Braden's face. "My suggestion is that we close ranks around you and gallop as fast as we are able towards the north crossing. We are too pinned in here, an attack could easily be deadly."

"But, would that not alert our stalker that we are aware of him?"

"When we closed ranks they were aware, sir. If my instinct is right there are far more than one man in those trees, and I do not believe mere following is their plan."

"Nor robbery, I take it?"

The captain shook his head. Braden swallowed hard. Who would want him dead? Braden was in total shock, entirely unsure of what to do. He just wanted this all to be over. He nodded to the captain letting him know he would do as the man thought best.

Klein spurred Braden's horse and his own at the same moment, and without order the other men all set out with them as they charged up the road. Braden hunkered low in the saddle, as Klein pushed him lower. Behind them Braden heard a loud splintering crash, and felt the swoosh of charging winds.

He glanced back between the soldiers and saw a pair of trees tumbling across the road, blocking off any escape to the south. A group of men came rushing out of Anwyn forest. Braden's heart stopped for half a second, then he tore his eyes forward and urged the horse on faster as his heart started up again, awakening those impulses he'd thought dead. He felt an itch to leap off his horse and take on his attackers, but that risked everyone. There would be a time to fight, he could feel it in his blood.

They rounded a bend in the road and came upon another blockade of trees so rapidly that the men before Braden lost their seats, thrown forward by the sudden stop.

Braden managed to keep his seat as men poured out of the forest and leapt up over the felled trees, blocking the road.

Braden's thrown soldiers took to their feet and began fighting. Klein had a sword out as did the rest of the soldiers around him. Braden drew his sword and prepared to leap from his horse.

"Stay back," Klein ordered and took a defensive stance in front of Braden.

They were everywhere. Braden counted ten men, but he couldn't be sure there weren't more, they moved so quickly. They weren't soldiers. They made no attempt to fight one to one, or even face to face. They leapt and slipped around

Braden's soldiers, with daggers and bows, and lances, managing to make small attacks against his men but suffering few injuries themselves. None of the attackers made any effort at all to harm Braden, focusing the totality of their attack on his guards.

Braden stayed back, on his horse with his sword drawn, waiting as the captain had insisted. But the more fighting went on, the more certain he was that he should be among the fighters. When the first of his men hit the ground, unconscious or dead, Braden could not stay out of the fray.

He dove into the battle, his blood surging as he and his men fought for their lives. But for every enemy injured, one of Braden's guards fell. He fought as the assassins closed in, these men clearly were not after prisoners.

When Klein fell and Braden was alone with men closing in on every side he heard a loud screech. Braden looked up towards the source and recognized the black and white falcon. One of Sorcha's pets. He felt a surge of hope race through his blood, he was saved, Sorcha would—

"Aaaa!" Braden cried out in shock as a dagger caught him in the gut. Braden dropped his sword, reaching out for the weapon lodged within him.

Braden looked back to his attackers, the man before him braced a hand at Braden's shoulder and gripped the hilt of the dagger.

"No, n—Ugh!"

The man yanked away his weapon. Searing pain tore through Braden. He shoved his hands at his gut to stop the heavy tide of blood pulsing out of him, stumbling backwards, unable to hold himself up as the world grew spotty and vague around him. They would kill him. The struggle was over for him. It was the last thought in Braden's mind before he struck the ground and the world darkened around him.

Asia could feel a number of interesting bits of magic in Stonedragon, but she was reluctant to go. They had a seer. She felt him, every time she delved into the seeing waters she felt him trying to alter their currants, trying to bend them to his will, trying to delve into their unplumbable depths. He was a powerful seer. Mother would want to meet him.

Asia should want to. She came here for seeing magic. But she found herself a bit afraid of what he would show her.

She was better at making her way alone. Alone she was strong and confident, and capable. But around others she was small. Her power pulled out all their needs and fears until she vanished beneath the tide of other beings. Alone was better.

What she needed now was a very specific sort of magic. She needed to get to Ever Spill. The cleansing waters of the Fairy fount could reverse Sorcha's spell on Owen. Perhaps even save Gavin, if he could be located. Asia just needed to steal a bit of magic, so she could get to the waterfall in the center of the Fairy realm undetected.

Fairy magic.

"Our magic will not work for you?" the little water sprite asked, hopping along beside Asia. She hopped from one pool of water to the next, sometimes splashing loudly but maintaining her form, other times allowing herself to be absorbed into the water before reforming in another pool.

Asia felt the child's joy at this ability. She didn't understand why Asia was so afraid of the power. She couldn't. This child had been raised to see herself as a part of the collective body of water sprites. But Asia had never been that connected to anything, even when she was mer. She'd longed then to be so much a part of something else, or someone else that nothing could tear her away. To be so connected with something that separation might kill her.

But that was before.

"They might," Asia shuddered. Considering the prospect of allowing herself to become water. Allowing herself to join the river and flow back to Ever Spill. She could make it in a few hours if that were the magic she stole.

But...what then? The water sprites had been banished from the Fairy Realm, there must be some safeguards against their magic entering the lands. And even if there were not, Asia's fear of this power was making it harder for her to understand. She doubted she could maintain it away from the collective, and she wasn't sure she could so easily build herself back into a physical body as this girl was.

"But I think I need something else."

"There is no fairy power so powerful that no other fairy can sense it," the child pointed out.

"I needn't be undetected at all times. Just enough to get what I want."

"Trying to have everything again?" Orla's sarcastic voice preceded her vaporous form appearing at the edge of a pool before Asia. The mist woman glanced down at the child and a half smile softened her features. "You are not allowed this far from the spring, Myrna, run along."

The girl stuck her tongue out, but obeyed. Spinning around, she leapt from one pool to the next, water splattering across the rocky ground.

Orla watched her go before regarding Asia. "You should go to Stonedragon Palace," the woman suggested in the same gruff tone she said everything else.

"Why don't you think I should help Owen?"

"Who said I don't?" Orla demanded militantly. "You need power enough to sneak into the Fairy Realm. So you need fairy power. Sprite power will be noticed, but you can pick and choose the power you take."

Asia bobbed her head from side to side considering. She was getting better at using other's powers when she was not near them. She was still able to do a bit of the illusion magic she'd stolen from the witch in Reethurn. It was how she'd convinced Prince Gavin she came with treasure. And how she'd tricked Prince Braden into believing he chased a woman in a cart, when she had in fact fled from him on a tired pony.

Just to see if she could Asia bent down and lifted a rock, she rolled it around in her hand and tugged out the bits of her mother's transformation power. She pushed and molded the rock in her hand until its hard form grew soft and malleable, then she opened her palm and revealed a wiggling worm.

"I suppose," Asia agreed and bent to free the worm.

Orla rolled her eyes. "If you can choose, then you can take enough power from the boy to get through the fairy shield."

"The seer?" Asia asked.

Orla shook her head. "No. You need Ferdy's power."

"They are friends of yours? Will you hel—"

"They are not friends," Orla interrupted.

Asia felt brittle all over at the quiet words. Calm, quiet, but so...powerful. Asia glanced down. Her own hands were solid ice, frozen in fists from all Orla restrained. Yet Orla was still vapor. Orla felt very powerfully about these people who were not her friends, otherwise her emotions would not have taken over Asia's form this way.

"I have never met them." Orla breathed slow and calm, carefully watching Asia's hands until the ice fell away and they were flesh again. "But as...water sprites we are all connected. Ferdy has trickster magic, he can be invisible, and weightless."

"But if he is a water sprite, the shield will keep me out?"

"Not with his sister in the Fairy Realm. She will feel his power and let you through. Then you can get what you need." Orla shrugged.

"How can you be certain?"

Orla looked away, in the direction of the palace but it was far too far away to be seen. "There is no magic stronger than the bond between siblings who love one another."

"Nor any force more destructive than that bond once it is severed," Asia countered, thinking of a legend from her home of siblings who broke the world once their love was perverted with jealousy.

"So don't sever it. Just borrow a bit." Orla didn't wait around for Asia to respond, simply evaporated, leaving Asia alone with her thoughts.

Braden woke with his whole body cold and stiff. He blinked but the world around him was murky. It hurt too much even to hold open his eyes so he let them drift shut again.

Braden groaned as he tried to pry open his eyelids a second time. He wanted it to be over. The pain, the fear, the struggle. The worry that he would be the betrayer, or be betrayed. He wanted it all to be over. But he was not ready to die. Some part of him longed for a lovely hum and soft smile, that he had yet to experience. He wanted everything else to be over, but even the parts of him that wanted to hold on didn't think he would ever find that hum.

Braden, you will find your love. You just have to wait. Rowan's voice commanded. Typical. Rowan couldn't even give comfort gently. Braden felt his lips tilting up at the order. Trust Rowan to disturb him as he lay dying.

Thump!

Something slammed against the ground just next to his head, shaking the earth, jarring his wound, and waking Braden thoroughly.

He blinked and opened his eyes to the dirty hoof and dirt spattered white leg of a horse. Braden rolled onto his back, looking up.

"Yseult? Rowan?" Braden croaked. "Rowan!" he shouted again. Slowly dragging himself up. He searched the ground around him.

Klein lay dead just feet from Braden, along with seven soldiers Braden barely knew the names of, and his page Wad. All of them dead. The bodies of their attackers had been moved, and the felled trees were gone, just vanished as though they had never been there. But there was no sign of Rowan.

"Where is she?" Braden asked the horse, dragging himself over until his back was against a tree trunk, he used it to help pull him higher. He felt so weak, and cold, and tired. But he couldn't just lay here. Rowan was in danger.

She was too headstrong. She would take on all of Braden's attackers and get herself killed.

"Rowan!" he shouted at the top of his lungs. But heard not a rustle of leaves in the distance. "Did she chase them off?"

Braden looked again to the horse and noticed something odd. It carried only one pack, and the blanket wrapped around its middle was lopsided and loose. Even the saddle straps looked loose.

"Where is she? Is she hurt? Does she need help?" Braden demanded, not sure why he spoke to the horse. She couldn't answer.

Braced against the tree, Braden slowly peeled his vest off one arm, panting and groaning from the stabbing pain it caused his wound. He lay back against the tree for several long moments, just catching his breath before he could pull it off the other arm. Once it was free he tried to tie it around his waist to stop the wound, but it was too small. With an agonized groan he balled the fabric up and stuffed it into his tunic, pulling his belt up over it as best he could to hold it in place. Groaning and panting and sweating, Braden tried to pull himself up the trunk of the tree.

But Yseult knew better. She knelt before him, so her body was touching his, lightly holding it up until Braden could throw himself crookedly across her saddle.

"Good girl," Braden whispered breathlessly. He looped the bridle around his arm, and closed his other arm around the horse's neck, holding on as tightly as his aching muscles would allow. "Take me to her."

Braden's eyes drifted shut as Yseult shot forward. He didn't see the forest they passed. Did not see the bird take flight in pursuit, trailed by mounted assassins. He just closed his eyes and held on as tightly as he could to the last strands of his life.

Patience

"I apologize," Rowan said, forcing herself to breathe deeply and try to slow down. It was a difficult feat to accomplish. Her heart was racing and her head was pounding; at last she'd made some progress, she wanted to build on it. "I did not mean to offend. But I am here on a matter of great urgency. Every second I waste people come closer to death."

"That is not so urgent," the dragon said as she rumbled slowly towards the waterfall. "For every one of you who dies another three pop up. And they were headed closer to death every moment you were with them as well. Sit down. Take your ease," she said in a gracious manner, sighing in contentment as the water rushed over her back. "Your business here will not be solved in a moment."

Rowan ground her teeth over one another. She turned slightly away from the dragon. She set her torch down in an obliging stone with a hole in the center that seemed to just be waiting for the torch. The cave was far too light to need it anyway. The walls were made up of some crystalline substance that carried a soft blue light all their own, and gave the room a misty, otherworldly quality.

Things were not going Rowan's way. She needed to move, she needed *dragons*. Plural. She needed help. Rowan angled towards one of the tunnels leading off of the large cave, watching the dragon out of the corner of her eye. She wasn't frightened of it. Nothing about the dragon but size felt threatening. Still, that could just be Rowan's natural overconfidence.

"Are you the only dragon here?" Rowan asked.

"Do you see any others?" the dragon replied with hints of amusement in her tone.

Rowan dropped her packs, fisting her hands at her sides. It would be just her luck that she would find only one dragon, and it would be an old cranky dragon who had no caring for the deaths of others.

"I came for help. I need numbers, allies of—"

"Your mind might have told you it was looking for dragons. But your heart knew better or it would not have led here."

"My heart didn't lead here!" Rowan shouted, yanking the pendant off her throat in frustration. "This did. And it led me on a wandering, time wasting path too. Was that your doing?" Rowan demanded, advancing on the dragon.

The dragon seemed to smile, entirely unperturbed by Rowan's anger or her right hand slipping to her sword. "You came for certainties. You came for *power,* and a better understanding of eternity. You came—to be sure you could beat her when you face your grandmother."

Rowan's heart fell like a stone from a cliff, plummeting into an abyss with no end.

She needed to move. Petal needed her to move. Gavin needed her to move. Everyone needed her to move.

There wasn't time for this.

"I thought," Rowan began, but the dragon cut her off.

"There is your problem. You are trying to fight your own nature. You are no thinker. Thinking didn't lead here. A thinker would have taken the whistle into a large field and blown. You are a creature of motion and instinct."

"Would blowing have worked?" Rowan demanded. She could still do that.

"A creature with no understanding of stillness." The dragon laughed. "I doubt blowing would work. You have too much fairy in you. Tanith is not overly fond of your kind, and she is the only dragon it calls."

"Are there only two of you in existence?" Rowan demanded rudely.

The dragon chuckled softly. "No. But it is fair to say there are few of us. Dragons do not reproduce as quickly as the rest of you. An egg gestates for at least thirty years, and sometimes as much as a full century before hatching. And with every generation we have more numerous enemies. Even decimated as we are." The dragon stretched out under the spray, with her neck laying out on the stony floor of the cave. "Know it long enough and eternity will teach you that urgency has always been a product of imagination and fear. Time is time. It doesn't move faster or slower because something is important or frightening. Take your ease a while, little warrior. The world will not end."

"Why did you lead me here, if I might be your enemy?" Rowan asked softly, her tone, her rush, everything ebbing. None of it was gone, but that speech seemed to call for quiet. And the dragon before her was a magnificent creature, that Rowan might want to marvel at were she not in such a rush.

"Ha," the dragon gave a tired sort of laugh. "I was here when the first of your fairy line took power. And later to see the first of your human line. I watched as the two feared one another and kept to themselves, and when they came together with a common fear, and set out to destroy my kind. What could you do to me that has not been done already?"

"But..." Rowan's tone was still quiet, but the tide of her urgency was rising again. And with it her need to have answers. "Did you lead me here to help me? Why would you?"

"I have no fear of death. All things die eventually. Die and become absorbed into the fabric of all that comes after. Thus before and after are ever and eternal. I am dead already, and so are you." The dragon's eyes were drooping shut, but her lips were tilted up, as though she knew Rowan found her meandering speech to be utter nonsense. "The world is full of scholars and fools who disagree with me, but there is only ever one reason that anyone does anything. Hope." With that the dragon shut its eyes completely and fell asleep.

Rowan wouldn't put it past her own luck for the dragon to die in her sleep now that Rowan had found her. She stood staring at her, but the creature continued to breathe loud and gustily. Her breath shaking the bushes near her head. Rowan rubbed the back of her neck, slipping the pendant back over her head.

She walked deeper into the cave, keeping an ear trained to that breathing lest there be any sign of a change. She might as well explore the rest of the cave, it was better than taking the dragon at her word that she was the only one here. Though Rowan felt rather certain it was true.

You came for certainties.

Rowan breathed out, despite her still plummeting heart. It wanted to sprout wings and soar upwards and latch onto the implication of the dragon's words, the implication of leading her here. But Rowan wasn't sure she could believe it, not just yet.

Maybe the dragon knew a way that Rowan could defeat Sorcha. Or maybe she just wanted to play with Rowan a while longer. There was no way to know unless she stayed.

As she wandered down the first tunnel, the lights off the crystals shifted from a warm blue into a pulsing green. The tunnel twisted away deeper into the mountain. And Rowan felt something large and powerful and warm, but...stuck. She moved towards it, hoping it was another dragon, but every step she took was harder than the last. The pulsing green light around her became somehow loud, and heavy, weighing on her, and screeching in her mind. When Rowan could not take more than a step without having to brace herself on the wall she turned around and made her way out into the giant cave.

She braced herself against the blue lit walls and bent forward, trying to catch her breath again. The dragon continued to sleep, the water continued to flow. Nothing but Rowan was any different than it had been a moment ago.

She shook her head. "Time is time," she said aloud. Her hand slipped down and into her cloak to find the burnt rose, but she found the lucky shamrock instead. Rowan closed her fingers around it and felt it pulsing gently against her palm. "I will come for you, I promise," Rowan whispered.

Slowly, as her breath returned to normal, Rowan made her way back to where she'd left her packs and she settled down to watch the dragon sleep. She might have been led here by instinct, or by an old dragon playing tricks, but she owed it to herself and everyone she loved to stay long enough to see if there was anything she could learn.

Scattered Blossoms

373 days until Roisin returns

Elish snuck out of her bed and made her way through the palace. She couldn't become invisible, like fairy could, but she could use the powers of the world around her as Petal had taught them. She needed to gather the other girls. She'd tried twice now, with Shay's help, to fix Queen Aya's son Owen. But with him in the hold of a fairy, and so little magic between them it wasn't working.

Elish was certain the reason the fairy would not let any of the girls together but Shay and Elish was because they knew together they had the magic to fight back. So she needed to get them all.

She'd seen Finnola and her family being forced into the dungeons, during the madness of that first day.

That terrible first day.

Shay still woke screaming from dreams of Prince Gavin shriveling into nothing before them.

She would wake up screaming *Uncle Gavin. Uncle Gavin.* As if he really were their uncle. As if they really were sisters. Every time she would run to Elish and throw her arms around her and sob, and Elish...couldn't help but see it too.

He'd hugged them so tight when they got back. Spun them around and kissed the tops of their heads and said how his family hadn't been complete without them. And he'd been trying to send them from the room when the Fairy queen cursed him. He truly had cared.

Elish shoved the aching, empty feeling in her stomach away and ran through the palace.

She needed to get to Finnola.

Ahead of her, Elish saw one of the fairy who was left to guard the palace, Varro. He began to sense her, turning her way. Elish did the first thing she could think of, she called the wind through the open window casement beside him.

It rushed in with a wild flurry, grabbing at the fairy's clothes and drawing his attention. As he was distracted Elish snuck down another hall. She was going the wrong way now, but it couldn't be helped. She had to hurry. Prince Ian would be here any day.

Elish's adoptive father was bound to take them away. Back to Heigh where they pretended to be safe. No one was safe anywhere until the Fairy queen was dead. Petal was still trapped with that woman. They had to help her.

They weren't little girls to just be taken from one place to another. All of the kidnapped girls were special now. They had no family but each other. Elish couldn't let anything happen to Petal.

She ducked into an alcove to hide and think. She needed to get to the dungeon. But there was no way to know how many fairy stood between her and her goal. Right before her was another open window. It was a small diamond on the wall, just big enough for her to fit through.

Elish's heart caught at the idea forming in her head. All of the girls knew how to levitate. But levitating wasn't the same as using magic to slow her as she sunk to the ground from four levels above. She could die if she did it wrong.

You need to learn fast and well, not safely.

Elish heard Petal's voice in her head and didn't hesitate to obey. She raced towards the window and pulled herself through. She heard feet behind her and threw herself forward. Her stomach dropped and she had just enough time to fill her lungs with air and blow it like a bubble around herself before she plummeted too far. She was about two stories down now, and hovering there. Now she just needed to get herself to the ground.

She couldn't think of a way to do it but to pull the air back into her lungs slowly. Shrinking the bubble. So that's what she tried.

It was working! She nearly laughed. Look at her, teaching herself magic. She was—

"Elish!" Shay's scream reverberated around the palace. Stopping Elish's heart, and stealing her focus. The bubble popped.

All she could think as she fell was that her sister needed her, and she was going to let her down. She hit the ground, and the world went black.

Petal sat with the crystal cradled in her hands as Sorcha taught her the desired spell, though she could not think why.

"Alright, my love, take a deep breath in and stretch your mind into the world. Don't ever let it leave you completely, think of it like pulling back the string of a bow. Not so taut that it will snap, nor so lax that it flaps about. Aim your mind for the bird in front of you and stretch yourself into its mind, take it over, bit by bit."

Petal cleared her mind, and let it float in a focused, obedient place. She didn't think of the plan, or her own reasons for wanting to know the spell of transformation. She just let her mind listen to Sorcha and do as she commanded.

There was a lark on the ground in front of her. It had a lovely voice, it sang out to other birds around it, calling for help, trapped as it was in a snare of the Fairy queen's making, so that Petal might learn this new spell. It had such a lovely voice. Like Finnola. Petal only hoped she'd gotten her song out. When Petal told Sorcha it was Gavin who conspired with her, Sorcha had done something to Finnola's voice, it sounded garbled, and choked, and would make no words. But surely it was just an effect of the moment. Surely Finnola would get Rowan the message, and Rowan would know what to do.

Petal shook out the thought and felt the jittery worry of it pulled off of her like a thin shawl caught in the wind. Only the worry wasn't caught by the wind, it was caught by the crystal, and the prince inside. Petal looked down, expecting to see him as a boy again, but today she saw a pulsing flame of power. A growing pulse of power. Did his magic grow every time he soothed her?

"My love," Sorcha's patient voice fell on Petal's ear as she crouched just behind her. "You must learn to focus." She laughed. "Just breathe."

Petal let her mind obey. She looked away from the crystal, and pulled in a deep breath. She focused on the lark before her, and let her mind stretch towards it.

"That's it. Now, do not be afraid to command him, he is yours. Every bird, every blade of grass, every fairy, are part of the Fairy queen's dominion. Their wills belong to you."

"But..." Petal startled and glanced over her shoulder at Sorcha. "*You* are the Fairy queen."

"For the time being, yes. But eternity knows all times. And if you are ever to be Fairy queen, then you are always to be Fairy queen, even in the time before you have taken on that role. It is why fairy respect the right of the challenger. Understand?"

Petal shook her head vigorously, her heart pounding. She was Fairy queen already? Would be Fairy queen one day? That made no sense. It was wrong.

Rowan was going to be Fairy queen. Petal was her spy, her emissary to the Fairy nation. Was Petal going to betray her? Was that why Sorcha loved her? Because Sorcha knew what was to come?

"Do not worry, my love. You needn't understand yet, nor even believe. Eternity will show you in its time. For now all you need to do is learn to control your subordinates. That bird belongs to you, it will do your bidding, it will carry your messages, be your eyes, become any beast you desire for it to be. If you can control it, even I will not have dominion over it any longer."

It was said so casually, Sorcha just walked away as if she had not just offered Petal a way to pass messages to Rowan, or her brothers, or anyone else colluding against Sorcha. Did she truly trust Petal so well? Or did she just think herself so powerful it would not matter?

Petal stopped trying to empty her mind and let all the worries and hopes and plans flood back in. If she could learn the spell she could turn the wolves human again. And fix Prince Owen, and any other human Sorcha had cursed when she was in Turrlough. If Petal could control the bird, she need not worry about Finnola finding her voice, Petal could use the bird to send her messages. She could use it to steal away with the crystal in her hand. Every day she felt more certain that she and this crystal should be far far away from one another. She knew how to free him. And he knew she knew. She felt him wanting out, she felt it in her heart. Every time she heard the wolves howl, or thought of poor Prince Gavin, just torn apart in a flash of light, ripped from the world as though he'd never been a part of it...whenever her mind drifted there, Petal thought of Prince Desmond wanting out. And worried that the longer she delayed, the shorter his life would be.

But she couldn't free him with Sorcha near. He was...full of power, and pain. His mother could easily turn that to her side. And Petal already felt drawn to helping him, as Sorcha wanted. How much more would she want if he were standing before her, asking her help? No. She could not free him here. But if she could get him away. Get him to Rowan, then she could free him, and maybe he would be on their side.

Petal knew Sorcha wanted to make Petal her heir, but knowing it was her desire, and knowing it was eternity's plan were two different things. Still...if she could transform the bird, what couldn't she do?

Petal let herself into the bird's mind, making sure to hold tight to herself as she poked around inside it, saw its family, its life, its soul. Petal felt it go from one more bird, to someone she knew and understood—

"Excellent," Sorcha's quiet voice quivered with delight. "Now, name him! Sew his name into his mind so you and you alone can call out to him."

Petal thought her mind was too full of the animal to come up with a name, but from nowhere she felt it, Nolan. It suited him, quiet, distinguished, strong. He was not a young bird, he'd had quite the life already. Petal felt Nolan warm with pride at the name she had given him.

"Marvelous! He is yours now." Sorcha's voice quivered with delight.

Petal opened her eyes, and blinked against the light, wondering what she'd turned the bird into, she hadn't been thinking of anything. But when she saw Nolan he was still a bird. She glanced back at Sorcha.

"I thought you were teaching me to transform him?" she asked, perplexed. Were they done already?

Sorcha leaned against a flowering bush behind Petal. The bush fluffed out around Sorcha like a settee, and the white gown Sorcha had been wearing grew a pattern of leaves and flowers like the bush until it appeared as though Sorcha had grown out of it like a larger than normal flower.

Sorcha waited until the transformation was complete, and grinned crookedly at Petal. "Stop shying away from your magic, Petal the Powerful. You knew how the ocean grows, without ever being taught. You knew how to command the ivy in your old room. Tell me, now that he is yours, how do you transform that bird into any creature your heart can conjure?"

Petal looked away from Sorcha to Nolan, then her eyes stole to the crystal in her hands. She remembered the stone Kermit had shown her just after she first came to the Fairy nation, asking her what he hid inside. She felt again that question he patted into her skin. Was she to be queen of the Fairy? Would she save them all? Did she have that power—and know it?

Petal's eyes lifted from the crystal to the bird before her. She was Petal the Powerful. All she need do was know what she wanted, and ask it of the bird, and it would do her bidding.

Sorcha was toying with her. Petal was certain of it now. She'd told Petal just the right thing to make her eager to perform the spell. Offered her power she had no intention of letting her have. But if Sorcha was truly right about eternity and Petal's place in it...well, she wouldn't be so casual if she knew all the power Petal had inside.

Petal smirked at Nolan. *Want to terrify the Fairy queen for me?* She asked the animal with her mind, and a bright pink flash of light filled the clearing. All she could see was the light, making Petal think of when Prince Gavin had been consumed in the purple light of Sorcha's magic. But she only had a moment for the light to remind her before sharp claws ripped through it. A giant wolf leapt over Petal's head, directly for Sorcha.

Petal felt a laugh bubbling in her throat, and let the crystal housing Prince Desmond fall to the ground so she could clap. But, so fast her mind barely comprehended it, a shadow slid between Sorcha, relaxed against the bush, and Nolan leaping forward to show off Petal's handy work, and slit the wolf's throat.

"Nooooooo!" Petal cried out in agony, too shocked even to move, as Nolan fell to the ground, bleeding out his life force. A tiny puff of pink light surrounded him, fading away almost as quickly as it had come, and when it cleared he was a tiny bird again, lying in a pool of blood bigger than his body.

"Dervla." Sorcha's voice pretended aggravation. "Why would you do such a thing?"

"My apologies, Your Majesty," Dervla said, her voice, her face, her every bit of self devoid of any emotion. "It was attacking."

Petal barely heard. She'd crawled to the bird's side, and sobbed running a finger along its wing. He was dead already. Dead. Petal tried only to use him for a little trick and he was cut down. She sobbed harder.

"Leave us, and send me a more observant guard," Sorcha ordered. She walked forward and settled herself on the ground beside Petal, pulling her into her arms. "There, there, my love, don't cry. He was happy to have served you, for however short a time. You must learn not to let these things eat at you so. You will touch so many lives, and very few of them will stretch on as long as yours. Have heart."

Petal felt Sorcha's lips against her hair, felt her magic rushing around inside her. Sorcha didn't know how to soothe like Mama did. When Mama's magic rushed through a being one felt safe and happy and loved. When Sorcha's magic rushed through Petal she only felt...itchy. Powerful and anxious to show it.

This was what power like Sorcha's brought. Petal made a new friend only to have Dervla kill it moments later. *Dervla!* Who Petal had begun to think of as a friend, despite the events in Turrlough.

Betrayed and disgusted Petal sobbed harder, and clung onto Sorcha with all her might. She couldn't save someone like Dervla. She couldn't save anyone.

Elish was pulled from her rest by the burning warmth of a fire. She ached everywhere, but she felt herself startle awake with the need to get to Shay. Shay had been calling out to her, then...she fell. Elish opened her eyelids just a slit and looked around. She was laid out on the table that had been dragged next to the fire in the great hall, and there was a mishmash of humans and fairy around her. Shay was sobbing in the corner so at least she was safe.

Pretending to be asleep still, Elish closed her eyes and tried to listen to what the adults were saying. But she could barely make it out. But words were just breath, and breath was just air, so...Elish focused on the air around them, and called it to her as gently and subtly as she could.

"Her back was badly damaged from the fall. It is a wonder she survived at all," a fairy was saying.

"Fairy can fix such injuries! I know you have fairy among you who can heal her." Elish thought that was queen Aya's voice, but it sounded so different, begging. Elish had never heard her beg, even when she spoke to the Fairy queen.

"We are to guard against such foolish impulses as turning on the Fairy queen. It is not our mandate here to heal humans who leap out of windows."

"She is distraught. She must have slipped," Queen Aya said, her voice horse with tears.

"The window was no less than five feet above the ground, Your Majesty, she did not slip."

Queen Aya let out a sob. "Please. Please. You have one of my sons, my husband is cursed to sleep. Gavin is *destroyed*. Please. Save my granddaughter. Sorcha promised those girls they would be safe here."

"From her—"

"Please! She is only a child. How can you be so cruel? I cannot lose her. What must I do? What must I promise?" Elish felt the loving desperation in Queen Aya's voice coating itself through her blood. She hadn't realized the queen cared that much. She hadn't truly been sure she cared at all.

"She is a child, but I do not think *only* applies to her. Be at ease, Your Majesty," Varro said snidely. "You needn't beg. We are not the monsters you would have us. Not only has she been healed already, she is also awake, and using the same sort of magic she saved herself with to spy."

Elish's eyes popped open and she stared right into the sharp eyes of Varro, the fairy left to guard Prince Owen. How did he know she was using magic? None of the fairy had known when they had done magic while kidnapped. He raised a brow at her.

Perhaps they had known. Known and...not cared.

"You should care more for your own life, child. Or if not that, for the worry you will cause those who do care." So saying, he vanished from the room and with him the two other fairy departed. Leaving Elish with Queen Aya, Shay and a few of the palace guards.

Queen Aya and Shay rushed over, both with tear soaked faces to close their arms around Elish.

"Do not ever scare me so again. I thought we'd lost you," Queen Aya sobbed.

Shay was blubbering so much it was impossible to tell what she was saying at all, but her arms clung so tight it began to hurt.

Elish wanted to sit up, and comfort them, or tell them to get off of her, or anything but what she did. She gasped for breath and an unstoppable torrent of tears exploded from her. Her arms lifted to hold onto her family.

Love Eternal

The dragon had been sleeping for hours. Rowan had made an inventory of her packs. And rinsed all of her clothes but the ones on her back in the rivet of water that ran off from the falls. It wouldn't clean them completely, but anything was better than as dirty as they had been in her weeks of travel. She wanted to bathe herself as well, but none of the clothes were dry yet and she would not put back on the same dirty dress that she hadn't even bothered to take off in the last three days. It was a terrible thought, but true all the same that she was looking forward to being clean almost more than she looked forward to saving her friends. The water in the rivulet was surprisingly warm, but that made sense of why the dragon liked it.

She made notes on her stolen map about how far she had traveled, and when the air became thin. Now that the initial excitement of meeting a dragon and thinking herself closer to saving her family had worn off, Rowan was disappointed not to have been the first human to reach this high on the mountain. It had felt so empowering. She never knew how badly she needed things to feel empowering, before this adventure.

Every once in a while, Rowan's eyes would wander off towards the tunnel of green light. Something was down there, and she wanted to know what. But she wasn't ready to try looking just yet. The other tunnel seemed to hold the same light as this cave. As the hours passed and Rowan was doing nothing but wait for the dragon to wake or her clothes to dry, doing nothing but munching on a few berries from an obliging bush, or wondering when the torch had gone out, she certainly hadn't noticed it, but it felt cool to the touch when she lay a hand against it. As hours passed with Rowan doing nothing but trying to stop herself thinking of everyone she was failing she stared more and more into the tunnel of green light. There was something there for her.

Rowan took advantage of the open space and went through her sword exercises. Twice. She would have done it a third time, but while she looped around the open space the bells at her ankle taunted her. "Save us. Save us. Save us."

"Alright, enough." Rowan didn't know why her mind seemed only to respond to commands spoken aloud, but it did. Perhaps she was too much the soldier. Or perhaps the fears just needed to be acknowledged.

They were headed closer to death every moment you were with them as well.

Rowan supposed technically that was true. But it was *different.* When she was with them they were together. When she was with them, if death came she was beside them to fight it off, or die alongside them. So much of her life she'd been away from Roisin as both of them grew closer to death. She'd worked to prevent it all the while knowing that even if she saved Roisin it didn't mean she would be there to see it.

Now Rowan was away from everyone she loved. And everyone she loved was in danger. It was so different. She didn't want any of them to move closer to death. She wanted them to stay, suspended in time until she returned to them.

But it wasn't to be. If she just picked up and left now as the dragon slept she would truly have wasted the journey. She had to trust that there was some reason she was here. She had to trust that some part of her had led here. And that it knew well that there was something here for Rowan to learn. She just wished she could be with her family still, or that she could let them know she had not abandoned them, or their cause. She just couldn't be beside them for a time.

Rowan pulled the burnt rose from the strap of her girdle and ran her fingers along the tips of its petals. She lifted it to her face and breathed in the scent. Its scent should have faded long ago, surely. But her magic had preserved it. She could almost see her mother's face in the scent. But she could clearly see the faces of those she loved who were yet living.

Rowan touched a finger to each of the thorns in turn. They had torn holes in her flesh as a child. Formed scars that defined Rowan as much as knighthood or sisterhood ever had. She was a scarred thing, a creature built of pains survived. Or she had been.

Rowan pulled forward the dragon pendant, it had melted away her scars. It had lifted them from her skin as though they had never existed.

But they had existed. Even now, Rowan could lay the rose against the exact spot where her scars had been because she felt them internally.

Thus before and after are ever and eternal.

To her mind the words were nonsense. But Rowan felt a stirring across her skin as power built in her, as instinct built.

"Don't think, Rowan," she instructed herself aloud. Rowan dropped the dragon pendant back to hang against her throat and walked to her now neatly ordered packs. She took the flute Gavin had sent her from its pocket. With the flute and rose Rowan sat back down. She brushed the rose with her lips before laying it on the stone. Rowan lifted the flute.

Rowan blew a long soft note into the instrument, then slowly shifted her fingers across the holes to create a tune. The rose lifted off the stone and began to spin around. It spun and spun like it was caught in a tiny local storm. It spun so fast its petals were ripped from the safe nest of their home on the flower and spun around it in lovely stretching loops like ripples on a lake.

It was a pink rose, though its color had faded some over the years. But as it rippled out, each loop of rose petals took on a different hue. There was a loop of sunrise colored petals, and a loop of yellow, and of white, and of pink with burnt edges. There was a single petal of deep red.

The loops spread faster and faster until all at once they vanished from the cave in little flashes of blue. The whole rose was gone.

Rowan lowered the flute slowly, too excited to notice the single yellow petal that appeared in a tiny flame across the cave—before vanishing into nothing. Caught up in the wonder, Rowan slipped her fingers into the pouch that had carried the loose petals that Petal had returned when she stole Gavin's letters. But those were gone as well.

Rowan smiled softly at the empty space where her most precious possession had been a moment ago. It was gone. She could not see it or hold it in her hand

and be comforted by the scent and the familiarity. But her heart pounded with a glowing warmth because she knew where it was. Just like her heart, the rose's home wasn't with Rowan, but with the ones she loved.

An Army of Roses

373 days until Roisin returns

etal lay curled up in a blooming bower in her new room in the palace. It was the only room that had called to her, save for the room that led home. She knew exactly where that room was, no matter where she was in the palace, or simply wandering the fairy lands, some part of Petal's mind was always watching the room that led home, waiting for her brothers to walk through it. She always knew how many steps it would take her to reach it, always longed to cross its threshold and run home. But she couldn't. She wasn't sure she belonged there any longer. She'd done too much bad.

So she chose a room that felt...safe. A room that opened into the Whispering Wood. All around, the trees held conversations. Whispering to one another, likely whispering to Sorcha. But even that was comfortable, there was nothing to worry about. Sorcha knew all. And anyway, ever since Petal stole Prince Gavin's letters and watched him be ripped apart by Sorcha's magic no one had visited Petal. No more petals were with her, none but the talisman at her throat.

She had no secrets any longer. Sorcha knew Petal still wasn't entirely hers. Knew Petal wanted to escape. Knew Petal was too weak to defeat her. She knew everything. And Petal was all alone. Every day more so, as Sorcha perverted or destroyed one cautious friendship after another.

Petal lay, curled up in a ball with both her hands wrapped around the talisman and her body draped in the fragrant blossoms that had grown down over her nest and listened to the wood whisper. Two of the trees were arguing over who was the eldest. One tree was singing to the moon. And the tree Petal lay in was chattering on about how many less stars there were from when she was

younger, and how she was convinced the stars died only when destiny had been changed, and she didn't like the sound of that. She was talking to Petal. And Petal listened, but she didn't care.

Her heart ached. Her power was scrunching tighter and tighter into her being, trying to be as small as it possibly could so that she could never be used to hurt or kill again. She wished she were an ordinary girl.

A low, crooning howl wove its way between the trees, some of the branches pushing the sound along because they loved the way its resonance rustled their leaves. Usually Petal would poke up her head and look for the wolf who was singing to her. But just now she lay on her back and ignored it. He howled again and again, and with every howl Petal felt something in her chest tightening, and fighting to break apart. She saw Nolan, the bird she'd transformed to a wolf, with his blood soaking into the ground and her heart burned.

Petal released the talisman and lifted her hands to cover her ears. The whisperers took heed of her anguish and shoved the howl back with such force they shook loose leaves and created a tiny tunnel of wind.

Petal shivered from the dance of the flowers that covered her, but no actual chill. And the howl slipped away. A new song invaded the wood, smooth and wandering, and full of power. Petal had never heard a thing like it. Her hands dropped from her ears, and she poked up her head, expecting to find a fairy sitting upon a near tree branch playing some instrument. But she saw nothing. Then from nowhere and everywhere at once a blue light swirled through the wood, as if it danced to the sourceless tune, and the scent of roses rolled over Petal.

Petal felt a sob break from her throat before she even understood what was happening. Then she saw them, swirling before her in a band of blue light, every petal she'd returned to Rowan took shape. But that wasn't all, more and more petals fluttered out of the light, swirling together and growing nearer. When the last petal slid out of the light, and joined its brothers and sisters, Rowan's most treasured rose with the burnt tips floated before Petal, sinking nearer and nearer to her chest until it had sunk into the talisman at her throat.

Petal gasped.

"Could I have just one petal from the burnt rose?" Petal asked.

"Petal, you may have the entire rose," Rowan offered with a wide charmed smile.

Reverently Petal's hand lifted to the talisman. And felt the power of Rowan's love sink through her like warmth on a chilly day. She felt it curling up around Petal's power, neither encouraging it to come out, nor trying to hide it, just laying there soothing, and loving. Tears ran down Petal's cheeks, as her heart beat, pumping that soothing feeling throughout her being. She was loved still.

Rowan's rose had shrunken some, to fit inside the talisman, but even so it did not fit entirely, some of its petals peeked out, hard and shiny as though they had grown out of the bubble taking its protective magic with them.

Petal let her tears fall over the rose, and with every tear its color seemed to grow more vibrant.

She was loved. Here was the proof.

Slowly the music retreated from the wood, and the scent of roses departed, and Petal's tears one after the next dried up, her fears fading away with them. She was loved. She was not forgotten. And Rowan, who had always been frightened of this place, and of her own magic, had stretched out her magic across the world to remind Petal of her love.

Petal drifted to sleep with her hands shut around the last rose from the burning of the garden and felt what she had been seeking so desperately from Sorcha, and magic, and everywhere but where it lived, she felt hope. And that could only come from home.

372 days until Roisin returns

Sorcha walked down the halls of her palace trailed by three fairy with a smile on her face and a slowly spreading feeling of calm. Admittedly, she had been quite miffed when she realized the Knight of the Rose had left her home, but Sorcha knew how to turn any situation to her advantage and this would be no different. She would still torture that girl for as long as she was alive, every second would be made a misery of doubt and betrayal. Every joy would be crushed under heartbreak a thousand times stronger.

Sorcha knocked at the door to the Whispering Wood. She quite liked that Petal had chosen it to be her room in the palace. It meant she was becoming more fairy. There was nothing human about this room, but there were many rooms in the palace that held human accents and Petal was slowly coming to reject all of that.

"Tallula," Sorcha said over her shoulder as she waited for Petal to hear the knock. The wood was quite large and Petal could easily be far from the door but the trees would carry the sound to her.

"Yes, Your Majesty."

"What are the children of Sigh Hill studying today?"

"They are learning to grow their heart homes."

"Indeed, how perfectly lovely. I think Petal would enjoy participating don't you?"

"Of cou—" Tallula cut herself off as the door to the Whispering Wood opened.

Petal looked up with a serene smile. "Good morning, Your Majesty."

"Good morning, Petal," Sorcha replied with a laugh. "Will I never convince you to call me Sorcha without specific instruction, my dear?"

"Surely not," Petal said with a coy smile. "It wouldn't be right. You are my queen." Petal tilted her head to the side and curtsied like the young women of the Fairy Court did, twirling around to create a breeze of flowers and leaves before sinking nearly to the ground with one leg stretched out behind her.

Sorcha was beaming with pride, but as Petal sunk towards the ground her talisman bounced against her collarbone and Sorcha's heart stopped. It had changed.

"Mama, don't you just love flowers?" Sinead's voice swirled through Sorcha's mind like the leaves and flower petals still aloft from Petal's curtsey.

"Of course, dear," she had answered absentmindedly, distracted as always with her quest to save her son.

"They can bloom even after they're dead; one petal calls out to another and another until they pull together and make an entirely new flower. An entirely new creation of power and love."

Sorcha had glanced back then, a bit disturbed with the worry that Sinead was too much like her aunt Nessa, too touched by nature to entirely grasp reality.

"What makes you say that, dear?" Sorcha asked gently.

Sinead looked straight into her mother then, a deep look, full of sorrow and power and strength. "I dreamt it. I dreamt that my power was blessed to a child through a single rose petal, but her love, and my love grew it into an entire battalion of roses that stood together to protect all who loved them."

A shiver had raced down Sorcha's spine. It wasn't fear, at least not of her daughter. But she was frightened for her. Sinead was very like Nessa. A queen needed more of toughness than of gentility.

"Well, my dear, that was a lovely dream. If you mean to make it true I suggest you go to your tutors and learn the art of speaking to roses. A queen needs to know all she can of all the fairy arts."

"Yes, mother." Sinead had bowed and left the room, and Sorcha had all but forgotten the moment until she'd first met Petal and seen that infernal necklace.

But now the memory attacked Sorcha and the chill ran down her spine once more. A different chill from the first.

Sorcha nearly cried at the mixture of pride and fear galloping through her blood. Had Sinead been stronger than Sorcha knew? She must have been, because the bubble that once held only a single petal had grown, grown right out of the walls of its bubble, a blossoming rose growing towards freedom.

Threatening Sorcha and everything she was working to do.

By the falls, she wished the child before her were truly Sinead, and not just her power passed on in a new being. She would reach out and hold her, spin her around and tell her how proud she was to at last see her power and her *will* growing strong enough to rival her mother's.

But she wasn't Sinead. And as proud as Sorcha was of her daughter's power beyond the grave, she wasn't pleased by the sight. It meant Petal wasn't as much Sorcha's as she'd thought. It meant Sinead was trying to rival her mother's power in favor of that aberration that caused her death. It meant that as with every other moment in her life, Sorcha was alone, fighting against those she loved.

Sorcha ground her teeth. She could see a slightly smug look in Petal's eyes. Petal knew what had stopped Sorcha's tongue. She knew what had angered her. Petal was indeed becoming more fairy, but as with every other one of Sorcha's children, she was fighting her mother every step of the way.

"Very proper of you, dear," Sorcha said coldly. "Now your queen has a task for you. Follow Tallula to Sigh Hill, you will take your lessons there with the noble children of the area."

"Children?" Petal asked with shock. "I have never seen any."

"When you were with the humans the children were kept away. Humans carry *disease* that our children are not prepared for. But you are no longer infectious." Sorcha watched the words sink into Petal, watched her eyes narrow with the first insult and widen with the last. But she merely bowed her head low, still in a curtsey.

"Run along." Sorcha flicked out a wrist, and Petal rose to do as she was instructed. Sorcha gripped her scepter tightly as the girl passed. Her rage ran up its staff in a crackling purple bolt of power. The light of it bounced across the surface of the crystal before sinking inside and setting off a dancing light show around her sleeping son. She watched to see if her rage might wake him though her love never had, but alas he slept on.

"All of my children will learn to mind me," she whispered towards Desmond. "I will set this chaos that *your disobedience* wrought to rights. Then you will see. You will see."

Yseult raced through the forest with Braden slipping around on her back, and trees darting into her path every few seconds. She'd only stopped running for a few hours in the night. Somewhere back there she'd lost the riders who followed them. But it wasn't Yseult's doing. The trees were on her side. They occasionally slowed her way, but they did much worse with the ones following her. Attacks, barricades, earth shaking dances of trees all managed to lose their pursuers. But Yseult pressed on. That hum was calling out to her. The hum Rowan had woken within her. The closer she grew to it the louder it sounded in Yseult's head, and the harder she pressed. She was almost there.

Braden hadn't stirred in a while. And blood had begun oozing from his side again. He was fading fast, so Yseult daren't stop. A swirling wind shook up the trees and the rich scent of roses filled the air. All around the lovely tune of Rowan's flute awoke the forest, until little white rose petals drifted off the sound to land on Yseult's back and Braden's hand.

The contact with the flower petal, like Rowan's kiss upon her shoulder, acted like a healing balm and an invigorating charge of power. Yseult pressed on faster than before. She was still tired, but now she knew she could and would make it to her destination. Rowan was not with her, but her magic still wrapped itself around the horse, defending her.

Even Braden groaned with more life than he had in a day, and the steady ooze of blood from his side slowed, as one after another rose petals coated the wound, sealing it up. They would make it.

Darling Girl lay a cup of steaming tea at Aunt A's hand. "Here you are Aunt A. It's awfully stormy outside don't you think?" Darling Girl leaned her face before her aunt she paused and reached out.

Aunt C caught Darlings hand. "That isn't a storm Darling Girl, it is your aunt."

Darling looked at Aunt A, seated at the table staring into the distance. Unmoved though there was food before her, and Darling had spoken to her. Aunt A was never still. Darling shivered. There was a wild wind beating at the windows and shaking even the ground. How could that be her aunt?

"What is wrong with her?" Darling demanded, the shiver eating up her insides.

Aunt C nudged Darling into a chair across from A and set a cup of tea before her. "Drink up. Nothing is wrong. A is simply a bit too busy in the mind to pay attention to all places at once."

"She is traveling in her mind?" Darling asked. "But usually she can speak to me still when she does that."

"Usually she is not also encouraging all of the forest to dance around and lose invaders at the same time," C said with a small chuckle and kissed Darling on the head.

"Does it hurt her?" Darling asked. She brought the cup up to her lips for a sip and at once the warmth sang through her, nudging the chill away.

"Darling Girl, to protect you gives A great pride, and eternal happiness. You are our joy."

"And anyway," B said a bit gruffly from the archway into the living room. "She greatly enjoys forcing things much bigger than herself to do her bidding."

They all chuckled.

Though the windows were closed a soft breeze of song filled the room, and the scent of roses enveloped them.

Aunt A blinked, and hers was the first hand to snatch a bright yellow rose petal from the air. She stared into her hand with a smile, as her sisters, and Darling Girl each caught a petal of their own.

"Ahhhh, at last! She is embracing what is hopeful in her power." Aunt A winked at Darling Girl and reached out for the raspberry muffin at her hand. She pulled off a little bite. "It's windy out! Who wants to go dance in the storm?"

Darling giggled, pulling the petal deep into her palm like a kiss.

Tempters

Rowan was taking poorly to stillness. She had to curl her fingers into her palms until her growing nails bit into her skin, to keep from reaching up to play with the dragon pendant. Her toes were curled tight in her boots to stop her crawling across the ground to reorganize her packs, or leap up and run through her exercises again. And that second tunnel was taunting her with all the things that it might hold. But she persevered. She was not going to move.

This couldn't possibly be harder than learning balance as a child. A shudder ran down Rowan's spine at the thought and she heard a man's voice coming from in the first tunnel.

"Stop trying to balance the staff," the voice said in a light, instructive tone.

Rowan wanted to look, but she refused to move. The words and the voice felt familiar, but she couldn't place why. It was probably another test, like leading Rowan all over her father's kingdom had been. The dragon wanted something from Rowan, and right now it seemed to be stillness. She could hold still.

She could. Rowan clenched her teeth.

"I'm helping you do it faster. It's you that needs to be balanced, lady knight."

"Bran," Rowan whispered as the voice fell into place in her mind. The knight trainee she had made friends with as a child.

She pushed up on her hands and peered over her shoulder towards the tunnel.

There didn't appear to be anyone there. But maybe he was in the depths she hadn't reached earlier. What if he was alive? What if he had never been killed in the Fairy Realm? Maybe he ran away from the fighting. Or maybe he was wounded and the dragon led him here to be healed. Or...

Rowan was on her knees now, with one hand at the knife stuffed in her boot, preparing to stand. Preparing to stand with a weapon.

You are no thinker. You are a creature of motion and instinct.

Rowan looked from the tunnel to her hand poised around the hilt of her knife. Her mind was offering all sorts of lovely, hopeful comforts. As her mind never used to offer. But even when her mind was hopeful, her instinct was untrusting. Her instinct was to fight. To move.

Rowan let her hand slip from the knife and slowly sunk back to the ground. She breathed out as she turned back to face the dragon sleeping under the water's spray.

"Now, Princess Page, I shall go defeat the evil Fairy queen, but do not let that end your training. I expect to find the kingdom's first lady knight when I return. They think we do not belong, you and I. But we know better. We are knights: loyal, brave, strong and honest, we march out to represent our nation."

Rowan shut her eyes. Bran. She hadn't thought of him in so long. The first friend she'd lost in this war. The first man to break her heart. Rowan had wanted so badly to live up to the faith he'd had in her. When he first left, when Rowan truly believed he would be successful and come home her hero, she'd trained harder and harder every day. She'd been all of twelve, and probably slightly in love with him. But more than that, she had just eaten up his belief in her, his similarity. They were both outsiders among the knights. A peasant and a princess were equally far from what a knight was supposed to be.

She hadn't thought of him in years. Not since she'd formed her company. But just the thought had her being flooded with old feelings. Old sorrows from losing him. Old desires to live up to his belief.

Rowan wanted to hop off the ground and run into that tunnel. She wanted to see him. To know he was alive and well. But she folded her hands in her lap and stared straight ahead with a heavy heart.

It wasn't him. Bran was dead. He had been dead for years. So many years more than she had known him. It felt so wrong that he was trapped forever in the moments they'd shared, while she went on.

Rowan's breath came in shorter and shorter bursts, she could not seem to pull it all the way into her lungs. And suddenly tears poured out onto her cheeks, shaking her body.

She didn't want to lose anyone else.

Rowan sat so for a long while. Her tears dried and the cave fell silent but for the rush of the water and the dragon's steady breaths. Hours passed and Rowan sat still. Every muscle in her body ached from the inactivity. Ached from the fear that in sitting still she was allowing others to be harmed. Her mind hummed with her grandmother's words. She felt like an aching ball of poison but she sat still. There was a lesson here and she was going to learn it.

The dragon had been asleep, forever. Or more likely a few hours. but it certainly felt like forever. Rowan decided to take a short nap herself. She shifted on the ground, unstrapped her sword belt and took the knife from her boot to hold in her hand, lest there actually be someone here other than her and the dragon. Rowan began to stretch out on the ground, and as she really should have seen coming, the dragon began to rouse.

Rowan let her head drop against the hard stone ground of the cave and groaned.

"What time is it?" the dragon inquired, stretching her long neck out as far as it would go.

"How would I know?" Rowan demanded. "Night. I arrived in the day and you've been sleeping for hours. But it's not as though I can tell in here. I could barely tell the hour as I traveled, and then I had the sun for a guide."

"My, you are cranky in the evening." The dragon stepped out of the water. "Dragons much prefer the night."

"Why doesn't that surprise me?" Rowan muttered. Yawning she shoved the knife back into her boot and forced herself to her feet. She felt exhausted and the tears she'd cried rather than freeing her of the suffering seemed to have weighted her heart down more. But she could rest later and address her feelings later. If the dragon was up, so would she be.

She needed to learn and learn fast, everyone was counting on her.

"Tell me, what do you miss most," the dragon prodded playfully. "Knowing the hour? Or the things you used to fill those hours with?"

Rowan opened her mouth to say something snide, she felt her pulse race like she was training with the boys. Heard Ardal's laugh. Saw Colum with his arms crossed, nodding his approval. Her breath left her; she had to fight with her entire being to hold back a sob. She didn't want to lose anyone else.

"Will this be another impulsive incident you later regret?"

"I left in the middle of the night!" Rowan exclaimed. "I barely spoke to anyone. I just left. I was certain that I had to go at that moment. So sure it was for the best and so...*angry*. And all of it for..." Rowan waved her arm at the dragon angry and sad, and so exhausted. "One dragon, who doesn't care if people die. And goes to sleep when I ask for her help.

"I always do this! I rush forward on instinct and people get hurt."

"Always?" the dragon asked patiently.

Rowan rubbed a crick in her neck. Her breathing was coming in heavy pants again, but this time she didn't feel tears behind it, just so much...fear. "All I did was share a bit of history with my father and he feels so betrayed that he hates me. And truly he is the least of my victims. I risk lives and nations. My friends lose limbs, childhoods, peace of mind. My instincts lead to pain and betrayal and death."

"Dear me, perhaps I shouldn't have led you here," the dragon remarked, pulling away a bit. "I'd no idea you were so powerful. You may yet find a way to ruin my idyllic life here in a cave, alone, for centuries."

Rowan bit her tongue, walking towards the first cave.

Loyal, brave, strong and honest.

She hadn't missed Bran in so long, but now she missed everyone. And missing him was so powerful a force that it was tearing her apart, revealing what she would feel if she failed. Over and over she would feel it, for all the people she loved now.

"I do not think I am powerful. Just..."

"Poisonous?" the dragon supplied when the word would not part from Rowan's lips.

Rowan spun to face the dragon. "How do you know so much about me?"

"Long ago. Oh, *so* long ago now, I had a decision to make: remain one with the world? Or become one with eternity?" She tilted her head from side to side, looking rather like a human shrugging. "I chose eternity. Now there are very few things that I cannot know."

Was that what it meant to unite with eternity? To then separate oneself from the world?

There was a fizzling in Rowan's chest, as the weight on her heart ebbed away. She had little doubt that it would remain gone, but the immediate sense of the fear was slowly being replaced with a feeling of lassitude. Like she was slowing down, inside and out.

"One thing that I have learned, young warrior, is that all death is important. But *far more* important is life."

"What does that mean?" Rowan asked tiredly. Someone else should learn from this dragon. Rowan was a straightforward woman.

The dragon smiled. "Do not fool yourself. It does not take a great mind, or a great poet to understand. It is simple, and I will help you to understand, tomorrow. Sleep. I promise the world will not disappear because you took your ease a while."

Tears pinched at Rowan's eyes again, but she was far too tired to refuse. "What is your name?" she asked quietly as she settled back on the ground. Her arms were too tired even to reach out for her knife.

"I am Oona. Worry not, nothing can harm you here." The dragon sat, circling Rowan with her body, it was like being cocooned in the warm embers of a hearth. Rowan shut her eyes and drifted to sleep.

A light of pure green moved out of the furthest tunnel, swirling around with individual spots of green. No, not spots, leaves and blades of grass, and fluttering insect wings. It moved towards Eachann as he sat watching Rowan sleep. He rubbed the petal she'd sent him between two fingers. He had not slept since entering the dragon's lair. It seemed harmless compared to the stories he'd heard of these beasts, but he would not allow something to happen to his granddaughter because he had failed to remain vigilant.

The mass of green grew closer, and Eachann could smell fresh earth. His heart pounded with anticipation. He knew who it would be before she took on her fairy form. And his breath caught at this—first sight of her.

"You look like your mother, in her younger days," Eachann whispered to this spirit, who was surely not his daughter, but held some part of her.

Sinead settled on the ground beside him, curled her legs beneath herself, and propped her elbows against her knees, making a childish resting place for her chin atop her hands. She grinned at him.

"I often wondered what you looked like, must I wonder forever?" Sinead asked.

Eachann startled, realizing that he was invisible still and that whatever force this was could sense him, but could not see through his spell of invisibility. He glanced to where Rowan slept with the dragon curled around her. The dragon was not asleep, but seemed to be using the water to peer into another place in time. Eachann's gaze moved back to Sinead's spirit. Clearly she knew where he was, what difference did it make if he was invisible or not?

Eachann knew enough about infinity wells to know they did not hold the true spirits of the dead. They held...echoes, the bits of self that were still so much apart of the living that they could not be shaken from the world.

Still. This was his daughter. He had longed to lay his eyes upon her face since the day she was born.

Cautiously, Eachann allowed his invisibility to slip away. Though his hands longed to lunge forward and take her's he did not even have to battle his own will to resist such pointless impulses. He'd been too long aware that what he wanted could never be.

Sinead watched him a moment, just stared deeply into his eyes. Then she sat up straighter and spoke. "You will not reveal yourself to her. You will not sleep for fear of the dragon turning monster in that one moment. And I think you will not join me in that tunnel no matter how long I ask you. Father, when did you give up hoping for the future?"

"I have a hope for the future," Eachann replied calmly. "I followed her here."

"Ohh, but I do not mean for the future of the world. I mean for a future of hopes and dreams and happiness. The sort of future you want her to desire."

"Why come to me as Sinead, and her as some...soldier from her youth?"

"Youth," Sinead laughed. "Bran was a soldier from her *childhood*. She could not have been more than twelve when she lost him."

"That isn't the point. I know what you are. You are the hungry well of the future, longing to know all, longing to gorge yourself on the hopes and dreams of all who enter so you can grow and spread and alter. Why not tempt her in with the face of her mother?"

Sinead leaned back, she looked down at her hands and at once they split apart into bits of nature, as if to float away, but they reformed into hands with no more cause than Eachann's sharp breath. She smiled softly, and looked over her shoulder to Rowan.

"My daughter is too much the pragmatist to be tempted into the future by one she *knows* to be dead. If she does not see it with her own eyes, that power inside her which she is only now beginning to feel promises her it can stop anything, even death. And it is not...*entirely* wrong. That soldier she had not seen dead with her own eyes, and he was an important part of her childhood."

"She never saw Sinead die."

"Yes, she did," Sinead argued, taking to her feet and crossing to stand between Eachann and Rowan. "That she cannot shut her eyes and see it makes no difference. She saw me die, with her own eyes. And that certainty lives inside her. And..." Here her tone turned so soft and sad it was hard for Eachann to hold onto his certainty that this was not in fact his real daughter. "Until she has saved your son, and stopped my mother's plans, she will not feel worthy to see my face."

Sinead burst apart in a cloud of green and rushed across the distance, to fall to the ground beside Rowan and reform. The dragon did not so much as twitch.

"She has such beauty in her, and unlimited power. But she feels unworthy to look on me." Sinead shook her head, rolling onto her side to look back at Eachann. "How can that be?"

"Are you asking as her mother? Or as the well of the future?" Eachann asked. "Do you want to know because you worry for her? Or because you feel the potential of her power and you do not understand how it was hidden from you, and Sorcha and every other seer in the world."

"Not every seer." Sinead sat up, dissolving again and rushing across the space to him. Taking shape once more with her legs curled under her and her chin on her palms. "Nor, entirely, from me. And you must stop thinking of us as separate entities. I am Sinead, but I am also the future. Her desires and worries as a mother do not have to contradict mine as a *force of the world*. Because in that girl over there, I feel the potential for a brand new well. I cannot make out its form or its purpose, but in her is power enough to match mine. But there is something about her...I can see her, but I still cannot make her out. I am missing something."

Eachann stiffened, his eyes were drawn not to the daughter he'd so longed to see, but to the girl he was here to protect. He'd felt Rowan's potential before and it was truly great, but he hadn't realized it was as massive as all that.

"How can a living being be one of nature's wells?" Eachann demanded.

"I am made up of all the dead beings, and all the potential they leave behind. Why should a well not be made of a living being?" Sinead smiled. "But I do not mean she would be one while living. Only that she has the potential to so alter the world that she creates a new well."

"And you want to stop her?" Eachann asked.

Sinead shook her head of green, leaves split off to shake around her like a halo. "I want to know her, and to know it. I want...to be sure this new well is a thing full of her best potential, not her potential for evil, and she *does have* potential for evil," she said slowly and pointedly.

"Everyone does," Eachann snapped. But his eyes lingered on Rowan. He'd long since felt the power in her, beautiful massive power, power she was only coming to understand. But that she had power enough to create a new well of magic that lived in the world and altered it; that was something he had not considered. That made her future far more dangerous even than what Sorcha had devised for her.

Sinead stood and held out her hand. "Will you look, Father? Will you help me know her potential more?"

Eachann leaned back against the wall, and shook his head. For good or ill, he had to put all his faith in that girl, but he would not risk letting any other force of power know the reaches of her potential. He was familiar with too many a powerful creature. They never did appreciate the beauty of a new power in the world.

"No matter how long you ask me."

Sinead smiled. "As I said." Her voice sounded light and amused. A long moment passed, before Eachann looked up and saw her looking on him with teary bright eyes, and her tone shifted. "Thank you, for guarding her so dearly."

"To my dying breath," Eachann promised.

Invader

370 days until Roisin returns

Darling was in the garden tending to her potato patch, digging up the weeds, roots and all, so she could plant them elsewhere and let all the plants live peacefully. She had the rose petal her friend sent in her pocket. She'd been carrying it with her everywhere. It was bright and full of hope, not emotions that usually described her friend. It was a lovely feeling to hold inside, knowing Friend was at last seeing all the beauty in the world, and in herself.

Darling almost never left the area within the protective ring of moss Aunt A had planted now. Not since Aunt B banished the last of the animals. Every once in a while all her aunts would take her out for a walk in the wood. But Aunt B was always so tense on the walks that bits of fear had started to work their way into Darling, and that wasn't her way. The only time she was truly allowed out was for her yearly visits with Friend in the Fairy circle; which wouldn't happen again for several months. But today as she hummed and dug, and hummed and planted and hummed some more it didn't feel frightening being stuck within this circle. It only felt confining. It felt like a smaller version of the life she'd always had, separate from the wide world.

There was something about this petal.

Darling pulled it out, holding it in her hand and staring at it, as if she could see the difference on its surface. It was tiny, but it felt so large. It was not drying out or crumpling, it was as though it continued to live, as though it was still connected to the rose it had been plucked from.

It was full of power. Full of determination. Full of—knowledge.

Darling didn't know how she knew it. But she knew that her friend was no longer in her home when she sent this. She was seeing a wider world. It was an odd thing they'd always shared, both their lives had consisted of tiny worlds, and once yearly visits to each other.

Her friend was seeing the world, and Darling was certain, desperately certain, that the wish they had made together must have bound them. They were two halves of one whole. So Darling's world could not be shrinking further and further towards the cottage alone.

If Friend's world expanded, Darling's should expand as well.

A breeze swept out of the wood, tugging the petal out of Darling's hand.

"Oh," she exclaimed and leapt to her feet gracefully. She chased after the petal with a quiet giggle.

Oh yes, her friend wanted Darling's world to expand as well. They were bound now.

You and I, ever two halves of one whole.

Darling was not a fool though, her friend might want Darling's world to expand, but her aunts did not. They were too careful of her, too protective. They wanted her to be the same girl she'd been when she came to them. They wanted her to always be safe and sweet and unaware.

Mother ruffled his feathers, and shook his wings in the apple tree he'd made his home. But he didn't rouse. The petal danced away, right to the edge of the moss. There it hovered, twisting over and over asking Darling to choose.

If she were being quite honest— which it was only recently that Darling even needed to consider, as she'd always been quite the honest child— but now there were times when she was not honest, even with herself. So she had to think on it. Staring at that twisting petal, a quite honest Darling must admit, no matter how much she would prefer not to, that her friend would want her to stay in the protective circle as well. She was vigilant and single minded in her protection of Darling. So much so that she would face danger and death all to keep Darling safe.

Darling could see in her mind that terrible vision of her friend dying on a field of battle. It terrified her, it was the fear of it that first taught her to lie. As she'd lied over and over to herself promising that it was only a frightening dream. But it wasn't. Friend had left her protective circle, of her own will, most likely to defend Darling. It was up to Darling to decide how much danger she was willing to let in, in order to keep her friend forever.

Darling grabbed a hold of the petal. And without a push of fate, or a second thought stepped out of her protective circle and into the wood.

At once she noticed a difference. It wasn't so much that the wood was darker than the protective circle. But the air was stiller, and so quiet. Darling shuddered. There was no breeze but she felt chilled. The shadows were longer here, and the trees felt dangerous.

Darling bent into herself as she walked forward, avoiding any contact with low hanging branches or brambled bushes. She had walked in the forest after Aunt A planted the moss circle. Why now did it feel so different? It wasn't even that there was a real visible change, except that the trees kept seeming to lean nearer without their branches even rustling.

Darling looked back. She could see her cottage, bright and happy. Mother was asleep in the tree, and she could still hear Aunt B's raised voice as she argued with the others about Aunt C's dream. The argument had been going on for hours.

Honestly, had they not been engaged in such a heated debate Darling would never have made it past the moss. But she had. And here she was hesitating. Afraid to face the wood alone. When she had never been afraid of anywhere before.

Darling looked out into the wood and felt a stirring both of fear and of destiny. There was something out here for her. Their argument and the wind, and her sleeping guardian were all conspiring to bring her into the wood. She only hoped they were conspiring with the good forces of fate. Darling steeled her shoulders and walked on, though the branches creaked, and the air chilled and her safe cottage grew further and further away.

"He came to me with a purpose. We need to trust the stranger," C argued with her arms crossed over her chest. Her throat still burned with the tears she would not allow herself to shed. B became utterly judgmental and unreasonable when anyone showed an emotion beyond anger. Lord, but that was tiring. C usually handled her sisters' quirks well enough, but it wasn't to be this morning.

As she'd slept she'd been held in Niall's arms again. She'd been home. They'd danced before the hearth in this very room and stars had surrounded them. But even in her dream she'd stopped herself saying his beloved name. She'd woken with the feeling of his arms around her but the longer the day went the less she felt them. And it was all because of another sister that he was gone. He'd fought on Sorcha's side! They all had. And what had it gained them? Niall dead, and all her sisters cast out of their home, forced to roam the world with no hope of ever returning. She could not even visit the tree beneath which her husband had been buried.

Niall.

She missed him so much. Missed saying his name. Missed his laughter. They were such an odd pairing, everyone had said as much. Cianna always at her artwork with her mind in the clouds of her imagination. While Niall was devoted very much to the moment at hand. He'd been a sentry, tasked with guarding a minor door of the palace, he would spend half his days alone. He'd done his duty well, but he'd never liked the solitude. And Cianna had been so surrounded by servants and sisters, and teachers, and guards that solitude quite appealed to her. But Niall dragged her with him into his world, where fairy danced on color and laughed loud and long, and had none of the ethereal grace and perfection in which Cianna had been raised. He expanded her world, never expecting her to fall in love with him as a result. He'd just wanted to be her friend.

"You can't keep the world out forever, not if you mean to bring it to life with your art. You need to know the world to do that."

She could recall arguing with him about that. Saying something like just because it wasn't a part of life that he understood didn't mean it wasn't life. So he'd shown her the world as he knew it. And he thought she'd fallen in love with that, and maybe she had, but she'd fallen in love with him first. She'd fallen in love with him forever.

"It's not as though your husband was ever known to see the future either," Bride pointed out in a condescending instructive tone she probably thought was helpful. Just now Cianna was more than sick of sisters.

"You know nothing of what he knew," C shouted, coming to her feet.

"Of course not," A said calmly, trying to sooth all the ruffled feathers as was usually C's role. "And nor is that the point. If C received a message from some force in eternity the form it took was merely the form it most—"

"It was not some nameless force. It was—" C gasped, catching Niall's name in her throat with a small sob. "*Him,*" C finished hoarsely.

A watched her sister fighting back tears and wanted to reach out and hold on tight. As she had just after Niall died, as they all had. Even Sorcha. But she could tell from the way C held herself that she wasn't after comfort now. She was after trust. And wasn't it strange that after all the years of working together every moment, of being together more than they had been even as children, it should still be difficult to give trust at a moment like this.

It wasn't that A lacked belief in the powers of eternity, or true love. Nor even that she didn't trust C's senses. But A couldn't simply trust that Niall was right and there was a man on a white horse headed to the cottage. A true love to someone inside, who could make his way past the barrier of both trees and magic moss, and the charm their great niece had built into the woods as a child. A couldn't trust that if such a person existed, and if such a person were someone's true love that she should then freely give over her trust to that person. It wasn't in her. Nor, she could see from her sister's posture, was it in B. C had long been the most open of them; well, open to new persons. B was the most open to new ideas and cultures. And A was...well, she was quite literally the most closed off of any sister. Even more closed off than Sorcha.

"The point B and I are making is not about him. It is about the message. We cannot promise to trust some man for no reason but that you had a dream saying we should."

"Can you not?" C demanded angrily. "Because the both of us trusted your dreams enough to leave the comfort we'd found off the island and return here risking Her Bitter Majesty's wrath."

"She has a point there," B remarked.

"And we remained on this island, so close to our home that we can taste it, but always out of its reach, *again*, because of your dreams," C continued forcefully.

"No," A argued, in shock. "That was because of our great niece."

"It was because her vision aligned with yours. B had different ideas. Safer ones," C dug in.

"How were they safer?" A demanded growing angry despite her intent to be the calm one. *Was she now to be blamed for everything?*

"They were safer because they did not rely on the magic of a child who was *afraid of magic,*" B argued. "A child to whom Her Relentless Majesty was seeking any and all connections."

"She made her a safe place. In a forest even Fairy could not tame. How is this not the safest place in the world?" A demanded of B, their other third forgotten as they sparred.

"Because it is only beyond Her Majesty's reach so long as she uses fairy and humans to seek it. But Her Crafty Majesty has many another trick up her sleeve. As the animals I banished are proof. And our great niece is only now showing *any* sign of the sort of magic it takes not just to make a safe space, but to maintain it," B said exasperatedly. "Admit it, C is right, you only trust your own plans and visions."

"I trust the both of you." A defended herself.

"For books and food and to share Darling with, but—" B broke off. She loved a good argument. Always had, and she was happy to spar with both her sisters at once over their equally ridiculous, though disconnected points. But all at once she realized what was missing. Darling.

She always played peacemaker when they began to argue heatedly. She couldn't bear voices raised for anything but laughter or song.

"Darling," B called out.

At once her sisters forgot their arguments. All three vanished from the room seeking their little girl. A vanished to Darling's room. C to the orchard. And B to the brook at the back of their home where they gathered water. But she was nowhere. As one they reappeared at the front of the house, and Mother, alerted to the crisis by their shifting energy, woke with a loud screech and took off from the tree. All three women followed after the bird.

"She could not possibly have been taken, I would have felt it," C insisted.

"Of course, she wasn't taken. Just as I predicted your foolish story, and promises of true love crawled into her head," B replied with dire certainty. She'd told C not to let Darling hear her dream nonsense. Darling was young, impressionable, and curious. She would be swept away by the adventure of it all and risk her life in the process. All because C had a pleasant dream.

"Mark my words, she's out here looking for her *true love.* Of all the nonsense," B grumbled.

"True love is not nonsense," C said; her earlier militant tone was not to be shaken.

Honestly B would prefer C go ahead and cry. When C became inflexible it inevitably lasted for weeks, when any normal person would let it go in hours.

"C, you've told the child that true love conquers all things. When we both know that to be an utter lie."

"How dare you?" she gasped.

"Did it save your husband? Did it prevent Her Majesty from losing all?" B pressed.

"True love does not stop death, nor does it prevent one from making terrible choices. But it lasts beyond all of those things."

"Exactly." B nodded magnanimously as C made her point for her. "It does not conquer all. At best it endures all."

"Enough, both of you." A shushed them. She'd made it a bit further ahead of them, and she stopped now, looking into the distance, her eyes narrowing with a look of suspicion B had not seen on her face since she met their other brother in law, Tyrone. That boded poorly for whomever she saw.

B took four long strides and caught up with A, only to freeze in shock. C joined them and looked ahead with a quietly gloating smile as Darling walked towards them leading a white exhausted looking horse with a man slumped over its neck.

Bride drew in a deep breath, and shut down every instinct that lived within her save one: suspicion. How likely was it that twice in their lives, by nothing but coincidence, she and her sisters should be in a place magically protected from all invasion and a man should make it through the magic by being near dead with injury? Impossibly so: thus, this man was here by design. The only question was whose?

B knew whose hand C saw in this business. But she was pleased to see that A was taking a more cautious view. However lovely it would be for C's true love to have reached out from eternity to give her a loving message, none of them could risk Darling's safety simply because it would make a more pleasing story.

Sorcha knew far and away too many tricks for this to be the hand of fate. B had no doubt now that the man Darling was leading to them, all but oblivious to her aunts as she watched over him, was quite likely to be a love enough to one of them that their spirit could feel his call. But that meant nothing but that he should be distrusted. No one knew love and all its perversions so well as Sorcha. She'd put Niall in Cianna's path. And Devon in Bride's, and she was bound to have put this unconscious man in their path as well.

It might be safest just to kill him and have done with it.

A stared down at the unconscious man. Her hands were fisted at her sides and her head pounded with worry and anger. She should not have healed him. They should have refused Darling. But while it would have been one thing to refuse Darling alone, it was another entirely to refuse both her and C.

What sort of lesson would it be teaching Darling to allow a man to die because he might be a threat to them? All of them wanted to be better than Her Majesty, to be better than their own frightened, angry impulses. But A's head pounded and bright lights flashed before her eyes as she tried in vain to search this man's head. His mind was well guarded.

A breeze blew in through the open window and A felt the ghost of a pair of hands rubbing soothing circles at her temples.

"Alma," Tristanah's soft voice feathered through her mind, soothing A's pounding head. How she had missed hearing her name. How she had missed hearing this beloved voice. "Sweet, why do you try so hard to know everything in the darkness? Mystery is a beautiful thing. If you know all life has to offer, then surely your life must be at its end."

"I do not need to know it all," A answered the echo of her old love aloud, though she knew well that she was not here. "I just need to know that we are keeping Darling safe."

"But of course you are." Tristanah laughed. "She isn't really alive."

The words startled A so badly she stopped feeling the pain in her head all together as her heart stopped beating. Was this how she truly felt? She knew the voice, the soothing presence, none of it was real, nor even a ghost, it was just her own mind calling forth a love she had not allowed herself to think of in years.

Even when they had been together, Alma and Tristanah had kept their relationship secret. Love between two women was forbidden in Tristanah's nation. And loving a human was not widely accepted among fairy. Everyone believed Alma hated humans so it gave their love the cover it needed to exist. Alma had not even told her sisters. Though she would wager heavily that Sorcha knew.

Sorcha threw them together, insisting Nessa use Alma as her ambassador to Creelan. As she had thrown Cianna and Niall together, as she had thrown Bride and Devon together, Sorcha once loved introducing a heart to its echoing beat. And A supposed Sorcha, so talented at manipulation, had also thought to have better control over Creelan, if Alma became involved with the king's sister. But it hadn't worked out that way.

Tristanah had never liked Sorcha; she thought her too manipulative, too involved in state business. Odd that she could not see how alike she and Sorcha were. Or perhaps she could and that was why she hated her. Tristanah had never approved of Fairy interference with her nation. Long before the war, she'd argued constantly with Alma over the messages she'd brought from Nessa. Tristanah claimed the Fairy wanted to control all the nations. She'd been part of keeping their two nations at a constant state of unease, largely over Nessa's concern that the Creelan nation was mistreating the Liadan by diverting its waters, and that they were destroying their nations lands with their constant mining for precious stones. Tristanah called it jealousy and fear of their nation's quickly growing power, and her brother listened. Sorcha would have known how to change her lover's mind, but Alma had not, and Tristanah had been a key voice in convincing her brother to join Tyrone.

True love did not mean, as Cianna believed, constant support and devotion. One could love someone but agree with nothing they did. One could be torn from their love by a divide between family love and romantic love. One could love and lose—even as their love went on living.

Alma was certain, to her bones certain, that Tristanah was alive. She was likely roaming the world as a wolf along with the rest of her family. But Alma had never sought her out. At first it was the anger over her role in this mess. But as the years passed, and Alma shrunk into A, and Tristanah became a cherished memory of a time gone by, A didn't seek her old love out for fear of ruining even the memory of being loved.

"One must be alive to be harmed," Tristanah whispered beside Alma's ear. Her memory deposited a gentle kiss on Alma's cheek and began to fade away with one last entreaty. "Wake up, sweet princess. I miss you."

Alma's eyes had never left the boy on the bed, but they left him now. She looked down into her palm at the rose petal her great niece had sent to her. It was powerful magic. It brought dreams of long dead loves and awakened dormant bits of one's soul, or secret wishes.

Alma observed the man on the bed. Logically she knew that he might be their great-niece's true love, or Darling's, though he was of an age too old for such an innocent child. But none of that meant he was not the greatest risk to their safety that they had yet faced. Love was always a risk.

It was strange that A had not realized until now that she was ready to risk again. Perhaps that was how he made it through all the barriers laid before him, not just his wounds, or the horse's tie to Darling, but some secret desire that lived in every woman in this lost cottage to experience the threat of real life again.

Petal listened to the other fairy children around her as she worked on her heart home for the second day in a row. Most of the children were keeping their distance from her. Not frightened exactly but...uncertain if she was friend or foe. Nestor had no such guards.

He was a fire fairy, the first Petal had met, apparently such a talent was rare. Three times so far he'd gotten angry with Conductor Web and had literally been consumed by a bright blue and orange flame. It was startling to the other children, but Petal had laughed. Nestor liked that, now he took up the pile of clay next to her and kept up a steady stream of conversation.

"You should make the mote breathe fire at unwanted guests," Nestor suggested.

His own heart home looked basically like the mound of clay with a tunnel pushed into it. She supposed he was trying to make a cave, but he couldn't focus enough.

"It's a bog, not a mote. There won't be any bridges," Petal said, thinking of her family cottage in Stonedragon, how it would feel when she got home. Since the whole rose arrived she was certain she would get home, it was a hopeful thing. When she got home she would shut the doors with her family inside it and shut out the rest of the world with a misty bog that sang in the music of crickets and frogs, and king fishers. "Just boats that only invited guests can find."

Nestor snorted. "You think you're awfully talented, don't you?"

Petal giggled at the sly rebuke and grinned over at Nestor. She thought it might be the best negative feedback she'd had since entering the Fairy Realm. Sorcha could critique plenty, but it tended to be far less...fun. She'd missed being around boys. Boys were never shy of giving an opinion, no matter how stupid it was. It reminded Petal of her brothers.

"Awfully," Petal agreed. She looked at Nestor's lump of mostly unformed clay, and back at him feeling out what he hid inside. He was very fiery, and quite used to being alone, but he loved company, and drama, and laughter. Petal let her power run out into his clay, transforming it with what she felt inside of him. It kept its cave like structure, but it grew eight arms, like a spider, and spots like a lady bug, on the roof, that opened to the elements, and its front door began to grow giant teeth—

"Petal!" Conductor Web stood over them with a sharp censorious tone. "That is not your home to build."

"I—" Petal startled, he looked so angry. "I was only trying to help."

"I like it!" Nestor smiled.

"That isn't the point," Conductor Web crouched near them, lowering his voice and softening his tone. "A heart home is something each individual must find for themselves. Whatever point in that journey Nestor is at, is the right one. By interfering—"

"When the future queen of the Fairy shows her favor it is not interference." Sorcha's cool voice circled the hill, and she appeared in a pocket of lavender light. At once everyone bowed.

Petal observed the queen carefully. She'd come with a purpose, to...disrupt budding friendships, or remind Petal of her place. Something angry. There was a raven at her shoulder. It looked only at Petal, and its gaze gave her shivers, like it knew something about her. Like it was trying to tell her something. Its gaze was far too intent to be merely bird.

Petal glanced around at the bent forms, and bent as well. Her stomach churned, she glanced sidelong at the home she'd grown for Nestor, he glanced her way with wide eyes, and wiggled his brow as if this was exciting.

Petal mouthed "I'm sorry." Nestor looked at her in utter confusion. But she felt badly. First she'd taken over his quest to build a heart home, and now she'd brought him to Sorcha's attention. Surely she would not punish a fairy child for being Petal's friend.

"My apologies, Your Majesty," Conductor Web muttered anxiously. "Of course, there was...no interference."

Sorcha stood over Petal, she looked down first on Nestor's heart home, then on Petal's. She examined it for several long seconds, then Petal's heart home began to change. Petal felt truly ill.

Sorcha changed the shape of the cottage, making it rounder, and longer, like a log. Then it sprouted moss covered branches, and giant ferns grew up on either side. The bog grew bridges, one golden, one made of daisy chains and one that was just large stepping stones protruding from the water. It was lovely, but it was nothing like home.

"Does that feel like interference, Petal?"

Petal nearly wanted to cry. Was that what she'd done to Nestor? Destroyed his home. She glanced sidelong at him and found him burning fiery bright, with all his rage aimed at Sorcha.

No. Sorcha came to destroy something. Petal had been trying to show Nestor what he had inside. She'd been playing with a friend. His fiery anger on her behalf let Petal relax a bit and she found her heart home intact inside her with a boat just for Nestor.

Petal stood and curtseyed. "Not at all, My queen," Petal lied sweetly, and then she went in for the kill. "My heart home lives inside me, where no one can alter it."

Nestor chuckled and his flame went out. Petal rushed forward, between Sorcha and the boy. She called out with her power and had the daisy chain bridge leaping off her heart home, and into her hand. Desperate to protect her friend, Petal grinned up at the Fairy queen and used the daisy bridge to wrap around her hair, pulling it to her shoulder as Sorcha liked it.

"Did you need me, Your Majesty?" she asked to distract her from the fairy at Petal's back.

Sorcha smiled knowingly. "Yes, my dear. Come along I would have you take luncheon with me, and my new pet."

Petal glanced at the bird, its eyes still boring into her, making Petal feel small and...hunted. She looked away at once and left the hill at Sorcha's side. Petal could feel the Fairy queen's anger as they walked away, and Conductor Web's relief, and even Nestor's growing dislike of the Fairy queen. Petal had won that exchange, and Sorcha didn't like it. There was a quiet angry power emanating from her that said she meant to have some revenge. Then Petal felt something else, near Sorcha, but not from her. Something enraged and frighted and—familiar. But changing.

Horror shook through Petal as she looked up to the bird on Sorcha's shoulder. It was looking right at her still.

It felt like someone Petal knew. It felt like someone with cause to feel she took part in *his* destruction. He felt angry with her. He felt like his whole being was being taken over with rage and resentment a peaceful heart rewritten into—a monster.

"Prince," Sorcha cooed. She lifted a hand and nudged the bird into the air laughing. "Stop frightening Petal."

The bird took off, and Petal could not tear her eye away from it. From him. Prince Gavin?

She'd thought he was dead. Thought the feather Sorcha had thrown at him was poison. But what if she was wrong? What if this bird was him?

It should be better, shouldn't it? But it felt worse. If that was Prince Gavin, it wasn't just his body that had been transformed. He was twisting inside.

"Don't fret dear, he's quite happy at my side. Like you are," Sorcha all but purred, so happy was she to be winning now.

Petal felt a pulsing at her chest, and lay a hand over her talisman. She still felt it promising she would go home again. She just wasn't sure any longer that it would be a good thing.

"Who was he?" Petal asked, couldn't keep from asking.

But she barely heard Sorcha's response. She didn't need it anyway. A rose scented breeze and a soft tune played high in the air. A pulse of power came from Petal's necklace; she watched the raven pluck a single red rose petal from the breeze.

He *was* Prince Gavin. He hadn't died. But—he most certainly wasn't alive.

Petal's gut churned and she felt an uncomfortable mixture of hope and fear. How was she to fix this? Sorcha always won.

You should make the mote breathe fire. Nestor's suggestion floated through Petal's mind. He had a point. When this was over Petal might like to hide from the world for a time. A very long time. With a fire breathing mote to keep her safe.

Unfamiliar Magic

369 days until Roisin returns

Asia entered the courtyard of Stonedragon Palace with a metal trader who'd found her walking and offered to take her along. It was apparently market day. In Turrlough when there was a market day the streets were a buzz of activity, bodies and noise long before the stalls were set up, but not here.

Since the man had given her the ride, Asia offered to lay out his goods, he pulled open the back of his wagon and rolled out two empty drums that he used to hold up a plank and begin laying out weapons, chain mail and roughly hewn jewelry. For the first few minutes between barking instructions at Asia and carefully unwrapping the cloth around each piece he laid out he seemed not to notice anything. And Asia as well was distracted by the pieces he revealed.

"These are no ordinary weapons," she said in wonder as she unwrapped a short blade with a heavy stylized metal hilt with knotted etchings laid into it.

"Nee, they're kingly pieces. Blessed too, my son works the metal, my wife blesses them with ash and sage burnings. The man who wields such a blade is twice blessed."

Asia knew a well practiced speech when she heard one and smiled, glancing side long to see if anyone nearby had heard the pitch. But the few people gathered around were mostly other tradesmen preparing their stalls. It struck her and the tradesmen at the same time. He paused, about to hand Asia another small wrapped item and looked around. There was something odd about this place.

"It is late for such quiet." His eyes wandered the area curiously before falling back on Asia and his table behind her. "Hey, you there, put that back!"

Asia spun around and found a little girl holding up an etched spear tip. She twisted it around in the sunlight, ignoring the tradesman.

He hopped out of the cart, but Asia was there already crouching in front of the girl with a broad smile.

"What do you need with such a piece?" she asked the girl playfully.

"To make myself a spear." The girl looked at Asia as though she were quite the fool.

Asia chuckled. "And what needs a sweet girl like you with a spear?"

"No one calls me sweet. I will be a knight soon. Rowan the Eternal said I could train with her."

"Did she indeed?" Asia said, fighting to hide her sudden disapproval with Gavin's love. She'd come to like the girl from his feelings and from the letters he thought he'd hidden so well. But this girl could not be more than nine, she had no business with weapons. She should be playing with other children and learning to read, and fantasizing about being a lady grown.

"Yes. Before." The girl bobbed her head to the side and looked up at the tradesman. "Is this one twice blessed as well, or only the dagger."

He grumbled, shaking his head. "All my pieces are twice blessed. But you've not coin enough even for a hair comb, which might actually do you good."

Asia was startled by the way he'd said it. It was similar enough to what she'd been thinking. But maybe this girl preferred a weapon to a lovely comb. Princess Rowan reportedly did. Why shouldn't other women? But...she was so little.

The girl lay aside the spear head and braced both her hands on her hips. "You don't know how much coin I have. Look around." She waved an arm at the near empty streets. "You'll not get a better offer than mine. The whole palace is asleep."

"Truly?" Asia walked around the girl. She could feel the people of the castle and they were...awake and moving about, but so unaware they might well be asleep. "What has happened to them?"

There was an...old, mossy, soporific quality to the air. As though something was creeping fog like out of corners and crawling over inhabitants one at a time.

Asia gasped for breath suddenly as a new, no two, new, vibrantly alive presences appeared behind her. She spun and found a pair of boys standing behind the little girl she'd been speaking to.

"You're supposed to be at sabotage," one of the boys said, clearly unafraid of being overheard.

The girl shrugged. "I heard him say twice blessed weapons, it seems like something the army could use," she replied, brazenly confident.

Asia knew at once that these were the two boys Orla had mentioned. Now she was near them she could feel they were very powerful indeed. But their power was different enough from both other fairy, and other water sprites that it might be easier for Asia to get hold of. They were a bit like her. She was a mermaid still, but she was in a human body, making her power different from how it had been under the sea. And these boys were human and fairy in one so their power worked differently than that of other fairies.

One of the boys had his attention solely focused on the girl, the other was regarding Asia as closely as she did him. This was the seer.

"Twice blessed, eh?" the trickster asked.

Asia could see him like a distant mist examining the wares on the table. Could hear the tradesmen bickering with the children impatiently. But her focus was caught entirely on the boy before her.

He was seeing things, and she could see half of them. They zoomed through his head, laid one over the other. She could see herself, a mermaid again, with a baby girl's face pressed against hers as she spun around. She could see herself walking along beside Owen as he grew older and older, and she aged so much more slowly. She could see herself hiding in an alcove, trying to restrain the power of the Fairy queen, only to be cut down by a sword through the back. She saw...so much. Too much.

Asia sucked in a breath. Now she had seen his power work she pushed back. Forced herself and the boy to see his possible futures instead. She saw him fighting as the water sprites did, made entirely of water he leapt from a river showering a field of fairy with shards of ice. She saw him curled up in a dim room of stone sketching over and over again the deaths of those he loved. She could see him as a man, rolling his eyes at something a tall woman beside him with a sword crown on her head was saying as she drew a knife and challenged his brother to fight. She could see him gurgling on his own blood as a giant wolf leapt out and gouged its teeth into his shoulder.

The boy jerked back, physically, as well as with his magic and before either could say a word the other boy was between them holding one of the weapons from the table at Asia's throat.

"What did you do to him?"

Keagan had never felt a power like that of the woman before him. Symphony. That was her real name. She called herself Asia here because mermaids were not allowed to reveal their true selves when they walked among humans.

Mermaids! Keagan had never really thought about such a thing, but he had heard legends. Apparently they were real. And she was here. And she had a power. A fascinating power. She wasn't an architect, or anything like it, anything like any fairy he knew of, she could just use his power against him. And she was fast with it. He'd only been poking around her thoughts, and seeing her futures for a few moments when she shoved the power back at him.

That one in the cell, sketching all his family dead. He had never seen that one before. He wasn't used to seeing futures that were just about him. It was startling, even more than the wolf ripping him apart. But that one...he'd felt it, like it was happening here and now.

Then Ferdy jumped to his defense, and Brigid stole a knife as well, holding it at the tradesman who was shouting at Ferdy. Keagan sighed. In a minute they would go from saboteurs to common thieves. It was one thing for Keagan to accept that he wouldn't be reaching Rowan, and throw his full support behind Rowan's Sword when they were actually working towards saving Stonedragon from the curse. But if they were just to become a gang of criminals—

"I'm fine," Keagan assured his brother. "She just...showed me a future I hadn't seen yet."

"That good, was it?" Ferdy said sarcastically, but didn't yet lower the weapon. "Who are you? What do you want here?"

"I am Asia," the woman said evenly, then her smile stretched and she disappeared from sight.

As soon as she turned invisible, so did Ferdy. Keagan could see his brother, sort of, he could see his energy back at the table of weapons, still holding out his stolen sword. Could Ferdy see other invisible beings? Interesting.

When a dagger lifted into the air Keagan smiled.

"You have to turn the weapon invisible too," Keagan said for a moment, feeling lighter than he had in months.

Asia reappeared before the table holding the weapon. She turned it over in her hand and lay it back down, giving a slight bow to the now apoplectic tradesman. He shook and caved into himself to get away from all the magic.

"That is a truly intriguing power." She glanced to Keagan with a brow raised. "Could I sneak up on the Fairy queen using his power?"

"I doubt it," Keagan replied then set his mind to sorting through her futures. He couldn't see her sneaking up on the Fairy queen at all. He wasn't even sure she truly wanted that. He saw her trying to sneak into the Fairy Realm, but not in search of Sorcha. If she did go near her it was mostly face to face and that didn't end well for her. But Keagan's mind played with the possibilities of Ferdy's power. He could see Ferdy sneaking up on Sorcha—and dying. Sneaking around to reach Petal—and dying. Sneaking up to distract the Fairy queen—and dying.

"You still haven't answered Ferdy's question," Brigid growled menacingly.

Keagan heard the byplay but his mind was caught up and his gut was twisting tighter and tighter as he watched his brother dying. He had been trying not to look at the future since Colleen suggested enjoying the present. Now that he had looked, Keagan couldn't stop. And all he saw, over and over was Ferdy dead. Knife in the throat. Poison spear. Strangled by vines. Ripped apart by giant wolves. Burned alive shoving Keagan out of the path of dragon fire. Over and over. Dead.

"I am here for magic," Asia said.

Keagan focused back on the here and now. Brigid had shifted so she as well as Ferdy was threatening Asia. The tradesman scuttled around the cart and crouched near one of the wheels. Asia looked unperturbed.

"I need to help restore the princes of Turrlough to their former selves."

Ferdy tensed. "You would be *Lady Asia* then?" Ferdy asked, derisively looking Asia up and down. What did he know that he hadn't told Keagan? "Tell me, when are you and Prince Gavin to be married?"

Keagan was utterly shocked. No one had mentioned a thing like that to him. How had Ferdy kept a possibility like that from him?

Asia shook her head, smiling. "He would not offer for me, though I am beautiful, came with wealth and passed his trials with great ease," she bragged. "There was another lady he loved," she reassured Ferdy gently.

Ferdy relaxed a bit glancing at Keagan, his eyes said he would explain later. "And what are the princes right now?"

"It is different for each of them," Asia said very carefully.

Keagan got the impression she was either hiding something, or did not properly know the answer. "You should never be near the Fairy queen." Keagan informed her. "She will be intrigued by your power, and if she cannot find a way to use it she will kill you. You cannot sneak up on her with Ferdy's power. Nor can you steal the water you want from the Fairy Realm."

"How do you know for sure? The future is constantly changing," Asia challenged as she walked around the table.

Keagan was unwilling to concede her point; the future might be constantly changing, but Keagan could see *all* its eventualities. If he couldn't, why had she even asked.

"There will always be fairy who can sense you," Keagan argued. "As you are neither fairy nor human, and would be trespassing on sacred land to steal sacred water, no fairy, whatever their allegiance, would hesitate to kill you. It would be better for you to return to...your home." Keagan finished without revealing Asia's secrets aloud, however deserted the streets were.

Keagan sighed, looking around. For a while defacing banners and chanting "Long live Queen Rowan" had helped weaken the curse on most of the palace's inhabitants. But not so now. Brigid was supposed to be about painting the rose sword on the walls of the soldiers barracks when she came over here. Ferdy and Keagan were to be look outs, and Colleen too, but she was no where around, she must have decided she didn't like this trick after all. Keagan should go find her. Not that she was in any danger. There was no one paying any attention to children running wild through the streets. No one was in any danger here.

"I am not going back there. And I am not leaving my friends to face this alone," Asia said, her eyes moved away from Keagan, taking in the quiet streets. A woman was walking by, laden down with buckets of milk for the palace kitchens, she was humming to herself lightly.

"Long live Queen Rowan!" Brigid shouted, but the woman walked on absentmindedly.

"What has happened here?" Asia asked.

"The curse," Ferdy said angrily. "It makes them forget things. First they forget Rowan. Then they forget the curse on her sister. Then they forget anything sad or frightening. Then they forget everything but the tasks they must complete to stay alive. Maybe they will forget even that eventually. And when the Fairy queen comes she will only have to step over their corpses."

Brigid lowered her weapon to turn on Ferdy. "No, they won't. We are Rowan's Sword and we will save them!"

Ferdy rolled his eyes, then he gave a half nod and his attention shifted to the blade in his hands. He gave a few practice slashes in the air, arced it before him a few times, and examined the carvings on the blade.

"The knot of Liadan," Ferdy said, his voice vaguely impressed. "Hey! How much for the blade with the Liadan knot."

"Take it," the tradesman whispered. "Take it and leave me be."

Ferdy dropped the weapon on the table with a clatter and marched to the side of the cart where the tradesman cowered. Brigid followed suit. Asia watched warily. She might know their powers, but she did not know them.

"I am Ferdy, son of Colum Keen, a knight of the King. I am squire to the crown princess. I do not steal." Then he laughed and shrugged. "At least not permanently. We have not harmed you with magic, quit hiding. Your future queen will have magic. And she will use it as she is now, to protect you. Our whole nation will be *four* times blessed, having a leader who is woman, human, fairy, and knight. Do not hide from magic just because you do not know it. Come to know it!" Ferdy just about shouted his last sentence in the man's face and Keagan was... impressed. His brother had a way about him, but it wasn't usually displayed in rousing speeches. Leading Rowan's Sword was waking a different side of his personality.

The tradesman stood slowly. He still shook a bit, but he regarded Ferdy with grudging respect.

Asia released a small breath. "You are quite the trio, aren't you? Children, but already soldiers. I would not have thought to approve but...You have such *valiant* hearts. Very well, I cannot simply abandon Owen and his brother. If I cannot steal the water, can you see a better strategy?" she asked.

Keagan considered her thoughtfully. She could still use his power, but she did not. It must frighten her, but he wouldn't let it frighten him. In the last minutes he'd seen his brother dying more times than he had in the months before. He needed to be looking, he needed to be working towards preventing that death.

Keagan dug deep, searching his mind for Owen and Gavin, searching his mind for a moment in the future when they were all together, when Asia was there, when they were themselves. There were so many futures, so many details to sort through. And they did not fall before him as he would expect. He thought it might be because he did not know Gavin and Owen well. Because he could look into most people's futures fairly easily.

"Is her power like mine?" Colleen whispered in Keagan's ear. She must be invisible beside him. He shuddered, worried she was siphoning the magic off of him because of something he'd done. "Is she another cipher?"

Keagan shook his head. He didn't want to answer Colleen aloud, but he sent his power after Ferdy's mind to alert him to her presence, so he at least would bundle up his larger feelings, as Keagan was trying to.

Keagan tried to focus on Asia's request, tried to bundle up his feelings, tried to see if he could find a way to make Asia useful in the future he wanted. There was so much rushing around him. Every time he tried to see Asia's future he kept seeing himself in that cell sketching death. So much death. Most of it Ferdy, or Pa. And the more he saw it the less he could tell if he was there from madness, or if he was there trying to reshape the futures he drew. Keagan started to feel faint. He slipped backwards.

Colleen grabbed him by the shoulders and shoved magic into him from the point where her fingers touched. She appeared beside him, startling Asia and the tradesman but no one else.

But what she'd done...that startled Keagan. He felt revived, filled with magic.

"Did you just give me magic back?" Keagan asked in shock.

Ferdy chuckled. "Told you her power was awesome."

Brigid and Keagan both turned dirty looks on Ferdy, but Colleen was looking at him as though he hung the moon and with her power coursing through him Keagan was able to see suddenly what it was about Asia that made her future harder to see.

She was literally of a different world, and despite her words to the contrary, she hadn't completely decided to stay away from it. She was an element of chaos, one moment tied to their cause the next disappearing into the sea never to be seen again. The things that sent her running to the sea were so varied he could not say from one moment to the next where she would be.

"Make up your mind," Keagan said to Asia. He slowly righted himself, removing himself from Colleen's hold, though he longed to stay that way, with her touching him, protecting him. He longed, but he shut that longing away, it was bad, it made her hide. "I can't see you helping him clearly yet, because you haven't decided who you are. But..." Keagan shrugged. "In many of the futures, helping him, or returning home, you begin your quest at Diddlyon."

"The other side of the island," Asia sighed, trying to fool all of them into thinking she hadn't heard the first bit of Keagan's speech. But it was eating at her.

"Eep!"

Every eye turned to face the tradesman. He'd opened his mouth to speak but been unable to make a real word.

"Yes?" Keagan prompted magnanimously.

"I...is...will she help Princess Rowan?" the man asked. "Does it help to save the Rose Princess?"

"The Rose Princess is the useless, sleeping one, Princess Rowan is the Blade of Stonedragon," Brigid corrected, making Ferdy chortle a bit more loudly than was called for. Not that it was marked by the soldiers watering their horses, or the maid with her head out a palace window, beating a rug.

"Helping Rowan means helping the Rose Princess," Keagan said impatiently. "Since Rowan's aim is always to save her sister. And..." Keagan bobbed his head from side to side, looking at the tradesmen. "Yes. If she stays it helps Rowan. Or at the very least it does not hurt her."

"I will take you," the tradesman offered. "So I can...get to know magic."

Ferdy nodded at him sharply. "Before you go, about that sword, and this dagger here, and...the comb with the eternity knot."

"You don't have that much money." Keagan approached the table.

"How do you know? He hasn't named his price. Anyway, the dagger was for Petal and the comb for Mama so I assumed you would help."

Keagan grumbled internally *you mean you thought I would pay for them and you could take all the credit.*

Asia chuckled loudly. "I always envied siblings. It shall be my gift to you both a reminder to guard each other well."

"You have money?" Brigid demanded doubtfully.

Asia smirked, she crouched on the ground and lifting a clump of dirt turned it over and over in her hands with her eyes shut, and magic of a kind Keagan was unfamiliar with biting at her fingers. She opened her eyes, stood, with her fingers still shut and moved to the table, her entire manner urging her audience to follow. When she opened her hands golden wing after golden wing fell to the table. There were well over twenty coins. Enough to buy several swords.

"Will they stay like that," Ferdy demanded, examining a coin.

Asia nodded.

"Excellent!" Ferdy said gleefully. The tradesman's well had a new and wild appreciation for magic.

"Girls, I know you care for your uncles, but you cannot help them by remaining in harms way. You must c—

"You didn't see it!" Shay shouted at the top of her lungs. It was usually Elish's place to fight, to protect them and speak for them. But in this it was Shay's place. She still felt such agony, her being reshaping, as herself was torn away a bit at a time. But she knew it wasn't truly herself she was feeling. It was her Uncle Gavin.

Elish couldn't feel this, Elish had trouble even feeling good things, she could not be expected to speak to this. Not when all she had managed to call their adoptive parents was "sir," or "ma'am," she hadn't ever called Prince Gavin their uncle, or Queen Aya their grandmother. Those things were easy for Shay to say, because even before Petal taught them magic, Shay had felt the love this family gave them. But not Elish. So it was Shay's place to speak for the heart of this family. She'd felt Uncle Gavin begging someone to take up the heart of the family, and make it strong once more. Shay would honor that request.

That was why she was objecting to returning to Heigh. She'd waited until they were away from the palace because the fairy were allowing them to leave, and they could not do much while confined in the palace. But they could not leave the battle altogether. There were other girls to free, their grandfather to wake, their uncles to save, and Petal to free.

"You didn't see what she did to him. To either of our uncles," Shay went on fiercely, though her eyes burned. "When we returned—when Petal's, and our uncle Gavin's plan succeeded and we were freed—He picked us up in his arms, and spun us around. He said he had been bereft without us, though he had barely known us before we were taken. But I could feel the truth of his words." Shay smiled though the words pained her, and she could feel the burning regret in her adoptive father, Prince Ian as well. "We had called him uncle because you had told us to. But on that day he was our uncle in truth."

"He loved you," Ian choked out, his voice hoarse and his eyes growing redder by the second.

"Then she came." Shay said. She felt around them for fairy spies, there was bound to be a fairy watching their trek to the sea. But she didn't feel any on or in this carriage, so she went on. "We were not in the room with him at first. We'd been preparing to flee with Uncle Owen, and Grandmother. But the Fairy queen sent for us, and we could hear them through the door. He was calm and in control of himself—until she brought us in."

"Then he grew afraid," Elish interrupted, adding to the story for the first time. Shay reached over and squeezed her sister's hand. They needed each other to recount such a terrible thing. Elish still shied away from speaking of it, or remembering it at all. Shay could not. She dreamt of it every night.

Across from them, their father knotted his own hands together, he needed reassurance too, but he had no brothers any longer to hold onto. He'd been more confident as he forced them to leave the palace. He'd arrived in a rush, convinced the fairy to release them, and without any more notice forced the girls into a coach. They'd not even had time for a proper good-bye with their grandmother.

All she'd said was "Bundled off on an adventure again, you wanderers. I envy you." But Shay had felt how much more she wished to say. She felt how lonely and afraid she was. There had been so much more to say, but she wasn't allowed. Shay had not felt until now that it was fear that had Prince Ian rushing.

"He was scared and his voice trembled," Elish continued the story. "He told the Fairy queen to send us away. He begged." Elish broke off, shaking her head. "*I* had not called him uncle. I called him Your Majesty. I had not thought of us as family, and he knew it, but he said, 'my nieces have naught to do with this. I am at your mercy there is no need to harm them.'"

"She laughed," Shay took over the story again. "She said 'they are not here to be harmed. They are here to say goodbye. I am not unfeeling, they have suffered already enough shocking losses, and you will leave them forever today, so they will have a chance to say goodbye.'"

Their father gasped and his fingers squeezed each other so tight they looked swollen and ready to split apart. But he said nothing. Shay could feel her sister wishing he would stop the story. Wishing she never had to hear it again. But Shay could not stop. They all needed to hear it. They needed to hold each other and go on as strong, loving family. Or all was lost. If they could not face the pain and go forward with love in their hearts then they were all lost.

"He hugged us both. And Grandmother, and uncle Owen. He kissed us on the head and said he was at peace with his fate, because we were home. But before he could say more the Fairy queen yanked him away from us with a spell. He slammed into a chair before his desk.

"'You will never be at peace,' the Fairy queen told him. 'You should have kept our bargain, but you thought you were so clever, you thought you could fool me.' She looked so angry as she spoke, purple and black and golden lights smearing the air around her. Then she lifted a black feather quill off of his desk and threw it at him."

Elish gasped now, as they all had then. But Shay could no more stop the story than any of them had been able to stop that feather. Elish shut her eyes, squeezing Shay's hand and blindly reaching out for their father's hand as well.

"It split apart in the air so dozens of feather's flew at him. Their sharp quill ends gouged into his skin." Shay saw it as she spoke. Her free hand rose to her cheeks. "In his face. His arms, and legs, his hands were pinned to the chair with the force of them. They drew blood, but as we watched the blood turned black, and became ink. It ran over him and everywhere it touched his skin shriveled up like a drying raisin. He was screaming in pain. We were all screaming." Shay gasped for air. She'd been speaking all in one breath without even knowing it, her words coming out faster and faster, determined to escape before she lost her nerve.

"We were all screaming," she repeated. "But his agony was so much louder. I still hear it when I sleep."

Shay heard their father sob sharply and looked out of her mind and into the racing carriage. He was crying.

"A bright pop of purple light filled the room. And when it was gone—so was he. All that was left were his boots, and a single black feather quill sitting inside of them. He was just gone. It was too much for Uncle Owen. He charged at the Fairy queen with an enraged cry. But she— winked and another pop of light took over the room. When this one cleared Uncle Owen seemed to have vanished as well. Then she stooped and lifted him. She'd shrunken him to the size of a beetle."

Shay stopped to banish a shudder. Elish and father were still crying. But Shay was not. This, speaking, being among those she loved, it was strengthening her.

"You cannot ask us to leave this place yet, Father. We have other girls to protect, and a family to repair. We cannot go until that monster is defeated."

Quiet filled the carriage. All that could be heard beyond the rolling of the coach wheels, and the passing wind was the heavy breathing of those inside. Father was battling something down, but he was not to defeat it. The cocoon of quiet was ripped apart by his sob. His hand flew from Elish's grip to cover his face.

Shay breathed in deeply and shifted to the bench with him, wrapping her free arm around his shoulders. One of father's hands reached up to close around Shay's in gratitude, and the other reached out again for Elish. He breathed slowly, calming in the arms of his family. Then he leaned his head in between them, and both girls took his cue, leaning near as well.

"You are my daughters. That makes you wanderers. Wanderers never run from injustice, but we do know when to fight head on, and when to try...different tactics." He infused the words with great meaning, his voice still raw. "Please come with me to your mother. She is waiting on the ship. I swear to you we will accept your help avenging your uncle."

Shay raised a brow at her sister. She knew Elish didn't always think of her as a sister, but she would soon. She couldn't do otherwise. They were in one another's minds and hearts now, even if not in one another's blood. Without batting an eye or twitching a muscle both girls looked at their father and gave a single nod.

Shay settled back in the seat and lay her head tiredly on father's shoulder. "He isn't dead," she said on a yawn. The story had taken a great deal out of her. "He was transformed into the raven that flew away. But the longer he is in that skin the less of him there is. The ink...it is...*eating* him. Writing over who he was to create someone new. Writing him into her servant."

Elish gasped anew. The last thing Shay felt before she fell asleep was her sister's horror at such a fate. She thought it worse than death. Perhaps it was, but if Shay knew anything it was the power of love to make a being anew. None of them was who they'd been born. They needed to get to Uncle Gavin, he needed to be saved, but Shay had no doubt now that they could do it, together.

Trust

365 days until Roisin returns

Braden woke with voices all around him, speaking in hushed tones. He could not quite believe he was alive. But he must be, he ached too much and his body felt too weak for him to be dead. How was it he'd never realized death might be quite the relief?

"Ro—" Braden coughed, unable to finish the word. His eyes weren't open, his throat felt dry, it was a mountainous effort even to stay awake, but he had to find Rowan. She'd been attacked. No. He had. Then Yseult showed up. Maybe they'd both been attacked.

"It would be better to save your breath for breathing boy," a tall woman said sharply. "You are not known to anyone here, nor are we known to you."

Braden coughed again, then held the breath inside his body, pushing it like a muscle into the parts of his body he couldn't seem to control. Forcing his eyes to open.

Two women stood above him, one seemed impossibly tall, and the other quite short.

"Who are you?" Braden managed to ask before his body was again beset by a fit of coughing.

The short woman shook her head, and a glass of water seemed to appear in her hand. Though Braden couldn't be sure, he was coughing so hard he couldn't keep his eyes open long enough to see properly. She moved in next to him, lifting his head and pressing the glass gently against his lips. Cool water ran down his throat, soothing him. When he'd had his fill she lay his head against the pillow once more and stepped back.

"You may call me Antidote, for death lay upon you when you came to us, and I have been your cure," the short woman said.

Braden opened his mouth, to say what he was not sure. It was all so odd. He needed to get out of here. He needed to find Rowan. But already his eyes were drifting shut and his mind was fleeing from him through a forest of wandering trees.

Her aunts weren't letting her see the man upstairs in her bed. They had not even wanted to let him stay in the room, or the cottage for that matter.

Aunt A, with Darling's help had healed the man, but as soon as it was done to the point where he would not die she had wanted to send him away. Though she knew perfectly well it would take days for him to heal enough even to wake, and longer to be able to prevent himself dying again.

It was only Aunt C's suddenly intractable nature that had saved the man a place in the house.

Aunt's A and B descended the stairs now, and Aunt C walked out of the den to meet them at the feet of the stairs. "Well? What did you find out."

"Literally nothing," A remarked sharply. They all spoke more sharply since the man came. And argued. And all of them were guarded. Darling could not go anywhere without at least one aunt dogging her steps. Even if she had to relieve herself an aunt stood by near enough that she could not escape.

Their worry was for naught. Darling wanted to be right here. Well, she wanted to be upstairs. In her room, with the man, discovering who he was, and why he was here, and why he and the horse both had petals like the ones that had come to her and her aunts. Was he sent by her friend? Or was he only known to her?

"His mind has been shrouded, and he is too weak yet to wake for more than a few moments together." B shrugged.

"Do you believe me now?" C demanded. "He was sent to us. We must trust him. We must care for him."

"He has been healed to the best of mine and Darling's combined abilities," A replied. "But my trust he shall not have until he has proven worthy of it."

"How can he do that while unconscious?" Darling inquired. She had yet to share with any of her aunts the fact that she had found petals covering the man's wound. She couldn't explain her reticence. Not even to herself. She trusted her aunts implicitly. And she knew if they were to send him away it would be for her good. Anyway, the petals should make them more trusting of the man. But she hesitated. She hid the petals in her palm and held onto the feeling of love and protection they carried.

Her friend had sent it to him, she was certain. More than that she was certain it was the reason he was still alive when they found him. Several petals had lain over the wound in his side, once Darling peeled them away he began to bleed again.

"Were his mind not shrouded I could have taken a peek and decided if we could trust him or not. But it is shrouded, so to be entirely honest, Darling, there is nothing he can do to make me trust him."

Darling laughed. "But if you know what he is thinking how would it then be called trust?"

Aunt B rolled her eyes. Aunt C beamed and Aunt A suddenly looked sad. She looked at the ground with her eyes clouded over.

"I suppose it cannot," she agreed. "I am sorry that none of you approve, but too often in life I allowed other people's trust to temper my caution and paid the price. I will not risk any of you. Even if that means loving no one but us four." Without looking at any of them she walked slowly from the house.

Darling wanted to run after her aunt and take everything back, but as soon as she stepped forward C shook her head.

"No, Darling. Let me. I forget sometimes that I am not the only one with a past to combat." She was nearly out the door when she stopped and looked at Darling. "You know your aunt has never once wandered around your mind, as she easily could. She has loved and trusted you always. This man is a stranger, and even if you and I trust him, it does not mean his presence is not a threat to our lives. I hope I have not in these past days encouraged you to doubt those who have loved you from the moment they met you. Whatever happens with the rest of the world there should always be trust in these walls."

Darling sank onto the cozy bench by the fire and opened her palm, staring into it. She looked up at Aunt B, the only aunt left inside. Darling held out her palm.

"I...I didn't hide it because I doubt you." She paused and her voice grew a bit choked. "I don't think. I just...I didn't want him to be banished before I even get to know who he is, or why he came here. Or how he knows her."

Aunt B approached and with a hand beneath Darling's lifted it high so she could see the petals that lay there, colored with the man's blood.

"Where did you find these?" Aunt B asked quietly. She lifted the wand from her belt and waved it at the rose petals. At once they lifted from Darling's hand to float between them.

"They were covering his wound. The horse had one as well, but it will not be parted from it."

"Indeed," B whispered, but she was only half listening. The air turned static and red lights danced around the petal. It spun around and around in the air, seemed to grow in number for a moment, seemed almost to make up an entire rose, then all at once the lights vanished, and the rose collapsed into petals again, they fell through the air to land in Darling's hand.

"Well," Aunt A's grave voice came from the archway. Darling had not even noticed them coming back in, but all her aunts were in the room now. "I cannot say I trust him implicitly, but it's clear our friend does. That I suppose is cause enough to let him stay a while."

C laughed.

B raised a brow, and nodded sideways. "For now."

Keagan had a very definite plan now. He'd finally figured out why he couldn't make the future come out right. He was trying too hard to keep all of the pieces together. They had to come apart to survive. If they were together Ferdy and

Keagan always fought together, always tried to keep one another alive, for themselves, and for Petal's sake. If they were together they wanted to be together. They wanted their family to be whole.

But they didn't need a whole family to defeat Sorcha. Some of the most successful defeats of Sorcha came with very few family members involved. They were more focused alone. What Keagan needed to do was leave, of his own will, and without fighting with his family.

Sorcha wanted to drive wedges between them, and that wasn't the sort of separation Keagan meant to have. They needed to be in different places, working with their own strengths, but they needed to continue loving each other. Just not to the exclusion of all else.

Mama was best here, working to hold the curse at bay, and helping Rowan's shield maidens. Pa, well hang Pa. Keagan couldn't work up the energy to think on Pa without getting angry. So it was just best Keagan left before he couldn't stand him at all anymore. And Ferdy was developing into quite the responsible leader of his army. He was good with humans. They listened to him, they respected him. Ferdy would be fine here. He would make sure Rowan had a legacy to come home to.

What Keagan needed was to get to Rowan, with enough power to show her the right path and help her take on Sorcha. He was of more use to her than he was to anyone here.

He just needed to...trick Ferdy a bit. Not in a mastermind way, Ferdy would feel it now, he was getting more perceptive. It couldn't be manipulation. It had to be Ferdy's type of tricks. The kind that came right out with what they wanted and even though you wanted just the opposite somehow tricked you into giving it.

Keagan leaned against the door to the barracks, trying to remember exactly how it had felt having Ferdy's power. Trying to remember how he'd made Rowan's box invisible, how he let the pieces become so much a part of him that they vanished with him. It had been an oddly startling feeling just vanishing like that. Knowing that no one could see anything you did, knowing that you could do nearly anything with impunity. It was *heady*.

It was a wonder Ferdy wasn't more of a terror with such a power. Wouldn't it be so easy to fall into doing all sorts of terrible things, knowing no one ever need know what you'd done?

But he didn't. Keagan wanted to ask Ferdy about that, but he shoved the thought away and went in to steal from his brother.

"I've a plan to get to Rowan," Keagan announced.

"Oh?" Ferdy did not even look up as Keagan came in. He had his nose buried in Devon's book on the Fairy. That startled Keagan. He hadn't thought Ferdy would actually read it.

"I...yes. We just need enough power."

"So you've said. Have you solved the problem of jumping to her when we don't know where she is?"

"We proved we could do that when we sent all the children into the castle."

"That was a disaster." Ferdy slammed the book shut and shoved it onto the bed behind him. "Brigid nearly got killed. And we knew exactly where we were sending them."

"The magic wasn't the problem, it was the children," Keagan argued, ignoring that his brother had a minor point. "This will be us."

"So I was right, that was your plan from the first? It had nothing to do with tricking the king?"

"It let us do both. Two birds, one stone."

"What do you want to kill birds for anyway?" Ferdy asked, but it was so casually said Keagan thought his brother must be relenting. Though he couldn't see into Ferdy's mind. Ferdy was hiding his thoughts.

"Well?" Ferdy demanded. "Are you going to leave me in suspense forever? You didn't burst in here to repeat the same old thing. What have you figured out?"

"Where we can get the power—*Colleen.*"

Ferdy held perfectly still, said not a word, just stared at his brother and Keagan was unusually unnerved by the quiet. He rushed to explain.

"She has an apparently unending supply of magic because she steals it from other people. But if you can steal it back for us, we'll have more than just our own power, we'll have some of Mama's and Rowan's, maybe even Sorcha's if Colleen ever came in contact with her."

"And what will happen to Colleen?" Ferdy asked, venomously.

Keagan felt a little slighted by the level of anger coming off of Ferdy, but he let it go. After all, he had no intention of stealing anything from Colleen. The plan was to make Ferdy help Keagan steal Mama's power and give up his own as well. The plan was to get Ferdy to agree to send Keagan out, just the way they'd both helped send Petal. Ferdy being opposed to risking Colleen was a part of that plan.

"Nothing. She was human to begin with, she'll just go back to being human," Keagan replied.

"But without the magic to hold onto and with half of her life missing from her memory. She isn't *just* human anymore. I'm not sure what she is, but it isn't just human. You have no idea what this could do to her," Ferdy argued.

"She'll be fine. I'm sure of it. But I'm not sure Rowan will be if we don't go soon. The dreams are only getting worse. She needs to know what I know."

"Is that all?" Ferdy said challengingly. "Why don't we send her a note. I'm fairly certain I can do that."

"Fairly certain isn't good enough! What if it never reaches her? What if it goes to Sorcha instead of her?"

"That's extremely unlikely," Ferdy dismissed. "We've no great connection to Sorcha, but we do to Rowan, and if we send it where we feel her it will go to her."

"She needs us! At least one of us. She needs to be able to adapt to the changing future. She..."

Ferdy laughed angrily. "So she needs *you*—to tell her what to do. Why, Kee? She's never listened to you before."

Keagan startled at the slap of the comment.

"What is it that makes you think you're better than her?" Ferdy pressed.

"What makes you certain she can do no wrong?" Keagan fired back, accidentally airing real grievances as his anger rose to match Ferdy's.

"I know she can do wrong. Just like I know you can see the future wrong."

"How would you know that? It's not like you can see the future."

"I saw it when I had your power, Kee," Ferdy snapped. Keagan was entirely shocked, and Ferdy could see it too. "Didn't think I could do it, did you? I didn't see everything, but I saw enough to know that you either see the future wrong, or you can't see it at all. There are too many possibilities for all of them to be right," Ferdy said flatly.

Ferdy and Keagan stared angrily at one another across the empty squires' room.

"You never told me you saw anything," Keagan said after a time.

"You never asked."

"I...assumed you would tell me if you had." Keagan looked away, wondering if Ferdy was slightly right. It had never occurred to him that his brother had mastered his power enough to see the future. Keagan hadn't really started doing that until he was nine, when Eachann came to talk to them about Petal going to rescue the kidnapped girls.

"What did you see?" Keagan asked.

"A few things." Ferdy shrugged. "I saw Rowan leaving, before it happened."

"You did?" Keagan demanded, starting forward. He'd never seen that. He'd seen futures where she had been gone for a while. But he had never seen the actual departure. "Why didn't you tell anyone?"

"The same reason you don't tell anyone all the futures you see, I was afraid telling it would make it true. Anyway, that wasn't the worst of them. The worst was a future where we win, but Rowan dies, and everyone is so fractured, and you are just..." Ferdy sighed, and glanced at the book beside him.

Keagan tried to sort through the futures, to guess the one Ferdy had seen. In any future where Rowan died people were fractured, that was to be expected. Her dying would upset any of them. But now that he knew Ferdy had seen the future it began to make sense of so many things Keagan had felt were off with his brother: Ferdy hiding things, his desire to stay even though he was as worried for Rowan and Petal, even Ferdy's commitment to leading the children, and so carefully when he tended towards recklessness. He'd seen the future where he and most of Rowan's Sword died, where Brigid died trying to protect Ferdy from an onslaught of arrows.

"Keagan, you're too—" Ferdy began just as Keagan was speaking.

"Are you still upset about Brigid?" Keagan asked right over his brother, and Ferdy fell silent. "I'm sorry, we shouldn't have used the littlest of the kids."

"It wasn't that you used them, Keagan. It was that you were dishonest about why. And you wouldn't listen to anyone's council but your own. Even when I told you we needed to bring them back."

"I needed to see how long our combined powers could hold out."

"I know!" Ferdy shouted. "Now! Instead of then. And you got what you were after, so it doesn't matter that it didn't really work. And it doesn't matter that other people have things to contribute, you only listen to you."

"Fine! What's your idea?" Keagan shouted. This wasn't how he'd meant to get here, but they were getting where Keagan wanted to go. "Because Rowan needs help. We need to get to her. You don't think we should take Colleen's power, whose then? Mama's? Yours?"

"Do you want my power, Kee?" Ferdy asked.

Keagan shook his head, discomforted by Ferdy's calm, knowing question. "No, of course not. I...we just need enough power to get to Rowan. And you don't want us to use Colleen's power."

"I would have thought it would be you who didn't want to use Colleen's power. Keagan, when things get hard your instinct is to go it alone, but I think that's wrong."

"Why is it wrong with me, but not with Rowan?"

"I never said it was." Ferdy shook his head, reaching behind him, he lifted Devon's book and fiddled with its pages. "You read this book and it makes tricksters out to be pretty powerless fellows, nothing like architects or guardians."

"You aren't weak, Ferdy," Keagan reassured, stepping forward.

Ferdy shrugged. "Maybe I am. I'm okay with that, because you know what... It isn't tricksters who start wars. It's the architects and the guardians. I don't need to be the most powerful, or the smartest, or right all the time."

"You aren't weak." Keagan repeated. "When I had your power...I felt a different kind of powerful. You could do anything you want and get away with it.

You could be an assassin, and no one would know. You are powerful. I don't know why you're always getting caught, you could get away with everything."

"I don't do it to get away with it. I do it for fun. There's no fun to be had by hurting people. That would just make you and Mama and Pa and Petal ashamed of me."

Keagan had his answer, but he couldn't say why it surprised him. Everything Ferdy ever did related to his family, making them laugh, shaming them when they'd done something wrong. Protecting them. But still it was shocking to have his brother's personality laid so bare before him.

"I...we don't have to steal Colleen's powers," Keagan offered. "If we just take a bit of Mama's and combine ours we can get to Rowan safely. We won't take much. Mama will be fine without it. She doesn't use magic very often anyway."

"But you're still determined we have to go to Rowan?" Ferdy asked. "There is nothing I can say to change your mind?"

"We have to go. Things have to change so we can all survive this."

Ferdy nodded silently. In the end, Keagan wasn't so sure he had tricked his brother. Or even that he'd really understood his power so much when Mama switched them. Maybe there were parts of that power invisible even to the wielder.

Stolen Center

Rowan stood before her sister's crib with her sword clasped in her hands and her body braced for an attack. She knew what was coming.

Sorcha.

But this time Rowan was prepared. She was a knight. She knew magic. She knew how to protect those she loved. She was a protector. A *protector*! Not a poison.

When Sorcha came Rowan would be ready, and she would defeat her.

The doors to the great hall banged open, the sound echoing around the vaulted ceilings. Rowan jerked her gaze that way, but the face before her wasn't the one she expected.

"You are disinherited." Her father spat out the words with a smirk painfully similar to her grandmother's.

Rowan shook her head, tightening her hands around the hilt of her sword. She searched the hall for Sorcha.

This wasn't right.

Sorcha must have put a spell on him. Father knighted Rowan. He believed in her.

"You may continue as a knight," he said magnanimously. "But any order you give will come from me."

Rowan opened her mouth to argue, but her voice wouldn't work. Her arms began to shake from the weight of the sword.

"You will not pass down proclamations, encouraging other women to follow you into the knighthood."

Her arms shook harder. Her father looked so tall. So big. Rowan glanced at herself and didn't know quite what to make of it. She was small. She was not the self she knew. Not tall or confident, or strong. She was a seven-year-old again.

She couldn't do it. She couldn't save everyone. She was just a child.

Rowan looked back at Roisin's crib with tears gathering in her eyes. But it wasn't just Roisin behind her. Petal was there, curled up in a ball, crying in a bower of ivy and flowers. Maureen was sitting alone with her light wilting. Peg and the women who'd been training as knights were battered and defenseless. Everyone was behind Rowan, looking to her for protection. Even Gwyneth and the boys and Braden and Rowan's knights. They needed her strength and she was failing them.

A thin purple mist drifted off Rowan and threaded its way between them all, sapping them further, like poison.

"They think they are following a queen," Father's voice reclaimed Rowan's attention. "But you are not one. And may *never* be."

Rowan dropped the sword and let out a sob that shook her from head to toe. Her body quaked so hard she woke herself. Rowan rolled aside, reaching out for the hilt of her sword. But it wasn't on the ground beneath her packs, and she wasn't in the forest.

"Awake at last," Oona observed, but her tone held back. She watched Rowan with concern.

Rowan curled her fingers into her palms, and tried to calm her raging heart. She felt weak and...helpless. Completely unequal to the task before her.

"Seems so," Rowan forced the words out though they emerged like a croak. Rowan stood, stretching. The dragon rose as well.

Rowan found her sword belt a few feet away and lifted it, strapping the belt around her waist once more. She always felt better with it at her waist. Always— except now.

She was nervy and anxious, and she didn't know what to do about it.

She walked towards the waterfall, needing a drink, and a moment to think.

When Father made his proclamations, Rowan had suffered a terrible shattering inside, she'd felt completely destroyed, she just couldn't explain it. He hadn't really taken any current power from her, and she had ways around him. But it had felt like the most dramatically painful moment of her adult life, and she hadn't understood why.

She understood now. He had taken her back, past the awkward fifteen-year-old who had allowed herself to be beaten and mocked trying to find her way in a world of men. Past even the ten-year-old who was a foreigner in her own skin, and carried the weight of the world on her shoulders. Dragging her all the way back to her weakest moment. When she had felt to blame for her sister's suffering, when she'd felt to blame for all the suffering in the world. When she'd felt poisonous, and truly believed the world would be better off if she'd never been born. He took her to the moment when she'd hated herself most, and this time, rather than being her hero and believing in her when she could not, rather than being the man who'd placed her sister in her arms and gave Rowan a purpose, rather than making her a protector—he was tearing all that away from her.

Her father had ripped into her and pulled apart the root of all her strength. Chopping her into a smaller, weaker form than she'd ever been before. And it had seemed as though he enjoyed it.

Gone was the man around whose faith she had built her courage. He broke it all in one fight, and Rowan didn't know who or what to trust any longer.

How odd it was. She doubted either of them would have imagined such a thing, but her father and that moment of faith were the center of her world. Now her center was gone and she was rushing around trying to save everyone to prove that she could be strong without it. To prove this was still who she was.

Rowan got the feeling that the dragon could read her mind. So it was odd how quiet she remained on the subject of Rowan's thoughts. What was she waiting for from Rowan?

Whatever it was, she wasn't likely to get it. Rowan may know now what was driving her anxiety. But it didn't change the cure. Rowan needed to rescue her friends. It was the only way she would ever feel comfortable in her skin again.

Rowan dipped her hands under the water and pulled out a great scoop. She swallowed three scoops of warm water before she turned back to face the dragon.

Oona. She was a magnificent being. Powerful, and inspiring. To just look at her it was easy to see why fairy might fear dragons. Her form would dwarf the largest fairy or human five, maybe ten times. Her scales though lovely glittering things, looked like impenetrable armor. And one of her teeth was easily the size of a human head. All alone her features were terrifying, but Oona had sat wrapped up around Rowan to keep her safe, though Rowan had been nothing but rude and demanding since she entered the cave. There was no reason to fear this dragon, and Rowan suspected that was true of other dragons as well.

"I am sorry," Rowan said after a moment. "I've been impatient with you."

The dragon laughed. "You are young. Youth is a time for impatience. I am old. Old age is a time for tolerance."

"Have you truly been alone here for centuries?" Rowan asked. She climbed carefully down from the rock stairs near the falls, watching the dragon the whole while.

"Sometimes one needs a bit of time alone to think."

Rowan laughed at the dry observation.

"But I am not alone all the time. Today, for instance, I have a visitor."

Rowan felt like there was more to the words than met the ear. Like perhaps they were some strange half truth, or some deeper meaning about the universe Rowan was meant to glean from them. But it could just be the way Oona spoke, or Rowan's suddenly uncentered self. Everything felt deeper now.

Rowan nodded towards the first of the tunnels, the one she'd made it part way down. The one where she'd heard Bran's voice. "Is that what's down there? Visitors from other days."

The dragon laughed. "Did you not look? I thought surely one as impatient as you would have explored my whole cave before I woke."

Rowan ground her teeth, already growing annoyed with her hostess. Why couldn't she answer a question directly?

"I heard a voice from that tunnel." Rowan tried again. "Are there any but us here?"

"There are, and there aren't." The dragon smiled, goading. "Are you hungry? We should feed you. Eternity is difficult to understand, if one is concerned with filling their stomach."

Impatiently, Rowan marched to a nearby bush and plucked off a handful of berries. The dragon snorted walking back to the spray of the waterfall.

"Nothing more substantial? I could catch you a rabbit, or—"

"No! I've given up meat." Rowan suppressed a shudder. She didn't want to see another thing skinned for her meal ever again. She didn't want to wonder about rabbit children made orphans or any other animal, for that matter.

Oona chuckled heartily, spraying the water from the falls everywhere.

"See what I mean, far too much fairy in you for Tanith to have countenanced."

Rowan raised a brow. "Fairy do not eat meat?" As she was saying it, Rowan thought back to the various meals she'd had in Maureen's home, and never once had she served meat. Rowan simply hadn't thought of it when she was there. The meals never felt lacking.

"No. They do not hold with killing anything with a heartbeat." Oona rolled her eyes. "All very noble I'm sure, and to each their own taste I suppose. But one animal to another, killing is killing. And fairy are willing to kill for other reasons than food, so their nobility seems murky."

"It isn't a matter of nobility to me," Rowan remarked. "Just disgust."

The dragon chuckled hard. "That tree has some nuts that are tasty, and they'll help keep your strength up. Don't worry, they don't bleed."

Rippling Reminders

367 days until Roisin returns

Colum adjusted the position of the royal guard on the large replica of the ballroom, and examined the room more closely.

"To be honest, Your Majesty, the plan was always to use forces other than our own. Forces not bound by your father's bargain with the Fairy queen. I do not think we should have your soldiers in the room at all."

Balder leaned in, bobbing his head back and forth. "If we are concerned that Sorcha has dominion over my nation we should not have servants or guests in the hall either. I might be as big a threat to my daughter's safety as the soldiers."

Colum grunted his agreement but did not voice the words. Instead he searched his mind for why this had never concerned him. It hadn't, had it? He could recall helping Princess Rowan finalize her plans for the night she would face her grandmother and free her sister from the curse. He could recall her decision to use soldiers of Turrlough, and he could even recall agreeing, but just now it made little sense. How were they to know the soldiers of Turrlough weren't equally vulnerable to the Fairy queen's sway?

He couldn't explain a number of things lately. He couldn't explain how he'd gone from showing the king Rowan's most likely paths, and advising on where to look for her next, to helping plan a ball. He couldn't explain why he couldn't seem to walk any closer to his own wife than three feet without some urgent need to be *here* taking him. He couldn't explain why the king was asking him for help. Because despite the many hours spent together now, it was very clear that the only thing to have changed for Balder was that Colum was now tolerable. There was no familial bond between them, there was not even friendship. So, it didn't make sense that he was allowed to be here every day. But here he was, and the longer the hours stretched at this table, the less sense Colum was able to make of any of the world.

And somehow, the less he worried about anything other than the Rose Princess.

"We should focus on happier things," King Balder remarked. "Roisin will be home. Were it not such a monumental moment for the whole island I would keep her all to myself."

Colum gave a quiet breath of a laugh. "Rowan would certainly prefer it so." Something caught in his chest at the words. Colum looked on all the plans for the ball and thought of the hours and hours Rowan had spent planning it out. Strategizing. Colum took a step away from the table.

Rowan planned this. Rowan knew just how it would go. It was not a celebration. It was a battle. But the soldiers were there for show, and to protect any bystanders. The battle was always going to be between Rowan and Sorcha. Roisin barely entered the plans because...because...

Colum's mind faltered over the answer, or shied away from it, a chill racing down his spine. The king spoke again, his words chasing away the chill with something else to focus on.

"Preferences aside, we shall have to share Roisin with the world at least for that night. So we had best plan it out to impress her, or protect her from all the attention that will be lavished on her."

"Yes," Colum answered, though part of his mind was still fumbling over that question.

A low note of music sang around the room, pulling both men's concentration off the plans. They looked up, seeking the source and a rose scented breeze fluttered through the window. Balder shuddered, Colum saw it from the corner of his eye, but before him he saw a petal floating. It twirled around and around in the air and before he even touched it Colum felt it waking parts of himself that he was frightened to face.

My little flower petal.

He saw Petal's special grin, the one that was only for her father. Saw her eyes sparkle with joy and power. His little girl. How many days had it been since he'd worried for her? Or even thought of her?

The petal twisted again, closer to him, hesitantly.

You think he is right?

He saw Rowan's eyes so lost. So hurt. Colum couldn't bring himself to reach out for the petal. As hesitant of touching it as the petal was hesitant of him. What was he doing here? How had he allowed himself to stand here day after day planning a ball that he knew, *knew* Rowan never intended to see? She meant to see a battle, she meant to see her sister safe. But she never expected to see a moment beyond that. And he was here planning for a ball that would happen only if she succeeded.

"Ugh, that smell." Balder waved a hand through the air, violently.

Colum's petal went tumbling towards the ground. Colum reached out for it, but it eluded him. When he would have stooped to seek it, the king pulled his attention again.

"It shall be almost impossible to have a ball for the *Rose Princess* with no roses, but I intend to fill the hall with enough other fragrant blossoms that I cannot smell that scent," he said with a shudder, and Colum saw the scared little boy Balder had been as a child. He saw the son he'd never known, never held or comforted. He had to help him. Colum's other fears slid away, but this was different, wasn't it? He wasn't hiding from them. He was putting them aside for a moment to help his son. That was as it should be. Wasn't it?

"I think we can manage that," Colum replied. "There are roses of no fragrance whatsoever. But perhaps," he spoke cautiously. "With your daughter returned to you, the smell will take on a more pleasant connotation."

Balder looked at Colum with a grateful smile, as a son might his father. "It just might," he agreed.

With their fears waylaid both men forgot bits of the wider world, and turned again to their plans. Forgetting almost entirely the music that had disrupted them, and the two rose petals that clung unseen to their clothes.

Ferdy was utterly torn. He knew his brother was trying to trick him. He knew Mama wasn't as indestructible as she had always seemed and could not afford to have her magic stolen. But above all of that Ferdy knew in his heart that if he let Keagan go on alone right now, the bond that had always held him and his other thirds together would loosen. So he must go with him. Or he must keep him here. But what Ferdy did not know was the more troubling.

He'd learned not to doubt his brother's abilities. Keagan could see almost anything if he set his mind to it. The fact that Keagan was so insistent that Rowan needed them gave Ferdy pause. What if Rowan *would* turn against them? Or what if she would just die without them? Ferdy didn't like to think that way, and he didn't like it when others did either, but Keagan could see almost anything. And he was more worried about Rowan than he was anything else.

Rowan had never had a bond like Ferdy, Keagan, and Petal had. Something so strong you knew it would be there even if the rest of the world was destroyed. She loved her sister, and they were surely connected, but Rowan lived in constant fear of something destroying that bond. She was close with Mama and Pa, but Rowan wasn't even sure of that bond forever. After she'd sent Petal to Sorcha, when Pa wouldn't speak to her, Ferdy had seen Rowan growing smaller and smaller, hating herself because she feared Pa hated her.

She was their daughter, but she wasn't. She was a sister to Ferdy and Keagan and Petal—but she wasn't. She was a sister to her own sister, but she wasn't. In all worlds Rowan stood apart. And it wasn't Rowan who was responsible for that. But it was Rowan who would suffer. She had a mind like Keagan's, not like his power, but like his mind, they couldn't look away from the bad. Perhaps, all alone in the world, the bad she always saw might grow so big that she couldn't see anything else, and that might turn her heart. Ferdy just wasn't sure.

And it held him back when he wanted to convince his brother to stay. It held him back when he wanted to tell Keagan that stealing Mama's powers might just kill her. It held him in a state of utter confusion so that he just followed along with Keagan, doing as he suggested, even though in his heart Ferdy thought leaving was the wrong course. They should be trusting in each other. Trust and love together was how their greatest magic had been performed.

"It will be easier to travel without the horses to feed and care for," Keagan said. "And we should take enough food for several weeks. Rowan's been gone some time, I imagine she will have run out of food."

"A map would be useful," Ferdy said absently, looking around the squire barracks.

It bothered Ferdy more than he would have expected that they had stopped training to be knights, that they were both openly flouting every code of knighthood. Ferdy knew his brother had never been as keen on the idea as Ferdy was, and that everyone just thought Ferdy wanted to play with weapons or compete with Petal's title, and maybe that was how it started. But when Ardal gave his speeches about the bonds formed in a company, and how they became another family who protected one another, and built a safer land even for those who could never fight, Ferdy had felt stirrings of pride, maybe even a calling. And now he was just letting that go, it hurt a little.

"Yes. And various weapons," Keagan went on. "Rowan took armor. There aren't any full suits in our size, but we could take chain ma—"

Music interrupted Keagan mid word, and a swirling gust of wind brought the scent of roses and a few loose petals drifting through the air. Keagan closed his eyes as he grabbed onto a petal, and his face lit up as it always did when he was solving a problem. But Ferdy kept his eyes open. He caught a petal in his palm, and even with his eyes open and that last petal floating before him, he saw a million moments go flashing by.

He saw his younger self on Rowan's back as she practiced in the old training ring. He saw her evil grin as she helped him play a trick, and her hungry expression as she sat with the family around the fire and Mama told a story. He saw Rowan surreptitiously watching Pa come home to the old hugs when Ferdy launched himself at Pa, and Petal floated to him, and Keagan just held him around the waist. He saw her longing to join in, but never knowing her place. He saw

Rowan's tears the day Petal rode away, and felt her arms close around him, holding Ferdy as tight as she could.

Ferdy stared straight ahead, as that last petal floated around and around as if it did not know where to go and he saw their lives together. He saw the proper place Rowan fit into, and he knew what needed to be done.

Keagan opened his eyes with a massive grin on his face. "I can feel her magic now. I know how to get to her. Come on!" All his lists and plans forgotten, Keagan leapt off his bed and raced towards the door. "We have to steal Mama's power now, and go while I can still feel her."

Ferdy stared right at his brother, and nodded. Then did what he hated most in the world, he lied right to Keagan's face.

"Alright, but we should get the supplies first, and have everything ready. I'll go for the food, you get the armor and weapons and we'll meet at the cottage."

Keagan vanished without another word, and Ferdy sighed. He looked down at the petal in his hand. Rowan needed to come back. But it wasn't Ferdy or Keagan who could bring her home. Nor should it be. Ferdy slipped the petal into his pocket and vanished from the room. Just a moment too soon to see that last petal float through the air and fall into the hands of an invisible sneak.

Colleen stared at the petal uncomprehendingly. She'd only really known Rowan a day before she left. There hadn't been much to their relationship except that Rowan felt responsible for her. But in this tiny bit of a flower, and that quiet drift of music she felt so much more. This petal could not have fallen into any palm but her own, it welcomed her, loved her, and hoped for *her*.

Wasn't it the oddest thing? The boys cared for her, everyone was careful around her, and her parents all but worshipped the ground she walked on, trying to make sure she stayed with them. But Colleen hadn't really felt hope like this. This hope transcended Colleen just being fine, it hoped that she would be happy, and healthy, and know her own heart. She didn't think she'd ever felt hope of this kind. It made her feel more connected to the boys than she ever had been before. She had to protect them.

Peg dove into a roll, coming up between two knights and yanked out blunted daggers to stab at each just under their armored sides. She managed it with one, but Cassidy caught onto her wrist and gave a great yank, pulling her from the ground. But Peg was far from beaten. She let her weight drop as he lifted her, so he bent at the waist from the shock. She swung her legs behind his knees, and sent him tumbling backwards. She landed atop his chest and shoved the dagger at his throat.

Cassidy held up his hands, laughing. Peg didn't move, her eyes boring into his angrily. She could hear Sean behind her using her fight to give the other women instruction, but Peg still didn't move.

"Sweetheart, either kiss me or kill me, or in a few seconds you won't have a choice," Cassidy said flirtatiously.

Peg was finding him to be quite the annoyance. To begin with he was smug, add to that he picked on her more than any of the other women and she was hard pressed not to shove that blunted dagger just a bit more firmly against his throat and drive out all her frustration with him.

"I always have a choice," she hissed and shoved away, coming to her feet.

She'd so wanted to beat him. To wipe that smug look off his face. When they were involved she'd adored that expression, it made hungry for his lips every time he smirked in the past. Now it made her hungry to slap it off his face. And he knew it too.

Michael handed Peg her other dagger with a nod. She walked to join the other woman. She could hear Cassidy and Michael having a whispered conversation, full of laughter. Everything was so easy to them, every thought so simple. Right and wrong, and blame all easy for them to assign.

Peg stomped, trying to block out the memory of her argument with Cassidy, the day he'd come back. How had he known anyway? No one else even suspected that Peg too had fought with Rowan before she left. Once they knew the list of all the men Rowan had argued with no one even questioned why she would leave. No one but Cassidy.

He'd come home, heard the stories and marched into the scullery seeking her out. For those first few seconds when she'd seen him standing there she thought he was after the comfort he used to come seeking from her. She'd even been willing. There had never been love between them, but there was plenty of fun. As frustrated as Peg had been since Rowan left, she could well use some of that comfort. But no, he'd come to fight. He'd come to protect his precious Rowan. As if she needed it!

"You just let her leave?" he'd accused in an ugly whisper, so unlike his usual easy demeanor.

"No one lets that girl do anything," Peg had hissed right back. "She just does it."

"And you didn't encourage it? You didn't say something ugly and blame her for everything that doesn't go your way?"

"*My way?* I'm not even allowed to have a way. I do as I'm *told*. What am I to her?"

"Her friend. She's never made a friend with a woman in her life, until you. She was so nervous about it, and careful like she isn't with anything. She was scared of losing you. You could have kept her here. Just like we could have if we were home. Did you even try?"

Peg had been shocked as much by his words as by the tears that sprung from her eyes. "It wasn't my fault. It was just an argument. I didn't know everyone else was gnashing at her on the same day. She just...we weren't allowed to train. She'd offered us this...magic and then took it away and she acted like it was nothing!"

Cassidy had stepped back and nodded, looking away. "Sort of like you treated the friendship she offered you like it was nothing," he'd said coldly.

Peg had swung out at him, and gave him a good punch to the chin. He stumbled back a bit surprised, then his eyes raked over her. "Guess you managed to get *your way*, without her around." He'd nodded once and left the scullery and every day since, when she faced him on the training field Peg had fought and fought to make him take back the words.

But it wasn't working. Every time she beat him or lost to him, she heard his words over and over and couldn't help but feel he was right. She'd fought with Rowan, in her worst moment and while Rowan lost everything, Peg had actually gained from the argument. It was wrong. And no matter how hard she beat

Cassidy's body, that feeling wasn't going to go away. She just hoped that wherever she was Princess Rowan was safe, and would return so Peg could try to set things right between them.

Peg watched Astrid and Bree take on a pair of knights between them. Cassidy stood outside the training area, instructing one of the village girls on how to hold her sword. He felt Peg's gaze and glanced up, raising a brow. It was halfway to taunting when a rush of rose scented breeze swirled around the gathering carrying an airy tune.

An array of rose petals darted out of the breeze to find Rowan's closest friends, her knights. Sean caught his and held it tight with a small, proud smile. Cassidy caught his and his shoulders relaxed for the first time since he'd returned. Odd, Peg hadn't realized he was worried. But they all were, weren't they? Ardal grabbed his and held on with his eyes shut as though he were praying. Liam laughed for the first time in weeks, as he pulled a petal off his cheek. All of them terrified for the force of nature that was Princess Rowan.

Even Maureen. She had held herself up like their general of late. But when that petal drifted into her hand, she shut her eyes, and lay it against her cheek and a soft glow of power settled around her, both glorifying her and revealing the cracks she'd been covering with mettle. She'd been as scared as anyone.

A bit of bright orange flew into Peg's field of vision, startling her. She took a few steps back in shock and stared at the petal. It was orange and yellow and just a touch of pink and it swirled around and around, seeming to follow her as she stepped away from it.

All at once a hand reached out and plucked the petal from the air. Peg looked up in shock and Cassidy lifted her hand from her side, laying the petal in her palm.

"I think this one is for you. Better keep it safe."

Peg closed her fingers around the petal like a promise.

Awakened Need

Colleen hesitated at the edge of the training field where women and men were fighting together. Grunting and punching and kicking and snarling at one another, as though it were normal. Colleen stood back a moment wondering what it was about the whole thing that felt familiar. Surely men and women did not fight this way in Turrlough? One night when her parents thought she was asleep Mother and Father would discuss how long they could remain in Stonedragon. It wasn't home, Pa had no work here, and surely they could not rely on the generosity of the crown princess when she was gone. But when none of those arguments were working Mama brought up these women.

"We need to be home, with proper women, before these radicals infect our daughter. Do you want Colleen to turn into one of those immodest women, running around in tunics and stockings and carrying weapons?"

"Perhaps if she'd had a weapon when the fairy came for her she would have felt safer and not lost herself to that fear."

Mother gasped and cried and Father comforted her, and Colleen lay on her bed with her arms crossed over her chest, trying to keep their worries and fears from crawling inside of her.

Colleen wished she knew for certain what desires were hers, and which ones were someone else's. She almost never knew. But as she inched forward she thought this one, this desire to help was hers and hers alone. The boys wouldn't like it. This was her desire, because she felt safest when they were around. This was her. It had to be. So Colleen walked forward to where she saw their mother watching from beneath the shade.

Once Colleen was near enough to speak her mind failed her, she had no idea how to say what she wanted to say. Surely she'd known how to speak before she was kidnapped. Why did nothing come back to her easily?

"Female fairy fight," Maureen said without looking over her shoulder, apparently having sensed Colleen.

It was unnerving, a shudder raced down Colleen's spine. But she didn't leave.

"I was raised watching it. But it was never a desire of mine. And somehow when I came here, when I stayed...I became someone who no longer knew what this looked like. I became so...human that it felt wrong to me for women to fight." Maureen glanced back at Colleen then. "You would understand, I think."

Colleen rolled her shoulders and took a step back. Her eyes darted to the fighters. Was that why it felt familiar? Had she seen fairy of both genders fighting together?

"Are male fairy not stronger than females?" Colleen asked her mind, her voice, herself far away. All that was with her in that moment were her eyes taking in the spectacle.

"Do these human men look so much stronger than these women?" Maureen asked, and her eyes went back to the fighting.

Colleen looked closer. The men were big, and muscular and strong, so strong. When they grabbed towards a woman Colleen gasped in fear, but the women didn't. And some of them were so small. The tiniest of them was somehow the least afraid, she slid between men's legs and kicked from behind, dove and danced around their hands. She was magnificent, and she was thoroughly exhausting the men.

"No," Colleen answered at last. "Not exactly."

Maureen sucked in a deep breath through her nose and nodded. "Not exactly. I believe I may have held Rowan back a bit. I was so afraid to lose her that I told her things were impossible when all they really were was frightening."

"But..." A level of urgency entered Colleen's tone that even she was not prepared for. "Sometimes people *need* to be held back. Sometimes they aren't ready."

Maureen spun around to face Colleen and reached out for her, but seeing Colleen's utter confusion she paused. Maureen pulled in another deep breath, stepping back, and dropping her hand to her side, and Colleen felt falling off of her a wealth of sympathy as Maureen tried to tamp down her own emotions to help Colleen.

Colleen thought the fear and the urgency she was feeling were her own. But she was never sure. Would she never be sure?

"Colleen, dear," Maureen said in a patient voice, like one used to an injured animal.

"I'm fine!" Colleen snapped, loud enough to startle people fighting on the field. They didn't stop, but most of them glanced her way, and a number of strikes missed their marks.

Maureen snorted, and nodded back behind Colleen, walking that way. Colleen followed, taking slow breaths.

"I am sorry. But it is bad enough not being certain if I feel what I feel," Colleen said, words just pouring out of her that she hoped were her own, even though they were by no means comfortable words. "It unnerves me to feel everyone shutting themselves away like I have, all to protect poor, delicate me. Do you think that people will always be so careful of my feelings?"

"Oh, my dear, *no!*" Maureen laughed. "All too soon being careful of your feelings will frustrate even the people who care for you. They will not mean to let it happen, but their feelings will overwhelm them, and then you. This time of respite will feel like a fantasy. I suggest you savor the space while you have it."

Maureen stopped with several feet between them and even more space from the people fighting. Colleen absorbed her words, and found herself oddly more intrigued by the return of everyone's petty feelings than she felt scared. Which wasn't to say she was not scared, she was, she might not be nearly as in control as people thought. She might go back to not knowing anything from moment to moment. But if certain people were with her, Colleen was sure she would be fine.

"Were you wanting to train with the other women?" Maureen asked.

Colleen shook her head. "I don't want to fight. I just...I want to know I'm safe."

"And..." Maureen began cautiously. "Is there something threatening that? Are you—"

"The boys," Colleen blurted out indelicately.

"What have they done?" Maureen demanded.

"No, I mean...They want to go to Rowan. But I think they need to stay here."

"Oh of all the ridiculous schemes. Go to Rowan. How? They do not even know where she is?"

"Keagan thinks he can follow the rose petals she sent back to her. They plan to jump to her the way fairy can, if they steal your magic for extra power."

"Steal my power?" Maureen shook her head. "Little fools. To begin with," Maureen slipped a finger into the belt at her waist and pulled out a petal. "I could tell the moment I touched this that Rowan sent petals all over the island. They cannot just follow one trail because it doesn't not have *one* trail, it has many. For all they know she will have moved when they arrive. Magic like this takes time, it reaches different recipients at different speeds. We may well have been the last to receive them. And if they think they can steal my magic they've another thing coming. Why must males turn utter idiots at the most inopportune moments?" The last was said more as a rhetorical lament, but Colleen felt words crawling out of her to answer.

"They're scared. Keagan sees the future, but he sees so much bad in it he stops believing in the good. Ferdy doesn't worry as much that your side will not win, but he is scared of your family being apart and the longer you are the more he thinks you will be in the future too. They don't know what to do, so they do anything that falls in front of them."

Maureen watched her quietly for a long moment before her lips stretched out into a smile.

"Turning sage, are you?" she asked like a joke, but her voice was choked with tears. "Yes, you may be right. My poor boys, they want so badly to fix the world."

They stood in silence so long Colleen began to grow uncomfortable. She hadn't thought herself uncomfortable with silence. But the longer it stretched the more she could feel Maureen's desires, large and small. Desires to heal the world, desires to help her sons, desires to have her daughters home. So much desire lived in that woman, but was never visible on her skin, she was as frighting for the depths of her desire as she was for the magic she possessed. All of it was a threat to Colleen. Yet Colleen didn't move, waiting to see if the desires would take her over.

"So what do we do?" Colleen blurted out.

Maureen smirked. "I should like your help with a trick, if you are willing. Be warned it will not be comfortable. You will have to put up with someone bundling up all their feelings so they can rescue you."

"Oh." Colleen laughed. So she was to let the boys rescue her, was she? Well, she supposed that was half the reason she wanted them here. "Yes, I suppose I can do that."

Ferdy marched into the king's office unnoticed, watching his father and this man who was apparently his brother. King Balder wasn't the whole reason Keagan was on edge, or that Rowan left, or that Pa was acting a fool. But the king certainly had a hand in all of those things. Ferdy didn't like this feeling eating away inside of him, that he was suddenly the healthiest, calmest, most reasonable member of his family. Ferdy was supposed to be the lovable fool. He wasn't supposed to spend hours worrying about how to keep his family together. Ferdy wasn't supposed to be the one reigning in his brother's wild impulses. He wasn't supposed to be unable to eat because his stomach was so tied in knots, and unable to sleep for dreams of everyone splitting apart—destroyed even if they lived.

Most of those jobs should be Pa's! And were it not for this—half-relative, who Ferdy doubted he would ever see as a brother, Pa would be paying attention to his real life. Paying attention to the people who would always love him, not just the ones using his interest to keep tabs on Rowan.

And that was all the king was doing. He didn't care about Pa. He didn't see him as a father and had no intention of accepting his friendship. But he would use Pa's desperation to fix a mistake of his youth, to take one more person away from Rowan. The king wasn't any sort of man, he was something else, something small and vile. Something unworthy. Another day Ferdy might have allowed this to continue. If Mama was well, and Petal was home, and Keagan was behaving himself and Rowan wasn't out in the world trying to prove her worth to everyone and make herself a place *in her own family*. If all of that were changed Ferdy would happily allow Pa to be distracted this way, knowing he would see his mistake in time. But there might not be time enough for Pa to see his mistake if Ferdy didn't act now.

Ferdy marched into the room impatiently. "Pa, I need your help."

His father didn't even look up, intently focused on— of all things—a swatch of fabric. What wild importance that fabric was meant to have Ferdy couldn't possibly guess.

"Can it wait, Ferdy?" Pa asked, rubbing the fabric between his fingers. Ferdy supposed it was a good sign that he recognized his voice, after all, Ferdy could feel the curse on him. And the curse was a thing of forgetting. It took away fear and pain at the cost of memory. You couldn't miss what you didn't remember.

"No. It's important. Your children need you," Ferdy bit out.

"What trouble have you gotten into now?" Pa actually laughed.

"None! But Keagan is going to get himself or Mama killed trying to fix your mess!" That was perhaps a bit more dramatic than accurate, but it wasn't beyond the realm of possibility and it had the desired effect.

Pa dropped the fabric and turned towards Ferdy in shock. "What did you say? How?"

Pa was squinting as if his head were in great pain. The curse still held him slightly in its sway though he fought against it.

Ferdy saw a bright flash of color on the leg of his father's hoes and glanced down. One of the petals Rowan had sent was clinging to his clothes though he ignored it. Seeing it clinging to him hardened Ferdy's heart.

"Don't let the curse take you like it's already taken Rowan's father. She needs you. Your family needs you." Ferdy reached out and pulled the rose petal off his father. He lay it in his father's hand, then pulled away from his touch, angry and unnerved by the fact that the curse had managed to take him at all. It never had before.

Pa closed his hand around the petal and his eyes drifted closed, the tension easing from his face. But not from his body, if anything his shoulders looked tighter and he seemed to be fighting against something new.

Ferdy's gaze slid past his father to the king. He expected to find him completely absorbed in his plans, why else would he have let go of Ferdy's remarks, but the king was staring at Pa with a look, part anger and part sadness. He felt Ferdy's gaze and glanced over contemptuously. They regarded one another silently. Until Ferdy relented. He could be practical, though it was hardly his preferred attitude.

Ferdy bowed to the king, if you could call him that. "I apologize, Your Majesty, I didn't mean that. I am just so worried about Mama and Kegan. We need Pa at home."

Pa's eyes had opened during Ferdy's apology. He glanced between Ferdy and the king, and bowed low.

"Please excuse us, Your Majesty. I shall see what the trouble is at home."

"Of course," King Balder said coldly. "Family must come first."

Pa said not a word, just lay his hand on Ferdy's shoulder to guide him out of the room. Ferdy preceded him at speed, fast enough for his father's hand to slip off his shoulder. He needed his help, but he didn't want to be touched by him.

Balder watched the pair leave and curled his hands into fists. *Don't let the curse take you like it's already taken Rowan's father.*

How dare he? Balder was his king. His king! And the boy showed him no respect. None of Rowan's followers showed him any respect. They hated him. Disrespected him. Thought him weak, and unimportant and—

"Ugh!" Balder slammed his hand down on the table in front of him. He could feel the rose petal that had been in his palm laying between his hand and the surface of the table and had half a mind to throw it into the nearest fire.

If Rowan wanted his attention she could come home where she belonged. Not run all over the world making more of his subjects flout his orders, and hate him. And for what? He'd punished her for a grand total of two days. It was nothing less than she deserved, but she made him look a monster by running away. It was always about what everyone else wanted. Always.

But it didn't have to be. Roisin would be different. She was his and Gwyneth's daughter. No fairy blood, no willfulness, no band of followers she would turn against her father. Roisin was his perfect little girl. And he would have her back in one year. Just one year more.

Balder brushed the rose petal off the table, and focused on his plans, unaware that the petal had other things in mind, clinging to his shoe.

Father and Sons

Ferdy was pacing around what was once the living room of the cottage. Now—Colum looked around—it wasn't even the same house. The roof was gone, eaten, it appeared, by an overgrowth of ivy and berry bushes. The floor was covered in moss and flowers and dirt. It wasn't the same home.

Colum ran his thumb along the petal in his palm as he fought off a swelling rage with himself. How had he let so many days pass without setting foot in his home? How had he let himself fall so deeply into the curse that he hadn't noticed the passage of days nor the changes that had come over his sons?

Ferdy looked thin, and angry, and weighty. And Colum couldn't call to mind the last time he had laid eyes on Keagan. He had seen Maureen every day, but always from a distance. Every time his feet moved towards her a fear would crawl over him and nudge him back into the castle, back towards the safety of those plans. He'd let so many things go in his desire to hide from all he'd done wrong.

As they'd walked to the cottage, Ferdy told his father the whole of the trouble, and not at all politely. He blamed Colum for the whole mess: Rowan's absence, Keagan's uncharacteristic behavior, his mother's illness, on which Ferdy gave no specifics. This room did not look like the work of an ill woman. An angry one certainly, but not ill. And he'd seen Maureen healing all manner of people on a regular basis. But what if Ferdy was right? How had Colum missed so much?

Ferdy spun, suddenly marching towards the door.

"We agreed to wait for them here, Ferdy."

"We cannot afford to wait. What if Keagan decides to steal Mama's magic without me? She isn't well, she cannot take that. What if Keagan tries to go alone and gets himself killed?" Ferdy shouted at his father, with no attempt made to hide his contempt. "He should stay here, but if it's a choice between him going alone or me going with him, I will go with him. Someone should be keeping your children safe."

Colum absorbed the words as he would a blow to the gut, with his feet braced taking the strike into him, but not allowing himself to express the pain. Not yet.

"You've been angry with me for sometime, Ferdy, would you like to address it now?"

"No. I'd like to go find Mama and Keagan, and fix this mess."

"They will come. You said you and Keagan agreed to meet here. Take a moment, tell me what you are feeling. You won't get a better opportunity. I am sorry that I have been distracted, but discovering King Balder was my son truly won't change anything."

"What world are you living in?" Ferdy demanded, shouting in his father's face. "It's already changed everything!"

"No, it hasn't. Not how I feel about you, and Petal and Keagan. I love you just as much today as I did before."

"Oh really, and how about Rowan?" Ferdy challenged, advancing on his father venomously. "It seems like it's changed the way you feel about her. She's *always* loved you— better than he ever will. But all it took was his having one argument with her, and you took his side over hers."

"Ferdy, that wasn't—"

"All she ever wanted was a place in *this family*. She was your daughter. Rowan was. She would do anything you asked, she fought with her father on your behalf. But you just threw her aside when she needed you most."

"Ferdy, what is between Rowan and I, is between us. Do not use her as a shield for your anger. Tell me what I have done to hurt you." Colum used the tone he used with soldiers, to no avail, Ferdy was too enraged for a mere command to reach him.

"You helped him break my sister's heart!" Ferdy bellowed.

Colum caught his breath, biting down hard on his tongue to keep in the tears charging at his eyes. He had, hadn't he? He'd broken Rowan's heart. Colum observed his son's wild intensity. In the past, when Ferdy would take up Rowan's side against any insult Colum thought Ferdy had a bit of a crush. But that wasn't it. He was defending his sister. And Colum hadn't even seen that.

Ferdy wasn't finished laying out Colum's sins. "Rowan should be *here*. Already Petal is gone, but at least she left knowing how much we love her, knowing her place. Rowan never had that. She should know that you love her no matter what. That you want her safe. That she belongs. Now she's all alone, with a broken heart, looking for dragons, all to prove her worth to you! And you know, *you know*," Ferdy's voice vibrated with anguish and rage. "That she's always planned to die doing this. You were supposed to teach her a better way. But you didn't see it when you made her think she was worthless. You didn't see Mama getting weaker every day . You didn't see Keagan feeling like he has to fix your mistakes. All you see is your new son. If Rowan dies it will be your fault!"

"Ferdy! Take that back this instant," Maureen gasped in horror from the doorway.

Colum couldn't stop the tears now. He gulped trying to swallow them again, trying to swallow his shame. He'd made so many mistakes.

You know that she's always planned to die doing this.

Colum curled his fingers tight around the petal in his hand, as the words sunk through him.

"No," Ferdy answered his mother, crossing to where she stood in the doorway.

"Ferdy," Maureen said, rage and sadness evident in her tone. "You have every right to be angry with your father. But you may not say things like that, ever. Rowan left of her own will. And she will not be dying, but if she did it would not be your father's fault."

"He's right," Colum choked out, the words weren't exactly clear, but he could see Ferdy and Maureen understand. And though Colum knew Maureen remained enraged with him her features softened and she shook her head.

"She did not leave because of you, Colum. She told me so herself. She had already forgiven you for the argument."

"Of course she had," Ferdy snarled. "What has that to do with anything. She forgives everyone but herself."

Colum nearly stumbled at the words. He could see Rowan standing in this exact spot, scuffing her foot on the floor as she told him she was sorry for ruining things, when all she had done was share a bit of shocking truth. Every bit of criticism, every bit of blame she took into herself and held onto. Ferdy was so right, Colum had failed her. Even before he discovered Balder was his son he'd failed her. Because somehow Rowan had grown up without ever learning that there was nothing she could do that would take his love from her.

Colum opened his palm and stared at the petal resting there. Rowan had never learned that such love belonged to her. But she had certainly learned to give it.

"Come sit down, Mama," Ferdy had his mother by the arm and was attempting to lead her to a seat, covered over in clovers.

"Stop that." She batted Ferdy's hand away. "I don't know what has gotten into you, Ferdy. But I will not be tolerating it."

"We both will," Colum said, trying again to speak. "Ferdy is right. I haven't been taking care of my family. And it seems in my absence he's become the man of the family."

"Oh, has he?" Maureen rolled her eyes. "And I suppose being a man means devising idiotic plans to steal my powers and use magic he does not understand to try and find Rowan? Huh?"

Ferdy startled. "It isn't my plan, Mama. It's Keagan's. That's why I got Pa. Keagan isn't behaving like himself."

"Keagan's plan?" Maureen demanded, flabbergasted. And for a moment the fairy light that had been burning bright around her shifted and he saw the exhaustion in her eyes, and the fragility of her skin. Ferdy was right.

All the wonder around them wasn't as Colum would have thought, an angry expression of independence. It was a desperate grab for her old self, for her stronger self. Colum crossed to his wife, and took her gently by the elbow.

"Come sit, love, we will discuss it all."

"What has gotten into the pair of you?" Maureen demanded sharply.

"We need to find Keagan," Ferdy said anxiously.

"I took care of Keagan," Maureen said, then sighed. "Of course that was when I thought the plan was yours."

"What did you do to him?" Ferdy asked cautiously. So cautiously Colum glanced over, and realized more he'd missed. Realized what a massive amount of fear this son must be feeling to ever betray his brother, even in his defense. Colum had a great deal to make right.

"I gave him another girl to rescue."

Ferdy chuckled. "You know all the best tricks, Mama."

"And don't you forget it. Oh, Ferdy." Her voice turned hoarse as she reached out for their son, allowing Colum to nudge her into a seat. "This isn't your father's fault. Or even the king's. We've all made mistakes and hurt one another. Even Rowan. But she is doing what she feels is right, and she would have taken you if she thought she needed you."

Ferdy shook his head, but didn't voice whatever it was he knew.

"Come sit, Ferdy," Colum said in a calm but guilt laden voice. "We will see about Keagan shortly. But first you shall tell your mother and I how you know where Rowan went, and why you have been hiding that from me as I searched for her."

Maureen looked between them. Ferdy just looked confused trying to pin point where he'd slipped up Colum would imagine.

"Did she tell you she was going to find dragons?" Colum asked.

Maureen gasped. "Dragons? She lied to me, she said—" Maureen cut herself off shaking her head. "No. She had her reasons. Rowan the Eternal knows what she is about and we will trust her to do it."

Yes. Colum nodded. But not alone. He didn't say the words just yet though. There were too many things to be said.

Ferdy sat across from his father, still looking more militant than Colum was used to even from such a headstrong boy.

Ferdy began shrugging, then almost as if he were battling the impulse to apologize he looked right at his father and cocked his head sideways. "I was sneaking around the king's bedroom to play a trick on him when Rowan went to him to tell him she was leaving. She took the dragon pendant with her, and told him she was done fighting for his love."

Colum's heart broke a little further. He tightened his hand on Maureen's, unaware until she gripped him back.

"I followed her to Braden's room. She told him where she was going and asked him to lie, because she couldn't take one more of *your* children into danger."

Colum's free hand rose and covered his mouth as hot tears burned down his throat. His poor girl. **His girl.** When had he forgotten that? His bright bundle of nerves who'd shadowed his steps from the first day he met her. His sweet, strong, selfless girl.

Colum leaned forward and kissed his wife gently on the lips. Then pushed to his feet.

"Ferdy, thank you. You are growing into a fine young man. Please keep looking after your mother and brother."

"Where are you going?" Ferdy and Maureen said in unison, though very different tones; Maureen's one of shock and confusion, and Ferdy's one of challenge.

"I have two more sons to speak to. Then I will go protect my daughter."

"What's happened to Petal!" Maureen shot out of her seat anxiously.

"Not Petal," Ferdy grabbed his mother's hand gently. Then he grew shy, scuffing his foot across the ground unwilling to meet his mother's eyes. "I called Rowan my sister."

Tears slid out Maureen's eyes, then she scoffed, giving her son a large kiss on the head.

"And what else should you call her, I wonder?" Maureen effected an air of nonchalance.

Colum's hand was a long while releasing Maureen's. "There is much to say, my love. Much to apologize for. Let our son look after you, you've looked after us all so well, it is time we return the favor."

Colum released his wife's fingers one bit at a time, and spun for the door. He had to fix things. He was out the door when Ferdy caught up to him. For a moment Colum thought he was to be threatened again. But Ferdy just looked around shyly for a moment before throwing himself against his father for a tight hug.

"I'm sorry I said it was your fault."

Colum closed his arms tightly around his son and planted a kiss on his head. "I'm sorry, Ferdy. I promise I will bring us all together again."

Keagan was on his way to the cottage with weapons and clothes, everything but what Ferdy was meant to gather. All they needed now was to steal Mama's powers and he and Ferdy could go to Rowan. He didn't know when he'd decided to take his brother with him, but ever since he'd left Ferdy, planning to take him along, that bit of his mind that was always wondering over possible futures had come across more and more positive ones. Maybe he'd been wrong when he thought that they didn't need to be together.

He stopped in shock, as he saw the gate to Rowan's garden open and close without anyone near. Not only had that gate not opened once since Rowan left, but also he hadn't seen a soul there. Ferdy would have just vanished inside if he wanted to go there. As would Mama, and they were the only ones in the kingdom who could even get in. The roses had grown across the gate and refused to budge. But before Keagan's eyes they had grown apart, opened the gate, closed it and grown back together.

That didn't bode well. The only person who should be able to make them do that was Rowan. She wasn't anywhere near here. Keagan could still feel her path.

Keagan hid his packs behind a cluster of bushes and vanished into the garden.

Keagan walked slowly down the rows, feeling for whatever invader was here. He noticed a rose on a bush before him, it was being stretched higher and higher, pulling its stem taunt. Suddenly it was plucked free and the stem snapped back, shaking the entire bush.

He moved slowly closer, holding his breath. The invader was invisible, but Keagan was not, and there was no way to know if the person was looking at him.

Or to know what it wanted. When he was but a few feet away she spoke—Colleen.

"I need more power," she said and the rose bud in her invisible hand was crumpled into a tighter and tighter knot. "If I have enough power I can save them all."

"Colleen," Keagan reached out for her softly.

She appeared before him with an odd expression. A gentle, unafraid, giving expression. It didn't look a thing like any expression she had worn in the last few weeks.

"Hello," she said sweetly, but her hand remained fisted around the rose. "Are you almost ready?"

"Ready for what?" Keagan asked, taken aback by her solicitous tone and eager smile. This wasn't how she'd looked at him when she hadn't known she was a cipher, but it was exactly how she'd looked at Braden.

It unnerved him. Keagan took a step back, trying to calm whatever it was in himself that she was latching onto. He didn't want to make her want him with his wanting. He wanted her to just want him.

"To go save everyone." She stepped forward for every step he took back. "Once I steal Ferdy's powers for you we'll be strong enough to do anything. Just us. Together. Isn't..." She shook her head, her eyes filling with trepidation. "Isn't that what you want?"

Keagan shook his head, stepping back again, and fighting the growing urge to say yes, that's exactly what I want. He knew he hadn't been thinking it. Certainly hadn't been planning it. But when she said it, it sounded so right. Had she been digging around in his secret hidden desires again and finding things even he wasn't aware of?

It wasn't as bad this time. At least, it wasn't his jealousy and insecurity she was pulling out. But it still wasn't good.

He was taking away her will. Even if it was unintentional, it was a terrible thing.

Keagan vanished to several rows away from her, forcing himself to breat—

She appeared before him and grinned. "Where are you going? You know you can't go without me."

Keagan was so shocked by the show of magic it shoved every other emotion out of him. And it gave him a second to build a wall between himself and his emotions before they all rushed back in.

"Colleen," Keagan said gently, feeling nothing but his concern for her. "Do you know where you are? Do you know what day it is?"

Colleen blinked over and over. "We can go away together," she said with a sob.

"Colleen, is that what you want? Do you know what you want?"

She looked around wildly, her eyes widening and both her hands clenching into fists together. She looked like she was fighting back tears.

"Colleen, it's alright. You don't have to do anything you don't want. Would you like to sit down?"

Her head was a tightly twirling storm of dismissal.

"Alright." Keagan nodded. "Do you want me to take you somewhere you feel safe? Or bring you so—"

She reached out suddenly and latched onto his wrist, the crumpled rose falling to the ground between them. "You."

"What?"

"I feel safe with you. Don't leave me. Please," she begged.

Keagan's heart fell. "I'm not going anywhere," he promised. Every single fiber of his being gave over to her.

He could be whatever she needed.

As soon as Colum returned, Balder could see a difference. Ferdy had his way, Rowan had her way. Everyone but Balder.

"Your Majesty," Colum said with a bow. "Might I have a word with you in private?"

Balder nodded, and together they walked to his private offices, Colum trailing several steps behind as was proper. He always treated Balder as was proper. He had even before this. Honestly, aside from having more private conversations, Colum's treatment hadn't truly changed at all. He was perhaps more attentive, but he had always been overly attentive for a subject. As they walked Balder recalled walking down these same halls towards the same office, but it was his father's office then, and it was Balder who trailed steps behind.

What must it be like to only be parent and child together? As Colum was with Ferdy. What must it be like to shout at your father in a flagrantly disrespectful manner with no fear of recriminations? What must it be like to be loved?

I will not be fighting for your love any longer.

When Balder reached his office he walked around his desk and took his seat as was proper, motioning for Colum to sit before the desk. Whether he preferred to stand or not, Colum did as his king had instructed. Rowan must see, there could never be anything like she imagined between them. This was reality. This was proper. Everything else was the fantasy of a child who did not like her life. A child who did not love her father, because he treated her as was proper, not as was... enviable.

"Your Majesty, may I speak freely?"

Balder stiffened. It was one thing for him to ponder Rowan's wild claims, it was another entirely for Colum to address them. Had he not made that clear weeks ago? Balder gave a tight nod and breathed in minuscule pulls.

Colum regarded him in silence for a long stretch then bowed in his seat. "Your Majesty, I must formally beg your permission to be relieved of your service."

Balder was so startled he breathed in a great gulp of air and found himself unable to speak around it.

"There is a young woman alone in the world, apparently seeking dragons—to save your daughter, and partially because of some things that I foolishly said to her. She should not be alone. Certainly not believing we are better off without her. Rowan meant no harm with the secrets she revealed," Colum said urgently, leaning forward and dropping all of the very proper pretense he had begun with.

"And it need not harm you. No one who was in that room will speak of those revelations elsewhere."

"Her theories," Balder snapped, regaining control of his tongue.

Colum drew in a breath, and bowed in his seat. "Of course, Your Majesty."

They were quiet for a long while, staring at one another.

"I shall be taking a small company in search of Princess Rowan to offer her our aid." Colum looked ready to depart, without Balder giving him permission, nor saying he was indeed relieved of his service. But Colum paused and his eyes found the ground, but his voice was as intent as his gaze tended to be, and as uncomfortable.

"Since I am speaking freely I shall tell you this. You were a lonely child, with no one you could trust, you quickly became distant, even with those who loved you. Rowan told me once that she was disappointed in me, because I could have been a father or even a friend to you as a child. I failed you as much as the parents you knew. She was right. I shall always regret how thoroughly I have failed you. Whether Rowan's *theories* are true or not." His voice grew laden with what sounded like tears and Colum cleared his throat. Once he had he looked up, and his intent gaze pierced Balder into place. "But I have a chance still to repair the damage I did with Rowan, and I must try while that chance exists. So I shall bring her home, because you also have a chance to set things right with her. Perhaps the best thing I can do for you now is to bring back into your life someone who has always loved you without condition."

Balder held up a hand to stop Colum. His shoulders were tight, his breathing was an agony of cracking rage. He wanted to bellow loud and long against everyone who thought they knew what was best for him. At everyone who always chose someone else over him. But he kept hearing Rowan:

I will not be fighting for your love any longer.

For so much of his life he'd felt like he had to fight for any little bit of love he was given. Any tiny bit of approval. He'd never meant to make his daughter feel the same. But she did.

It woke such fear within him because he didn't think Colum meant Rowan might not let him fix his mistakes if he didn't go now. No, Colum was saying he had to go to Rowan before she died and there was nothing left to be done. Before she died.

He shuddered and felt from the back of his mind a lovely peaceful place where he could hide. He heard music, and could nearly see the torches crackling with light. He should go back to his plans for the ball. That was safe. Roisin was safe. She would always be safe, his little rose.

I will not be fighting for your love any longer.

"You may take any knight you choose. Any supplies, any weapons in my armory, and any amount of time. But return to me before you set out. You are not relieved of my service. You shall be carrying with you a message from me, to *my daughter.*"

Colum bowed low, his eyes full of all the understanding Balder wanted to impress upon him. With nothing but a nod Balder dismissed the man. He didn't relax until Colum's footsteps became tiny distant things. Then he slumped in his seat and buried his head in his hands.

Growing

Maureen sighed, laying back against the chair and the growth of clovers that covered it. At once the clovers cuddled her face and Ferdy appeared at her side with a cup.

Maureen quirked up an eyebrow at her son. "What's this?"

"Just a bit of water, have some while I make you tea."

"I am not dying of dehydration. I am tired." Maureen shook her head, refusing the water. Not that she was opposed to drinking it, she could stand a bit to drink. But she didn't like the way Ferdy or Colum were fussing over her all of the sudden. Just look at what she'd done to their home, and neither of them so much as remarked on it.

Was it possible they were so oblivious they did not notice foliage on the furniture and a missing roof?

Now that she'd begun feeling a bit better, a bit less like she was unraveling from the fabric of the universe, *now* they were concerned with her health! Wasn't that just like a man? And a *half*-man. She snorted.

Ferdy was staring at her militantly, refusing to budge.

"What has gotten into you?" she muttered.

"I saw you," Ferdy choked out. "When Pa said Prince Gavin had died, you came here." He nodded towards the room.

Maureen's heart clinched in her chest, and she took the water from her son, reaching out for him, to pull him near. Ferdy stepped back, and though she could see clearly he was indeed sad, and worried, he would not accept her comforting.

"It is my turn to look after you. I was even before Pa said," Ferdy rushed out.

He was still angry with Colum. Well, so was Maureen. But that didn't stop either of them from loving him.

"I lent some of my magic to your...project." Ferdy looked around.

Despite the fear and sorrow within him Maureen saw his light, a smile painting his features gently.

"Is this how the Fairy Court looks?" Ferdy asked almost absentmindedly but Maureen knew he was thinking of his other third.

"A bit of it." Maureen nodded "But in truth it is more similar to the modest homes in the fairy nation. Similar." She repeated, thinking that none of those homes had walls of bricks or furniture hewn from metal and carved from wood.

Those homes were grown. But as much as Maureen had begun to miss the home of her childhood, she couldn't part entirely from the home where her children had been born. She liked the brick walls, and the deep hearth, she loved that when they were all within its walls and the doors were closed she could block out the entire world and just hold onto her loves. This was her home, and she wouldn't part with it, she just needed to add a bit more of herself to it. Not her old self. But her—*whole*—self. Fairy would always be a part of her, however removed she was from that nation.

"I like it," Ferdy said after a long, empty stretch of silence. "It's fun! Almost alive enough to frighten people."

Maureen chuckled.

"Rowan would have liked it too. It's like what she did with her room. Keeping the human bit, and letting in eternity."

"She called me Mama before she left. Did you eavesdrop on that as well?"

Ferdy shook his head.

"It is a moment I shall cherish, burned into my heart from all the years of waiting to hear it. She is your sister. But if she does not know that in her own heart, it is not only your father who is to blame. It is me as well."

"You don't need to try and fix us, Mama." Ferdy shook his head. He walked to the cold hearth, and began arranging logs "He needed to hear what I said."

"As you need to hear what I am saying. It is good to defend those you love, but it is equally important to forgive them. And to know that we are all composed of mistakes." Maureen ran her fingers through the plants around her. "It was a mistake of mine that this was not a part of your home before now."

"And Pa's too."

"Do you think so?" Maureen chuckled. "I suppose he had his hand in it. But not by intention. He knew only the human world, how was he to know that I was shutting away a part of myself? Had he known, he would have wished to see it."

Ferdy lay down the log, he angled his head backwards with searching eyes. "How do you know?"

"Because he loves me, as I love him. Completely. Fears and flaws and wondrous beauties all together. It is how he loves you, and all your siblings, even Rowan. And it is how—" Maureen sighed, accepting the truth even as she forced the words out, and accepting that she had a share in her current difficulties with her husband. "He will now love the king."

Ferdy stiffened. Maureen well understood but she kept speaking, knowing that the hearts that belonged to her children had always been bigger and more open than her own, and that she needed to help them remain so.

"We must make an effort to do so as well. It will not be comfortable, nor easy, but we must do it. For your father's sake, and for Rowan's. And for your own as well."

"Mine?" Ferdy scoffed. He struck the flint three times before a tiny spark leapt into the kindling.

"Yes. Yours," Maureen agreed tiredly. She allowed the clovers to caress her face, giving her love. "It is good for you to stretch, and to seek the good in people even when it is not easily apparent. I hated Balder when Rowan was first born, but..." Maureen looked at her son with his back towards her and his head down. He was listening, but when a thing was hard Ferdy tended to hide from it.

"On the day that you were born Rowan wanted to be with us, as she had been with Gwyneth when her sister was born. But her father had forbade her from coming to my wedding because I was a servant, and I tried to settle her into the fact that she could not be here. Her sister had been kidnapped—" Maureen paused, thinking over Rowan's confession about the memories she had stolen.

Maureen had long felt a wrongness to that particular memory, but she had not picked at it, knowing Rowan must have changed it. But now every day she felt a little closer to knowing what had changed. She was certain now that Roisin had not been kidnapped, but had in fact been protected. Now she felt certain she knew by whom. All she could not explain was why. Why would the royal triplets have taken Roisin and not Rowan?

Maureen shook herself. "Her sister was gone, their whole family was inconsolable I could not imagine that her father would relent. But just before you were born there was a knock on the door. I heard them from my room, King Balder had brought Rowan and asked your father's permission to wait with him until you were born."

"She was here when we were born?" He asked quietly, and his body slowly twisted around to face his mother.

Maureen beamed softly. "Where else should your sister have been?"

Ferdy and Maureen shared a warm regard for several long moments.

"She was here. And so was...your brother. He sat with Rowan and your father while a midwife attended me. He waited the whole day, though the three of you took far longer and made your mother far more tired than was necessary."

Ferdy chuckled, well used to the old lament.

"And when at last Keagan came out, though no one had told her he was the last of you, Rowan vanished from her father's side and into my room." Maureen laughed her mind drifting out of the moment and into the past.

She had been so tired and too overcome with wonder to do anything but stare at her three beautiful children all lined up beside her on the bed. Then Rowan appeared. A human midwife had attended Maureen, because there were no fairy to attend her. When Rowan appeared the woman had nearly fainted. But Rowan hadn't noticed, and Maureen had laughed, so pleased to have her there. Rowan stretched out her neck, craning to get closer as she examined the triplets with wonder.

"She said," Maureen choked out the words, overcome with tears of joy. "'I could feel their light burning, Maureen. Aren't they the most amazing eternal things in existence?'" Maureen reached out a hand as if to trace Rowan's face like she had that day. And her eyes fell on her son as she did. "And so you are."

It took her several long moments to clear the tears from her throat, and let the memory burn within her, relighting her fires as no amount of nature over taking her home could do. That love was their past, and it would be their future.

"So, being as you have such greatness within you, it behooves you, my son, to find the best in others, and help them to see it as well."

Ferdy stood slowly, crossing to her, he leaned on her chair and stretched his arms around her, laying his cheek against her own. And his love as well wrapped around that fiery memory within, keeping it safe.

Colum found several packs shoved hastily behind a group of bushes. Upon inspecting them he found several pairs of squires uniforms, chain male, blankets, and a small arsenal.

At least his sons intended to be prepared for any eventuality. With little effort, Colum lifted the packs and slung them over his shoulder. They were near enough to the rose garden to assume that was where Maureen had laid her trap.

He felt oddly calm about that. In the past he would have fought with her about it. But he didn't know that he felt a right to argue with anyone about anything just at the moment. He'd let his entire family down. And when he'd looked around their cottage so alive with nature, but more with Maureen's magic he realized he'd been failing them in more ways than he knew. All these years he'd felt sure he honored the fairy part of his children's heritage, but if he hadn't honored it enough in his wife that she felt comfortable putting Fairy into their home, he could not have been honoring it properly in his children. And he certainly hadn't with Rowan.

She trained as a human. This last year he'd encouraged her to use more fairy magic, but it shouldn't have been such a hurdle, she should have known all along there was beauty in her magic. And he was certain now that she did not know it.

How could she? Even Maureen did not seem to know its beauty, and they were so alike.

With a sigh, Colum knocked on the gate. It was overgrown with rose vines, everywhere the eye looked there were thorns and flowers. But though he'd pounded his hand right next to a tangle of thorns his hand was uninjured. This was Rowan's magic. Her lovely powerful magic, but she couldn't see the wonder of it, how it could guard, but not harm even as it blocked one from entering.

"Keagan." Colum knocked again. "I know you are in there. We need to talk."

Keagan appeared beside Colum, glaring militantly.

"What is it? Colleen needs me right now."

Colum refrained from making a comment on that point. He regarded his son for a good long while, as Keagan's militant expression revealed what lay beneath it, fear and hurt and so much worry. This son carried far and away too much for an eleven-year-old. He was a man already, though he was in a child's body still.

"I will be leaving shortly with a company of knights."

"Do you need to get a special goose for Princess Roisin's birthday ball? Perhaps one that will lay golden eggs at her feet?"

Colum laughed. It was the type of snide comment one might expect from Ferdy. As Ferdy's lecture earlier was more what one might expect of Keagan. They had taken on more than powers from one another when their mother switched them. Colum smiled, it was oddly good to see, despite all the negatives that had brought him here.

"To find Rowan," Colum answered the sarcasm with calmness. "But you will stay here. And while I am gone, you and your brother both will take care of your mother, not attempt to steal her magic."

Keagan gasped, utterly startled. "He told you?"

Colum nodded once. "Yes, he did. And we should both be grateful that your brother overcame his natural desire never to break your confidences in order to protect this family. I needed to hear what Ferdy said."

Keagan struggled under his father's regard, his militance folding slowly into his being.

"What was that?" he asked.

"That I have not been taking care of my family. That I was to blame for Rowan leaving, and you being willing to risk your mother's life to repair my mistakes."

"I wasn't going to risk Mama's life," Keagan said defensively.

Colum nodded his head to the side. "Ferdy thinks you would. He thinks your mother is unwell. Even if she is not, did you know for certain what would become of her without magic, Keagan?"

Keagan shook his head, his eyes filling. He moved jerkily away from the garden gate, pulling his father with him.

"We, all of us, need to care for the people we love. I am sorry that I have been failing lately." Colum dropped a hand on Keagan's shoulder, staring into his son's eyes. "But do not follow my example."

Keagan nodded again and again, clearly battling back the tears he did not want his father to see. Colum dropped the packs, and knelt, taking Keagan's face in his hands.

"Let it out, son. There is no shame in tears when worry fills your heart."

Keagan shoved his head into the crook of his father's neck to cry, and clung tight to his neck.

"I keep seeing bad endings, worse and worse every time. Ferdy dying, you dying, Rowan—Petal. I need to fix it." Keagan sobbed.

"No, *we all do*. It cannot be on you alone. Nor Rowan, nor any of us. We all hold a share in bad endings or good. What you must do, is learn to trust in others."

Keagan hiccuped. "Ferdy said I was going after Rowan because I didn't trust her to stay good, but...Gavin is gone, and I know Braden is lying to us, and there is so much bad in the world. It wouldn't make her weak, or bad to give in to that. It would make her...normal."

Colum tightened his arms around his son as the fear dug into him as well. "I know. That is why I must go find her. She needs to know that she has a place in this family and that we will love her no matter what. So I am counting on you to hold this family together while I am gone. Alright?"

Keagan nodded. They both took a few extra moments to bundle up their fears before they separated. When Colum took to his feet again his gaze fell on the slightly ajar gate to the rose garden and the young woman peering out. She darted back the moment she saw him looking. Colum sighed.

The girl was a full six years older than his son, and suffering from the sort of wild loss of self that affected a being for the rest of their life. And Keagan did so love to save people. As Colum had in his youth. Perhaps he still loved it. But he stared now at the gate overgrown with thorns and roses and it reminded him of his home overgrown with moss and berry bushes, and with sunlight streaming in through its missing roof.

Rowan might never have lost herself, but he wasn't entirely sure that she'd yet found herself either. And he knew the incredible loss of self Maureen suffered in the past. All these years later, Colum was only now realizing that it was not his place to hide that pain and fear from her, it was only his place to sit beside her and come to know it with her.

Colum nodded at the gate. "That girl in there, it is good of you to be her friend, and give her what help she asks. But...do not mistake her fear for weakness. Trust her to care for herself."

Keagan looked taken aback. "She is frightened. She said she only feels safe with me."

Colum bobbed his head from side to side. "I am not saying to abandon her. But think of all she has gone through. She doesn't need saving. When she must have been more terrified than you can even imagine she made herself so resilient that no one could hurt her. Even if she had to lose a bit of her old self in the process, that is an action of incredible strength. Perhaps you should trust her now to feel the fear, but not lose herself to it. Knowing that you are there to help if she needs, but that you trust her to care for herself as well."

Keagan was quiet for a long while, considering. "That was strong, wasn't it? Not like Rowan or Petal are strong, but—"

"We've all of us our own strength and each has its own beauty. Do not lose sight of that."

"Alright, Pa." Keagan nodded. "So...I should leave her alone?"

Colum shook his head, smiling. Pleased at last to give fatherly advice not mired in his recent failures. "No. Speak to her, tell her how impressed you are with how she saved herself. Ask what she wants. Be her friend. But do not stifle her confidence with your worry for her."

Keagan smiled. "I can do that." He reached out suddenly and latched onto his father's hand. "Pa, the night Rowan left—" Keagan's voice broke and he appeared to be fighting against something massive. "I think Petal was here. I didn't tell Ferdy because..." He scuffed his foot a moment then looked up with all the fear written plainly on his face. "I had dreamed of Petal helping Sorcha do something bad and Rowan turning on her. Then Rowan left, and I felt Petal and all the futures I saw were worse and worse, and now Gavin is dead. What if...what if Petal helped her kill him?"

Colum felt everything inside him splinter and held his breath lest it split his being apart entirely.

Petal.

It all went back to the moment Rowan knighted Petal and sent her away. He'd been terrified, and lost, and aching since that moment. And somehow in the few days he'd spent planning with the king all that fear had gone away. He'd felt so comfortable. That comfort weakened him as nothing else in life ever had.

"Petal might have come here to do something less than good for Sorcha," Colum said, choking on the words as they left him. "But she would not help her to kill. And nor would Sorcha need such help. Rowan knows that. Of all of us Rowan knows what Sorcha's curses do to a being. We will put our faith in both of them. But we will not hide from these fears, because it is not the having of fears that weakens us, but the hiding from them."

Colum could see the fear in his son's eyes still, and part of him longed to rip it away, but he did not try. "Go settle things with your friend. But come home tonight for supper. We should all eat as a family before I leave."

When Colum walked back into the house, Maureen cast Ferdy a look. He vanished to give them a moment alone.

A moment alone. They hadn't had that in weeks and as angry as she'd been with him she'd missed him every moment. Even angry she preferred to be near him. But that must not be true of him, or else he would not have stayed away.

He always preferred to stay away with his anger. And she preferred to fight.

Colum approached her slowly now, his hands shifting uncomfortably at his sides. When he reached the hearth where she was stirring the stew he lay a hand on the mantel, slightly overgrown with ivy and shook his head. The ivy at his fingertips crawled over him gently.

"You were always a spectacular creature," Colum said, facing the ivy. But as he spoke his face drifted towards his wife and she could see the regret and the love in his gaze.

Maureen wanted to be moved by the sadness in his voice and simply forgive him, simply go back to how things had been, but she didn't think that could be the way this time. She watched the ivy caress her husband and felt in herself all the times she had bent out of her own shape hoping to please him better. And perhaps he had never asked, and would not have had he known. But nor had he noticed. And he had not bent himself to accommodate her. She could, and did forgive him, but they could not go back. They must go forward, and the only way to do that was to have the truth between them.

"It has been weeks since you even attempted to speak to me, but you think flattery will win you my favor?" she asked, in a voice of quiet curiosity.

"I have no right to ask your favor. I know that. But I look at all you've done," he stretched his neck back observing the missing roof, "and it seems as important that I remember to tell you what I have forgotten in the past. That you are magnificent in every way. And I am honored to be your husband."

The words burned through her and Maureen bent her head to hide her tears.

"Maureen, love, I am so sorry. I shut you away from your Fairy self, didn't I?"

Maureen looked up, despite the tears, shaking her head. "You would have to kill me to do so. You just...you were so fully human, and I wanted to be a credit to you, so when you shut yourself away from nature I did the same. And I worked to stifle my tricks so as not to draw attention to you. But that is over now."

"As it should be," Colum agreed. His free hand rose gently towards her own. "My love, there is no part of you that would bring me anything but honor. I am sorry that I failed to show you how truly blessed I am by every part of you, magic, and tricks, and kindness, every piece of you."

His hand locked around hers, and Maureen let the ladle sink a bit into the bubbling pot, as she was pulled gently into her husband's arms. He lay his head against the top of hers, all his muscles clenched tight against some emotion.

"I..." Maureen fought to find the words to express what she was feeling. That she loved him, that she'd missed him, that she was glad he'd seen some of his fault in the matter, but that addressing the reasons for their distance was no longer enough to solve their dilemma entirely.

"You cannot leave again," Maureen said against his shoulder, but her words were unyielding. "If you are angry, if I am angry, if you are frightened or ashamed. You cannot leave my side to feel what you must." Maureen's intensity grew and grew as she spoke, her pain clawing its way free and demanding to be expressed. She could hear a slight whine of wood stretching as it was pulled apart, but didn't care how her magic was changing the house. She only cared about expressing herself.

"You will feel it *here*. With your family, as you promised. You will fight with me, or cry with me, or—"

Maureen shoved out of Colum's arms, her face damp with her tears. "You made me a vow and you *will* keep it. You will not give into that curse, you will not pretend that Rowan's revelation affected you alone. I cannot know everything you feel, but I can stand beside you and help you to face it. That is marriage: burdens shared and pain halved. When I was at my lowest you stood beside me and grew into my heart, but I wonder now if I ever grew into yours."

"Of course you did. Maureen, there is nothing in the world I love more than you. I was ashamed."

"And when I was ashamed, I was ashamed at your side!" she shouted back. "You wanted me to bring my weaknesses and flaws to you, to share them with you, but you will not do the same with me."

"It is not as though I did not have to force your secrets from you," Colum said, his tone growing gruff with frustration.

"It is not as though *I* ran away from you, every time something went wrong. "

"No, you just keep your own council when you think something will upset me. And you passed that habit onto Rowan."

"Oh, so I absolve you of fault in her leaving and you want to blame me?" Maureen fairly well screamed and a great crack sounded above them.

As one her gaze and Colum's swung towards the ceiling. Another roof slat splintered and was devoured by the encroaching wildlife.

Colum let out an involuntary laugh. More of a snort really. Maureen swung to face him, and watched as he dissolved into wild laughter.

"What will happen when it rains?" he gasped between laughs. "Will the house be flooded or turn into a boat?"

Maureen raised a threatening eye at her husband but couldn't help but be drawn in by his boyish smile. He did have such a sweet smile. She found herself half grinning half glaring, as Colum reached out for her again, this time bracing himself on her and leaning his head against hers.

"I was not blaming you." Colum sighed. "Certainly not for her leaving. No, that blame lays all with me."

"It most certainly does not," Maureen said tiredly.

"Look at all this." Colum laughed. "It is wild, and beautiful and has a life all its own. This is what fairy magic does. I stifled it as much in Rowan as I ever did in you. I asked her to use fairy magic, but to think only as a human."

"And I helped you," Maureen admitted guiltily. "You had never seen the like of this, but I had. I was still so...*angry* with my past. Angrier than I even knew. I forgot the parts of it that I loved. I forgot to show her the parts I love." Maureen raised her hands to either side of Colum's face and pulled him back just enough to stare into his eyes. "You are not alone. Not in your triumphs or your guilt. Share with me," Maureen begged. "I cannot feel everything that you do, but I know what rage and guilt and fear, and even joy you must be experiencing, discovering you have another son. I know how hard it must be to reconcile with the fact that he is your son, and your king, and the boy who has spent his life blaming you for his suffering. It is yours to feel. But if you would only speak of it with me, and with our children we can all come to an understanding of it together. Rowan did not keep her own council about this secret because it upset her, or because she thought it would you. She kept it because she feared it would drive an even bigger wedge between you and Balder."

"But I let it drive one between Rowan and I instead. I let it drive a wedge between her and her own father."

"He did that, Colum," Maureen said shortly. And caressed his lips lightly with her own to soften the blow. "Being his father does not make you responsible for his actions. But more than that, what is done is done. Let us look forward."

Colum nodded. "I have missed you, my love. I think I had forgotten how much I need your love to make me strong."

"I do not think you should go," Maureen whispered and pulled her husband near, unsure where the words had come from. She knew she did not want to part from him again as soon as he returned, but there was more. A chill ran through her blood, and exhaustion sunk through her making her wonder if Ferdy wasn't right. Maybe all this magic hadn't made her well. Maybe it had only hidden the trouble.

Colum locked his arms around her, kissing slowly down her neck. "I do not want to either. But the boys are worried for Rowan." Colum paused, and swallowed heavily, a bit of tension raced through him. Maureen began to wonder what he was hiding from her now. But he breathed out, and kissed her neck once more before pulling his head back to look at her. "And for Petal. Keagan worries one or both of them will turn on the other."

Maureen breathed out shaking her head. "Then you must go. But do not go in fear. What worry you carry will guide your path, or what hopes. Follow hope."

Colum kissed her brow. "I shall go only to bring them home to see your handy work."

Maureen laughed softly, giving over to his attempt to lighten the mood.

"What does happen when it rains?" he asked again, with a Ferdy like grin.

Maureen rolled her eyes but sent a bolt of her power into the air, calling forth a tiny shower of rain. At once the ivy eating away at the roof leapt out across the gap, different strands of the vine criss-crossing like a woven basket to make a canopy above them. The rain pattered against the leaves and the faintest scent of it enveloped the room, but beneath the canopy Maureen and Colum were safe from the storm, locked in the arms of their beloveds.

More Important is Life

"What did you mean by all death is important but more important is life?" Rowan demanded the moment she'd swallowed the last of her breakfast. She'd eaten much more than she would have expected, berries, nuts, some bark and there was even some fruit, Rowan felt fuller than she had in days. But her impatience was not so easily sated.

"You must learn to take your time." Oona shook her head, but answered all the same. "I meant that it is more important to live than to die."

"And what does that mean?" Rowan asked. Riddles and puzzles had never drawn her much. And as impatient as she was now, they held no appeal at all.

"Quit thinking. Thinking left you convinced you've destroyed the lives of your friends. Thinking left your spy, Braden, afraid he'll never find love. And your father disowning you, and Ardal trapped in a cave from chasing down the wrong answers. Thinking is ripping Keagan apart, and leading Petal towards her most destructive impulses. Thinking left Gavin vulnerable to attack from the Fairy queen. What all of you need to do is believe."

Rowan thought her heart might have stopped. How did this dragon know so much about Rowan's life? How did she know so much about everyone? Rowan had not said any of their names to her.

Rowan's heart started back up at a wild pace. Hard as she tried to ask her questions calmly they came out in an anxious rush. "Has the Fairy queen gone to Turrlough? Do you know what she's done there? Is Petal alright? Is Gavin...alive?"

"You don't obey well, especially for a soldier," the dragon remarked, studying Rowan like she was a great puzzle. "You are too consumed with death," she said in a careful, impatient voice. "All you see is Gavin's death, Petal's death, Sorcha's death, Roisin's death. Your own death. And because death is all you see, your feet walk straight towards it. You can make your own future. Why do you want it to be deadly?"

"I don't!" Rowan shouted. "That is why I came seeking you. So I can save them all. So no one else has to die! I don't know how to save them all alone. Is it wrong for me to worry for the people I love?"

"Yes." The dragon spoke more patiently for Rowan's outburst. She walked around Rowan in circles. "Because you only worry. You forget to love."

"I love them."

The dragon shrugged. "You must have faith that all will end well, in order for there to be any chance that it is so."

"Wh...I...That doesn't make any sense!" Rowan shouted. "I should just sit around believing and then everything will work out? How is that better than working to make it right? And how am I meant to trust you with something as massive as the fates of those I love? I don't know you. And you don't even care! You said I shouldn't worry about these people because three new ones would pop up for each who died," Rowan screamed, waving her arms around. She had no center and she was trying to find one. She'd so desperately hoped this dragon could lead her to a new center, but nothing she said made sense, and the longer they just talked the worse the world became.

"I don't want three new people. I want the ones I have!"

Oona stopped circling and stretched her head lower, but further back, so that both her eyes were level with Rowan's. "*Good*. That is a beginning. That desire you are feeling, to have the thing you love, that is life."

"That is exactly what I've been talking about this whole time," Rowan growled, frustrated.

"No, it isn't." Unperturbed by Rowan's mood the dragon lifted her head, smiling. "You were talking about saving what you love. Not keeping it. There is a vast difference."

Rowan planted her feet to keep her balance as the dragon moved and made a current in the otherwise still room. Rowan was trying to save the ones she loved, not keep them? It was similar to the admonishments she'd heard all her life: that

Rowan needed to learn to enjoy the years of waiting, that she must plan for the future. It was similar and different, because Oona didn't just want her to plan, she wanted her to believe in the future. Believe that it would happen.

"I don't know that I can...stop fighting for them, and trust that all will work out," Rowan said honestly.

"Oh." The dragon shook her head. "There you go thinking again. I do not mean you give up on fighting. I mean you fight for the right things. Not just that they continue to be alive, but that they live, that you live with them. That you are a part of the world you are creating."

Rowan shut her eyes and tried to find the right way to want. The right things to fight for. A new center.

"I want...to bring the triplets together again. I want to have both my sisters with me, and love them, and laugh with them. And I want to form a new company of knights that is entirely composed of women. And I want for Gavin to be alive..." She broke off, opening her eyes, prepared to fight with the dragon, knowing those weren't the words she wanted. "I want to meet him."

The dragon was glaring in a sharp-toothy way that made Rowan gasp for breath. She felt her heartbeat, and it was lighter than it had been in the past year. Unconsciously, she began to rub a hand over her chest.

"I have felt his heart beat inside mine, and I want to go on feeling it," Rowan whispered, ashamed still to want things that so clearly served no one but her. "I want to be loved for who I am. I need to have the people I love in the world, so that I can know who I am. And I'm afraid if I do not hurry Sorcha will stop me. Please, will you help?"

Oona opened and shut her mouth a few times, shaking her head. "Well, that is not a perfect understanding, but you must start somewhere."

"So...you will come with me? You will help me rescue—"

"Stop. Breathe. Think," Oona instructed with a half smile. "You know your plans must change. You were not brought here for a horde of dragons to march out and fight *your* war. I will help you, but not in that way."

"First, it's don't think. Now it's think?" Rowan demanded. Her heart began to pound again. Harder and harder, seeming to pound in her head more than it did in her chest. "Fight for those you love. But don't *worry* about them while you're doing it. Are you just toying with me? That is a very dangerous thing to do right now. I need help! I know I cannot save them all alone. Do you want me to choose, is that it? Because I can't...I will not do it. But if you are toying with me I will find a way to destroy you. You are right in front of me. But they *never* are. And Sorcha never is." Rowan's hand twisted painfully around the rose hilt of her sword and tears bore into her eyes. "Everyone I love, and everyone I ever used to build myself out of are gone, or threatened, or have turned their backs on me. I am no one any longer, but a single minded need to save them, and the warrior I was built into."

The dragon had drawn back to watch her silently with her mouth agape. As Rowan's words dissipated from the air the dragon began to smile. The smile expanded and became laughter. It started out small then grew, shaking the floor. It grew larger and crawled up the walls. But it did not stop there. The dragon laughed so hard that water sprayed out of the falls, and bits of the mountain broke off and fell from the roof of the cave. Rowan jumped out of the rockslide of hilarity filling the cavern.

Rowan landed in a muddy spot of ground and got pummeled by some of the smaller flying rocks. Dirt and stones, and even a bit of water fell on Rowan. She lay under the onslaught, seeing over and over in her mind her father as he'd been in the dream, and all those faces behind her. She needed to be strong enough to save them. But she felt so small. She was so small. Why had she ever thought she could do this?

As the dragon's laughter quieted she leaned over Rowan and looked at her lovingly. Without saying a thing she opened her jaw and moved nearer Rowan. It should be terrifying, all of those teeth closing in on her after she'd threatened the dragon. But Rowan didn't fight, she didn't startle, she only lay there hoping if she died the ones she loved would be safe.

But the dragon wasn't looking for a meal. She closed her teeth gently around Rowan, and using her mouth like arms, she lifted Rowan from the ground and carried her to the falls. She deposited Rowan gently under the warm spray of water and took several steps away.

"It's alright, brazen warrior. I will help you. You needn't believe in yourself all at once. With all things time. It will come to you."

The Day of the Rose

366 days until Roisin returns

Balder watched Colum ride away from the window of his suite overlooking the courtyard. Colum's whole family was there to wave him off, and most of Rowan's court, even a few of the women training to be knights. All the people he cared for. Even Gwyneth was there. Perhaps if Balder had accepted Ferdy's invitation to dine with their family last night he would have been invited to see him off as well. But Balder wasn't going to let them manipulate him. Colum was not his family.

Balder marched out of the room, he had better things to do. Tomorrow was the last Day of the Rose before Roisin returned, it should be the grandest ever. Balder was sure no one cared that he was not there waving Colum off. No one had missed him last night and they wouldn't now. No one ever missed him.

Of their own accord, his feet led him to the portrait hall. He stopped before his mother's portrait.

"That all began with you," he said aloud. "If a mother does not even want her child, who else will?" Balder turned his back on her as she had turned hers on him.

He walked on, flatly ignoring his father's portrait he walked instead to the portrait that was made in honor of Roisin's birth. He stood beside his throne with a hand on the back of Gwyneth's throne, where she was seated with Roisin cradled in her arms. Rowan stood a step down and to her father's left, at the very edge of the painting. She had her head back and her eyes staring right at the viewer, but she had not done very well at standing so for the portrait.

It was painted before Sorcha came. Before everything changed. Rowan had been too excited to keep still. Every time Roisin had cooed, or yawned or cried Rowan had to be beside her. Balder had considered having Rowan hold her sister for the portrait, they were so sweet together. But that wasn't how things were done. A king's heir was depicted in a pose of power, not mooning over their sister. A king's heir stood separate to mark them as above the rest of their family. Balder had heard his father's voice in the back of his head reminding him of his place, reminding him to teach Rowan hers.

He laughed bitterly, his father would have appreciated Balder making Rowan his heir. Other kings were not so confident that they would let a mere girl be their heir. It was a mark of extreme confidence to do such a thing, and to announce to the world that any husband she took would be merely a consort.

His father would have liked that. But his father would not have let Rowan forget her place for a moment. He would have been quite pleased with her training among the knights, crown princes generally did. His father would have liked Rowan. But she would have hated him. She would have chaffed as he told her what an honor it was for her to be allowed her birthright. She would have fought him every day as he tried to simultaneously make an heir of her and remind her of a woman's true place. They would have fought constantly. And his father would only have liked her better for it.

Rowan was exactly the sort of heir King Flint had wanted. Confident. Bold. Honorable.

Balder's eyes drifted to the right where Rowan's individual portrait hung. It was done when she turned twenty. Though she'd loudly expressed how pointless she found the tradition, she'd agreed when Balder pointed out that every crown prince on the island had a portrait made before he was crowned. In the portrait she stood with her head thrown back dressed in her armor with a hand at the rose sword hanging from her belt. She wore a flagrantly challenging expression, mostly because she had disliked the portrait artist.

The man had spent much of the time giving her suggestions of more lady-like ways she might be depicted. Even teasing that she should at least let him change the sword to a bouquet of flowers, and the armor to an extravagant gown.

"Maybe it could become the fashion," he said flirtatiously; unaware Balder stood behind them. But Rowan had not noticed the flirtation at all.

"I'd much prefer women in armor become the fashion," she'd snapped.

Balder had smiled and not bothered entering the room. Rowan had that man well in hand. He never needed to worry about her. She never needed him.

Balder shook off the memory. Rowan always thought she knew best. But she didn't understand as much as she thought. She ought to have listened to him. She ought to have learned a lesson, any lesson that Balder wanted to teach her. Not the ones his father would have wanted but the ones he wanted. She should have learned that there was value in being obedient, and in listening to those who had lived longer than you. She ought to have learned the value in minding one's king.

Balder turned slowly to the wall behind him. To Roisin. The last portrait of her in the palace left unmarred by Colum's brats. At once Balder's worries began to slip away. It didn't matter that no one else had ever cared to have him in their lives. Roisin cared. Roisin was three in the portrait and she gazed out at him with all her love and excitement. He'd had to sit just before her talking to her the whole time her portrait was painted or she'd gotten frightened. But she'd sat so well with him beside her, so sweet and obedient. She wore a soft white cloud of a dress gazing up with a sweet smile. She was perfect. She was not the sort of girl to need to challenge everyone around her. She had a gentle heart. One had only to look on her to know she would be a perfect princess.

"Your Majesty," a servant called out from the end of the hall.

Balder glanced back and nodded for the servant to approach. The man came forward with a slaver containing a letter. Balder lifted the massive and recognized the crest of King Alistair of Anwyn. Odd. Balder had not received official correspondence from the king in years. Perhaps he was pressing again for an official match between Braden and Rowan.

Balder was in a bad enough mood he might just agree. He'd allowed too many important decisions to be taken out of his hands as concerned Rowan. She was his heir, he was her king. If he wanted to organize a marriage for her she would curtsy and thank her liege for his consideration.

Balder forced out a puff of air glancing again at Roisin's portrait. She was always a comfort. Soon she would be home and things would all be well. Perhaps that was what the letter was about, a gift for the Day of the Rose.

When Roisin was home all would be well. Just a year now. He should have the bards prepare a tale for her, so she could know what had happened in the years of her absence.

Balder was barely paying attention as he read. It did not even engage his attention to read that Braden was missing. He thought snidely that perhaps all the royal children of the island were running away from their parents. And wondered why Alistair thought to bother him with it. Balder had better things to worry about than being blamed for a missing prince.

Annoyed with the letter, Balder cast it aside and walked out of the portrait hall in search of the royal bard.

365 days until Roisin returns

Keagan watched from the back of the throne room as the king ordered his servants about with a level of glee one generally reserved for celebrations. The Day of the Rose had never been a celebration. It was bad enough that Ferdy had invited the king to dine with them before Pa departed, and told Keagan about how Mama wanted them to try and at least be friendly with the king. Keagan had only let that go because the King had not accepted. But now Pa had left Keagan with the task of delivering the king his personal gift for the day.

He wanted it given in private, before the processionals of gifts arrived, which was why Keagan stood here, hidden in the shadows of the predawn throne room. He didn't think the king deserved any gift. And Pa had known it too.

"Rowan is one of your sisters, and that day is set aside to honor a sister she misses very much. We all know how much that day has hurt her in the past, but I truly believe she would want us to try to comfort her father in her absence. Are you man enough to do this for me?"

Pa loved throwing that word around as manipulation. The trouble was it worked. Keagan wanted his father's approval. He wanted him to look at him and call him a man. Even when Keagan was enraged with his father he wanted that.

"What do you mean there are less gifts than usual?" King Balder demanded in a tone of great offense. "This is to be the grandest Day of the Rose ever!"

"I am sorry, Your Majesty. But with Turrlough in mourning neither their royal family nor their citizens sent any gifts. From the nation of Anwyn we have a few gifts from citizens, but the royal family has sent nothing. And—"

"And!" Balder screamed enraged that there could possibly be more.

"There were some rumors of citizen's of Anwyn being turned around on the roads by the king's soldiers."

"Over this nonsense with Braden?" The king dismissed, annoyed that the world was conspiring to ruin his plans.

He seemed a bit off. When the sun had set, last night marking the beginning of the Day of the Rose, King Balder had sat next to Queen Gwyneth for the recitation of his daughter's birth as usual. But he'd seemed confused when Gwyneth, for the first time ever, told the story as it had actually happened, with Rowan blessing the Rose Princess and choosing her name.

Keagan moved slowly away from the wall, he envied Ferdy's ability to vanish completely. Keagan had to sneak around in truth.

"So the boy hasn't returned home, I've never seen any sign that he likes his home. Why else would he spend half his year here? We've no use for him until Roisin returns for him to marry."

Keagan paused, that sounded—odd. The king had been trying to marry Rowan to Braden for years. Perhaps Balder was not close to Braden, but he knew Rowan cared for Braden. That, if nothing else, should make him worried for Braden if he had indeed failed to return home.

Why hadn't he?

Keagan's own parting with Braden had been fraught. Braden had seemed truly shaken when Keagan said he would be their traitor.

That had been Keagan's intention, but now Keagan didn't know how to feel. Perhaps Braden had just gone to the Fairy queen to betray them. But what if he'd been so worried Keagan was right that he ran off somewhere to hide. Or was injured? Braden was Keagan's oldest friend. He didn't want him to be hurt. He hadn't even wanted that when he spoke to him. He'd just wanted to...be able to trust him. He wanted him to be his friend still as he hadn't seemed recently.

"Why hasn't Braden made it home yet?" Keagan asked, abandoning his plan to hide until the servants were gone. "He left here weeks ago."

"He is probably just hiding," the king said. He was responding to Keagan, which Keagan supposed was something, but he did it almost as though he were responding to a passing servant. His eyes looked right through him, and none of Keagan's concerns even nudged his consciousness.

"Don't you think Rowan would want us to be sure Braden is safe?"

"What?" The king glanced at Keagan as though he were insane. And even though Keagan knew it was probably something Pa would say was bad, Keagan poked into the man's mind.

For a man who'd seemed so giddy he had an awfully quiet mind. There was a soft, pleasant tune playing in it, and a little girl calling him Papa. But there wasn't much else at the surface. So Keagan dug deeper. There was a frightened angry pocket behind a heavy, barred and chained door. Keagan was sure what he was looking for was in there. So he pulled at the chain. But the king fought him, both with his mind holding fast to the chain, and with his words aloud.

"What business do you have here, Keagan? This isn't a place for children."

"My father asked me to deliver you his gift for the Day of the Rose," Keagan answered, but internally he was fighting against the king's mind. He was stronger in there than Keagan would have expected. He fell victim so often to the curse.

Keagan stopped fighting as the thought struck him. Keagan examined what he could see of the king's mind. Roisin, soft music, laughter, peace. But nothing real. No Rowan. No Sorcha. No worries.

Keagan shoved the small wrapped package into the hands of the king, though he should not touch him without permission.

Keagan could not stand on ceremony now. Not when the king had once again given in to the curse. Keagan knew precisely what was behind that door in Balder's mind now. He didn't even need to unchain it to slip inside.

Rowan—shoved into a corner and locked away. Rowan with her eyes filled with tears, but her head high, standing between her sister and death. Dying to save the Rose Princess, all the while knowing her father loved Roisin more. Rowan—cut down again and again.

Keagan hated this day. He hated this man.

"It's a carved rose," Keagan informed the king coldly. He spoke on in anger, trying to remind the king of the daughter he'd forgotten—*again*. "It is a match to the one on *Rowan's sword*. Pa said he carved it for Roisin at the same time as he made *Rowan's*. He thought she would like sharing something like that with her sister. But he never knew what to put it on. So Mama added it to a special leather girdle that she made herself."

Keagan felt the king's mind trying to make sense of the words but refused to stand around waiting to see if he would succeed. He vanished, hoping ugly tasks like this were not what it meant to be a man. Because he didn't like it one bit.

Darling Girl woke with the dawn. It was different sleeping outside with Aunt A. Sweeter and sadder at the same time. When she was waking she half expected to feel Vincent brush her awake with the back of his bushy tail, but all the animals had been banished from the forest. All but Mother. He sat on the branch directly above where Darling's hammock was hung, watching over her. He'd waited for her to wake, she could tell. As she sat up he screeched high and loud, and fluffed out his feathers around him with a good morning shudder.

"Right you are, Mother," Aunt A said in a sleepy voice. "Happy Birthday, Darling Girl."

Darling giggled. She wondered if Mother had truly been wishing her a happy birthday. And if so, how had he known it was her birthday. He hadn't been with her on her last one. Not even a full year he'd lived among them, but he felt like family to Darling Girl.

"Thank you, Aunt." Darling rolled out of her hammock, curling her toes into the dewy damp ground and glanced up at the window of her room. Where the man she'd rescued was still sleeping. "Do you suppose he will wake today?" Darling asked.

"In fact, I am quite certain he will not," A said ominously then rolled out of her hammock, with a bit more of a plop than Darling, and so much more energy. She smiled broadly. Always when the sun was on her face, and Darling was beside her Aunt A had a smile on.

Before either of them could say more Aunt C came walking out of the kitchen bearing a tray with a pot and four mugs. Aunt B followed her out holding a table. She set it down under a tree and walked back into the cottage for chairs as Aunt C laid out her tray.

"Good morning, Aunts," Darling sang out loudly, and couldn't help another glance at her window.

"Ha," Darling heard Aunt B grumbling. "Getting up before the sun, nonsense."

Darling smiled, because she did love them best when they were being themselves, and Aunt B hated mornings with a passion.

"How do you know the man will not wake?" Darling asked Aunt A, turning her way slightly. She didn't notice Aunt C before her until Aunt C took Darling by the shoulders and kissed her on the cheek.

"Because if he interrupted our last birthday keeping you all to ourselves, he would find us all quite angry hostesses," Aunt C answered for her sister, and Darling forgot all about the man.

"Your...last?" Darling whispered and tears burned at her eyes.

"We agreed to make that announcement together," Aunt B very nearly shouted, approaching the hammocks and haphazardly dropping the stools she'd carried on the ground.

"I...I knew you were all preparing for me to leave, but I hadn't thought it would be quite that soon." Darling said. She hadn't really thought of how soon it would be. She knew, it felt like she'd always known that one day her life here would come to an end and she would go into the real world. Sometimes she had even wanted it. Desperately. But right now, with all of them surrounding her, and the words, *the last,* hovering between them all like a choking billow of smoke, right now it felt terrible. She never wanted to be parted from them. Never.

"Your real family have been missing you for some time," C said, but her voice was so choked it sounded like the voice of another woman. "We cannot be selfish with you forever."

"No. Not forever," A agreed. "But today we surely will be."

"Yes, we will," B grumbled and stretched her arms forward to pull Darling into her arms alone.

Darling laughed a bit against her aunt's chest, but her tears fell as well. *The last.*

The Phoenix Theory

Under the warm stream of water Rowan slowly calmed. The water was like that cleansing, soothing. Rowan appeared to relax, but her tears continued to fall, helping her release the things she'd held onto.

"It is so quiet here," Rowan spoke into the spray of water. "All I can do is hear their voices. And think of all the things I've done wrong. As I searched for you I fought off the frightening thoughts with motion, or speaking aloud. But I could still hear the words like they were a part of my blood. So I would say over and over again 'you will find the dragons, and when you do they will help you, they will know how to fix things.' I thought you would fix everything I had made a mess of."

At the edge of the water, Oona watched Rowan as she had once watched her own children. It had been years, so many years since she had such a young thing around her. She had forgotten the doubt and the guilt that were so much a part of growing up. How had she grown past that?

Oona glanced over her shoulder to their other companion. Rowan's silent, invisible guard. She nodded her head sideways to ask if he wanted to answer this new fear Rowan was expressing. But he just watched. A good sort of guard for the girl, he did not interfere, allowing Rowan to set the road and see what she needed to see on her own, but without actually being alone.

Oona returned her gaze to Rowan, her newest student. She should have tired of this by now. None that Oona had led here over the years had ever really listened, and none had stayed. But...she never did give up on the beautiful creatures who wanted to make a better world. She just hoped this one was as capable as she seemed. Despite the doubts tearing her down.

"One cannot fix the past," Oona said quietly. "One can only be reborn from it."

Rowan wiped the water out of her face, and stepped out of the spray.

"I was a mother four times over once." Oona went on. "And four times over I lost my children. I lost their children—every one. And for every loss, I was reborn. Everything dies, but it comes back to us."

Rowan walked slowly out of the hot springs, shivering as the human parts of her reacted to the change in temperature. Were she only a fairy her body would respond differently, it would adapt. There were even humans who lived in enough harmony with nature to do the same, but this girl was still very much a child of her upbringing. Her body expected to be cold, so it was. But that was something she would learn with time, for now...Oona would help her feel the warmth her body expected.

Oona yanked a branch off of a tree with her mouth and plopped it down in front of one of the boulders she had knocked loose with her laughter. She dug deep into her being, where all the love and loss lived. Where the fire lived. She dug deep, and expelled a bright stream of flames, setting the branch ablaze.

Rowan's breath caught and her eyes widened with that same lovely wonder they'd held when she looked at Oona and asked if she was eternal too. Then, like the creature Oona had come to know from years of watching, Rowan shut off her wonder, trying to understand the lesson in Oona's words. Trying to prepare for her great battle. Always trying to improve, this girl. It should make Oona more hopeful. None of the others had been so intent on self improvement. But this girl was so certain she was flawed that she doubted her own instincts, be they bad or good.

"You don't mean actual death do you?" Rowan asked. She leaned against the boulder and stretched her arms out to the fire to warm them.

Oona shrugged. "What makes one death more real than another? Eternity exists in one moment, and in every moment combined. You understand too much as a human."

"No," Rowan said slowly, far more calm for her wild outburst.

It really had been a delight to see. She pent so much rage in. Oona doubted even Rowan knew how much she held in.

"You mean, I cannot go back. I am never the same again so it is like being born over and over."

"Yes. And no," Oona said with a smile. Knowing this girl disliked the duality. Too focused and literal was she to appreciate the magnificent fractal that was life.

"*You* hold too tightly to the past. When one is reborn, one can carry the lessons, but not the guilt. Rebirth *lightens* one, so they may fly. You, Rowan the Eternal, are very much a creature of the ground, held down because you will not *let go.*"

Rowan looked vexed and impatient as she tried to puzzle out Oona's words. She shivered and pushed away from the boulder, walking to where her packs lay.

"What are you doing?" Oona asked.

"Finding something dry to wear."

"Why?"

"I'm cold. I will warm up faster in something dry," Rowan said exasperatedly.

"And I take it you thought all those things just then."

"No," Rowan shrugged. "I felt cold so I came over here to fix it."

"Instinct." Oona nodded with a smile. "And look, you haven't killed anyone."

Rowan grumbled as she shook out a dress that had been lying over a rock to dry. "Give it a moment. It always takes a moment."

"Maybe you are seeing connections where none exist," Oona remarked. "You are still thinking. You need to simply get up because you are cold, and fix it the way instinct tells you. You need to look into the expanse of stars and beg them to *make her eternal too,* just because the moment calls for it."

Rowan let the dress drop to her side as her gaze returned to Oona.

"You know even that?"

"I know eternity."

Rowan's voice shattered pitiably as she asked. "How does it end?"

Oona moved her face low, so across the foot between them their eyes were level. She smiled. "It doesn't."

"Will I defeat Sorcha?" Rowan pressed desperately.

"You did yesterday." Oona shrugged. "But you have not today. And we will have to see about tomorrow. Eternity is a sea, it keeps churning and every time you encounter it, it changes."

Rowan shivered again. Turning her back to the dragon, she stripped off her ruined wet dress and kicked off her wet shoes. She wiped as much of the wetness as she could away with the wet dress and quickly pulled on the dry one. She lay a fresh pair of stockings out but did not pull them on. Instead she pulled a brush from her pack.

With the brush in hand Rowan walked back to the fire on bare feet. She sat on the boulder and pulled her long braid over her shoulder. It was wet and matted, there were bits sticking out here and there. With a sigh, Rowan put down the brush and set to untying the leather strap that held it all together. It didn't look especially comfortable to untangle. Not for the first time in her life, Oona was glad to have been born a dragon.

"You are too human," Oona repeated. Shaking her head at Rowan.

"Was I not too fairy a while ago?" Rowan grumbled, annoyed.

Oona ignored the snide remark. "Fine, think. But think of the right things."

"Which are those?" Rowan said between her teeth as she tried to untangle a particularly gnarly knot from around the strap.

"The thoughts you banished while you sought me. You can only let things go when you confront them. See the truth or the lie of them and put them into their proper place."

Rowan stopped untangling and looked up at Oona, and Oona could hear her thoughts so clearly, she might as well have spoken aloud. *All four of her children died, probably at human hands. And her grandchildren too. Why would she want to be reborn after something like that? I would want to die.*

"Do you not want to die already?" Oona responded to Rowan's thoughts aloud, startling the girl. A heavy silence held the space a moment.

"I did want to die," Oona said. "And I did. Over and over. That is how I am here now. Death freed me to live again. To be here, when you needed someone to show you the way. Tell me." Oona moved closer, her voice and her stare intent.

"What are the things you cannot banish? What makes *you* want to die? I promise —I will understand."

Rowan looked down, her fingers had gotten tangled up in her hair. Oona worried that perhaps she was pushing the girl too far too fast. She could feel how wildly unstable Rowan's emotions were; angry, frightened, heartbroken...lost.

The trouble was, Oona knew the answers to too many of Rowan's questions. Haste would be of no help to her, but there was not much time for leisure either.

What makes you want to die? I promise I will understand. The dragon's words echoed around Rowan's head.

Rowan hadn't really thought of herself as *wanting* to die. She wanted to live, she'd even begun to believe that she would live when the battle was over. But... there were moments when she had wanted to die, and they lived inside of Rowan. They were a part of her makeup as much as this hair was.

Why were these called the ends of her hair? These bits were with her when she began. The origins of her flawed self.

"She died so I could live," Rowan whispered, untangling her fingers from the hair. She did not need to say her mother's name, Oona would know.

Rowan's fingers moved slowly up the braid. "And here, when I first felt my father's fear of me. Here where he burned her garden. And here where my grandmother called me poison, and cursed me to *kill* my sister." Rowan gasped. "I had only just met Roisin and already I loved her dearly, but my grandmother spoke her curse and I could see myself killing my sister. I can never escape that. It has altered me completely."

Rowan looked up at the dragon, begging understanding, begging her to take that part of her away, it would help so much to be rid of that moment. But the dragon said nothing and in the silence other moments fought to be expelled.

"Here where I threatened my great aunts. Here where I gave them my sister, out of fear. Here where I did not see, or did nothing to stop my family from being taken over by the curse."

The list grew and grew as long, maybe even longer than the braid her fingers climbed. "Here where Eachann told me that I was little in power, age, and understanding. Here where I proved him right, banishing a man in a fit of temper and making an enemy for life. Here where I rejoiced again and again over frightening my stepmother. Here where I asked my friend to risk his life as though it was a game?" As she spoke Rowan's voice grew in volume and intensity and the dragon watched so silently that Rowan nearly forgot she was there.

"Here where I put an entire nation at risk to have a friend in this struggle. Here where my father asked me to *die*. Here," Rowan stopped and her voice broke. "Here where I asked the world of Petal. Here where I broke her father's heart and splintered their family. Here where I threatened my stepmother's life. Here where my knights returned, broken men for my answers. And here where Braden learned to fear me." She paused, staring at the braid, everyone learned to fear her eventually.

"I saw nothing as two brothers drifted apart. I nearly destroyed Colleen, a wounded child, because of my own fear. And here—where I abandoned Eachann like my father would abandon me. And here I celebrated a truth that would make my father hate me, and told him in a cowardly way, in a room of *my* friends. Here where cherishing my letters with Gavin risked him and everyone he loves. And here— where I lied and I left because I could not stand having destroyed Petal." Her voice broke and tears fell from her eyes. "Here –"

Rowan broke off, with the braid still grasped in one hand she bent to her sword belt and yanked out the dagger, she sliced clean through her braid.

"Here where I doubted Petal," Rowan said in an oddly flat voice. The severed braid clasped before her. Rowan stared at it, frozen for a long moment. Then with a giant gasp she cast it into the flames before her. Wanting more than anything to kill the memories.

Rowan looked into the fire in horror as if to cry, but burst into laughter instead. She lifted her left hand to what was left of her hair at her neck, and fell forward at the waist under the power of her amusement.

Rowan had never felt quite this light before. She laughed even harder.

Apparently pulled along by Rowan's near hysterical burst of humor, Oona began to laugh as well.

It was a while before they settled. It happened slowly for the dragon, but suddenly for Rowan. She had laughed for some time watching her hair turn to ash, but the moment the last bit of hair curled up in flames, turned black, and crumbled her hilarity stopped.

She stared into the flames where her hair used to be, not even aware that her right hand was pulling through the hair at her neck.

"I don't think that's what you meant," Rowan said at last.

The dragon sputtered, cutting off a laugh by biting her own tongue.

"Maureen is going to kill me." Rowan shook her head, looking down at the knife in her hand. She giggled at the sight then looked back up at Oona. "Is that it then? Am I reborn?"

Oona couldn't fight the laugh any longer. "You tell me?"

Rowan sighed, her hand was still running through the bit of hair that she had left. "It's so much lighter… I never realized how heavy it was."

Rowan looked back at the fire, thinking of how it had consumed her hair, consumed the weight of all she'd carried. She smiled. Her past had been consumed by flames. She played with the new ends of her hair. No, its new beginnings. Rowan let out a shuddering breath, rolling her shoulders. She pulled the rest of her hair out of the bit of braid it remained in, and shook her head. A smile blossomed slowly over her features.

"It's like the scars," Rowan said, rubbing her thumb over the spot where her scars used to be. "The ones the pendant melted away. They're gone...but I can still feel them."

"When you need to," Oona replied. "Only when you need to."

"I think I could fly now." Rowan's voice drifting over the air lightly.

"Then I will have to teach you. And," Oona broke off smiling broadly. "For such a small woman you are a bit dramatic. I'll have to teach you to breathe all that fire you hold inside."

Rowan looked up at Oona, a grin lighting her face. If she could not have a dragon by her side, perhaps Rowan could become one.

Awaken, Charming Prince

362 days until Roisin returns

Braden woke slowly. He knew he was awake, though he could still hear the lovely hum of a woman's voice like the vision Sorcha had shown him. He must have had the dream again, but he couldn't remember it, it was just the hum, floating through him, making him feel safe. Braden fought the part of his mind that was stirring. Fought the yawn he felt on his lips, and his groaning muscles. He didn't want to wake. He didn't want to see the blood that must be dripping down his body. He just wanted to lay here with her voice in his mind, soothing him. He wanted to see her face, and know peace.

But already daylight was heating his eyelids, and he felt his body shifting towards it as one does after a long, deep rest.

Braden groaned, and blinked. But the hum did not go away. He examined his surroundings in surprise, sitting up with a start and yanking the covers to his neck. He was not on the south road, bleeding his life away. He was most assuredly not home in Anwyn Palace. Nor was he in Stonedragon. Where was he?

It was an odd room. There were animal footprints painted on the walls, and bits of wood, rocks, a snake skin, even some empty egg shells scattered on the tops of dressers, and along window sills. The room was full of frilly soft sheets and pillows and curtains. It was soft, but it was odd.

Braden looked down at the bed, and jumped again, noticing the lacy sleep dress he wore. That most certainly wasn't his. Where were his clothes? His sword? Where was he?

Braden slipped out of the bed as quietly as he could, and went on a quiet search for his clothes and weapon. Every drawer had women's garments, and none of it in a size appropriate for him. Whomever had gifted him their sleep dress was not the occupant of this room. Braden was on his hands and knees searching beneath the bed when it occurred to him that he had been stabbed in the gut.

He felt the pressure and sting of the blade sinking into his flesh. Felt the excruciating pain of climbing onto Yseult's back, and the jarring jab of every stomp of the horses hooves. He should be dead. He should be in excruciating pain. Glancing around for observers, Braden pulled up the sleep dress to examine himself, but he could find no wound site. Nor even a scar.

Braden let the gown drop as thoughts fell one after another out of his head until it was empty of all but two things, the woman's hum, and a growing fear.

What was this place?

The man in Darling's bed still hadn't woken. Aunt A said not to worry, that his body had been through a great deal and it simply needed time to become itself again. Roisin hoped that was so, but the longer he slept the more she worried that she had saved him from death only so that he could sleep his life away. What sort of life was that?

Roisin was anxious for him to wake, for several reasons. She had nearly as many reasons as her aunts. They just weren't the same.

It had been decreed by an eerily unanimous tribunal of the aunts that:

> *No one was to mention Friend, neither by name, nor to reference any relationship to her.*
> *No one was to share with the man that they too had been gifted magical rose petals.*
> *Everyone should pretend they were citizens of Anwyn and resided in one of its forests.*
> *Under no circumstances should Darling be alone with the man.*

The last decree was the most galling. She could understand why they shouldn't trust the man, but why should they not trust Darling? She'd said just that, to which Aunt B of all aunts had laughed and laughed.

"Darling Girl," she'd said, still chuckling a bit. "I wouldn't trust you as far as I can throw you."

It was clear that all of Darling's aunts agreed that Darling was just a bit too eager to speak with the young man, and generally too trusting, and possessed of ulterior motives regarding Friend.

That they were right about some of those things did nothing to stop Darling feeling offended. It was unendingly frustrating. They just didn't understand. They knew everything, or most everything. While Darling knew nothing. And here was a chance to know more about the real world! To know more about Friend. Perhaps even to learn her name, even if only to see it written. Darling could keep the name locked up in the most secret part of her heart if need be. She just needed to know it. She needed to know so much. Every day the hunger to know more of the world grew.

Soon, Darling was going to leave this place; so soon that it kept her up at night with a mixture of terror and joy. She was going to go into the real world and learn her true name, find her true place, her true family. And it felt lovely, and awful in the same instant.

She'd spent many a secret quiet moment, not plotting to see the man, as her aunts suspected, but staring at the portrait Aunt C had made for her birthday. It was the secret project she had been working on so long. A painting of Darling and her three aunts all together. Just the four of them alone. As they would never be again by this time next year.

For so long Darling had wanted to know *so many* things. Why she was hidden? Who her family were? Why they had not come with her? Where she belonged?

But for every one of those questions there was a fear she could not shake. Fear that the evil she hid from would never be defeated. Fear that her true family were not the ones of blood any longer. Fear that her first family had gone on without her and wouldn't truly want her with them. And worst of all, fear that she had been separate from the world so long, and found such powers in herself that she no longer fit anywhere but here. She wanted to know the world, but it terrified her as nothing ever had, she wasn't sure she would ever be ready to leave this place.

But upstairs, asleep in her bed was an...innocuous way to know more of that world. Someone to ask where she fit. Someone to ask what sort of world Friend lived in. What the flowers looked like? And what sound was made by trees that could not pick up their roots and go for a wander when they felt like it? She could ask him about her friend's beaux for surely she had many. She could ask if he was one. She could ask everything she'd ever wanted to know.

But for her protection the aunts were forbidding her asking anything. She had to pretend to be someone she was not, living somewhere she was not, knowing even less than she already knew.

It was a torture of protection.

Darling had walked out of the moss circle and into the world knowing full well she was walking closer to danger. Now her aunts would deny her even that!

A breathy whinny at Darling's shoulder startled a giggle out of her.

"Well, good morning, beautiful lady. I am sorry I did not see you there." Darling leapt down from the tree branch she was sitting on and petted the horse's nose, rubbing her own against it.

She framed the horse's face in her two hands so she could stare straight into her eyes.

"Have you seen the world? The danger and the beauty? Do you know my friend?" Darling whispered in the horse's ear.

And, special creature that it was the horse nodded and nudged the pocket where Darling kept her own rose petal.

Darling giggled in delight. She hugged the horse around the neck and whispered in her ear. "She loves us both. Do you go on adventures with her? Isn't she the most fearless, exciting woman in the whole world?"

The horse nodded slightly but also seemed to give Darling a vaguely incredulous look. Darling didn't mind the horses lack of enthusiasm. She spun away, humming her favorite tune and plucked the horse an apple, holding it out to her so she could have a bite.

"Your pardon, good lady, if I might beg one answer of you," a voice called out from above and behind Darling. She glanced back to her bedroom window and saw the man leaning out, very awake, and standing, an excellent sign.

"Where am I? How did I come to be here? And who are you?"

Darling beamed up at him. "To which question would you like your one answer?" Darling teased.

He blushed.

Darling plucked a second apple without looking, and held it out to the horse in the same manner. All the while she stared up at the man in her room. Her heart beat wildly and she felt like she could leap from the ground and float all the way to him. At last, he was awake.

"Shall I bring you some tea? Then we may speak." Darling didn't await an answer. Any moment her aunts would realize he was up and go interrogate him before Darling even had a chance. She ran into the house as quietly as she was able.

"B, he is connected to our great niece. She sent him," C argued quietly.

"She sent the horse," A countered. "He rode it."

C and A were in an unsteady truce about the man upstairs. But every day that passed without him waking felt like a day closer to Sorcha finding them, as far as B was concerned. She was always Sorcha in Bride's mind. Bride could think of herself as B if necessary, and her other sisters as A and C. That was no trouble. But even trying to force herself to think of her elder sister as "Her Majesty" took concentrated effort. She was Sorcha. Wiley, playful, *hungry*—Sorcha. She'd always been so hungry, and so talented. But she never did get what she needed from their parents. Alma and Nessa were the only daughters who could even garner their father's attention, with so much of his time devoted to studying eternity. And Mother...Mother was too much like Sorcha to ever give her what she wanted.

It was always Nessa to give love in the old days, when they were girls. Nessa had been like their second mother, and Sorcha their mad aunt. When they were together, when their parents were not around, then all of the girls were happy and hopeful, and loved.

But then Mother and Father would speak to their children, and Sorcha, who had always been the most talented of them would be all but starved of attention, as Mama tried to draw the best out of all her girls and Father would only speak to his favorites. Sorcha had gotten so hungry, and taught herself more and more, to attract their attention.

"I thought we settled this when we saw the petal she sent him," C said impatiently.

"You settled A's concerns."

"Some of them," A clarified.

Bride felt her muscles tightening, not with the tension growing in the room, but with the tension growing in her mind. She wished, oh how she wished Sorcha would just stop this. Stop fighting eternity, stop punishing her sisters and herself by extension. Bride had...adored her sister. Nearly worshiped her. Sorcha knew so much of the world, and what she didn't know she sought out. She didn't dislike dwarves, and leprechauns and humans on the basis of their species. She didn't call Bride nearly human behind her back, because she could never focus her magic without a wand of willow in her hand. Sorcha loved variety, loved different, loved life.

When they were children.

But all the things that had made Sorcha Bride's favorite big sister as a child made her nervous now. Because Sorcha's love, and openness and wonder had been transformed to anger, a closed heart, and power over others. If that boy upstairs had ever, even for a moment, met that sister, then he should not be here. Because Bride was certain Sorcha had continued to expand her powers. There was surely something in him that connected him to Sorcha. So Bride didn't want him anywhere near Darling.

"But if anything I am more concerned now. C—" Bride cut herself off. She'd been about to use her sister's name, her real name, her full name. Knowing full well the trouble it could cause. This was just the sort of thing she'd been concerned about with the man's presence. He was an unknown factor, a rogue wave, a tornado, a volcanic eruption in their otherwise calm lives. He needed to leave before he irreparably changed the harmony between them.

"She'll fall in love with him," Bride said flatly, not her true argument, but...it was a part of it.

Love at such a young age was an all encompassing monster. Darling would be altered forever by love.

"She is a bit young," C admitted. "But why shouldn—"

"Do not start in again with that drivel about love and its power. C, she's naive, she has never known true heartache, or jealousy, or possessiveness, or anger, or betrayal. She knows nothing of the darker side of love. And that veil in his head says plainly he is someone's spy. Let us assume the happier of the two options and say he does not work for—Her Majesty," B forced the name out with a heavy sigh. "If he has that veil it can be assumed that he is expected in her presence at some time."

"In fact, I can even feel the imprint of her magic across the surface of the veil." A nodded. "She has tried to see past it."

B waved a hand hoping C would begin to see reason. "Even were all cases the best, Darling should know more of the world before just loving the first man she encounters."

"Just because your love betrayed you does not mean Darling's will betray her," C argued gently.

"He did not betray me," B disagreed calmly. "He simply did not share my feelings. I long since came to terms with that. I am not relating this to my past, but to your's, and our eldest sister's, and—Her Majesty's." If her sisters noticed B hesitating every time she addressed Sorcha they gave no sign of it. "When Darling loves, I want it to be love, not proximity and curiosity. She deserves better."

Silence fell between them, and in the absence of their own voices they all heard the young man upstairs, heard Darling responding flirtatiously, though she had no prior experience being so.

Cianna nodded heavily. "She is bucking against the restriction. If we do not allow her some room she will rebel, in truth. Let me go. I will...camouflage myself and watch them."

The others nodded and C made her way up the stairs, painting herself like a canvas so she blended with each surface she passed.

B watched her go, but her heart was far from settled and for the life of her she couldn't think of how to properly address her concerns with her sisters. Though they had been beside her all these years, it only now occurred to B that there were chambers of her heart still secret from them.

She was still humming. It filled his mind. Promising him peace and safety. And she was so lovely, and gentle and good. She was perfect.

Over the last year Braden had learned to be suspicious of perfection. He couldn't explain how he was alive. Or how he'd come to be here. He didn't even know where here was.

He remembered an attack. He remembered the bird crying out above him, and a searing pain, and darkness and cold closing in around him. Death, he thought. Then he remembered Yseult showing up, and climbing onto her back. Then nothing. This was a trick. He didn't know its purpose, but it must be one of Sorcha's tricks.

That sweet voice humming to him, and that lovely feeling of contentment that coated his being from the moment he saw her, they were tricks as well. He needed to know to what end. And if he was in some strange half-world between life and death, or …he knew not what. All he knew was this was not real.

Braden searched the room for something he could use as a weapon. Clearly his weapons had been taken from him for a purpose. To trap him, to have him at a disadvantage. He grabbed the sharpest thing he could find, a flat rock from the woman's collection.

He heard a noise at the door and moved across the room to open it, shivering at the air fluttering under his sleep dress. No wonder women were of such delicate constitutions if they were constantly contending with drafts. When he opened the door he saw no one. He leaned out slightly, and felt another quiver go running down his spine. He jerked back, looking around him, and shoved the door as he went.

"Ouch," he heard a young woman's voice exclaim.

Braden spun back, the rock gripped tight in his palm. "You weren't there a moment ago."

"I was climbing the stairs," she said patiently, but with a mildly reproving tone that reminded him of his sister when she felt she was owed an apology. She was younger than he'd taken her for at a distance. But he couldn't let that fool him, Fairy could appear years younger than they were. Her appearance of sweetness could be a trick as well.

He eyed the lack of tray, "Oh, and what of the tea you promised?"

"I put the kettle on, it takes a moment." Now her eyebrow went up. But after only a moment she relented and smirked. "I am sorry." She waved at his nightdress. "Your horse had no packs, so you had to borrow from us."

"Yseult?" Braden asked cautiously, trying to feel out this new tactic of sweetness. What did she want to know from him?

"Is that her name? She is lovely. I thought all knights rode stallions. Are you not a knight?"

"I am a knight," Braden ground out, unconsciously crouching into an attack ready pose. "Where am I? Who are you? Where are my things? How did I come to be here?"

"I will explain it all to you, I promise," she said sweetly and tipped her face up towards him in an innocently coxing pose. A tingle raced through Braden, telling him to trust her, to give her whatever she wanted. To do something so she would smile at him again.

Those were precisely the sort of feelings he had when he looked on Sorcha. Braden clenched his muscles against a strange wave of exhaustion at just the thought, he had to hold out. What if this was Sorcha in some disguise, trying to steal some knowledge from him? What if she had found a way past the veil in his mind and this was all a trick she'd planted in his brain?

"Answer me," Braden growled.

She drew back slightly, and her eyes grew larger. And when her answers came they were in a flat informative tone. "I am called Darling Girl. You are in my home. The horse brought you to me, so that my aunt and I could save you."

"Darling Girl?" Braden rolled his eyes. "What sort of name is that?"

"The only kind you shall be given," she returned in an injured voice.

Braden had a sudden flash of memory, of a short woman and a tall woman standing over him. Neither was this girl, but the short woman had called herself Antidote. And now he was speaking to *Darling Girl*, who was trying flirtation to manipulate him. They were all playing some game to him, he just hadn't sussed out its purpose yet. He refused to allow himself to be moved by her play at pique. "Where is here?"

"Perhaps you should sit, you look a bit...uncomfortable," she suggested in a solicitous voice.

Braden was beginning to sweat, his face felt hot, his head was pounding and he couldn't seem to get in enough air. He was trapped in a prison, designed to look like that beautiful vision he'd had of the future. He had to escape and get back to the real world.

So he could die in a puddle of blood in Anwyn forest, making sure Rowan was alive.

Braden lunged for the girl, grabbing her by the arm and shoving a rock against her throat. "Where am I?"

The girl screeched, but before he could even feel guilty for the attack he was thrown across the room and back onto the bed by a force he couldn't explain. A woman...*manifested* between him and the girl.

"You will not find us so easy to overpower. This young lady deserves a good deal of the credit for saving your life. You should be bestowing all your thanks and charm on her, not your rage. Rest. You are overtired."

"I..." Braden tried to speak, tired to apologize, or ask again where he was. But he could no more make his mouth work than he could make himself sit up. He fell, quite literally, fell straight to sleep.

Forever Drafts

owan lay on her makeshift bed of blankets trying to sleep. The dragon was settling under the falls for her rest and it seemed to Rowan the best way to adapt to her schedule was to force herself to sleep whenever the dragon did. But forcing oneself to sleep was harder than it seemed.

Her fingers kept curling through her shortened hair and a million thoughts raced through her mind. She wanted to be up, running through exercises, marching out to challenge Sorcha. Anything really other than laying on the ground during what felt like midday trying to sleep.

She could still smell the slightly acrid scent of the braid she'd burned. She could see it, curling up and turning black, in her mind's eye. Maureen used to comb that hair. When Rowan was little she would gather it all together between her hands and rub her face in it.

"Oh, what a wonderful rag this makes," Maureen would tease as she pretended to mop up her brow with it. Or her voice would turn quiet and far away. "Your mother had lovely hair, but not like yours. Your's is wild, like sheep fluff, or dandelion wishes twirling through the air. Your mother would have adored your hair, she would have made you sit in front of her all day just to play with it."

Rowan remembered pretending to be anxious to get away, begging Maureen to hurry up. But it was always pretense. She would have sat for hours letting Maureen play with her hair because she felt so...loved and peaceful when she did.

It was rash cutting it off. That hair held good memories as well—

"You are thinking far too loudly for me to get any rest," Oona grumbled.

"Would you prefer I get up and exercise?" Rowan asked dryly.

"Yes."

Rowan very nearly did it, but despite the dragon's sharp tone she doubted Oona was serious. She just wanted Rowan to be quiet. Oona liked her routine, Rowan supposed.

"What do you do here when you do not have visitors?" Rowan asked. She had liked some of the solitude while she traveled, but she missed having people around. She didn't think she could stand to stay in such solitude forever. It would be torture being alone with her thoughts.

"I use the waters to watch the world. I look into the past, and the present, occasionally the future. I come to know eternity, and occasionally lend a hand to... my favorites," Oona replied with a small chuckle.

"Am I one of your favorites?" Rowan asked. "Is that why you brought me here?"

"Oooh, yes." Oona shifted under the falls so her body was under it, but her head stretched out and lay on a rock across from Rowan. "I have been watching you with interest nearly from the time you were born. For most creatures I like to watch their lives unfold, I like to watch them blossom, and add to the great work of art that is eternity. But sometimes I am too curious to resist a peek at possible futures. I was too curious with you."

"You know my future?"

"I know...its potential," the dragon corrected. "I have watched you live and love, and die a thousand ways. I have watched you defeat your enemies, and be defeated by them. I have watched you defeat yourself with fighting so hard you failed to recognize when the fight was over," the dragon chuckled. "You are a creature with a great deal of fight inside. Sometimes I have seen that fire burn so brightly that you died, consumed in it—but your fight lived on so powerfully that others took up your mantle and fought in your place."

Rowan didn't much like the sound of that. There seemed to be rather a lot of dying.

"But," Oona said just when Rowan was beginning to feel a lack of air. "I have also seen the potential inside of you to transform all of that battle into something far more powerful. I have seen you turn enemies into friends, and inspire some of the ugliest souls in eternity to repair themselves. I have seen you inspire wonder, and magic, and unity. Sometimes through your death," the dragon said casually. "But sometimes through how you live your life. But most of all what I have seen from you was a hungry, curious heart. Like my own was once. And I wanted to meet you, to talk with you, to know what, if anything, entering this cave would change in your path."

"What has it changed?"

Oona smiled tiredly. "Well, it has shortened your hair."

Rowan snorted, and stifled a yawn.

The dragon yawned as well. "Don't go looking for your end before you have truly begun," the dragon advised. "And don't worry about what was lost in the fire, it was only hair. The memories remain with you."

The dragon shut her eyes and really in a matter of moments was deep asleep. Rowan yawned again, but rather than making her feel tired that second yawn seemed to pop a bubble inside her and bring her fully awake. She sat up. If Oona could use the waters to see into the present, surely Rowan could as well.

Slowly and quietly Rowan stood and crossed to the stream that ran off away from the dragon. Rowan sat at the edge of the stream and curled her legs under her. She stared at the water for several long moments but it looked like nothing but ordinary water. Maybe she should drink it. Maybe she should wait until nightfall and ask the dragon how to go about it. But Rowan felt...tingly. She felt her own power nudging her to *make* this discovery. Magic was so much more wondrous when she came to it on her own, in the quiet hours when others slept, or when she sat on the edge of a mountain looking off at the sunset, or wandering into her garden and found a doorway to another world.

Rowan stretched out a hand and began stirring gentle circles in the water. Around and around and around, watching the water ripple out from her fingertips. Slowly, her fingers faded from her vision. The ripples began to meld. And another place revealed itself to her.

It was a meadow, there were hills and trees in the distance, and around her a group of about fifteen fairy children. Rowan had never seen so many fairy children. And Petal was among them. They were spread out on the meadow, each with a mound of dirt before them and an adult fairy walked between them giving instruction.

"Today is just a draft, do not be afraid to rush into it, and try all your ideas at once," he said with a grin. "Let all the dreams of your heart pour into that ground, and imagine what can be. Maybe you want to create a home like the world has never seen before, maybe you want to create one that reminds you of your favorite memories, a castle, a cottage, a bog. Do not let anything limit you today."

A boy raised his hand, and the teacher crossed to him. "Conductor Web," the boy said when the fairy stood above him. "Mama said any heart home we make will have a doorway somewhere within Fairy Cache, even if it is only a draft. So, should we not want to make our best work?"

"If it is in your heart it cannot be wrong, Weever."

"Yes. But sir, it will be here *forever*," Weever exclaimed.

"Everything you do will be here forever. Not just your heart home, and the things you can find in Fairy Cache, but your actions as well. They will touch the lives of those around you and remain forever, reshaping each life that comes in contact with them."

"Conductor Web," a little girl interrupted, waving her hand in the air. "If our homes will all have doors in Fairy Cache, does that mean the finished version? Or will there be doors to each stage?"

As everyone spoke and fretted Petal worked. Rowan watched the cottage Maureen's family had lived in take shape, but there was a moat around it, and trees growing out of the walls, and the door looked a bit like the gaping mouth of an alligator. Rowan grinned. She wondered if Petal's imagination would nudge the real cottage to change from such a distance. Maureen had certainly been altering it, it was only fair that Petal should have a bit of sway on it as well.

Conductor Web chuckled at the girl and looked around at the sea of nervous faces. "Weever, when you go home do tell your mother what a disruption she has proved today. Auburn, there will be a door to each stage of your heart home within Fairy Cache. But not in the public halls and the keys to those doors shall belong to you, and all of the doors will reside within the final stage, once it is complete, so that you can walk through and see the growth. One is not beautiful because one is perfect, one is beautiful because one develops. Please, show us your worst. So that when you show us your best, we are all astounded."

The meadow, and the children, and Conductor Web began to fade away, the last things to fade from sight were Petal's heart home, and the smile on her face.

Rowan swayed, exhausted, yawning before she even knew she was seeing the cave around her. She blinked several times, because the world was fuzzy, and raised her hands to rub her eyes.

"You ought to sleep now," Oona instructed. It took Rowan several seconds to clear her eyes enough to find the dragon wandering around on the other side of the cave. She looked like she'd been up quite some time. "That was quite the feat, seeing into the near past on your first try at the seeing waters. But it took most of the day, and a bit of the night as well. Sleep. We'll get to work when you wake."

Rowan couldn't think clearly enough to develop a response. And didn't even crawl over to her makeshift bed. She just lay backwards next to the stream and rested, imagining Petal's power stretching out to change her home. Altering the world.

The Cache of the Fairy

361 days until Roisin returns

"The prince was allowed to take his daughter, and fairy we're following to be sure he left but—"

"But?" Sorcha asked impatiently.

Brook drew in a deep breath beside Sorcha. They were walking down the hall to Petal's room. Sorcha was in a calm enough mood that Brook's hesitance was unexpected today, and Sorcha couldn't explain it.

"Well, they boarded the ship, but we are certain that the family never reached Heigh. And another girl went missing from her village."

"Stop!" Sorcha threw up a hand coming to a sudden stop, her heart, her breath, everything frozen on angry teeth inside her.

"Tieve!" Sorcha shouted. Now she understood. She turned her gaze on Brook as they waited for the caretaker of Fairy Cache to appear. Brook sunk back with her eyes on the ground.

"Your Majesty," the sweet, questioning voice of Tieve preceded her appearance in the hall. She appeared before Sorcha at a bow, this woman who appeared all of six, though in truth she was nearing four-hundred-and-seventy. "How may I be of service?" She rose and smiled up, patient and solicitous.

Sorcha waved at the door to Stonedragon. The *altered* door to Stonedragon.

"When did this change occur?"

Tieve stepped towards the door. Once an arched door of cold grey stone, it was now being slowly covered by intersecting vines of daybreak roses. Tieve reached out and caressed a single blossom.

Sorcha squeezed her scepter and felt her magic dive angling into the crystal atop it to keep from striking out at the ancient woman before her. No one struck out at the caretaker, least of all Sorcha. Already this woman had cause to criticize Sorcha since the exterior of the palace must be hidden now.

Sorcha had never liked her and the fact that she'd been aging backwards for the majority of Sorcha's life only made her that much more annoying. Every year she looked younger and more innocent while the palace festered.

"Should we hide the blight, Your Majesty? Would it not be easier to repair with light cast upon it?"

Sorcha all but growled at the memory.

Tieve at last turned back to face Sorcha with a slight smile.

"Only this morning, Queen Sorcha." Tieve nearly appeared to smirk as she answered Sorcha's question. "Your granddaughter is reaching out as she has not before, making her presence known to the Fairy."

Sorcha saw steam rising around her. She could feel Brook growing anxious, but Tieve was calm as ever.

Sorcha hated the woman. If it would not cost her half the fairy, Sorcha would stab her with the infinity poison tucked away in her private chambers, and watch the woman wither and writhe in agony.

Sorcha bit back the words of protest. No other fairy but Petal ever called the Knight of the Rose her granddaughter. But if Sorcha argued with her Tieve would win simply by refusing to change the door. The palace made its own choices.

Sorcha swept around the woman. Enough was enough. She would destroy that girl, her every bit of power. She would show the fairy just how human and how poisonous that girl was. And the palace would repair the door. On its own.

Late at night she marched towards her study. She was certain she knew where that poisonous knight had disappeared to now. There were few places as fortified against magical intrusion as the well of the future.

Oona's home.

That dragon always was a meddler. In the past, Sorcha had not cared. She'd even helped her for a time. Displeased with Nessa for bending to Tyrone's fear of dragons and conspiring with humans to see them destroyed. Nature did not make mistakes; just because dragons were not loved by fairy did not mean they should be destroyed. Banished from the island fine, but eradication was wrong. Every creature nature created had a place in the world.

So Sorcha had gone behind her sister's back, making sure Flint's bride would be one who would help the dragons he tried to kill. But now Oona was interfering in Sorcha's plans.

Oona always had played favorites.

You should be content with fairy powers, Sorcha. You are an unrivaled force already, but I fear dragon magic will drive you mad.

Drive her mad. Ha. Sorcha was perfectly sane. And she'd learned all that dragon had refused to teach her on her own.

Sorcha let her magic race down the hall in each direction, watching to be sure she wasn't seen. This door was known only to her. It had been even when Nessa was queen. Even Tieve didn't know it fully; she could feel its existence, Sorcha couldn't prevent *the caretaker* knowing that, but its form Tieve could not make out and it moved about the palace constantly so none but Sorcha could find it.

When she was sure she was alone, she fit the end of her scepter into a notch on the wall, revealing a door that had not been visible before. Sorcha pulled the door wide and walked into the dim, obsidian cavern. At once, from deep in the cave a fiery light illuminated the sharp glasslike walls, making them flicker.

Sorcha walked deep into the cave, and heard Quion moving around, his chain dragging across the cave floor. But she had no need for a dragon tonight.

Oona ought to feel guilty for her refusal. Sorcha never would have needed to hold that baby dragon captive if Oona had been willing to help. But Oona was jealous of anyone who rivaled her knowledge of eternity. She'd wanted Tyrone dead for the same reason, because he was a threat to her power.

Now she would help that Knight of the Rose. Offer her powers she'd denied Sorcha. Offer her succor and encouragement, all in an attempt to kill Sorcha. Well she could just keep trying. Sorcha was smarter than her. Sorcha had more powers than fairy, more powers than humans, more powers than dragons. Sorcha had seen and studied and now understood more types of magic than any creature in existence.

Sorcha found the slab of obsidian that served as a desk and lifted the bundle of letters Petal had stolen for her. She'd not really had much use for these but to show Petal where she belonged. But now... Now Sorcha was glad some instinct had told her not to burn them at once. Prince was proving difficult to fully command, even as a bird. These would help.

Sorcha untied the pack of letters and flung them apart. They scattered about the room and Sorcha lifted her scepter, releasing a sliver of magic to slide between the letters and find her one that stood apart, one that had power both from Gavin and from that girl. To find one where he'd shared his soul.

A letter flew into Sorcha's hand, she unfolded the well worn pages and read.

> *Dear Rowan,*
>
> *I have some news for you, but it will have to wait for another letter, as today is special; today you were born.*

Sorcha's hands clenched around the page. Born. Such a lovely, mild word for the violence that brought that aberration into the world, and destroyed Sorcha's daughter. Sorcha nearly rent the letter to pieces just for the affront, but she forced herself to breathe. To calm, and to read further.

> *I have decided that I tell you far too many sad stories. So I shall tell you a funny one today. But you must keep it a secret. No one outside my closest family knows this story. With good reason, my mother would kill anyone she heard repeating it, and she is a very gentle woman.*
>
> *The story goes like this: When my father was a boy, he had two older brothers and so was certain he would never be king. So he could be incautious—*

Sorcha skimmed the story. She was familiar with most of it. Embellishment aside, Sorcha actually quite liked their love story in the past. But when she reached the last lines of the letter Sorcha released a small chuckle, at last something worth the reading.

> *Since I know you think I invent all my tales, I offer you this proof as a birthday gift. My mother's bells.*

Sorcha wondered just what that Knight of the Rose had shared of herself to inspire such personal revelations from Gavin. His mother's true heritage was a secret kept only between family. Sorcha only knew it from the delving she'd made into the mind of the young couple when they'd met during the war. But the Knight of the Rose was not sweet, or caring or...anything that should inspire such trust from Gavin. Was it just him? Was he so trusting of everyone but Sorcha? He'd clearly trusted Eachann, Sorcha could feel him on every bit of that palace when she'd been there. Honestly that had made her angrier even than Gavin's failure to keep to their bargain.

He trusted Eachann and that girl, and nationless fairy. He trusted that magical woman he'd played fiancé with. He gave himself over to belief, especially when that belief was held back from him.

I offer you this proof.

The Knight of the Rose was forcing him to prove himself; over and over. And he just ate it up.

Sorcha smiled, spinning the letter around before her. After a moment she cast the letter aside, it fell in with others littering the ground. If all Prince wanted was to prove his worth to the girl, Sorcha was happy to give him another chance.

Men were too easy. Sorcha leaned back, sending a pulse of magic out through the cavern and into the palace; calling for her new pet.

Anyone who knew of Sorcha's, sometimes called vindictive, nature would assume she hated Thaddeus and his bride. After all they had taken sides against her. And they had raised their children to distrust Sorcha, and fight her at every turn. But the truth was, she quite liked them. She was endlessly intrigued by their continuing love. Aya should not have been the sort of woman to accept the life she had in that palace. She should have rebelled, she should have...killed her own husband rather than let him languish as he did under Sorcha's sleeping spell. But Aya bent. She bore up under hardships, and...boredom. She sat by her husband and continued to love a man that could not give the emotion back. It was astounding. Sorcha often felt bad about the lengths to which she had to punish the couple. They should be happy.

She did not, however, hold any such feelings for their offspring.

A flash of purple light delivered Prince into the room, flapping and screeching and looking anywhere but at her. His eyes fell on the letters scattered about the ground and he dove for them.

Sorcha chuckled. "Can you feel it, Prince? All the passion, all the heart, all the longing you put into your letters? Your love never did the same."

The bird moved about the ground, gathering the letters neatly together. Shuffling and rearranging them until they were in some proper order. Sorcha smiled at the exercise, it was sweet. Hopeful. And revealing. There was still a great deal of Prince Gavin in the bird. She would not have expected quite so much.

Perhaps it was his mother's magic working on him. Preserving him. Wanderers did tend to have a certain resilience. Prince found the ribbon that had held the letters together and between beak and talons tied a gentle knot around the letters. He clamped a talon tight around the ribbon, and beat his wings to rise off the ground, hopping forward a bit when he did not have enough momentum.

"Come here, silly boy." Sorcha chuckled. "Wherever do you think you can get with those?"

He obeyed her command at once, though he would not look on her. Flying to her seat and depositing the letters on the obsidian table beside Sorcha.

He sat atop the letters, guarding them, his talon digging deeper and deeper into the pile. Sorcha ran a pair of gentle fingers down the bird's head and leaned in so her lips touched just over his ear holes; she kissed him gently.

"Your destiny hasn't changed, Prince," she whispered and watched his talons tear deep into the pages. "Go find her, so we can torture her together."

At Sorcha's order his talons slid open, releasing the letters. He took off into the air. He flapped before her, with his gaze locked on the letters as if he wanted to stay. Sorcha sent him off with a wave of magic.

He might not want to, but that bird would do Sorcha's bidding. And that girl, and her...inability to love like him, would help Sorcha make Prince's transformation complete.

Needed

360 days until Roisin returns

Darling Girl sat in the tree, rubbing her arm where the man had gripped her two days ago, before Aunt C put him back into a magical sleep. It didn't hurt. Aunt A had long since healed it. But she could still feel it. No one had ever grabbed her like that, no one had ever frightened her like that. Her heart had stopped and she'd thought for a moment that she was all alone. She thought he would kill her before her aunts could get there. She still felt sick from the fear. And so...stupid.

Not only would her aunts *never* leave her alone. But he hadn't been trying to kill her. The man was as frightened as she had felt. He thought he was being held captive. He thought they were enemies. He came from the real world. And the real world, it seemed, made you doubt every show of kindness.

She'd seen that in her friend. Not the violence, but the doubt of any love. More and more Darling Girl dreaded the real world.

When she'd first lain the man on her bed to convalesce she'd thought him so lovely. His face was smooth and gentle in his sleep. And his hair was soft as rabbit fur. He'd looked so much like, and so different from what she'd expected that she was dying to know him. She thought the real world must be lovely, if it sent her such lovely things.

But now she was unsure. All of her aunts had tried to help her understand his fear. This place was foreign to him. How could he know she was a friend. But Darling had never been mistrusted before and she did not like the feeling.

She heard a screech of her window opening and looked up. He was trying to climb down. He had long stockings covering his feet, but wore nothing else besides the sleep dress. Where could he possibly expect to get that way? He would freeze before ever he got out of the Enchanted Forest.

He was almost to the ground. Darling Girl looked away as the wind tugged at the dress, and he fought it down, barely managing to catch his footing.

"Why, Yseult?"

"Ack!" He shouted and lost his footing completely. He fell the last foot from the trellis, and conked his head on the side of the house. He let out a curse Darling Girl had never heard and gripped onto the trellis with both hands, fighting down more of that violence she'd witnessed in him.

Darling Girl felt the pain in her arm again, and her heart beat harder. She scrunched her body closer to itself, shivering.

He noticed and took a deep breath. He shook his head and his eyes filled with confusion.

"I...didn't mean to...hurt you, before. Are you alright?"

Darling nodded, watching him cautiously. She managed to uncurl herself a little, but she was still too edgy to uncurl completely.

He could tell, she saw him fighting through his own confusion and violence. Trying to find his better self.

"Some charming prince I've proved to be," he said in an almost pained voice. "I seem to do the wrong thing more often than not." He sighed. "Yseult is not mine, she belongs to a friend. A lady knight."

Darling Girl beamed beginning to relax. She'd known her friend loved the horse, but she hadn't realized the horse belonged to Friend.

"She said if a woman could be a knight, a mare could be a warhorse. She claims she named it Yseult so there would be no doubt in anyone's mind that it was a mare. But I think she just liked the love story surrounding that name."

"About the knight who falls in love with the woman he is escorting to marry his king?" Darling was truly enthralled now. One of her feet leaned out of the tree to touch the ground and her body bent towards the visitor.

The man nodded, and beamed at Darling. Then he tilted his head ever so slightly, and Darling felt a change in him. Or not so much a change, as she felt another layer to his gentle entreaty and softly shared story.

"Darling," he crooned coaxingly. "Do you know where my things are? I must escape. I'm needed elsewhere."

"Needed by this lady knight?" Darling asked.

His eyes narrowed as he dropped the pretense. "Who do you work for?"

"No one," Darling replied at an utter loss. Who did anyone work for?

"I won't lead you to her." He advanced on Darling with that violent fire back in his eyes. But he stepped on a twig and howled in pain. That only served to make him angrier. But this time Darling was not afraid. She saw Aunt B walking into the garden.

They'd been watching her the whole time, hadn't they? Knew perfectly well she was talking to the man, talking to him alone, and about Friend, and they let her. Because they trusted her. But they stood by to keep her safe. How could any other family be truer than this one?

"I won't betray her. You can tell So—" The man choked on the word, grabbing at his throat.

Aunt B walked forward and stood between them. "A name is a powerful thing, boy. You will not utter any others here." With that B lowered her wand and the man stopped choking.

He looked between B and Darling, his rage palpable, and his desperation. He truly thought he was needed, didn't he? Darling thought about what she knew of Friend, she was strong and valiant, but more than that she had powers even she didn't understand. If the horse was hers she had sent it to this man when he needed it, and she had sent them both to Darling to look after. Friend was well.

As soon as she thought it Darling had a terrible flash of her nightmare, Friend bleeding on a battlefield with men dead all around her. Fear shuddered through Darling's being, and a few tears sprung from her eyes. Aunt B lay a hand on her shoulder and pulled Darling nearer.

"What is the matter, Darling Girl?" her aunt asked.

Darling looked at the man, she had trusted him implicitly until he woke. Since then she had felt sympathetic, frightened, angry and friendly towards him. He was so different from every person she had ever known. All she had ever known was trust, but she didn't know now if she should trust him, he kept threatening her, but he knew her friend, and she seemed to trust him. Darling looked up at her aunt.

"What if he is right?" she whispered.

Aunt B shook her head, and kissed Darling's nose. Darling felt oddly shy of the affection with that man watching. Her eyes kept darting to him, though her aunt was comforting her.

"Have you had the dream again, Darling?"

Darling shook her head.

"Have you seen her dead another way?"

Darling shook her head again.

"You will find eventually that fear and love can combine and make one feel all important, and necessary to the continued life of the one you love, but just because we feel that way doesn't make it true."

"She is magnificently powerful." Darling beamed at her aunt. Then she spun to face the man with her head in the air superiorly. "Your friend is a knight. She can take care of herself. And anyway, you will be no use to her dead, you ought to come in and finish healing, *Prince Charming*."

Aunt B scoffed at the name. But the man released a breath, and as he watched Darling walk by him. She would swear she saw both more trust than before, and more fear. Wasn't that odd?

Braden sat at a table in a neat kitchen, still wearing a sleep dress, and only now did he truly examine his surroundings. The home was warm, if small, and welcoming. It looked like the inside of a tree, which made sense, as he was clearly in the presence of fairy. Exclusively female fairy, the worst kind in his experience. But he began to doubt that they worked for Sorcha.

But he couldn't be sure. It was just too similar to the cottage of his dream. Darling Girl was too like his fantasy woman. Too many things were too perfect for him to trust.

"I would have my clothes returned to me whatever their condition," Braden said sharply. He sat on one side of the table directly across from Darling Girl, as one of the women, the one who could become invisible, served him a thick welcoming stew.

He had to bite his cheek to keep from diving face first into the bowl.

She said nothing to his remark, but paused before moving away and gave him a sharp look. "You have not eaten in over a week. You will want to begin slowly."

Braden fisted his hands in his lap, refusing to eat until everyone had food, as manners dictated. When Darling Girl was served she looked sharply at Braden, then in a sweet, instructive tone looked up at the woman serving.

"Thank you, Aunt."

The woman laughed and bowed her head slightly to the girl, moving off to serve the other women. Both of whom thanked her politely before she sat.

"Are we on the lands of Anwyn?" Braden asked.

Darling Girl opened her mouth to reply, but it was the one who called herself Antidote who spoke first. "Yes."

"Good." Braden filled a spoon to the brim and lifted it into the air, giving it a moment to cool as he made his next statement, intending to shock the room. "I am your prince, B—"

His lungs closed and he dropped the spoon with a clatter. Looking to the end of the table where the woman with the wand sat. She held it out with a brow in the air.

"Will it make things clearer to you, boy, if I tell you to call me Bailiff. You are a prisoner here. This is not your palace. And in this cottage no true names are spoken."

"You would do well to mark her even outside the cottage," the yet unnamed woman said. "You were brutally attacked, and left for dead. Should any be seeking you, your name would be an easy way to find you. Fairy, you understand, have powers of perception beyond those of humans. Even human princes." She tilted her head aside at the last statement, smirking.

Bailiff lay down the wand and Braden could breathe again. He didn't know what to do for a moment. Then Darling Girl nodded to his food.

"Are you not starving? Eat."

Braden lifted a spoon to his lips and closed his mouth around the warm, soothing brew. At once he felt that same feeling of peace he'd woken to filling his bones. One bite had his stomach growling hungrily, demanding more. He forgot for a moment the need to be on his guard. The need to discover who these women truly were and just ate.

He was halfway through with the bowl before he realized the others were just staring at him. He began to shove the food away, afraid of being poisoned. But the unnamed lady laughed, and simply ladled more soup into the bowl.

"Why save you only to poison you? We had simply forgotten how entirely oblivious a man is with food before him."

At this the other women laughed, and Darling Girl looked between them.

"Is he quite normal?"

Had she never met a man? The thought came and went as even the worry over poison could not overcome Braden's hunger. He was starved. And he needed his strength to escape.

359 days until Roisin returns

Keagan's direction had been to head towards Mount Kieran. No easy task for a group of fourteen soldiers with no real cause to be on the lands of another King. They followed the Liadan as far as it took them on Stonedragon's lands, then crossed into Anwyn's lands at a less guarded area near a wood. They were doing their best to be circumspect as they made their way, they couldn't afford to draw attention to themselves.

He felt certain Rowan had been avoiding roads as they were. As he went he considered all the aspects of a knight's training that he had ignored with Rowan. She had never been taught to make camp, or hunt. She had never been taught to prepare food, or how to know poisonous plants from safe ones. He felt in his heart that she must be alive. But the further along he went the more he realized he hadn't properly prepared her for the world. Just for the fight. One fight.

He had to find her. If for no other reason than to tell her how much more there was to life.

They were well into Anwyn's lands and there were too many villages and patrols for them to move quickly. Scouts were sent ahead pretending to be travelers to decide the best routes. More than once they had been forced to spend an entire day hiding in some glen or bit of wood while soldiers passed.

"There seems to be an unusually large amount of military activity in the region," Colum's scout reported. "They were searching every home in the village four miles up the pass. No one would say what they were looking for, but they weren't polite about it."

"Do you think they've received some sign of us passing?" Colum asked. They made an effort to clean after themselves at each nights encampment, but as they traveled there was no way to move quickly and cover one's tracks.

"I don't think so," the man said. "They were searching such small areas it wouldn't make sense that all fourteen of us and our horses could be concealed."

"Very well. We will keep moving, but remain vigilant."

"Sir, I hesitate to suggest it, but we may want to skirt a bit nearer to the Fairy border," the soldier suggested.

Colum felt his heart leap at the words. Had he been waiting for someone other than him to say it? He knew his heart wanted to be as close to Petal as he could be, but not only could they not possibly find their way onto Fairy lands, but he also doubted even if they could that they would ever find themselves near to Petal. What was more, the border fairy were nearly all tricksters, placed there to spin humans about and make them lose themselves in the woods. They might set the group back several days, or divide them completely.

He couldn't let Rowan down that way.

Already Petal is gone, but at least she left knowing how much we love her, knowing her place. Rowan never had that.

"No." Colum heard the choked nature of his own voice but did not try to conceal it. "We cannot risk it. We will keep to the outskirts of the villages, looking for any sign of the princess, and keep at least five miles between us and the border of the Fairy Realm."

Colum pressed on. He was tired. This was far too long in a saddle for such an old man. But he had a daughter to find and he could not stop until he'd done it. He needed to rebuild his family.

Dressed in Armor Made of Pain

"*D*ragons do not just use the magic of nature, and eternity to fuel our power," Oona was saying as Rowan leaned against a boulder to listen, they hadn't gotten to the flying, or breathing fire portion of learning yet, apparently the dragon wanted to give a history lesson first.

Rowan was unusually calm about the whole thing. Watching her hair, and her pains burn up in the fire had been...unexpectedly cathartic. She wasn't anxious. She wasn't crushed under guilt or fear. She was just here, learning what she could, until she knew how to help the people she loved.

"We feed our magic with our own pain. A single dragon is born with access to all the pain, and suffering, and lessons of its ancestors, and in this way we become stronger with each generation."

"Truly?" Rowan asked doubtfully. "I would think you would become weaker with each generation."

The dragon smiled. She stood at her full height, and stepped into the dancing lights of the cave. When she stood, bathed in light her scales which Rowan had originally taken for a dusty grayish color, glistened like iridescent stones, one moment looking green, the next bluish or purple, even red. She lowered her head so it was directly across from Rowan.

"You still do not understand pain. Look at my scales. Soldiers tried to pierce this hide with spear and sword. Some were even successful. Traders tried to rip the horns from my head to make potions." As she spoke, different sections of her scales caught the light, and it was as though Rowan could see the violence upon the creature. Her heart broke for Oona, such a gentle woman. But Oona smiled.

"Do not fear your pain. Do not fear the creature who is stronger than you. Do not fear what you might suffer at their hands. All of it will become a part of you. And it will be—*terrible, wrenching, destructive agony.* But when that agony has passed, you can take that pain and shape it, and beat it, and fire it, and forge yourself a suit of armor through which no weapon can penetrate. *You* are the forge of your own destiny, your own emotion, your own impact upon the world. What others do to you might harm you, but what you do with that harm belongs only to you.

"Every one of these scales I made for myself from a pain I had suffered, or a pain my ancestors had passed on to me. Dragons did not always appear this lovely. We looked like...very large, horned, four-legged turkeys."

Laughter exploded from Rowan with wild shock. She'd been sinking lower and lower with every word the dragon said, aching for Oona's losses, and thinking over her own and the...poor way she had responded to them. She spent so much of her life feeling like she was a creature of Sorcha's making, but...it wasn't so. She was a creature of her own making, and she had been allowing Sorcha's anger to mold her.

She could have been happy.

Well, she could have been happier.

Rowan continued to laugh, much softer as the dragon moved to sit across from Rowan.

"You seemed to need that." Oona smiled.

"I did, thank you." Rowan beamed at her, but she was still too deep in thought for the lightness to remain. "How do I change?" Rowan asked. "I have spent so long looking at my pains and thinking of myself as this terrible creature that Sorcha was making into her weapon. I fight, and I race to try and stop her, to try and be someone else, but whenever she hurts me, I do what she wants. I lash out at those I love, or I pull away from them. I sent Petal. It always comes back to that. I knew it was wrong when I did it, but I hoped it was right too, but how can it be?"

"Very easily." The dragon dismissed. "If killing one human saves one hundred then it is right to do so. But it is still wrong, because killing is wrong, whatever the reason."

Rowan cocked up a vaguely annoyed brow. And the dragon responded by wiggling her eyebrows at Rowan.

"You are looking at life as if every action you take will be tallied and counted when your life is done and someone else will determine if you were bad or good." Oona shook her head. "Don't wait for someone else to decide for you. Do good. Do as much good as you can, and when you do bad make amends. Give more of yourself to the world. But the only way to do that, is to take the pain that lives within you, whether it is pain you have caused yourself, or pain others have inflicted upon you, and transform it.

"Let us take a more practical approach," Oona said impatiently. "I see your brow furrowing with thought again and we have already established that is not how you learn best."

Rowan tried to be annoyed at the comment, but it was a bit amusing. And honestly, she preferred a practical application to a philosophical conversation in most cases.

"Right at this moment, what pain do you feel most acutely?"

Rowan shrugged, she'd burned up her pains. Her hand rose to the new beginnings of her hair and twirled it through her fingers, the short cropped hair slipping away from her.

"What about sending Petal?" Oona suggested when Rowan did not rush to answer her. "Latch onto that pain. Feel the regret, feel its impact on those you love. Feel the loss, and the fear that you have changed the world forever with that choice."

Rowan caught her breath, it wanted to lunge from her as a sob though she'd thought all of this addressed already. She'd thought she was better. But...Rowan *had* changed the world forever, there would be no going back to the way it used to be. So that pain could never truly leave her, could it?

"Shut your eyes, and imagine that pain before you like a glowing disk, it swirls with emotions made into colors, it is warm and malleable. Take it into your hands and shape it like a piece of scaled armor. Work it with your fingers until it is tough and strong, and impenetrable. That moment will always be with you. So make it into a place of strength, a piece of armor that reminds you of all the pain a single action can create, so that you do not ever take so large an action without considering all the ramifications."

Rowan didn't feel the sort of lightness and happiness the dragon had shown as she spoke of where her scales came from. But she did feel the power of holding onto the mistake rather than hiding from it. She tried so hard never to think of it. Tried to shut that part of herself away. But if she held onto it, if she looked at it, she could be better than she ever was before.

"Hmm." The dragon sounded amused, maybe even pleased. "Open your eyes, little warrior."

Rowan opened her eyes and looked down at herself. Her right hand and forearm were covered in iridescent scales that formed a gauntlet and bracer.

"Ha." Rowan chuckled lightly. She punched her right arm with her left, the left bounced off with what felt like a million shrilly singing bones. But her right hadn't felt a thing.

"It's actual armor. I made armor!" Rowan exclaimed, still shaking out her left hand.

"Do you feel as heavy inside?"

Rowan looked up at the dragon shaking her head in wonder.

"But..." Rowan looked from her scaled hand back to the dragon. "How long can I maintain this? This is magic, isn't it? Will I be scaled forever? If I go into battle will I need to stop before I enter the fray and shape every piece I wear?"

Oona chuckled hard. "My word, but you do rush ahead of yourself. You will not be scaled forever, that was an adaptation dragons made over generations. You can maintain it...well, I do not know. It is not a lack of magic that would make it leave you but choice, or a power so jarring you forget your own strength, or... something else that I have not thought of yet." The dragon shrugged and smirked at Rowan's narrowed eyes. "Yes, it is magic, but not in the way you think of magic still. You think of magic as separate; it is in you, it is in you always, *whether you can find it or not.* Even when you fell unconscious from exhaustion, still the magic was in you. You simply did not know how to reach it.

"You would have to spare some thought to pulling on this armor before, or during a battle, but once the pieces are formed they will remain so unless you reforge them, so it is only a matter of calling them to the surface, not rebuilding them a piece at a time."

Rowan smiled wide. Now that had some serious potential.

The dragon groaned. "I was teaching you this to help you improve your inner self, not so you could have a new suit of armor to make war with. Ugh. Just as I said you are not a creature who is served by thinking."

Rowan grinned.

Magic Remnants

356 days until Roisin returns

Petal knew perfectly well she was being followed, she even had a fair idea of who it was, but she didn't alter her course. She was going to meet the wolf family. If Dervla tried to kill someone today, Petal would just have to stop her.

She knew it was a bit wrong of her to be so angry still with Dervla over killing Nolan, when it had clearly been an order from her queen. And Petal wasn't nearly as angry with Sorcha. But Petal felt betrayed. She was trying to help the Fairy as much as she was trying to help Rowan, and no one was learning the lessons. Dervla needed to learn to say no. Of her own will. It couldn't all be on Petal or Rowan. If it was then it didn't matter who the Fairy followed.

So Petal was angry. But she did not try to send Dervla away, because despite the betrayal in that moment Petal still believed Dervla would not betray Petal's secrets. And this was going to be a secret.

The Fairy queen was busy with something, she'd not seen Petal in three days, and Petal had used that time to teach herself a new trick. She learned to make fairy remember only what she told them.

So she'd told the guards at her door that she was sleeping and they believed it, even as she walked away. She'd told the moss and trees she passed that she was another fairy out for a silent walk, and they'd all believed. She could do the same to Dervla once this was over. Or she could gamble, see if she was right about Dervla only following Sorcha's direct orders.

Petal wasn't sure which she would do. But she had some time to decide yet.

Petal crested the rise of a hill, with open fields all around it, but only once she was at the top did she recognize where she was. The old tree that had housed her and the other girls. Petal felt her cheeks lifting and ran towards the tree.

She'd missed it. Petal ran to the entrance and threw open the door, racing up the three steps until she came into the wide circular room with the—

All of the cots were gone. There used to be sixty-one of them but there were none now. Petal walked into the center of the room and tilted back her head to stare up into the impossibly high tree. She remembered doing this when she first came. Staring up and up and wondering if the tree went as high as eternity went long. The room began to exude that stinging fresh scent Petal loved when she'd lived here, it was welcoming her back.

She smiled around her old cell.

"I've missed this place," she said aloud. Walking further into the room she saw the scratched up floor and gathering of leaves, fur and twigs that must make a bed for one of the wolves. There were other nooks like it around the room. Four in all. "I was so scared when I came here, but...there were times when it felt like the safest place in the world and the most daring all at once, isn't that strange?" Petal said. She wasn't really asking the wolf she could feel behind her, or Dervla, she was just talking.

She'd felt the wolf follow her in, but she hadn't heard it. He was very quiet. It was only the one wolf right now, the eldest. Lorchan, if Petal remembered the family right.

Not so strange, you are the most beloved and protected child in the world. Petal heard the wolf's reply in her mind and spun around, shocked. *But anytime we face our fears we feel daring, do we not?*

Petal had expected to feel the wolf's response. Feel if it was connecting with her words, or just with her power. But she had not expected to hear a voice in her head. Nor had she expected such a philosophical nature. And such a human voice. What she felt from this wolf was so different from the others. He felt human in everything but body.

And his body...he was the exact shape and coloring of a grey wolf, but so large. His head would reach as high as Petal's did if he stretched his neck up. He was massive. He could devour her, if not whole, than in two or three large bites. Petal shivered.

She watched the man-wolf pace the room like an animal would. Petal knew this was one of the wolves she'd been sensing since she helped Sorcha curse Gavin. But Malachy was the only one she'd ever felt this near and he howled and growled and felt nearly true wolf. Not so with Lorchan. He paused and hunched a bit lower, rolling his shoulders from one side to the next like a predator about to pounce. He was trying to unsettle Petal's observation of his more human nature.

Why did you come here? Lorchan asked.

"To see," Petal answered softly. Her heart was pounding like wild and she felt tingles all over her skin. Tingles of excitement. This wolf was *dangerous*, and he didn't like Petal quite as much as his brothers and sister did. But Petal was not afraid.

For one thing, she could now see Dervla hiding in the shadows against the wall. But mostly...she was Petal the Powerful.

This was the room where she'd taught human girls magic. This was the room where she'd made forever bonds. And faced her fear of being alone, of growing up, of being Petal the Powerful. Here she was strong.

Maybe that was why Sorcha made her take a room in the palace. The palace dwarfed Petal, but this giant of a tree *stretched* her.

"To see if I could fix you with my magic," Petal said, tilting up her chin. "Why did you come here?"

The wolf mewled almost a laugh. *To see.*

"The same thing?" Petal asked brightly.

Lorchan took to pacing again, wandering the edges of the room. As he approached Dervla's hiding place the fairy disappeared completely again.

No. Dervla had just moved, slipped into another shadow further up the tree. Wasn't that a neat trick? She wasn't flying. Wasn't clawing her way up the tree, she just sat on the shadow like it had a corporeal form.

"How old are you?" Petal asked when it seemed the wolf would not answer her previous question.

It's hard to say now. I was older than you when we changed. I remember that. I remember our home. And the day the Fairy queen came. His gaze shot to Petal and the wolf growled. *You may change my siblings back, if you have the power to do it. I promised them I would see them human again. I promise it as I fight them back from the brink of turning true animal—as our father did. So I will not stop you, if you wish to turn them back. But I will keep this form.*

"Why?" Petal asked in shock. "Do you not want to be yourself again?"

The wolf shook its head, turning his back on Petal.

I never lost myself. I know every moment of my life. I have only stopped counting the way humans do. This is me. He growled, showing all his teeth as he approached Petal. *And the fear I smell off your* queen *whenever I am near, tells me this form is the one I will need for my vengeance.*

Petal's eyes darted briefly to where Dervla still hid. She hadn't moved. Wasn't trying to kill the wolf, but that didn't mean she wouldn't if Lorchan kept talking of vengeance against Sorcha. Of course, he wasn't speaking aloud, so perhaps Dervla couldn't understand him.

"I ...cannot help you with that," Petal said. She didn't know why she shied away from making such an offer. Surely if she offered to help Lorchan she would be able to watch him more closely. It was not as though Petal expected Sorcha to live through this.

Petal walked to the side of the tree where her cot used to sit, to the place where the ivy had grown in, stretching a hole large enough for Petal to fit through. She couldn't remember what she thought this was when she came. An adventure maybe. To save the girls and be more powerful than the queen of the Fairy. But she didn't think she'd really understood that this was a battle. Not fought between armies, but no less deadly. Sorcha or Rowan would survive in the end. One of them would be queen of the Fairy. And the other would be dead. It was the only way. At least the only way either of them saw.

Petal toyed with the ivy.

She hadn't thought of this as a battle. She hadn't thought of herself as setting out to help kill a woman. But that was what she was doing. So why hesitate to offer such help to Lorchan, who clearly had reason to seek revenge? Did she want

Sorcha to live? Sorcha who showed Petal wonders and terrors with the same smile. Sorcha who doubted every love.

Petal looked at her hand, curled round the ivy, but saw the crystal there instead. She could feel Desmond's heartbeat against her hand and she knew as much as he had been angry with his mother, as much as he disagreed with her. He wanted her to live. And...Petal wanted to help him. She wanted him to wake to a beautiful world, a peaceful one, a happy one.

The necklace at Petal's throat pulsed. Petal looked down at it and saw the rose glowing bright, felt the power of it soothing through her. Rowan's mother wouldn't want Sorcha killed either. She wanted the same sort of world for her brother that Petal wanted. And she wanted it for Rowan as well.

Petal turned to face the wolf, a bit more confident now in what was right, though no more sure how to achieve it.

"What sort of revenge are you seeking?"

It doesn't matter. The wolf growled. *I do not need your help. My siblings are drawn to you, not me. What I came to see, little girl, is if you will be a help to them, or a hindrance. I came to decide whether or not—I should eat you up.*

"Oh, is that all?" Petal smiled broadly. "And have you decided?"

The wolf snorted, a large gust of air that blew up bits of dust and dirt from the floor. *Are you not afraid to be eaten?*

"I am less afraid of being eaten, than you are afraid of returning to your old form, and not knowing what to do."

The wolf pulled up his head and his maw ticked up at one side like a sly smile. *That...is not my fear.* The wolf gave a bark, but in Petal's mind she heard it as words. *Malachy, get in here.*

The youngest of the wolves bound into the room racing straight at Petal with his maw wide and no sense of caution about him. Petal was too startled to vanish from his path. He would hurt her if he wasn't careful.

Lorchan pounced on his brother, grunting and snarling in a warning way that Petal could feel the meaning of, but could not hear in her mind.

Malachy was too much wolf for his brother to communicate with him any other way. Petal felt her heart sinking. Now that he was near she could feel there was almost no human left in this wolf. What would become of him, if she changed him back?

When his brother was calm Lorchan climbed off of him. Malachy lay on the ground making begging noises as he looked between his brother and Petal.

It will eat away all that we are eventually, Lorchan said. Only then did Petal pull her gaze away from the young wolf. Lorchan was staring at her in a deep, unsettling way, and behind him Petal could see both of the other wolves, Grendel, their sister, and Ebon. And on the ground behind them, wrapping her way around their shadows was Dervla.

Petals heart stopped for a moment. She was utterly terrified. They were so large, and so full of pain and rage and slowly shrinking humanity. How could she possibly expect to fight them all off. Lorchan tilted his head up, showing his teeth and it should scare Petal more, but his words sunk through her consciousness. This was his fear. Not being aimless as a man, but becoming animal completely, and being drawn to someone and willing to serve them as Malachy clearly was.

Petal stepped forward and settled on the ground near Malachy, stretching out her hand for him to sniff like other dogs. But he didn't sniff, he bumped her hand up with the tip of his nose and his tail wagged happily.

This isn't safe, Grendel told her brother with a growl, but Petal understood. *He has no control, he could hurt her.*

Look at her, Lorchan argued. *Does she look scared to you? You are the one who said we should meet her.*

Yes. You and I. Not Malachy. Lorchan, he is nearly gone. Grendel's maw snapped loudly, her teeth making an uncomfortable leap in Petal's blood.

And she thinks she can bring him back. Lorchan insisted, not once taking his eyes off Petal. He kept a battle stance with a low growling that was clearly aimed at keeping Malachy in line.

Petal felt her heart pounding again. What if she couldn't bring back their brother? Grendel was very angry. Perhaps the angriest of any of them. She was a beautiful wolf, dark silver more than grey, but she had a huge claw scar marring her right shoulder. And a smaller slash over her eye. She had been through much. They all had.

Well, have you seen, little girl? Can you fix him? Lorchan demanded.

Petal couldn't focus her magic enough with all of them crowding her, and arguing. She didn't know what she could possibly do for them, if they did not give her space.

Petal looked into the toothy, salivating mouth of the wolf above her. *To see if I should eat you up,* his taunt tingled through her mind like a shiver.

Give her some space, Ebon, the only silent wolf up to now, said.

Petal glanced up and found him across the room, lying in his own bed. Dervla was now slowly dragging the others back by their shadows. If Petal didn't miss her guess, Ebon could sense Dervla. Dervla was...helping.

Petal let out a breath. "I am Petal the Powerful," she whispered, and shutting her eyes, laying her face against that of the youngest, wildest wolf. "I am Petal the Powerful."

Malachy growled low.

Asia and Jaron stopped in a small village only a few miles from Turrlough Palace and began setting up to sell his wares. Asia would have preferred not to do this in each town, village or small gathering of people they had passed since leaving Stonedragon, but Jaron had been kind enough to offer his escort, so she could exercise patience. Despite the fact that she could have been in Ulm already had she traveled by boat, but she hadn't suggested as much mostly because the seer's words were still haunting her.

You haven't decided who you are.

Asia liked focusing on other things, like her interesting traveling companion. In the weeks of travel she had been trying to read his mind without much success. She could sense no magic from him, but his mind was so empty it should be a spell.

There were other odd things about him. He'd neither gone home to inform his family he would leave, nor sent any of the coin she'd given him home. And he seemed incredibly comfortable with long travel. Strangest of all he appeared suddenly entirely comfortable with magic, but had not once asked her to transform anything into gold. She'd first suspected he was biding his time, but it seemed not so. He provided them plenty of food and clothes and coin as they went by selling his goods.

He was a much easier oddity to focus on. Especially today, with the palace only a few miles away. So close she could feel Aya and Owen. She wanted to run to them, she felt in her heart that they would welcome her back with open arms despite her having fled when they were in danger. But she was terrified that if she went to them now she would put them in more danger. She couldn't bear it if she was used to hurt them, the way she'd been used to hurt her mother all her life. They were better off without her.

Asia finished feeding the pony and rounded the side of the cart, only to dart back behind it again. She recognized the couple Jaron was bartering with. They were the parents of one of the kidnapped girls, Gavin had brought them to dine in his home when he was trying to frighten Asia away.

"It is lovely," the woman was saying, as she examined a comb. Asia could not recall her name, but she remembered her sobs, and the aching in Asia's own chest as the woman spoke of lying on her daughter's bed at night, longing for some way to bring her home. "She used to love such things. She would let me comb her hair and arranged it like my own." The comb clattered to the table and Asia heard muffled sobs.

In Asia's chest she felt her ribs beginning to pull, stretching so far they cracked and splintered from the pain in her heart, so full of love, but so overwhelmed with longing still. Asia crouched low, and peeked out from behind the wheel of the cart, watching as the woman was turned into her husband's arms so she could sob.

"Our daughter was taken from us, years ago," the man explained. He must think he looked composed, but his voice trembled, and Asia could feel his quaking inside her own being, so helpless.

"But she has been returned! It is a blessing. Such a blessing," he said heavily, as though he would share nothing of the pain. Then other words came spilling out. "But...she is changed. Not ours any longer. She is watched constantly by fairy and says her work is not done."

The man grew animated and his wife backed out of his arms, calming as their full truth began to unfold before this total stranger.

"How can she have work undone? She is a mere child." The wife took up the story. "She does not want to be with us. She wants the other girls who were taken with her. She is home. But she isn't truly home. And no comb or bauble will fix that!"

Asia had to fight back her own tears now. Her own rage. Since she'd been made human her rage with her father had carried her, or her love for Aya and her sons had distracted her. But now Asia had a flash of memory of her mother and it ate away at her confidence, feeding her rage.

She felt herself throw her arms around her mother in a tight hug as other girls did, but her mother cringed, and shook her off. Pushing away all of her daughter's affection. She felt again like the ugliest creature in the world, and not by her own doing, but by the way she'd come into the world.

Born ugly by something beyond her control, or her ability to repair. All of Symphony's rage and pain rose up in Asia as she listened to this couple, she wanted to race forward and tell them the right way to treat their child. Wanted to demand that they love her despite any change that had been forced on her by the world. To tell them to support her, and cherish her, and help her do whatever work she needed. But before she could move, Jaron spoke.

"The comb is yours free of charge, but for one favor. When you give it to your daughter, hold her tight. Tell her how you have missed her, and tell her—*her time will come*. If she has a task to complete then she will do so. Promise to be at her side when she does."

The woman exploded with sobs again and her husband lost a fair amount of his own. But Asia felt...soothed. And more curious than ever about this man. She watched him thoughtfully all day, tried to delve time and again into his mind. But she found nothing, and it only made her more curious.

Later that night, Jaron told Asia a story, almost as though he knew she was wanting to know more about him.

"I have two brothers and one sister. I have always understood my brothers better than our *baby bird*. When she was all of fifteen she fell in love with a man who was not from our world. None of my brothers nor my father approved. But she loved him, and he promised to stay in our world, so we let them marry. But he didn't stay and when he left he carried her away with him. And she...*smiled* as she told us that was the meaning of love. Giving yourself over to another being. But we fought, and we...sent her away with anger. Later we tried to mend the breach but it was never truly the same. She didn't trust us. So much so that even when her husband was gone, and her world was under threat, she did not call to us for help." He stared into the fire and for a long while he said nothing and Asia could not understand why he shared the story. Then he looked up, almost as if he'd heard her magic poking around his mind for the answer.

"I could not let that couple make my mistake. We fight so hard to make people into who we want them to be, that we fail to see the beauty of who they are until it is too late."

The words settled into Asia; she felt bonded to him, for the first time in this travel. She didn't speak the words but she suspected he knew. Whether of magic or...simple understanding, Jaron was a special man. She was pleased he was willing to take the journey with her.

Petal felt her heart stop at that growl but didn't open her eyes, and didn't allow herself to move away from the animal. Malachy was nearly all animal.

As an animal he was free. He only had to think of warmth and food and staying close to the pack. With the pack he was happy.

Petal let her magic race through him, trying to find Sorcha's curse. Trying to find why it was affecting him more than his siblings. Most everything she could see was a meal he'd chased, or the joy he took at howling against a thunderstorm, trying to be louder and more powerful. Then she felt herself. Petal startled. When he smelled her he felt more excitement than he did from a hunt, and more joy than he did in a thunderstorm, and safer than he felt with his pack.

He felt about her like she felt about Braden, maybe more. It was unsettling, frightening. For a moment, Petal wasn't sure she wanted to help him at all. She didn't know him, he didn't know her. How could he feel so towards her?

Petal opened her eyes and pulled her head away a bit. Swallowing she looked at the wolf. He watched her like a happy puppy, his tail wagging and his eyes begging for her attention.

Petal looked around the room, her eyes fell on Grendel who still looked heartily angry, and worried.

"I...I cannot find any memory of being cursed in his mind." Petal shook her head, unsure if she should voice her other concerns.

You do not want him thinking about that when you are near. Grendel growled, low and pained and her words drifted through Petal's mind. *When he thinks of that he...cannot fight his wolf side at all. It sends his being into a rage of pain and desperation and he will try to kill anything near him.*

He takes refuge in the wolf to fight the wolf rage. Ebon gave a bark. *Even before the change he was different from others. His joys were simple and wide and his pain was wild and uncontrollable.*

Petal took the words in thoughtfully. Unaware that she was petting a hand from the top of Malachy's head down his neck to sooth him. She just did it. She could feel him growing ill at ease with all the focus on him.

Her gaze drifted back to the animal and she continued to sooth him gently. His bright loving eyes startling her again.

"Why does he love me, when he does not know me?" Petal asked quietly.

Doesn't he? Grendel asked. *He has always had a better sense of one's heart than the rest of us. He ran when Sorcha came, hid under Father's throne, already making noises like the wolf he would become. I think he feels in you a safe harbor, a magic that will always protect him.*

If you are worried he will...attack you with his love, do not be. Lorchan said dismissively. *Human or wolf his love is a pure devotion, nothing else.*

Petal glanced at Lorchan, he was growling still, hunched over his brother and Petal unmoving. She'd taken it for him protecting Petal from his brother's more wild side, and that was likely a small part of it, but he was also protecting his brother. He didn't want to risk Petal hurting him.

Petal felt her tears dropping but paid them no heed, her magic was pulsing out of her, powerful and full of hope. This was what she had missed, having her siblings around her, protecting her, loving her, willing to risk anything to keep her near.

The pulse of pink light spread out from Petal, touching every crevice of the room, and every being within it. As one, the wolves threw back their heads and howled low and smooth. Dervla pulled herself into a shadowy corner, and her eyes overflowed with tears as the light pulsed.

When it dissipated Petal looked around the room, hoping to find four humans and one fairy, but her heart dropped, it hadn't worked. Perhaps she was not more powerful than Sorcha after all.

"Do not feel too—" Lorchan broke off, looking down at himself, his still wolf self. "Did I? Am I speaking aloud?"

"Yes!" Petal stood excitedly.

Don't go. Malachy latched onto Petal's hand with his teeth closed softly around it. He hadn't spoken aloud, but for the first time Petal heard his voice in her mind, and she could feel a bit more human in there as well. The human before the curse.

Petal bent closer, running her free hand over his head. "I am not going, just checking on your brothers and sister."

Malachy opened his mouth, releasing her hand and wagged his tail excitably. Petal beamed at him. Slowly, Petal crossed the room, towards the other wolves. She moved first to the wolf she knew the least, Ebon. As soon as she lay a hand on his head she felt her magic racing through him, it was changing him, changing them all, a bit at a time. But her magic had to do battle with Sorcha's. And Sorcha's spell had been there longer. Sorcha's magic was a part of their makeup now.

Petal stepped back and her eyes went not to the wolves, but to the corner where Dervla still cried silently.

"My magic is doing what it can, but it will be up to all of you to do the rest." Petal turned then to face Lorchan. "You will need to decide which is more important, your vengeance, or being with your family. And you will need to battle the curse inside you. But if you find it in you to change, my magic will guard you through the process, and make it safe."

Lorchan moved away from his brother to stand before Petal. For a long moment he only stared at her, then he bent his front legs and lay his head before her feet. One by one the other wolves did the same.

"We are in your debt, Petal the Powerful," Lorchan said. "Anything you need, have we the power to give it, we will."

"Welcome to the pack," Grendel said brightly. Then lifted her head to let out a long smooth howl. One after the other, all four siblings howled in welcome.

Petal smiled. She had missed being part of a family.

Eternity Wells

owan and Oona couldn't seem to get on a similar sleep pattern. Every time Oona laid down to rest, no matter how much work, or worrying Rowan had done that day, no matter how tired her body was, she could not sleep. She'd been here three days and four nights now. She felt a need to press on, but she hadn't managed yet to breathe fire, or fly, or much of anything worthy of justifying this journey.

Oona was teaching her many things. The most exciting so far was to walk through flames. She had to pull on the armor she'd made of all her fears and pains like a dragon's skin, and simply step into the flames, but she was not burned. It was fascinatingly hopeful using what Rowan had considered her weakest parts to protect herself, and having it work. She *loved* walking through fire! She would do it all day, every day if she didn't have other needs here. It felt like a promise that no matter what she had to go through, it would make her stronger one day.

But now the dragon slept, and there was no fire to walk through. And though Rowan had tried twice to visit her family, something was preventing her. Something about this cave, whenever she tried to cast her senses it felt like she was having to dig herself out of the mountain just to find the world. It exhausted her, and she never even found them.

"Good morning, Lady Knight," Bran's, recently familiar, voice said from somewhere in Rowan's mind. "Conquered the world yet?"

Rowan didn't look nor open her mouth, but she heard the reply as though it came out of her mouth. "I can't conquer anything."

Bran laughed. And Rowan felt air whoosh over her head like he had swung a quarterstaff above her. "You can do anything in here."

"Anything?"

"Think of it, and it's done. Do you want to defeat Sorcha? Bring me back to life? Meet your *handsome prince*?" he said the last with a playful laugh, as though mocking Rowan's taste in men. "You can do any of it. You can do all of it. Over and over until you get it right."

Rowan lifted her gaze and watched a bright green glowing Bran walk into the tunnel of similar light. He'd tried to entice her into it twice before now, this ghost Bran. And twice Rowan had resisted. Once trying to learn the stillness Oona wanted from her, and the second time, simply trying to resist that part of herself that always wanted to fix something in her past. There was no going back. She knew that. Everyone told her that. And surely if there were a way to move back through eternity and fix the bits you didn't like Sorcha would have done it long ago and Rowan would never have been born.

But tonight as she watched this spirit she was rather certain was *not* her old friend walk deeper into the tunnel, Rowan couldn't come up with a reason to resist. What was the harm in seeing what that tunnel held?

Oona lifted her head off the bumpy ground and watched Rowan venture into the second cave. She lifted a brow. That was generally the beginning of the end of her visits. Guests saw, they began to question, they began to worry and the world could be resisted no longer. To be honest she was surprised Rowan had resisted this long. She was a curious creature. But also one of iron will, it was an interesting battle to watch.

Oona glanced at Rowan's traveling companion. He was not asleep either, and there was an aura of worry dancing around him, but he didn't follow her in.

"Why didn't you try to stop her?" Oona asked.

The fairy made himself visible, watching Oona warily. For her part Oona was quite unperturbed by the prejudice she felt in him. Other dragons would be hurt by it, enraged and long to change it. Oona...well she was less dragon than she used to be. Less fire, less desire. She was old, and quiet and well settled into the truth that strange was frightening until it was no longer strange. And that some responded to fear with rage.

"Why didn't you?" he asked, with a quiet provoking tone.

Oona smirked. Yes, she thought he might be a bit like herself. Not prone to answering questions.

"She would have to look eventually. And I confess, I am as curious as she to see what she makes of that cave."

"She is not familiar enough with eternity to enter an eternity well and come out full of understanding," the fairy commented.

"Is she not?" Oona replied, rousing herself enough to stretch. "Then why ever did you let her enter this one?"

"She cannot be forced to things, least of all forced into giving up her quests. She was so at war with her fairy half that she marched up this mountain like a human and was dying for lack of air. Yet still she would not turn back." The fairy smiled, his look mingling pride and worry. "The little queen is nothing if not committed."

"I believe stubborn is the word most often used." Oona smiled. She liked his nickname for the girl. "Tell me, why have you not revealed your presence? I think her outburst of the burning hair made it quite clear she would welcome the sight of you."

He shook his head. "She needed to do this on her own."

"But she is not."

"Yes she is. That I am here does not change what she has done. It has only prevented her from being alone. And…" The fairy shook his head. "Too often in the past I looked to comfort and heal the aches of one I loved, when I should merely have sat beside her, and seen what she needed. It is perhaps the most difficult thing I have ever done, watching that girl shoulder pain after pain and doing nothing to shield her from it. But she will know her own strength. She will know what impulses are need and which are want. She will thrive."

"Ha," Oona laughed. "Why do you swing so wildly from one extreme to the next?" She shook her head. "I think perhaps you believe you have passed nothing of yourself onto your granddaughter. But that erroneous opinion that there exists no middle ground, *that* you have given her. It is part of what stops her flying or believing, and all of what sent her fleeing her home."

"Didn't you want her to leave her home?" he countered.

Oona shrugged. "She has more paths to success for having left. But she always had paths to success. Try as she might to block them with thorn and fire and fear, Sorcha cannot destroy every one of those paths. And it's well that she knows it." Oona smirked. "That is why I brought your *little queen* to the well of discovery, so she might know their number. And—" Oona nodded to the hall. "Seeing the well of the future, truly seeing it, that is important."

"Bran," Rowan said softly as she followed him deeper and deeper into the green tunnel. It was pulsing loud and heavy, weighing on her steps like stones upon her back. She bent forward and her steps were slow. "Are you dead?"

He looked over his shoulder, walking tall. He grinned. "I lay bleeding in what looked like an endless field of green grasses and red poppies. Everywhere my blood fell new flowers popped up and brushed across my skin. All around me were other soldiers, dying, crying out for those who loved them. I couldn't look on them, nor could I look at the flowers so I looked up. I sought the death birds. Have you heard of them?"

Rowan nodded, and realized that her steps were easier now, if she looked into his eyes and listened to his voice, though she was weighed down, she was not hindered by the weight.

"I searched the sky for them, and I thought for a moment that I saw the flapping of black wings, felt something tugging at my soul, but before it entered my sight, I saw you. You smiled at me from the sky, reminding me of the promises I had made to you, ordering me to sit up. To fight. To live."

He stopped speaking for the longest time and Rowan stared at him expectantly.

"I saved you?" Rowan demanded impatiently when he did not continue the story.

He shrugged. "What does it mean to save someone, lady knight? You did not charge onto that field and stop my bleeding. Nor kill all those I fought. Neither you nor I nor anyone else has defeated the Fairy queen. I do not know any longer what it is. But nor do I think I am entirely dead yet. What I know is that I am surely not living, and right now, neither are you. One cannot live separate from the world."

"You didn't used to be philosophical," Rowan said angrily. This was not Bran. If she were being honest, she hadn't even truly believed it was him the first night she'd heard his voice. He was long dead. And someone, Oona, Sorcha, eternity itself, someone was playing a game with Rowan.

The weight returned as Rowan fought against falling victim to whatever trick this was. And this green projection of her old friend smiled with Bran's lips.

Rowan stumbled forward. Logic told her to turn around. Even instinct suggested it. But she was determined to beat back this new oppressor. She forced her feet to move faster than the spirit before her, though her skull pounded and her breath felt thin and she was bent so far forward she was nearly crawling. Rowan came to a space devoid of light. She hesitated to enter the unknown. Bran came up at her back and gave her a push.

"It's you who needs to be balanced," he said with a laugh.

Rowan let out a shout as she tumbled into the pitch, down, down, down.

She didn't seem to be stopping. She couldn't feel a thing around her. She reached out for something, anything to help her.

She heard a tiny ping, like something glass striking a rock. Her lucky charm! Rowan opened her hand and wished with everything inside of her that she could close that clover in her hand and see Petal's beloved face.

The talisman dropped into Rowan's waiting palm.

As soon as Rowan closed her fingers around it the black filled up with pockets of green light, and in each pocket, another view of Petal. Rowan looked to the one nearest her and felt it growing closer.

Petal lay on her back beside a lake, Ferdy and Keagan were swimming, laughing and splashing one another. Petal wasn't really watching them, she looked at the sky, and her fingers played with the grass beneath her and she smiled. When her brothers tried to goad her into the lake by splashing her Petal just giggled. She flicked a bit of water off of her and every other drop that had fallen on her leapt up to follow suit, building one upon the other and rushing off after the boys as a giant wave.

Rowan giggled. That was the Petal she remembered. Sweet, powerful, devious Petal. The pocket of light faded away and another drifted closer.

Petal was alone, far older than now, perhaps fifteen. She wore a long red traveling cloak with a hood up covering her hair. She walked through a dark overgrown wood, with gnarled trees, and no clear path. It was growing dark around her as the sun set, but she walked on. When the moon took the place of the sun, a howl sounded in the distance, and Petal smiled slowly. It wasn't a smile of joy, or amusement, there was a great deal of sadness in it, but also comfort. She knew that howl. She tilted her head up towards the moon and it bathed her features in soft smooth light revealing two long scars along her chin where she'd been clawed. A wolf claw?

Petal let out a low crooning howl all her own, as if to let the wolf know where to find her. She dropped her head and walked on, alone.

The pocket backed away, taking a shiver from Rowan as it went. She didn't think she would want to see the next pocket, but she looked all the same.

Petal was dancing with Braden, there were tears on her cheeks and filling her eyes, and on his arm Petal's hand was clenched tight as if to hold him with her.

"Petal, I am sorry that I do not love you that way. You are like my little sister."

"I have never been like a sister to you," Petal snapped bitterly, as more tears raced from her eyes. "Why does everyone love her better? What is so special about her? All she has ever done was be protected and cost lives. I saved her. Rowan saved her. All she did was live."

"I do not love Darling because she survived the curse."

"That isn't her name."

"It is to me. And it would be to you as well if you would only get to know her. Rowan would want you to."

"All Rowan ever wanted was for her sister to live and she died seeing that happen. I nearly died seeing it happen. I want nothing to do with your *Darling* now, or with you." Petal shoved out of Braden's arms, and ran crying from the room, as Roisin slipped forward and took Braden's arm softly.

Rowan gasped and the pocket collapsed on itself. Rowan was shaking from head to toe. She continued to fall, and her eyes stung. There was no end to this tumble.

Rowan had never really imagined what it would look like, if she died saving Roisin. She'd never wondered what would become of the ones she loved. But she couldn't bear for it to be how she had just seen it. She couldn't stand for Petal to be heartbroken and alone, and all but take up Rowan's place, feeling like everyone loved Roisin more than her. She had to make sure that didn't happen.

Another pocket of light floated her way. Rowan braced herself. They were most certainly getting worse each time she saw them, but now that she was seeing, she had to see.

Petal was on a throne next to Sorcha. Sorcha listened to complaints of a human before her as Petal ignored. She had a rose in her hand; one at a time she plucked the petals from it, ripping them into tinier and tinier pieces and casting them into the wind. It took Rowan a moment to realize it was the rose she'd sent petal that was being destroyed. The burnt rose that Rowan had treasured all her life and sent to Petal to show her how much she was still loved. All of a sudden Petal looked up from her task and stared out of the green pocket of light straight at Rowan. Her huge eyes were cold and nearly lifeless, but when they pierced Rowan through this void they sparked. She glanced at the rose in her lap and back up.

"I used to think you didn't know what it would cost me," she said with an angry little laugh.

Beside her Sorcha shushed the man and watched Petal with a gaze alight with excitement.

"But Sorcha was right all along, wasn't she? You just didn't care. No price is too high, if it saves the Rose Princess."

Rowan jerked away and fell violently onto the stone floor of the cave. Her head struck a jagged rock and pain skittered across her skull with dancing jabs. That last vision of Petal...it could well be tomorrow, or this very second. She needed more from Rowan than talisman's and symbols of love. She needed to be protected the way Roisin was, she needed to know that Rowan loved her just as much as she loved Roisin. She needed to come home.

Rowan pushed herself up. She needed to leave. As she stood her head swam, and her body tilted towards the black again. A hand at her shoulder caught her.

She looked back slowly, her body tensing for a fight. It was still Bran, but he was not preparing to push her. He raised a brow.

"What now?" he asked. "Are you going to save us all? Or hide here like you hid in your palace?"

Rowan didn't like that she could feel his hand on her shoulder when he surely wasn't there. She didn't like that he taunted her. But worst of all she didn't like that she wasn't certain who or what he was.

Rowan shrugged her shoulder out of his hold, tightening her fingers on the lucky charm. Rowan looked down at it, but instead of seeing an orb with a clover floating inside, she saw Petal's five-year-old face. *"It's much better than their gifts. It will bring you luck."*

Rowan felt the sickness that had filled her as she sliced through her hair and tore off the piece of her being that had been weak enough to doubt Petal's loyalty, the part of her that had forgotten why she had entrusted such a dangerous task to a child. Not just for Gavin, and not even just for her own revenge. She'd trusted Petal because of all the beings in the world Petal's heart had always felt the most incorruptible. She could do anything.

Rowan just had to have faith enough in Petal's goodness, not to run headlong into one of Sorcha's traps and make things worse in the process.

The talisman in Rowan's hand began to glow a soft mossy green and another pocket opened before Rowan. Petal stood with a group of girls neatly lined up behind her to make a triangle. They each wore capes with pointed hoods of different colors, making them look like a patch of bells. Petal bowed at the waist, then took a knee and the girls behind her followed suit. They had all the precision of a well trained army, but the wonder of diverse souls.

Rowan watched herself step forward. She wore a crown like the one Gwyneth had designed on her head, and her stockinged legs were covered by a thigh length tunic, and she wore an extravagant train behind her.

She stopped before Petal and bent forward to kiss her head. "Beloved sister, Petal, Duchess of Stonedragon, and—" Rowan paused to smirk at the array of girls behind Petal. "General of the Survivors, on behalf of a grateful nation, I thank you."

Petal looked up at Rowan and quirked a brow in a vaguely sarcastic fashion that reminded Rowan of when she used to faint to stop her brothers fighting.

Rowan could feel her vision self preparing to say more, but the light faded away.

As the vision passed Rowan looked on the strange spirit before her; she smirked heading towards the main cave.

"I cut out my doubts only days ago. You will not shove them into me so quickly."

Bran laughed. Rowan walked away from the laughter. The further out of the cave she went the less her head hurt, the less the air of the room weighed upon her. When she made it out of the cave, exhausted because her hopeful self still had to battle the part of her nature that very much wanted to rush out into the world and rescue Petal, Rowan found Oona rumbling around the cave humming, as she laid out some nuts and berries and leaves for Rowan's breakfast. Rowan smiled and resigned herself to no sleep today.

Love and Fantasy

353 days until Roisin returns

Braden had been awake for a full week now. But he had not been allowed out of this room very often. He ate like a king, but for the lack of any meat. However, oddly he'd not missed it much. Custodian, as the third woman chose to be called, was an excellent cook. By far she was the woman most comfortable with Braden's presence, but even she would have odd moments of mistrusting him.

They kept Braden from wandering too far by keeping his clothes from him. Based on their relative sizes he had to assume he was wearing only Bailiff's clothing, it was a bit unsettling. It was also annoying that they had taken to calling him Prince Charming at every turn and making jokes about his manners, or lack thereof. He could not get straight answers out of any of them, but they had stopped questioning him. He was beginning to feel safe here, and only wished he was allowed more time with Darling Girl. Apparently having threatened her twice was too much for her family to countenance. He was only allowed near her when the rest of them were present.

Every morning at this time she tended her plants, and Braden would sit at the window and watch. He knew she could feel him. Every once in a while he would see her tilt her head to the side and her eyes would crawl backwards shyly, but eager to see him all the same. She was sweet, and innocent, and...darling.

He had found paper and charcoals in her room and this morning he was sketching her as she hummed. It was so like his vision. So exactly like it. But for the presence he felt behind him.

"Am I dead?" he asked in a whisper, not bothering to turn around.

"Is that what has you so on edge, Prince Charming?" He recognized Custodian's voice. "No. You are not dead. Antidote and Darling Girl saved your life. As you have been told several times."

Braden lay the sketch aside, and spun to face the woman. "I was shown my future once, a woman I could love, who would love me. I would swear that is her voice," he pointed over his shoulder, unsure why he was speaking the truth to this stranger who would not even share her own name with him. "I would swear this is the cottage I envisioned. But...how is that possible?"

Custodian lay down the neat stack of sheets she'd brought in and sat at the edge of the bed.

"Many things are possible that seem not so. But I do not think this is your time yet."

"What do you mean?"

She shook her head. "Before you came I had a vision of my late husband, telling me to trust a man who rode in on a white horse. I had not seen his face for so long, and I have missed him so entirely that no part of my being doubted. I was certain you *must* be trusted. I was certain he had come because you would find your true love in this cottage, as I had found mine in him. But...if our Darling Girl is your true love, it is not a true love of today. She is *too* young. And you are too angry. Your hearts may belong together, but they must first belong to yourselves and yours is not yet your own. Her Dark Majesty is in there. So as much as I trust you to be ready one day, I cannot trust you with her now. She is too precious to me. To us all."

She stood, patting the pile on the bed. "When you leave remember my warning. Endeavor to own your own heart."

She was all the way to the door before she spun around with one of her rare sharp looks. "And the drawings remain here."

Braden ground his teeth at having yet one...no *three* more masters. But before the rage could truly take him he heard her hum again. Darling Girl. He looked out the window and found her for once staring right at him. Their eyes touched, held, and all the anger within him melted away. Here he could be happy. Here he could be at peace.

Someone called her and Darling Girl skipped away into the cottage. He supposed she was quite young and unworldly. Were she human he would guess her to be no more than fifteen, but he wasn't sure she was human. And anyway, he'd offered for Rowan when she was fifteen.

And...he admitted to himself, Rowan had been much older at that age than Darling was likely to be at twenty. Darling was too young, but Braden still felt cheated. She was his fantasy. He knew it, but he couldn't have her.

Braden turned back into the room and moved to change his own sheets as the woman clearly expected. Something he'd never done before.

But as he lifted the pile he realized it was not what he'd thought. They were clothes. New clothes that Custodian had clearly sewn herself, of a perfect size for him, light and incredibly fine. So soft it felt like it was slipping through his fingers.

Two days ago Braden would have been dressing as fast as his fingers could move. He would have been sneaking out the window and rushing through the forest. But today he hesitated.

He could be happy here. Did it really matter that outside of this bubble the world was still moving? And people were still dying? How powerful was he really in the grand scheme of things?

350 days until Roisin returns

Dressed in proper clothes the man looked—quite different. Dashing. That was the word in romantic tales, and at last Darling understood what it meant. It made her heart race to watch him move about the room. He wouldn't be still; for the past few days he'd been *exercising*, preparing to leave. She knew it, her aunts knew it, but no one tried to stop him. Darling supposed she'd known she couldn't keep him forever, but despite being attacked by him twice and his not being nearly as sweet and charming as she had imagined a man being, Darling still quite liked his presence. She liked the variety of it. She liked the things she could get him to tell her. Her aunts had relented a bit, and were allowing Darling to question him about Friend so long as she did not allow the conversation ever to stray to her name, or where she was now, or her plans for Her Majesty.

They were all around the fire now, Aunt B had a book in her lap, Aunt A was sharpening her axe and Aunt C was weaving and Darling was interrogating the man as subtly as she was able about her friend. *Their* friend. Darling's heart fluttered, they shared a friend.

"Are there many other lady knights besides the one you know?"

"She is the only one. Well." He bobbed his head from side to side as he paced before the fire. "There are other women training to join her in the knighthood. But she is the only true woman knight. Do not say it is a path you wish to follow?"

Darling paused in her questioning. She had not thought of that. True, she had asked Friend once to train her, but nothing had come of it, and Darling had forgotten all about it. She began to assure him that she was merely curious, but he spoke first.

"That is no path for a woman like you. You should live a simple peaceful life, like you have here. Doing womanly things and—"

"Are you saying your friend is not womanly?" Darling demanded.

"I...she. No of course not," Prince Charming fumbled. "She has many womanly qualities, but I would not say her knighthood is one of them."

"Oh, and what are they? Of which of her characteristics do you approve, *Prince Charming?*" Aunt A asked, the sting of her blade against the grindstone striking the air like sinister music.

"Well...She loves children. She wants to have seven of them."

Darling laughed, unwillingly charmed. "Truly? Seven?"

"Yes," he nodded enthusiastically, staring at her smile in a way that made her whole being tingle with excitement. "She was a terrible dancer before, but she has much improved, now she is quite graceful."

Darling smirked into her lap. "Did you teach her to dance?"

He laughed. "No. I tried, but we weren't friends then. We met just before her sixteenth birthday and my presence necessitated a ball in her honor so we danced, but it was apparently the first time she ever tried."

Darling looked around at her aunts and laughed. "When she was sixteen was the first time she *tried* to dance. How different her world must be, if they do not dance at every opportunity."

His eyes darkened and his words became laden with thought. "Her world has always been a bit grim. But I suppose her desire to be a knight has as much to do with her never dancing. She looks down her nose at frivolous endeavors."

Aunt B looked up from her book to give Darling a warning look, they were straying too near sensitive subjects. So Darling asked instead about his home. He was much less eager to speak on that subject, his eyes became cold and angry. Darling felt chilled by them. Until—without prompting to do so, he changed the subject back to Friend.

"My home is more beautiful. And its people are not constantly battling the grip of a dark depression. But her home feels more like a home. I mean…" he shook his head with a sad, fiery smile. "I know I do not belong there, but I have friends there. And because she loves me I am always welcome."

As he spoke he came alight with the fire of his love and his true self shone through. Darling had always considered love a soft, comforting thing. But not so with him. With him it was bright and wild and almost painful. He loved Friend. That was what she saw when he spoke. For no other topic was he so alive.

Darling watched, unsure what the feeling growing inside of her was. She was happy and sad, and unreasonably hungry for that feeling to be directed at her, *not* her friend. But she could not explain why. Friend deserved such a love. She deserved more love even. But Darling longed to feel a love that—wild.

Left Behind

Rowan dreamt of flying. She was dipped between tree branches, then carried up over their tops or twisted low along dusty empty roads. It was a lovely feeling, being weightless, but she wasn't in control. She saw a group she thought were fairy, playing some sort of game with rings and tree branches and wanted to go nearer, but the dream pulled her away.

She flew on and on until the forest grew dense and she could see the base of a mountain up ahead. Was that—

Rowan jerked awake her hand curled around the dagger she kept under her packs. She swung it out as she sat up, half expecting some intruder had found her in the cave.

"I told you, you are safe here. Am I so hard to trust?" Oona's calm voice came from behind Rowan.

Rowan's breathing slowly evened out as she looked around the cave. There was no one here but her and Oona. She lowered the dagger to the ground.

"I trust you," Rowan said simply and was a bit surprised to find it entirely true. In the past she would not have trusted such a creature at all, for Oona was clearly full of secrets. But Rowan implicitly trusted her. Everything she did was in Rowan's best interest, or in the best interests of the island. "The dream...it just...I don't know. It didn't feel like a dream, it felt—" Rowan's gaze drifted to the green lit cavern, "—real."

"Then it very likely was," the dragon replied nonchalantly. "What did you see?"

Rowan shook her head, trying to catch onto the beginning bits of it as they slipped away. "I was flying. Over the Fairy Realm first, I think. Then I was being flown over my own path through the woods, towards Mount Anwyn."

"Um," Oona grunted, bobbing her head to the side. "Seems someone wants you found. I wonder who," she said, her voice bubbling with amusement.

"Sorcha," Rowan supplied. Rolling her shoulders to wake her sleeping muscles Rowan pushed slowly to her feet and crossed to where the dragon sat before the second cavern, the one Rowan had yet to enter.

"She cannot find you here. As I said none but those I invite can find this cavern."

"But if she suspects where I am, being unable to enter wouldn't prevent her preparing a trap for me," Rowan pointed out. As she walked forward, the dream slowly faded from importance. Oona was more curious. The dragon had laid out a breakfast for Rowan as she frequently did, but this time it was right at the mouth of the second cavern. After her experience in the last cavern Rowan was a bit cautious of this one.

She would enter it, but she wanted to know what it was and what the other cavern was. She wanted to know many things, more and more the longer she was here. The more she wanted to know, the less she felt the urgency of leaving. It should feel more urgent after the futures she'd seen in the green cavern. But it felt less so. Being here, learning more and more began to feel more important than saving anyone. Anyone at all.

"Wouldn't be much of a trap, if you saw it coming. Don't worry little warrior, you are a single minded weapon of defense. No trap Sorcha can spring will get in the way of your saving those you love," she said with false gusto. "Wasn't that the way it went?"

Rowan raised a brow. "Something like that. What is in there that you want me to see?" Rowan nodded towards the cave.

"A better question, to my mind, is why curiosity hasn't driven you there yet? What if it holds a horde of other dragons all eager to do your bidding and fly out to destroy your enemies for you?"

"I never said I wanted you to do all the fighting for me. I just...I cannot be three places at once and I wanted someone I was..."

"Willing to risk losing?" Oona suggested. "A soldier you cared nothing for to face the lances while those you loved remained safe?"

Rowan didn't like the words one bit. She liked even less the feeling that they might be true. Why had she thought she could ask creatures she had never met to take her part in a war they had no part in? What made her think that was acceptable? Yes, she thought they were stronger than humans, she thought Sorcha feared them. But she knew it would risk their lives. Why hadn't that mattered more to her?

"What's in that cave?" Rowan asked again, this time with more force, but also more trepidation.

"Nothing so dire. It is only a cavern. Guest quarters as it were. Most of my visitors have stayed in there for privacy."

Rowan looked skeptically in the direction of the cavern, then back to Oona. "Then why do you want me to go in there?"

"Tell me, little warrior, what spirit from your past led you into the well of the future? It is always so. A ghost, or a memory draws you in, shows you good and bad and worse. Who drew you in?"

"Bran," Rowan answered. "He was a soldier I—"

"Oh yes, I recall. Your first boy love." Oona chuckled.

"What?" Rowan blushed. "I was a child when I knew him, and Bran was..."

"Sweet, and thoughtful, and he listened and he liked you. Such a man is an excellent first love. That he could not have been a lover does not make him any less a love. You surely mourned him a good long while. Hating nearly every other soldier because they had not accepted him, because they were not he. An interesting choice to lead you."

"Whose choice?" Rowan demanded.

"Do you know." The dragon looked up thoughtfully. "I am not sure? I believe sometimes that eternity is the combined force of all life forces coalescing and so it shifts and wrinkles and sways changing as each life adds its say. Other times I believe eternity is a life force all its own, devouring all the life-forces in the world and spitting them out new. I have not found that answer yet. Which is how I know I will be here a while longer."

Rowan reached down and collected a handful of the berries the dragon had laid out.

"You do not want to know what I saw?" Rowan asked as she threw a few berries into her mouth.

Oona shrugged. "You saw possible futures. That is all one ever sees in the well of the future, until they decide if they will rejoin the world or unite with eternity."

"What do they see once they make up their minds?"

At that the dragon smiled. She nudged Rowan towards the guest cavern. "When one is ready to know that answer, one simply knows it. Go along, take a peek into our shared past, it will help you."

Rowan stared the dragon down. "You said I came here for certainties. To know how to defeat So—"

"This will help. Some things have to be felt, before they can be told. Go. Look. Feel. Save questioning for later."

Rowan walked forward slowly there was a glow to the cavern of similar blue light to the large cave. When Rowan rounded the corner, half expecting there to be some ghost in here as well, she was quietly surprised to see just what Oona had said, guest quarters. There was an old, hastily made bed of blankets covered over with dust and spiderwebs. And a collection of packs in the corner, even some old clothing scattered on the floor. Apparently the dragon could not fit into this cave to tidy up. That made Rowan smile.

She'd spent so much of her life with all the tidying done for her, that dirty things vanishing and returning clean had seemed to be the way of things. But now that she'd had to scrub her own clothes in rivers, and march on for days without bathing...now the human parts of her childhood began to feel somewhat magical. It made her feel more real, more human to go about the room, lifting old moth eaten clothes and shaking them out, rolling them up into neat bundles and laying them alongside the cot of blankets.

The first things she lifted were tunics and stockings, none of it remarkable until she lifted a heavy swath of velvet, shaking the rich fabric out she realized it was a woman's gown. And not just any woman. To own something so fine she must have been very wealthy, a noble perhaps, or royalty.

Rowan chuckled softly. She didn't know if she should be offended not to be such an odd princess after all. Or pleased to not be alone in this longing for more from life than a tower and a fine gown.

Rowan folded the gown neatly and laid it beside the other clothes and moved over to the packs. The first one was quite old, and thin. It held mostly clothes, from some man, not a soldier, all his clothes were functional but not protective. Deep at the bottom she found a single letter. Unfolding it Rowan sat down with her legs curled beneath her to read. Her heart caught for a brief moment before the words were revealed, caught with a wildly unrealistic hope. Imagining that the words on the page would be Gavin's.

Her left hand rose of its own accord to rub over her heartbeat. She missed him. She had been far longer than this without a letter in the past, but this was different. She hadn't felt the tearing since she entered this cave. But nor had she felt Gavin's heartbeat. She hoped it was just the magic of this cave blocking her from feeling his heart. But she didn't entirely believe that.

She tried to shake off the feeling and read, but her heart still pounded too hard for her to forget. So hard she barely read at first, longing to go back to the well of the future and seek out some knowledge of Gavin this time. But Oona thought there was something for her to learn here and she needed to at least try.

> *My darling,*
>
> *Do you remember when we lay on Glavel hill and stared up at the stars. We were so young, and already my heart belonged only to you. You listened as I invented world's that we would discover. You believed when I said I would meet dragons and giants. You believed when I swore that this world would not break me into just another lady still and silent beside her husband.*
>
> *You own my heart, my darling, because you have always believed in me. Please listen to me once more.*

When I said I wouldn't be broken, I forgot that my father knew me too well to try beating me down. He knows to destroy those I love to break me. He would hunt you to the ends of the earth. He would hunt us, should I run with you.

It would be a glorious adventure. We could see other nations, meet magical beings, sleep under the stars. I would follow you anywhere.

And your mother and brothers would suffer his rage in our absence. My sisters would be beaten and broken or forced to wed in my place. They are not like us. They have always needed us standing between them and the horrors of the world. So this is my choice. Not my desire, but my duty and my honor to stand between you all and my father's wrath. I will be married when this reaches your hands. I know what rage you must feel for me, what pain, but please, my darling, do not mourn me. Carry me across the world where I cannot go. Count all the stars. Be free, for you will carry my heart with you always.

With all my love,
Liadan

Rowan let her hands drift into her lap with the letter. *Liadan.* Was there truth in Gavin's story after all?

"She was a wild thing, unsatisfied with one view." A voice like the one that had comforted her as she traveled sounded in the cave. It was different here, both further away and closer. Sometimes she forgot to worry for him, or Petal, then she would grow quiet and have to fight the urge to rush out and save them. Now here was Gavin creeping around corners, nudging her with memories and wishes.

Rowan felt an odd kinship with the woman in the letter. Wasn't that backwards? Shouldn't she feel a kinship with the love Liadan had written to? The one who escaped the tower, and saw the world, met a dragon. Met the same dragon! Yet in her heart some part of her was Liadan still.

Trapped in the tower. Cutting herself off from everything she desired in order to protect others. Crying every day until her tears formed a river and cut across the island to find the sea.

Rowan lay the letter aside, more curious now she dug into the other packs. The next pack held mostly weapons and maps. One weapon in particular caught her eye. Rowan lifted the curved dagger, swishing in through the air, admiring the weight and balance of the weapon. It had an almost sickle shaped blade, the handle was a perfect fit for Rowan's hand, and a spike protruded from the end of the handle. It was an excellent weapon for close quarter fighting, but Rowan had never seen the like on any of her knights. She was sorely tempted to take it.

What were the chances of this guest coming back for their weapons?

As Rowan replaced the bag, the curved dagger sat on the ground beside her.

From another pack she removed a veritable cascade of under dresses, girdles, over dresses, and full gowns. Rich fabrics, with detailed embroidery and even one with gems sewn into the collar. Whoever this woman was, she was wealthy, and impractical. Who ran away with so many expensive gowns and no weapons?

Who runs away with no food? Rowan taunted herself.

Rowan was about to toss the bag aside, with its contents still strewn across the ground, but the pendant at her neck flashed, casting a beam of colorful light into the bag, illuminating a bit of brown leather. Rowan reached deep, past a wrinkled gown of soft silk and her hand closed around a small leather journal.

It reminded her of something familiar. When she pulled it out she realized what was familiar. It looked like one of Danu's journals.

"No," Rowan whispered aloud. Why was Rowan being constantly pulled to connections to the parts of her family that she had never known?

Her eyes found Liadan's letter on the ground.

She was always stumbling upon odd connections. It woke an uneasy feeling beneath Rowan's skin. That old feeling of destiny she had never trusted.

Steeling herself for some profound revelation, Rowan opened the journal.

I should go back. I am needed.

A shiver raced down Rowan's spine as the fated feeling built within her.

Balder needs his mother. He is so sweet and soft. The king hurts him constantly with his coldness. I miss his little arms reaching out to me. I miss his shy smile. I could not have let those poor babies rot away in the caves and dungeons my husband held them trapped in. But they are free now. Why do I stay?

My home is out there. My loves are out there. But in this cave I feel so...free. I have never felt free before. I did not even know I could feel so. All my life when I watched my father train men to go into the world and become more brutes, I felt small. I felt weak and afraid, so I fought them. I made them all despise me. But even that wasn't enough to free me. Flouting my king was not enough to free me. Freeing the dragons was not enough.

But here. Away from the world—I can breathe. Oona will teach me to understand eternity. She has offered me so much. I want constantly to sob for the beauty of it. And she offers it all freely. There is nothing she requires of me if I wish to stay.

I sleep without fear. I spend my waking hours as I choose. I wear clothes of the long-dead—male visitor of a dragon and have all but left Queen Danu behind. But Queen Danu was a mother. Should I remain here I am a mother no longer.

I should go back. Why can I not nudge myself out of the cave? My freedom should not be so hard a thing to give up, to see him loved. I know he will not be loved without me beside him.

Rowan slammed the book shut shuddering with rage and resentment and sadness. She felt it pressing down on her, as though the weight of her grandmother's failure were her own. It wasn't the same. Rowan wanting to be loved for herself and arguing with her father when he lashed out at her, it wasn't the same. She knew it had hurt him, but it had hurt her too. Was she meant to just forgive and forbear everything because he had been hurt in the past? She didn't know that she could. Yet his pain weighed down on her. The weight of wanting something for herself and knowing what it cost others pressed down on her.

She should have left already. She came for dragons to aid her. When she knew she would not be getting it she should have left. And it was only partially for magic that she had stayed. Part of her had stayed because she wanted something here, something she had yet to find.

Rowan tossed the journal beside the letter, she wanted to scream. Here were two women who'd made the opposite choices, and for the life of her Rowan couldn't see which choice was the better. Danu was eventually found and sentenced to death. And Liadan cried herself a river over all she'd given up. How was either choice right?

Rowan leapt to her feet, involuntarily lifting the curved dagger as she went. She ran out into the main room of the cave.

"Did you bury them?" Rowan demanded. "All your guests, where did their bodies go?"

Oona laughed. "No guest has ever stayed. If they did I would teach them to live as long as I do."

"You can do that?" Rowan asked in wondrous shock.

"Of course. The magic isn't in the dragon blood or even the fairy blood. It is in everything, the air, the ground, the water. One simply finds a way to connect with it or one doesn't. It is true that from generations of connecting to it dragons and fairy are born with a more organic connection to eternity. But anyone can learn. And both fairy and dragons can be born without the connection."

Rowan nodded slowly, puzzling through the things she'd begun to feel in that room. She twisted and spun and played with the blade in her hand as she walked.

"None of them could resist the pull of the world," Rowan said thoughtfully.

"They could not resist life," Oona corrected.

"And it cost them that very thing," Rowan remarked.

Oona chuckled. "Everyone dies eventually. Dying is not the cost of life, but the *promise* of it."

Rowan jerked to a stop, staring at the dragon. Oona smiled a soft, sad smile.

"I am contented with my cave, little worrier."

"Warrior," Rowan corrected.

Oona shook her head. "I have seen and felt and suffered enough life to know its draw, and I turned my back to it. I study the world and eternity, but not to take part in it, only to understand it. I lead my visitors here because I feel that same hunger in them, and I wish to feed it. But if one has it in them to *live*— to truly live and at their end to *die*—one should. There is beauty in impermanence. Imagine if your sister were truly preserved in a crystal like that vision that drove you from home. She would be safer. But she needs to break free. She needs to scrape knees, and break hearts and feel the profound pains that change one, and help one relate to the world. She needs to be unsafe or it would be as though she was already dead."

Rowan jerked as her breath was yanked out of her body. She thought of all the banister decorations with Roisin's face, and the roses cast into the fire on her birthday. It had always felt morbid. Rowan had hated it, but she had never realized that her own desire to keep Roisin "safe" was just as dangerous. Rowan rubbed her right palm where her scars used to be.

My sister won't have scars. She will be perfect.

Rowan looked around this safe cave she'd shut herself into and a heaviness settled in her heart.

"You...sent me in there so I would see I need to leave?"

"Oh no! You are overthinking again." The dragon smirked. "No. I am not at all sure that you have the sort of death I mean in you. You see death as a violent strike cutting short a life. What I mean is the sort of death one earns with a well lived life. In here, out there, training, or writing, or learning to use magic, *you* are a being of single minded focus. You are as lacking of life as I am. And you were so long before I led you here. No, I sent you in there to see the pointlessness of overthinking. Though apparently you were not quite ready for the lesson." The dragon laughed softly, nodding to Rowan's hand. "At least not entirely."

Rowan looked down at the blade in her hand and back up at the dragon. "It is alright if I keep it?"

"Ashira will not be coming back for it. She is long dead."

"This belonged to a woman?" Rowan asked with a grin.

"Indeed. It is called a thorn. The people's army of Maltuba carry two weapons, a staff, they call a branch, and the dagger they call the thorn."

"Nothing for fighting at a distance." Rowan commented, staring at the thorn. She'd known there were women in the army of Maltuba, but they hadn't fought a war of any kind in over two hundred years. Most people assumed the women were only a part of the army for show.

"To kill one's enemy one must first see oneself in their eyes. Such is the weight of all killing."

Rowan felt the words fall through her like a stone. "That is why they have not fought wars in so long."

"Indeed. Their first queen built her legacy well."

"Ashira was their queen?"

"Ugh, no. Why do you persist in thinking? It will not serve you well. She was a mere soldier. Like you," Oona said snidely. She leaned her face near Rowan, her eyes laden with challenge. "One cannot lead a nation from a cave, nor even from beside their father, however proper a place that may be for them to stand. Stop overthinking your choices. Make them and live with them. Every guest I ever had stole something from those who came before them. You stole a weapon. You can stop to wonder what that says about you, or you can fit it into your belt knowing that you will know the answer when the time comes, and use this time to learn what you must."

Rowan spun the blade around in her palm with a slight smile and shoved it in her belt. "Alright." She felt an urge she could not explain but she didn't question it, she just moved towards it, better or worse. "Before I left Stonedragon, I was trying to teach myself a specific spell," Rowan said carefully. "One that is said to be known only by the Fairy queen."

Oona tilted her head to the side and an oddly impressed half smile tilted across her features.

"Can you teach me to use the window spell?"

"Why?" Oona challenged.

Rowan shook her head. "I don't know. I just know I need to know it."

Oona smirked. "Very well."

Traps

346 days until Roisin returns

"Sir half the food vanished in the night," a soldier reported, red in the face from shame and frustration. "There is no explaining it. We are keeping a full five miles from the border at all times as instructed, unless the border has changed."

"Or unless being as Anwyn and the Fairy are closely aligned fairy are allowed to cross the border without repercussion. Or unless fairy simply have no fear of human retribution. Or knowing us for Stonedragon's soldiers they are toying with us. There are many explanations. What should concern us is preventing it again. Tonight we double the watch. Do not clear the area of brush, add more, the noisier the better. We set a trap, something shiny and important that will compel the fairy to steal it."

Several soldiers exchanged glances. "Sir, you wish us to...harm fairy?"

"If they are attacking us," Colum said sharply. "I am not planning to kill the fairy, only to capture it."

"Of course." The soldiers agreed and set about packing for the day's journey ahead. Colum busied himself with the same tasks, but kept an ear out to hear the men, talking amongst themselves.

Apparently it was something of a shock that a "fairy-lover" would tell humans the way to capture fairy. Colum's hands slowed as he worked. He hadn't hesitated a moment to teach these men some of the tools to catching a trickster which he had learned from training his own son. Because they were his men, and this trickster was a threat to them. He had never in his life put his men in jeopardy if he could help it.

But perhaps he should have taken more pause. He'd thought only of this moment, not how they might use the knowledge in the future. Were these men ones he would later have to guard his children against? After all, he'd seen since his sons became squires, surely he should have been more cautious.

Since Colum saw what Maureen had done with their home, he'd been considering his failure to encourage Rowan to love her fairy half. But had he failed equally to teach that love to his other children? There was so much he needed to do. So many reasons they all needed to be together.

Gwyneth was in her solar weaving with the other gentlewomen. She missed having Maureen join them, but did not know how to ask her to return. Maureen had taken on quite a bit, essentially leading Rowan's knights, and her shield maidens, healing anyone who needed it, and trying in vain to keep Ferdy's army of children in line.

Ferdy had half the squires causing mischief now. As well as most of the small children from anywhere near the palace. And the word was spreading. Last night a pair of horses had been stolen by children and by the time the sun was up six more children from further villages were here to join the army of the future queen: *Rowan's Sword.*

It was rather sweet. Gwyneth liked watching the army of children. All of them away from their mothers, as her daughter was. But Gwyneth no longer had anyone to talk with about such things. Maureen had seemed to truly understand her. But ever since Rowan had shared her secrets in the rose garden things had changed between them. She knew Maureen still cared, she was still all things polite. But so many things took from her that it seemed an effort for Maureen even to smile most days. Her lack of spirit was having a disheartening effect on Gwyneth.

"I told my husband, the king has kept us safe this long, he will not let Anwyn attack."

"Let Anwyn attack?" Gwyneth looked up from the pattern in shock. She hadn't truly been paying Lady Hilda any attention.

"Yes. They have threatened war if King Balder does not present them with their missing prince," Hilda said as though Gwyneth was pitiable. "Didn't you know? I thought the king told you everything."

Gwyneth opened her mouth to defend her relationship with Balder, but she stopped. She had never liked Lady Hilda.

"Excuse me." Gwyneth stood. She glanced around the room of weaving women. Rowan had given this task to her, and it needed to be done, but Gwyneth was slowly coming to realize she could do things to help Rowan without being asked. She had things to offer. "There is a slightly more pressing matter I must attend to. Please continue without me, I shall rejoin you as soon as I am able."

Gwyneth marched out of the room in search of her husband. She did not find him in his study where a guard directed her. But she found his correspondence on the table.

> *King Balder of Stonedragon,*
>
> *Be of good health. This is the second attempt I have made to contact you regarding the fate of my son. We received word via advanced rider that he was heading home on the thirtieth of May. It is now nearly a month with no word of him or his escorts.*
>
> *When first I wrote I merely sought your help in discovering his path. Your lack of response has made me concerned in other ways. If you are possessed of any knowledge as regards my son and his wellbeing I advise you to share it. I have dispatched soldiers to search for him along his every possible path on my lands. I hope to hear from you before they reach your border, either to announce you are returning my son to me, or to offer your assistance in finding him.*
>
> *We have all been sympathetic and offered our aid as you sought to find your youngest daughter. Now is your opportunity to*

*make good the promises of peace between us. Return my son. Or
expect the peace between our nations to be at an end.*

> *In earnest faith,*
> *King Alistair of Anwyn*

"My word," Gwyneth breathed softly, allowing the letter to drift to the table.

"My dear, here you are." Balder entered the room with a small chuckle. "I went looking for you in your solar."

"To discuss the letter?" Gwyneth said hopefully. Her head lifting with pride that he would seek her council.

"What letter? Oh, that nonsense about Prince Braden. I have it well in hand."

"Your men are looking for him? Should we inform Rowan's knights as well? They are his friends."

Balder looked momentarily taken aback. "There are plenty of men seeking him. I am sure they will find him languishing in some convenient village, hiding from his responsibilities."

Gwyneth startled. "Perhaps Braden is not the most ambitious of young men. But he has never seemed unwilling to perform any task put before him. There is no cause to criticize him. Are you truly not worried? He has been missing nearly a month. And he is one of Rowan's allies."

Balder turned away.

"I know you are angry with her. But what if Sorcha discovered their connection and sent someone to harm Braden?"

"I am not angry with anyone. But nor am I concerned. Alistair has never shown any love for his youngest son, he is trying to rattle me."

Gwyneth stood with several feet between her and her husband with sadness building in her heart. He'd forgotten again, hadn't he? "Balder, promise me you have men looking for Braden. And that you wrote too Alistair to tell him so."

Balder looked her over derisively. "You do not understand much about leading a nation, dear. Go back to your tapestries, they are coming along quite well. You shall trust your king to do what is right."

"I do trust you," Gwyneth said, her chest tightening with every word. "That is why I ask for your word. It would do me no good if I did not trust you."

Balder smiled as one would with a small child. "Gwyneth, my dear, I promise you, Braden will be found. Of course I would seek him out."

He looked so much more himself that Gwyneth shook off her worry. She walked into the arms her husband held out for her and allowed herself to shrink into them so her head lay against his shoulder.

"Of course you would. I am sorry. For a moment I worried that..."

"What did you worry?" he asked gently, kissing the crown of her head.

She had always felt so safe with Balder. But now, though she did not feel threatened, and she could not place her finger on what it was about him that had changed, his safety no longer felt like *love*.

"Just that the curse was making you forget things."

"No. Never." He kissed her head.

"Why were you seeking me?"

"Ahh," he said excitedly. "The bard has finished his first of thirteen songs and I thought you should hear it."

"Thirteen songs?" Gwyneth asked at a loss.

"One for each year Roisin was away, so she might know what happened in her absence."

"Oh!" Gwyneth's heart caught with the beauty of such an idea. For a moment she forgot that she had been avoiding the topic of Roisin's return in fear of the curse taking her.

"That is lovely. What...does he sing of Rowan in the song?" she asked cautiously, rather than asking if Balder had forgotten his eldest daughter.

Balder laughed. "Come hear the song and you can ask that he add any story or friend you think he should." Balder coaxed, leading Gwyneth from the room. She went along, cautiously. Balder did not seem himself. Gwyneth couldn't help thinking she should send that letter to one of Rowan's knights just to be safe. But she followed her husband, and long before she reached the throne room, his steady stream of conversation had melted into a soft sweet tune in her mind.

The moon was high, and the trap was set. Colum had given himself first watch, but when nothing happened and his relief team woke he waved them off. He would be exhausted tomorrow, each day seemed longer and heavier than the last, but he must be the one to catch the trickster.

He was beginning not to trust his own men. He would have preferred to take Rowan's knights. But they had not been especially fond of him, and they were needed in Stonedragon. Ferdy, Keagan and Maureen alone might be able to hold the curse at bay, but it would take its toll.

It was better that Colum be with men he didn't trust, than men he didn't trust be guarding his family.

Since they had brought little gold the prize was the last of their ration of food, surrounded by a pile of weapons. It would appear that they were trying to guard it from stealing hands, but the blades were a lure. The fairy wouldn't be able to resist such a blatant challenge; and he had iron chains on hand to bind it, once it was caught. Colum just hoped they were dealing with only one fairy.

Colum hefted the weight of the iron chain. He could recall when King Flint forced all his soldiers to turn in their steel blades, much easier to wield for the lighter weight, and passed out iron, because iron had been a humans best defense against fairy; it weakened their powers. If you could get iron around a fairy, it couldn't get away.

Colum had been eager for the war to be at an end, eager to find Danu and be sure she was well. So he'd thrown himself headlong into his king's cause, unconcerned with killing fairy because at the time it had seemed anything that wasn't human wasn't worth the same concern. He'd been like that before, hunting dragons for his king. Now all of those men were behind him. Colum was willing to hurt other creatures if they attacked his family, but outside of that he felt they all had the same right to life. But would he have ever come to such realizations were they not forced on him by life? Would any of these men?

He hoped so or else the world was doomed. Rowan could show them. Rowan had always known the value of a life, any life was no greater or less than another.

Loud whining and hooves pounding woke most of the men as someone invisible released their horses and frightened them away. The men jumped and ran towards the chaos, shouting and adding to the cacophony. Colum smiled. It was a clever trickster. He stayed right where he was against a tree.

When one of the swords slid slowly away from the food Colum threw himself forward, wrapping the chain around the first thing he grabbed, a wrist from the feel of it. He looped the iron around twice before the fairy lost hold of its invisibility and appeared before Colum.

It was a young boy. Probably a few years younger than Rowan. He smirked and cocked his head to the side.

"Well, aren't you a clever human?" the fairy taunted, all bravado.

Colum could hear his men behind him, some still chasing after the horses, others regrouping and heading his way.

The ones who came back circled Colum and the fairy, drawing weapons.

"Those aren't necessary," Colum said casually. He didn't feel casual though. His heart was pounding, and his bones ached. He looked on this child, knowing full well it may not be a child at all, and all he could think of was a story Maureen had told him years after they met, just before they were married.

She'd come to see him after visiting Rowan on her birthday. Rowan had predicted he and Maureen would have children and Maureen had seemed almost as enraged as she was afraid. She'd nearly refused to marry him.

"I will not bring more children into this world!" she'd shouted, pacing about the room with tears in her eyes.

"Do you mean the world, Maureen, or the human one?" Colum had asked, because there was something in her tone that made his skin crawl with shame. He didn't even know why yet, but he knew it was shameful.

She'd looked at him and her eyes had priced him with their fire and their fear. She'd curled her hands at her sides and turned away. "I don't know what I mean. I am just far too old to be a mother."

He'd crossed to her, sliding his hands down her arms gently, and holding her with her back pressed against him. "You are as spry as ever. Tell me, love. There is nothing of your life I do not want to know, even the bad."

"I thought I wasn't her anymore," Maureen said so quietly. "The little girl I once was. But as I walked here I found myself looking in every shadow for someone who would harm me. I never told you how I met the Fairy queen. I was so young then. Maybe eleven. I was playing tricks on humans who strayed too near to fairy things. I was so eager to be like the other children. I didn't for a moment think of the danger."

"Children never do," he said when she stopped speaking. He didn't want to know this, not really, but she would be his wife, and it would be his place to heal her wounds. Or so he'd thought then.

"I felt so grown-up," she said with a pained laugh. "Then a human caught me. He was a soldier, huge, and furious because of the mess I'd made of his camp, and the fish I'd dumped back into the river. He just had me caught with his hand at first, and I was terrified as I'd never been in my life. I didn't even think of yelling, or trying to vanish back to my family. He would have come with me if I had, but they would have been there to protect me. Then his friend came over with iron chains, and I started crying because I knew they would kill me. I was so afraid, and so alone."

She'd been held captive for days, forced to be their servant, threatened with death. Colum felt rage boiling beneath his skin, just thinking of how she'd cried as she spoke of waiting for her family to come for her, constantly worried that she wouldn't live long enough, because humans hated fairy so much. In the end, it wasn't her family who rescued her, it was Sorcha. And Maureen had felt her life was owed to Sorcha from that moment on. She'd done everything Sorcha asked of her, even shutting away her fear. But when Rowan spoke of the children Maureen would have, all of that fear came back. She could take the fear for herself, but not for her children.

So Colum had promised her they would build a better world, and that just the presence of their children would make it a better, safer world. And he truly believed it had. But it was not a good enough world by far yet. Colum had more work to do if he was to keep his promise.

"We won't harm you," Colum said to the fairy now, trying to keep his tone neutral and calm. "But nor can we allow you to steal what is ours."

"What can a man own, if he is trespassing?" the fairy asked cockily.

"Were you sent alone?" Colum countered.

"I wasn't sent at all, this is my doing." The fairy notched up its chin.

"Why are we talking to it at all?" One of the soldiers asked. "If you will not kill it we should tie it to the tree and take our leave."

"*He* has a name," Colum said sharply. He glanced at the fairy. "I am Colum of house Keen. What is your name?"

The fairy observed Colum like a rare curiosity. "Tyce," he answered after a long stretch.

"Tyce, are you doing this for the Fairy queen? Does she know where we are?"

The fairy shook his head. "I was not sent by the Fairy queen. I have never even laid eyes on her glory. But I cannot say what she knows and does not. You are human, I am fairy, this is simply the way of things."

Colum nodded. "For now, perhaps. But it needn't be so. No matter who your queen is—or mine."

Both the fairy and Colum's men were looking at him like he was mad. If Colum must teach it one human and one fairy at a time he meant to make them all see what could be between them.

"Did you happen to play any tricks on a lone traveler who passed this way sometime ago? A woman traveling by horse?"

The fairy shook his head. "Human women tend not to travel alone in these parts. Who is she to you?"

Colum wasn't about to answer that question. The boy may not have performed this trick for Sorcha but there were many fairy who would aim to win their queen's favor by telling her of Rowan's location.

"I shall accept your word that you will not steal from us again, and release you. If you are willing to give your word," Colum offered.

"You would trust the word of a fairy?" The fairy and two of Colum's soldiers asked in unison. Tyce winked at the men.

"I would," Colum confirmed.

"Why?" the boy asked with a challenging expression Colum had seen on a number of young squires over the past year.

"Because I have found tricksters possess a deep sense of honor. Sometimes even deeper than other fairy. And because I wish my children to know that their father has as much faith in their fairy half as their human one."

"Humph." The boy snorted. Then he gave a slight bow. "You've my word I won't steal from you again."

"Thank you." Colum bowed in return and unwound the chain.

"You must be joking," one of the Colum's soldiers, Taggart, challenged. "He isn't one of your sons. And your trickster son is known to raise all manner of trouble."

"Ferdy has never once played a trick for which he was not willing to suffer the consequences. Nor have any of his tricks harmed anyone," Colum snapped. Taggart looked militant still, but a few of the other soldiers looked...perhaps intrigued. Nevertheless all of them knew who was in charge. When the chain was unwound from the fairy they stepped back.

"Colum Keen," Tyce said with an odd smirk. "I shall remember you." With that the fairy vanished.

"Wonderful!" Taggart said snidely. "We have half our rations and half our horses, but at least your sons will know you trust fairy."

"Go look for the horses," Colum ordered.

A loud whistle had them all jerking around. Tyce was standing just outside of the camp holding the reins of the six runaway horses. "Thought you might need these." He chuckled at the expressions of the other knights and vanished before anyone could reach him, leaving the horses behind.

Colum smiled. He knew he was right about tricksters.

Breath of Flames

"There is too much for you to learn, we must give up on flying," Oona remarked impatiently, as Rowan fell for the fifteenth time today, bruising herself and cutting a gash in her arm.

Rowan ground her teeth more to keep in her annoyance at failure than to fight against the pain. She ached all over. At first Oona had told Rowan to build herself scale armor in order to protect herself should she fall. But the fourth time Rowan failed to fly she lost control of even that magic and bruised herself, making Oona frustrated.

Rowan was more than a little embarrassed that she was the only thing that could unsettle this ancient woman. Oona eventually told Rowan to wear her human armor when trying to fly. It helped keep her from being seriously injured. But it made no difference. Rowan couldn't fly.

"It was the least of our needs anyway," Rowan said, intending to sound bland and dismissive. But the dragon clearly noticed her frustration, she shook her head.

"With all things time, little warrior. You will learn when you are ready."

"Oh? Have you seen me flying in the future?" Rowan rolled her eyes.

"At least as many times as I have seen you falling," Oona teased. "You do not take to it as well as you might like."

"Too human?"

Oona shook her head. "Come, use that frustration to good purpose. Feel your rage of failure, let it build inside your gut, let it burn."

Rowan shut her eyes and tried to call those feelings forth as fire. She felt her whole being growing hot from her center out. She lifted her face high and opened her mouth to spew out the heat, but all that left her was a pitiful cloud of smoke that immediately sunk towards the ground.

Oona stifled a chuckle.

"Even that won't fly," Rowan muttered, annoyed, but not enraged. The odd contentment she felt here was the problem. "At home I likely would have done this by accident a hundred times already."

"Then there is nothing stopping you. Those feelings live in you, access them."

"I am reborn, remember?" Rowan said spinning around with a sarcastic brow raised.

"Are you?" Oona chuckled. She observed Rowan curiously, then nodded her head sideways. "From your guilt perhaps. But rage is different. You cannot simply cut out the rage. Think of the things that made you too angry to speak at home. Think of your father disinheriting you."

Rowan paused with a hand caught up in her curling hair. She hadn't really felt it curl like this since she was a child. Hadn't really felt it at all. Her fingers slid away and tried to think about being disinherited. But her mind shied away from the moment.

It kept on calling forth what she knew now, of her grandmother Danu, and her father's lifetime of unhappiness.

She tried to focus only on her feelings, not the moment, but the anger she felt at the loss of the future she'd been working towards: of leading her people and making her father proud. The loss fed her rage. It built inside her, she felt the heat again. She breathed out and a tiny flame, just large enough to grace the end of a candle, hung in the air a moment then shuddered away with a tiny pillar of smoke.

"What about your friends taking his side?" Oona suggested, her voice laden with humor.

Rowan shrugged, unable to come up with rage at that anymore. "I might have overreacted. He is their king."

"If you are going to be so reasonable I will wonder who you are. We need you to breathe fire, not rainbows. Quit hiding from the feelings."

"I am not hiding."

"Yes, you are. You are afraid the guilt will return with the anger. You are afraid to be weakened by it, and be unequal to the task before you. Hiding helps no one." The dragon shoved Rowan backwards with a mere flick of her tail. "Get angry. *Feel.* How did you feel when your father was so awed that Braden had *bent to your will*? Or when he implied Gavin has not waited for you? When he threatened to force you to wed Braden?"

Rowan's hands clenched into fists as heat built inside of her. Her being raging against those moments. Filling up with unspoken words and grievances.

You will be his.

Her mind wanted to bellow something loud and long, but Rowan wouldn't let it. She didn't want to go back to that feeling. She didn't want to feel *unwanted* again.

"I cannot be forced," Rowan bit out, and spirals of smoke escaped with the words. Her being burned. The thumb of her right hand, rubbed again and again over the missing scars as if to soothe her burning being.

Rowan didn't like this. She felt smaller than the fire building inside her. Smaller than the fears Oona wanted to pull forth. She said she was after rage, but she was after fear. Every bit of the flames scorching the air came from fear. Her heart pounded hard, and her chest rose and fell with rapid, aching effort.

"Doesn't it eat you up inside, knowing what Sorcha showed Braden?"

"What?" Rowan almost separated from the flames. *Almost.* Somewhere within the flames grew stronger, and she couldn't say why. "Why should it?"

Oona lowered her head slowly, her eyes full of challenge and pity. "Because he will love her more than you."

"I don't care about that," Rowan said, almost desperately.

"He was yours first. But he'll be hers forever. She'll be his whole world—He'll forget about you." The words were achingly soft as they ripped through Rowan, and woke a wealth more flames.

"Don't you want to be loved like that?" Oona spoke the words from Rowan's old nightmare. Rowan's entire being shuddered, the flames built so strong inside her she felt like they might burst out of her skin instead of her lips. "He'll forget about you. They all will. Just like your father ha—"

"No, he WON'T!" The words came out in a blinding hot stream of flames. They tore across the dragon, and Rowan's heart pounded with fear for her along with every other fear she already suffered.

But Oona was unharmed. When the flames dissipated she leaned her warm head right next to Rowan's tear soaked face and caressed her with it gently. "Good. Good." The words were breeze soft, but Rowan jerked away shaky and more afraid than she'd allowed herself to be in years.

"I won't do that," Rowan insisted her words as soft as an avalanche. "I won't kill my sister! Certainly not over a boy that I have never wanted."

"You did not want him for a husband. But you wanted him for a friend. It won't matter that you do not want him. Not when all she will have to do is smile and all the people who should love you will fall under her spell. You will bear it as your subjects love her more, and your enemies. Then it will be your father who loves her more, but you have always known that, and though seeing it will be a new torture, that will burn inside, it will not break you. But Braden, and Maureen, and the triplets, your knights, they are *yours*...what will become of you if she steals their love as well?"

"I won't kill my sister," Rowan said again, but the words lacked any power. "Tell me I won't do that." Rowan demanded, a tiny stream of flames escaping her again, though she had not even felt it building.

"Brothers and sisters fight. They love one another, and they resent one another. You are not so different from other children. But all Sorcha needs to do is find a way to manipulate one of those resentments and she will make you her tool in your own suffering. That is why you must learn to breathe fire. Let it loose. Express your rage and your resentments and your fears, tiny wounded warrior, so they cannot be used to control you."

Rowan let out a little sob. Bending into herself, she shuddered as she forced herself to stop hiding from the fear she'd silenced earlier. The fear she fought with every mile she'd ridden from her home. The fear that her father never would love her for who she was. That no one truly could. No one knew the whole of her. Rowan hid herself for fear of being despised for her selfish desires and resentments.

Rowan let all of that ugliness, all of that fear build inside of her. If they were a part of her, they could serve her purpose. She could make a weapon or a shield from the parts of her being that she loved the least. She had to, there was no other way.

Burning with a fire a hundred times as hot as any human or fairy could make, Rowan breathed out a sharp blade of flames slicing a path through the air. She drove it into the heart of the falls and watched as the water boiled up and evaporated around the flames.

When Rowan at last cut off the flames, breathing deeply, the shaking had stopped. She was still afraid, and angry. She still felt smaller than the flames within, but she knew the way to defeat the fear now.

"Sorcha has no idea who she's challenged."

"No," Oona said airily, taking a step back and observing Rowan with a bit of surprise. "No, she does not."

Escape

344 days until Roisin returns

Braden found his boots hidden behind a pile of wood in his room. They had not been here all along, of that he was sure. He knew when he found them that he couldn't stay any longer. He needed to find Rowan. Maybe he wasn't necessary to her survival as Bailiff had said, but he was her friend, and he knew from experience how important it was to know your friends wanted you alive.

He needed to find her and remind her that there were people who loved her, especially after the way she'd left home. She didn't know how many people regretted the way they'd parted. She didn't know what her flight had inspired among her citizens. And he had a feeling she still didn't know about Gavin. She ought to hear it from a friend.

Braden snuck out the window again. He'd hidden a few rolls of bread the last few days, and a sheep skin of water. It wasn't much, but he hoped it would see him out of this deserted part of the forest to a village.

"Do you want to marry her?"

Braden slid down the last several rungs of the trellis, getting scraped and bumped along the way. *Again.*

He sighed, laying his head against the wall of the house, and turned to face the soft voiced dream of a girl he was being forced to leave.

"Don't you ever stay inside?" he countered with a soft smile.

"You have my room," she said reasonably. "I sleep there."

She nodded to a hammock strung between two trees, and Braden felt a fool. How had he not noticed this? It was right below the window. He could have watched her sleep every night. Stored up a thousand memories of her.

"You haven't answered my question," she said in a small, shy voice.

"Would that make you jealous, Darling?" Braden said coaxingly. He walked nearer to her, waiting for her to look directly at him. But the closer he came, the more her eyes became tied to the ground.

"That isn't my name," she whispered. "You don't even know my true name."

"Nor you mine," he teased. She was holding a small pile of blankets, apparently preparing herself for bed. Braden reached out and played with the fringe, so near her arm, watched her stiffen and begin to blush. He smiled deciding to make it easy for her. "She is my friend, nothing more."

"Nothing more?" She looked up then, and her eyes were so hopeful. For half a second Braden was filled with an all encompassing fear. He saw in her eyes the same sort of expression Colleen had worn when she looked at him. Colleen's love wasn't real. What if Darling's wasn't either? None of these women had real names, what if this was all in his mind?

She was looking at him with those lovely wide eyes and he longed to lower his lips to hers, and wrap her up and run away with her into the night. But he looked around this lovely safe place. She belonged here. She should stay safe. The world should bend around itself to build a case to preserve this jewel.

Braden lifted his hand and ran a single finger down the slope of her cheek. She shivered and drew away just a step, looking at the ground again.

"I can tell that you love her. And she must love you, if she sent you her horse. Does she want to marry you?" Darling's tiny question fell towards the ground.

"Ro—" She cut him off with a finger pressed to his lips and electricity charged through him. They froze neither of them able to break the contact for a moment. Then she spun away, her breathing heavy. She threw the blankets onto the hammock and began throwing fruits and vegetables into a pack.

"No names," she reminded him breathlessly, with her back to him.

"She has never wanted to marry me," Braden answered, because he felt sure she needed to know. "She fancies herself in love with a prince she has never met."

"Does she?" Darling Girl spun around, delighted. "How romantic."

"What is romantic about that?" Braden asked in disgust.

"Well," Darling shook her head, and her eyes took on a distant dreamy quality. "Their hearts can pull to each other across the wide world, and build hope inside them. He could be anyone. He could be perfect."

"Only until they meet. Then he's as real as anyone."

Darling gave him a patiently superior look. "Why does she think she loves him? If they have never met?"

"They write to each other." Braden shrugged.

"Oh." Her hand clutched her heart. Braden would never understand women.

"Then they have met. Their hearts have met, even if not their eyes."

Braden rolled his eyes to show her just what he thought of that.

Darling moved off again, collecting food, and humming as she went. She moved as though she was dancing. He didn't know why he scoffed at her belief in the romantic. She was his dream, and here she was even better than he'd imagined. Why shouldn't Rowan's love be the same? Why did he want Rowan's love to be less special? He did not want to marry Rowan. But for so long he'd thought of her as his friend, and his eventual bride, it was rather galling that she could love someone more than him after all he'd done for her. It made him...resentful.

Braden startled at the thought. Custodian was right. He was too angry for this lovely girl. Not just angry with Rowan, with his family, with Sorcha, with the world for keeping him from this place. He was far too angry. He didn't deserve Darling Girl. But her little jealous comments and concerns meant that she too felt what was between them. Just this once he wanted to forget about the world.

Braden walked up behind her and lay a gentle hand on her shoulder. "May I have this dance?"

She looked at him for the longest time, her eyes wide and hopeful, then she shook her head.

"You shouldn't tarry," she said, and a grin covered her face. "Bailiff will be along shortly to return you to your cell. If you mean to escape this is your chance."

Carrying the pack and lifting the blankets from the hammock, she walked out of the little garden, towards a post where Yseult waited, holding at least two other sheep skins of water and another pack of food to add to the one she carried.

She was helping him escape.

"Why are you helping me?" he asked.

She shrugged. "You want to get back to her."

"She is...my brother in arms," Braden laughed. "I need to be sure she is safe."

Darling tied the second pack to the saddle, and rolled up the blankets to slip into the straps. "I understand."

It was lovely watching her work. Like she was his wife sending him off on a quest. Making sure all of his needs were properly cared for, her eyes averted to hide how much she would miss him, how much she wished him to stay.

"Dance with me," Braden said again. "Let me hold you in my arms just once before I leave."

"No." It was quietly said, but he could hear that she was flattered by the request.

"Why not?"

She looked over her shoulder at him then with a lovely playful smile on her lips. "It wouldn't be as romantic. Now you shall ride away wondering just how it would feel to hold me in your arms and our hearts shall long for each other across the distance. Pulling us together no matter how far away you ride."

Braden laughed. She was perfect. Better than perfect, she was a living dream. He wished he could stay. He wished he could hold her. He wished so many things.

Braden took the reins she held out to him, and as her hand pulled away he saw a rose petal, dotted with blood lay in his palm as well.

"It was on your wound, many were." Darling's fingers gently traced the air above the petal making Braden's pulse race. "I think your friend sent them to keep you from dying until we could find you."

Braden stared at it simultaneously appalled by the idea that not only had these strangers saved him, but Rowan as well, and also...so immensely grateful that his heart hurt from the feeling. Rowan truly did love him, didn't she? Sometimes he wondered.

"Thank you for keeping it safe." Braden slipped the petal into a small pocket on the tunic Custodian had sewn for him. He lifted a foot into the stirrup and pulled himself onto Yseult's back. He looked down at Darling Girl and smiled. "And thank you for finding me. It was wonderful getting a chance to walk through the evening air, with my dream come to life."

She blushed at the little compliment, but appeared too overcome to speak. So Braden turned the horse away from the house and galloped off into the forest.

"We should leave the forest," A said as she watched the boy ride away.

"He cannot find his way here again." C countered. "And...he is her true love. It was bound to happen. The nurse's blessing said Darling Girl must find love."

"It said she must earn it," B countered, not to be out argued, even when no one was arguing with her.

"One could safely call saving his life, having *earned* his love," C replied.

"It is not his love, or hers that concerns me," A interrupted. "He is our sister's man. I feel her power all over him."

"And our great niece's," C pointed out.

"Yes. But who of the two of them has spent their life manipulating and perverting love?" A shook her head. "Her Majesty means to find Darling Girl through him. I have told the trees to move about constantly, confusing him, but I am not sure it is enough."

B laughed. "I told the horse to ride him in circles for a while as well."

"Then we are well protected." C commented. "Anyway, Her Majesty knows where we are, she simply cannot find us. He may be partially her man, but when he returns for Darling, he will be his own. Trust me. He is her love. And I will not allow Her Vengeful Majesty to so pervert love that I can no longer believe in its power. All will be well. You will see."

A and B watched their sister walk back into the house without a word. They would stay in the cottage a while longer. But caution was too much a part or their makeups to let them simply trust love.

Challenges of Magic

owan braced one hand on the wall of the guest cavern regulating her breathing, rolling her muscles and waiting. When she heard Oona screech, a sound oddly similar to a small eagle, Rowan launched herself forward.

A flaming wall of debris blocked her path, but Rowan didn't hesitate, she raced through the inferno, headed towards the falls. Flames heated her body, and singed her hair, but she was protected from most of the damage by the armor of pain turned scales that she had built herself.

Rowan had to fight not to laugh. She loved this.

As Rowan leapt up to clear a small fissure on the cave floor, Oona's tale came out of nowhere and knocked Rowan down, she landed on her back, amid the flames.

Rowan rolled away from the fire, afraid for no reason. She still had her scale armor so she was perfectly safe. But...lying there in the flames she felt like she was a rose tossed into the bonfire on the Day of the Rose. For a moment she was terrified of dying alone, consumed in flames.

So she leapt to her feet and ran for cover as Oona began to pelt her with a little shower of flames.

"Hey, you haven't taught me that," Rowan complained as she ran. Oona's flames had flown out as one stream, then split apart in the air like a shower of arrows. It was amazing! But it wasn't fair that the dragon was holding Rowan back with magic she had no way of knowing.

This was a sort of test, to see how well Rowan could use dragon magic while in motion. Rowan's objective was to reach the falls, Oona only had to keep Rowan back. It was a test Rowan had to beg the dragon to give her. Oona thought the whole thing silly. Rowan would know what she needed to know when she needed to know it, or she would die. It was all very simple to someone who'd lived for centuries. But Rowan wanted the test.

Honestly, Rowan wanted the fun! She hadn't had fun like this in so long.

Oona chuckled. "We could fill four of your lifetimes with the things I haven't taught you."

The dragon breathed more flames. These curved like a whip around the bolder Rowan crouched behind to flash right before Rowan's face like a toothy, gaping mouth.

"You'll have to imagine, invent or discover most of it on your own, eager warrior."

Rowan, who loved to run, loved to fight, loved to be in motion, stood still and stared deep into the mouth of flame. It shifted and writhed, but never dissipated. *It was so beautiful*. Could Rowan make something like that?

Rowan set fire to her insides, not with fears and pain as she learned to use, but to her wonder and to her imagination. She set it alight and fanned it so smoke rose within her. Rowan tilted her head back, and breathed smoke upwards. It rose out of her like a column, but as it grew high the smoke dipped and rolled and rumbled, forming eerie clouds that blocked the bolder from Oona's view.

Rowan laughed as she stepped confidently into the mouth of Oona's flames. Rowan stood within the flames and rolled her neck, loving the heat pulsing across her skin, loving the echoing heat within her being. Ooooo, she could do anything she wanted, couldn't she?

Unlimited.

Rowan raced around the bolder. The clouds blocked her sight as much as Oona's, but Rowan could hear the falls up ahead. She raced towards the sound.

More balls of fire flew through the air, pelting Rowan, and the ground around her. Rowan raced around them where she could, but several struck her directly, burning and jarring with the impact though they could not do serious damage.

Oona's tail swung through the air again, but this time Rowan felt it coming. With a rush of air her tail shoved at Rowan's clouds of smoke, slicing through them.

Rowan ducked and rolled away, still on track to reach the falls. As she rolled to her feet Rowan shouted out a stream of flames directly at the dragon.

"Dragons like heat." Oona chuckled.

Rowan ignored her, she wasn't trying to hurt the dragon, just distract it. She was nearly to the falls, a few feet more—

"Aaa—ghh—" Rowan cried out, fumbling even to make noise as she fell, drenched in mud from the stream. It was in her mouth and nose, it tripped her feet, and as she fell it lay upon her as heavily as a fallen wall.

Oona had dipped her tail under the water and used it to throw water and mud over Rowan. Rowan struggled to shove it out of her mouth and off her eyes. She couldn't even get rid of enough of it to yell at Oona.

"That is how you combat dragon fire," Oona informed Rowan, wearing a superior smirk. She sat back comfortably under the falls as Rowan slipped and slid and fumbled even to find her feet. Clearly Rowan had not passed the test. It seemed she was a bit unmatched against the dragon.

For now.

"The window spell is really terribly simple," Oona said with a yawn settling under the spray of the waterfall. It hadn't escaped Rowan's notice that they had trained more in the last day and a half than they had in the rest of the time she'd been here. Oona was pushing. Growing as rushed as Rowan had been upon finding the cave. It should make Rowan nervous, clearly the dragon knew things Rowan did not.

But Oona's haste was making Rowan calmer, and more curious about this creature. They wouldn't be together long, and Rowan wanted to know her.

"All eternity is connected. Therefore all beings are connected. One simply has to find the being they want to inhabit and enter their mind."

"Of course," Rowan said dryly. "Why didn't I think of that?"

Oona chuckled. "We've well established thinking is not your talent, knight."

Rowan settled on the ground, taking a deep breath, she began to think about how everything was connected, and tried to sort through who—

"Oh stand up and pace. Twirl your thorn," the dragon said exasperatedly. "You are trying to think again."

Rowan grinned and obeyed. She quite liked the dragon, insults and all. She paced slowly, spinning the thorn around and around in her hand, every time it turned she watched the deadly beauty of its arc. It was so lovely, but so clearly deadly. It spun and Rowan saw her grandmother's face as she cursed Roisin in the arc of the blade. Sorcha was never far from Rowan's conscious thought, but Rowan was never sure she understood her.

The blade twirled again but it seemed further away. She could feel the thorn, could vaguely see it, but her being was reaching out for other eyes.

Rowan began to see a misty image before her, a clear blue sky, and white clouds, it was indistinct, but endlessly peaceful. Rowan saw a slender hand laying against a puff of white cloud. But...something was...fighting her. The blue of the sky darkened at the edges, as it fought to shove Rowan out. But Rowan wasn't done yet. She shoved with her power and with her being, fighting to get inside that mind. She could see like the frayed edges of a tapestry, a hand stretching towards her, holding out a crystal.

A small hand, soft and...maybe familiar.

The dagger clattered against the stone floor of the cave and Rowan stumbled back several steps. She felt light headed.

"Sorcha!" Oona's shout reverberated around the cave, shaking the ground. She was out from under the falls and fully awake, towering over Rowan, looking equal parts horrified and impressed. "The first time you use the window spell you use it to enter the mind of your greatest rival— the *queen of the Fairy*! Are you mad?"

Rowan lay a hand against one of the dragon's flanks to steady herself and crouched to lift the dagger, smiling to herself. She hadn't seen much. But she'd done it, otherwise Oona would not have known, would she? Rowan had used the window spell on Sorcha.

She lifted the blade and slid it into her belt, her dizziness shifting into a tingle of heady pride.

Rowan notched up her chin, taking several steps back to better see Oona's face. "Now she knows." Rowan shrugged, unsure if that was true, Maureen hadn't known when Sorcha used the window on her. But Rowan had certainly felt like someone was fighting her. "Or at least I do."

"Knows what?"

"That spell is said to be a power only the Fairy queen can wield. Now I know that at the very least I have power enough to deserve that role," Rowan remarked.

"*My word,* but you are arrogant," Oona said in an awed voice. "I knew you were a bit, but...this level is very nearly impressive. For one who spent her whole life fearing power, you are becoming quickly fond of it."

There was nothing in Oona's tone to imply censure, but Rowan felt it still. She took another step back, and forced the pride of having...

"I beat Sorcha! Why shouldn't I enjoy that?" Rowan shouted at the dragon, and herself at the same time, as doubts began to grow within her. "All my life she has been tearing me down. Winding her way into my closest relationships and distorting them. She used Maureen to spy on me against her will so I began hiding things— from *Maureen!* Sorcha tricked my father into telling me he would prefer I die than Roisin." Rowan broke off a moment as she heard tears in her own voice. "It isn't as though I didn't already know it, but she made him *say it* to my face. I have spent my life frightened that she would always be more powerful than me, that there was no way for me to ever defeat her. All I did was...see that there is a way. What is wrong with that?"

"Who said there was anything wrong with it?" the dragon asked patiently. "You should love your powers. You should be pleased when you see what you can do with them. I was merely galled at the inexpressible magnitude of your arrogance to make such a choice." Oona tilted her head to the side a bit and nudged her head up slightly in question. "What do you think is wrong with it?"

Rowan released a breath, turning away from the dragon. What did she think was wrong with it? Nothing. Why would she?

Rowan felt that tingle of heady power dancing across her skin, but with a slightly sickening effect now.

"I...Braden has been afraid of my power. I remind him of Sorcha. I suppose sometimes I remind myself of her. Then...in the forest when I was on my way here. It took everything I had not to crawl inside the minds of my father's soldiers and change their very natures and bend them to my will." Rowan clenched her fists at her side. "I suppose I worry that I will like the power too much and try to change the whole world to suit me."

There was a slight snort behind Rowan. Slight for a dragon. It blew Rowan's cropped hair and the skirt of her dress forward, but it did not affect Rowan's footing.

"Far be it of me to stop someone from wanting to keep an eye on their thirst for power but— you could not now or ever truly alter the nature of those soldiers, or anyone else. You might manage to control another's mind enough to force a task on them. And we know for certain you can steal a memory or two. I suppose if the memory were profound enough the removal of it might alter one's inner nature, but not the way you mean. There is no magic in the world that can change one's deepest self. Only one's choices can do that. If there were a way, Sorcha would have destroyed you years ago. There would never have been a Fairy war and all the world would simply bend to her power as she wants...some days."

Rowan spun to look at the dragon at that remark. A heavy sort of curiosity settling over her.

"What...does she want other days?" Rowan asked quietly.

"Hmm." The dragon moved slowly back to the falls. "Sorcha has always loved power. For every bit of it she found or used she wanted more. But she didn't truly relate it to power over others until she was hurt again and again by those to whom she gave her trust." The dragon looked off into a corner of the cave, and Rowan had to bite her tongue to keep from asking if the dragon had known Sorcha personally, or if this was all what she'd gleaned from her knowledge of eternity. Maybe she should ask. But Rowan was always at war with her curiosity about

Sorcha. She didn't want it to become what it had been in the past— a longing for there to be love between them.

"Until you were born, I would say most days Sorcha wanted to have someone love her unconditionally."

The words struck Rowan, and she felt her fingers curling in to find her scars. Were they so similar?

"There are still days when that is all she wants. But...it is unlikely she would recognize such a thing now, even were she to have it. Years of hoarding power has confused love and unflagging obedience for her." There was a long stretch of quiet, heavy with thought. Then Oona looked up from in the falls with a soft smile.

"Do not think about that too much, arrogant warrior," Oona instructed with a smile. "Already I feel you wanting to take on responsibility for her pain, and it isn't yours to carry. It isn't anyone's. It is good that you be...aware of your love for the power blossoming within you. Your fairy half and your human half may yet prove complementary to one another. But do not be so cautious that you forget to feel the joy of the power. You should have joy in all your gifts, and awareness of all their potential costs."

"It's me that needs to be balanced," Rowan said quietly. She peered over her shoulder to the green cave where Bran had led her. The well of the future.

"Oona," Rowan said, her eyes once more finding the dragon. "Who led you into the well of the future?"

Oona sighed and her eyes grew large and sad. "My son, Hyde, my youngest. He stood in the archway grinning like a fool and dared me to chase him. He was always too eager for his own good, that one. When first I stayed I understood so little. I thought he would stay with me. I thought it would be as though he were living. It was not. Still I stayed. In here, I thought, I shall never feel loss again." Her eyes looked up and pierced Rowan with that same look of tearless pain. "It seems no matter how many times I learn the lesson, eternity has more to teach me."

The dragon lay down beneath the spray and shut her eyes. Rowan stood just where she was a while longer, watching the dragon. She didn't feel ready to rest yet. Maybe it was that lingering tingle of success. Or maybe it was the way Oona's eyes lingered on her as though she knew Rowan were about to die and wanted to stop her. Whatever the reason Rowan's mind wasn't ready to rest.

Was she arrogant? Was it arrogance that led her to choosing Sorcha's eyes to see through? Rowan worried that it was worse than that. She worried that the child part of her that once wanted to earn Sorcha's forgiveness and be one another's family had more to do with the desire.

Rowan always wanted the love she could not have.

Like Sorcha, apparently.

Rowan followed her feet towards the other caves. She thought at first they were headed towards the guest cavern. But she walked into the green hallway instead. She could feel the pressure of it trying to shove her back, pushing down upon her. But she walked on. She didn't know who or what she was hoping to see today. She just knew she had to be in here.

She felt a presence beside her. On instinct her hand wrapped around the hilt of the thorn and she swung around with her blade, stopping just short of Bran's neck.

He seemed unperturbed by the threat. His eyes slid down to the blade and back to Rowan's face blandly. "And here I thought you saved me."

"Why did you try to lead me in here?"

"So you could see something that wasn't in front of your face for a change." Bran shook his head. "But you would resist even that."

"I saw Petal."

"Because she was part of your purpose here. Because her gift was in your hand and your love for her was in your heart. She was right before you. Think bigger. Wider. *Wilder*." Bran spread his arms wide, still unconcerned with the weapon at his throat. "This is the well of the *future*. Any future. All futures. Remember that baby you foresaw in your father's arms? See its future. See Brigid's future. See the future of that baby you blessed with a quill." Bran laughed. "See the *quill's* future. See the future of another land. Another people. Look beyond your face!"

"Why?"

He cocked his head to the side. "For a girl who believes she can set her own limits you set them awfully small. Have you such little use for yourself?"

Slowly Rowan lowered the blade to her side, and slipped it into her belt. She looked down the hall, felt its pulsing power, heard a voice whispering "limitless."

"I have plenty of use for myself. I have curiosity enough to look. And hunger enough to stay to see it all." Rowan said slowly. Then her eyes found Bran again and she smiled. "Seeing what is right in front of my face isn't setting limits. It is experiencing eternity in one moment."

Gently, Rowan lifted her hand and gripped Bran's upper arm the way she did with her knights back home. He hadn't been alive when they'd developed that gesture, that secret hug between friends. But he raised his hand and gripped her back.

"I am sorry you are dead, my friend. I have missed you. And I have tried to keep my promises to you," Rowan insisted.

Bran smirked. "I am pleased to hear it, lady knight. Never say I didn't offer you a peek at what is ahead for you."

"Death, or success, or utter surprise, I shall see my future when I reach it," Rowan said confidently.

Bran's laughter lingered in the hall, long after he vanished, taking the weight of the room with him. Even the pulsing light was gone.

It took Rowan a moment to realize what she was seeing. Her breath caught as she walked up to what had appeared to be solid walls before. The tunnel stretched high and wide, as large as the cave she and Oona trained in. And the walls were filled with hundreds of alcoves, nearly everyone had a pulsing fire and resting in each flame, a single dragon egg. One egg was roughly the size of Rowan's torso and formed from scale like iridescent skin. Hundreds of eggs waiting to hatch. Waiting to change the world.

Rowan laughed in shock. "The well of the future indeed."

Wrestling Fears

336 days until Roisin returns

It took Braden over a week to exit the forest. The trees moved. He'd swear he went around in a million circles. The forest could not possibly be as large as it felt while he was in it.

It had only taken him until his second night away from the cottage to realize that he had never been in Anwyn's forest. He was in the Enchanted Forest, which made escape all the more difficult. What he couldn't explain was why the women had felt the need to lie about that as well as their names. There was something very otherworldly about that cottage, and yet he'd missed it from the moment he left.

He had always considered himself very much a man of the human world. He was not overly fond of fairies or their magic. He had no interest in finding magical creatures. He liked ordinary things, women in their place, men in theirs. Good food, good company, and time enough to pursue his passions. Magic had never entered into his desires.

But that cottage was clearly magical. It was in nearly every way removed from the human world. The women were all fairy. They lived without any company but their own, and despite the incredible comfort and peace of their lives, they lived like criminals. They trusted no one, they would not allow for the use of proper names, nor so much as ask what was going on in the rest of the world.

They were fleeing something. But Braden could not bring himself to care. If Darling Girl loved them, he was on their side in whatever crime had sent them fleeing.

He just hoped when this was all over Yseult could help him find his way back. Otherwise he would wander the woods for the rest of his days searching for them. No wonder the forest was reputed to devour a hundred men a year, any man would go in looking for them? Who wouldn't allow themselves to be eaten in hopes of finding that cottage once more? He would.

He wondered if they'd been there forever. If they waited for every wounded man and nursed him back to health. He wondered how old Darling Girl truly was. He didn't care if she was a hundred or twenty, he loved her. He had to go back.

"They were real, weren't they?" Braden spoke to the horse, needing his question voiced to the universe. "I wasn't trapped between life and death, and having visions of perfection, was I?"

The horse, who had been walking slowly up the south road in the direction of Anwyn, stopped and looked askance at Braden. Her expression said clearly that he was an idiot. She reminded him slightly of Rowan in that moment. Rowan wouldn't sit around worrying about things like that.

He didn't want to go home. He'd left the forest to find Rowan. The trouble was he had no idea where to begin looking.

"Can you take me to her? Do you know where she is?" He found himself reluctant to speak Rowan's name aloud. Having been choked three times, and warned at least twice as many by the women of the cottage had not done it. But he felt Darling's finger against his lips shushing him, and the word would not come out.

He didn't need to voice her name. Yseult pulled at the bridle nodding her head. Then her ears pricked up, and her every muscle went stiff. She yanked the bridle out of his control and darted back into the Enchanted Forest. Braden fought her the whole way, but the bullheaded horse was just like her mistress and wouldn't listen.

She dragged Braden unwillingly behind a clump of trees. Braden was about to yank on the reins again when he heard the unmistakable sound of horses' hooves. Many of them.

Braden ducked down closer to the trees so he was nearly leaning against it, only then noticing that the sleeve of his tunic, which he had originally taken for a very soft blue color, was blending in with the foliage around him. Rather than wonder at it, Braden yanked the hood of the tunic over his head and pulled the blanket free of his packs to lay over Yseult. They blended right in with the forest. Well enough to watch an entire garrison of soldiers passing. Braden and Yseult were hiding for the better part of an hour, as mounted soldiers, several wagons of weaponry and supplies, and battalions of foot soldiers marched down the road. Towards the border of Stonedragon.

Those were Anwyn's soldiers. Marching on Stonedragon. What was going on?

When it had been quiet for some time, Braden pulled the blanket off Yseult's back and rolled it up slowly. Was his father going to war with Rowan's?

He ought to reveal himself to the army and demand answers, but he felt very cautious of such a move. He'd been attacked on his father's lands. Traveling with a contingent of his father's soldiers.

"Take me to her. Before I change my mind," Braden instructed the horse. He held onto the reins to help keep his seat, but made no effort to direct the horse as she raced out of the forest and up the road.

Petal and Sorcha walked down the slope of a little hill, towards the sea. There were a few children playing along this stretch of beach, with their parents watching or playing along with them. They were much younger than Petal, the children of Petal's age were at their lessons now. Petal had been excited when the outing was offered. But she didn't seem as enthusiastic now that the moment had come.

Sorcha thought that might have something to do with their feathered companion. Petal was holding the crystal with Desmond inside, had even asked if she might. But Prince was perched where the crystal usually rested, his claws digging into the scepter to hold him in place.

Petal tightened her hold on the crystal, drawing comfort from Desmond. It would not take much time now, every day Petal grew closer to Desmond. She just needed something. Some little push.

Sorcha nudged her gently. "Go on, say hello. Go play."

Petal paused, stretching out the crystal.

"I trust you with him," Sorcha said gently. She settled herself atop the hill to watch.

"Aren't you coming?" Petal inquired sweetly, but Sorcha noticed her eyes carefully avoided the bird that had hopped off the scepter now and was pecking at the grasses on the hill.

"No dear. When a queen is present play ceases. I will not hinder your joy. Go. Play."

Petal turned her back on Sorcha and ran down the hill with a giggle. Sorcha leaned back on her hands. She'd so rarely done this with her own children, watched them play.

"Do you know, Prince, I must thank you. She is a new chance at motherhood. I will get it right this time. She will be strong, she will be powerful, and she will be *loyal* to those she owes love."

The bird pecked at Sorcha's hand viciously. She drew it away with a laugh, and healed the little gouge easily.

"Oh, don't pout. Why I've let you out three times this week to find your love, to show her anything you want of my kingdom, and my movements. I will let you prove your worth to her. I will let Petal free Desmond for her. I am endlessly generous. It is you who should have thought more carefully about what you desired from life."

Petal was making all the children scream with laughter as a hand of waves scooped her up and threw her into the air so she splashed back into the water with a giant crack.

Petal glanced up the hill and waved with a broad smile.

Mama, look! Look, I can make the whole garden dance with me.

Sorcha waved at Petal, her mind laying Sinead's little face over that of the sweet girl before her.

"I will get it right this time."

A loud screech heralded Bran's return. Sorcha glanced up to see him flying towards her. Prince shot off the ground and flew at the other bird. They tussled in the air, each taking a few nips out of the other.

"Sorcha! Your Majesty, watch," Petal cried out.

Sorcha heard her with one ear, but her eyes were caught on her struggling creations.

"Boys, that is enough." She lifted a hand into the air, and though Prince continued to try and take a bite or two out of the other bird, Bran ignored him and flew right to Sorcha's hand.

Once Bran was with her, Prince, as ever afraid to lay eyes on Sorcha, landed on the hill and went back to pecking at the ground.

Sorcha remembered then that she'd heard Petal cry out and glanced her way. But she was just splashing in the waves with the other children.

Bran ran his head against Sorcha's cheek softly, showing her what he'd come to share.

Braden had left the Enchanted Forest, well rested and healed, and wearing fairy silks.

Sorcha's hand clenched angrily in the grass. Her sisters were helping him though they must be able to sense her on him. Fine. Sorcha wanted him alive until he could lead her to that cursed Rose Princess, so all they'd done by helping him was help Sorcha.

Bran screeched apologetically.

"Do not worry," Sorcha replied, running a hand down the bird's head. "You won't fail me again. Follow him more closely, show Sir Donovan where to arrange his display. And be sure to give the troops their orders in...ten days should do it, I think." She threw the bird up in the air and he vanished in a flash of purple magic to speed him along. "What do you think Prince, can you—"

"Your Majesty!" Petal cried out again. Really, she had the worst timing.

"One moment, my dear." Sorcha held out her hand, looking at the raven before her. He hopped on obediently but kept his eyes on the ground. Sorcha saw a little something red clasped in his beak but when she tried to take it he rolled it into his mouth defiantly. Sorcha chuckled. "I've something special for you to show her now. Prove your worth, show her how far you are willing to travel just to find her."

She nudged the bird into the air, but didn't use magic to speed him along. Every time she sent him out, that girl's bond with the bird grew. He was in her mind, in her dreams. Sorcha giggled to herself. Any day now, Prince would nudge her out of that cave.

Sorcha watched the bird flying away for a moment. When she glanced back down the hill, Petal had already left the ocean. As Petal walked her soaking clothes blew out around her, drying out with the steps. She settled on the ground beside Sorcha and gave her a vaguely disappointed smile, before holding out the crystal.

Sorcha took it with a bit of regret, but Petal couldn't possibly expect to have all her attention all the time.

Petal stared off into the distance. "I think Desmond likes the sea," Petal said softly. "The crystal began to glow a soft misty sort of blue when we were jumping through the waves. Like he was waking up— I called you. But you didn't see."

Sorcha opened her mouth to speak, but the words were choked by the past.

I did make them dance, Mama. I did. Sinead's petulant voice filled Sorcha's mind. *I called and called but you didn't look. You never look.*

335 days until Roisin returns

Colum was risking getting nearer to the border now. Not just because of the way things had gone with Tyce. But because there seemed to be a distinct possibility that Anwyn's soldiers were looking for them. The soldiers had stopped searching villages and moved into the forest. The journey was taking much longer than Colum would like. They'd reached Mount Anwyn and were skirting its feet along the border of the Fairy nation to avoid Anwyn's soldiers.

And they were being followed. But not by any human, nor a fairy. A bird followed them. A large black and white eagle with a fluffy face the size of a man's. Everywhere they went, it went, for two days now. Colum was fairly certain now that Sorcha knew where they were. What was not clear was what she would do with that knowledge. Colum worried that she was simply following them to see if they would lead her to Rowan. He couldn't let that happen. But nor could he just turn back.

Every day Colum had to fight the urge to march into the fairy lands and demand someone lead him to his daughter. Either of his daughters. But he felt so much closer to Petal here. And he was so tired. When he pulled himself up into his saddle it felt like it took hours, the only way he made it up was promising his body it was just a little bit further. Once his family was together again, he could let go. Just a little bit further.

Papa.

Colum searched the area for the source of the words but he couldn't see anyone.

Papa. Aren't you coming to get me? Please. Don't you want to see me before you die?

Colum's breath caught, but he pressed on. It was a trick. It had to be a trick. He was not dying. He was just tired. The eagle cried out high pitched like a laugh, but Colum pressed on. He wasn't dying.

Know or Alter

Rowan was flying low over a field of barley, tilting her wings from side to side and allowing the stalks to tickle her feathers. She dipped low into the crop, weaving between them so quickly it was as though she knew the way. She did. She knew exactly where she was going. Her heart was so full as she flew through the stalks, so at peace.

All at once she shot straight up. Out of the field with only bright blue sky and burning sun before her, up, and up. She looped through the air, and evened out to a steady glide, headed straight towards a small citadel. Oh how she'd missed it. Its dark twirling turrets looked lonely today. Her heart grew slowly heavier, black banners of mourning hung from all the windows of the keep. Something terrible had happened.

A violent flash of purple and a terrified scream tore at the fabric of the dream, jarring Rowan. Then it faded and she was flying once more. Closer now to the keep.

She saw its flag, two knotted stalks of barley, the crest she'd become as familiar with as with her own over the years. The flag of Turrlough.

Rowan felt a violent clawing at her heart as something cried out. Her? Or the bird? Or both of them? She nearly shook herself awake with the pain, but something wouldn't let her.

Turrlough vanished and the bird was flying with Rowan through the forest of Mount Kieran. It felt different now, Rowan felt the sensation of flight, but didn't connect to it as she had when she'd been carried through the fields of Turrlough. She just went along as the flight brought her to her own route up the mountain. It flew her through caves she'd searched. Closer. And closer.

Rowan jerked awake. Her heart ached like a claw had dug into it and her breath was as rapid as if she were mid fight. Her hand closed around the hilt of her sword beside her, aching to leap to her feet and fight an enemy. To fix whatever had gone wrong.

Someone had died in Turrlough.

Rowan rubbed the heel of her palm against her heart and fought the fiery fear building up inside her. It was Gavin, wasn't it? She'd never seen him with her own eyes, never sparred with him, never floated down Liadan with him. She'd built so much of her life around the promises of someday. Of one more year.

What if one more year is all some of us have?

She'd been callous with Braden's concerns hadn't she? She hadn't really cared because it was always one day more for her. The future was—

Rowan glanced up and saw Bran's ghost watching her from the mouth of the cave. He raised a brow, offering to show her. The desperate beating of her heart longed to look. Longed to walk into that cave and know for certain if Gavin was alive for her to save. For her to see.

Rowan leapt to her feet, obeying her instincts and nothing else, she began gathering her belongings. There was plenty more to learn here, but there would always be more.

It was time to go.

Oona woke to the sounds of the girl packing, the bells at her ankle tinkled reverberating off the walls and out of the mouth of the cave. If she thought leaving would make it harder for Sorcha's new servant to find her she was very wrong. In here each tinkle of the bell, each beat of her heart had to travel nearly ten times as far just to pass a moment. Rowan was far safer here.

"You could stay," Oona offered, even though she'd known before Rowan reached her cave, that Rowan would not stay. It wasn't in her.

Oona watched the girl running around with that resolute look back on her face. With her short hair tickling her face, and the thorn sticking out of her sword belt.

It had been so long since missing had been fresh. It had been so long since she had to consider once again if she had made the right decision when she decided to step out of the world and remain in this cave—forever. Her life was lengthened both by time and by loneliness. Instead of a life shortened by the mass of feeling that accompanied all experience.

Every time she grieved again, she wondered if this time would be different, if this loss would at last force her to give up this quest to know eternity.

"Sorcha cannot make you kill your sister if you never leave this cave." Oona increased the enticement.

"What about the others? Gavin, and Braden and Petal. Who will protect them?"

"So arrogant." Oona shook herself, rising slowly to step out from under the falls. "There is always someone else. Perhaps one of them. Who is to say Sorcha will not just let them alone if you disappear?"

That stopped her. Rowan turned in the midst of stuffing her last gown into her packs and looked at Oona with a raised brow. "You are."

Oona shrugged sideways. In truth she could not answer that question. She could say it was one possible outcome of Rowan remaining in the cave. But another was that Sorcha, knowing where Rowan was, became so enraged she hurt the girl's family more, to force her out. There were no certainties. But before Oona could set about explaining that she felt Rowan connecting with her share of eternity in a new way. Rowan shook her head, not even bothering to ask the question tickling the tip of her tongue.

Rowan smiled. "Maybe I could never be made to hurt Roisin here, but I could never look in her eyes and tell her she is my sister. I could never wrap my arms around Petal again, or have Maureen frame my face with her hands the way she does when she tells me she loves me." Rowan's smile was a soft, dreamy thing. "I could never see any of them again if I stayed."

"You can see anyone," Oona corrected. To be sure Rowan truly understood all of what she was giving up. "How do you think I knew you before you came."

"But you didn't. Not really. Not the way I need to know them. You knew my name, and my past, even my fears. But you didn't know I was funny. Or how arrogant I am. You didn't know I was mad enough to chop off my hair in a rage and laugh as it burned. You didn't know I would steal the thorn. I need to know all of them. Their secrets and desires and hopes. And I need them to know me."

"Humph." Oona shook her head, she'd known it was pointless. Rowan was too bullheaded, and too young. Despite all the pain she'd felt already, she still had too much hope for her life to give up on it and stay here. "You are right, I didn't know you were funny. But the madness I was well aware of. It runs in your family. It may be the most profound thing your grandmother ever left to you."

"Sorcha is mad?" Rowan said doubtfully.

"No, it would all be so much easier if she were. I meant your other grandmother, Danu. Who but a mad woman would risk her life and the lives of those she loved to save something that scared her half to death? Who but a mad woman would choose to stay here as long as she did, when she had love in her heart and a child at home? She was a creature of deep loves and desires. She wanted to understand eternity as I did."

"Why did she leave?"

Oona shrugged. "She was a young mother and a novice at exploring eternity. She tried to look in on her son as an adult, despite my warnings. What she saw was who her son would become without her influence to temper his father's. She saw much more of the king in him than she had believed possible and she could not allow it to come to pass."

"Then the king truly is his father?" Rowan asked, her voice half shocked half angered.

"You were not wrong." Oona smiled at this girl, still so literal. "Colum is the father of his blood. But the king is the father of his rearing. You cannot ask him to destroy that bond, however imperfect. Even the worst parents can leave their children with some fond memories."

Rowan swallowed her rage and nodded. Oona was sure it must be a trick of the light, but she thought she saw the girl's hair grow as the guilt grew inside her. What an interesting creature she was. Oona wanted to know her almost as much as she still wanted to know eternity.

"So," Rowan spoke slowly, puzzling as she spoke. "She left to fix something she saw, but wound up creating the very circumstances she'd seen?"

Oona gazed at the girl before her and felt Rowan's heart expanding with empathy and love to encompass people she had never known, to forgive some of her father's failings that had led her to leave. Ohh, how Oona would mourn this girl. She was something special. "Sometimes we must learn the hard way that we can know eternity, or we can alter it," Oona replied to herself, really. "Never both."

Rowan tilted her head up and smiled sadly. "Then I must choose to alter it. I would never be content just watching."

Oona laughed. "This I believe I have known about you from the time you were shoving away your nurse's hands so you could learn to walk on your own."

"I cannot be controlled," Rowan said proudly.

"Well, you do not make it easy," the dragon corrected with a chuckle.

"Oona," Rowan said hesitantly. "May I come back, when this is all over?"

Oona turned away smiling though her heart ached. "It shall be the thing I most look forward to."

There was a long quiet stretch as Oona moved about the cave, collecting berries and nuts for the girl to take along with her.

Then out of the quiet came the question Oona most feared hearing.

"Do I defeat her today?"

"You can know. Or you can alter," Oona replied without looking back. She couldn't look on that eager young face, so daring and alive, knowing what lay ahead for her. Traps and challenges, and blood draining away. Loves killed. Magic stolen. So much pain was ahead for her.

"Well," Rowan laughed. "I used to think my mother knew all that lay ahead for me with her mother. Knew it and sat in a thunderstorm so I would be reminded to never give up. That may or may not have been her intention, but it is very much who I am now."

Oona turned to watch the girl for the first time since she was too small of a child to understand, burning fiery blue with the light of her own eternity. She had never appeared more fairy than she did in this moment, and Oona felt again how truly blessed she was to have found this cave, and lived this long, and met this beautiful girl, no matter what her ending was.

"Unto my dying breath," Rowan said, speaking the first words of the oath of knighthood. Then she made the words her own. "Neither man, nor fairy, nor eternity itself will be master of my fate."

Oona's laughter shook the cave, and her heart burned with love for this girl. "Oooh, arrogant warrior, I shall miss you dearly."

In The Forest

331 days until Roisin returns

They were heading up into the pass of Mount Anwyn. Braden couldn't think how Rowan had expected to find dragons here, but he allowed Yseult her head. She seemed to know where she was going. A few days into the journey he noticed something odd. They were following the trail of several mounted men.

Braden felt his unease grow the further on they went. Why had he not once asked the women who rescued him what day of the year it was? He had a feeling he'd been in that cottage far longer than he'd believed. When Yseult led him to a little outcropping overlooking a small clearing Braden took her nudge for a hint and dismounted. He removed the blanket again and hid Yseult beneath it before pulling up his own hood and finding a comfortable enough spot to lay down at the cliff's edge and watch.

A rather large part of his mind wanted to call him a fool for following the orders of a horse and for believing she had some sort of predictive powers. But he hadn't been laying down five minutes when people slowly trickled into the clearing. Men on horseback. The same men who attacked him on the road.

Braden wanted to look back at Yseult and ask how she could possibly have known, but he held still, forced even his breathing to be as small as possible lest any of them sense him.

Braden lay quietly for a long while, watching as the assassins filtered in, and milled about. What were they all waiting for?

Suddenly, out of thin air, a large armored man appeared flanked by two fairy.

The horses at the edges of the gathering whinnied uncomfortably, all around birds took to the air. Every human in the circle tensed.

"I don't see my package?" the armored man called out in a challenging, familiar voice. Braden was certain he'd heard it before, but he couldn't place where.

"He could not be followed," one of the assassins said, stepping forward to take the blame.

"Why not?" the knight inquired mildly.

"The horse was too fast, and the trees kept moving before our eyes."

"Then you should have been closer."

"If we were closer we would have to have been on top of them. We'll take our payment for the attack and be on our way," the leader of the assassins put in. "We've been waiting far longer than is advisable and I lost three men getting out of that forest."

"The Fairy queen does not reward failure." The knight turned around and Braden barely restrained a gasp. Donovan! That was the knight Rowan had banished, the one Sorcha had enlisted to kill Rowan.

Before it could all sink in Donovan had drawn his sword and struck down the assassin nearest him without any warning. He gave a great cry as nine men attacked him at once.

It was carnage. Donovan had killed three men before even one managed to get a blow in. Brutal, ugly deaths. He drove his sword through one man's eye, shattered another's knees to bring him low then chopped off his head. Blood and screams filled the air, and Donovan...smiled. One of the fairy stayed where he was even as Donovan began to suffer wounds, but one could not. It leapt into the fray, killing the assassins as well, far more quickly, and gently than Donovan.

When Donovan was alone facing off with the leader of the assassins Braden held his breath, it seemed Donovan had finally met his match. The man threw daggers with a speed Braden had never seen before, and had struck Donovan twice in the throat, and once in the armpit. Donovan was slowing down. He lumbered forward, looking as though he would fall over dead at any moment. He threw his sword, it arced through the air and struck the last man square in the chest, hurtling him backwards. He landed several feet away and blood gurgled out of his mouth as he lay dying.

Donovan chuckled, pulling the dagger from under his arm. Blood spewed out of him, and dripped from his mouth. Then the still fairy walked forward and lay a hand against Donovan's shoulder.

His wounds healed themselves at once, and the fairy turned away a look of such rage and disgust on his face it was clear he didn't approve of this servant of the Fairy queen. But he kept the man alive. He kept that monster alive.

Donovan rolled his shoulders, and smiled evilly. He and the fairy vanished from the clearing.

Braden lay a good long while, unable to breathe. The assassins hadn't been after him, not really. But somehow Sorcha had known that a near dead Braden could reach the cottage, and the four fairy who hid there. Braden thought of all the times the women had stopped him speaking his name, Rowan's, Sorcha's; they knew their hiding place was tenuous. He was a threat to them but they'd brought him in and saved him. He had to make sure they remained safe despite that risk.

For surely Sorcha was not done trying to reach that place, and those women. Braden needed to be very cautious. They all did.

Braden glanced back at the place he knew Yseult was hiding. He could not see her because of the blanket he'd been given. He hoped the women had equally magical tools to conceal themselves while he came up with a way to protect them.

330 days until Roisin returns

"Did you know, in the Fairy realm it is possible to be in more than one place at a time?" Petal said as though imparting a secret.

She sat on her father's saddle as he moved about, rolling up his blanket and gathering his rations.

"Your mother has never said so," Colum replied with a smile for his little girl. She was teasing him. She had a sly little slice of a smile on her lips and her eyes were twinkling like stars.

"Well," she shrugged. "It isn't true for *everyone*. But I can."

"You are a special girl," Colum agreed. He tied the last of his gear to the saddle and held out his arms for his daughter to hop down.

She pouted and crossed her arms over her chest. "You still aren't coming for me? Truly?"

"Not just yet," Colum said heavily. His heart broke more and more every day as he had to refuse her again. It wasn't her. That's what he told himself, but it felt like her. And he wanted to go to her so badly.

He'd taken to moving his sleeping roll further away from the other men since the first time Petal had visited. None of the other men could see her, and he couldn't afford to be seen talking to the air. They trusted him, but not implicitly. He needed his men's trust. Because it was clear someone was trying to manipulate them.

It wasn't only Colum who'd seen odd things. Several of his other men reported seeing long dead comrades beckoning them into foggy patches of wood. And their path had become so scarce of animals they were barely able to hunt enough food to survive.

"Do you love her more than me? Is that why? She's older, she's trained as a knight. And she isn't surrounded by the enemy. I need you. She just wants all your attention."

"Petal," Colum sighed fighting not to allow the words to sink into him. This wasn't his daughter. Petal didn't feel that way. Petal knew how much he loved her. "Fairy aren't the enemy. If I knew a way to get to you I would turn the world on its head to make that happen. But right now Rowan needs me. When she is with me, we will come find you together."

"I don't want her to find me." Petal turned her back to him. "This is all her fault. If she'd never been born everything would be better."

"Don't say—" but she was gone, vanished from the horse, taking Colum's breath with her.

She wasn't real.

Yet his hand slipped by the horse and his feet walked towards his vanishing daughter. He didn't want to let her go. Not that way.

"Petal."

Sorcha had her eyes on Petal's talisman again. She did that more and more lately. The talisman disturbed Sorcha, but she also grew...softer sometimes when she saw it.

Right now was not one of the soft times; her hand kept clenching and unclenching around her scepter. Petal thought it might have to do with the door to Stonedragon. Every day it grew more roses, and the more it did the more fairy began to question Sorcha. The talisman was making Sorcha nervous today, reminding her of that door, and Petal was just fine with that. Sorcha ought to feel a bit of the unease she caused others. She ought to ache from her heart out with fear. Ought to lay awake at night longing to be someone else.

Petal rolled the crystal around in her palm as her mind danced with pleasure at Sorcha's discomfort.

A bird swooped between them, startling Sorcha, but not Petal. Petal had seen it coming, and anyway it was a huge eagle, not the raven. Try as she might to believe that what had happened to Prince Gavin wasn't her fault, Petal couldn't see him without feeling badly. The only bit of hope she had was the red rose petal the bird carried in its beak. The bird was very careful never to let Sorcha touch it. If there was still enough of him for Rowan to reach him, then there might yet be a way to restore him.

Petal's stomach knotted. She hadn't been able to fully repair the wolves yet. Sorcha's spell was too strong. And...it seemed likely that her hold on the raven was even stronger.

The magic tied us together.

Prince was at her hand so often, doing her bidding so often. The more evil he did for Sorcha, the more he became truly hers. Just like Petal.

Petal's stomach roiled and a chill ran down her spine at the thought, but she shook it off. Enjoying Sorcha's discomfort didn't mean she was becoming like her.

Petal would find a way to fix Prince Gavin. If indeed there was any of him left in the bird. There must be a way. Rowan loved him so much, Petal had felt it all over the letters she'd stolen.

"Come here to me, my heart."

Petal remembered taking Rowan's hand in her's and whispering the words. She remembered the rush of love she'd felt as the spell called forth Rowan's chest of treasures. Remembered the soft crinkled paper and the ribbon that bound them all drenched in love and hope.

Love and hope that Petal had stolen. Doing evil for Sorcha. Becoming every moment more closely tied to Sorcha.

Sorcha ran a hand down the eagle's head, reading its thoughts, Petal supposed, or seeing its memories. But it did nothing to improve her mood.

"Well," she said with a bit of a bite. "It seems we will need to leave sooner than planned." Sorcha glanced up at Petal. "My dear, I have a treat for you."

Her voice didn't sound especially treat-like, but Petal smiled broadly and widened her eyes waiting for Sorcha to explain.

"How would you like to visit an old friend?"

Petal glanced from the bird back to Sorcha.

"It has not been so long since I saw the other girls," Petal said hesitantly. She couldn't afford to scream *No! Don't go anywhere near my friends!* But that was how she felt inside. "I cannot say I've missed them yet."

All of Sorcha's earlier unease vanished in true amusement. She laughed light and breathless and the air around her burned with a lovely lavender light like a fresh blossom of spring. She looked so lovely, so innocent. Petal had no idea how she managed it. A moment before Petal had been afraid of her, now she felt like this must be the kindest, gentlest soul in the world.

"Oh, Petal, my dear, I do love you. No, no. We are not going to see the girls. The king of Anwyn is in need of my advice and I thought to take you with me. How should you like to see Prince Braden again?"

"Braden!" Petal's heart leapt. She could see Braden. Everything under her skin felt light and fresh and happy! She hadn't seen him in so long. She'd missed him. He worked for Sorcha so she couldn't object to Petal befriending him. Petal could have a friend again. In Petal's palms the crystal began to burn, its surface thinning out. It pulsed softly, nudged Petal, it knew she knew how to open it, and something in her excitement made it think she would do it now.

Petal swallowed. She didn't dare open her palms lest the Fairy queen see. But there was something in Sorcha's eyes. Something, even when she looked soft and kissed by goodness, that whispered of secret knowledge. She already knew, didn't she?

She already knew Petal could open the crystal and was refusing to. Why didn't she force the issue? Petal glanced to the bird still at Sorcha's hand, but she didn't see the eagle. She saw a raven. She saw it as though it were pecking its way out of Prince Gavin's body. A man of nearly six feet, reduced to a bird of less than one. Maybe Sorcha was forcing the issue.

Maybe she would take Petal to see Braden, and turn him into a bird so Petal would free her son.

The crystal turned solid again.

Petal nodded enthusiastically. She allowed her eyes to fill with tears, pretending they were only for the joy of seeing one she loved again. Pretending that she felt no fear at all. "I would adore seeing him." She raced forward, hiding her face in Sorcha's dress as she hugged her tight. "Thank you, Your Majesty."

Sorcha kissed the top of Petal's head, returning her hug gently. "My dear girl, you know Mama only wants you to be happy." She was hugging Petal so tightly she must have felt her startle, but she did not let go. And Petal cried silently harder.

This was the second time Sorcha had called herself Mama when she spoke to Petal. And the second time Petal's heart had almost wanted to curl up in the word. She missed Mama so much.

329 days until Roisin returns

Petal hadn't been back in two days. While he had been certain it wasn't her when she was right in front of him, the longer it went with her gone the more Colum worried that it had indeed been his daughter. How was he to know that she hadn't learned some new and impressive powers among the fairy? How was he to know that the time away wouldn't make her remember her home as uglier than it had been? Fear could change a great many things.

Three of his men were missing. Just vanished in the night with their packs and horses though other men had been awake and guarding the camp. Several of the men blamed fairy, and Colum had to admit it was a possibility. They were closer and closer to the border every day. An unnatural fog made travel much harder. Colum wasn't even sure they'd gone anywhere, the trees all looked the same. And surely if they were properly traveling they would have reached the mountain by now. He felt like nothing had changed.

Nothing but Petal's absence.

Colum held up a hand and the men behind him stopped at once. They looked as tired and frayed as Colum felt. No one slept through the night anymore. One man would hear his friend's voice in the cry of a bird, another would swear he saw a dead sibling beckon him. And the flock of birds that followed them had taken to swooping down and stealing food right out of their hands. But across the border were animals a plenty to hunt, and bushes covered with the ripest berries they'd ever seen.

Colum wouldn't have believed it had he not seen it with his own eyes. But the border between kingdoms was a visible, living thing. The trees moved differently. Light fell with purpose and artistry into the Fairy Realm, making lacy patterns on the ground. Animals looked healthier, and fog shaped itself into beings or tunnels —calling out. Everything about the Fairy Realm called out to one and beckoned them nearer. There was no mistaking the Fairy Realm and the human one.

He had his horse poised to cross that border, to try and enter the Fairy Realm though he could not explain it with logic. He wasn't here to find Petal. They all knew where Petal was. And just because one fairy had looked on Colum with favor didn't mean the entire nation would. He had no way to reach her. He didn't think it was Petal who needed him most right now. It was Rowan. Except—

What if she helped Sorcha do something bad? Keagan's voice broke with fear, and that fear crawled into Colum. And the further into him that fear dug the more inviting the border appeared.

He needed to cross that lovely, magical border. There didn't seem to be any possible outcome but that he would cross it. How could there be? His little flower petal was out there.

Colum heard the growling first. It was low and threatening. He could tell his other men were hearing it too, many a blade slide from its sheath. A pair of wolves, impossibly large...materialized stepping over the border from the Fairy Realm. They only appeared when they were on the human half of the border, their tails and hind legs still hidden over the border as though that beautiful vision was only a mirage painted between them and another world. Maybe it was.

The wolves advanced on them slowly, the horses grew skittish, stomping at the ground and walking backwards. Colum led the horses backwards slowly, keeping his eyes trained closely on the wolves.

The animals snarled, showing huge sharp teeth and wrinkling their snouts menacingly.

"Move back slowly," Colum ordered and felt his men beginning to obey. The further back they moved the less magical that border appeared.

Colum shook his head, looking around. It looked like the exact same camp they'd been in the last time Petal had visited. If fairy could trick him into thinking he saw his daughter, why not trick them all into thinking they were still searching when they hadn't moved at all?

"We need to put more space between us and the Fairy border," Colum ordered. They moved further and further from the wolves, but the animals didn't pursue. Odd. Were they trying to keep them away from the Fairy border? Were they fairy guarding their home from invaders? Or was there som—

A group of three birds dove for the wolves, screeching high and angrily.

One of the wolves leapt clear out of the Fairy realm, leaping over another wolf to guard it from the attacking birds. It threw back its head, chomping at the birds and howled a loud warning cry.

Colum was half tempted to wade into the fray and defend the wolves from the birds. Or perhaps the other way. He couldn't know who was on his side. But looked at his men and jerked his head east. The men turned their horses and began to flee.

But a cry rent the air. A human cry.

Colum spun back to see the largest wolf writhing on the ground as one after another the birds dove at it, taking giant bites out of its skin.

"Flee," the wolf cried out, in a woman's voice. The second wolf obeyed.

Colum couldn't just leave her. He didn't know who she was. But he had to protect her.

He leapt off his horse and raced towards the wolf with his sword drawn. He swung for the birds, and quickly enough more swords entered the fray. Colum didn't look to see which of his men had come to help. It didn't matter. The more birds they injured the more the trees filled with birds. Every kind of bird of prey, some diving in with talons raised to attack the men, some diving for the wolf, others just calling out taunting cries from the trees.

Colum's men formed a circle around the wolf, when they'd cleared the birds from her back and aimed their fighting towards the sky. Colum crouched over the wolf, only then noticing the two dead birds on the ground beside her. She was covered with bloody patches of fur, and her eye had been clawed. Her breathing was heavily labored but she was still alive.

She forced herself back to her feet. She had many wounds, but none looked mortal in nature.

"Are you alright?" Colum asked. Too caught up in the moment to even notice how odd it was to be talking to a wolf.

"You do not need to save us, Father of Petal," the wolf said in a woman's voice, and Colum's heart stopped. "We were saving you."

The wolf's ears pricked up and her fur stood on end. She faced across the border and began growling. She howled loud and long. But not loud enough to drown out the scream that came from across the border.

"Papa, help!" Petal's voice.

Colum charged forward.

Though he'd heard a million stories about the Fairy nation guarding itself from men, nothing held him back. When the wolf leapt up to stop him it was tackled by a group of vultures. He could hear the violent struggle behind him. He heard the clanking metal of his soldiers following. But nothing mattered. Nothing but Petal. He had to get to Petal.

Rowan walked out of Oona's cave late at night. She should have expected as much, she was finally on the dragon's sleep cycle. But she didn't let it bother her. She'd known she needed to leave now, so she had. There was snow falling and covering the ground but she wasn't cold. And though Rowan remembered being barely able to breathe towards the end of her journey she had no such difficulty now.

It seemed she'd been learning things from Oona that she hadn't even realized. She could feel that the change was in herself and not the air. The air was just as thin as it had ever been, but Rowan wasn't fighting to draw it in now. She was letting it come to her. It was like that first night when she'd sat for hours and hours trying to learn to be still. The dragon hadn't meant physical stillness. All her life Rowan had been moving, in her mind if not her body. Fighting to get to that future where Roisin was home and safe, where Sorcha was defeated. She'd been under the curse as much as anyone, she just couldn't see it. Her whole life revolving around one moment, every day that passed being counted towards an eventual future she didn't know for sure was coming. But when she just let go, when she was still the air came into her lungs, and the way revealed itself to her, and she found connections she wouldn't have dreamed possible.

Oona had helped free Rowan from the curse. She wanted to turn around and thank the dragon, but the moment she left the cave its entrance was swallowed up by solid rock. There would be no going back yet. Yet.

Rowan smiled, as she added one more thing to the list of hopes for her future. Return to Oona's cave. She made herself a little bed for the night and settled in to try and sleep.

She had a long way to go tomorrow. And she would need all her strength, because she had a feeling the Fairy Realm would be fighting her as much as fairy secrets ever had.

Rowan felt a clawing in her chest, and lay the heel of her hand against it, rubbing it as hard as she could.

"I am coming for you," Rowan said quietly, her hand running circles over her aching heart. "But I have to go to the Fairy Realm first. I need to see it. I need to know it. But I will come for you. So...stay alive, please."

Rowan lay a while, waiting for her mind to call up that Gavin phantom as it had on her journey up the mountain, but nothing happened. She fell asleep, with one hand still guarding her heart.

Shield and Sword

328 days until Roisin returns

Gwyneth and the other gentlewomen were presenting their progress on the various tapestries to the king when the message came. Since there were four tapestries needed and each woman had her own style, Gwyneth had made all the designs then divided the work between the gentlewomen. One tapestry was all but done, because it had been worked on by Maureen as well as Gwyneth and two other women. The others were well on their way, they would be ready when Roisin returned in three-hundred and twenty-eight days. Less than a year. Gwyneth's heart pounded with excitement. She looked back at her tapestry hung from the alcove so everyone could see how far along it was.

As the king addressed the two armored messengers from Anwyn, Gwyneth examined her own tapestry. Roisin lay in the arms of her protector. Her... Gwyneth's mind knew the girl in the design was important, she knew she should know who she was, and why she'd allowed her daughter to be held by a mere child at such a moment. But she simply couldn't reach the knowledge. Every time she tried a soothing music in her mind grew louder and louder, distracting her. She could see dancers moving across the great room with torches lit and so many smiles, such utter peace. But that tapestry kept distracting her. To the left of the alcove was a balustrade with a carving of her daughter's cherubic face from when she was only three.

Gwyneth turned to look at it, there was something wrong with it. Gwyneth walked closer and closer, trying to place what was the matter. When she was right on top of it, she realized it wasn't a carving of Roisin at all.

"Rowan!" Gwyneth gasped. She'd forgotten Rowan.

They all had. Gwyneth looked between the gentlewomen who had suggested she change the design of her tapestry so Roisin lay in her mother's arms. None of them knew Rowan. Not one. But...Gwyneth looked on the tapestry. It was the strangest thing, she hadn't remembered Rowan either. But as she worked her face into the tapestry she felt safer. She felt Roisin was safer in her arms. So she couldn't part with the face of a girl she couldn't even remember.

Gwyneth didn't realize there were tears on her face until Lady Donna lay a hand on her arm sympathetically.

"My queen, what is wrong?"

"Rowan. We forgot Rowan."

"Who, my lady?"

"Rowan!" Gwyneth shouted at the top of her lungs. "My husband's eldest child. Roisin's sister and protector."

"Gwyneth," Balder handed the message to one of the soldiers, who looked on him like he was mad, as he crossed to his wife. "What is wrong, darling? Are you well?"

"Yes, I am well. It is the rest of you who have given in to the spell. Balder, look at that, look at your daughter." She grabbed him by the arm and led him to stand before the tapestry.

"She is lovely. She will be with us soon my love, only three-hundred-and-twenty-eight days left to wait."

"No. Not Roisin. Rowan! Your eldest. Your heir. The daughter who has spent her life trying to protect our little rose and bring her home. The daughter you disowned. Please."

"Gwyneth, you are overtired," Balder said in concern. He turned to face the gentlewomen of the palace. "Lady Donna, Lady Hilda, see your queen to her chambers and see to her comfort. She needs a rest."

Gwyneth jerked out of her husband's arms and approached the soldiers. She yanked the massive out of their hands. She had not read two lines before spun on her husband.

"Balder." She tried to sound patient. "There are soldiers camped at our border. King Alistair is threatening *war*. He says you've missed his deadline to negotiate, twice! Tell me you have our armies ready. Tell me you have sent an emissary to Alistair to negotiate."

Balder laughed. "Alistair is posturing. He would never break the treaty."

"He is!" she shouted. "He says you have. Do you even know if Braden is alive?"

"Of course he is." Balder's tone grew impatient. "Gwyneth, you need a rest. Go with your gentlewomen, or you will go with your guards."

Gwyneth froze; she stared at him, everything inside her shut down for a moment. "With guards? Why?"

"You are causing a scene."

"Corpses littering your nation will make much more of a scene! The curse has you. Fight it. It is more frightening, I kn—"

"I am a king. There is no part of my reign that frightens me. If you are afraid you should have more faith in your king. Guards, escort the queen to her room."

"No. Balder, you must remember Rowan. All of you. Remember Rowan, crown princess of Stonedragon, Knight of the Rose. Remember her! It isn't too late!" Guards grabbed Gwyneth by either arm and lifted her off the ground carrying her from the room.

She did not stop screaming, trying to remind anyone she passed of the girl they'd forgotten. When they reached her suit of rooms the guards threw her inside. She stumbled over a chest and struck her head on the ground, but she leapt to her feet, a bit unsteadily and raced for the door even as the guards were slamming it shut. She yanked it open, but the men stood there with weapons drawn. They didn't say a word but it was clear she was stuck where she was.

Gwyneth shut the door again. Only then realizing she had the letter from Anwyn's general in her hand. She had to get it to Maureen and Rowan's knights. Someone must do something, before the nation was invaded and destroyed. She had to keep it safe for Rowan. Rowan had kept them all safe for so long. Gwyneth sat on her bed, her head was pounding and she could not stop crying.

Rowan would know what to do. Rowan would fight the men and escape. Rowan would never have been taken by such men. Gwyneth simply wasn't like Rowan. But there must be something she could do.

Gwyneth stood with the letter clasped firmly in her hand and paced around the room, looking for a weapon, trying to think like Rowan. Rowan was fearless. Rowan's heart wouldn't be shattered because her husband didn't listen to her, and locked her in her room for causing a scene she—

Gwyneth stopped pacing. No. Rowan wouldn't even have married a man with power over her. But her heart had been broken by her father. It had been broken when he asked her to die instead of Roisin, it had been broken when he didn't listen to her secret, and lashed out. How had Gwyneth seen these parts of her husband time after time and never really understood? He'd never struck her, never struck Rowan so anything he did had seemed so much better than her own father. But Balder should be better still. He should listen. He should respect that others had something to offer.

Rowan had had her heart broken by her father again, and again. That was why she ran away. For the same reason Gwyneth had had an affair with a married king, because she needed to be somewhere where her heart was safe. Because she had to make sure he couldn't break her again. All these years Gwyneth should have related to Rowan far better than she did. Perhaps Rowan was also saving people in the process of running away. But she'd run away from her father. And Gwyneth hadn't seen it.

Gwyneth walked out onto her balcony, looking into the distance. It had never occurred to Gwyneth to go away, alone. Did it occur to other women? Or was it just the Rowans of the world who realized they might be stronger alone? Something soft brushed her fingers, Gwyneth looked down at the climbing rose vine. She'd hated these roses from the beginning of her marriage. Before they began taking over the palace she'd hated anything that reminded her of the woman she'd displaced. Then they began climbing the palace walls and Gwyneth had at last a reason to be rid of them. She'd even convinced Balder to burn the garden. But it wasn't enough. Almost as if the other woman was taunting her, showing her that this would never truly be her place the roses came back, again and again, climbing by Gwyneth's window and winking at her.

Gwyneth cradled the blossom now. And cried even as she was laughing. "I am sorry. I never allowed myself to think of you, only myself. And look at this mess.

You have such a strong daughter. She protected us all for so long, even me, and she must hate me."

Before her eyes, the rose wound itself out of Gwyneth's hand wrapping around the balustrade. And more vines joined it, wrapping around one another and the balcony. Covering the walls. Gwyneth looked to her left, the wall was completely covered with vines of roses that had linked themselves together in a way that looked precisely like a trellis.

"Ohhh." Gwyneth reached out and tugged down on a rose vine. She held tight and dropped her weight towards the balcony floor. But the vine wouldn't budge far enough to let her fall.

Gwyneth's heart pounded with fear and...excitement. Disentangling herself, Gwyneth ran back into her room to search for a sturdy pair of gloves; already her hands were bleeding. But she didn't stop to clean them. Rowan wouldn't.

When she had her thickest leather shoes and gloves on Gwyneth stuffed the letter into the bodice of her gown and walked back out to the balcony. She took a deep breath and held it in her chest. She lifted one leg over the balustrade, holding the railing tight. With a pounding heart she lifted the other leg over. She slipped around slightly as she was setting down her second foot, but a pair of rose buds slipped through her girdle and yanked her flush against the balustrade.

Gwyneth released a breath, shutting her burning eyes a moment to fight back the fear. She could do this. She had to do this. Gwyneth stretched out her right arm and grabbed onto the vines climbing up the wall. She tugged again. But it held steady and there was nothing to do now, but trust that the little girl from the tapestry wasn't done saving them yet, or climb back into her room and fail everyone.

Gwyneth fit a foot into a little hole of rose vines, and released her weight from the balcony, pulling her second foot to meet it.

Ferdy lay back on Rowan's bed, waiting for Gwyneth to make it in through to the missing wall. Honestly, he was impressed. When he'd seen her hanging off the palace wall he hadn't thought she had it in her. He'd waited, expecting her to give up and call for help, but she hadn't. Not once. True, she'd cried the entire way. And talked to herself a little. But it would be pretty terrifying for someone with no magic, and she'd been thoroughly cut up by the thorns.

When she all but fell into the room and crawled away from the open wall of Rowan's old room Ferdy clapped, startling her so badly she screamed.

"Don't turn all helpless now," Ferdy commented with a sideways grin. "You just saved yourself."

Gwyneth collapsed against the wall with a hand at her chest, but slowly a smile spread across her face. "I did, didn't I?"

"Yep. Of course I was already on my way to rescue you, but— hey, now you know."

Gwyneth had a sudden burst of energy; she leapt to her feet and shoved a hand into the bodice of her gown wincing as one of the thrones stuck in her glove cut her chest a bit more.

"I need to speak to Rowan's court. It's urgent."

"Yeah. We guessed that when you ran through the palace screaming about remembering Rowan before it was too late. Mama sent me to fetch you." Ferdy crossed to her and held onto her wrist. "Shall we go?"

He didn't wait for a response. Just vanished with her from the room to the rose garden where Rowan's assembled forces were waiting.

Ardal was finding his place among the other men again. He was no longer their leader, that role was being filled quite efficiently by Maureen. But he was slowly earning their respect. He needed Rowan to return so he could earn her forgiveness.

But at the moment he was simply working to preserve her legacy. Word had reached the Knights of the Rose, through the scattered network of women that composed Rowan's shield, that soldiers from Anwyn were making camp at the border between nations. They had already blockaded any trade by land, or by

Liadan, but had yet to take any further aggressive action. Twice soldiers had been dispatched from their regiment to King Balder, yet none of Stonedragon's forces were preparing for battle.

All the Knights of the Rose were assembled in Rowan's rose garden. As well as five representatives of Rowan's shield maidens. Peg had insisted they be present, Ardal would have insisted himself had she not done so first. For a woman who'd looked down on Rowan's forceful habits in the past she was surely making a wild turn around. She refused to wear gowns, and as far as he could tell no longer performed her duties in the palace. Rowan would have liked that.

Ardal probably wouldn't have invited "Rowan's Sword" to the meeting were it his place to decide. It was composed of young squires, and all manner of children ranging in age from seventeen to seven, and was led by Ferdy and Keagan. The sword was a wild bunch, luckily only five members of the army were present.

It amused Ardal that they had ranks. Ferdy and Keagan split the title of general, while Colleen was a lieutenant and Molly and Finn were captains of the saboteurs and infantry respectively. He supposed they had been doing more than their share to fight the curse before Ardal and the knights, but this didn't seem the right place for children.

When Ferdy appeared with a badly scraped up queen in toe Ardal began to laugh quietly. Sean glanced his way and raised a brow.

Ardal shrugged. "I was just wondering what would happen if we just unleash the children on the Fairy queen."

Sean grinned.

"What on earth happened to you?" Maureen asked as she was laying a hand on Gwyneth to heal her.

Ferdy gave his mother a sharp look then glanced at his brother. The pair watched their mother with concern. Was something wrong with Maureen?

"She climbed across the east wall of the palace, at the fourth floor, held up by nothing but rose vines," Ferdy answered in a wildly impressed voice when Gwyneth struggled for words.

"And why didn't you help her?" Maureen asked sharply. "I sent you to get her."

"And spoil her grand rescue of herself?" Ferdy shook his head. "That would have been cruel."

"Yes," Keagan agreed and a soft lightening of his features took a few years off his sometimes old face, he nearly looked like a child again. Nearly. "She needed to do that."

Gwyneth nodded with still teary eyes. "I did. Thank you, Ferdy. But...we haven't time. There are soldiers camped at the border and Alistair is threatening war if we do not return Braden to him in three days."

"We already knew about the soldiers," Peg commented.

"And that Braden is missing," Keagan added.

"We knew that?" Ferdy asked.

Keagan shrugged. "I knew it. I...I want us to be able to trust him, but I don't know if we can."

"Well *if* we can, and we don't go looking for him when he's missing, he would have a fair amount of reason to turn on us," Ferdy snapped at his brother.

Keagan looked at his feet. "I've been looking," he said in a small voice.

Ferdy rolled his eyes and slung an arm around his brother's shoulder. "Now we'll all do it. I...I should have told you before..." he mumbled. "Rowan asked him to lie to us before she left. So she could make good her escape without you and I following."

"You know where she went?" Keagan demanded.

"Not the location. But I know she's trying to find the dragons," Ferdy replied.

"Oh." At this Keagan seemed to brighten even further. "You should have told me. All but two of the futures where she has dragons on her side result in us winning."

"You put too much faith in your power," Ferdy said darkly.

"What else should I put it in?"

"*Us!*" Ferdy shouted. "I've already told you that."

"Then why didn't you tell me about Braden?"

"Because you would have still wanted to go with Rowan, and we shouldn't."

"She needs us." Keagan looked desperate. "Both of our sisters are out in the world *all alone.*" He shook, fighting off tears. Ferdy clenched his fists a moment before releasing a sigh and pulling his brother into a half hug.

Ardal recalled how focused and certain Keagan's power seemed to make him last year. But it wasn't certainty, was it? Like forgetting Rowan, for those who fell victim to the curse, trying to control the future was a safe place for Keagan to hide from his desperate fear. Poor child.

"We need you here," Colleen said quietly. "Not just me, everyone. Rowan's shield maidens, the people you keep trying to wake up. You're needed here."

"She's right." Maureen stepped forward and lay a hand on each of her sons' shoulders. "Rowan said it before I was even pregnant with you. She said I would have three children, a girl and two boys. *The boys will stay, and she will go away. She will go to the fairy court.* And I asked her why; Rowan said, because I will ask her to. I think she is asking you to stay here as well. To protect her home."

"A fine point," Ardal interrupted when it seemed the boys might start fighting again. "We need to stop an invasion, and somehow find a missing prince."

"This is Sorcha's doing," Colleen said out of nowhere. The whole group of them were gathered around the bench and the tree Rowan was born under, but Colleen had set herself off a bit from the group so as not to absorb their emotions. Everyone looked amongst themselves to see who she'd pulled that thought from.

"Why do you say that, Colleen?" Maureen asked.

Colleen shrugged. "Anwyn never declares war. Even in the past." At first she spoke hesitantly, but the more she spoke the higher her head grew and the closer she grew to the gathering. "They are comfortable. They have no reason for war. They deal very closely with the Fairy queen—she wants war."

"For what reason?" Liam asked. "More and more of our citizens are falling victim to the curse, the king has fallen to it. Why start a war now?"

"What has changed?" Ardal asked quietly. Waiting for someone to provide the answer he already knew. Rowan was gone. And while it was true that the king had fallen victim to the curse, and even some of Rowan's closest compatriots. It was not true that by sheer number there were more people falling victim to the curse.

Rowan's shield maidens, and the network of female informants were proof of that, and the army of children. Somehow Rowan's leaving had woken those who had been victim to the curse in the past.

"Rowan is gone," Keagan said, and his eyes went wild, peering through various futures, Ardal supposed.

"What difference does that make to the Fairy queen?" Nora asked softly, leaning near her grandfather. Before Ardal could answer Peg spoke.

"She is not here to torture for one. Perhaps she does not know where Rowan is. For someone so intent on hurting her, that would be most unsettling."

"And..." Queen Gwyneth spoke up then immediately silenced herself. Everyone looked to her waiting on her comment. "Rowan will learn more away from the palace than she ever could here. She will be alone with the responsibility for her survival. She will succeed or fail at each task on her own. She will have to truly know her power."

"You think we stifle her power?" Cassidy demanded, outraged.

Gwyneth nodded sadly. "It is a human thing. A woman thing. We keep our women close, teach them just enough to always need someone there to guide them. A woman is taught to rely on everyone around her for a sense of her worth. Alone, Rowan will have no one to rely on but herself. It will give her a strength she never could have learned here— if she succeeds. And as long as she has been gone...well she clearly has not given up."

There was a long silent stretch, Rowan's shield maidens nodding their agreement. Her knights sank a little with guilty feelings as though they should have seen and changed this already. Perhaps they should. But now was not the time to be concerned with the past. Rowan the Eternal had gone out into the world and she would come back, stronger and wiser than ever before. Just like they could all be strengthened by these new experiences. Ardal closed his hand around Nora's. He wouldn't have thought to train his granddaughter in the past, but falling victim to the curse had shown him the mistake he made not recognizing the power of ordinary women. His mistake had improved him.

"Let us say that is true," Sir Michael said skeptically. "How would starting a war change anything?"

"It would bring Rowan home," Gwyneth said, more confidently this time. "Word will reach her and she will come back to save us." Gwyneth looked down at her gloved hands, peeling them away. "I escaped my room by these roses." She waved at the roses growing up the wall of the palace.

"I have hated them since I moved into the palace. And Rowan has protected them from me all that time. Today they saved me." Gwyneth went on. "Rowan allowed me to see that I had a strength I did not know. I truly understand her for the first time today. She needs to be out in the world, like I needed to hang off the palace wall."

"I take it, from your flight through the palace, and confinement to your room, that the king has once again forgotten Rowan?" Ardal asked, though his mind was on others the curse might try to ensnare with their desire to hide.

Gwyneth nodded. "Somehow forgetting her has made him oblivious to everything else. He is not even concerned with the threat of war. He says Alistair is posturing."

"He is not posturing." Ardal looked between Rowan's knights. In the past he would have simply ordered them to rally as many soldiers as they could to their cause and head to the border, but it wasn't his place now. And it might be wiser to get the word out through Rowan's Shield. Ordinary women of uncommon strength.

"I can..." Keagan looked around cautiously. "I knew he was forgetting her since the Day of the Rose. It made me angry, so I didn't help him, but I can make him remember. It might not make much of a difference though. He hasn't just been taken by the curse. He chose to be taken by it. He doesn't want to remember Rowan."

Ferdy clenched his fists at his side and a bright light burned around him. Keagan didn't look any less impressively angry. And Maureen settled on the bench heavily.

"What is he afraid of?" Maureen asked her son.

"He thinks she will die, because of what he said. He lives her dying over and over. So he locked her away in a part of his mind where he never looks."

"Coward," Sean bit out. But there were tears in his voice.

"We can rally the forces without him," Peg said, looking among the other shield maidens.

"We can. And we can find Braden without him," Maureen agreed, looking among them all, then her eyes fell on the roses growing up the wall. "But if we are truly to preserve Rowan's legacy she will want her father to be a part of it."

Maureen took a deep breath and looked back at her troops.

"Alright, there is no time to waste, and fortunately we've forces enough for there to be no such need. Keagan, you and I shall remind the king of his daughter. Peg, you and the other shield maidens spread the word to everyone near the Anwyn border to pick up arms and prepare to defend their homes, then call up as many forces as you can from the ocean borders, male and female, send them here to be trained and disbursed as needed. Knights of the Rose, you will seek out Prince Braden. Do not let any soldiers of Anwyn, nor any fairy stop you. Until we know the prince is safe he is your mission."

"Are we making no efforts at diplomacy?" Declan asked, eyeing the children. "You cannot mean to use the children for such a cause?"

"Diplomacy isn't really our mandate," Ferdy remarked slyly. "Now if you want a coup, we're your team. King Ferdy has a nice ring."

Colleen giggled and a round of laughter sounded among most of the gathering, Keagan didn't laugh, too busy watching Colleen jealously, and Maureen simply regarded Declan with a sharply raised brow for the interruption. He relented, bowing his head to apologize, and Maureen released him from the power of her glare.

"If Sorcha is after getting Rowan home, diplomacy will not work. Once we remind King Balder of who he is and what he owes his children and his nation, he is welcome to try diplomacy. But *we* will make no such efforts. Bringing Braden home is for his safety. We are preparing for war." Maureen gave them barely a moment to absorb the words before turning to her sons.

"Keagan, before we wake up the king you and Ferdy, and Gwyneth will work to wake as many citizens as we are able to from the curse. We will show Sorcha just what power can be brought to bear by citizens who *love* their queen. Then Ferdy, you need to be about recruiting far and wide. We need Rowan's sword in every village, waking every citizen we can."

Ardal caught Maureen's eye.

"What?" She snapped impatiently, clearly realizing his desire to speak. Of everyone, Maureen remained the angriest with him for having forgotten Rowan. He felt the weight of that shame whenever he looked on her, but now was not a time to focus on mistakes, only on what they had taught him.

"If we can spare one knight I believe someone should be sent to Turrlough. That nation is hiding from Sorcha the way the curse victims do. They need to see their own strength." Ardal squeezed Nora's hand again. "Even in ordinary humans there is strength to battle Sorcha's curses."

Maureen's features softened. Towards him for the first time since he'd woken. Her eyes darted between only Rowan's four original knights: Sean, Liam, Cassidy, and Ardal himself. She jerked up her head when her eyes fell on Cassidy. "That will be your duty, charmer. Do not let them shove you from their borders until they know that hiding serves no one," she ordered.

There was a long silent stretch. With an impatient wave of the hand, Maureen had the garden gate swinging open.

"Well, you have your orders, get moving," she snapped.

Ardal smirked. Maureen made for *quite* the effective general.

Old Friends Made New

The further down Mt Kieran she went the more she wondered about the passage of time. She felt like she'd been in that cave for a week. But the air was so warm, and the plants were so full and overgrown, she began to suspect time passed differently in Oona's cave.

She'd said something about stretching time out so she could live longer. But Rowan had thought she meant stretching her own life out, not actual time. But it didn't matter. Rowan had gone into that cave, and stayed as long as she had stayed, all that was left was to live with it.

When Rowan made her camp for the night she decided to try and visit her family. Her magic had that massive feeling back, and she had no fear of what she would see today. Whatever it was she would find a way to make it something beautiful and powerful and strong. Just like her fears and her scars everything could be made better with time and effort.

So Rowan danced. She spun in circle upon circle with the music from her bells reverberating around the little clearing she stood it.

She went first to the boys.

Ferdy and Keagan were sneaking through the courtyard, followed by a band of small children, all carrying artwork from the palace.

"Sabotage is all well and good," Ferdy whispered to his brother. "But a coup would have been more fun. I still say King Ferdy has a nicer ring to it than King *Balder*."

"Of course it does," Keagan agreed pleasantly. "But King Keagan sounds much more dignified."

Ferdy smirked at his brother's back. Rowan was about to leave them to their fun when Gwyneth stepped through the crowd of children, holding one of the banister decorations in the shape of Roisin's head. This didn't bode well.

She stopped in the middle of the courtyard next to a giant pile of other Roisin art work, and the children one by one added the pieces they carried.

"Citizens of Stonedragon, wake up!"Gwyneth shouted.

"If you were going to yell why were we sneaking?" Ferdy said loudly, not to be outdone by a mere queen.

"Do you want your princess returned, or merely more images of her? Fight the curse by my side. Remember your crowned princess, only then can we have our rose home." Gwyneth dropped the banister ornament into the pile and took a torch from the hands of a small child, Rowan thought might be Brigid. With a shudder, Gwyneth dropped the torch onto the pile of art and turned away unable to watch as it burst into flames.

Rowan caught her breath, and found herself back on the mountain side, with little bushes around her. She stood still a moment taking it all in. That the people of Stonedragon had quite literally forgotten her was not such a surprise. But Gwyneth setting fire to all that art—that was world shatteringly astonishing.

Gwyneth loved those. Why had Gwyneth, of everyone, remembered Rowan? They were never close. Rowan had a twinge of discomfort at the thought of all those images of Roisin being destroyed. She'd hated them all her life. Hated the feeling that it was as though they were honoring a dead girl. But now they were all just gone. Her home wouldn't be anything like she remembered when she returned.

She didn't quite know what to do with that thought, so she decided to make another trip. She would visit the people who always remained the same, safe and loving. Maureen and Colum.

Rowan began to dance.

Braden heard the bells ringing before he saw Rowan. His heart relaxed for the first time in days. It was an oddly painful feeling having his heart unclench, blood and air raced in like knives, but he didn't care. He'd found her. If her bells were ringing she was not dead yet.

He and Yseult made their way into a little clearing and saw her spinning. She spun and spun, oblivious to the world. Braden leapt off Yseult's back and approached Rowan. She was wearing her armor, and she seemed unhurt, but oblivious. She just kept spinning no matter how shallow her breathing became.

"Hey! Wake up." Braden shouted, he didn't want to say her name, what if someone was listening. "Wake up," he bellowed right next to her face. "You eternally annoying pain in the—"

Braden didn't know what else to do. He swung his open hand hard and slapped her across the face.

She gasped for breath and stumbled back. But almost immediately she yanked a knife from her belt to threaten him. Rowan was leaning against the mountain with her eyes shut and her dagger arm warding him off. Then she tilted her head to the side and peeked at him. She smiled, and stuffed the blade back in her belt.

"Braden!" She jumped forward as though she'd not been about to pass out a moment before and threw her arms around his neck. He flinched but caught hold of her. "I'll get you back for that."

Her armor crashing against him hurt. But Braden laughed in spite of himself. He'd never been hugged by someone in armor. He didn't want to repeat it either. There was something different about her.

"I'm so glad to see you," Rowan exclaimed. "You don't know how much I've missed this face." She pushed out of his arms, glancing around the clearing. "I don't know why that wouldn't work? I am still on Mount Kieran, so I didn't go anywhere. Did I bring you here? I must have done the spell wrong. I felt like I was being pulled in different directions."

Braden didn't follow the half of what she was saying, but he shook his head. "You didn't bring me. She did." He indicated the horse.

"Yseult!" Rowan exclaimed like a different, more excitable woman and raced by him. Clearly time alone had made her...*female.* He was sure he didn't like it.

When he wasn't struck in the face by her flying braid he realized what was so different.

"Where has all your hair gone?" he asked rather stupidly even to his own ears.

Rowan, who'd been hugging her horse, glanced back at him, still with an arm slung over Yseult's neck. "It went and burned up in a fire," she answered. "Whatever shall I do without all that dead weight on my shoulders?"

She was teasing, he could tell. "But...you had so much of it."

"I know," she said with a massively relieved sigh, the sort expelled after reaching the end of a particularly arduous climb. "I think this suits me better."

She really was different. It was all Braden could think. A different Rowan than he had known. What happened while he was in that cottage? What had become of the world?

"Well, it won't get in your way when you're fighting," Braden said, by way of a compliment.

She shook her head. "Never again."

It sounded like there were a wealth of other meanings in that statement but Braden didn't delve.

"I'm glad I found you. I've been looking for you. When she found me," he nodded to Yseult. "I thought perhaps you were hurt."

"I am unharmed. I sent her on when we could not climb the mountain pass together."

"Unharmed," Braden scoffed. "Of course."

Rowan looked a bit surprised by his tone but didn't reply. Braden felt badly, it was not that he wanted her to be in danger, but here she was with short hair and a bright smile, entirely unharmed and he'd left his fantasy to save her. It was typical of her. Braden changed the subject.

"Did you find dragons then?" he said a bit bitterly. "Will they be joining our cause?"

"I found one," Rowan said with a secretive smile. "But she will not leave her home."

"Well." Braden sighed heavily. "My news is not good either. As I was seeking you we stumbled across...the knight you banished, he was meeting with a group of assassins the Fairy queen had hired to kill me."

Braden broke off a moment and Rowan took a step forward in concern. A small part of Braden was annoyed to have to relate his story of near death when she was perfectly fine, as always.

You are too angry. Her Dark Majesty is in there.

Hearing those thoughts race through his mind now only made him that much angrier. He didn't want to be angry. He wanted to be worthy of the girl with the soft smile and sweet voice, who refused him a dance because it would be more romantic.

"Where did you go just then?" Rowan asked in a softly curious voice.

Braden looked up. Rowan's head was cocked to the side the same way Darling Girl did sometimes, and Braden suddenly saw the resemblance. All the curious things he had not understood about that cottage and those women fell into place.

Darling Girl was the princess of Stonedragon. She was Roisin.

Arrrrrr! Braden wanted to be shouting. But he was not. He wanted to be throwing things or fighting someone! Of course his love was someone else caught up in this mess. Why couldn't he just love an uncomplicated shut-in from some hidden corner of the woods?

"Bra—"

He held up a hand to stop her speaking. "A name is a powerful thing."

"So it is," she said softly. Rowan regarded him with heavy concern for a long moment. Then she took his hand in hers, drew in a deep breath and blew out a long thin stream of smoke. It wound around like a snake, circling himself, Rowan and the horse. A soft breeze blew through the area, causing the smoke to billow out like the sails of a ship, rising high above them so nothing could be seen beyond it. Braden heard a screech as the smoke curtains rose, but could not see the bird it came from.

Braden couldn't breathe. Not at all. It wasn't until spots appeared before his eyes that he remembered a need for air. This was a different world entirely, wasn't it?

"Tell me everything, the smoke will protect our words." Rowan settled, pulling him to the ground beside her.

"It seems you've had quite the adventure without me," Rowan said after Braden's story.

He hadn't said her name, or in any way implied he knew her identity, but all Rowan needed to hear was that four women without real names in the Enchanted Forest had saved him for her to know who it was. Honestly, she hadn't even needed that much. Between the vision Braden had told her about before she left Stonedragon, and Rowan's own vision in the well of the future, all Rowan had needed to hear was "a name is a powerful thing" to know he'd met her sister. Rowan had wondered how it was possible that Braden was meant to love her sister when they'd never met, but that wasn't a hurdle any longer and Rowan still couldn't quite believe it.

Roisin. He'd been to the cottage, stayed with her for weeks. All Rowan ever got were moments stolen once a year. Weeks. She couldn't believe she'd been in the cave so long. Her mind wanted to dwell there, but there was too much rolling around inside her.

She kept thinking of the violent stream of flames Oona had pulled out of her talking about how much Braden would love Roisin. How much everyone would.

Shouldn't she feel the fire building in her now? She didn't. She was jealous—she could acknowledge that. She wished she could have had weeks with Roisin. But a bigger part of her was caught up in the magnitude of all she'd missed. And this was only with Braden. She'd known Gavin and Petal were in danger when she went into the cave, but somewhere along the way the urgency had faded from her mind and the world went on without her.

Braden had nearly died. Met Roisin. Been healed. And escaped the Enchanted Forest. It didn't seem possible. That cottage was supposed to be protected from everyone. Not just from Sorcha.

"I spent the longest time so sure it was all a trick, that I was dying somewhere and...*your grandmother* was trying to make me betray you somehow. It was too lovely to be real. She was too sweet, no one is that sweet." He snorted. "Asia told me I would doubt it if I met the woman of my dreams."

"Asia?" Rowan asked, it was the first name Braden had been willing to voice. And though Rowan had gone along with the aunt's insistence that names were too powerful to be spoken whenever she was near Roisin, Rowan began to feel a little uncomfortable with the practice.

Her power was unlimited. She should not give in to fear. Hiding names felt like fear. But Braden had nearly died. His power was not unlimited. She could be cautious for him.

He looked more uncomfortable than he had before. "She is...a woman I met last year, in Ulm. Your prince brought her to the birth celebration," Braden said slowly. "He said she'd been staying with his family. She had apparently passed the princess trials."

"Oh." For a moment Rowan felt nothing, she was a void, empty, boundless. Then the bubble popped inside her. "*Oh,*" Rowan snorted. "There is no proof he's waited for anything else," she quoted her father and giggled painfully, leaning forward.

Wouldn't Father be pleased to be right? Unconsciously she began rubbing the heel of her hand against the breastplate of her armor, right over her heart. But her hand met with steel and paused.

Her heart hurt. Clawed at her, but she fought against giving in to the feeling and the need to rush out and find Gavin. She didn't feel his heartbeat in her own any more. She didn't even know if he was alive. So why should it hurt additionally that he'd been courting someone else? But it did. It ripped at her heart anew.

Don't you want to be loved like that? Wouldn't you like to be beautiful?

Sorcha's voice slipped through Rowan's mind. She felt the fire now. Hot, and enraged, it obscured what she was afraid to face—the worthless and unlovable feelings inside.

"Even when he said it," Braden interjected. "It seemed like he was playing a part."

"What does she look like?" Rowan found herself asking perhaps the least important question.

"I...I don't know. What difference does it make?"

"That pretty, is she?" Rowan laughed. She felt something intolerably close to tears building in her eyes and stood to pace. "Well, good for him. Like I said, if you, if h—" Rowan's voice shuddered, she forced herself to breathe deeply, but she couldn't quite bring herself to say it. "If anyone thinks they've found love far be it of me to deny them."

"I don't think it was like that. But there is something else."

Rowan looked at Braden, trying to force away the unworthy and useless feelings coursing through her. Why couldn't he have waited? Why couldn't he have come to her? Why did Sorcha have to...but this wasn't Sorcha, was it? It was just some pretty, uncomplicated girl. Like they all wanted.

Don't you want to be loved like that?

Of course she did! How could she want anything else when all her life she'd watched open, uncomplicated love doled out to everyone but her?

"Your grandmother went to Turrlough," Braden said carefully. "Knights went looking for you there, but were turned away because the palace was in mourning."

"For Gavin?" Rowan finished Braden's thought as a breathless question. Braden nodded.

A talon gouged into Rowan's heart, digging in and shaking her heart back and forth, refusing to be budged. Rowan's hand pressed in harder, and harder still, against her armor, trying to force the pressure through, to soothe the ache.

She felt the anguish that had shaken her when she dreamt of flying by the castle Turrlough, the banners of mourning. She'd known even then, hadn't she?

Rowan just stood there.

Know it long enough and eternity will teach you that urgency has always been a product of imagination and fear.

Rowan wanted that to make sense right now. Wanted it to make it alright that she'd been in a cave with a dragon learning to breathe fire, and find inner balance while Gavin had been dying. But nothing could make it right. Her hand rubbed harder.

She had stopped feeling his heartbeat long before she'd entered the cave. But still she'd marched on. She'd wondered, and she'd feared, but she'd gone on for the only reason anyone ever did anything—

She'd hoped.

Rowan's eyes found Braden. She couldn't find the words to voice aloud the myriad of feelings running through her, so she did what had always come more naturally.

She lifted the thorn from her belt and moved around the open space, practicing the motions required of such a blade.

"You never finished telling me about Donovan. He was meeting your would-be assassins," Rowan prompted.

Braden accepted the change of subject in his stride. "They mentioned a deal with your grandmother."

"Marvelous. More enemies." Rowan leapt around low hanging tree branches, and over stumps, bringing the blade up against the throats of imaginary attackers.

Braden shook his head. "He killed every one of the assassins."

Rowan gave a small snort as she jumped over a little mound of rocks, landing on her knees with the knife pressed against a tree branch. "They couldn't have been very good assassins if they failed to kill you," she teased.

"This isn't a joke. There were fourteen men and he killed them all. And one of them lodged knives in his throat and beneath his arm. Killing blows. But—"

"A fairy healed him?" Rowan asked with a bitter sort of humor, unsure if she wanted to laugh, or cry.

Braden gave her a concerned look. Rowan shrugged and stood, slipping the thorn back into her belt. She really did like that blade. She hoped Oona's next visitor liked the flute she'd left behind.

Why had she left the flute? Had she known before she left that Gavin was dead? The talon clenched tight. Rowan shuddered from her heart out. Rowan shook off the thought and answered Braden's unvoiced question.

"It would have been foolish to assume my grandmother had him working for her, but would fail to see he lived to face me. She wants me to face all my mistakes."

Saying the words aloud had an odd effect on the grief trying to eat at her. It paused. It made her wonder. Sorcha wanted Rowan to suffer, she wanted her to *face* every mistake. She wanted everyone to look her in the eye as they told her they loved someone else more. She would want Rowan to see Gavin with his Asia, and Braden with Roisin, and Father with Roisin, everyone with someone better than Rowan to love.

"I don't think he is dead," Rowan whispered.

Braden looked pitying for a moment. Then he just shook his head. "I hope you're right. But it's you I am concerned with. That...monster killed fourteen men and laughed at what should be mortal wounds. He is unstoppable. Why aren't you more concerned?"

Rowan felt tears in her eyes and smiled shaking her head.

There are no limits set on who or what you become.

Rowan couldn't explain her lack of boundaries. Not with the way she knew Braden felt about magic. And honestly it wasn't the only reason she was so at ease with thoughts of Donovan. She supposed she never had been afraid of her own death. That it seemed was one thing Oona hadn't changed.

Rowan didn't want to die. She wanted all those parts of life she'd ignored. But she wasn't afraid of failing to get it. If she died for the people she loved, it would be worth it.

"He isn't here. But you are, and you are safe." Rowan lay a hand on Braden's shoulder and smiled. "I shall take the moment to appreciate that. Because I am so grateful you are well, brother." Braden nodded, with no words apparently.

Rowan wandered away. "What we do from here is what we must think about. If the Fairy queen has tried to have you— *nearly* killed and followed once, it stands to reason she will continue to do so until she finds what she wants, a—"

"I know I cannot go back," Braden said, his voice sharp with rage. "I knew it as soon as I saw that monster in that forest. She needs to be protected. They all do."

"If it helps," Rowan said sympathetically. "I do believe you will find them again. Some things are inevitable," she said with a sad little smile.

She didn't think Gavin was dead. She felt a certain fated likelihood that they would meet. But she began to understand that all her worry in the past that he wasn't quite real, or that he might be bad. It was the part of her that still felt the future, warning her not to hang all her hopes on meeting him. They would meet — but it would likely be a painful meeting.

Braden watched her for a long silent stretch, feeling out the things that were unsaid between them about where he'd been hidden. She wasn't certain he knew, but she was certain he had an inkling.

"I think you should head back to Stonedragon," Rowan said with forced brightness. "It will be safest for you."

"And you."

"I cannot go home yet." Rowan shook her head. "Tomorrow I head into the Fairy Realm. There you cannot follow. She will know if you are on her lands."

"Then she'll know you are there too!"

"Most likely," Rowan agreed.

"Don't go. Go to Turrlough. See for yourself if Gavin lives." Frustration at last pulled names from him. "See if Sorcha even did anything there."

"Oh, she did something. Something twisted and evil as that is all she can do. I am sure I will make it to Turrlough eventually. I owe it to them to do what I can to protect them, after their alliance with me is what caused her rage. But...you are right, I have changed. I am not the old Rowan the Eternal." Rowan spoke her name with no fear. Let Sorcha send who she would, Rowan could protect herself and Braden both. "I cannot carry her guilt, or her fears. I have been nothing but an armored mage wandering the world since my escape, and it has taught me more about myself than I ever knew before. And there is more I want to learn. I want to see this aspect of heritage that *I* have denied myself. I could have known it so long ago, but I shoved it away in fear. Tomorrow I face that fear. But you should go home. We will just have to find a way to be sure you do so safely."

"Where is home?" Braden asked, bitterly.

"Where you are loved, my brother. As you are in Stonedragon. Get some rest. We'll talk more in the morning."

Conquered Fears

Maureen walked beside her son through the palace. She was so angry, with Balder, with Sorcha, with her sons, with everyone. Even herself. She wondered what would hold her up should she ever lay this rage to rest. But it seemed unlikely to happen any time soon.

When they entered the map room, Maureen let loose a stirring wet wind that swept everyone but the king from the room, screaming and struggling to find their feet.

"Mama!" Keagan chastised.

"Do not take that tone with me," Maureen said absently. The wind swept the doors shut so they were alone with the king.

He didn't look afraid as a man she'd threatened should. He looked annoyed, as if she frequently swept aside his visitors. As though he was accustomed to her powers, when in fact he had rarely seen them.

"Mama, you are not well," Keagan said so gently. "If you want magic done I will—"

Maureen cut her son off with nothing but a look. "You weren't worried for my supposed illness when you were conspiring to steal my powers." She saw him startle as the words struck home, they should have spoken of this more fully before now, but she was too angry. *Keagan!* Of all her children, she never worried that Keagan would do anything so reckless. She was so angry with herself that she couldn't speak to him, even to give him the chastisements he deserved. She should have seen him growing reckless. She should have known. He should still be her gentlest baby.

"You would do well to remember, you are not an adult. Your knowledge of eternity does not make wiser than those around you," Maureen lectured. "Wisdom is a thing of experience, prudence, and understanding."

"Maureen, Keagan, to what do I owe this pleasure?" Balder interrupted their low, tense conversation, apparently done waiting.

Maureen spared the man an angry glance. "To your own faults and nothing else." It enraged her to have to do this. Enraged her that she must find a way to swallow her justifiable rage with this man and treat him as family. So many things enraged her.

Keagan started hesitantly forward, but Maureen caught him with a hand at his shoulder. He looked up at her in uncomfortable hesitance. He didn't quite look like himself.

She didn't want him to lose himself, but she couldn't afford to be anything less than firm with him right now. He was in as much danger as the man before him of falling victim to something so much larger and more frightening than himself. Maureen hadn't brought Keagan to fix Balder's mind, she didn't need him for that. She needed him here for himself. She needed him here to see the power not of magic but of heart, the one thing that connected human, and fairy, and animal, the thing that connected every creature of nature and eternity. All had hearts to guide them, if they would but listen.

"And which of my faults have you come to lecture me about now?" Balder demanded.

Maureen looked not to Balder, but her son. "Pay attention."

She stepped towards Balder. Let all her magic fall back into herself, and spoke not with magic, but with the love and the rage and the fear in her heart.

"In my life time I have pitted you, disliked you, hated you, and for a while forgave and even cared for you. But I do not think either of us has ever truly understood the other, but for one moment. That one moment when you came to my home, during my confinement, and took up my hand to beg me to save your daughters. Such fear lived in both of us that we could no longer hold walls between us, we could no longer hide ourselves. I *know* how great is your love for your daughters, *both* your daughters. And from that day forward any rage I felt towards you was only for how poorly Rowan knew that love."

He jerked, and shuddered. But he didn't leave. He couldn't. His heart held him in place, weighing him down even as the rest of his being fought to let the curse keep him.

"It is terrifying that she is out in the world without us. It is appalling that she is out there, unknowing of all the love that lives here for her. Your's, her people's... even my own." Maureen admitted the words torn from her with a dry sob. "There are so many layers to my love for that girl that I never voiced, as much in fear of losing her, as in fear of your reaction. But no more. Neither of us can hold back any love from that girl. Whether she is here or no, it can reach her. *It will* reach her. But only if you let yourself feel the fear. You are afraid she will find others to love as mother and father. And you are right. She has. She is *my* daughter. She is *Colum's* daughter. But she is yours as well. And if she finds yet more mothers and fathers you and I shall celebrate them. We shall embrace them, and honor them for the love they have given *our girl*."

There were tears running down the king's face, he opened and shut his mouth again and again.

"The only way you or I, or anyone could ever offer her protection was not with armies, or magic, or evils locked away, but with love to shield her when evil strikes. Because it will strike, again and again. Whether she is at your side, or a thousand miles away. Remember her. Shelter her in your mind, build your love for her, and hers for you into a coat of armor to hold that curse at bay. Because the only way you can ever truly fail your daughter, is by failing to love her."

Balder gasped and he fell sideways, held up by the map table next to him as he cried.

Keagan had a deeply focused look about him, the air around him fizzled with the fragile mist of his power as he fought to understand what his mother had just done. He looked so delicate, so lost. She wanted to pull him into her arms and hold him, promise to hide him from all of the evils he could see in the future. But she couldn't do that. She could only love him, every part of him, even the faults that were so like her own that they enraged her. She slid her hand down to rest gently on his shoulder. He jumped, looking up with a face awash with tears.

"He's back," Keagan gasped. "He remembers. You didn't even use magic. How did you know?"

She leaned down to kiss her son gently on the head. "The same way I know that you are losing yourself to your power in fear," she whispered. "Because the love in both of you is hiding. Let it out. Please, my dearest. Let it out. I will love you no matter what, but I want so much more for you than the fear will allow."

Rowan sat awake for a long while after Braden fell asleep, there were too many things on her mind. She could imagine Oona telling her she wasn't a thinker, but it didn't seem to stop Rowan from doing so. She doubted Braden would believe her if she told him that she'd been as shocked as he at how happy she was to see him. It had just taken her over. She'd been missing so many people. Worrying for so many people. When she saw him standing there, alive and well, joy had completely enveloped her.

He looked peaceful sleeping under a blanket that hid all but his head. Rowan grinned. It looked like Braden's head had grown up out of the ground. Rowan would love a blanket like that, or a tunic like his that blended in with anything it passed, thoroughly camouflaging him. Rowan had shed her armor in preparation for sleep, she just wore her quickly deteriorating gown with scorch marks and holes, and likely a fair amount of dirt. The cloak Maureen had sewn her was still in her packs, it had been torn once as she rode and Rowan refused to wear it again. She didn't want to ruin it. But unlike Braden's tunic, Rowan's cloak was sentimental and beautiful, but it was made of human fabrics. It had no power but love.

She wondered at that. Perhaps Maureen simply didn't have fairy fabrics to work with, or didn't know how to make such things. But it seemed to Rowan for as long as she could remember Maureen had seemed like a human with very special gifts. Why was that? Fairy had many things in common with humans, but what was separate was...special. That blanket and that tunic didn't even pretend to be human. Light and soft and unreasonably warm and magical.

Fairy things. Gifts from her aunts.

Rowan loved and trusted Braden, more than he knew. But she had to make sure he returned to Stonedragon as much for the secrets in his head as for her love for him. If he was truly destined to love Roisin, no matter how much it would irk his pride, he would allow Rowan to help him remain safe.

Some things are inevitable.

Rowan rubbed the heel of her hand over her heart. It was easier without her armor in the way. She felt it on her skin, and the talon seemed to as well, relaxing its grip, though still refusing to be budged from inside her.

The palace was in mourning. For Gavin.

So what? Stonedragon had spent years in mourning after Roisin was cursed. Perhaps he was merely cursed.

Rowan lay her head against the tree. Maybe she wasn't a thinker. It was disheartening.

You need to simply get up because you are cold, and fix it the way instinct tells you. You need to look into the expanse of stars and beg them to make her eternal too, just because the moment calls for it.

Rowan looked into the heavens intending to beg them to make Gavin eternal, but what came out was not what she intended.

"Please, don't let me have ruined his life," she whispered, her voice clogged with tears so desperate she barely recognized it. "Let him be happy. Let him be free of all this."

She closed her eyes, shaking her head as a few tears rushed down her cheek, and the talon in her heart dug in more viciously than ever before. Rowan groaned from the pain unable to do anything but hold onto her heart and ride out the agony.

"Alright," she whispered when she was able. "Then let him be safe."

The talon relaxed.

After a time Rowan leaned against the tree, rubbing her own heart and the talon inside it, wishing she knew how to fix this, or even what there was to fix. But she had no idea.

She had to deal with what was in front of her, that was all she'd ever been good at, dealing with the problem of the moment. Rowan stared across the camp at her friend.

The best way to get Braden home would be to take him herself. Magically. She could vanish with him and Yseult, and cut her travel time down considerably. But her path didn't lead home. Everything inside her said as much. If she knew where Eachann was she could ask him. But she had no idea if he'd returned to Turrlough or not. If he'd been there when Sorcha came he might not even be alive, and Rowan had never—

"I am right here, little queen."

Rowan spun to her left, and there, relaxing on a low hanging branch of a tree, as though he had been sitting there forever, was Eachann.

He grinned, reading her thoughts as always. "Perhaps I have sat here forever."

Rowan smiled wide, immensely pleased to see his face. Her grandfather.

"Have you been with me this whole time?" she asked.

It must have been he who stole her blanket on the mountain! Who kept her moving when she was dying for lack of air.

"I was heading to Turrlough when I sensed Sorcha there. I could not return with her present so I sought you. I caught up to you in Anwyn forest."

"Why didn't you reveal yourself?"

"I was not entirely certain I would be welcome. And it became clear that this was a journey you needed to take of your own will. Though perhaps not entirely alone."

Rowan blushed and looked away. "I talked to myself rather a lot."

Eachann shrugged. "As the dragon said, you inherited madness from your human relatives."

Rowan chuckled. "You followed me even there?"

"Into the cave of the monster and back."

"What about your fear of them?"

"*For you*, I conquered my fear. And I am better for it," he bowed in the tree. "So I am to escort your prince to Stonedragon?"

"If you are willing."

"I would much prefer to stay with you. But since you mean to enter Fairy I cannot follow you." He paused, looking at her in that heavy way Colum or Ardal would when a task was dangerous. "But I have come to *know* your power. You can find what you need in Fairy alone."

Rowan took the praise in, but did not know precisely what to say to it. She was only now coming to understand her own power, it was lovely that he had such faith in it, it felt lovely that she was growing so confident in it, that his words didn't feel like mere flattery, this felt like truth. She looked into her lap for a long while and in the quiet uncomfortable thoughts crept out. "Do you know what Sorcha did in Turrlough?"

"I do not. But whatever it is lingers across the entire nation, not just the palace. And." He tilted his head down towards her with a gentle smile. "I too doubt he is dead. A dead man has little use, but her magpie nature finds a purpose for every living being she collects."

"Do I remind you of her?" Rowan had to ask it, absolutely could not hold the question in. Though the tingles of fear dancing in her blood weren't entirely sure what answer she wanted.

Eachann shook his head, smiling broadly. "In very few ways. I told your young king once that you draw one in as your grandmother does. But she never would have looked into the stars and begged them to release one she loved."

Rowan gasped, and the tingles in her blood raced all together to her heart, warming it. Soothing its pains.

"You made the offer, that he does not wish to let go is no one's doing but his own." Eachann said softly.

Rowan leaned her head against the tree. "Well then, I shall not blame myself if he is tortured and maimed."

"These pains are but little prices to pay, if the reward is your love."

Rowan blushed and looked away. That seemed a very grandfatherly thing to say. Seemed the sort of thing Maureen would say. Why was it so strange coming from Eachann?

Quiet descended and out of the quiet crept thoughts Rowan had managed to shove away earlier.

"Did you meet her?" Rowan whispered. "That woman who was living at the palace."

"I did not," Eachann said as though that would be the end of it.

Rowan looked up with a curious eyebrow raised. And her grandfather gave her a fond, quiet smile.

"He did not trust her when she entered his home, but family tradition prevented him sending her away. He thought for a time that she might be in league with Sorcha, but it was not so. I do not know precisely what led to it, but I know he took her somewhat into his confidence."

"So...he trusted her in the end. Do you think..." Rowan faltered. She didn't want to know what she wanted to know. What if she discovered that Gavin loved this girl? What if it changed the way she felt towards him? Worse, what if it didn't? What would it say about her if she kept clinging to the hope of a perfect love, when she knew the person she was hoping for loved another?

But she couldn't seem to keep the question inside.

"Does he love her? Do you think he offered for her?" Rowan forced the words out in a rush.

Eachann was a long while in answering. When he did, his tone was so flat Rowan thought he must be hiding something. "I know he made his mother a promise that he would consider such a match. I know that he was very disquieted by the promise. And I know that after he received his floating letter from you, all of that disquiet changed. He loves you, little queen. Of that I am sure."

Rowan leaned back feeling comforted, but distraught still. Surely Eachann's assurance should be enough. Why then did she still feel jealous of this woman who had passed the princess trials and lived with Gavin, and went out in the world on his arm? Why did she feel saddened by the idea that even if he did not love this woman, he had taken her into his confidence? Why did she feel guilty for feeling...angry that here again was another sweet, uncomplicated, beautiful woman that she must eventually stand next to and hope someone chose her above? Why couldn't she have one person in her life whose love was pure and uncomplicated and had never even considered another?

Well enough is never quite enough for you, Maureen's voice taunted. Why did Rowan need everything to be so perfect? Colum had loved another before Maureen, but it didn't stop him loving her now. Why should it stop Gavin?

Rowan was thinking too much. Oona would not approve, but she couldn't seem to stop, and the more she thought the further from rest she grew.

"Was she very pretty?"

"Indeed," Eachann replied without hesitation.

Rowan gasped with a little laugh. "You are supposed to lie."

"Why-ever for?" Eachann asked, genuinely confused. "She was lovely, and very sweet, wanted to be a comfort to him, and she certainly appeared uncomplicated. Though I imagine she would have proved as complicated as other women. Why should any of that matter. *She* is not the woman he wanted. The woman he wanted is so complicated that he had to write to her constantly even to get her attention. She had been angry at him for months and rebuffed even his friendship for a time. So much so that he began to doubt he would ever earn her forgiveness or her love. The woman he loved was one who could never be described as uncomplicated, one he would have to fight for, and bend for, and certainly wait for, because he knew she was worthy of *all* he had to give."

Rowan couldn't speak. She held back tears with fists clenched at her sides and her tongue clamped between her teeth.

"The woman he loved had already made him a better man and king. She had already dragged from him powers of comfort and understanding he had not known he possessed." Eachann shook his head. "There was something about him when we first met. I would not have called him worthy of you then, but his spirit and his hope both were difficult to defeat. It is that trait of his character that first made me believe he might win your love."

Rowan snorted, trying to shove away her urge to cry with humor. Her heart just ached so much, and as beautiful as Eachann's reassurances were, Rowan still felt heavy doubt inside. She never measured up.

"You think I need him as my hopeful balance?" Rowan teased, swallowing the tears.

"No, little queen. Because you are difficult to convince of a thing—be it good or bad." He smiled with gentle patience. "I can imagine hundreds of men who might love you, but you would never believe them. Just as you have been told time and again that the path you are on leads to death, but still you are unconvinced." His eyes lit up with pride as he said it and Rowan was *moved*. It was powerful having someone love what was generally viewed as one of her biggest faults.

"I have always been stubborn," Rowan agreed. "I was born in a storm, you know?"

"I do not know the tale," Eachann said sadly.

"No." Rowan watched him thoughtfully. "I suppose you don't. I on the other hand have heard it all my life. Maureen tells it to me every year on my birthday."

"And you are quite tired of it?" He grinned softly.

This was her grandfather. She had to keep reminding herself, not because she did not believe it, but because there was still so much they didn't know about one another's lives. But here was something they shared completely. Neither of them knew much of anything about Sinead. It seemed he might know even less than she. Rowan shook her head.

"I think I could bear the tale at least once more. If you would like to hear it," Rowan offered shyly.

"It would be my honor."

Rowan settled more comfortably against the tree and began the story with the words Maureen always used.

"I was born into a raging storm. My mother had gone out into the rose garden, as she did every day, to be among her friends. They smiled, always welcoming, a sea of roses of every different hue. She sat among them as the sky grew dark and the wind grew wet. And Maureen at her back begged her to 'come inside' and have her child in a bed 'as is proper.' But my mother wouldn't back down. She said 'my daughter is not just some insipid princess, to be petted and groomed and made a tool for a man's ends. She is a child of the earth and the air. She is a fey creature, and she will be born in the light and the air and the storm if need be," Rowan spoke, unconsciously adopting even Maureen's posture. Pride and love holding up her shoulders.

It struck Rowan as strange that she had heard this story so many times, but only in the telling of it was she truly seeing it. She knew so much more about her mother's life now. Even that statement, that rallying cry Rowan had built into her makeup must be seen a bit differently. It didn't change how Rowan saw herself, she just understood as never before what pain her mother had been in. It was a heartbroken wish, that credo. A wish for her daughter's life to be happier than her own.

"My mother was always a gentle creature," Rowan continued, the words fell from her lips even as her mind ate up the story with her new understanding. "Delicate as a wisp of spider thread and charming as a baby's laugh, but on that night, with her back to the blazing fire of the rowan tree's leaves, she was as firm as any mountain. She called for my father, the king, and told him what would be. That I would be queen of his people and would choose a king to sit beside me. The wind grew fierce and cold, and the rain came down in waves, shedding tears for what nature knew was to come. But still my mother would not move. Her girl was something special. Her girl would not be frightened by a little storm." A soothing sort of affinity with her mother and that moment filled Rowan as she spoke.

"And so it was, in the hour of my birth, the winds raged to welcome me, and the rain fell to bathe me, and thunder and lightning shook the very air of the world, for here was a special child. And my mother laughed for the joy of it, saying that even her own powerful mother was born in a bed as is proper for a princess, 'but not my girl.' When my mother held me in her arms, her fire blazed more brightly than the strongest flame. She looked into my eyes, my eternity, and came to know me in an instant. She told me that I was perfect and named me for the tree that sheltered me as I was born. And we gazed into each other's eyes, of one mind in that moment, and she whispered her last words, 'You are loved, you are beautiful, and you are eternal. You are my beautiful love.' Then she shut her eyes to this world, leaving it to me and became one with eternity."

Rowan reached the end of the story as she had always heard it, and fell silent. Eachann was looking into the distance. It was too dark to make out his face, but Rowan was certain he was crying. She had certainly cried a number of times herself.

She wasn't crying tonight, though telling the story had made it so much richer. She could see now all the details Maureen had kept hidden. Even her own anger and grief in that moment were masked by her words of joy for Rowan. Maureen always worked so hard to let Rowan know she was loved. It even struck Rowan as she spoke that the story would likely play out differently were her father the one telling it. It was, like every other story in life, a moment captured from one perspective. She supposed it would make her a fuller, better person this ability she had now to see other sides. But she wouldn't part with this perspective for anything. It had helped to make her who she was.

"Thank you," Eachann said, startling Rowan from her thoughts. "For the joy you gave her when you were born."

Rowan gasped and tears ran down her cheeks unexpectedly. No one had ever expressed it in just that way. She'd always known her mother wanted her, loved her, desired her more than she desired her own life. But that Rowan had brought her joy, right then, when she was heartbroken, and dying. No one had ever said it that way. And it wasn't until hearing it that Rowan realized how much she had always needed to.

Rowan shook her head, brushing away the tears. "Her father and her daughter." Rowan waved between them. "And we know so little of her but other people's stories."

"And each other," Eachann added. "There are bits of her in each of us, and flowing down into each life we touch."

Rowan nodded, it felt like the sort of things Oona had been teaching her. "Eternity." Rowan felt her exhaustion building as the words soothed away old aches. "Eachann, thank you. For being difficult to defeat yourself. And for following me and showing me another piece of her I needed to know."

"It is my great pleasure, granddaughter, to know you and to share your journey."

Rowan smiled thinking she ought to say something more, but before words could make it to her lips, sleep took her over. As she was drifting off she wasn't worried about things left unsaid. Eachann would know. He always knew her thoughts.

Battle Forged Heart

327 days until Roisin returns

Rowan dreamt of flying. She swooped low over the south road, flying past row upon row of Anwyn's soldiers, following them to yet more soldiers building camps along the Liadan, on Anwyn's side of the border with Stonedragon. She arched skyward and flapped over the river. Swooping slowly over every one of Stonedragon's border villages, circling every farm or playing child. Showing Rowan every unprotected piece of her home. Her heritage. Her responsibility.

Rowan woke with a start. She leaned forward and glanced around her little camp. Despite the dream she didn't feel afraid. Perhaps confused, but mostly she was comforted. Braden was alive, Eachann had followed her. She wasn't alone.

She glanced at the tree where Eachann slept and smiled. It was good to know some members of her family were stubbornly committed to loving her. Perhaps others were out there loving her as well, and she just needed to look closer.

She walked quietly away from Eachann. And Braden, who slept curled up next to Yseult.

"Traitor," Rowan muttered in the horse's direction. Yseult poked up her head and gave Rowan an incredulous snort.

"I know I sent you," Rowan responded. "But you weren't meant to choose a new friend." She relented and winked, walking further away.

There was a little stream nearby. Rowan headed that way. She stretched as she walked, and listened to the light tinkling of the bells at her ankle. Absentmindedly she rubbed the heel of her hand over her heart, it wasn't aching yet, she just felt closer to him that way.

She stepped across the brook as easily as the bird had flown over Liadan in her dream. Perhaps that was all it was, a dream. Otherwise…what could it mean?

"The Fairy queen had something she wanted you to see," Eachann said from right at her shoulder, startling Rowan.

She spun on him, barely resisting the urge to punch him in the shoulder. Eachann smiled at the direction of her thoughts, raising an eyebrow as if inviting the violence.

"More troubling to me than what she showed you," Eachann went on when it was clear Rowan would not strike him. "Is how the thing was managed. She has not reached your mind so directly before."

Rowan shrugged. She didn't particularly care about that at the moment. "If she wanted to show me, that implies what she is showing me is real."

Eachann bobbed his head back and forth.

"I need to see for myself."

Eachann smiled. "As I've said, you are difficult to convince."

Rowan smirked, and without another word began to spin. She hadn't tried to visit her father since she'd been traveling. Too angry, and too hurt even to try.

She'd never tried to visit him before, had she? As though she was unsure that the sort of love they shared was enough to pull her to him.

But this journey had taught her more than just magic, and a lighter connection to the world. She knew now the power of her own love. It didn't matter if his love would reach out to her, Rowan's love for him was strong enough to find him. Hers was unlimited.

Rowan felt her father's heartbeat, felt the little chill of cold that never quite left the palace, no matter how many fires were lit. Felt the familiar solidity of the stone floor beneath her feet.

This was different. She'd never had this many physical sensations before, as if her body were truly there. *Unlimited.* She wanted to shout and wave, see if she could be seen, but Rowan saw all the serious faces gathered with her father around the map table and the excitement of her growing powers were brushed aside by the need of the moment. She felt her ears pop as the sounds of the room opened up to her.

It was an odd group. Ardal, Maureen, Keagan, Gwyneth, General Feibar, and Vance were all surrounding Father. Rowan wondered why Colum was not with them. She knew her father and Colum did not get on well, but he was not close to Maureen or Keagan either.

"We must plan as though Prince Braden will not be recovered before the deadline," General Feibar said.

"Indeed," Vance agreed. "Even were we to find him in time, we cannot assume that the soldiers camped at our borders will simply accept him and march away."

"No," Father said. "We are preparing for invasion. But we cannot give up on finding Braden and ascertaining his safety for ourselves."

"I dispatched the Knights of the Rose to find him," Maureen said sharply. "And Rowan's shield maidens will seek out any information they can of him while alerting your citizens to the need to take up arms until your forces arrive."

Father looked at Maureen with a slight tightening around his lips that Rowan was well familiar with. It said plainly shut your mouth and stay in your place. Rowan started forward to get between them but he just breathed deeply.

"Good." He looked away from Maureen. "The soldiers have been dispatched already. My citizens will only need to hold out for a short time."

"Your Majesty," Ardal spoke up. "I know you do not expect to be able to use Braden to gain peace in the immediate future. But I do not think we should *ever* use him so. If his father would use him to start a war he cannot be safe in his own home. And he is one of Rowan's closest friends. We must protect him."

Father's lips tighten again, but slowly he lifted his right hand from his side, and opened it, staring into the palm. Rowan walked closer and saw the rose petal she'd sent him lying there.

"I suppose we must expect war, rather than only an invasion. I don't know that our nation is ready for war. All we have prepared for for years is a ball."

Gwyneth until that moment had remained silent and off to the side, at Father's comment she broke in with a loud, unladylike snort, followed by explosions of laughter.

"Perhaps Anwyn's soldiers—" she gasped, giggling too hard to speak for a moment, "—would care for a dancing war."

Keagan shook his head at her and glanced back at the king. "We might not be ready, but this is our home. We will protect it."

Father nodded. The room was beginning to look vague around Rowan, light and dark shifting and melding before her. But Rowan heard her father's last comments even as he faded from her sight. "What I don't understand is if Sorcha meant this to bring her home, where is Rowan? Do you think she is still alive?"

Rowan stumbled back a step as she came back to her body. Eachann was there with a hand at her elbow to steady her.

"See what you needed, little queen?"

Rowan nodded, breathing deeply. She didn't feel weak, or lacking in power, just unsteady.

"We are going to war with Anwyn." Rowan glanced back to the camp where Braden slept. Annoyed with him for no reason, Rowan yanked a cone out of an obliging tree and threw it at her friend.

"Braden, wake up!"

"Ow! Ro—" He cut himself off, rubbing his shoulder even as he sat up. Spotting Eachann he jumped up in earnest, and spun in circles, looking for more fairy Rowan, supposed. "Where did he come from?"

"The mountain of Kiloth on Ether originally," Eachann said dryly.

Rowan jerked towards him in surprise, a million questions flooding her mind. He was not from Great Island? She supposed she knew there were fairy other places, but how was she to know he was one of them when he had not told her? Why did she never know anything about her relatives?

"But if you mean more recently," Eachann went on, casting Rowan a glance from the side of his eye, a smile tilting his lips. "I have been following the little queen invisibly for months."

"Months?" Rowan demanded answers to the most pertinent question as usual. She'd thought weeks had passed, not months. "What is the day?"

"Three-hundred and twenty-seven days until Roisin returns," Eachann said with a little half smile for the way Rowan, and truly *most* of the island, counted the days.

"*So* long." Rowan shook her head. She had entered Oona's cave with three-hundred-and-seventy-four days left to wait for her sister's return, and she'd lost forty-seven of them without even realizing.

Rowan's stomach fell away leaving a yawning emptiness inside. She'd lost so much time. And it had been wonderful, and inspiring, and frustrating and so illuminating, but—it was just gone. She'd missed Roisin's birthday. Gwyneth's too, not that she generally cared about that, but—she'd missed so much.

Shouldn't it feel wonderful to know that a month and a half of waiting and worrying had passed like a week to her? It didn't. It felt like she'd gone to sleep one night and woken up forty-seven days closer to death.

The thought struck Rowan in her empty, roaring stomach and forced her to gasp for breath. Had she always thought of it so? Truly? Even when she'd thought she was planning for the future? Had she always thought of the day Roisin returned as her own final day on the earth? Because that was what it felt like now. Like she'd blinked and leapt closer to her own demise.

"Why did you hit me?" Braden demanded rubbing his shoulder.

Braden's voice startled her out of her thoughts. She glanced up at him, rolling her eyes at his petulance, but part of her felt bad for the pain she'd caused him and wanted to heal it.

Braden stopped rubbing his shoulder with a little leap away and stared at Rowan with wide frightened eyes.

"Did you just heal me? Without even touching me?"

Did she? Rowan felt excitement racing through her, chasing away that heavy empty feeling. She hadn't been asleep in that cave, she'd been learning, and growing. She had been getting strong enough to hold onto this world for longer than the three-hundred-and-twenty-seven days she had left. Rowan opened her mouth to share a bit of that with Braden but his horrified expression stopped her words. Rowan shook her head.

It was enough that she had the knowledge of her own growth. She didn't need him to know it.

"Heal what? The cone barely nudged you. We have important things to worry about. Our fathers are going to war, apparently over my father's failure to return you to them."

"That is nonsense. My father doesn't care that much about me," Braden scoffed.

Rowan swallowed, wanting to reassure him, but unsure how to but with lies. He would see through lies.

"I heard my father talking with advisors," Rowan said flatly. "If you are not returned before tomorrow, your father's armies invade."

"Then it is another game of —Her Majesty's making," Braden said bitterly. "I was attacked on my father's lands by men who report to her, and my father is in league with her. This is her doing."

"I agree. But that does not mean your father doesn't care," Rowan insisted. "Only that he is under her spell. And it does not lessen the threat. We need to get you back to Stonedragon today."

Braden laughed incredulously. "If the threat is imminent I should return to Anwyn. Where I can avert the war."

"If she means us to go to war we will." Rowan pointed out. "You should go where you are safest."

"Stonedragon is your home, not mine. Once they realize I lied for you whatever friends I had there will turn on me." He swallowed, looking away. "The safest place for me is in that cottage, but I left it to save you. And you are never in any real danger. *You* don't need anyone to protect you." He laughed bitterly. "I shouldn't have left, but I did and—" He looked up and his eyes bit into Rowan with fiery rage. "We both know I cannot go back. Don't we?"

Rowan startled. Surprised both by the resentment of his tone and the realization that Braden knew Rowan understood where he'd been. His words were a dull knife digging into her flesh. *You are never in any real danger.*

"This needs to end before I can go back. So if I go anywhere but with you, it should be to Anwyn, to do my part."

Rowan felt her right hand settle over the hilt of her sword, rubbing the place where her scars used to be over the rose. She couldn't voice aloud that just his acknowledgement that he knew who Roisin was made her more worried about his returning to Anwyn. Sorcha might be there, and she had more ways to get at Braden than through the thoughts Rowan and the boys had concealed. If she manipulated Roisin's location out of him, or if she nearly killed him again so she could follow him...well, this was all over if Sorcha found Roisin before Rowan had a chance to stop her.

He should go to Stonedragon. There he was safe. There Roisin was safe from the secrets he knew. Once she knew everyone was together Rowan would find a way to stop the war so she could—

Laughter rolled through Rowan's mind, loud and rumbling, shaking loose every other thought.

Still so arrogant? Oona's voice asked.

Rowan glanced sideways, Eachann was smiling at her. Apparently he agreed with the dragon.

Rowan closed her hand over the rose hilt and shut her eyes. She was used to thinking of herself as the curse thwarter, and Sorcha stopper, the savior.

But without her there Father was listening to Maureen and Ardal, Rowan apparently had shield maidens, and *Gwyneth* was helping the boys battle the curse. Without her around Yseult had rescued Braden, and Roisin had healed him. The fight continued without Rowan there to drive it. And Sorcha *wanted Rowan* to go home. She wanted Rowan to be...limited. By her fears and doubts, by all the things she didn't know about the world. Sorcha wanted Rowan doubting her friends and riding in to rescue them when she wasn't needed.

She wanted Rowan so worried for her loved ones that she never knew the fullness of life.

Rowan stared at Eachann and questions that had lived in her since she discovered he was her grandfather, questions that had nothing to do with war, or Braden or Roisin, or anything worrying her now, came out of Rowan's mouth.

"Why did you never come to my mother? All those years you were banished, you didn't even go to see her when she moved to Stonedragon, did you?"

He shook his head, his eyes clouding over. "I could not. Sorcha did not just banish me. She cursed me, and it prevented me going. I could not have even gone to you of my own volition. Only at another's behest could I circumvent her spell."

Rowan smirked. "And that is why you beat Gavin's first messenger, so you could take his place?"

Eachann smiled confirming Rowan's suspicions. "He was well paid for his troubles. And at last it afforded me a chance to meet my family."

Rowan was glad she'd asked. His answer soothing little hurts she hadn't even known she had.

"You must wish there had been a way to meet her instead of me," Rowan said just shy of a whisper, and heard Braden gasp, only then remembering he was watching.

"I wish, little queen, that I had been able to meet you both— together."

"That would have been lovely." Rowan smiled though her eyes stung and her heart pounded painfully. She tore her eyes from Eachann and looked back to Braden, even now her heart pounded with a desire to rush ahead, to rescue, to be the hero. But this moment was the moment she was living, and it was important too.

"You are loved in Stonedragon, Braden. What I heard was my family worried for your safety. Preparing for war, even as they sought you. Once they found you they meant to keep you with them, *where you are loved*. Knowing you lied for me will not change that. We are your family."

Braden ran his tongue around his teeth edgily. After a moment he sighed and nodded. "Thank you. You are my family too. So...I will do what I can to protect them from Anwyn. And they can do what they can from Stonedragon. With luck we shall all meet again in a few weeks well and safe. If you have some way to get me home tonight I may even prevent a war! Aren't I heroic?" he said sarcastically.

"I have been asked to guard you on your way," Eachann put in, ignoring the last comment. "If your way leads to Anwyn I should be able to get you home by their midday meal."

"How lucky, I was just feeling peckish."

Eachann laughed.

But Rowan was too heavy hearted again to give in to levity. She glanced sidelong at Yseult. She'd rescued Braden from certain death on the side of the road, at the hands of men who likely worked for his father.

"Safe has never been a word to describe a spy," Braden said, for once following the course of her thoughts.

"No," Rowan agreed. "But brave is. You are a brave man, brother."

"So how does this work?" Braden asked Eachann

"I touch you," Eachann explained. "And extend my magic around you, making you as light as air and carrying you as far as I am able before the magic begins to falter. Then I take a short rest and we travel again. I estimate with your size it should take me about four trips to see you home."

"How many trips would it take if I were Gavin?" Braden said with a challenging brow up.

Both Rowan and Eachann laughed.

"Will you be able to stay in Anwyn once you've delivered him?" Rowan asked Eachann, changing the subject. "Sorcha may be there, has she barred you from their lands as well."

"She has not. However, her finding me there would do your friend no favors. I shall take him close enough to get home; then see to my own safety as I have these many years."

Rowan nodded. That didn't feel right. Nothing felt right. She wanted everyone she loved safe and together.

"Would you deliver a message for me, to Stonedragon? Explaining why I cannot come home yet, but letting them know I am safe. You might even be of help to them."

Eachann's smile said clearly he knew she was trying to manipulate him into safety, but he nodded.

"Will you be safe?" Braden asked. He reached into his tunic and pulled out the petal Rowan had sent him, holding it up to her. "You sent me this, didn't you?"

Rowan nodded.

He stared at it a moment. "You're going after her, aren't you?"

Rowan said nothing. *Yes.* Her mind was screaming out. As much as she needed to know anyone was safe she was worried most for Petal. She'd sent her off in anger and haste and fear, and she couldn't stop the growing fear that it was exactly what Sorcha wanted. She didn't doubt Petal. Petal was as unlimited as Rowan. But it felt like she'd plucked Petal out of her safe, loving garden, and plopped her into brambles of doubts and resentment and fear that Rowan had grown up in.

Yes—she was going after Petal. She was going to do everything she could to set that mistake right.

But she was also going to the Fairy Realm for something else she needed to find there. Rowan didn't know what it was, but she knew there was something for her on that path.

"Do you know, I think you are easily the stupidest woman of my acquaintance."

Rowan giggled. "What was it you said to me? 'There are qualities more desirable than intelligence.'"

"And you have none of them. It's just lucky you're a princess."

"Look at me," Rowan teased, pointing to her frayed and not quite clean clothing and her messily cropped hair. Then she sent her magic out into the trees around them, and had branches lifting her scattered bits of armor and depositing them at her feet. He should know her power, even if it sometimes frightened him, because it was what she would use to protect him as much as she could. "I am no insipid princess. I am a force of armor and sword, loyalty, and magic. I am something new."

"Humph!" Braden scoffed, rolling his eyes, but his breathing was tight with his discomfort. "As I said, you haven't even one of the desirable qualities. You know modesty is a quality those princess trials seek. You've heard of modesty, haven't you?"

"I think so," Rowan grinned quite liking their little game. She could feel Braden meaning some if it, not all. He loved her, but he was also uncomfortable with her power and her pride. But she liked those parts of herself. "It's that one where you pretend not to be special, right?"

Braden laughed. "That's the one. It doesn't hurt to flutter your eyelashes either."

Rowan shook her head, she bent and lifted the skirt of her armor, strapping it around her waist. Eachann came and began assisting her with the straps. She nearly laughed, for weeks as she traveled she'd done this alone, how many of those had he traveled with her, and offered no assistance? She couldn't say why that pleased her, but it did.

Braden stared at her for a long while as she put her armor on, one piece at a time.

"The first time I met you, you were dressed in that armor. It swallowed you then. It doesn't now." He laughed. "Do you know, you still look like a princess to me."

Rowan looked at him incredulously.

He shrugged and laughed, making no attempt to explain the statement. He waved the rose petal at her before slipping it back into his tunic. "Thank you for the token, my lady. And good luck to you."

"And to you."

Braden said no more, crossing to Yseult; he began whispering to the horse about keeping Rowan safe. Rowan watched him from the corner of her eye as Eachann finished tightening her last strap. He smiled at her in a way that made Rowan a bit self-conscious despite what she'd said to Braden. Or perhaps because of what he'd said.

You still look like a princess to me. What was that supposed to mean?

"I will do everything in my power to see you meet your son," Rowan said to Eachann, to change the subject and remind her of what was ahead.

"We shall all be a family together," he agreed. "And I shall tire you both with long stories of my past. The good and the bad."

Rowan grinned at that optimistic outlook. She wasn't known for her optimism, but perhaps she could be.

Wasting no more time talking she used her limitless power to pull together a patch of fallen leaves, and lay them together like stones on a wall, until they built a neat little sheet of paper for her letter. Then she lifted a white feather with a black tip from the ground for a quill. Just lifting it sent an odd chill through her. She searched the area but could not see the bird it must have come from. And she *knew*, somehow that it was not the bird she flew with in her dreams. But she also knew this feather came from one of Sorcha's servants.

She glanced back at Braden and Eachann. She wished she could make them both go to Stonedragon where they would be safer. What if Sorcha knew? She always seemed to know. What if it wasn't birds telling her secrets? What if she was in Rowan's mind and had always been? What if she knew all?

Eachann looked up from where he stood eating a bit of fruit from one of Braden's packs. He raised a brow.

Rowan laughed at herself. No. She would never be known for her optimism. But she might find a way to be happy despite that. After all, she was unlimited.

 Shaking off the fear, Rowan lay the quill against the page and glowing golden ink flowed out, inscribing her message.

When the note was written she rolled the dragon pendant into it and handed it to Eachann. They didn't say more, none of them had words left. Eachann and Braden vanished together, leaving Rowan and Yseult alone.

Alone Rowan was not so comfortable with this plan of leaving the battle to her family. She knew it was likely the best course. But she wanted to be there with them. To see them safe with her eyes, and her sweat, and her power. She wanted to shield them, but she needed to be elsewhere. Petal needed her, and what was more, Rowan needed Petal.

Keep it close. It will bring you luck. The wind seemed to whisper Petal's old instructions.

Rowan slipped open the little pouch that carried her clover and closed her hand around it. She thought of the rose she'd sent to her loved ones, split apart and gifted to them all. Rowan closed her fingers around the clover.

"Keep one another close," she whispered into her fisted hand. "Together you can do anything."

Rowan felt the power building inside her hand, all around the trees began to shake. Wind built rustling around her, until it could not be contained to her camp

—It exploded, reverberating from her to rush across the world. Off to shield those who needed her.

Rowan crossed to Yseult. Rubbing her nose gently across the horse before she mounted. "I have missed you," she said from the horses back. "Now, are you ready to finish this adventure we started?"

Yseult yanked up her head and whinnied enthusiastically.

Rowan nudged her towards the slope of the little stream. As they left their camp area, passing through the lingering mist of Rowan's smoke spell from the day before, Rowan heard a high pitched screech. She jerked around in her saddle.

There was a black and white falcon perched at the top of a tree, staring right at Rowan. When she'd passed through the smoke screen it dissipated, and the bird looked around the empty clearing and back at Rowan. It jerked its head once, gave another loud screech, and took off into the air.

Rowan watched it flap away, off to tell her grandmother what direction Rowan was headed no doubt. A tiny pit grew in Rowan's stomach worrying for what her refusal to go home would bring down on her family. But she wouldn't alter her course. She had put her trust in her family, and that trust would be their shield.

Balder looked up, searching the room, for a moment he thought he'd felt Rowan. He didn't want to say anything, it felt too foolish, but he saw Maureen looking about too, their eyes met.

She nodded. "I felt her too."

"Rowan?" Keagan demanded. Then seemed to shrink his eyes grew distant and he lost that natural confidence that had been so annoying to Balder. Balder knew that look well. Keagan felt left out, less, because he had not felt her. But Balder had seen over and over how much his daughter loved that little boy. He wasn't less. He just...hadn't felt Rowan. That didn't make their love less, it only made his focus different.

Balder wanted to reach out and lay a hand on the boy's shoulder, reassure him that Rowan loved him as much as anyone. But...this was his half-brother, and he knew well that Keagan didn't like him. He had plenty of reason not to.

"Yes," Maureen answered. "She was here for a moment, so she knows about the war."

"Do you think it will shake her from her path?" Ardal asked.

He didn't appear as much concerned as Keagan about not having felt Rowan, only on the mission of the moment. But Balder had noticed a change in the man from their past dealings, a quiet shift, he was serving his role here, but all was for Rowan now. If that shift told Balder anything it was that he too must feel slighted by not having felt Rowan.

Balder had been reluctantly accepting all the help around him, though it grated at his pride, though he wished to do it all on his own. Serve his nation, protect his people, preserve his daughter's legacy. But understanding the others around him settled some of his oldest and most closely held fears.

"It will not shake her," Balder said before Maureen replied. He glanced at her to see if she was angered by his taking over, but she simply allowed him to speak, her face expressionless. "If she has seen us all together, her court working to preserve her home, then she will press on with whatever it is she needs, as we do what we must—together."

"Well said," Gwyneth piped in from her corner. She smiled at him gently, but he noticed she had not tried to speak to him alone, or see to his comfort. She stayed well back.

Surely she knew it was nothing but the curse that had caused him to confine her. She couldn't possibly be afraid to anger him now. No one was ever afraid of that.

"Indeed," Ardal agreed. "So let's get back to it. I keep feeling as though we've forgotten some asset, but how could we have. We are using everyone from farmer to shepherdess to child."

Balder's gaze drifted from Gwyneth to Maureen, and as his hand rubbed over the petal in his palm he saw his daughter before him, arguing the value of her women's conscription when he would only allow her five women to train.

"Father, they are an asset. I know they can resist the curse! Why do you refuse to see the power of women?"

"What about a woman of power," Balder whispered the phrase Maureen had threatened him with the night before Rowan left.

"We are using women," Ardal remarked. "Rowan's shield maidens, and every woman they rope into her service now."

"That is not what I mean." Balder's gaze settled unshakably on Maureen. "What about your magic? Yours and the boys? Can...is there any way it can add to our arsenal? I have seen you do such things with water. Could you not...flood the river? Make it impassable for a few days?"

"She can't!" Keagan shouted, and blocked his mother.

Balder saw in Keagan that same fear Balder had felt as he saw Rowan limping bloody off the training field again and again. The maddening desire to protect what he loved. He wanted to back down, because he too felt it was wrong to risk a woman, any woman. But the Rowan in the back of his mind was forcing his lips to part.

Maureen beat him to it.

Rolling her eyes at her son as she spoke. "The Liadan is sacred water. No single fairy can do that. Not even three. But..." she swallowed heavily and looked away. Her eyes met no one and her voice was far away and hesitant when she spoke again. "Since Sorcha banished them from the Fairy Realm nearly all the water sprites of the island have taken refuge at Dragon's Breath. Together...they could do it."

"Will they help us?" Balder asked. "Is there something I might offer them in exchange for assistance? Do you know any of them?"

Maureen's eyes skated very carefully past her son as they rose to meet Balder's, and he saw in them a fear not unlike the kind that had lived in him when the curse took him over. He nearly took back the request. But Maureen's eyes hardened, and he—saw Rowan.

Maureen was so right. She was Rowan's mother. It was clear in her stance as some unnamed pain fell over her. Rowan was her girl. She had helped forge the fiercely independent, dauntless, heavy hearted daughter that Balder had driven away.

Maureen gave a heavy nod. And Balder felt a welling of fathomless gratitude that Rowan had such a mother, of love and strength, and selflessness.

"I will go to them. I can make no promises, but I can ask."

"Thank you," Balder bowed, wanting to say so much more than those two words but not knowing how.

Maureen nodded. But that her heart was still heavy no one could miss. Such was the true power of women, Balder thought, to persist in the face of such relentless pain. He only wished he knew such power in himself. He needed to learn it, or he would be no good to either of his daughters. For surely all their pains were far from over.

Wily

It felt like, and apparently it was nearly true, that no time had passed since Eachann had touched Braden's shoulder in that camp on Mount Kieran. But they were already halfway down Mount Anwyn just outside a little village Braden thought might be Charisse, a mining town.

Eachann was resting in the shade of a tree but Braden was too anxious not to move. He paced around and all the anger inside him swirled. He rubbed his shoulder, but could not feel the spot where Rowan hit him with that pinecone. She had healed him. With barely a thought, and five feet of distance between them, but she hid it because she knew he didn't like magic.

He hated the feeling that she was right to have hidden it. He didn't like magic. Hers, Eachann's, Keagan's—*You betray us in half of the futures that you are a part of*—he hated Keagan's powers. He even hated Antidote's power though he knew it had saved his life.

He was so angry. All the time. Angry with everyone. In his home when Sorcha was present, magic thickened the air, and made every conversation one teetering at a jagged edged cliff. His Father nothing but a willing slave to the Fairy queen's whims. His brother was at war with his desires to serve her, and to be his own man. His mother—Braden wondered what had become of her in the past months. She was always so delicate and Sorcha's visits dragged her to the ground so she seemed to crumple into dust motes and blow into corners. She must be distraught.

He worried for her. But even that angered him. He wanted to be like this new light Rowan, who performed magic with a smile and laughed in the face of death. They might as well have traded places.

Braden should have told her what Keagan said. It was eating away inside of him. But he couldn't say the words and risk that she would stop him helping her as he must. He must help. He needed to see Darling Girl again. His brief time with her couldn't be all he was allowed. He...deserved to be happy. He deserved to be with someone who simply loved him. He deserved his true love. He'd earned it.

Braden kicked a tree root, and rather than stomp around thinking a moment longer, he spoke.

"Why do all of you have such epic faith in some grand love between...that prince," Braden fought to keep from saying Gavin's name. Anyone's name. "And our friend?" Braden demanded.

"*Epic faith* seems a bit of an overstatement," the fairy replied blandly, not even bothering to open his eyes. "Would you prefer we think of you as the little queen's fate?"

Braden growled and paced away. "I just don't see where it comes from. He has done nothing for her. He sits at home with his comfortable, whole family, and his happy uncomplicated nation."

The fairy peeked through one eye now, a grin growing on his lips. "My, but the two of you understand little of the other," Eachann remarked. "He was constantly concerned over your presence with the little queen, when you spent such time in the proximity of her grandmother. And you assuming the Fairy queen's lack of visits to his land left him safe. His father is cursed. Young girls of his nation are kidnapped. Large numbers of his citizens begin to leave, or revolt. Even when a few of the girls returned home he had to put down an uprising of citizens trying to steal them to interrogate. His life is a constant wash of little troubles. It is true his family is not under the constant influence of Sorcha's spells as yours are. But they are not free of her ire, nor her curses."

Braden sighed. He leaned a shoulder back against the tree and looked down towards the village. "He won't understand her the way I do." Braden shook his head. "No, I don't want to be her husband. But I don't want her with someone who will look on her anger and her pain and fail to understand that she will never be free of them. She looked happy, but it was because she isn't home." Braden laughed, speaking as much about himself as he was Rowan. "When she gets home she will have to face all of the people who betrayed her. All of the people who put her sister first. She will be full of those rages and sorrows that so characterized her before. How could he possibly understand that? To him, family is a loving thing, full of devotion and protection."

Eachann let the air hold the questions aloft a moment. Braden waited, because he could tell this fairy had some insight to share. He must, he was Gavin's servant after all.

"Your love will understand only what truths you explain to her," Eachann said, apparently sensing the deeper fear in Braden's words. "But it will help to understand them first yourself. It would help I think to know that...you are special. Not quite the special child the Fairy queen expected your father to have when she met him, but special indeed. You can resist her in a way none of your other family members is able. And none of them was given the gift of secrets. You cannot know what pains they suffer within, doing her bidding against their own wills. It is possible they have truly given in to her, and shut away their loves so they could do so without dying inside, but you can never know, unless you try to see from their perspectives."

Braden deflated, slumping against the tree. "I want someone to...protect me despite the risk to them, to love me more than they fear death."

Eachann smiled. "They do." Eachann shook his head looking away. "They already have. If you want not to betray them, you must find a way to see it. Because even as you resist her, the Fairy queen is working on you, finding new chinks in your armor to exploit."

"How do you—"

Eachann shrugged. "You are a spy. And a furiously angry one. And I—" he shrugged, "— was the traitor once. I recognize the signs of a man doubting those around him, to distract himself from his *self doubt*. Remember what you are fighting for, it is the only way."

Braden was nodding, about to say more when Eachann turned to his side and pillowed his head in his arms. "Go steal yourself some human clothes. Those will give you away. I need to rest."

Braden ground his teeth at the order, but he straightened and headed towards the village to obey.

Asia and Jaron were nearing the border to Ulm. In each village they passed they saw more fairy wardens than the last. They were barely a day's press outside of Ulm in the forest shadowed by the wall.

Jaron threw Asia a wink as he was setting up his table, and nodded towards a pair of fairy watching them with open mistrust.

"Did I tell you my wife blesses each sword with a drop of water from Ever Spill? She was given a vial by a fairy she rescued from a group of human soldiers."

"Thrice blessed!" Asia clasped her hands over her heart.

She felt more than saw Jaron grinning. She felt the fairy approaching. One seemed very nearly enraged by the audacity of such a claim, the other only vaguely bored. The closer they came the more of their powers Asia could feel. The angry one felt fiery inside. The other was calm and earthy; his power seemed to tend more towards healing than his current role of guard. Asia felt around his power gently, it might come in handy if she could understand it well enough to use.

"Your wife was lied to," the fiery fairy bit out. "Fairy do not share the waters of Ever Spill. None would even be allowed."

"How dare you," Jaron cried out. "My wife saved the fairy, and the fairy blessed her with the waters."

"I've no qualm with the idea a fairy gave your wife water," the fairy said snidely. They were gathering quite the crowd of observers, but if fairies were near the cart no people would approached it. "But it was a trick, it's what fairy do. She probably gave her nothing better than pond water."

"The fairy was male!" Jaron said in entirely false, but easily believably high dudgeon.

Asia bit back a snort.

"Even less likely to have given the waters," the fairy replied with an ugly smirk.

The distraction was proving quite useful, though Asia couldn't imagine Jaron had called for their attention, only to get Asia a chance to find a new power to toy with. She was coming to understand the nature of healers. It was not, as she suspected connected to their understanding of time, and ability to undo harm. But rather a relation to their own hearts and a desire to...preserve the lives around them. Not just anyone could heal, because healers had to give over bits of themselves. They could easily shorten their own lives in the process.

"If you don't believe me, prove me wrong. Hold the blades, you will feel the purifying magic of the waters. You will. You will!"

Asia glanced sidelong at Jaron. What was he up to?

The angry fairy grasped the sword nearest him on the table. His mouth was open to speak but he paused and tilted his head to the side. Asia leaned closer. Was it true? There were human and fairy across the island who would give up their homes or...children if they were quite mad, all for a chance to touch power like Ever Spill was reputed to possess.

If the swords had touched such power why not tell the world?

The sword began to glow. Asia felt something shifting in the air, not around the sword or the table, but in the distance. She didn't realize what it was at first. Then she felt it. There had been three little girls among the people watching. Three little girls who felt magical though they were only human. As soon as Jaron provided them a distraction, they left.

Not ran, not walked. They...vanished, as fairy could.

Asia smiled internally, fighting with every bit of her strength to keep from turning her head to look at Jaron. She was quite sure now, that he was also magical. But for some reason it was a magic she could not touch. This bore closer study.

"Eh," the fairy said tossing aside the sword as if only a moment had passed when in truth a full minute had. "It's nothing but ordinary metal. Your wife was tricked."

"No," Jaron said aghast, and yanked the sword to his chest. Then his eyes pierced the fairy. "You lie. He's envious I tell you. These weapons were blessed by the water's of Ever Spill!"

At once a chorus of interested voices called out among the humans. They rushed to the table. The fairy backed away to allow the fools to buy what they would, but the angry one threw Jaron a cold snarl. Jaron winked at the fairy over the heads of the people examining his wares.

Asia was too busy helping the people to see the fairy backing away, but she heard the earth fairy's amusement.

"A human tricked you into helping him sell his goods." The fairy chuckled. "We have been among them too long."

Asia smiled at the table. Jaron was just a bit wilier than all of them.

Braden half expected to be met with assassin's at the palace gates. His heart was pounding so hard and his entire body aching. It wasn't until that moment that he realized how much of the anger was fear. Not until the gates were opened to him and he entered. He walked slowly forward, wishing he had a weapon. Wishing he had—magic. Not just the gift of secrets, but a power like Rowan's or Sorcha's. A power to decimate his enemies with thoughts.

As if conjured by the thought a giant brute of a man stepped into Braden's path with his hand resting casually over the hilt of his sword. Sir Donovan.

"Prince Braden!" Donovan said with unsettling animation. "We had nearly given up on your return."

"I...had no idea you cared so deeply for my well being," Braden said, only half sarcastic. Trying to understand this monster better.

This man cut down fourteen others, and laughed as he did so. Could such a man care about anything? Was there a human man left inside?

"Anything that worries the Fairy queen worries me. Therefore I must share her great relief as well," Donovan replied with a grin.

The terrible thing about that smile was that it looked human. It looked like a man lightly returning another's verbal jab. Being smiled at by such a man should be frightening but it made Braden more confused.

He thought about Eachann admonishing him to consider other perspectives, and Asia calling him a mirror spirit. Braden wondered if he'd ever really looked at another person's perspective. He wondered if he'd ever really tried to see more than what was right before him.

Donovan nodded down the hall, and soldiers of Anwyn stepped aside so Braden could proceed him. Another time Braden would have been so enraged by the displacement of his people he would have been too angry to think of anything else, but now he thought. He thought...and his thoughts were *private*. He could do or say anything he wanted on the outside without ever revealing what was within, couldn't he?

"Has her Gracious Majesty been here the whole time I was recovering?" Braden inquired. But inside his mind he was looking at his soldiers, noting their anger. He'd never wondered if it angered them to be displaced, to be serving—not their king—but one of his allies as though this was her nation.

"Recovering?" Donovan said casually.

"Yes. I must speak to my father as soon as possible. I was viciously attacked, very nearly died."

"How terrible," Donovan said without a trace of humor in his voice.

"We must set out a search party for the men responsible. They killed my entire traveling complement. I am miraculously fortunate to have escaped with my life."

"We are all most blessed by your return. Come, the Queen is in the garden with your parents, they shall all be overjoyed."

"As I will be to see them." Braden watched the eyes of every soldier he passed. So much rage, so much resentment. None of them liked Donovan or the fairy any better than Braden did. They could be assets.

He needed to find out just how many more allies he might have here, right under his nose all these years.

Leprechauns

owan had found fruit, vegetables and some bread in the packs Braden had left on Yseult. More gifts from her sister and aunts. She munched as they rode through the forest. Rowan supposed she ought to mind the quiet again, with so much to worry her.

Gavin, if he was still alive, had been cursed by Sorcha. Her family were threatened by war and she was just riding away from them. Braden knew where Roisin was and Rowan had let him go where he wasn't safe, and where, if Sorcha were present, the secrets he kept were not safe either. Everything should worry her.

Yet Rowan felt certain that this was the right path for her, and perhaps for everyone.

After a while the trees and the ground, even the sounds began to change. The trees would sway more, as the wind rushed through them, not just their branches, but their trunks as well, and Rowan swore she heard laughter. The ground started playing with Yseult, annoying her by slipping and sliding beneath her feet, trying to make her trip. It seemed they were entering fairy territory.

Rowan had expected some sort of physical barrier. But what she felt wasn't a barrier at all, it was a...fog. The sort of thing that turned one about, had you crossing the same thirty feet a hundred times before ever you realized you were going in circles.

Yseult was not liking this barrier at all. She was very near to growling at the trees and ground. Rowan had her moving at nearly a crawl's pace so she could keep nudging the horse towards the fairy she felt.

"Awfully tall," a voice grumbled from behind the bushes near Rowan.

"Umm. And not terribly bright," another voice remarked.

"She looks almost full human, but for those pointy ears," a third, older, voice agreed.

Rowan sent her magic out, feeling for the fairy. She'd heard three voices, all male. But she felt several other fairy nearby. She didn't think she'd quite crossed the border into the Fairy Realm, but she supposed here in the mountains it was less of a border and more of a matter of settled territory. Rowan decided not to address them. But she listened as every second Yseult grew more tense.

"Do you think she knows where she's headed?" A female this time.

"When do humans ever know where they're headed this close to the border?" the first voice inquired.

"She doesn't even appear to hear us speaking. Most humans notice that," a new male joked.

They all laughed. Rowan grinned reluctantly.

"Alright then," Rowan asked, looking around for some sign of the fairy she sensed. "Are you the border guard? I must admit I hadn't exactly expected there to be this many fairy at the border."

"This isn't the border," the first man said, poking only his head out of a tree just before Rowan, with a disdainful expression. Yseult grunted stamping at the ground impatiently as Rowan forced her to stop. "This is the sovereign nation of the leprechauns."

"The what?" Rowan asked, at a total loss.

"*Humans.* Are you saying you have never heard of Leprechauns?" The woman asked, but made no effort to reveal herself.

Rowan shook her head. "I have heard of you, but I was under the impression you were simply another order of fairy. I'd not heard you had a separate nation."

"Order of fairy," the head in the tree scoffed. He disappeared.

Rowan drew in a deep breath. In the past when someone spoke to her that way she grew so annoyed at being thought of as stupid that she would fight with people and shove them away, and fail to see what there was to learn. But she'd come into the Fairy Realm knowing it held things that she did not know. Things she wanted to know. So Rowan fought those old familiar feelings of frustration and dismounted, holding tightly to Yseult's reins as she looked ready to bolt or to fight. Yseult didn't like this place.

"I apologize," Rowan said tightly. "I clearly don't know as much of your nation as I should. I didn't mean to trespass. May I...continue through this way so I can enter the Fairy Realm."

"This is the Fairy Realm, tall lady," a man said snidely, the same voice that had teased about her not hearing. He stepped out into the clearing with Rowan.

She sighed. He was a good deal shorter than her, shorter than most humans. Shorter stature had a tendency of making one distrustful of her. Which was annoying, it was not as though she'd asked to be tall.

He smirked at her and cocked his head sideways. "You're even a bit *stout* for a fairy, but don't count on that to be an advantage. I will still defeat you."

"I am not an attacker. I simply asked safe passage through your land," Rowan remarked slow and calmly, valiantly battling her annoyance. "If I must take a different path..." Rowan sighed. She still felt like this was where she was supposed to be. "I will leave if I must."

The head poked out of the tree again staring at Rowan incredulously. "I thought you said you'd heard of leprechauns."

"She doesn't know this is fairy land, Fayz," the man in front of Rowan tilted his head back with an eye roll. "I assume when she says she's heard of us, she means she's heard the word. That or she lies."

"She is right here," Rowan growled.

"Yes, we can all see you," The woman said, pulling aside a bit of tree so Rowan could see her as well. "Tall and stout, hard to miss."

Rowan had a sinking feeling they were all heads shorter than her. She hadn't much considered her height as she traveled, only when Oona called her small. Now Rowan wanted to laugh because the difference in perspective reminded her of her father waxing philosophical about there being no inherent goodness in the world, only a matter of what one had known.

"Alright, stout lady, a quick lesson before we fight," the man before her said in a less than friendly, yet fairly unthreatening tone. "Leprechauns are a fairy nation, within the Fairy nation. Another group the Unnamed king wished to expel. We were too unsightly to be seen by humans and called fairy."

"Why?" Rowan crossed a few feet to tie Yseult to a tree. In the tree she saw another older fairy looking at her like a fool. But she turned back to the man with her in the clearing.

"Height." He waved at himself. "We looked too similar to dwarves, people might wonder if we were related to those ground dwelling all-but-humans."

"Charming. His words or yours?" Rowan asked sarcastically. Beginning to be amused, not by the story, but by the man telling it. It seemed her fairy heritage had as much ugly in it as her human heritage.

"His." The man cracked a smile. "The king cast us out, but we, despite our stature, or because of it, were better suited to the high mountain and settled here, starting a small war with the king for the right to make our own nation. Before the battle was settled Meave unseated her father, and granted us our own nation, still *technically* under her dominion, but allowed separate governance as long as we pay in gold each year for the right."

"Hmm." Rowan wanted to ask why not just welcome them back into the nation, but the look on the man's face implied he disliked interruption.

"We did not immediately accept this deal," he went on. "So she challenged our leader to a single combat to decide the matter. When she beat him, we accepted. So this is Fairy land, as we are fairy. And the tradition developed that if you wish to pass through our land, wish to ask our assistance, wish to do anything in Leprechaun territory, you fight one of our warriors."

"Fair warning, stout lady," the woman called out.

Rowan bit back a growl.

"None but Meave has ever bested one of our soldiers. Most of us think he let her win, because he didn't want to rule all the fairy," the woman finished.

Rowan nodded sideways. "Sounds like a smart fairy."

The trees shook with leprechaun laughter, but the man in front of Rowan watched her with quiet intense eyes. She felt vaguely uncomfortable with that stare. It wanted something from her and she wasn't entirely sure what. Rowan was tempted to say she would just turn around and make her way around their territory, but the man in front of her raised a brow.

"Scared?" he challenged.

"What happens if I lose?" Rowan asked, looking away from the man. His stare was causing an uncomfortable tingle down her spine.

He grinned, pulling a knife from behind his back. "Don't lose, and you won't have to find out."

The ground beneath Rowan rolled, and she stumbled forward. The man was racing at her. Rowan vanished behind him and kicked out, but she missed. For a short man he was very fast, he was all the way across the clearing.

Rowan smirked and pulled the thorn from her belt, and took on a battle ready stance. Again the ground rolled, but this time Rowan was braced for it, and braced for him to charge at her. But he was even faster than she'd guessed, she saw him move, then he was just behind her, like he'd vanished, but Rowan felt the rush of air as he passed her. He kicked the back of Rowan's knee and sent her tumbling into a roll. She came up on her knees and searched the clearing for him, but before she'd found him he was rushing in from her right. He leapt into the air kicking straight for her shoulder.

Before Rowan had time to move her magic responded, sending out a pulse that shoved him back. He fell to the ground a few feet away and rolled back to his feet, grinning.

"At last, fighting back a bit," he called out, then ran so fast towards her he all but disappeared.

Rowan shoved back up to her feet as fast as she could, but she was nowhere near as fast as him; she wouldn't be even without the armor she currently wore slowing her down. He shot by her before she was fully up. Something that felt like a kick in the gut sent her stumbling back. But in truth he moved too fast for her to see.

Rowan tried to sense from what direction he would come but he was moving so fast, and the fog of magic around them was disconcerting. She shoved the thorn back into her belt and used her magic to yank her quarterstaff off of Yseult's back.

Spinning it around her in an arc. Hopping to hit something.

"You fight like a human," her challenger taunted. The ground beneath Rowan gave a sudden jerk, and kicked her hard in the ass.

Rowan landed on one knee and one foot, with aches all over her body and enough frustrated rage to focus her skill. She vanished to her feet on the other side of the clearing, and sent her magic into the ground. Thorny vines shot up all over the clearing racing at the man.

He laughed and threw his knife in an arc at the nearest vines. They fell to the ground as he raced around the other's diving for him. He was too fast even for that.

Rowan raced at him. When Rowan threw up a leg to kick him in the gut he used it like a spring, leaping over it to punch her in the face. Rowan took the hit, but managed to latch onto his arm and with both their momentums combined threw him towards the waiting vines of thorns. They caught him for only a moment, before tree branches yanked the vines away, freeing him.

Rowan was grinning in spite of herself and rushed back into the battle.

She landed a few good blows, but he was certainly landing more. Rowan had never fought anyone so fast. Even Ferdy didn't have this speed. They both lost their weapons. But they didn't seem to notice, fighting with hands and magic and anything they could reach. When he kicked Rowan, head first into a tree she fell to the ground dazed and couldn't regain her feet.

She could see him approaching. One of his eyes was bloody and puffy, his nose bled, and his arms had scrapes and dirt all over them. He looked about like she felt. But he was going to win, because she was too dazed to see straight, she could attack him and hit nothing at all. Rowan felt her power building up. What would happen if she lost? She knew nothing about them. What if they killed her? What if they hurt Yseult? She couldn't give up.

Rowan dug deep, stirring up all her doubts and fears and regrets and setting them alight. When he was right before her, Rowan let out a shout or rage, and expelled a stream of fire, aimed over his head at the branch that Yseult was tied to. The tree caught fire and screams exploded all around her, leprechauns ran out into the open to try and douse the flames that were climbing incredibly fast up the tree.

Yseult reared up, kicking wildly at the leprechauns all around her. They jumped back and Yseult raced to stand between Rowan and her challenger. The leprechaun she'd been fighting had dove for the ground at the explosion of flames and lay there laughing his head off as his compatriots managed to douse the flames, all of them together using magic to build a bubble around the flaming tree.

"Now you use dragon magic, and again in a *human* fashion," he said, laughing harder and harder.

It was a bit fuzzy, and it hurt to focus her eyes enough to see, but once the bubble was around the tree for a few seconds the flames went out, leaving smoking burnt limbs. The bubble popped. That was interesting magic. The leprechauns turned slowly away from their work dousing the flames and gathered around Rowan and Yseult. Rowan latched onto the bit of bridle she could reach; if she had to fight them all, she would find a way.

"She will certainly make for an interesting queen of the fairy if she wins." The woman said looking Rowan over still with a fair amount of derision, but what might be grudging respect.

They knew who she was? Rowan held her breath a moment, unsure if she should expend her power to heal herself, to make for a steadier escape, or try to vanish with Yseult.

The bloody leprechaun on the ground held onto his side as he laughed. "She would be the first queen since Meave to lower her dignity to fight one of us. And had a grand time doing it." He winked at Rowan. And despite a slightly uncomfortable flutter at the look, she felt less threatened.

"Although she doesn't lose with dignity," he added.

"I didn't lose at all," Rowan said, and coughed on something acrid in her throat. She spit out a bit of blood and laughed to see it. She rolled her neck and began sending her magic out to heal her wounds. "This was a tie."

The leprechaun on the ground sat up slowly, watching Rowan as she healed her own wounds. He looked Rowan over with heated eyes and a smile Rowan could only call flirtatious. "Want to settle it now?"

Rowan smiled back at him, and felt herself blushing. "What, and lower my dignity to a tradition you clearly made up."

"It isn't made up," the oldest man among them grumbled. "Just rarely honored."

The man before her smiled and bowed his head, laying a hand over his chest. "I am Zain. Welcome to Fainwood."

Family Reunions

Maureen had not allowed either of the boys to come with her to Dragon's Breath. There was too much she would need to explain, and she knew, *knew*, there would be anger and pain and so much resentment in this, first meeting with her old family. She didn't want that to be her sons' first experience with other water sprites. They would be loved here. And she was certain and they would love the other water sprites. But if they came with her now and saw the justified rage thrown her way— her sons would answer that rage with some of their own in her defense.

So today she was alone.

The closer she grew to the hot spring the more power she felt. Magic flooded the air and Maureen realized there was so much she had missed. All these years she pushed this family and magic from her mind so she would not miss them. But all the feelings bubbled up inside her now.

It wasn't only magic she was feeling. She could *feel* the laughter, and innocence that had made up her childhood. She could feel the bond of every water sprite together as water, but individual in heart. She could feel family, love, longing, even sorrow. So much sorrow. This was a place as heavy as it was blessed.

Oh, how she'd missed it.

Maureen stopped a ways from the springs. She could just make out the rainbow steam and layers of seeing pools up ahead, but she wasn't quite ready to walk forward.

She felt a tingle of massive power, long since departed, in the air. Rowan's power. She'd passed here.

Maureen wondered if the sprites had even shown themselves to her. She doubted it. It wasn't their way. Rowan would have had to draw them out. And Rowan wouldn't have known how to do it. Might not have done it even if she knew the way. Rowan was still so uncertain among fairy.

Maureen took several steps away, to a large old oak and pressed her back against the trunk.

It had been so long since she'd truly felt what it was to be a water sprite, since she'd truly felt as though she was one of them. She'd felt separate for too long. No water sprite was ever entirely separate.

"Orla, Maureen, come here dear hearts." Her mother's long banished voice lapped gently over Maureen's mind. She and Orla had been fighting over some toy but now they rushed to their mother. "I want you to listen, and listen well, not only with your ears, or your minds, but with your hearts. No toy, no weapon, no place can ever belong to just one being. All are of eternity, so all are connected. Lock hands."

Orla looked at Maureen out of the corner of her eye and rolled her eyes. Apparently she'd heard this lesson before. She held up her right hand grudgingly and Maureen took it in her left, uncertain. As soon as their fingers closed around each other Maureen felt a shock. She and her sister must have held hands a hundred times before. But this time was special. This time the clasped fingers didn't just touch, they melded.

Maureen stared at their watery hands in shock. She'd known how to make herself water. She'd even learned how to join the collective, allowing her being to be absorbed into a river or a lake so she held no form of her own. But this was new.

Maureen giggled softly, reaching out with her free hand to run a finger to the bundle of water they created, half vapor, half water, able to hold its shape in the air without any solid thing directing it.

Orla smiled. Her big, bright tsunami of a smile that drowned out every mediocre joy around it. She leaned in and whispered in her sister's ear.

"Keep your fingers knotted, but pull away your palm for just a second. When you feel me press back, do the same."

Maureen obeyed. Their hands formed a little watery pyramid for a moment then Orla winked and slammed their palms back together. A little shoot of water spurted away from their hands and hit their mother square in the eye.

"Orla!" Mom shouted, but the sisters were too busy giggling to worry about her tone.

Maureen opened her eyes. She shoved out a heavy breath. Today was not about her. It was not about her sister, or her parents, or the years she'd been away. Today was about preserving Rowan's heritage and saving lives.

She forced herself to move away from the tree and cross the remains of the meadow until she came to the guarding trees that blocked the spring. Once she parted the tendrils of weeping willow branches, Maureen felt the power of the spring rush over her, waking parts of her being she hadn't even known were asleep.

Braden was led out to the interior garden, no one noticed him at first, which allowed him the chance to observe. He was more watchful now than he had ever been as a spy. He just wasn't watchful of Sorcha. He was watchful of his own servants, and his family. And either things had changed in his absence or he had never seen the truth before. All the human guards who stood in Sorcha's presence looked captivated, overtaken, but not all of them appeared happy with this. Some were aware of her power and struggled against it.

His father, as ever appeared Sorcha's willing slave, but perhaps seeing the human in Donovan helped, because Braden saw a bit of human in his father now. He looked small, and frightened but whenever Sorcha looked on him he appeared so relieved, seemed to grow in size, and in confidence. He might well have given over to her completely years ago, because now he was entirely lost without her.

Mother was the biggest surprise. He thought of the conversation they'd had before he left, about love, and how she came to be queen. He was so used to dismissing his mother and her wildly desperate, delicate moods as nothing but female frailty that he hadn't really listened. He'd heard only the bits that angered him, and ignored everything else. He hadn't even asked what her real name was. He still couldn't quite reconcile her story with what he'd known of her all his life, but he began to believe her story was true. She was a servant forced into the skin of a princess to save his father's pride. She was in every way at a disadvantage here. But now...Braden was so used to her cowering in corners, or wearing her head towards the ground with deference, that it was startling to see her looking the Fairy queen directly in the eye and speaking with firmness in her voice.

"I know my son is alive. You know it as well. Tell me how a war will do anything but make any road he is on more dangerous."

Braden was about to race forward and defend his mother from the queen's ire, but in his absence, with his mother finally speaking her mind, Sorcha didn't grow angry. She smirked.

"Sometimes a bit of danger is a good motivator, my dear. Especially when one is off hiding from his duty as your son must be, if gone so long by choice."

"Perhaps he is only hiding from—"

"Mother," Braden raced forward, ignoring Donovan at his side and racing to close his mother in his arms, as was appropriate for one who'd barely survived a heinous attack. In the back of his mind he began to wonder if his mother's rage might not be part of what had the guards—even those directly in Sorcha's presence—fighting. A mother's love was a powerful force.

"Braden!" His mother leapt to her feet, she did not smile as he expected, nor immediately embrace him back. When she did he felt *rage*.

Her arms vibrated with restrained rage as they rose and lay softly against the back of his head, pulling it into the crook of her neck.

"My boy," she said softly. "You are...back."

There was something off in her words. They didn't sound entirely certain. He didn't feel her doubting who he was. There was no question in them. There was only anger and regret. Did she not want him home?

Braden drew back and looked into her eyes. "I've missed you, Mother. I am so glad to be back at last." It was only as he said it that Braden felt what was off in her words and his. *Back.* That was what they both said, that he was back. Not that he was home.

Yes, she regretted having him back, because she knew this wasn't his home. She cared more for him than her own safety. How had he never seen it before?

"I was so afraid I would never make it home," Braden said. *And I still fear that,* his mind finished.

His mother lifted a hand and laid it against his cheek. "I never doubted it for a moment."

"Indeed she did not," Sorcha said, bringing this little reunion to its end.

The Fairy queen had not risen. She smiled up at him in what appeared to be genuine pleasure, if also a bit of amusement.

"Nor did any of us. Fairy and human together have been scouring the lands in search of you, and at last you have returned. Without even *one* sighting of you. Miraculous!" Her smile tilted and a brow lifted. Braden swallowed. "My dear boy, wherever have you been?"

Braden set his mother's arms aside, allowed a shudder to run though his whole being and sat at the feet of his Fairy queen, taking her hand in his own.

"My queen," Braden said passionately and kissed the back of her hand. "I hardly know where to begin but to say..." Braden hesitated, preparing to voice the story he and Eachann had concocted between jumps. It might undermine that rage he felt in his guards, and their fight against Sorcha, but it couldn't be helped. It was the problem of the moment, then the problem of the future.

"I felt your magic pulling me back to life as I lay bleeding on the road. I felt your power...tying me to this world. If I am alive, and home. Though others tended me, it is all your doing that has made it possible."

Sorcha, Fairy queen, leaned forward, her free hand running along Braden's cheek. She tilted his face up all the further and leaned down to bestow a soft kiss beside his ear.

"My dear boy," Sorcha said so softly her words brushed across him like a gentle breeze rustling the long scraggly hair beside his ear. "I could not allow death to take you from me."

Yet. The word poisoned the air, though she had not spoken it. Braden felt it, and from the shudder shaking his mother, she felt it too. Oddly though, for the first time in months, Braden felt entirely himself. He felt more confident, more present, more hopeful.

Having his enemy before his face, lying to her, hiding things from her, plotting against her. This had become his skin. He had missed it so much.

Braden smiled. Sorcha smiled. Other beings faded into fog. He was home.

Orla felt her sister closer than she'd been in...forty years? It had been so long she'd nearly stopped counting. She'd given up on ever seeing her again years ago. About ten years ago. Or maybe only two. When Orla had felt her niece leave Stonedragon for the Fairy nation she'd thought...*hoped* that Maureen might come to them for help.

Maureen knew they were here. Orla could feel her sensing them. She was not so little fairy as to miss that. Maureen knew they were here, and she chose not to come. Orla wondered if her sister hadn't come to feel about other water sprites the way the Fairy queen felt. That they were lesser, and unworthy.

One should not be able to feel so about their own kind. But look at her, even now stomping across the low pools as if she were a human when she could easily have cast her body apart as water and joined the spring.

She looked so different, so old. Orla would not have known her, if she could not feel her heart even from here. Orla made her form of a thinner and thinner mist the closer Maureen came, fading to the very back of the hot spring so she could not be discerned from the steam rising off the largest pool.

Maureen walked up to the shallowest of the pools and slipped her feet out of her human shoes before stepping into the water. At once her eyes drifted shut, and the faint fairy glow about her grew brighter. She'd been needing it. For a long while from the look of her, but still she had not come. As stubborn as ever. The water rose up to Maureen's claves soaking the rim of her gown so it was pulled down heavily. Human clothes. Human shoes. Human habits. Perhaps she wasn't a fairy at all any longer. Her sister was much heavier of heart than the waters would allow one to feel, and so old.

"Matron of the water sprite, I beg your presence," Maureen bowed.

Orla rolled her eyes. If she were still truly water sprite she would not feel the need to beg. She would walk into the water and demand the collective reveal themselves.

"Don't be so dismissive. You do not know why she is here," Delaney splashed the words through Orla's mind before pouring herself over the side of the largest pool like a little waterfall and taking the shape of a small girl on the ground some feet from Maureen.

Of course we know why she is here, Orla thought bitterly, *for the humans on the point of war.*

Just because Orla didn't look into the future didn't mean she failed to understand her sister's motives. The other water sprites always wondered at Orla's unwillingness to look into the pool of the future. She never looked. She had no desire to see the future. It only held more pain. Why look on it in advance? She would suffer her pains soon enough.

"Sister sprite," Delaney said holding out a hand with a smile on her face. "You are ill. Why have you stayed from the water so long? You must know you are ever welcome among us."

Maureen swallowed and looked away from Delaney in shame. "I had no right to come. It is my fault you were cast out of the Fairy Realm."

Delaney laughed. "This spring may be our home, but we own no more claim on it than anyone else. Have you forgotten so much? You should have returned. You are weakened, and aged prematurely. Do not punish yourself for the actions of others."

Maureen threw a hand to her cheek and her face darkened in shame.

"But I do not think you come now to renew yourself, do you?" Delaney asked and other sprites took shape all around the pools.

Orla could feel the welcome from many of them, but there were plenty who resented Maureen. Plenty who looked on Maureen with the rage she deserved to feel. She'd left. Left them all so much longer ago than the moment she blamed herself for. And she was not even returning. She only came because she wanted something from them.

Maureen shook her head and steeled her shoulders. "No. I came to beg your assistance."

"From *lesser* fairy?" Orla spat, entirely unable to restrain the words.

"It was never I who called us lesser, Orla." Maureen shouted, her eyes searching the crowd for the sister she could not make out. At least she remembered Orla's name, such a kindness that. "I would have been speaking of myself."

"Ha." Orla let her face alone take shape, emerging from the mist so her eyes could pierce her sister, and so Orla's youthful face compared to Maureen's aging one could add to her discomfort. "You have not been fairy for a long time, I think. And you've not been a water sprite since you ran off to serve your princess."

"Orla," Delaney glanced over her shoulder and up to the high spring behind her. "Your sister has come home after many years, now is not the time for recriminations, but the time for welcoming."

"It is because of her that we are not allowed to go home," Vale snapped from her pool to Maureen's right. She threw Orla a nod as if to say the words were meant in Orla's defense. But Orla felt no camaraderie at the statement. She only felt rage, and neither Vale nor Delaney nor anyone else had a right to come between the sisters and their argument.

"The Fairy Realm is not our home, the sacred waters are. Anywhere the sacred waters flow we are home," Delaney instructed the gathering.

"And one must not forget," Murphy called out in Maureen's defense, always in her defense. "That for several long years we were the most honored wild fairy, because of Maureen's friendship with the Fairy queen of now."

Maureen was blushing, over that rather paltry defense from the boy she had been promised to when she was a young girl. *Promised to.* Orla rolled her eyes, they were no more than ten when they made the pact to marry. And both of them had long since found other partners, but one word from him and Maureen was blushing from childhood memories and pulling her grey hair forward as if to hide her wrinkled face.

"I am sorry that I could not return to Sorcha when she threatened to cast you out. I could think of no way to fight her. Still, I should have done something for you. I could not leave Rowan in a world with no fairy."

"As I said," Orla said looking her sister up and down derisively. "You are no fairy. So you failed even in that."

Orla and her sister locked eyes despite all the space and bodies between them. Rage and pain and regret grew so thick it nearly formed a solid wall between them. When Maureen made no more apologies Orla could stand no more of this reunion. Maureen hadn't so much as said she missed her sister. She wasn't here for family, or love, or community. She was here for help with her humans.

Orla sunk into the hot spring, sloshing around violently so the waves would keep the rest of Maureen's words away from her.

Maureen stared at the place where her sister had vanished. She had crackling pain in her chest that urged her to throw herself into the spring and drag Orla out so they could lock hands again, as they would as children, anytime the world was too hard to bear alone. She'd missed Orla so much. Somewhere over the years she'd forgotten that there was a time when they had been close, when they had been friends. It was only as Maureen got older and made so many more friends than Orla that they had grown apart.

Then Sorcha entered the picture and took Maureen with her into a whole other sort of life. And...Maureen had been angry enough with all of her family at first that she hadn't even missed them. By the time her anger dissipated they hadn't wanted her back.

"What help have you come for?" Delaney said, startling Maureen's attention back to her. She looked like a little girl of about ten but she must be well over a hundred now, she'd been matron all Maureen's life.

Maureen had forgotten how much the water could rejuvenate. She must look ancient to them. Even to a woman more than eighty years her senior. Orla hadn't appeared a day over thirty though she was Maureen's older sister by seven years.

"I was sent by the king of Stonedragon," Maureen answered at last. "The nation is on the point of war with soldiers dispatched by the Fairy queen. But King Balder was so trapped in her spell that he did not even prepare his forces."

"It seemed odd that he cared not at all for the coming decimation of his people," Delaney said with a dry sort of humor Maureen was not used to from her.

"The king offers, in exchange for your assistance, to set aside land around the spring for you to make your own nation. And to declare the portion of Liadan which borders his nation a sacred site, under your control. Ordering his citizens to follow any laws you make regarding its treatment."

"My my," Delaney tilted back her head and regarded Maureen curiously. "That is quite the offer. He will displace many citizens. How much was at your suggestion?"

Maureen shrugged. Most of it. But Balder had been unusually open to her suggestions. And Maureen was certain Rowan would happily have made such an offer.

"He has plenty of land to resettle them. And their lives might be cost without your help, so it is a fair exchange. But you would do well," Maureen said a bit sharply, feeling Rowan all over this spring, and knowing full well not one sprite had spoken to her. "To consider that you will be defending the first home of the future Fairy queen. I know in my heart when she is crowned she will welcome the sprites back into her nation—" Maureen's tight speech was cut off by not only Delaney's laughter, but several other sprites as well.

"We have watched her. She is not much fairy. I doubt she will ever be queen."

Had the sprites begun to use the seeing waters regularly? That was dangerous. It could easily cause one to untether from the present. When she was a child they had lived in the waters of the Liadan, healing waters. So all water sprites, whatever their fairy gift, had a passing talent for healing. But the seeing waters were different. They were tempting magic, even to those who knew the threat of looking, and being stuck, unable to look away.

"Then you are confused from looking too long, and living too little," Maureen snapped. "Rowan the Eternal is more than fairy, more than human. She

will rule the Fairy and when she does she will make a place for the water sprites, though you are unsure of her, and too cowardly to help her people. You should ask yourselves if you will deserve that place. It is the duty of those who serve eternity to defend all life. I may have failed to defend you in order to raise her, but raising her has served the greater good. What do you do but hide?"

Maureen spun around, yanking up her shoes she began to march away.

A giant wave of warm water fell over Maureen, causing her to stumble and drop her shoes.

Delaney appeared in front of her. "You always were hot tempered. It is good to see you have not changed so entirely, sister sprite. What is it this human king would you have us do?" she asked, tilting her head to the side with a wide wash of a smile.

"Flood the river," Maureen snapped. "Perhaps even disable the bridge, to slow the progress of Anwyn's soldiers until his own forces reach the front."

"He would not have his enemies drowned?" Delaney asked with some derision.

Maureen sighed. "It has been the council of his advisors that the soldiers approaching now are not to blame for their current actions. Rowan, if she were here, would save as many of them as possible. So no." Maureen bobbed her head to the side, feeling just now like she would like them drowned very much, it would put an end to the problem, for a time at least

Delaney smirked. "Very well. We will do as he asks, and more."

"What more?" Maureen demanded.

"Whatever more we see fit." Delaney chuckled. "A knight, and one of your temperament, but she hesitates at killing her enemies." She shook her head. "If you prove wiser than the waters, she will make for an interesting Fairy queen. Send us one of your sons as a messenger. It might do them good to be among fairy."

Maureen ground her teeth, but she'd seen this request coming, so she only nodded. It would have been a different matter if her parents were still alive. Then she would have offered. But she worried about sending either of her boys here just now. Too much was changing already in their worlds. She couldn't let Keagan so near the seeing waters with him relying so heavily on his magic, and Ferdy was so easily wounded.

Maureen glanced back to the pool where her sister had vanished. "Do not let Orla take her anger out on Ferdy."

Delaney shook her head. "That is not anger. It is pain. You need to forgive and fight for your sister's love, at least as much as she needs to do the same for you. Love may well exist without us deserving it, but that does not mean we should not try with our every breath to be worthy."

The matron of the water sprites vanished as so much mist.

Maureen felt the waters of the pool sinking into her skin, reviving bits of her power that had indeed been very old, and very tired. She should not have stayed away so long, but perhaps, just perhaps Rowan's path had taken her away as much to reunite Maureen with her fairy side, as to help Rowan finally claim her own.

Perhaps Rowan by some design of her open, powerful, child mind was setting more right in the world than just the curses Sorcha had laid. She had such power. Such heart.

A Danger to Others

Once Rowan and Zain were both healed the leprechauns led Rowan further into the woods to where they lived. Yseult was much more settled now, once she crossed properly into the forest the ground stopped rolling and the trees stopped needling her. She was a horse who liked to have her bearings, Rowan would also guess that Yseult preferred having the leprechauns in front of her where they could be seen.

Rowan wasn't quite sure what to make of them. Or the things they told her as she walked. They seemed to be a people at ease with lying and manipulation. Rowan's lack of knowledge about fairy history was a gap they could exploit to great advantage. And she didn't know how closely they were aligned with Sorcha. They were under her dominion if their own stories were to be believed, but not as strongly so as some other fairy.

The lone woman who'd watched the fight was named Yas she explained to Rowan that the leaders of the leprechauns tried with each new generation to convince the Fairy queens to fight them, but all had refused. The leprechauns never meant it as a challenge to the throne, but they viewed it as increasingly insulting that no queen would submit herself. Rowan's willingness to fight made them more disposed to be friendly towards her. But friendly, and friends were different things.

Yas looked to be in her middling forties but with fairy it was hard to tell. She had black hair partially hidden beneath a colorful bandana and wore loose billowy clothes. Rowan had first thought she was wearing a skirt, but it was in fact a very wide legged pair of hose. Her blouse as well was loose and covered over with a scarf tied at the waist and a vest. All of the leprechauns were dressed in many-layered, colorful clothing. Several wore belts or scarfs dripping with gold coins of various origin and denomination. Rowan spotted the swan and trout of Anwyn, the crossed bars of Turrlough and some golden wings from Stonedragon.

"Are the coins significant?" Rowan asked Yas.

The woman glanced askance at Rowan. "Road leprechauns wear them. Trophies of particularly impressive swindles." Her tone challenged Rowan to take exception.

Rowan chuckled. And her eyes rushed ahead to examine the coins at Zain's waist. Apparently he had been a "road leprechaun" for a time. Rowan supposed that referred to the leprechauns she'd heard of, who found travelers and offered them short cuts or magical assistance in exchange for gold, but whose assistance was less than honest. In Rowan's opinion such a role suited Zain much better than his current one.

Zain, who Rowan took to be about thirty-five was the current leader of the leprechauns. Their chief. One was chosen by the nation once every ten years. This was his first year serving. Yas was convinced he'd only won by being attractive and friendly, although she would concede that he was a decent fighter. Rowan found the concept of a chosen leader interesting. It was equal parts dangerous and hopeful.

But she didn't know that she approved of Zain as a leader. When they'd fought he'd had all the seriousness of a Cassidy, overly confident and all for the fun. She loved Cassidy, but couldn't imagine him as the leader of her company. He took nothing seriously. Why would a group choose such a leader? And the unnerving tingles Rowan felt whenever Zain looked her way made her cautious as well.

As she walked, leaving one hand on Yseult's flank to guide her, and with one ear listening to the talk around her Rowan sent out her power. She used the window spell to slip into the mind of that man Fayz who was up ahead, whispering with Zain.

"Are you sure you want to break bread with her?" an older man asked. "The Fairy queen cannot deny us the right to let pass any who meet the challenge. But bringing her into the wood. Dining with her...We have lived at peace the Fairy queen for decades, will you risk it all over a decent fighter with pretty eyes?"

"They are pretty aren't they?" Zain smirked. "Don't worry so much, Grandfather. This is a calculated risk."

"Oh?" Fayz demanded. Rowan could feel the anger in him, he didn't like her at all.

"The seers aren't sure who will win this struggle for the throne. It pays to know who we might be dealing with," Zain remarked.

"Ha," Zain's grandfather scoffed. "She fights like a human, be it with weapons, fairy magic, or dragon fire. And she didn't even beat you. That girl is just an annoyance to the Fairy queen. Sorcha will win."

Rowan let the spell go, settling fully into herself. She'd never much liked the sneakiness of the window spell. But it did have its uses. Rowan couldn't afford to just trust everyone who fought her and invited her to dine. Nevertheless, as Zain had said, it paid to know who she would be dealing with once she was queen.

Rowan happily accepted the meal of wild vegetables and braided bread with olives inside. It was the first proper meal she'd had since leaving home. When they offered her a thick fruit filled pie for dessert, she nearly begged to stay forever. It was marvelous. She'd missed food, *good food* so much.

When dinner was over and the leprechauns were sitting in the evening air with the older members of the group telling stories and the younger children playing Rowan sat back and just enjoyed. It felt like the best times among her knights, when they would all sit around laughing and joking and lying about one another.

She missed them, missed being part of a company. Having companions lighter than she was who would defend her with word or sword, and unto death.

The sun was just setting behind Mount Kieran, and Rowan was tempted to look in on Braden to be sure he was home safely, to see if he would stop the war. She doubted he could. Sorcha meant to bring Rowan home. Men would fight and die, while Rowan was listening to silly stories and passing her hours in peace.

You are never in any real danger. Braden's accusation burned through her mind. She wasn't in any danger.

Rowan felt her skin heating and a tingle racing down her neck, she looked up. Zain was watching her with bright, interested eyes again. Rowan wasn't quite sure what to do with such blatant interest. She couldn't say that she'd ever felt a thing like it. Her pulse raced and her skin was hot and she felt like smiling. She looked away. She couldn't make sense of herself, why was he effecting her this way, when no one but Gavin ever had?

Even Gavin hadn't really. Only his letters, only her hopes. But Zain looked at her and she felt...beautiful. She hadn't realized attraction would feel this exciting. Even from a stranger.

But Rowan didn't like it. Or she didn't like *that she* liked his eyes on her. She didn't like that she'd set out this morning worried over what Gavin must be suffering, but now, whenever she thought of him heard her father's voice.

That is no proof he has waited on anything else.

She'd lied saying she didn't care, knowing full well they both knew it was a lie. And when Braden mentioned that other woman last night, Rowan had lied again and said it meant nothing. That woman's existence had made Rowan feel ugly and unlovable again. It made her think of her father's affair with Gwyneth, made her wonder how she was ever meant to compete with women like that. A woman who could just be a comfort to him, could stand beside him and let his work and his needs be the most important thing in her world. The more she thought of it, the angrier she was with herself for wanting Gavin to be alive and well, for wanting to save him when he—had someone better to love.

So why did it feel like there was something wrong with her for being so easily flattered by Zain's glances.

A breeze shook up Rowan's cropped hair. No. Not a breeze a gust of air as Zain rushed over to take the seat next to her by the fire.

"You are far too thoughtful for such a lovely night," Zain said lightly. "Have a mead."

Rowan took the flagon, but didn't drink immediately. A few of the leprechauns took up instruments and began playing a bright playful tune. Rowan watched as children and adults began to dance together. She wondered if it was like this in the villages around Stonedragon, or if this was unique to these people. It was lovely.

"What did you mean, about using dragon fire in a human way?" Rowan asked.

"Well..." Zain bobbed his head from side to side. "We all have different ways we connect with Eternity, don't we. Dragons feeling the suffering of their every generation cannot help but take a long view and thus use magic in lingering ways, or very sparingly. It is the reason so many of them were killed. They could have gathered together as groups and laid waste to your entire human ancestors in a few days of fires. But they were only willing to fight the ones who came after them directly."

"I didn't use the fire until it was a last resort," Rowan pointed out, without taking her eyes off the dancers.

"No." She could hear the smile in his voice and felt her own lips lifting in response. "But you attacked the tree with it. A tree that had done nothing to you."

"I was freeing Yseult."

"Human." Zain agreed. "Willing to hurt one innocent to free another. A dragon would have just attacked me." He laughed as Rowan's hand tightened around the flagon. "Fairy look on magic as an extension of the self, but not the physical self, as humans tend to view it. We look on it as an expression of the inner self." As he was saying it, a little honeysuckle plant climbed up the log Rowan sat on and wound around her head, making a little crown of flowers with one trailing strand down Rowan's neck, before the rest broke off and it rushed away.

Zain grinned. "Your inner self isn't just a battle, stout lady. Why do you let the world convince you it is?"

Now Rowan couldn't take her eyes off him. He had lovely eyes flickering light brown full of mystery and intrigue, offering Rowan all sorts of adventure. Her heartbeat pounded and her breath grew thin and just for the moment she didn't fight the feeling. She just did what instinct told her.

"I want a rematch before I leave," Rowan said.

Zain threw back his head and laughed wildly. "Was there ever a woman who knew more thoroughly how to ruin a lovely mood?"

"Have you never met my grandmother?" Rowan asked, raising the flagon to her lips for a sip as his words made her self-conscious. She wasn't used to... flirtation. Of course she would do it wrong.

Not that she was trying to flirt with him. ***She wasn't.***

Zain grinned. "Only briefly. When I went to swear my loyalty to her as the new leprechaun chief."

He said it with a brow raised, as if challenging Rowan to get offended.

"If she were to call on you today and ask you to raise armies to march against me, would you?" Rowan asked, mildly curious. Having fought him, she knew what a threat a full army of leprechauns could be, but she felt very safe among them.

Zain leaned back thoughtfully. "I do not know. She has not asked. Are you asking?"

"No." Rowan shook her head. "I am done asking those I barely know to fight my battles. But...if you truly are a *sovereign* nation, if you follow the will of your collective being, then I would hope you would at least take pause and decide, as a collective being, if her will is deserving of your lives. Even now she has dispatched men to kill my citizens in an attempt to bring me home. Too many shall die in my name for me to ask this of others. But asking that you...think twice, that I will do. That I am willing to face you in combat for the right to address your nation and ask."

"Very well," he nodded, serious now, but Zain's eyes burned across Rowan's skin too warmly not to be flirtatious. "At first light. I suggest you get some rest, stout lady. I have seen you fight now."

"As I have seen you." Rowan agreed.

Zain bowed. Before she saw it coming he lifted Rowan's hand, and deposited a breath stealing kiss on the inside of her wrist. "Until tomorrow."

Rowan nodded, unable to speak with tingles racing through her. Why had she always thought she couldn't like a man who was shorter than her? She didn't notice the difference when he was holding her hand.

Zain released her and walked away slowly, throwing sly looks over his shoulder.

A screech split the air and Rowan jerked her head towards it. There was a raven perched in a tree across from her. It stared at her with burning, focused eyes. Rowan suffered a very different sort of shiver, cold and foreboding. Shaking off the feeling Rowan stood, resolutely turning away from the bird to go find a place to bed down for the night. Why would she care if Sorcha saw that?

Although...it might be a danger for the leprechauns sheltering her.

"I shall answer seven questions. Four of them honestly. Two dishonestly. And one so vaguely it could be either true or false," Jaron said playfully as they were loading up the wagon. The fairy and humans were a ways off now and the evening was quickly darkening into night. They might well just make camp here.

Jaron had sold nearly all his wares today, but between arguments and bargaining it had taken many a long hour. Asia didn't think the fairy had realized yet that the girls were gone.

She wanted to ask why Jaron had helped those three when they had met with other returned fairy captives but not helped any of those. But she didn't dare ask such a question. Even if she would have to guess if he were answering truthfully the fairy might still hear.

Someone else might take it for a game. But Asia knew he was both offering to share with her, and testing something about her. She was also fairly certain that he was not a citizen of Stonedragon. And it seemed to her now that she must be serving some purpose of his, or he would not be taking her where she wanted to go.

"What purpose did I serve you in Stonedragon?" she asked, trying to get at his deeper motives.

"Ohhh, the way you word that, I am wounded. Was I not of service to you as well? Should one neighbor not assist another?"

Asia carefully wrapped a heavy bracelet in a swath of fabric and placed it atop the small pile in the back of the cart. That was not his answer, honest or otherwise.

When she said nothing he laughed. "I knew not what to ask the half-fairy but I knew they had information for me, your questions were of help. As was the chance to see them interact with another of magic, but magic of an unfamiliar kind."

Asia moved back to the table, selecting a knife to wrap this time. She wrapped the cloth around and around it, added another cloth and lowered her hand to her side, allowing the knife to slip down in the cloth so she might sneak it into the folds of her dress. She still felt that she could trust Jaron. But he had been lying to her for weeks.

Jaron stepped in front of her and took the cloth wrapped knife from her hands. He unwrapped it and held the knife out, handle first. Asia startled, nearly jerked away. She did not have a firm grasp on his magic, but she had not thought it included mind reading.

He smiled. "You are a better liar than thief. That little girl in Stonedragon could teach you a trick or two."

"She stole something?" Asia demanded.

"The spearhead," Jaron nodded. "But...it seemed to belong to her, so I let it go. Here, guard yourself if you like. I mean you no harm."

Asia took the knife by the hilt. It was odd to realize as her hand slid around the grip that she'd never been terribly afraid while traveling among humans. They might be bigger, or hold weapons, but she had knowledge. So much more knowledge than they. She knew of whole other worlds, she had studied their world in ways few of them had ever did. She'd never felt a need to arm herself, she had magic to feel when others intended her harm and she...avoided them. She ran if one was stronger then her and meant her harm, because she was prudent. It did no one any good to be overconfident. As her hand closed around the hilt of the knife she felt like Symphony. Felt like the self she'd been born.

Symphony—despite every fight with her father, or her forced husband, despite her magic, despite every bravado filled word she'd ever spoken, despite her near fifty years of living—Symphony was terrified. Every moment afraid to be shaped into someone new. Afraid to speak. Afraid when she was silent. Symphony was terrified. But Asia was free.

Asia wrapped the knife quickly in cloth, and tossed it on the pile, wondering what Jaron would see of the struggle within, the struggle between the two women who were both a part of her. She'd longed so much to simply be reborn. To take on human form and be an entirely new being, but she couldn't. Symphony came with her.

"Umm. Why did you pick me up on the road that day at all?" she asked to change the subject. A useless question, she realized the moment it was out of her mouth.

"Och, you looked quite lost, I couldn't leave such a poor defenseless girl all alone."

Asia rolled her eyes at him. Though she suspected that was his first lie, and should appreciate that he'd lied about something so pointless in the asking. She had three truths yet to seek, she'd better make good use of them.

"Who are you to Gavin and Owen?"

"What can a man be to two other men? Surely not the same thing to both? But..." he shrugged. "I have often offered them use of my wares, and they in turn have given me great heart. And I swore to my mother to do good turns to those who had done good turns to me."

Asia sighed. Apparently she needed to try that a different way. "What do you want in Ulm?"

"Why, to help you of course."

Now she was growing frustrated. "Are your wares blessed at all?"

"Surely they are. By my love's hand, and by the gifts of every hand they touch."

Asia considered that a moment. He wouldn't tell her his connection to Turrlough, at least not exactly, there were words in that little speech, words he had not needed to use that stood out for it. He had not *sold* Owen or Gavin any of the weapons, but had allowed them to use them. And they were blessed, he said, by *the gifts of every hand they touched*. Then there was the odd mention of his mother. It felt like a hidden message, but she could not think what and she had only two questions left to discover it.

So far he was most willing to speak about Stonedragon, and she still felt there was something to his being there, on the road, and the game he'd played with the children pretending to fear magic when he clearly had some. Even his asking if helping Asia would help Princess Rowan.

"Why...do you want to serve Princess Rowan? She is not your queen."

"She is no ones queen yet," Jaron smirked at Asia trying to trick him with two questions in one. "I would not say it is my aim to aid her, but she means something to those who mean something to me, so if I can help her while helping them, I shall."

"How do you hope to help them from Ulm?"

"Ah, but that would be eight questions, and I am a man of my word."

"You answered only six!" Asia all but shouted. "I asked after your aims in Stonedragon, What you want in Ulm? If your wares are blessed—"

Jaron lay a hand on her shoulder, halting her list. "I think it likely the question you forget, is what young Brigid stole from me."

"I—" Asia felt her arms reaching up to strangle the man before she realized she was doing it. She grunted in frustration and turned away to pack the cart, her movements sharp and nearly violent. She'd never thought of herself as violent before.

"Did no one teach you when you set out in this life, you cannot trick a trickster?" Jaron asked behind her sounding light and unaffected by the...need. That was what frustrated Asia. She *needed* to help Owen and Gavin. They had been like the family she never had, she could not allow the world to destroy that.

"There is no point in fighting him, Symphony. I tried, so long I tried. But your father has you by your fate. Fight fate and your every energy is fed into it. Just... accept."

Never.

Asia fought that side of her nature that she knew to be wholly Symphony. She'd told Gavin not to fight his fate, told him to believe beyond it, because when she was with them, when she had Owen's wide open heart to bask in, and Gavin's overpowering belief to marvel at, and Aya's immeasurable strength...when she was with them Asia believed beyond fate. But when she was away from them, when the days stretched on and she began to think she would never see them again. Out here Asia was slipping back into Symphony.

And Symphony was never any use to anyone.

True Fairy

326 days until Roisin returns

Rowan woke from an unsettling dream with the honeysuckle crown Zain made her in her hand. Feeling around with her magic, to be sure she wasn't observed Rowan carefully folded the flower crown up and closed it into one of her packs.

They were the first flowers a man had ever given her. Rowan felt her lips lifting against her will and leaned in for one last sniff.

She knew it was silly to get a tingle down her spine at just the thought of them. Zain was probably only as serious with his flirtations as Cassidy was with his, but...

Rowan had a sudden flash of her dream from last night. She and Zain had been walking hand in hand down the halls of Stonedragon Palace. When she'd begun to feel nervous, when she'd heard Sorcha's voice taunting her from up ahead *~wouldn't you like to be loved like that?*

Zain had lifted Rowan's hand and deposited another tingly kiss in her palm. She'd glanced down at him. His eyes were warm and loving, and she'd felt beautiful. She'd walked into her sister's welcome home ball with a smile on her face. She'd danced, and laughed, and hadn't cared at all that so many of the people who had been uneasy with Rowan all her life fell instantly in love with Roisin.

When the moment came that Rowan had the spindle in her hand, and Roisin was reaching out a finger towards it. Zain's voice had drifted through her mind, soft, and comforting, and curious.

Your inner self isn't just a battle.

Rowan shook off the dream, and stood, stretching. Gavin had written her things like that over the years. And Maureen had said them. Even Roisin had. Rowan had never realized how powerful a feeling it was to be wanted.

It was unsettling how much she wanted to keep feeling it from this near stranger. She couldn't afford the distraction. Yseult was just stirring, Rowan ran soothing hands down her friend's mane as she woke. Rowan slipped a hand into one of the packs Braden had brought searching for an apple. She munched on her prize enjoying the crisp sweetness then held out the rest for Yseult.

"We'll be on our way shortly, I promise. But I need a rematch with Zain."

The horse head butted Rowan in the stomach, giving her a side eye, doubtful look.

"They seem to respect fighting," Rowan said defensively. Knowing full well she had quite enjoyed the battle, and was looking forward to trying it again. "I need to show them what I am capable of so they respect me. I don't know enough fairy history or traditions to properly fit in, but I can show them that I am willing to learn."

Rowan felt a tingle down her spine and glanced around. She didn't see the raven. And she felt no fairy in the immediate vicinity, but she got the feeling someone had been watching her. She shook her ankle to have music to follow back as she cast her senses, but just the jangle of bells sent a searing pain through her chest. She reached up to sooth that claw in her heart but hesitated.

It had been that searing pain that woke her from her dream. She'd been holding out the spindle, Zain's words had flowed through her mind, and her magic had transformed the spindle into a posy. She'd felt so at peace. Then that claw dug into her heart and yanked her away from that feeling.

She was attributing that claw to Gavin. Had been since she first felt it. But... wouldn't Gavin want that dream for her? The man she'd been writing to these past years was constantly telling her she was not the cause of this battle, telling her she was wonderful, special, inspiring, *good*. Would Gavin try to steal that peace from her, just because there was a different man at her side? That...didn't seem right. It certainly didn't seem fair.

The bells had fallen silent now, and Rowan didn't know if she wanted to set them jangling again, because either the claw in her chest wasn't Gavin, or Gavin wasn't the man she'd thought him to be. And the bells—Rowan could still close her eyes and call up the day before she left Stonedragon when she lay on her bed and set the bells ringing and saw his face. When she traveled in her mind to Gavin and he *sensed* her.

Rowan had loved him for so long, but perhaps she was too good at pretending that feeling was something else. She'd had to fight it for so long because some moments her feelings for him were so strong they threatened to make her forget everything else. When Gavin had said her name, when he'd sensed her presence Rowan thought he felt the same. She'd believed in those, beautiful inevitable things he'd written. She had locked the hope for that up so tight that it felt like perhaps her love alone would protect him and that claw was proof she could, proof he still lived. Still cared. But now that claw was stealing peace from her. And what made Rowan angriest was that she felt guilty over Zain's little flirtation. And she shouldn't have to.

She should be able to smile and laugh, and blush and dream sweet dreams about a man who liked her without feeling ugly. Something began to feel hot, burning inside her, fire. Anger.

Rowan lay a hand against Yseult's side, and fisted the other. She had more important things to focus on. She needed to focus on her purpose here. So she sent her power out, not her eyes but her ears. Sent them seeking anyone who was speaking of her, or Sorcha, or anything important.

"We cannot let her address the lot of us," a man was saying in low, anxious tones. "It is treasonous to give honors to the one who plans to usurp the queen's throne."

"She is the heir to it, not its usurper," Zain defended casually. "We honor *Meave's* traditions."

"The Fairy queen has never acknowledged her as kin," someone pointed out.

"Oh…" Zain laughed. "That is princess Sinead's daughter. There can be no doubt."

"Then why does she know nothing of our traditions? Why does she not *feel* when she is on Fairy land? A true Fairy queen would know." The first man's voice again, and growing more forceful by the second.

"Hobal was the least of us." Rowan recognized Yas's voice. "His magic was weak. He knew the ways, but could not keep to them. Yet, when he led the leprechauns we were our strongest, because we respected the journey all make."

"Aye."

"True. True." The men agreed.

"Are you saying that you trust her?" Zain asked doubtfully.

"I am saying we should not doubt her ability to become Fairy queen. *That* is why we should send her away."

Zain laughed. "Did you elect me only to suddenly assume I'm incapable of the job? The Fairy queen has been informed, via my messenger, that her granddaughter is here. And that she will be facing the challenge, in hopes of addressing my people. We are a sovereign nation, and what we do on our land is our business. Our bargain only promises our annual gift and that we not take up arms against the Fairy queen. Which the young lady has not asked, and I would not do without agreement from my citizens. Have faith in your chosen leader, friends. I am not endangering our people. I am giving them all the choices our nation affords them."

Rowan let the spell go. She was under a little den created by tree branches and moss, away from most of the village. The mountain sloped down from here so Rowan could see down into the Fairy Realm.

The Fairy Realm that she was already in.

Why does she not feel *when she is on Fairy land? A true Fairy queen would know.*

Rowan sighed and began to brush Yseult down by hand when she stumbled across a brush in the packs Braden had taken from the Aunt's cottage. A true Fairy queen would know. Like a true knight would have known to bring food for the journey. Like a true crown princess of Stonedragon would have known what her people suffered.

Were there truly those just born with knowledge? Magic had always come more easily to the triplets than it had to her, but even they weren't born knowing all of it. And if they were, what was the point?

Yseult neighed loudly and stamped at the ground as Rowan began combing as aggressively as she was thinking.

"Sorry," Rowan muttered. She pulled the brush through the animal's hair more gently. "I set out on this journey with one goal, and things have changed so dramatically. My goal hasn't really changed, but...I have," Rowan whispered. Laying the brush back in the packs, she patted Yseult three times, and pulled out another apple for her. "Or I thought I had, but here I am, as ever with the same—

"Do you always talk to animals?" Zain's playful voice sounded from over Rowan's shoulder. "Not that I mind, I talk to animals all the time. But the ones I talk to answer back."

Rowan took a deep breath, steeling herself for that smile before she looked. He had a lovely smile, so open. She turned and found him sitting on a little rock ledge behind her camp. Rowan supposed she ought to feel annoyed, or betrayed that he had gone behind her back and informed Sorcha of her presence, but in fact it made her approve of him more as a leader. He was seeing to the safety of his people, that was what he should do.

"Tell me more about your system of rule," Rowan asked rather than respond to his question. That Yseult didn't answer aloud didn't mean the horse failed to answer, but Rowan saw no need to have that conversation.

He smirked. "What do you want to know?"

"How is a leader chosen?"

"One can nominate oneself, or an outgoing chief nominates you. Perspective chiefs present their vision to the collective and a vote is held."

"So there is a limit to how long one can rule?"

He laughed. "There is a limit to a term, ten years, but one can have multiple terms. Why, stout lady, do you want my *throne*?"

"Can you not elect women?" Rowan countered.

"We can and we have. Yas had the last three terms. And my grandfather before her. We do however limit the office to leprechauns, if you truly were seeking another people to lead. "

"I was not. I am just curious." Rowan thought about everything Yas had said yesterday. She didn't entirely approve of Zain. Rowan wondered if she had been unseated by him. One would look at another style of rule and feel they knew better wouldn't one? "The system is foreign and interesting to me. If your unseated chiefs remain a part of the society, does it not run the risk that people will begin turning to them out of familiarity and comfort, and ignore their new leaders?" Zain opened his mouth to respond, but before he could Rowan was speaking over him. "Do unseated chiefs never become angry, and try to undermine the rule of the new one?"

"I wouldn't say never," Zain laughed. "But no one tries to do major harm. It would harm the entire collective."

"So you have never had a ruler seek that role solely for their own glory?" Rowan asked, disbelieving.

Zain leaned back considering. "I suppose we have. There are always rulers we look back on with shame. But we look back on them with shame at our failure to see their faults. We look back on them as a lesson for how to better protect ourselves in the future. As a *collective* we learn a lesson. Does anyone learn a lesson from your ancestor kings who were selfish?"

"Just their family, I suppose," Rowan said, still considering the pitfalls and benefits of the leprechaun system. She was well acquainted with her own kingdom's system. "So, even when a leader is bad, they are not able to truly damage your collective society?"

"Ahhh. I did not say that." Zain leaned forward, on his knees with a deep thoughtful expression. "Any leader can harm the entire collective. So every leader must constantly weigh what choices they make for the whole, against the cost of losing the whole. But, because we are a collective society, even when a leader damages us, we can undo the damage. We can repair our way of life, *together*."

"Interesting." Rowan swallowed, taking in the weight of his words. He'd chosen them carefully. Rowan wondered if he could, as she did, sense when someone was looking in on him, because it felt very much like he was explaining why he had told Sorcha where she was.

"Well," Rowan said and cleared her throat when the word barely emerged. "That will all be good to know when I address your people later."

Zain laughed, hopping off the ledge that had left him a few feet above her. Even standing before several heads shorter his presence was no less unsettling. Rowan didn't like it a bit.

"What makes you think you can win? Are you planning to use your magic in a fairy way now?"

"No," Rowan snapped. His taunts putting her back up, and setting her more at ease. She was far more comfortable fighting expectations. "I'll use my powers my way. If you think it's too human, then prepare to be defeated by a *stout* human."

Zain roared with laughter. Rowan could feel other leprechauns moving nearer to see what was going on. It was mostly younger ones, but Rowan felt Zain's grandfather's very disapproving presence.

"Why do those words offend you?" he asked, softly serious.

"Because I've only ever heard them used in insulting ways," Rowan bit out.

"From me, never," he shook his head, his eyes warming by the second as he gazed deep into her eyes making Rowan feel overheated. "You wear your build well. I would not have you different." He reached out suddenly and took her hand, depositing a kiss within.

Rowan felt her pulse skip and something soft, very nearly sad unwound within her. She wanted to curl up in the praise, so she pulled her hand gently, but firmly away.

"If you are trying to flatter me to keep me from beating you, it will not work," Rowan forced the words out, annoyed with herself because she couldn't say for certain that was true.

"I just like unsettling you." Zain smirked. Apparently uninjured by her withdraw. "It brings such a lovely rose color to your cheeks and makes me think you like me."

Rowan had to literally bite her tongue to keep from giggling. *Giggling*! She battled down the urge, but couldn't fight her smile as easily.

"Tell me, *stout* lady, has no one ever remarked on what an impressive goddess you are? With that height, and that wild hair and that fire around you?"

"We should stop talking and fight," Rowan said, forcing her muscles to clench up, and her mind to shut him out. He was a charmer. Like Cassidy was a charmer. Their words never meant a thing, and she knew it. But she was eating it up like a starving woman.

"Very well, but I must warn you, I will not hold back just because you are a stout human," he said in a falsely commiserating fashion. "I respect your people too much."

"I will not hold back either." Rowan tilted her head up higher as she spoke. "But mostly because I like to win."

Zain chuckled, the leprechauns behind her chuckled. She could even feel Zain's grandfather lightening with amusement. Rowan let out a sigh of relief as Zain walked away, she didn't know exactly what was coming over her, but she liked his words far too much.

Ferdy was having the time of his life. It was the most fun he'd ever had without one of his siblings. The water sprites were teaching him all sorts of new things and happily answering his questions. And since he and Keagan were keeping up a continual conversation in their minds Keagan was learning the new things too.

Ferdy wasn't sure Mama was right about sending him instead of Keagan. Keagan was still very upset. He was hurt that Balder had sensed Rowan, and Mama had, and Ferdy had, but not him. He felt slighted. But Ferdy didn't think it was because they were closer to her. Keagan's mind was just...never quiet enough to be in the moment. This place, these fairy, they might be just the distraction Keagan needed to pull him into the present.

"When you flood the river in Stonedragon, will it flood the whole way across the island?" Ferdy asked the group of fairy preparing to do just that, when they saw any movement from Anwyn's soldiers.

It had been decided not to do it unless Anwyn's soldiers attempted to invade, otherwise it would be like the water sprites declaring war on Anwyn, and they weren't comfortable doing that.

"No. The water may rise a little further up the river, and sink some closer to the sea, but it will only flood where we make it," Patrick, by far the most informative of the water sprites, responded. He didn't look much older than eighteen, but Ferdy could feel he was much older, probably older than Mama.

He was the one who told Ferdy about the restorative power of all the sacred water sources for water sprites specifically. He said there was a hidden fountain, the fifth sacred water source, that had been lost for centuries, and if one drank from it every day they could in fact live eternally, be they human, fairy, or mole rat. But no one knew where it was. Water sprites however could have their life span doubled, or even tripled if they lived in any of the sacred waters of Great Island. And even humans and animals could use the specific powers of each of the sources, to see, to heal, to cleanse, or to travel.

Mama had talked about some of this, but it had never felt as real as it did now. Ferdy could feel it. He'd been trying to use the waters to check on Petal, or Pa, or Rowan, but it was difficult. The others said he should start smaller than people Sorcha was watching, or people who might in fact be in the Fairy Realm. And it seemed logical, so Ferdy flatly ignored it. Anything worth doing was always difficult.

"We're at least seventy miles from the bridge, and we're not even at the river," Ferdy said with bits of excitement and glee coating his voice. "What if the soldiers are crossing the bridge already? Will you know? How quickly can you get there? If I were vanishing it would take me two jumps at least."

Patrick smiled. "There are sprites keeping watch. If we were vanishing it would take us as many jumps as well, though...when pressed one can cross a much greater distance than is strictly healthy. But we aren't vanishing, we're joining the water. Once we become water fully...it only takes a matter of moments for us to be nearly anywhere that water is."

"Truly." Ferdy's mind spun with possibilities. You could travel the entire world with such a power. Why did they stay here? "Can you move other things as quickly, or just yourselves?" Ferdy demanded. That promised to be an exhilarating ride if they could do it.

Now Patrick was laughing in earnest. "Do you mean you?" He laughed again. "We could move you quickly, but not that quickly. Far faster than ships would carry you. Have you ever seen the rapids of the Liadan?"

Ferdy shook his head. He never went anywhere.

"They cover several miles before reaching the bridge we'll be flooding today. Those waters move a boat five times as fast as it can go at any other point in the river. And we could move you *ten* times as fast as the rapids."

Ferdy grinned broadly, rubbing his hands together. Now this promised to be an excellent adventure. Just as soon as Petal was back. Keagan would enjoy it too, but not as much as Petal would. It would be excellent.

"So how exactly do you do it, you know, flooding the river and moving fast? Do you become part of the water, and with your added selves make the river overflow?"

"There aren't quite that many of us participating in this part of things," Patrick laughed. "Yes. We become water, and join the river. But then we must also use our power over the water to raise the levels, to pull as much of the waters to the places we want them. It takes us working together, even the sprites who will remain here will lend their powers to the effort." Patrick hesitated a moment, his eyes glance around the area looking for objection. "If you like, I can show you a bit here, and you can join us. But if there is danger you must stay well back from the fray."

"I am trained to fight," Ferdy said, offended.

"Not as water. If you cannot agree—"

"I can agree," Ferdy said quickly, not about to lose this opportunity to see what becoming water felt like. "But..." he hesitated looking around. There were sprites rushing all around, some were entirely made of vapor, some looked like streams of water. Only a few had fully recognizable human form.

"Will I be able to turn back into myself?"

It was their leader Delaney who answered. He'd not seen her a moment ago, now she rose from the water between Ferdy and Patrick, a stream of water, in the shape of a young girl.

"Being a part of the collective does not mean losing the self," she said sweetly. "But if a human body of flesh and bone is a part of how you define yourself, then it might be a difficult transition to make."

Her tone was sweet and informative, but Ferdy felt a bit of testing, perhaps even judgement in it. He wasn't sure the judgement was directed entirely at him, but he didn't like it one way or the other. Yes, a physical body of flesh and bone was a part of his identity, how could it not be, it was all he'd ever known. He supposed if the water were made up of Keagan and Petal he would be willing to shed the body easily enough, but...he was part of a group of thirds, not a whole collective of strangers.

"The choice would not be made now, you understand?" Delaney said with a small sideways smile. "Until one has reached adulthood they have a time of exploration, in which I can extend the power of the collective to them so they might see what it is to be one of a whole. However, if you ever chose to be fully water sprite, and join our collective you would not have a body of flesh and bone. You could build yourself one of magic, but it would only exist for a few hours, or a day at most, before you would have to return to the waters."

"But..." Ferdy hesitated; her words were intriguing, but as exciting as the idea of being water, or vapor and aging so slowly it didn't really seem like aging at all was, there was something a bit scary about her words.

"Yes," a woman of vapor, behind the rest of the group spoke up, before Ferdy could finish the thought. She waited until his eyes were on her before she finished what she was saying. "To become a part of the collective, you must be fully water sprite. It would mean abandoning your human half."

"How could I?" Ferdy asked, equal parts appalled that such a thing was possible and curious about the particulars.

Delaney cast the mist woman a sharp look then glanced at Ferdy. "We can talk more later. There is movement at the borders. Patrick, join the others."

"But he said I—"

Delaney held up a hand and though it annoyed him to do it Ferdy shut his mouth for her obediently. "Orla, Murphy, bring the boy and see he stays safe if we meet opposition."

"I am not a nursemaid," Orla, the woman of mist snapped.

"But you are a part of the collective, and you have your instructions." Delaney remarked and rather than waiting around to be argued with fell apart like so much water.

A bit of the water splashed over Ferdy's face making him shudder, it felt like it was clinging to him.

"I don't need a nursemaid," Ferdy said, throwing the woman a snide look. But he couldn't help another shudder. The water that had splashed over his face and arm felt cold and clingy—and it was spreading.

Orla moved closer. "It will work better if you do not fight it. I thought you wanted to be made water."

"I..." Ferdy looked down at his wet arm in shock, it was being...eaten away by water. It was terrifying, and exhilarating. Ferdy's heart was pounding so fast and hard it seemed it might leap out of his being. Maybe it would—when his skin was gone entirely and he was just water.

Kee, he thought, *you have to try this!*

Battle

Peg it turned out, was not especially gifted at following orders. She'd left the village she was meant to be in. Maureen had not precisely given up on the border towns, but she had known there wasn't proper time to fortify them so Peg was to help fortify the places that had a chance. And she had. She'd set them about packing off all their children for the palace, or the coast and the elder children had all been sent to harvest early whatever crops they could to stock up for the coming days, while the adults were arming themselves and laying out traps for invaders. Everything in its place. She wasn't needed there.

But Swallow Fell, the town a mere seven miles away, might need her. So Peg stole a horse and rode. When she was nearly there she saw a sheet of smoke before her that could mean only one thing. The soldiers had crossed, and they were burning the town. All because King Balder had not been ready to defend his nation.

Rowan would have protected them. And Peg had chosen for herself the role of Rowan's Shield, which meant she should have been here to protect them as well. Peg heard screams and swords and tried to urge the horse forward, but this was no war horse. He kicked up his front legs into the air, tossing Peg backwards. Even before she'd hit the ground the horse apparently sensed its freedom and bolted away.

Peg lay a moment, aching and winded and terrified. Then she heard another shout. She charged to her feet and ran towards the smoke and the heat and the screams. She ran towards the battle and her heart raced ahead of her. Her mind slipped clear and neither fear nor regret could make their way into her conscious thought.

She ran through the smoke towards the village, choking a bit as the thick, singed air, coated her lungs. It was madness. Peg had never felt nor seen a thing like it. Smoke, screams, weapons slashing, one soldier lay on the ground as a group of three women beat on him with broom handles and ladles. It should be amusing, but there was rage, and horror in their screams as they beat at him, and on the ground nearby was a body, unshielded by armor, and bleeding into the soil. The air was a putrid mix of smoke, a sweat and blood. Her short sword was in her hand, but Peg stood in the melee of fighting bodies and could not move.

This was different from defending yourself. It was different from training with the knights. This was—

"Aaaaaa!" A young woman's cry split the air as a soldier's blade sliced open her side.

Peg launched forward straight for the soldier. He didn't see her coming, too busy preparing to slice the defenseless girl again. Peg shoved between them kicking the soldier off balance, striking him in the side of the knees. Peg raised her sword high, and jabbed it towards the gap where his breastplate and shoulder guard met. Her blade nicked his skin before he struck it away with his broadsword.

"Run," Peg called back over her shoulder but focused her attention on the soldier before her.

His sword fell heavy on her, nearly dragging her down. This was what the training was good for. Peg swung her sword down away from his blow and stepped back and sideways, making him come to her. He struck out again with a heavy two handed blow that would come down on her shoulder hard but she jumped away. She was faster, lighter on her feet.

He grunted in frustration and tried kicking at her instead, his sword still raised to block the vulnerable spot Peg had already exploited. His raised leg provided her another target, she jabbed her weapon into the slats between leg straps. She gouged deep into his muscle and the knight bellowed in pain as he fell. But he managed to bring down his sword in a glancing blow on Peg's shoulder as he went. Even a glancing blow from a broadsword was powerful enough to send her tumbling to the ground with a bloody wound.

She landed next to a body and glanced aside at it. It was the girl she'd dove in to rescue.

"No." Peg gasped, the ground was warm and gooey from the girl's blood and she lay still with her eyes wide open and her chest still.

Peg rolled over and kicked out towards the knight crawling away. "No!"

Leaping to her feet Peg rushed forward and brought her booted foot down hard on the man's arm. He howled again and released the weapon. Peg lifted her blade ready to stab it into the man's eye or mouth or ear or any flesh she could find. But hands feel on her shoulder, grabbing her back.

"Leave him," a woman shouted and tried to drag Peg away. "There are others. Those three will kill him."

The women with brooms and pans and ladles ran over as another woman latched onto Peg's good arm and dragged her deeper into the village, towards the thickest part of the smoke, and the loudest screams of metal and human agony. Her stomach turned as she ran and she tasted bile in her mouth, but she ran forward all the same. There were other soldiers to kill.

Orla didn't like being left to watch over her nephew who didn't even know who she was. But even less did she like what Delaney and Patrick were trying. They wanted to trick Maureen's children— at least one of them— into becoming fully water sprite. And Orla didn't think they were doing it out of the goodness of their hearts, or a desire to have him among them, or even in the hopes of bringing Maureen home.

It was all politics.

After Maureen left several of the waters sprites gathered at the pool that showed the future trying to decide if Maureen was right about *her Rowan* being the next Fairy queen. For her part, Orla could see that happening as likely as not, but then, she never looked in the pool of the future. The others weren't sure, but they all saw the benefit of having one of the girl's closest friends and servants as a member of the collective. Like flooding the river now, it was calculated. Nothing to do with right or wrong, just best for the collective or not. Orla remembered when Delaney wanted water sprites to be the flowing symbol of all that was good in Fairy, protecting all of nature, all of the world that they could.

That wasn't what they were doing now. Still and all, at least they were doing something. Orla hated this sense that they were still water, turning foul in the air and the heat.

Orla watched as Delaney's spell covered the boy from head to toe, his eyes took on a half horrified half exhilarated light and he grinned, and she could feel his mind reaching out for his brother.

"Orla!" Maureen had shouted out for her sister the first time she'd turned water. There was no fear in it for her, she'd been raised with it. But she was joyful, and at that time all of her joys had to be shared with her sister.

"Orla, look at me." Maureen spun around and around, a little girl of water standing amid a cluster of flowers on the river bank, casting droplets on the ground.

"Watch this!" Orla challenged, smiling at her sister.

She always challenged Maureen to run faster, swim farther, laugh louder. And when she got it, when Maureen was laughing so loud that birds took off and all the grown-ups came running because her laughter sounded exactly like shrieks of fear, then Orla felt her heart beating hard and her blood turning light and misty with her effervescent joy. Only then.

Orla made her arm into a sword of ice and sliced towards her sister's watery arm.

This time Maureen did shriek in fear, falling to the ground in her haste to get away from the sword. She hit the ground with a thud, and what had been mother's spell fell away, leaving Maureen back in her flesh and bones.

Orla dropped her sword arm to her side and rolled her eyes at her sister.

"Maureen, I wouldn't hurt you. I was just going to show you how you can let ice move through you. It's amazing, you get all tingly and cold but only for a few seconds."

Maureen had stared at her sister's sword arm for a moment more, then her face dropped. "Mom's spell is gone. If I tell her she'll be angry."

"Eh, not with you. She's only ever angry at me." Orla leaned forward, holding out her free hand of water. "Come on, I can do the spell too."

"Really? Already? But you haven't made the transformation yet."

Orla grinned. "I'm really good at making myself vapor. I followed Delaney and the elder class and I watched her teach them the spell."

Maureen giggled. "Can I go with you next time? I can't make myself vapor, but I can be invisible."

"Of course," Orla agreed readily. "Tricks are always more fun with you along."

As soon as the boy was completely water he forgot about wanting to see the others flood the river, forgot his fears, forgot everything but playing with the spell. He scooped up water and shoved it at himself like he was trying to see if he could be molded into a new shape like clay. Then he sunk into the water, and rose. But he did it all wrong, instead of spreading himself out, he bent at the knees.

Orla smiled, he had a bit of his mother in him. Murphy was being exceptionally quiet. Orla glanced over and found him watching her and not the boy. Was she shortly to be treated to another of his lectures on healing the breach with Maureen, as if it was her doing.

"Come on." Orla grabbed the boy by the shoulder, then she felt the water for where half of the collective had gone and cast her watery cells apart. She pulled herself and the boy back together some seventy miles from where they'd been moments ago. Well, not quite that far. She kept him well back from the action.

He was gasping and struggling at first as if worried he'd drown. Were he in his human form he might well have, the river was very deep at this point, but he wasn't in a human form right now.

"You can't drown when you're water," Orla snapped. *I wouldn't hurt you.* Her mind added, but she wasn't about to say that.

"Oh...yeah." Ferdy didn't exactly seem offended by the rebuke. He just examined himself and his position more carefully.

He hadn't noticed the fighting ahead of them yet. But Orla couldn't tear her eyes away. She sent her power into the water, lending her magic to the fray as the water was shoved up onto the north bank of the river, catching the men nearest the banks and carrying them forward on a giant wave. That was easy. The water was rising, the banks were flooding, the humans were fleeing.

But in the trees nearby were fairy. Fighting on Anwyn's side.

Earth and air fairy, soaking the water up, or shoving against it with a force of wind. It was a battle. They had waded into a battle once more with *fairy*.

Orla pushed herself out in front of the boy, preparing with her magic wrapped around his ankles to drag him under the water should the fairy notice them. Should the fairy fight in earnest, rather than just holding the water sprites back.

"Hey are those fa—"

"Quiet," Orla hissed, and shockingly the boy obeyed. Maureen never obeyed commands.

Orla remembered the last time the collective had faced off against fairy. When Sorcha's forces had driven them from their home in the Fairy Realm. Those fairy had done far more than push back water sprite magic. They'd come with yarrow root for slicing through the water with blistering pain, and magma shoots that forced sprites back into their flesh and bone as it burned their beings away. Those fairy had killed.

Orla had her hands clenched as she watched the struggle. No one was killing. Not yet. On either side, but Orla felt the order rushing through the water, Delaney wasn't willing to leave it to chance. A great wave of sprites fell across the bridge, shattering it apart, then all of the water sprites washed away from the river, and back to the hot springs.

Orla didn't breathe until they were all back at the hot spring. She waited for the others to start shouting that they should not have gotten involved. Or to suggest running again. They all remembered their last battle with the Fairy. They had all lost someone.

Orla saw her mother dying. *She took on a flesh and blood body that Orla had never seen before. And Orla had watched as she screamed, and her eyes alone were made of water, weeping in agony as the magma grew up her leg all the way to her chest. She'd barely been able to speak, in such pain. But she'd managed the same two words she always said to Orla.*

"Protect Maureen."

As if she ever, even after all they'd been through needed instruction to do that. Orla would never allow fairy to do such a thing to her sister. Their mother had probably just been in too much pain to think of a thing to say. She'd said those words to Orla so often. It was probably nothing more than a memory, but Orla couldn't shut them out. She never had been able to.

Orla wondered now if Maureen even knew that their parents were dead. Did she know how their mother had died? Father at least died of illness. But not Mama.

Delaney stepped out into the center of the mass of bodies flooding the top pool, so many water sprites taking form, in every pool and on the formerly dry ground around it. With all of the pools crowded with bodies the water began to spill over the rocks to the ground. Delaney would have been dismissed in the human world, she looked so like a child. But here her age was known, her wisdom and experience were trusted. Here the world waited for her words.

"It would have been nothing to promise if we did not face fairy," Delaney said at last. "I feel with you the worry, the pain and the memory. But this will not be like the moment we were cast out. I cannot promise you that Sorcha will be dethroned by the Knight of the Rose. But what I can promise is that this battle, unlike the one forced on us when we were cast out, or the war before over Sorcha's throne, this battle will be *just*. Not one of us shall perish if we can help it, but nor will we turn away. We all knew such a battle would come one day."

Orla began to feel badly about her earlier doubts towards her leader. Perhaps telling Ferdy about his heritage was not meant only to gain them a favorable ally. Perhaps they were only sharing what they loved, unaware that Ferdy, as a child of both worlds had equal cause to love each.

Sprites began to vanish as Delaney sent out orders through the water. This one to watch the river. Another to guard the spring. Groups to practice water battle. And another to seek out a place of hiding for the children among them.

Orla moved forward to join her group and practice water battling though it was a skill she'd long since mastered, but her nephew caught her hand.

"When you were cast out, because Mama wouldn't return to the Fairy queen..." Ferdy hesitated his voice laden with regret and sorrow. "Some of you were killed?"

Orla gave a short nod, only realizing as she felt his hand tighten on hers, that she'd built herself a body of magic, a full form on which he could see plainly all her expressions— or her scars. She nearly cast the thing apart, but she saw him growing small and wanting to hide as if it had been he who had killed them. Orla shifted her body sideways, so he could not see her back where her burns must stand out as testament to the ugliness of that moment. He shouldn't feel that.

"Those who came to cast us out had spent their lives believing us *worthless*. So when given the permission they were cruel, even monstrous. And for this their eternities shall be filed each with ugliness and pain. But...it was *never your mother's doing*." Orla forced the words out. She felt tears welling in her eyes and fought them. "None of those deaths are on her hands. Those monsters would always have found a way to let loose their evil."

It hurt so much to speak aloud the truth she would keep from her sister at any cost, that she'd never blamed her for that suffering. It hurt nearly as much as it hurt to stand before a boy who she'd loved, and watched grow up in these waters, without him ever knowing who she was to him.

"Come along," she said, clearing her throat. "We'll show you how to fight like a water sprite. You should be prepared."

"It was only a squadron of about forty, and we'd seen them coming," the mayor of Swallow Fell explained to Peg now that the battle was over. "It went better than we could have hoped. If the whole army had crossed we would be gone."

Peg nodded hollowly. The battle hadn't lasted long after she'd come. Not that her presence turned the tide. The people of the town were fighting, and water fairy that Peg was loath to trust had been putting out the fires which were not the city itself but the crops that lined the river. But the fairy had not stayed around to be thanked or trusted, they just put out the fires, broke the bridge, and left. Absorbed back into the river.

Peg wanted to be more comfortable with such magic but she wasn't. She wasn't comfortable with anything. Not today.

She felt sick still, though she'd vomited twice since the killing had ended. Every time Peg saw a new body her empty stomach threatened to explode again. There was nothing noble or honorable about this. Was this truly what war was?

All told the villagers had killed about six of the soldiers which in itself was quite impressive when few of them were trained for battle and the soldiers were all heavily armed and armored. Anwyn's soldiers had killed well over twenty of the villagers, it would have been far more had not the village seen them coming and prepared.

"We set up corridors of attack." The mayor went on. "All our weapons were given to the men, and the women pelted the injured soldiers with rocks, sticks, anything they could find. All of the children were snuck out on foot two nights ago. They should be well on their way to the Narrow Hills already."

"Why there?"

"I assumed the soldiers' aim would be for the palace. The hills, being on the way to Creelan would be a very unlikely road for them to take."

Peg nodded again. She didn't know why the mayor was telling her any of this, as if she was someone who mattered. As if it really made any difference.

Peg had failed. The king had failed. These people should not have just been fodder to slow an invading army.

"The purpose of a queen is to be a shield for her people." Peg said barely aloud, wondering at the words. If they were true, where was Rowan? If that were true for a queen, why was it not for a king? Why had Peg ever thought that she could change the world?

The mayor lay a hand over Peg's, she startled jerking it away and going for her sword. But the man stepped back, holding up his hands in surrender.

"It has been quite the troubling morning. I am sorry. I...I was only going to say...she is not yet our queen. But even so," he nodded sideways, towards the river. "Fairy we do not know saved our crops, and shattered the bridge so more men could not reach us. A woman she conscripted into service came to our aid, and we were forewarned enough to get our children to safety, and to save many of our homes. No shield can prevent *every* harm." He held out a palm and showed Peg a single shamrock like the kind that had flown to all of Rowan's allies yesterday.

Peg gasped, tears streamed down her face. The mayor stepped slowly forward, extending his arms as he did, but he moved too slowly. Peg threw herself into the arms of this stranger and sobbed. Today they were not strangers. Today they were kin. And he was so right. Even though she was not here, Rowan's power and her influence were working to protect her people. They just had to work together to see it.

Future Fairy Queen

There was a battle ring off at another edge of the village. Rowan hadn't properly toured the whole thing last night. As she wandered through in the light of day she found herself wildly curious. The homes were widely spread out, there was a farm in the center of the village, and animals that wandered about. Rowan saw a rabbit running through the garden with a tiny head of butter lettuce in its mouth and a child chasing after it yelling about putting it in the stocks. She grinned, that might well be a serious threat.

If animals could answer back, they might well be subject to the same laws? And if fairy didn't eat animals then it wasn't under threat of death, but a public humiliation might be in the offing.

There was a particular area that caught Rowan's eye. An old tree, burnt to a white cracked husk sat in the center of a tiny hill, surrounded by a rock wall. There were no walls anywhere else so that alone was intriguing. But from each branch of the tree groups of prisms were hung. They varied in size and shape, and there must be hundreds of them, catching the light and casting beautiful rainbows down the little hill, into the crevices of the wall.

"Plotting to steal our treasure?" A man asked from Rowan's right. It was Zain's grandfather, Hazam, one of the four men leading her through the village.

"Simply admiring the beauty."

"Ha. Imagining how you'll make us share more when you're queen more like. But I wouldn't place any bets on your winning the throne."

Leprechauns travel by rainbow light
Deep into caverns only they see

*There they pile their gold up high
For power to grant one's wishes three.*

Rowan snorted. Maybe she knew more about leprechauns than she thought. She'd assumed that old song was just a legend to tempt humans. Perhaps the old stories held as much truth as they did intrigue.

Rowan didn't comment. She walked to the ring. When she and Yseult stood alongside the ring Yas crossed to her.

"Would you like help donning your armor."

Rowan shook her head. "No. Thank you." She just barely remembered to add her thanks.

In a normal battle the armor was a help. But Zain was too fast. The armor slowed her down. At least, her metal armor would.

She shut her eyes, drew in a deep breath, and felt her pains. Everything from her father's fear, to women calling her mannish, to these fairy saying she was too human, and that claw tearing her out of her peaceful dream. Every single pain she laid across her skin as a scale. Right down to the first gauntlet and bracer she'd made from her regret over sending Petal to spy.

She heard oohs and ahhs from the younger children of the village, felt them crowding around. When she opened her eyes with her body covered over in purple and blue iridescent scale armor she saw that their crowd had doubled in size. And Zain at the opposite side of the ring was grinning.

"You can't intimidate me with dragon magic," he called out.

Rowan smirked and stepped into the ring. Zain took his place as well, grinning. When she was sitting across from him, or when he held her hand, that smile could do things to her stomach that she'd honestly never felt before. But not now.

Oh she liked it, and it tingled. But this wasn't just an exercise or a challenge. This was proving her worth to people who didn't think she had any. This was a test of leadership. This ate every other feeling and fed them back to her—as power.

Zain and Rowan charged at one another. Neither held a weapon today, not that it mattered, at first neither one could get near enough to the other to land a decent blow. Rowan was mostly taking defensive moves. With his speed when he landed a blow it felt like three men were landing one at once, so she wanted to avoid the pain for as long as she could.

He didn't seem to tire, no matter how much she kept him moving. Usually she would tire but she didn't today.

When Zain feinted to run around her, and instead slid across the dewy grass to knock her off her feet, Rowan was surprised enough that the move worked. She fell backwards, but managed to vanish before she could hit the ground. She reappeared behind him and kicked out, but he was racing across the ring already.

You are a creature of motion and instinct. A creature with no understanding of stillness. Oona's words laughed through her mind as Rowan prepared to race across the ring again.

She was going about this wrong. She'd learned things from stillness. Learned to be a creature of both instinct and consideration. Learned to balance her arrogance with her good sense. She not only could beat someone as fast as him— she was going to.

Rowan stood just where she was and smirked in Zain's direction. "Is that the best you've got?"

A few of their observers laughed, mostly the children. But it gave Rowan a little boost of confidence. She always had had a better effect on children. Zain didn't respond with words, but he launched himself across the ring so fast Rowan couldn't see him after half a second.

Rowan blew out a stream of smoke to hide her and even things up. Then she stepped forward, slowly, not rushing just because he was. She felt the air for him, felt with magic and with the senses of her skin.

She kicked out with her right leg, and clipped him in the shoulder as he ran by her. He spun around as soon as her kick landed and kicked out catching her in the gut. As with yesterday the one strike landed like three, but the dragon scales absorbed most of the impact. Rowan staggered back, but kept her footing. He was rushing at her again, she could feel it, straight on.

Rowan hunched, held perfectly still until he was right before her, then she launched herself forward. Their bodies crashed into one another, with enough force to send both hurtling away. Rowan landed on her back and immediately rolled to her feet. She couldn't see him, the smoke hadn't cleared away. But that meant he couldn't see—

Something slammed into the back of Rowan's knees, knocking her to the ground at a kneel. It wasn't him, at least not his body. He was running back and forth across the ring, clearing away the smoke. He'd used a tree branch, or some other plant to attack her.

Rowan leapt up and started racing forward, angered by the pain. The bells at her ankles jangled loudly. In her metal armor she would never have heard them, but she heard them now. *Unlimited. Unlimited. Unlimited.* They chanted.

Pure instinct sang through Rowan like a bell reverberating as it toned. She cast herself apart. Raced with her physical body towards Zain from behind, and projected another self before him.

There were gasps from among their avid audience, but Rowan barely noticed.

Zain was attacking the projection, attacking nothing but air, and Rowan managed to grab him from behind, yanking him by the shirt, and slamming him with all her might to the ground. He gasped as the move stole his breath. Rowan threw herself atop him, with one hand holding him down, she yanked the thorn from her belt and pressed it to his throat.

For a moment everything was silent.

Then cheers and laughter and shouting exploded from their audience.

Neither Zain nor Rowan moved. Both panting for breath with their eyes locked. His face was getting closer and closer, and it was all her doing, but Rowan couldn't seem to make herself stop. Her heart pounded with as much excitement as she felt at a battle but this—it wasn't about a battle. She was going to kiss him. She was—

A congratulatory slap on the shoulder had Rowan rolling off Zain, and jumping to her feet.

Zain lay where he was for a moment, and began laughing. He covered his face with his hands. Rowan turned away, hiding her hot face. She couldn't help smiling as she was cheered and danced around by children, and congratulated by a few adults. She could barely catch her breath. She just hoped they attributed it to the battle.

"How did you make two of yourself?" one little girl shouted.

"I...can cast my senses different places."

"The looking glass?" an adult commented. "That isn't meant to be perceptible to others."

"I meant it to be." Rowan notched up her head. She honestly couldn't say how she did things, she just did them. And anyway weren't *true fairy* meant to just know such things.

Hazam smiled, and gave Rowan a deep bow. "You've a bit of your grandfather in you."

"You know my grandfather?" Rowan asked, thinking of Colum.

"Yes. Eachann Elderhorn and his brother Tyrone hid here for a time," the man bobbed his head sideways. "Before they managed to invent themselves a royal lineage to have descended from, and set out to trick a queen."

A number of the older leprechauns laughed. Rowan was completely thrown.

"What do you mean invented a royal lineage? They tricked Sorcha, Nessa and all of their sisters? And Queen Ashling into believing they were someone other than themselves?"

"Indeed. A better pair of liars I've never encountered." Hazam grinned. "They would have made excellent road leprechauns."

"And you...helped them?" Rowan asked with a shocked grin. She knew so little of Eachann's life. It was hard even to recall he was her grandfather half the time. What a life he'd had. Rowan truly looked forward to their next meeting perhaps she could convince him to tell her some of his stories before the battle was over.

"Of course we helped," Hazam said bemusedly. "A pair of sprites wanting to steal the throne of the Fairy who called them all lesser. Determined to defy the entire world if need be to be seen for their full value." He nodded at Rowan, to indicate how he thought her similar to Eachann. "We understood. And we helped."

"And *paid* deeply for it," Yas interrupted the playful tale sharply. "We were many before. Now we are two-hundred-and-ninety-six here, and a few scattered more throughout the world. You won the right to speak, princess." Yas bowed as though deference was what Rowan had been after with the fight. "But do not expect us to risk what life we have here to aid your cause."

Rowan slowly folded the old pains from which she had built her armor back into herself, so she stood before them in her road battered clothing, torn and dirty from constant use. She looked nothing like a princess. She might look more like her scarred self now than she did with those scars made into dragon armor. She let them see her as she was.

There had been a time, not even months ago, when learning of a nation of Fairy that Sorcha did not control might have prompted her to come here seeking more soldiers, but no more. She did not think she was owed their allegiance by right of birth, or right of battle. She only wanted a chance for them to know the sort of queen she would be.

"I did not fight to gain your assistance in any battle." Rowan glanced around. Her eyes fell on Zain. She'd felt him close behind her, but hadn't allowed herself to look, he'd not said a word to her yet. But when her eyes fell on him he was looking at her with more admiration than before. Rowan's stomach flipped and she forced her eyes away. This was her chance to say her piece. To get to know the first of her fairy people in any way she could.

She let her eyes fall on as many faces as she could, and fought for herself in the far more frightening way than with weapons.

"I mean to challenge my grandmother for her throne. I cannot claim to know much of her life prior to when she cursed my sister, but I am told she was once a good queen, and I have no reason to doubt it. But I do not believe the same can be said of her now. I do not ask for your assistance. All I ask is that if she seeks your aid in our coming struggle, you answer not as subjects to their ruler, but as a sovereign nation to an ally, considering first what *you* believe to be right."

Rowan swallowed heavily and her eyes found the ground for a moment, but she lifted her head again, and met the stares before her. "I didn't always recognize the weight of such requests, but I do now. I understand this is no small thing. I realize that it might prove as dangerous as asking for your aid. So I shall make you a promise: *when* I am queen of the Fairy, whether you have served Sorcha in the struggle or not, I shall endeavor to...extend the hand of friendship to your nation. And our association shall begin from there."

There was a different sort of quiet now, heavy, thoughtful. And Rowan had no idea how to break it. Zain solved that problem neatly. He walked in front of Rowan and raised her hand, bowing over it.

"I look forward to the day, stout lady." He winked and pressed his lips to Rowan's hand.

She didn't even try to fight the smile that crawled over her face, or the flutters in her gut. She would look forward to seeing him as well, when battle and worry were over and she could...understand him and herself and the world better.

Rowan jumped when a vine of honeysuckle leapt up from the ground to wind around her wrist. The end of the vine snapped off and raced away and Zain popped his eyebrows.

"You've lost your crown." He winked. "A lady as magnificent as you ought always to be adorned with flowers."

Rowan yanked her hand back and rolled her eyes for good measure. But she left the flowers right where they were. She had always loved the smell of honeysuckle.

Bonds

owan felt more confident in her path after meeting the leprechauns. Her first encounter with a purely fairy culture had gone better than she expected. There were plenty of them who still disliked, or more likely distrusted her, but she had shown herself willing to participate in their traditions, she'd spoken her piece, and had tried to pass by them peaceably.

Rowan snorted at the thought, her way of passing among fairy peaceably was to fight with their leader in one-on-one combat. She could get used to that sort of negotiating. Maybe she should establish such traditions when she became Fairy queen.

It was odd thinking such things over and over again as though they were certain. Uncomfortable, but she had to keep thinking like that. *Because death is all you see, your feet walk straight towards it. You can make your own future. Why do you want it to be deadly?* Rowan hadn't especially embraced the lessons when Oona was right before her. But they had opened Rowan up to the need to embrace the moment. To ask Eachann the question in her heart that served no practical purpose. To...flirt with a handsome man who found her attractive. This was how one lived, wasn't it? By experiencing the moment they were in, not building their life towards one future as though it was all that mattered.

She could make her own future. She would. It would be beautiful. Not one fight, or one purpose, but a long, exciting adventure.

The further into the Fairy Realm she went the more Rowan saw to excite her interest. It helped that she was more sure of her way now. She'd asked for specific directions to Fairy Cache as she left. Which honestly was a moment of embarrassment she expected to relive several times, but she had done it, and it couldn't be undone.

"A Fairy queen, even only a future one, would know the way," Hazam, had said with a cautious expression. All of the nearby leprechauns had nodded, some even laughed. "Even Tyrone knew when he left, and he never claimed that throne."

Rowan fought the blood rushing to her cheeks, she would not blush in front of them over her lack of knowledge.

"It is interesting to think," a woman at the back of the crowd had commented. "That if she manages to take the throne, Tyrone will still have his original goal. A sprite will rule the Fairy."

That startled a great many gasps from the gathering. Even Rowan was shocked. She was a sprite? The woman stayed well back from Rowan, and her eyes took her in with a quieter sort of consideration than her elders. She seemed to be in her later thirties, and was the tallest leprechaun Rowan had seen yet. Her expression seemed more intrigued than anything else.

"That may be the goal he claimed, but...I think we all know differently now, Twill," Hazam replied.

"We cannot know anything from a dead man," Twill remarked sharply and stormed away.

Yas watched the woman go before turning to Rowan. "A Fairy queen makes the way," she informed Rowan harshly, then her tone softened. "But that does not mean she knows she is making it as she does so. Stop worrying about where your road leads and follow it. You will find what you need, whether it be what you are seeking or no."

Fairy, human, dragon, everyone had some message of belief for Rowan to learn.

Rowan had found it odd that Zain made no comment on the issue. But she'd seen out of the corner of her eye the way he was taking in the debate. He wasn't any more sure of Rowan than the others, was he? But whenever his eyes fell on her Rowan couldn't doubt his attraction.

"A queen *makes* the way," Rowan whispered aloud now, leaning low over Yseult's neck. They weren't moving very fast through the forest, it was too dense for a proper canter, but Rowan didn't feel anxious. She would get where she was going.

She rode, and the bells at her ankle jangled rhythmically; Rowan felt her mind drifting away. She felt someone's heart calling out.

She saw the pulsing pink light before anything else, and Rowan's heart sped up with excitement. *Petal.*

Rowan didn't see Petal at first, she was in a garden. Bright colored flowers were laid in neat rows along a stone walkway, and large trees cast scattered pockets of shade. There were benches of smooth marble under one of the trees and the path curved ahead with bushes trimmed into the shapes of different sea creatures. It was lovely and peaceful, but nothing Rowan would have expected from the Fairy Court. Then she spotted Petal. She sat on the ground with her legs folded under her, rocking back and forth with her hand wrapped tight around her talisman.

"Petal," Rowan called out as she raced forward.

Petal heard Rowan's voice and jerked her head up. She couldn't possibly be here.

But...Petal leapt to her feet, Rowan was here. Here! Well, some of her was. Petal watched the wispy shape of Rowan race forward. She looked different. Her hair was short, and her face seemed longer and she was...here.

How was she here?

No!

Petal's eyes searched the garden. She couldn't see anyone, but she knew Dervla was guarding her. Dervla might be on Petal's side, but she would tell Sorcha if she saw Rowan. Any fairy would.

"Petal, you can see me?" Rowan asked, reaching out. Petal felt Rowan's fingers just barely graze her arm and her heart clenched up. Tears threaten to overpower her.

Rowan was here, and trying to hold her. She didn't hate her. Petal gasped. But she didn't dare cry, didn't dare speak, or show how happy she was.

Sorcha would know. And everything would get so much worse.

Petal hadn't slept since she'd been in Anwyn. Sorcha hadn't shown her to Braden and his family yet, she was waiting for something. Petal lived in constant dread of Sorcha turning Braden into a bird as well as Gavin. One of them Rowan might be able to forgive. But if Petal stood by while Sorcha transformed, and destroyed all of Rowan's friends, Rowan couldn't possibly continue to forgive her. Petal couldn't possibly forgive herself. If Sorcha knew Rowan had come…if she knew Petal had wanted her here…She would be ruthless.

Sorcha could be calm as she cursed. Cold and calculating, and dangerous. But she was at her most vicious when someone threatened her relationship with Petal. Sorcha was liable to kill everyone Rowan loved if she knew about this.

Petal drew in a deep breath and dropped her hand to her side.

"Why are you here?" Petal asked coldly. "If you think you can hurt me you are wrong. The Fairy queen *always* protects me." Petal tried to alert Rowan to the danger with her cold words. "Just because you cannot see them, does not mean I am unguarded."

Rowan let her hand fall to her side and her eyes scanned the area before falling on Petal's face again.

"I've missed you," Rowan whispered with teary eyes.

Petal scoffed, her eyes slicing cruelly across Rowan, though she longed to reach out and hold her. "I haven't missed you. With you I was nothing but a tool. But with Sorcha I will be a queen. I will be *Fairy* queen. And you will be nothing."

"Petal the Powerful," Rowan smiled softly. "There is nowhere in the world where you could be only a tool. You are the best of us." Rowan bowed towards Petal. Rowan's lips began forming words: *I love y—*.

But before she finished the last word her body jerked backwards and faded away.

Petal held her breath. Held in her tears. Held onto her talisman. Rowan never had power enough for that sort of spell in the past, but she'd found it. She found magic enough to come to Petal. For several long moments, Petal shut her eyes and held the moment close. She missed home so much. She missed Rowan even as she was with her.

She wanted to be held so badly she thought she might break apart. But she couldn't.

"Dervla," Petal called out, her voice cracking slightly.

The fairy appeared before Petal with her expression as usual masked in the light. But Petal felt Dervla's heart reaching out.

"Yes?" she asked softly.

"Why did you not attack her? She intruded on me. Aren't you meant to keep me safe?" Petal demanded sharply, as if she were still watched. She must assume she was always watched.

Dervla shrugged. "One cannot attack a projection. But *do not worry*, one of Her Majesty's birds was sent to...deter her from intruding again."

Petal felt her eyes widened, burning angrily. "Deter how?"

"However he can." Dervla replied casually. "One imagines the falcon will merely be an annoyance, to a knight. But she will know she cannot intrude on you unmarked."

Petal sucked in a deep breath, and tried to appear merely annoyed. It wasn't the raven, that's what Dervla was telling her. That...and that she thought Rowan would be safe.

Petal felt the rose protruding from her talisman brushing her palm like a kiss. Rowan would be safe. Petal would be safe.

Petal the Powerful, there is nowhere in the world where you could be only a tool. You are the best of us. Petal clenched her hands at her sides, and fought the urge to cry. Sometimes she was so angry with Rowan,

and Gavin, and herself that Petal forgot how very much she missed Rowan. And how very much she loved her. This was such a scarier life than she'd imagined when she set out to be a spy. But her heart burned and her talisman pulsed, she could still be her. She could do this.

Petal felt the warm glow of sunlight shifting through the shade to close around her like a hug. Her breath caught. She glanced up looking for Dervla, feeling her magic in the light, but she couldn't see the fairy before her, she'd disappeared into the light she cast.

Petal stood in the light, and let it enfold her. She was loved.

Rowan flew backwards through the air as Yseult reared up. She landed on her back, half in shock, but she was too well trained to stay down. It was not a coincidence that Yseult had thrown her while she was visiting Petal.

Rowan rolled into a crouched position and drew the thorn from her belt, searching the area. Yseult was neighing wildly, and fighting against a pair of trees that were pulling at her bridle and saddle. She kicked out, and bit at branches, growing more and more angry with every second.

Birds kept swooping down to bite at her.

Rowan leapt to her feet and rushed into the fray. The thorn was too curved to aim true when throwing so Rowan dropped it and drew her sword.

She swung it towards the birds, knocking them off course and tried to send out her power at the same time to the trees. But these trees fought back, unlike the rowan trees, these were not on her side. They shoved Rowan's magic back towards her, leaving her unsteady. So she slashed at the trees with sword rather than magic.

Before anything could be thoroughly injured one of the birds swooped down, just out of reach of Rowan's sword, flapping its wings to stay level. It let out a loud piercing screech and at once the branches let go of Yseult and the other birds flapped away.

Yseult was too angry to leave it at that, kicking at all the trees around her. Rowan kept her protective stance as she stared at the bird. It was the same one she'd seen on Mount Kieran as her smoke shield faded away. It flapped again and again, the current brushing up a swirl of leaves. Suddenly it flashed with a bright purple light and the bird was gone, leaving a man in his place.

A human man.

A...familiar human man.

"I—" Rowan opened her mouth to speak, but shock caught up her tongue and she could do nothing but stare.

"Come now, Princess Page, it isn't nice attacking defenseless birds and trees."

"Bran?" Rowan whispered. Her grip tightened on the sword and she felt her muscles tensing.

"It is good to see you too," he replied with a broad smile. "You've grown into quite the knight. If a bit of a temperamental one. You were in no danger."

"Bran?" Rowan repeated, unable to move past that. It was Bran. Bran who had been dead since she was twelve. Bran who she had mourned. Bran who's spirit she had spoken with in Oona's cave.

She'd wondered if he was alive then, but had dismissed it, it felt too hopeful. But this *wasn't* hopeful.

"You... Have you been alive all this time?" Rowan asked. "Have you been working for the Fairy queen?"

He smiled, raising his head in pride. "She is a great lady, Rowan. We were wrong to attack her. You should get to know her."

"She does not want to know me," Rowan snarled. "She is trying to kill me."

Bran laughed. "She is a queen defending her throne. A throne you are attempting to steal. If you left her alone she would do the same with you. But do not worry, Rowan. I promise. She does not want you dead."

Rowan advanced slowly on the man before her. "You helped her attack me. I was thrown from my horse."

"You may have a bruise or two. But it is nothing you cannot heal, is it? She had to warn you not to trespass."

Rowan stared at Bran, at a loss. He was...spellbound. It was the only explanation. He knew who he was, knew who Rowan was, but willingly served Sorcha, put Rowan, *his friend* in danger for Sorcha.

"Bran. I am sorry you were ever sent to attack her. But she is manipulating you. Using you to hurt me."

Bran smiled. "For you I lay in a field dying. For you I clung to life, determined to kill her. But the Fairy queen..." His voice softened lovingly and his eyes took on a glazed tinge. "She saved me. She forgave my attack and pulled me close. She blessed me with my life, and this power."

"She made you a bird that she dispatches to do her bidding!"

"She gave me the power to become a bird, or a man. She gave me a purpose. I serve her of my own will. Stop fretting. I am happy. That was your worry, wasn't it? Friend."

Until that moment he had seemed like a brightly oblivious version of her friend. Even when saying he nearly died for Rowan there was no malice in his tone. But now Rowan heard anger. Now she heard resentment.

"Of course I am afraid for you," Rowan replied carefully.

"For me, or of me," he nodded to the sword in Rowan's hands.

Rowan stared at him, half her mind shouting that she should not lower the sword. Shouting that he was a threat, that he was manipulating her. But the other half of her mind just saw her friend.

She'd been with Petal. She'd been nearly able to hold her. But Petal knew the danger better than Rowan, Petal shoved Rowan away with words to protect herself. Petal was changed and heartbroken and alone. All alone with Sorcha.

If this were Petal, even if she was here to hurt Rowan would Rowan stand before her with a sword in hand? Would Rowan go after Petal with weapons if she began serving Sorcha in earnest?

Things happened to captured men, little queen. They do not always turn against you, but they never come back as they were.

Eachann would want her standing here with her sword aimed at her old friend. Probably Colum and Ardal would too. Even Maureen would worry more for Rowan's safety than Bran's feelings. But though Rowan was not the one who had sent him, it felt like her doing that had brought him to this place.

Slowly Rowan lowered her sword, sliding it into its scabbard. She reached a free hand backwards without looking, and waited for Yseult to rub her nose against it. As the horse nuzzled Rowan's hand, she felt her calming.

"I am sorry. I have thought you were dead for so long," Rowan said. "I have missed you for so long. I am a little...bewildered."

"I am not offended." He laughed. "Nor frightened. Though I have seen you fight, and you are *incredible*. We did it." He grinned. "Both of us showed everyone who thought we could never be knights exactly what we're made of. You lead your own company. And I serve the strongest, greatest woman in the world."

Rowan tried to smile, stepping slowly forward. She had to help him, but she had no idea how. And now that her sword was sheathed he went back to behaving as if he held no resentment for her.

"Is it you who has been showing me the armies of Anwyn marching on Stonedragon?" she asked. "Doesn't that worry you?"

Bran shrugged his shoulders. "I've shown you nothing. Are you sure you didn't imagine it?"

"I am certain. Bran, the Fairy queen is attacking Stonedragon to get me home."

"Was it the Fairy army? I thought you saw Anwyn's soldiers."

"She is using them."

Bran laughed. "You are operating on false information, Rowan. You sound like the other humans all wanting to blame fairy for their mistakes of leadership. The Fairy queen is even now in Anwyn trying to help King Alistair come to a peaceful resolution. But she was not there when the soldiers were dispatched."

"You are...with her so often?" Rowan asked.

"I am with her whenever she has need of me."

"What did she need of you today? If not to put me in danger?"

Bran nodded aside. "You were hurting Petal, making her uncomfortable. You will not be allowed to harm that girl. She is special. She will be the next Fairy queen. Queen Sorcha has deemed it so." His head was raised like a herald proclaiming a king's word, then his head bobbed and his demeanor shifted to taunting. "And she thought you should know..."

"Know what?" Rowan asked when Bran dragged out the comment.

"That there is nowhere you can go where she cannot know of it. The leprechauns aren't your allies, they told her of your visit."

It was taking everything in Rowan to remain calm. She wanted to grab him and shake him and tell him to be himself. She remembered him as light and playful, but so warm. So helpful. The man before her felt counterfeit. He had Bran's face, and his lightness, but none of his heart.

"I remember once," Rowan said, focusing on drawing out the man she'd once known. Or...discovering if there was any of him left at all. "I was trying to climb up a wall, Colum had said I must know how to scale a keep wall." Rowan laughed, shaking her head, remembering all the levels of training Colum had tried to force on her before he would allow her to hold a sword. Every time she passed another he made up a new one. How had she not realized sooner he didn't want her to be a knight? She shook off the thought and focused on Bran.

"There were squires across the courtyard watching and teasing. I was pretending I couldn't hear them, but it got harder and harder to climb, and I felt like crying. Then you came striding over, with this huge smile on your face. At first I thought you would fight the boys, and make them apologize, but you," Rowan beamed, "grabbed the rope beside me and said—"

"Race you to the top," Bran finished for Rowan with that same huge smile on his face.

The muscles around her chest unclenched and she could feel herself relaxing though she felt sadder than before. He was still in there. He was still him, he was just lost.

"Yes. It was so much better than if you'd defended my honor, because you helped me see what I could do. You believed in me," Rowan said with tears in her voice.

"I still do." He walked forward, taking Rowan's hand. She forced herself not to startle or try to push him away. This was her friend. This was her friend, and he needed her. "I told you, I am not here to hurt you. She doesn't want you harmed. She just wants...to decide what is done with her throne. Is that so wrong?"

"Of course not," Rowan said heavily. His words sent an angry shiver down her spine.

You are disinherited.

No one wanted Rowan to have their thrones.

"Bran," Rowan began hesitantly. "Do...you know Petal well? Is she happy?"

"I have never spoken with her. But...she is graced by the love of the Fairy queen and beloved by fairy of every nature. She is the happiest child in the world. You should be so proud you sent her."

I haven't missed you.

Rowan's free hand clenched into an angry fist. Bran saw it and laughed.

"It has been good to see you, Princess Page. The Fairy queen truly hopes you enjoy this glimpse of her kingdom. But you should know, the fairy have instruction not to engage with you, and Fairy Cache is hidden. Only the Fairy queen can make the path wind to it."

He grinned, then a bright purple flash fell between them, and he was a bird again.

He flapped before Rowan for a few moments more before he took to the sky, flying away.

Rowan felt as though whatever power had held her up simply fell away as he vanished. But she didn't fall. She didn't scream. She didn't cry. She stood where she was with her fists clenched and her heart pounding with sadness and regret. But she felt like she'd collapsed within.

After several moments Rowan felt the nudge of Yseult's nose against her shoulder. She spun around and wrapped her arms around the horse's neck.

She had been *so close* to Petal. So close to reaching her, holding her, telling her she was loved. So close to everything she'd needed to do since she ran away from home. Even with Petal pretending coldness it had been such a comfort to see her. To *be seen* by her.

So what did Sorcha do? Send her an old love to mourn once more. Show her how small she was, how tiny her triumphs were in comparison to Sorcha's. Rowan wanted to scream. She tightened her hold on Yseult.

"She is so close to defeating me today," Rowan whispered. "I cannot let her defeat me."

Rowan pulled away from the hug, running her hand down Yseult's nose. Every step Rowan took forward, Sorcha tried to shove her back. And she had so many tools.

Bran was alive.

Alive! It should be wonderful, but it was at least as terrible as it was lovely. He was alive and he was part of himself, but not all. How many other soldiers had survived the assault only to serve Sorcha years later? Or was it only Bran because she could feel his connection to Rowan? Rowan had no idea how to save him. What if the same happened to Petal?

You should be so proud you sent her.

"Alright." Rowan turned away from the horse, searching the clearing for the thorn. She found it and slipped it into her belt, crossing back to the horse. "Alright," She said again. "I won't let her defeat me. She wouldn't have sent him to taunt me if she wasn't afraid. We're going to Fairy Cache, the Fairy queen makes the way. So—I'll make the way. And give Sorcha a real reason to fear me," Rowan said with her head thrown back and fire in her words, but a dampened heavy heart.

Shifting Futures

When Rowan chose to make camp for the night she and Yseult were both more settled. Rowan was a little less marveled by her surroundings, but she was trying to be. The queen made the path to Fairy Cache.

The Fairy Realm had a living queen. Rowan could feel fairy, fauna and flora alike poking their heads up in interest at Rowan, but none of them were sure of her. They would answer to her if they must, but they were waiting for her to prove herself. Waiting for her to...force them into the shape she wanted in order to make her path. But Rowan didn't want to force the trees and the ground and the squirrels to love her and answer to her, any more than she'd ever wanted to force her people to love her.

Rowan laughed at herself a little as she ate some braided sweet bread with fruit and nuts baked into it that the leprechauns had given her. Yseult poked up her head to look at Rowan.

"I want it to be fate," Rowan answered the horse's expression with a laugh. "All my life I've fought against anything that felt too fated. Now I want ruling the Fairy to be fate. I want—" Rowan laughed again. "I want to just know. It has always seemed like fairy, *real* fairy just knew everything. Where their powers came from, how to use them, where they fit in the grand scheme of life. But what if they don't? What if there is no grand scheme? What if there is only the world as we know it, and the world as it could be?"

Yseult stared at Rowan. After a long silent stretch she shuddered and neighed, all but rolling her eyes.

"I've missed our philosophical conversations too." Rowan chuckled, absently turning the honeysuckle cuff at her wrist. With each turn the smell floated up towards her stronger than the last.

When the scent had all but enveloped her Rowan looked down at the flowers, and Zain's grinning face popped into her mind. His eyes so intent they made her shiver even now when they weren't before her.

"Maybe I don't want it to be fate." Rowan lifted the flowers to her face, though the scent already surrounded her. She smiled at the tightly racing beats of her heart, and this...first little bit of joy she'd had from the Fairy Realm. "Maybe I just want to see more of this land I have denied myself so long. Maybe I am making the way, but I am making that way show me as much of this realm as I can see first."

She ran the flowers slowly across her cheek, trying to dismiss the little voice within that said she should not be enjoying herself, or exploring, or flirting, or having an adventure. She should have one goal. Everything else could come after her sisters were safe, and Sorcha was defeated.

Merrymaking is something you *have the luxury of every day,* Peg's old chide scuttled through Rowan's brain. She'd felt so guilty at the time. All the time. Like she truly was stealing something from Roisin by enjoying any moment. She'd felt guilty every time she smiled or laughed, or wanted anything for herself. And the days had stretched, every hour more painful than the last. But since her time with Oona, it wasn't that the guilt went away, it just fit into a quieter part of Rowan, and the days before her, though they might hold pains, held other hopes. They held hopes for joy within the pain.

So Rowan shoved that voice away, and embraced the urge of the moment.

Rowan looked into the trees. She could feel fairy watching, listening, weighing Rowan's worth as a queen.

Rowan threw herself backwards, urging the ground to soften and cushion her fall, *asking* it to. And it did. She asked for help, the ground was glad to aid her.

"Tell me, where is the Whispering Wood? Where are the Laughing Hills?" Rowan spoke with her eyes closed, sending the words out with her magic, to the fairy listening nearby. Her voice softened. "Where are the places my mother loved? I should like to see some of them tomorrow, if you will guide my path."

Rowan didn't expect an answer right now. So she allowed sleep to take her slowly, and the oddest thing floated through her mind, Colum's words to her as they danced at her birthday ball.

You do not have to be a queen. *When you are ready to claim yourself, as much as your new role, you will be* the queen. *The only one of your kind.*

Darling was walking in a hazy field. The air felt damp, and smelled heavily of poppies, and all around her she heard muffled sounds of metal striking metal and people grunting. She shivered. She didn't want to be here. She wanted to wake up. She couldn't be back here. This was where Friend died.

She tried to clear the air before her with her hands but a thick fog lay across it that she could not move away, every time her hand brushed through the fog it brushed by another rose petal. Darling's heart pounded hard with fear. It couldn't be both of them now, could it? Friend and Prince Charming. The only people Darling knew outside her aunts, the only people who loved her. They couldn't die. Neither of them.

Darling heard voices, and moved towards them, begging with everything that was inside of her that Prince Charming not be there, that Friend not be there. Darling had changed things. She must have changed them for the better.

"Please," she begged, aloud and in her sleep. "She and I, ever two halves of one whole."

She could feel herself thrashing in bed, felt her body calling out to her to do as her heart wanted and escape the dream. But she fought it. She needed to see.

She could be brave. She wasn't a knight. She couldn't go into the world. But she could do this. She could look so her aunts could find a way to fix it.

"Colum!" Friend's voice called out. Then cried out in pain.

Darling raced towards the sound of her friend's voice. But before she'd reached her an air shaking growl made Darling tumble back. Flames flew into the air, burning away the fog.

There were people everywhere, men. Soldiers with their weapons drawn attacking one another. But they stopped with the fire, struck as still as Darling.

Darling wanted to move, but she couldn't. Her friend was bleeding again, dying again. Blood drained from her side and her face was anguished. There was a man before her with a bloody sword poised to strike her down, but he threw it away in horror when he saw Friend. Friend swayed forward, and the man dove to catch her.

"NO!" Darling jerked awake.

Her aunts were all around her at the foot of the bed. Darling looked among them, unable to find the words, but they clearly all knew.

Her friend was dying, in the arms of one she loved. Darling felt something wet in her hand and looked down, she gasped and tears streamed down her face. Rose petals—wet with blood—were scattered atop her sheet. So many petals.

325 days until Roisin returns

Flooding the river and destroying the bridge had bought Stonedragon time to get some small amount of their forces to the border towns before very many soldiers could get across. But there was already a small squadron of Anwyn soldiers on Stonedragon land. And apparently fairy were helping the soldiers cross now that the bridge was out.

This news was delivered not by falcon messenger, or even Ferdy, though Keagan had used him to verify it. It was delivered by fairy. The same fairy messenger who had always brought Prince Gavin's letters. The same fairy messenger who had first suggested Petal go to the Fairy Court. The same fairy messenger who could not be in a room with Mama without fighting with her. Or he had not been able to, until today.

Mama was acting oddly. Ever since she'd gone to see the sprites, or maybe even before that, when she'd helped the king remember Rowan. Keagan could tell she was still angry, but so much more she was guilty and heavy and so tired. Keagan couldn't believe he hadn't realized before Ferdy how ill Mama truly was. Her exhaustion was the only excuse for her...calm and grateful treatment of the fairy. It was unsettling.

Keagan didn't trust Eachann. Not at all. He could feel the world shifting back to one of the bad futures with his arrival.

That was the bad time. Keagan heard his own voice in his head.

That terrible future flashed through his head. Ferdy's wide, empty eyes, the blood covering his chest, the holes in his throat from Sorcha's scepter. Keagan shuddered and forced himself to refocus on the present.

Keagan couldn't say for sure that it was Eachann's arrival that caused the shift towards bad, but they certainly coincided. Every future that tumbled through his head showed either Ferdy or Pa dead. And Rowan was bad in half the futures now, when she'd only been bad in a handful before. This was very bad.

"So Braden is back home safely?" King Balder said slowly. "And I am simply meant to trust this information from you?"

The fairy smiled tiredly. "Make of the news whatever you wish. It was merely a mild reassurance. That he entered the palace of his own will and in one piece I can attest. That Sorcha still has use for him, and is thus unlikely to kill him, I believe. But his home is far from safe, as it was from within those walls that came the order to attack him. And he is not Sorcha's man."

"What makes you so sure?" Keagan asked, stepping forward militantly. He'd never liked this man, but he'd always felt as though he was serving eternity. Something had shifted in him. Kegan wasn't sure who he was serving now.

The man tilted his head to the side and examined Keagan quietly. "You tell me, mind reader. For in truth I cannot say I know whence came my certainty. I could not penetrate the boy's mind, by a spell of your doing. But...perhaps it was merely that the little queen trusted him."

"It is so easy for you," Keagan said, tilting his head to the side as his power crawled around the man's mind, his history. "Switching allegiances."

"No, mind reader, never easy. Though I do admit—it was often done."

Mama rushed forward, no longer patient. "You say Rowan sent you. Do you know where she went? Why did you not go with her?"

The fairy, who oftentimes started the battles between himself and Mama today surprised Keagan, perhaps everyone. He reached out for Mama's hand and bowed over it. "I could not follow your girl there. She went to Fairy. She said she had things there to learn."

Mama did not fight to take back her hand, just nodded again and that heavy regretful essence settled around her once more. "Many things."

"Do not fear," he laughed. "I trailed her as she dauntlessly walked into the nest of a dragon, as she fought her way up a mountain, as she resisted her own desire to return and end this war. She is feeling eternity's greater purpose. The child *you all* raised," he said, lightening with the words so he appeared to rise off the ground. "She can do anything. Even a centuries old dragon believes so."

"She found dragons?" Keagan asked when everyone just sunk into the knowledge forgetting things needed doing and knowing and planning, and sorting. Dragons were a part of far more good endings than bad.

You are losing yourself to your power.

Keagan shuddered at the echo of Mama's entreaties. He couldn't listen. His power was all he had. It was the *only* way he was useful. He couldn't reach Petal, or Pa. Ferdy was fine among sprites or the humans. And Keagan couldn't figure out how to help Mama. And everyone—Even Balder could sense Rowan, but Keagan could not. His power was the only way he could help. He could find the future they needed to live and guide them to it. He wasn't losing himself, he was saving himself, and the rest of them. It was the only way.

"She found one. A dragon named Oona," Eachann said, far too thoughtful for such a simplistic answer.

"The lonely one!" King Balder said aghast startling the whole room not so much with the interruption as with the fact that he might know something pertinent.

Keagan was being unfair. Balder must know *something* pertinent.

"You've heard of her?" Ardal asked.

"Yes, my mother told me stories of a dragon named Oona who would come to her in her dreams and help her to find the way to lead dragons out of captivity. She called her the lonely one, because she lived alone in a cave protecting the future, but to do it, she could never join the present."

"The very one," Eachann said calmly. "She was quite fond of your daughter, taught her new magic and—"

"But Rowan isn't returning? And the dragon is not coming to help us fight?" Keagan asked, redirecting the conversion once more. He could feel the many adults of the room wanting to spend long emotional hours picking apart the man's words, but at the moment they had a war to thwart and another to start. They needed actionable military information. Keagan needed to know which path they were on!

Ferdy's bloody face flashed before Keagan's eyes. His heart stopped and the image vanished.

The fairy smiled at Keagan and shook his head. *Careful,* the man thought. *You can lose yourself to the future. Then how will you guard those you love in the present.*

Ferdy startled. He didn't like having someone other than his siblings in his head. It gave him a shudder. Was this how the others felt when Keagan poked around their heads?

Keagan, he heard Ferdy's voice in his head. *You alright? Your mind went dark.*

I was just startled. Keagan lied. *Eachann is back, he took Braden to Anwyn.*

At least we know he's alive! That's good. Don't suppose it will end the war though, Ferdy thought.

Seems unlikely. I'll tell you the rest later. Keagan brought the conversation to an end so he could focus.

"Perhaps her letter will help you understand more," Eachann held it out to King Balder, rather than Keagan, though he was looking at Keagan. "She asked that I deliver the prince to safety, then deliver this, and help here in any way I could."

"And just why," King Balder said, suddenly awakened to his fatherly distrust, and all from his umbrage that the man offered him help. "Did Rowan allow you to travel with her? Or think we would be willing to trust a self professed turncoat?"

Eachann shrugged, continuing to hold the letter out as Balder had not taken it. Another twenty seconds and Keagan would take it himself.

"She did not know I traveled with her until a few days ago."

"What!" Both king Balder and Ardal bellowed, advancing on the man in anger.

Eachann laughed. "She trusts me to help because she knows my love for her is all that drives me. My desire for us to be family. And you should trust me because you trust her, should you not?"

"Family," King Balder spat the word as though it were disgusting.

"He is her grandfather," Mama interrupted. "Sinead's and Desmond's father."

King Balder startled and grasped the letter. But all of the sudden Eachann would not release it, holding Balder's eyes though the man was a good foot taller than him. Odd, Keagan never really thought of the king as tall, and he did not seem to much intimidate the shorter man. Balder didn't know how to wear his height, did he?

"I was never father to my children, not for a single moment," Eachann said intensely. "So every moment was a failure, but it was also so ordinary a thing by the time they were small that my failure could no longer disappoint them. You would have surpassed me in fatherhood for even spending one moment with your child, but you will I suspect also far surpass me in wounding your child, because she harbors still—after every pain—such hope for you. I hope you live up to it. I will stay, whether you welcome it or no, because I serve her cause."

Balder was fluctuating between rage and sorrow ready to lash out at this man threatening his power. Oh he did not like that at all. He didn't like any of them leading him, especially not Keagan, but he was taking it because he'd fallen victim to the curse while they had fought it. But here was one more man making demands on his power, Keagan briefly wondered if this would be the thing that broke him. For surely he would break. Few and far between were the futures in which Balder was anything but another spellbound victim when Roisin returned.

Careful, the fairy thought to Keagan again, *see the now, or you will never know any future.*

Eachann released the letter which appeared like a bundle of yellow leaves laid together. King Balder unrolled the letter and gasped as the dragon pendant fell into his hand stinging him. Rowan had sent the dragon pendant to her father? Keagan had never seen that happen before.

Keagan glanced from the king to Eachann unnerved and intrigued. This man was no architect, but he seemed to understand something of Keagan's power.

"What does she say?" Ardal demanded ahead of Mama which Keagan found odd, until he glanced over and saw she was reading it from beside the king. Ardal was simply too low to do the same.

Keagan was vaguely surprised at himself for having forgotten the letter, but Eachann was...interesting. Keagan still didn't trust him, perhaps not at all, but he was worth closer study. He must know a great deal about Sorcha, if he was father of her children.

King Balder slipped the pendant into the pocket of his robes before reading the letter out, at first sharply, but his tone softened slowly.

"Dear Father,

I cannot return home as yet. I know it is Sorcha's aim in starting this war, so there must be more out here for me to find. But I have every faith in you, and those I see you have pulled around you to defend our home.

I cannot regret having left, as there was much I needed to see on this journey. It has helped me to understand myself and my role far better. But I do regret the haste with which I left, and the words of anger I exchanged with so many.

I am returning the dragon pendant to you as I have no use for it any longer, but I am certain that you will one day, be it soon or in the far distant future. There are many things to say, and many stories to share but they shall have to wait.

Eachann will have either returned Braden safely to Anwyn or carry him to you if something went wrong. But know that Braden chose to return to his family to help us all, and try to end the war. He lied for me, to give me time to make good my escape, as a friend and brother would. Do not blame him for this. And please put your trust in Eachann and make him welcome in our home. Too often in the past I was so focused on my task that I failed to respect that others, as well as I, have a part in this struggle. All others. Let him find his, as you must find your own.

And please convey my love to everyone. I love and miss you all.

We will be together again soon.
Rowan—"

When he finished reading, the room fell quiet and though he'd heard similar things said time and again, and though he'd sworn he was listening when he heard them, Keagan felt for the first time like he was truly beginning to understand the words.

Too often in the past I was so focused on my task that I failed to respect that others, as well as I, have a part in this struggle.

They all had parts to play. And every time one of them found their part, more of the futures got brighter.

The Fairy Realm

Yseult hated the Fairy Realm, she didn't like the shifting trees that bowed low and parted branches to lead Rowan in different directions. She didn't like the animals that darted in front of them, only to pause, looking the pair over, then hurry on their way. She didn't trust anything.

But Rowan was enjoying it. Perhaps she should be more suspicious. She never used to simply trust that someone would lead her in the right direction. But she was more confident in herself, her power, and her path. Rowan was doing what she should for her sisters, but she was also doing what she should for herself, and her people, be they human or fairy. So she found it easier to go along on the adventure, without a need to direct it.

She felt sure now that the trees, and the animals, and the softly caressing wind were leading her where she'd asked to go. The trees led Rowan to a little cliff low on Mt. Kieran's southern face, too thin for Yseult to pass. Rowan slid off the horse's back, letting the reins hang loose; as uncomfortable as Yseult was, she wouldn't leave Rowan.

Rowan walked out, right to the edge of the cliff and a great rush of air flew up at her, she laughed wildly and leaned into the wind as her hair shook around her. At first it felt like it was simply a playful wind welcoming her, but after a moment she heard a voice within it. Petal's voice.

Rowan would love this. She loves high places. She would stand on the very edge, unafraid.

Rowan leaned further into the wind. Petal had been introducing her to the Fairy Realm, helping them to get to know Rowan before she came.

She is human, but she is fairy as well...That is why she sent me. As her emissary. To let you know, even though she could not be here, that she loves the Fairy, and she means to care for you all when she is able.

The wind gave Rowan a little push, shoving her back from the edge before it rushed around her, bending the branches of the trees and the blades of grass and the arms of bushes, all bowing before her.

Rowan stepped back, and bowed in return, her heart burning bright with the welcome.

The breeze blew off, clearing a path through the clouds so a beam of bright sunlight shone down over the Fairy Realm. Rowan stood with just inches between her and the edge and stared into the heart of the Fairy Realm. There was so much to see, and she wasn't even seeing the half of it. She knew off towards the north west the Fairy Realm touched the sea. And she knew somewhere to the west were Ever Spill and Fairy Cache. But what was before her was so massive, and so lovely she couldn't imagine the sights she was missing being better.

There were forests of dancing, likely whispering, trees. And a bundle of sliding hills, that looked precisely like a basket of bread rolls. There was a wide clear lake that caught the sunlight and reflected it back. Rowan watched its glistening light, long enough to see a giant snake-like creature lift its head high and spin about in the light again and again, before it suddenly ducked its head into the lake, and pulled out some wriggling creature Rowan was too far away to make out.

She could see little fairy running through a rambling patch of bushes shaking berries loose to be caught in glistening nets. There were birds of every kind flying around, and butterflies swarming at the crest of a hill.

The butterflies swirled and swirled in a funnel that seemed to call to Rowan ~ *come see.*

Rowan took one last moment, committing the beauty of this world to her memory then raced back to Yseult so they could go see the view from that hill.

As Rowan and Yseult set off down the mountain, a bright blue butterfly with glistening wings glowed between a pair of trees, marking their path. Rowan led

Yseult that way, and saw a dotted path of butterflies ahead. Guiding her to her mother's favorite places, just as she'd asked.

The butterflies led Rowan to the Laughing Hills where they convinced her to lay on her back and go rolling down, laughing all the way. When she climbed back to the top she found Yseult waiting at a tense ready. Rowan wondered if it was herself who had changed or the horse, because Yseult's tension felt unwarranted to Rowan. They had usually been in such perfect sync before.

Fairy *were* reputed to trick travelers, show them great beauties until they became so lost that they wandered forever. But Rowan didn't think that was happening to her.

Rowan twisted the flowers at her wrist, they still felt alive, as though they had never been plucked from their vine, and every twist brought another breeze of fragrance.

Rowan was not being lost. She'd asked for something and the fairy were showing it. That didn't necessarily mean they would follow her, or that they wanted her for a queen. They could be doing it at Sorcha's urging, showing Rowan everything that she would never allow Rowan to have. But Rowan didn't think so.

So she went along when a pair of tussling bear cubs stopped at the base of one hill and bowed to Rowan.

"Come on. The Whispering Wood is this way," one of the cubs called out.

Rowan and Yseult followed.

They chased the bears through a wide field, dotted here and there with trees and bushes and everywhere with tiny wildflowers or dancing grasses.

It didn't feel like a trick. It felt light. It felt free.

It felt like...they had loved her mother, and they adored Petal. So by extension they loved Rowan, and were willing to share with her.

It was odd that Rowan felt more welcome here than she had at home. It must be something to do with how she was responding to the realm herself.

"Perhaps it is because Stonedragon was never your home. This has always been your home, Fairy queen."

The words danced at Rowan out of the shuddering leaves of an aspen nearby. Shivering across the air in a nearly familiar voice. Rowan sent her magic into the tree but could sense no fairy hiding inside it. It was unnerving to have her thoughts answered by a nameless, faceless force. A force that Rowan thought she should know, but couldn't place.

Rowan was not the only one to hear the words. When the voice called her Fairy queen, the trees in the field bowed and the flowers of the bushes exuded stronger fragrance and the wind swirled around Rowan again and again. Yseult danced around in a circle uncomfortably.

Rowan didn't know what to say to the voice. Stonedragon was her home. And while this was a beautiful welcome, it did not escape Rowan's notice that it was largely animals and plants that were doing the welcoming. It was a welcome laid by Petal, perhaps even by Rowan's mother. All it would take was a word or a threat from Sorcha to change it. Sorcha was *allowing* Rowan to see the land, Bran had said as much. But it wasn't home just because it was welcoming her.

If anything, the voice woke Rowan's need to press on. Friend or foe, Rowan couldn't let it trick her into forgetting that her purpose here wasn't to find a home, but to free her sisters, and end Sorcha's quest of vengeance.

The bears had run on without her as Rowan paused to listen to the voice. Rowan turned Yseult in a slow circle. Wondering where she meant to go now. She could see the mountain stretching up behind her. A dark deep forest on one side of this clearing, ambling hills on another and what looked like farm land ahead. She wanted to see all the places her mother loved. But she needed to find a way to free Petal.

Fairy queen, the voice had called her. Had it meant to recall Rowan to the purpose of making the road and finding Fairy Cache? Rowan looked up the slope of Mount Kieran, she remembered Maureen telling her that Fairy Cache sat high on the mountain's western face. So logically if she meant to find the palace she should head that way, but logic didn't necessarily describe the things made by fairy.

"No." The voice interrupted Rowan's thoughts again. It was a woman's voice, a bit playful, and very curious. As if she were testing Rowan. Was it her mother?

"Fairy are creatures of the wild and whimsical. Creatures of the passionate, and peaceful. But rarely creatures of the logical. Where is the fun in logic, or the challenge?"

Rowan smiled at the voice, as it shook out of a nearby berry bush. Rowan didn't mind the company. But nor could she stop her mind from trying to place that voice. It wasn't Sorcha. It definitely wasn't Petal. Nor Oona. There was something very present, and yet not quite alive about it.

"A fairy cannot be whole or at peace away from nature. It is why you felt so much more yourself in the room with the missing wall. All of nature loves the Fairy, for fairies serve nature, and nature in turn serves them. That is why the trees bow, and the winds dance, and the flowers draw you nearer with their scents. They welcome you not as future queen, but because they love and serve you now. They believe you are here to stay.

"Are you?" the formless woman asked.

Rowan opened her mouth to say yes, of course she would stay. Then the implications hit her.

Do you ever mean to come back? Rowan heard the voice of the woman she'd rescued in Stonedragon, months ago. Rowan had been absolutely certain when she told her yes. But if she defeated Sorcha today, if she took her throne, and freed Roisin from the curse, and Petal from her spying... If Rowan stopped the armies of Anwyn by taking away the ally who manipulated them into war. All of that would mean staying here. This would be her home—forever.

Rowan hadn't thought that far ahead before. She didn't know what she'd thought would happen after Father disowned her and she ran away in the night. Had she thought to fix everything and just go home and train with her knights and struggle with her citizens for the rest of her days? What had she thought would happen to the Fairy?

Before Father disowned her she'd been trying to think of herself as the future queen of the Fairy nation. But apparently she hadn't quite succeeded. Even now, even when she'd told the leprechauns her plans she hadn't envisioned what her future would look like.

Whose voice was she speaking with?

It wasn't her mother, was it?

Rowan felt a flurry of tiny snowflakes dancing in her veins. She shuddered and took in the world around her with a different eye. Not the eye of a long absent daughter welcomed home, nor of an awestruck traveler admiring the wonders of another world. But with the eye of a future queen surveying all that was her's to protect, to preserve. To serve.

Was she here—to stay?

Petal was having tea in a small garden all alone. Well, no one was visible, but she was certainly guarded.

She held her talisman in her left hand and her tea cup in her right. The cup had a delicate rose pattern painted around it. As she sipped Petal could smell the roses blooming and feel the petals brushing against her fingers. The tea even tasted rosy.

Petal set the glass down and gazed into its rose-gold translucent fluid. She saw the halls of Fairy Cache. The door to Stonedragon was completely covered in roses now.

Petal giggled softly as she saw fairy stopping in the hall to stare in wonder, perhaps even in fear. The vines had left the door and were growing up the walls and along the floors of the palace. Petal felt the soothing warmth of the tea spreading out inside of her, as the roses were spreading out in the palace. Felt comforted and strengthened as Rowan's magic wandered the halls of Fairy Cache, making a place for herself in the heart of the Fairy.

And it was working. It wasn't just the palace welcoming her. Petal could feel fairy softening towards her. And breezes speaking to her. It wouldn't be long now.

Finnola must have gotten her message to Rowan. Petal's plan was working. Rowan's power was growing. Very soon Petal would complete her mission, and all of this would be over. Very soon.

Rowan didn't try to decide where she was going, she just urged Yseult forward, and followed where she led. Her mind kept whispering that she was letting Yseult lead because she was as uncomfortable with the prospect of staying here forever as the horse was.

She liked traveling. She liked seeing what the world had to offer. She liked it as much as she'd ever liked training to be a knight or learning to breathe fire or—

"Or settling into that role your father took from you?" The voice broke into Rowan's thoughts again. It was odd that she was not trying to urge Rowan in any particular direction, but was clearly trailing her wherever Rowan went. Was Rowan still headed towards Fairy Cache through this dark forest?

Rowan stiffened her spine. She thought...cutting her hair, and burning away her past that had cut out her anger. But Rowan felt so many mixed emotions. Part of her wanted to race forward, find the palace, shove Sorcha from her throne and take her place as Fairy queen. She could show her father, and everyone else who never thought her capable. But another part of her felt like this was an adventure, and when it was over she would go back to her room with the missing wall and take up her old self with more confidence. But she began to doubt that was even possible. And she wondered why she would want it with all she'd overcome.

She'd overcome the men who thought she shouldn't be a knight. She'd overcome her fear of the women who thought she was unfeminine, and arrogant. She'd overcome her own fear of ruling. Her fear of her people. She'd come to love Stonedragon, its people, its lands, her place among them.

If she never went home, what was the point?

And who was to say if she decided to never leave here, and fought to end Sorcha's reign and loved and embraced her place here fully, that someone wouldn't come along and shove her out of this role too?

Rowan's right hand fisted and she rubbed her thumb across the spot where her scars had been. She was scared again. Maybe she'd cut out the rage, and the guilt, but she hadn't cut out the pain, or the fears that grew out of them. Thorny fears beneath her skin since birth it seemed. Fears that she wasn't worthy, fears that she couldn't be loved, fears that what she wanted would always be taken away.

How was she ever meant to put all of that away?

Rowan waited, quiet inside and out for an answer. From the voice, from the trees, from the claw digging into her heart again, or the honeysuckle at her wrist exuding that sweet scent. But nothing answered her.

All around the little wood the light fell differently. It barely made it between the dense branches of the trees, just decorating the ground with the same sort of fractured light that entered the palace of Stonedragon—home.

It was still home.

That didn't mean the Fairy Realm never could be, but it wasn't yet. It also didn't mean she wasn't going to fight for this land, because she would. She was.

Rowan saw the trees bend up ahead, heard whispers among them and pulled Yseult up to a stop.

They think you are here to stay, the voice had said.

Forever. Rowan let the word sink through her. Imagined what it would be like to never return to her room with the missing wall. Never train with her knights. Never lead a company of women. Never...

Rowan had this image, this tiny little fantasy, that she only ever looked at when she was all alone. Of a time when Roisin was home, and Petal was home, and Rowan was finally able to meet Gavin. And everyone: Maureen and her family, and Father and Gwyneth and Roisin and the Aunts and Eachann and Gavin, and the kidnapped girls and Rowan's knights and anyone she'd ever known or loved were all together. There was a fire in the hearth and they were laughing and telling stories and there was so much love in that room and everything was peaceful and bright, and when the sun was about to rise they all walked out together to her mother's rose garden and Rowan shattered the wall apart in a sprinkling shower of magic and for just a moment, as the wall was bursting her mother would be there smiling at her—so proud. And that happy place surrounded by love and family was where she lived the rest of her days.

That would never be. Would it? There was nothing realistic about it.

If she became queen of the Fairy it would be her place to serve them, and represent them, and be what they needed. They would want to see Rowan immerse herself in their world and their people. And she would very likely do it, because she would want their love as much as she had ever wanted Father's love, or her subjects' love.

If Rowan were to rule the fairy she couldn't surround herself with humans, and bring her company of knights. If she relied on her knights the fairy would come to view that as Rowan loving her human half more. And even if she could make the fairy understand, the Knights of the Rose were men of Stonedragon, they wouldn't want to abandon the lands they'd fought for all their lives and come live in the Fairy Realm.

Perhaps Maureen, Colum, and the triplets would come, but even with them there was no certainty. The boys had known no home but Stonedragon and Rowan had no idea how Petal would feel about these lands after the battle was won. By choice or no, Petal was trapped here now, and all prisons must leave a mark.

Rowan might well be entirely on her own. Braden would never come with the way he felt towards magic. And Roisin having returned home would be locked in Father's and Gwyneth's arms, never to be set free.

And Gavin—

Rowan looked down at the honeysuckle winding its way out from beneath her bracers to curl atop it. Her cheeks heated and she felt that tingle all over her body again as she'd felt in that moment when she nearly kissed Zain. Fairy would want her to marry another fairy. And perhaps that truly would be for the best. Rowan ran a finger along the buds.

For so long if she managed to imagine a future, Gavin was a part of it. But she made his life worse. He was...captured, or injured, or cursed because of his connection to her. She knew Eachann had said those were little things to suffer, and she had liked the sound of the words, the way they felt inside. But they weren't little things. If the claw was Gavin he'd been trying to steal peace from her. Something had changed between them, and it wasn't a little thing.

He was crown prince of his nation, he should marry a woman who could sit beside him and be a helpmate, a consort. Their years of letters notwithstanding, there had never been any promises made between them, and Gavin was too hopeful not to have made them if he truly thought they would come to be. There were no promises. Only wishes.

How had Rowan even thought it would work?

The clawing in Rowan's chest grew hot like tongs pulled from a furnace, smoldering as they dug into her heart no matter how hard Rowan ground her heel against her armor. This could never have worked. Rowan felt a few tears go rushing down her face, but ignored them, trying to sooth her burning heart. Like that lovely image of the future Gavin was a fantasy. And those parts of her who had doubted, and pushed him away, they had always known it. She had just... forgotten for a time, and hoped.

This place would be her life, its people her people. There would be new subjects to get to know. New customs to explore. And whispering woods to wander through. Maybe even fairy soldiers to train with, and so many other things she had never really imagined before. Like—other loves. It wouldn't be anything she'd ever pictured for herself. But that didn't make it bad.

It wasn't nearly as exciting as just wandering through and seeing what she loved in this fairy world. But that didn't mean it couldn't still be beautiful. Maybe it would even be an adventure. She could find a way to...love this role too. She must, or she would not deserve it.

Yes, Rowan supposed, she was here to stay. She brushed away her tears with the cold metal of her gauntlet and forced herself to ignore the searing pain in her chest.

Rowan leaned forward, caressing Yseult's neck.

"I doubt I ever will learn to fly," Rowan whispered. Then nudged Yseult on. "Come on, we'll have years to explore. We have a castle to find."

This acceptance wasn't precisely a morose feeling, but nor was it the lightness with which she'd entered this realm. *Queen* was weighty title to bear.

New Beginnings

"Well." Jaron looked from the river back to Asia with a brow in the air.

"Well, what?"

Jaron indicated the river. "The only way to enter Ulm is by boat. You wish to enter Ulm."

"Do you think I have hidden a boat beneath my dress?" Asia asked snidely. They were not quite their easy selves since he'd refused to answer her questions.

"I think one of us has the power of transformation, and she ought to use it on this cart, and perhaps her dress as well, *Lady Asia*." He gave a mocking bow.

"What will you do with the horses?" Asia asked rather than agreeing. It was a good idea. She was exceptionally angry still and her temper wasn't serving her well. It had never served her well. She fought and fought and fought and the more she did the tinier her world became as her father crushed her.

Asia took a deep breath as she walked around the cart, running her hand along it, feeling its nature. She wondered if the power of transformation hadn't stayed with her longer than other powers did because it was so closely tied to her own. The source of both powers was the same, understanding the nature of things. Transformation sought to understand so it could better transform while her power sought out natures so—

Well she wasn't sure what.

"Animals are easy. You've only to whisper in their ears to run for safety and they will see to the rest," Jaron said.

"Or you assume they have, because they are gone from your sight and thus no longer your worry."

Jaron chuckled. "Seems you're better acquainted with the natures of men than reported."

"What reports?"

"Did I say reports? I meant impressions." He smirked at her a good long while and Asia's rage built.

She wanted to lash out, she wanted to rip the beard from his face as if she would be able to know him better if only she could see his full face. She wanted to tear apart whatever magic he had that she couldn't understand she wanted—

Asia's hand slid off the boat as it was now a boat, changed in a massive pop of raging energy. She'd wanted to take from Jaron, wanted to change him, and she'd changed the cart instead. She hadn't even been thinking as she'd done it, and look what she'd made.

It didn't even appear to be made of the same wood as the cart had been. The boat was long and thin, with oars on either side, and a seat right in the middle suited for a queen. The seat had a shaped back that sloped and crested like waves on the ocean, there was a canopy above it that looked like the underside of a jellyfish, replete with little flittering ribbons, thick and curled or thin and hair like. In a rage she'd let loose magic and brought the sea to land.

Asia's fingers curled into her palm and she sucked in a breath.

This is the most important rule: you can never *let the humans know what you are. You can never even hint at it. Were humans to know of the mer our peaceful existence would be at an end.*

Asia felt her mother's voice in her mind like a shiver. Fear. Always Mother's voice was a fragile frightened thing, and always when she heard it Symphony grew smaller, hiding from that same fear.

Symphony did. Asia on the other hand reached out to touch the ribbon tendrils from her jellyfish canopy. It was lovely. So lovely her old home. How had she never realized that every time she allowed herself to hide, she'd seen a little less of the beauty around her?

Asia raised her head, and felt a sigh escape her. The young seer was right, she hadn't chosen her path yet. The sea kept coming out of her when she least expected it, but Asia was teaching her so much about Symphony that she'd never known. Perhaps she should stop fighting that part of fate.

Her journey began in Diddlyon, that's what the boy said. Now she needed to get there. They were almost at Ulm's borders, but the capital city was still several days' journey within the nation.

Asia let the magic fall over herself, shaking out her head. Her hair fell down in a thick wave as she wore it under the sea, and her dress turned a soft airy fabric suited to such a seat. She looked like a princess again, she knew without looking at herself. With a brow in the air she regarded Jaron, no longer angry with him. He had never been truly the source of her rage, it was that impotence she'd felt building up inside her, the same as she'd lived with all her life. But she wasn't impotent. She didn't know her role yet, but she knew she had one, and she meant to face it with her head held high, and her fear pushed into a dark cavern within.

"I suppose you will have to take on the role of my servant." Asia nodded sideways even as her magic was rushing over Jaron, and giving him a neat little livery of cool teal blue. "Be about getting that on the water, we haven't all day."

Jaron bowed with the dignity of a man who'd spent his life in service, but as he stood straight again he winked. The man was a consummate performer.

Good. Asia breathed out and settled her being into her new role. She was a performer as well, now she just needed to find her stage.

Finnola had sobbed herself to sleep the first night she was back. She still woke up with dreams of what the Fairy queen had done to her. What she had done to Prince Gavin, and Papa. That woman was evil.

Finnola remembered the first moment she'd looked on the halls of the fairy palace. Her heart had stopped and she had felt such wonder, and pride. Her people had made this. It was endless, it was alive, it held all parts of the world within its walls, but contained none of them, it was just...connected to them.

"That is why we call it Fairy Cache," Mama had told Finnola and her brother Quinn one night when they were little. Littler. She'd been telling them stories of the fairy nation that they would one day return to. "Because it holds the greatest treasure in the world, a connection to the *entire* world. Turrlough is a lovely land. And we are honored to find safe harbor in it. But in the Fairy Realm lies the key to knowing every nation. One day, when the Fairy queen is dethroned and the revolution begun by the great Tyrone Elderhorn is truly successful, all fairy will return home. All fairy will finally have a chance to see the whole of the world."

Neither Mama, nor Father, nor Quinn had ever seen inside Fairy Cache. But Finnola had stood in the waterways that flowed through it, and walked down the halls that held doors to every nation, and jungle and mountain the world over.

She had felt so honored. She had been so excited. Then the door opened to Turrlough, and she smelled the barely and the wet earth, and she felt the air of *home*. Turrlough was home. The Fairy Realm was still home to her parents but this place was home to her. Her heart had burned with joy to return to it.

Until that joy was yanked away.

Finnola watched her mother now, sweeping the floor of the dungeon they were locked in, keeping it neat and tidy like she was a human. Hiding her magic away, to fit in. In the past it had bothered Finnola that they must always hide who they were. But now...Finnola was angry with fairy.

No human realm is as beautiful, as alive. The Fairy queen's words sliced through Finnola's mind. Reminding her, that her power was still inside Finnola, altering her. Stealing from her.

Had Finnola not stepped through the door to Turrlough before she heard those words, she might well have agreed with the Fairy queen, but she didn't now. And she never would.

Turrlough was a quiet nation, the farmers and shepherds and cobblers, and fishermen all worked together to keep their nation running. All of them had known Finnola and her family were fairy, but they had loved and embraced them. They had tried to hide Finnola the year the other fairy came to take her.

This was a beautiful land. In every way. Not just to look at. The Fairy Realm looked lovely, it looked alive, it looked prosperous. But it was...a festering hole.

Finnola never wanted to return. But Petal was still trapped there, and Finnola hadn't held up her end of the bargain and delivered Petal's message to Princess Rowan of Stonedragon.

Finnola looked at her mother. Wondering what she would think of Finnola's mission. They—she and Papa both had wanted for there to be no queen on the Fairy throne. That was why they fought alongside Tyrone, because he promised to give the throne to the people. Promised to make this an age of the sprite, and the leprechaun, and the common fairy.

If Finnola helped Petal still, she would be helping the cause of one who wanted to be Fairy queen.

I am Petal the Powerful, and I serve the Fairy queen that will be.

It had seemed a cute little naive idea at the time. And Petal was so persuasive. As persuasive as the Fairy queen could be. Magnetic.

Now Finnola didn't know who was wrong or right. She just knew she loved Petal, and wanted to help her get free. And that she was useless now.

Quinn came over and slung an arm around Finnola's shoulders.

"You are home. It is all any of us has wanted for years. He was so happy. So happy that you were free."

Finnola looked up with teary eyes. She wished she could make him hear her thoughts, like Petal could, but whenever she tried everything in her grew garbled. The words she meant to say became other words with no rhyme or reason to their order. It was the same when she wrote, and worse if she tried to speak.

Finnola shuddered, remembering the Fairy queen's hand under her chin, and her eyes boring into her. She'd sent Petal away and called all the girls to her, with Finnola standing right beside her, in that lovely room of sky and clouds.

"Did you know you had a traitor in your midst?" Sorcha asked the other girls, holding Finnola to her side.

The other girls had looked amongst themselves, disbelieving at first.

"This girl is fairy. Her voice whispers to me. Her soul belongs to my nation. Her power belongs to me," she said sweetly and watched with glee as the other girls began to grow frantic. "But do not worry I will protect you from her treachery."

"If she serves you, why would you care to stop her?" Daniella stepped forward to demand, always so headstrong and defiant.

The Fairy queen smiled at Daniella as if she truly liked her. *"She did not serve me out of love, or duty. I told you, her power belongs to me."*

"You cannot hurt her," Daniella insisted.

"And I shall not. I shall simply stop her ever being a traitor again." Sorcha winked, and spun back to Finnola. *"You, Tattle-tongue, will tattle no more. You belong to your queen, and you will remember that forever, every word on your lips, every thought in your mind, every flick of your pen is mine to give to you. You will learn loyalty."*

Finnola buried her face in her brother's shoulder and cried. How was it possible he didn't blame her? She did. She saw Petal trapped with the Fairy queen, saw Papa dying on the ground. How could he not blame her?

"It's alright," he said again and Mama's arms closed around her as well. "Everything will be well. We are together."

Finnola cried harder.

They might be together. But...they weren't their own. They were owned by the Fairy queen, and it seemed the only way to undo her magic was to help another who would own them. Finnola sobbed.

The door to the dungeons opened and Queen Aya descended the stairs. She crossed the room slowly and heavily, coming to a stop before Finnola and her family. Finnola stopped crying.

Queen Aya stretched out a hand and lay it on Mama's shoulder. They looked into one another's eyes silently, as Finnola and her brother both grew uncomfortable, waiting to know what horror faced them now. She couldn't be here for Mama, could she? Mama had done nothing wrong.

At last Queen Aya spoke. "I have convinced our fairy...*guardians* that you are no threat. If you remain in the palace, and follow their rules you may leave this dungeon. Come, please, join me. We shall be a comfort to each other."

Finnola felt like there must be some hidden meaning in the words, but she couldn't find them. She looked at her mother and brother. They nodded, and as a family they stood, leaving the dank dungeon behind.

Lost Hopes

Gwyneth was overjoyed! It must mean something terrible about her. A war was coming to her home, but she didn't care. She had opened up the entire old family wing of the palace. Even the nursery that had spent years untouched. All of it was full of life now. Every day more of the nation's children were flooding into the palace for protection as word reached the villages of what was to come.

She loved it! Loved the noise and the chaos. Half of the children were screaming their heads off, but they were here and alive and she was going to guard them all, as someone else had guarded her daughter. When Roisin was first born, before Sorcha came, before her world was shattered, Gwyneth had imagined filling this wing with children. So many children. They would laugh, and sing, and —*glow* with all the love she was giving them.

But that was before. Once Sorcha came and cursed her child all Gwyneth could see was how her love would be taken from her, how that beautiful life would be cut short. She'd hated Balder then. She hadn't exactly realized it, she'd just known that none of her love could go to anything but her daughter. And the more she loved Roisin the more she feared, and the more she feared the more the idea of other children was abhorrent. So she'd gone to the midwife in the village where she'd grown up for help.

The woman had said no at first. She'd looked at Gwyneth with such disgust. But a week later a messenger arrived for Gwyneth with a letter from the midwife, and a charm to prevent conception.

It was a brief message.

Wear it always to prevent a child. That choice I offer to every woman I meet. I apologize if it seemed not so. My anger with you was in feeling you had given up already on your daughter living. Do not do so. Hope is necessary should goodness have any chance to prevail.

Gwyneth was certain she'd burned the letter, years ago. But its words lived inside of her. She finally understood what the woman meant. Gwyneth had given up. When she'd suggested sending Rowan, when she'd shouted at Balder, when she'd hid away in this nursery letting no one invade her time with Roisin, she was already mourning her daughter.

This room had needed life and hope for so long. But that had never needed to come from children of Gwyneth's making. They just needed to be that loveliest of things, voices of hope for the future.

Maureen walked into the nursery and hesitated beside Gwyneth in the doorway. Gwyneth toyed with the charm at her wrist as she stared at the children and waited for Maureen to say whatever she was here to say. Maureen was still angry with Gwyneth, or at least she was not as friendly with her. Perhaps it was all this mess of being forced into the role of general of Rowan's many forces, but Gwyneth thought not. There was a deeper something troubling her.

"Ferdy sent word that the water sprite children are being taken to the southern coast to hide. These children might be safer there as well."

Gwyneth's hand clenched around the bracelet. She'd only just found all of these children.

"But...all of the children in one place, won't that make a very obvious target? Anwyn has ships after all."

Maureen examined Gwyneth searchingly, she glanced at Gwyneth's hand clenched at her charm, and back to her face. "You do not want them gone? They are overrunning your palace. We are already understaffed with so many of the women taking up arms. Between laundry and cooking alone there will be no time left for the servants to do anything at all."

"I do not mind. I shall assist them. And my other gentlewomen as well, even the bigger children. These are the children of my nation. Who should protect them but their queen?"

Maureen stared a moment more before swaying her head aside in a motion that stopped just short of a nod.

"The water sprite children may come here as well. We can find the room," Gwyneth offered.

"I will pass your generosity along, but I imagine they will prefer the coast. Fairy are stronger in nature." She moved slowly away. Gwyneth simply could not allow things to continue so between them.

"She will come home, Maureen. Do not give up hope now."

Maureen paused, but did not face Gwyneth as the pained words left her. "Which she?"

"They both will." Gwyneth moved around before Maureen with firm words and her head held high. "*All three* of our girls will. Our children will be brothers and sisters, and though they be nearly grown they will still fill this room with laughter and singing and light. Such light Maureen, do not give up."

"I have not given up, Gwyneth. This...weight is not giving up. It is exhaustion. I tell myself not to look for them, any of them, but then I lay alone in my home and it is so quiet that my power goes seeking them. I do not sleep for seeking. At first, though I could not find Rowan, nor Petal I could at least find Colum, but I cannot now. I haven't given up. I have hope. But I have such *fears* as well. If he is lost to my magic it means Sorcha has him." Maureen shook her head and the tears that had been building in her eyes sprayed the air.

"I would once have said she would not hurt him, because he was my love, and she cared for me once. But it isn't true. She will do anything to hurt Rowan. *Anything.*

"I believe they will come home. I believe Rowan will persevere. I do," Maureen insisted. "But what will they all have lost before they reach us?"

There were no words to say to such a thing so Gwyneth did the only thing she could she stepped forward and pulled Maureen into her arms, holding on as tightly as she was able, trying to pour into Maureen all the hope she could.

Yseult stopped without warning, shaking Rowan's seat. Her armor clanked and scraped as Yseult began turning around and around in a circle.

"Shhh." Rowan leaned forward, running a soothing hand along the horse's neck.

It was completely quiet around her, but for the rustle of trees, yet Rowan felt a weight on the air like many bodies, like anguish and confusion, and exertion. The hairs on Rowan's arms pricked up and her right hand slipped down to the hilt of her sword.

"Press on. Follow the way the trees lead you," the formless voice instructed.

At once a group of aspens leapt up and pointed their branches down a particular path. But other trees were...fighting. The aspens waved and waved, trying to draw Rowan's attention to a clear path with little animals waving in welcome, and even a few fairy peeking out to watch. While another group of trees lifted up their roots and made an opening into a massive field of flowers.

As Rowan looked into the field, one of the aspens raced by Rowan and Yseult with a shuddering wind and planted itself in the opening to block the field from view. An oak beside it stretched out its branches trying to pull the aspen away.

Yseult agreed with the voice, and was backing slowly towards the path with animals and fairy, but Rowan leaned forward.

She could swear she heard swords clanging in that field. That *empty* field. Something was out there.

"Press on. Pass it by magic if you like. But do not enter that field."

Yseult backed further away from it, and Rowan was sure she should let the aspens, and the voice, and Yseult have their way. The field looked impossibly wide, with its grasses seeming to wave Rowan forward, and bright red poppies winked in the light. It was welcoming. It called to Rowan more from this fight to keep her from it than anything else. Rowan tightened her hold on Yseult's reins pulling her to a stop.

She heard it again, the familiar clang of metal on metal. Rowan felt her pulse racing as it did before a fight. There was something for her in that field.

A poppy caught the light, bright red and swaying and Rowan heard Bran's voice from when she spoke to his spirit in the cave.

I lay bleeding in what looked like an endless field of green grasses and red poppies. Everywhere my blood fell new flowers popped up and brushed across my skin

"It's a basin of the lost, isn't it?" Rowan asked, staring between tussling tree branches into the green and red field they were fighting to conceal, or reveal to her. Some trees trying to protect Rowan, and others trying to serve Sorcha.

Could Rowan truly be sure which were which?

The fairy often lost travelers in such basins if they dared to cross into their realm. That must have been what happened to Bran, and the other soldiers. They'd entered the Fairy realm, marched into such a basin and been lost, or killed, or captured and turned.

Rowan slid off Yseult's back. She could feel the fairy she'd seen on the path behind her pressing closer, but she ignored them, training her ears towards that field instead.

The voice had not answered Rowan's question, but she asked it another. "Are there more of them out there? My father's soldiers? Lost and unaware of the years that have passed since they left home."

Still the voice would not reply. Which Rowan supposed was answer enough. She could hear them clearly now, swords striking swords, men grunting, crying out in pain. Rowan took another step forward, and felt her right arm tugged backwards. She glanced down, and saw that the honeysuckle had unwound at her wrist, and lay like a hook halfway around her, the rest stretched out, trying to tug her back to the saddle.

"It isn't safe now," the voice said at last. "When you are queen you can free any human you like."

When she was queen. Rowan paused, staring at her wrist, and the tugging blossoms, at Yseult's stiff posture, at the fairy out in the open now watching her.

When she was queen.

How many men would have died by then? How many turned? Rowan had no idea how long her battle with Sorcha would last.

"Are you..." A young male fairy edged closer to Rowan, speaking hesitantly. "Are you a queen of man?"

Rowan cocked her head to the side, shaking it slightly. That was an odd question.

"Do you know the knight, Colum of Keen?" the fairy pressed, moving closer though other fairy tried to pull him back, or shut him up.

Rowan's heart stopped. She let her gaze rest with that boy alone. How did he know that name?

Rowan hadn't seen Colum any of the times she'd traveled. Had something happened to him? Had Sorcha found him? Killed him? Turned him?

Colum walked forward, wrapped an arm around Rowan's shoulders, pulling her to his chest. "My granddaughter."

Rowan felt all the love and the joy and the *rightness* she'd felt in that moment. *Her grandfather.*

Rowan's heart pounded and her eyes narrowed on the fairy around her. Several of the fairy vanished from the path, and a wind rushed around with a magical feel to it that reminded Rowan of her smoke screen. These fairy didn't want Sorcha to hear what the boy was saying.

"He is known to me," Rowan said quietly intense.

"Press on!" The voice insisted, shaking the trees with its force. "You tarry here at great cost."

The young man edged close to Rowan. "I think, such a man as he, would wish you to heed the Fairy Mother and press on."

"What do you know of Colum?" Rowan demanded.

The Fairy Mother, the title shuddered through Rowan. Meave. She was speaking with the mother of Rowan's fairy line. How was that even possible? Maureen had said she still led the fairy, but Rowan always took it to mean her legacy led them. Not that her formless voice invaded the air around them and told them what to do.

"He caught me stealing, but freed me for only the cost of a promise not to do so again. He said he needed his children to know he loved their fairy half."

"When? Where did you meet him? Is *he* out there?" Rowan took another step towards the field. The flowers at her wrist would not stop tugging her back, and now the boy's hand closed on her arm as well, stopping her.

The boy shook his head. "No one is out there. If you go out there, you will not be there either. There is a powerful curse upon that valley. It is all but impossible to find what you are seeking there, even for a fairy."

"Where. Is. Colum?" Rowan asked with intense precision, her eyes boring into the fairy.

"I tried to warn him away. Even the curse-wolves tried to warn him away."

Rowan shook off the boy's hand, but the flowers would not let go, tugging her back.

"You are no use to him out there," Meave's voice snapped. "Find Fairy Cache. There is little the Fairy queen cannot do. But you must claim that throne."

Without thought Rowan's left hand yanked out the thorn and sliced clean through the honeysuckle, it fell from her arm in two pieces and lay upon the ground as Rowan marched towards the field, stowing her dagger, she drew the rose blade.

"That way leads only to death!" The fairy mother shouted.

"I am difficult to convince," Rowan said as she waded into air so dense it was nearly solid. If Colum was out there, she was going to find him. Sorcha could not have him.

Useless

324 days until Roisin returns

Ferdy got the distinct impression Orla didn't like him. She'd brought him along to learn to fight then went out of her way to avoid him. Murphy was good fun though.

He'd shown Ferdy how to control the water from outside of it. Making it a giant scoop and or a slashing wave, dragging it away from a particular spot, or making it spray at another. Ferdy could only do it with a very small amount of water. Murphy explained that it took a great many sprites working as one to truly alter a sacred source like the river.

"That is part of what makes it such good practice for a boy needing to learn fast," Murphy was saying. "If you can nudge the Grey Lady, imagine what you can do with an ordinary stream."

"Do you not like salt water? Are you afraid of it?" Ferdy asked.

"Of course not. We can do with salt water what we can with any other type of water. But...we tend to keep nearer land than the further stretches of the ocean."

"Why?"

Murphy seemed unsure. "Because we do."

Ferdy shook his head. He wouldn't have been able to listen to rules like that if he had been raised among them. He would have had to know why. He would want to go out to the furthest, deepest stretches of the sea and find out why water sprites didn't go there. Even if it killed him.

"Humph." Orla's grunt came from behind Ferdy and he felt the misty air she liked so well taking shape.

He hadn't wanted to tell Murphy, but he honestly found Orla a more interesting subject of study. She could turn to mist, her hands had turned to ice during the battle, then she'd taken on a body of flesh and blood, all in a matter of moments. She was a talented water sprite, Murphy was a soldier. But Orla's humph hadn't sounded particularly promising.

"Now you seem like Maureen's son," Orla remarked. "She never liked rules either. It's what got us all into this mess."

"Orla," Murphy said, his voice low with warning.

Her mist rushed forward and spun around Murphy again and again, only her face retaining a discernible shape. "What? Do you think you and the others can tempt, and coax and show him only the good and one as wild as he will not go out and die as a result?"

"We are watching over him, and teaching him."

"Your family got up and left without struggle, Murphy. They never saw battle. I saw it. You cannot protect *anyone* in a battle. You can only fight until the fighting is over."

With a suddenness that both shocked and thrilled Ferdy Orla abandoned Murphy and stood before Ferdy entirely composed of ice. She nodded towards the forest.

"Has your mother ever told you how she met the Fairy queen?"

Ferdy shook his head. There was so much angry, heartbroken power coming off this woman. It wasn't just a story to her. It enraged her, ate her up inside with...guilt. That's what she felt like, guilty. The way Keagan had been when Colleen was pulling out his insecurities and feeding them back to him.

Ferdy was silent, waiting for the woman to speak.

"Maureen and Murphy were tricking fishermen along the river, stealing their catch, turning them about. Harmless stuff. But your mother...she was wild, always had to push just a little past what was allowed. So she saw a pair of soldiers intimidating this little boy, and decided to exact revenge for him."

Ferdy notched his head up, that sounded exactly like Mama, and exactly right.

"She kept appearing and disappearing before them, tricking them into the Enchanted Forest."

"Do you mean vanishing?" Ferdy asked.

"No. She made herself invisible," Orla replied impatiently.

"But...she's a healer." Ferdy shook his head in shock. Did Mama have powers like his?

"Now." Orla shrugged. "It was always a part of her nature, but when she was younger she embraced her trickster powers more."

"She was a trickster? Like me? You can...change powers?"

"It was always a part of her, like I said. But yes, I suppose one can change powers if they want it enough. Anyway she led them in a little ways. Even fairy can get lost in that wood. But she stayed near enough the river that she could feel it. But apparently even getting them lost wasn't enough. She tried to steal their weapons. But by now the men knew they were being tricked by a fairy and they were enraged. They caught her."

Ferdy gulped and his stomach dropped. He didn't want to hear this.

"They wrapped her hands in iron, because iron saps our powers," Orla said heavily and Ferdy began to see little fissures in the ice that formed her body, they started near her chest and grew outward. She shivered. Telling the story was— hurting her.

"Maureen shouted and screamed and cried out for help, but they just laughed, tied her to the back of their horse and carried her away."

"Where was Murphy? Why didn't he help?" Ferdy demanded with a racing heart as fear and rage built inside of him. He kept telling himself that Mama was fine. She must have escaped. Mama could do anything. But he felt the pain in Orla's words and he knew there must be worse to come.

"I—" Murphy opened his mouth to respond but words failed him.

"He'd run off as she led the men into the forest. The forest was forbidden." Orla threw a dark look Murphy's way. "Forbidden because it loses fairy and human alike. Just because we can find your way out, doesn't mean we can find our way to what we seek within. And Murphy has always been an obedient fairy."

Ferdy felt heat rising off of his skin as he looked at the woman before him, there was steam between them, but he didn't know if it came from him or Orla.

She was telling the story and it was hurting her, but she told it all so lightly, as if it were a joke. As if any pain Mama ever suffered would be forgiven.

Ferdy had been trying to make friends with her, because Mama told him this was her sister and they had been separated for years. He was trying to be *careful* with her, because she must have suffered pains like Petal. But Orla could smile as she spoke of Mama's pains. It wasn't right.

"Why didn't *you* help her?" Ferdy growled.

"How was I to find her?" Orla laughed. "Do you know how vast that forest is? It took Sorcha three days to find her, and she had all the power of a royal fairy at her disposal."

"How did Sorcha know to look?" Ferdy asked.

Orla shrugged. "Murphy told her."

"I—" Murphy started to speak.

"And what did you do?" Ferdy demanded drowning out whatever Murphy would have said.

"What I was told. That's the point of the story," Orla snarled, her icy being beginning to evaporate into steam. "Your mother broke the rule and was punished by eternity itself, kidnapped and bound by humans for three days. If someone says water sprites don't do something— *don't* do it."

Ferdy looked between the pair of them. If he had his tongue he would give his aunt the lashing she deserved, but Mama had made him promise to be kind to her.

Neither of us knows what she has been through, Ferdy. But we know whatever it was she had to face it without her sister beside her. Be kind. She is hurting.

"You're useless." Ferdy vanished with the words. He didn't want to train anymore. He went back to the hot springs to wait to be needed.

Rowan stepped into the field with her sword drawn and her heart pounding. She stepped forward and...everything before her eyes vanished. No flowers, no grass, no light. She walked through air that was humid and heavy, and smelled sick with blood and bile.

If you go out there you will not be there either.

Good job listening, Rowan. Good job thinking it through.

Well, Oona said she wasn't a thinker by nature. She told Rowan to trust her instincts. She also essentially implied that Rowan would die in this cause.

Rowan shoved the thoughts aside and just walked forward. She could feel so many bodies, but she couldn't see them, or hear their voices. The sounds of swords clanging were dampened by this unnatural fog. But she couldn't stop. She had to find Colum. She had to find anyone who was out here. No one should be trapped like this.

What if he was out here because of her? What if he thought Rowan hated him? She'd been so angry when she left. She hadn't even said goodbye, but she didn't hate him. She couldn't. Even when they fought he was in her heart. He was her grandfather, and for so long...her very best friend. She couldn't let anything happen to him.

She could accept that she was never going home. She could accept that her fantasy would never be. But Colum had to be in the world. Everyone she loved had to go on. They had to.

A light darted into Rowan's path. Tiny and bright red, like a flame. It flashed, urging Rowan a different way than she had been going. She stopped and stared at it, it flashed again, and moved further back.

I know what you are looking for. It seemed to say.

Rowan walked slowly towards the light. She followed it on and on, though her feet felt as though she was walking in a circle and her head began to ache from tracking that flame. Everything took so much more effort than it should. Her arms felt weighted down, but Rowan didn't dare lower her sword. Her feet were like led and the armor tried to drag her into the ground as it had not since she'd first worn it at fifteen.

Keeping her eyes open, and her ears listening was a massive effort. She felt more than heard the bells at her ankle shake with every step forward. So far away, so long falling. It felt like they took hours to lift and to fall.

She couldn't go on this way. Everything was so heavy and she wasn't finding anyone. She wasn't helping anyone. Rowan wanted to cast her senses ahead of her in search of Colum, but the weight of the air was draining her power.

"Unlim..." Rowan tried to speak and could not even finish the word her tongue weighed too heavily in her mouth.

That way leads only to death!

322 days until Roisin returns

Keagan had a new focus; instead of trying to find a place in the future he busied himself trying to find everyone's true purpose. The one that made the future glow brighter, the one that made them glow brighter. If everyone had a purpose maybe this was his, leading everyone to their purpose.

He'd thought briefly that Ferdy might already have found his. He seemed to glow brighter among the water sprites, but he also glowed bright when he was leading his army, and...he'd been shutting Keagan out of his mind recently. Or maybe Keagan was shutting Ferdy out. He didn't know.

Keagan had taken a room near the top of the palace, far enough away from all the activity of new children in the palace that he could think. He took his charcoals and parchment and just sketched, waiting for a sketch to call out to him, to show him a person's true path. Somewhere in the midst of trying to find bright futures he'd started seeing dark ones again.

He had started by sketching his brother's death at the hands of Petal's wolves, or at the hands of squires the Fairy queen turned on them. Or wrapped up in vines that slowly choked the life out of him. Or...over and over again, Ferdy laid out on one of the pools at the hot spring or the shores of the river with his head bleeding and his eyes wide. No one had killed him. He was just dead. Before Sorcha or Petal or Rowan or anyone could kill him, Ferdy was just dead. And the future darkened with his loss but—in a few of the sketches—Ferdy glowed bright. How was that possible? How could death be anyone's purpose?

Keagan couldn't stand it. He didn't remember the last time he'd eaten or been outside, or even been back to help the adults plan for war. He just sketched. A knock sounded at the door, but Keagan ignored it. He was sketching Petal. He could feel her now. She was out of the Fairy court. In Anwyn, he thought. She could escape, he felt her knowing she could get away, but refusing to leave. He thought she stayed because she had yet to complete her mission, but he wasn't sure that her mission was so important.

He'd seen Desmond in a few of the futures. His presence was neither so powerful nor so distracting to Sorcha that he was necessary to the cause. In fact, in several of the futures he took his mother's part, and in others he just got in the way. If Sorcha was defeated he could be freed. Short of that Keagan didn't think he was necessary. All he did was get Petal cursed, or hurt, or dead.

The knock sounded again.

Keagan ignored. He dragged his charcoal in a slow, smooth wave, filling out his sister's hair. She lay outstretched on the ground, with one hand clawed over her heart, her eyes wide and pained and her last agonized scream dead on her lips. She'd dove between Desmond and his mother in this sketch. Saved the useless prince. Well, not really. Sorcha only cursed him worse after Petal died. In her rage Sorcha set her son on fire, he died in agony next to Petal.

"I did warn you to be careful of the future." Eachann's voice so startled Keagan that he drew a violent slash through the image of his sister. He jerked to his feet.

"What are you doing here?" Keagan demanded.

"I did knock."

"And I did not respond!" Keagan shouted back. "Why bother knocking if you do not mean to abide by the response?"

"But you made no response." The fairy smirked. "I worried you were unwell. I see I am right. Come, take some air with me, you need space from this."

Keagan glared. Who did Eachann think he was anyway, meddling in everyone's affairs?

"Well, I admit I am no Keagan. I have not your vast knowledge of the future, but I suppose I am old and set in my meddling ways. You have time yet to escape such pointless patterns."

Keagan nearly growled at the man, but then his eyes slipped around the room, scattered with sketches of death and he remembered what he'd seen when Asia tried to understand his power. His heart raced. He looked from one sketch to the next, all the deaths drowning the few happy sketches he'd made. Keagan's chest rose and fell, but he couldn't feel any air in his lungs he tried to pull for air harder.

A hand came down gently on his shoulder.

"All life leads to death," the fairy said gently. "And you are seeking out endings. Fear not, there are as many paths to happiness, you simply...cannot seek them in such a way. Come. Walk. Breathe and for a moment look only at the world around you."

Reluctantly, Keagan followed the fairy out of the room. His feet crunched over a piece of parchment, it clung to his foot. Keagan looked down, shaking it off. The paper slid away and Keagan saw his brother's wide empty eyes, and the gaping wound at his temple. He was so bright. Shuddering Keagan crossed the threshold, pulling the door shut behind them.

"My brother had your gift," Eachann said. He was leading Keagan up what remained of the place stairs, towards the roof. "He could see so much of the future, such detail that I believed he could not see wrong. I followed him because so often in life I was uncertain what was right or wrong and I thought his knowledge made him certain. It is only in recent years that I have realized he was as unsure and as frightened as I was. He was just fighting so hard to appear unmoved by his fear that he...walked right towards it."

The further they grew from the room, the better Keagan's lungs worked, and the calmer his racing heart grew. Calm enough that he didn't just hear Eachann's words, he felt them. He felt his fears building up, all the deaths he saw overtaking his mind so that he pulled away from Mama and Ferdy, and even Petal. He pulled away because he was so afraid to lose them; he shut them out so he could find the way to save them. And no matter how many bright futures he saw, he still saw so much death that he pushed them away again.

"I cannot let her take them all," Keagan said quietly.

Eachann nodded. They reached the door to the tower roof. Eachann pushed it wide. There were guards posted at key points around the perimeter, but after glancing Keagan and Eachann's way they went back to watching the distance. Eachann walked to the side nearest the north and looked out in the direction of Anwyn, though it was far too far to be seen by the eye.

"On a clear day like this one," Eachann said. "You can see the foul air rising off of Anwyn and know she is there. Plotting and manipulating and twisting people into what she has determined are their proper roles. My brother knew things and this made him gifted at manipulation. But Sorcha had less knowledge of eternity, but more knowledge of the hearts of those around her, and she knew how to turn them. Were she as young at this study as you, you might well have been a match for her manipulations. But she has spent her life trying to outdo a master, and proved equal to the task. You cannot beat her merely with knowledge of eternity. It would take a far trickier mind than yours even to hide what you know from her."

"You think she is in my mind?" Keagan asked, a bit thrown. Ferdy had suggested as much, but Keagan had taken it for his brother grasping for a happier alternative than Keagan being right.

"I think she doesn't need to be. You try to twist eternity, she feels it, and alters her course to meet you."

"Hmm." Keagan took a deep breath. The air was so much crisper here than in the castle. It was colder inside, dark, and the coolness sunk into the stones and stayed. But here in the light and the air, he could breathe and he could...think. Out here he was awake.

Keagan could tell this fairy wanted him to just stop trying to change the future, but Keagan didn't know that he was capable of that. He felt them all heading down deadly paths he couldn't just let them die without a fight. But perhaps he could change his focus. Pick one person to help. One person to save, the way Rowan had.

Rowan always picked Roisin. And more often than not no matter who else died that princess lived. Maybe...Keagan could do the same. He could save Petal, not just from death, but from growing so angry and twisted that she didn't know good from bad any longer. He could save her from turning on them as she did in more and more futures lately. But even if he could get to Petal he didn't think he could convince her to come home if she hadn't completed her mission. No one knew how stubborn she was as well as Keagan did. She wouldn't stop.

"You have a tricky mind," Keagan observed. "Can you trick the Fairy queen?"

Eachann laughed. "If I were that close to her she would sense me, and I would put your sister in far more danger. I...I was never able to trick her before."

"Weren't you?" Keagan asked, not so much trying to push the fairy to do what he wanted, but truly curious to know. "She thought you were on her side, until the moment you betrayed her."

"Because she had taken me for granted. My power was nothing she could not master, so she paid me no heed. I was nothing to her. But now—"

"What if one was nothing. If one was immensely powerful but equally absent she might not sense them at all," Keagan said with a bit of a laugh. Maybe Ferdy was right. Maybe Colleen's power was awesome. Maybe even she had a purpose.

Keagan almost never sensed her. He still couldn't see her future unless she happened to be standing alongside someone else he saw. Colleen could sneak up on the Fairy queen. Colleen could reach Petal. And Petal could come home.

He saw it again and again. All the ways Petal could come home. She was much brighter with a friend at her side. Keagan did not bother explaining a bit of his thinking to Eachann, he just vanished, off to find Colleen. Turns out the fairy was right, the fresh air really had done Keagan some good.

Basin of the Lost

The closer she grew to the light the more control Rowan felt over her limbs and lungs. She could see no better. But it did not feel like years between lifting each foot, and laying it upon the ground. And she no longer felt she was walking in circles. But she didn't think it was because of anything she'd done. She was either leaving a specific part of the spell, or worse, it had wrought its work and Rowan simply didn't know what it was yet. Perhaps years had passed. Perhaps...

A whoosh of air had Rowan ducking to the ground. She heard a pair of swords meeting above her head but still could not see the men who wielded them.

"Colum," Rowan called out, and shoved to her feet, keeping her head and shoulders as low as she could and tightening her grip on her sword.

There was no answer. If Colum was here he could not hear her. But the light was flashing again, trying to lead Rowan on. She followed slowly. Feeling the air for bodies. It was warmer where the men fought, sickly so. As though they were feverish, their bodies thickening the fog and adding sweat to the murky air.

A body rushed out of the fog at Rowan's left, slamming into her shoulder and sent her spinning. Rowan managed to keep her feet. The man who'd slammed into her let out a loud angry cry and charged at Rowan. She ducked around the heat of him, searching for the light she'd been following. She'd lost sight of it. There were people all around her, but Rowan had no way of knowing who they were. They had no way of knowing who she was. They might not even be real.

"I am Rowan, crown princess of Stonedragon, and future queen of the Fairy. Announce yourself," Rowan shouted, not thinking it would work but having to try.

She felt the bodies around her closing in on the sound of her voice.

Rowan's heart pounded so hard she could see its pulsing in her eyes. She searched and searched the fog for the light.

A man was right before her, he was still for a long heavy moment, but she could feel his energy, his focus falling heavily upon her.

"Liar!" he shouted and charged her. Rowan held still, breathing deeply, preparing to vanish around him when she felt his heat. He was nearly on her. Rowan let loose her magic to vanish.

His sword unchecked by her own, shoved up under the straps of her armor and sliced into Rowan's shoulder. Rowan shouted out in shocked agony, and kicked with all her might. The man stumbled away taking his sword with him. She hadn't vanished. She hadn't vanished! Why hadn't she vanished?

She felt men rushing at her and tried to shove them all back with a pulse of magic, but nothing happened.

"Get back!" Rowan shouted. She swung in a circle, knocking blades away with less than her usual strength as the pain in her shoulder grew worse and the weight of the sword seemed to treble.

A few of the men knocked into one another and turned their manic energy on attacking each other instead of Rowan. Rowan could not see any of them, but in her mind each one became one of her knights. Her pulse raced with the need to save them. And to escape. Something was wrong with her magic, she couldn't see, and now she was injured.

A sword glanced off her right gauntlet. Rowan kicked out and tried to send her magic into the ground to make it roll, but nothing happened.

"Colum!" Rowan shouted. "Liam. Cassidy. Sean. Paul. Tom. Anyone! It's Rowan. I'm here to help you."

Rowan shouted as loud as she could then crouched low. She felt the whoosh of air rushing above her scooted around the bodies she felt, holding the sword with only her left arm. She searched the air around her for any sign of a face, or the light that had led her this far.

How was she to wake men who had wandered here for who knew how long fighting shadows? How was she to tell them that she was a friend? How was she to free them from the spell when something was wrong with her magic?

A man tumbled backwards and fell over Rowan's crouched body, knocking her over as well. He kicked out, knocking into her injured shoulder his foul epithets sounding louder than her shout of pain. Rowan didn't recognize the voice, but all that meant was that he was not one of her knights.

His kick sent her sliding across the ground. She barely managed to hold onto her sword. She slid to a stop alongside a pair of fighting knights. Her arm aching and her heart pounding. Something warm and wet struck her face. Rowan peeled it off her face and held it before her eyes. The bright red of blood leapt out at her. Blood soaking a single rose petal. There could be no doubt now, these were her men. Fighting unseeing and ripping each other apart. The air thick with sweat and fever and blood. Thick with death.

Rowan shoved to her feet and swung her sword up between the men before her.

"Stop!" She cried out.

The two swords knocked apart by her interference turned on her. She could feel all of their energies drawn to her own. And tried to...pulse even brighter, drawing them near. "You have to stop."

One after another swords and legs and bodies hurtled against her. She felt the strikes, most absorbed by her armor but each sapping her of energy and shaking loose more blood.

You were talking about saving what you love. Not keeping it. There is a vast difference. Oona's voice rumbled sternly through Rowan's mind. A bit late to stop her entering this field...and Rowan didn't know that she would ever have done differently.

Off a bit in the distance she saw again the flashing light. It moved from one spot to the next, flashing. As if trying to wake everyone. Or as if it too had become lost.

Rowan raced forward shoving through the men, racing towards that light. She had to get to it. When she was nearly on top of it she heard the voice she'd been seeking, and her heart clenched up with fear.

"Take me to my daughter," Colum shouted, pounding his sword over and over against the sword of the man before him.

"Colum." Rowan held her sword with her bad hand and dropped it to her side, reaching with her good arm to grip onto his shoulder, tugging him to face her. "Colum its m—"

"Aaaaagh!" Rowan shouted in shock as he swung to face her and jabbed his blade between the straps joining her armor along her right side.

"Lies!" He shouted. "You will not use her voice to fool me again!"

"Colum," Rowan gasped, his sword still stuck in her side.

Rowan dropped her blade and both her hands rose to grip his sword. Trying to shove it back, even as he tried to push it further against her.

"I'm your granddaughter. Pleeeease—" Rowan shook, shoving with all her might. She kicked out and he stumbled away. The sword ripped free of her flesh, yanking another pained howl from her.

Rowan dove to the ground. She felt him raising the sword again. She stuffed her fist into her mouth to stifle the sobs she could not seem to stop. She felt so much blood pouring out of her side, and the air stung across it angrily. She was shaking and weak, her wounds pulsing with fiery agony, but— Colum was before her, dying, and killing, and entirely unaware of himself.

That way leads only to death.

Rowan swallowed a sob, nearly gagging on gigantic bubble of it. She heard a great cry to her left and a man fell to the ground beside her.

It is you in my nightmare... Roisin's words from Rowan's birthday floated through her mind and time seemed to slow down. She felt more than saw another man fall to the ground just in front of her.

You are wearing your armor. There is blood dripping out the side and you are crying. There is a man dead in front of you and another on the ground beside you. Then you fall to the ground and whisper a name, and your eyes close.

Rowan could feel the thorn in her sword belt. Felt a presence above her. Colum's presence. She could stab him from such a position. As he as well could easily kill her.

Roisin said she would die so. Oona as much as said it with her refusal to answer. Braden, the boys, even Maureen had been terrified of that vision, but Rowan never paid it any heed. Now she would die here. And what broke her heart was that Colum was here as well. That these men would go on fighting, that Bran had lain in a field like this. That Rowan had brought them all here, and had no way of saving them. The flashing light was growing closer. Rowan saw it in the distance, but her mind showed her a million moments outside of this one.

She saw Colum sitting on the fence post outside the old training ring, smiling at her. She saw him running a finger down the side of Maureen's cheek until she looked his way, then kissing her gently. She saw the old welcome home hugs with all three of his children climbing on him in their own way. Saw him watching Rowan on the field as she fought with his knights. His rage when she sent Petal. His arms around Rowan when she cried, when he forgave her. Dancing with him at her birthday ball. And that burning, sad, but loving look on his face when he found out about her father.

My granddaughter.

Every moment blazed within her. Every one they had ever shared, bad and good alike were their history, their love. They set her alight within. She forgot the pain and the fear and even her desire to save them. She just felt—alive. She felt the moments that made her love her life and herself. She wasn't going to lose that.

Rowan threw back her head with a shout and set the fog alight with a bright hot plume of fire. The fog burned bright blue as Rowan's love wrapped round the spell and devoured it. All around were shouts of terror as the fire ate away the air.

When the flames dissipated and the light of day fell across the field, sad, heartbroken gasps came from the fighting men.

Rowan looked up at Colum, gripping his sword tight between two hands and bearing down on her—all at once recognition slid across his face, and wild helpless horror followed.

"Rowan!"

He dropped his sword and fell to his knees before her. Gasping and gurgling as tears poured explosively from his eyes.

"Colum," Rowan whispered. Her eyes fell shut and she swayed forward, lightheaded and weakened from the wounds and the release of magic. It didn't matter. Colum was here and he was alive. She was safe. This was her grandfather.

Interrupted Healing

Ferdy was still avoiding his aunt and Murphy, he let Patrick train him but only at the hot springs. He didn't like it here anymore. But it wasn't just his aunt, and the story bothering him. He'd felt...fuller, from the moment he came, and he thought at first it was just being among other fairy, such a new experience. But that wasn't it. He'd only realized what it was when he felt Keagan shutting him out of his mind more every day and when he continued to feel full even when he began to resent the fairy around him.

He was feeling Petal. She was out of the Fairy court. He didn't think she was necessarily any closer than she'd been, just less...blocked. Wherever she was, he could feel her again. But it felt so different he hadn't even known it was her at first.

That made him angry. Every day it made him more angry. He would look at his...angry aunt, who from what he could tell had few if any friends among the other water sprites. He imagined Petal returning home so. Returning so different that it wasn't her home anymore and he and Keagan weren't her thirds anymore. It made him angry that he wasn't going to her. But he couldn't. He couldn't go to her anymore than he could go to Rowan. They had their tasks and he and Keagan had theirs. Stonedragon was literally under siege. He'd heard the fairy whispering about the soldiers who had made it across the border into Swallow Fell, they'd killed people, and burnt farms, and they were headed towards the palace. Ferdy and Keagan were needed here to protect their home. But Ferdy wished he could go to Petal, he wished she were home. He wished they were all together and the longer it went without that the more he worried that it would never happen.

He'd said such terrible things to Pa before he left, and Rowan had left so sad. None of it was right.

"Are you intending to avoid me forever?" Murphy asked in a tiny voice, plopping up onto the side of the hot spring to sit next to Ferdy's hand in a body of water. A liquid body that was only the size of...Ferdy's hand. Ferdy was unwillingly intrigued.

Water sprites could change their size as well? Excellent!

But he hated this man.

"Your mother is perfectly well," Murphy said as though that were the issue.

"She wasn't then," Ferdy growled, and turned away from the tiny man.

"Clearly you know little of your mother as a child. Maureen was fearless." Murphy laughed and splashed back into the hot spring before Ferdy, taking on his usual size, heads above Ferdy.

"That's the point." Ferdy jerked forward, his hands fisted by his sides, but longing to punch the man. "She isn't now! It changed her. She was scared and alone, and kidnapped by humans, but none of you came for her."

Murphy held his ground before Ferdy for a long silent moment, his gaze fixed on Ferdy's clenched fists.

"Apologies aren't owed to you for that, Ferdy. Only to your mother, but I do not think they will make a difference to you. You are enraged. And useless for it." He observed.

Ferdy seethed. He was useful. That was why he was here. He was here helping.

"I doubt all that rage is meant for me, but..." Murphy waved his watery arms wide. "Come get your revenge."

Ferdy knew bating words when he heard them, but for once he didn't care. This wasn't a squire he could get expelled from knight training for fighting with. Or his brother still so on edge. This wasn't the aunt he wasn't allowed to fight with. Or Pa who he had to love no matter how angry he grew with him. This wasn't someone as untouchable as Sorcha. Maybe he wasn't where all of Ferdy's rage was aimed, but some of it was surely aimed at him, because this was the man who'd abandoned his mother, when she was Petal's age, so she was all alone facing horrors he would never know.

Ferdy rushed forward recklessly. He charged at the man of water and crashed through him, sending a spray of water in all directions.

Ferdy caught himself on the other edge of the spring and spun around looking for Murphy in shock. Surely that hadn't—

Murphy reformed out of the water before Ferdy. "Is that the best you can do? Patrick must have taught you something about fighting like a water sprite."

Ferdy raced forward again, but this time as he ran he sent his power into his fists making them as solid as ice. He pummeled his icy fists through Murphy's watery body, but it simply shifted and reformed around the strikes so Ferdy was wearing himself out. In frustration he slammed both of his fists into the water at his sides, imagining a geyser shooting into the air.

The moment his hands hit the water—his power hit the water carrying all his pent in rage—it worked. All the water in the hot spring shot into the air, throwing Murphy high five feet, ten, maybe more, and Ferdy flew up along with him. Ferdy felt his stomach drop, felt shocked laughter bubble up in his chest. Murphy's physical form vanished, joining the rest of the water as it fell. And Ferdy was plummeting back towards the hot spring.

He saw other water sprites looking on in horror. He saw his aunt racing forward. But he was too shocked by what his own power could do to be afraid. He'd don—

The world split apart. Ferdy felt the cracking of it in his head, but he didn't have the wherewithal even to make a noise. The world was screaming bright one moment and entirely black the next. It hurt. Everywhere hurt, he opened his mouth to gasp for breath and water and blood rushed in. There was blood in the seeing waters, that couldn't be good. The water came in and it—carried him away.

Ferdy lay in a body so much larger than his own, it felt heavy, he thought his legs and torso might be under water. His limbs were so weak. He felt cold for a moment, but even that was fading away. But he couldn't sleep yet. She was shouting at him. She wanted him to look at her. He opened his eyes, blinking once, twice.

"Wake up!" Rowan shouted. "Colum!" Rowan screamed.

One of his eyes opened just a tiny crack. "It's alright, Rowan. I love you. This is how it should be. It's al—"

"NO." Rowan shouted right in his face. "No. Do you hear me? You are going to live."

The world went black again.

Colleen had been left in an odd position in Rowan's Sword. She was meant to be directing the older children to help care for all the new children flooding the palace for protection, but there was a bit of a problem with that. Not all of the older children wanted to listen. She wasn't sure the boys were aware of the growing resentment among their forces. The older children didn't love how much Ferdy and Keagan took it upon themselves to direct them. When the forces were small it was easier, but the more recruits they gathered the more the elder children tried to take charge. Most went along because the boys were powerful, and because they liked the trouble they got into, but now that Ferdy was with the water sprites and Keagan was consulting with the adults all the time. Some of the older members of the army had...created their own faction. They weren't doing as Colleen said anymore.

She had a feeling she could make them do what she wanted. Some days, she felt powers like Keagan's growing out of her, telling her how to make this person do what she wanted, or how to make that person look like a fool so the others stopped listening to him. But she wasn't doing it. Every time she consciously felt the power and resisted it she felt stronger. She felt more...her new self. She still wasn't sure what being Colleen used to mean, but she was beginning to discover what it meant to be her now.

Things were even going better with her parents. Their desires had always been the hardest to resist, but they bundled them up so tight and were just trying to get to know her. And every day it was easier.

Her mother and father both had started helping with all the new children in the palace. At first that they were frightened seeing all of the children without their families would bring back fears from the Fairy Court, and Colleen had feared it herself. But that hadn't happened. Colleen couldn't remember the Fairy Court at all. And these children, as scared as they were, they knew they were among friends, among people trying to protect them.

It wasn't the same. Colleen liked helping. She was able to keep the younger members of Rowan's army helping here as well. Just this morning she'd been helping a shy little boy make friends among all these children he didn't know and her mother had crossed to her, and kissed her gently on the head.

"I am so proud of you. You are such a strong, good woman."

Colleen had felt...like she was burning and floating and sparkling from inside. It had felt so much stronger than when she was stealing powers to protect herself, it had felt like—she was coming to life again.

Then Keagan appeared before her. She could feel so much off of him. He was so afraid. Inside, he was like her, always afraid of something, always uncertain of who he was. He was trying to bundle his feelings up tight, and she wanted to reach out and hug him, promise him he would be alright, but she didn't. Resisting him was like resisting magic for her, challenging, but so empowering. Because so much of her felt like she owed this little boy her life and wanted to give him anything. But that was where the trouble came from. She needed to know if it was a power, or if it was her. And if she could resist, it was her.

"Come to check on the army?" Colleen asked. Ridiculously pleased with herself for sounding normal.

Keagan stared at her like he would pick her apart, and his smile stretched the longer he looked.

"Ferdy's right about you, isn't he? Your power is awesome, and you're strong."

Colleen took a step back. This wasn't right. Keagan tried to heal her. Ferdy tried to make her embrace her cipher side. It didn't bode well, not the question, nor the smile on her face, nor the fact that she could feel him intentionally letting his desires loose.

Her breath caught as she felt what he wanted. Fear crawled over her skin and she felt herself wanting to be smaller, to be invisible.

He reached out suddenly and his hand caught on her arm.

"I'm sorry. I know it's scary. I wouldn't ask it if I could see another way," Keagan said so sincerely. He thought it was heartfelt, didn't he? But it wasn't. He was like her. Not like new Colleen, he was like cipher Colleen. He didn't even know if what he was doing was his own will or the will of his power. He was so like her.

She glanced down at his hand on her arm, but she was invisible. He was holding nothing. She was nothing again—because *he* wanted it. Keagan who had so badly wanted her to be well before. Keagan who both her cipher half and her new Colleen half wanted to help, because he had such a pure heart. He was taking her new self away.

"You are the only one who can do it," he whispered.

She could see what he saw. Saw herself slip into his sister's room. Saw her take Petal's mission and make it her own. Saw herself an invisible nothing steal from the Fairy queen and slip away. But wait, the Fairy queen hadn't seen her, hadn't felt her. Colleen was nothing to such a woman. Maybe she slipped in when she was asleep, maybe she slit her throat.

Colleen felt the warm blood on her hands, felt the woman's life drain away, felt Keagan so happy, so safe, so content that nothing else mattered. She could give him what he wanted, what he needed. He would never have to hide in the power again. But...she couldn't feel herself. She couldn't feel her desires, she couldn't feel when her mother kissed her on the head.

Colleen took another step back. Then another. She pushed the magic off her skin and stood before him visible so he could see her lift her head. So he could see her eyes bore into him with anger and betrayal, and...strength.

"No." Colleen shook her head. "I won't do that for you. I'm just beginning to find me and I'm not giving that up."

"You wouldn't be. I just need you to be a cipher for a little while."

"You don't know that I could come back. You don't know that I won't lose myself right away and forget my purpose. Do you even care? I thought *you* cared," Colleen said bitterly.

"Colleen." He shook his head. "That won't happen. I *need* my sister home," he begged and his voice broke. "I need her safe, and you are the only person who can do it. You can fool the Fairy queen! You can make a projection of Petal that walks and talks and fools the Fairy queen into thinking Petal is there when she isn't."

"That isn't the only thing you're thinking about," Colleen hissed leaning nearer. "I can feel what you really desire."

He startled, and his cheeks began to darken with his blush.

"I won't murder for you."

"Oh." He startled again.

"You think you can come to me with these ugly desires and I will just have to do what you want, because I'm nothing." Colleen glared him down with a force she could barely credit herself with having. "That I don't have any will of my own, that's what you think. But I do. I am not yours to command. I said no, Keagan. Now go away, before this *nothing* makes you."

"Colleen, that isn't what I think. I know you have a will of your own. That's the only way this would work. If you were a slave to other people's desires sending you away would be pointless, maybe even risky. I know you ha—" Keagan's words stopped, but inside he screamed.

Colleen stumbled back from the force of his fear, the force of his desire. Something was wrong with Ferdy, and Keagan was calling out for his other thirds.

He vanished.

Colleen let the wall hold her up as she sobbed, and her insides warred. Something was wrong with Ferdy, and Keagan was crying out in agony, slipping into that place inside where he wasn't fully himself. He would truly be like she was soon. Without his siblings Keagan would lose himself. Colleen glanced back towards the nursery. Her mother and father were playing instruments, making the children sing.

She wondered if they had ever done that with her. She couldn't remember it. But was that because it had never happened, and this new life had changed them as much as her? Or because no matter how much she became her own person the one she'd been would never come back to her? Colleen cried harder. She wanted to be stronger. She wanted to be her own, fully her own. But she could already feel herself edging away from that little bit of self she'd been carving, edging towards the safety of the abyss. Keagan needed it. And if he needed something she knew she could give it. Whether she wanted to or not.

Orla cradled her nephew's body, lifting him out of the hot spring, to lay on the ground.

"Get me water from Liadan," she shouted at whoever was nearest. Then turned her rage on Murphy. "What were you thinking! He is too young to think of consequences."

"He'll be fine, Orla."

"He isn't full fairy, he can't just crash over the rocks like a spout of water. Or heal from minor injuries on his own. He has too much human for that." Orla quieted, laying her ear against her nephew's heart. It was beating. Far too fast, maybe faster than her own. But at least it was beating.

He's alive. He's alive. He's alive. She had to keep repeating it to herself. It felt like the day Maureen was kidnapped all over again. It was her fault.

She shouldn't have let Murphy goad the boy into fighting, he was too reckless, just like—

Ea came back with a flagon of water from the river and moved to pour it over Ferdy's wounds, but Orla took it from her. Gently she poured the first half of the flagon over the wound and watched as the huge gushing gash in his head grew back together bit by bit.

He'll be okay. He has to be.

Before the wound was fully closed Ferdy bolted upright! He threw a hand against his head, moaned loudly and tilted to the side. Orla grabbed onto his shoulders to steady him.

"Pa," he managed an agonized whisper, his face turning grey so he looked like he might vomit. "Pa," he repeated, begging.

Murphy sat on the ground beside Ferdy, putting an arm around his shoulder. Orla moved back slowly, Ferdy's begging expression tearing a hole through her.

"Ferdy, do you know where you are? Come have a little of this water." Murphy lifted the half empty flagon.

But Ferdy only shook his head, beginning to cry, his eyes never wavering from Orla. Barely able to breathe from the look, Orla dipped her hand into the seeing water, and let her essence drift apart, joining with the water to do what she never had before: look.

The future slammed into her, vibrant and painful. It commanded her. Pulling at her heart with love, and pain and wildly raw grief.

"HEAL HIM!"

Orla jerked her hand out of the water. She leapt up unable to speak what she was feeling. She was shaking from head to toe and she could not make her mouth work no matter how she tried. His father was dying. She had to try and help. Orla nodded to the boy, she saw him understand, relaxing into Murphy's hold, and she cast herself apart as mist.

She reformed at the river, feeling around for other sprites. "Maureen's husband is dying. Help me." She said no more, unsure if anyone would follow her. She'd never really been close to anyone—no one but Maureen. But she dove into the river, rushing along as fast as the water would allow and she felt herself gaining speed as one after another, other sprites joined her. Though they did not know all. Though they knew they were headed towards the Fairy lands from which they had been banished. Lands they could well be killed for returning to, still they followed. They had to get there. They had to help.

Her mother's constant entreaty rolled over and over though her head as the river rushed.

Protect Maureen. Protect Maureen. Protect Maureen.

Protect Maureen—She loves too well.

Grandfather

owan didn't pass out as she expected to. Her head slid forward and was caught against Colum's shoulder. His squishy shoulder. Her eyes shot open.

"Rowan," he couldn't stop saying her name. "I nearly killed you. I nearly killed you."

Rowan opened her mouth to reassure him, but cut herself off with a terrified shout. "No!" Rowan shoved Colum's body aside and spit a tiny stream of flame into the air. A falcon was diving towards Colum's back, with its sharp beak primed for a bite.

The flames flew right beside the bird, and Rowan jumped to her feet. Bran took human shape in a flash of purple light, his sword clasped between his hands. Rowan yanked out the thorn, not much defense against a broad sword, but it was all she had. She'd felt faint before, but as she leapt to defend Colum all of that faded to the back of her mind.

"Bran, you don't have to do this."

Bran snorted. He kicked out, just barely missing Rowan's stomach as she jumped back, but the ground was so slippery with blood and sweat she stumbled a bit, keeping her feet, and Bran took advantage, rushing at Colum, prone on the ground, all out of fight.

Rowan drove between them, sliding to her knees and stabbed upwards shoving the knife into Bran's side. Bran stumbled back. His sword fell to his side, as he threw a hand to his wound. His eyes bit into Rowan in shock. "You stabbed me. I thought we were friends."

Rowan shook her head, blocking Colum. "You must stop, Bran." She begged. "These were your friends too! Colum believed in you."

"They are *your* friends." Bran countered, enraged. He dropped his sword entirely, and pulled the dagger out of his side. He cradled his gushing wound dropping the dagger to the ground. He looked around the field of bleeding, groaning men. "How many friends will you be responsible for killing before you stop?"

A bright purple light enveloped him and with a high *klee-klee-klee* she rose into the air, a small trail of blood following in his wake. Rowan let out a small sob of air and dove at Colum. She turned him over gently, so she could examine his wounds. Her heart wouldn't stop pounding and her side ached, and everything was wrong.

"Colum," she gasped, heartbroken. He was bleeding in several places, not even wearing metal armor, he only wore light weight leather, which had been stabbed through in several places. He looked colorless, and his eyes were wildly bright like one in a deep fever and there was sweat soaking his entire body. He was dying. Colum was dying.

Rowan spared a quick glance around the rest of the field and saw most of the men were the same, bleeding, and likely feverish with infection. Nearly dead and all at the hands of their friends and comrades. They were all soldiers of Stonedragon. Rowan recognized their faces, if not their names.

"Help me take this off you," Rowan said, shoving at the leather over Colum's shirt. He looked terrible, she needed to heal him. Then she would heal the others. "I need to see your wounds."

"No." He shoved her hands back gruffly.

"Colum!" Rowan shouted, fighting him, but every move made her ache stronger and her blood flow faster, she was faint again, but she couldn't let herself feel it. She could not fight him and heal him at the same time.

"Rowan! I nearly killed you. And you would have *let me*. I stabbed you!" He sobbed a wrenching broken sound and tears streamed from his eyes. He grabbed onto both of her shoulders. Rowan gave a little helpless grunt as the move jarred her shoulder wound.

Colum looked to where his hand lay and more tears slid from his eyes, he moved his hand aside gently so it wasn't brushing her wound and gazed into her eyes with fervent pain and love. "You have to love yourself, Rowan. You have to know how much we all love you. There is nothing you could do that would make us stop loving you! But *you* have to feel the same way towards yourself. You have to protect yourself! Even from me! Do you understand?"

Rowan felt her tears falling as well. She couldn't speak, she nodded, and they sat there on the bloody ground gripping each other. "I promise." She said after a moment. "Now help me heal you."

"Heal yourself first," he growled.

"You're dying."

"Heal yourself, Rowan," he ordered.

Rowan shut her eyes and tried to send her magic out to heal her wounds. But nothing happened.

"I can't." Rowan's eyes shot open again. In a rush she laid a hand against his shoulder and tried to send her magic after his wounds. But nothing happened. "It isn't working," Rowan shouted frantically.

She thought it was the fog stopping her magic, but the fog was gone. She looked around wildly. Injured feverish knights were holding each other up and moving in closer around them.

"It has to work." Rowan pressed her hand against him, clenched up every muscle in her body, searched every crevice of her being for the magic, trying to force it out and into him, but she couldn't reach it. She couldn't find it.

"It's alright, Rowan," Colum whispered. He pulled away from her a bit and reached into his vest, pulling out a blood dotted letter and shoving it at Rowan. "It's alright. I got to see you one more time." He lay his hand against her face with the letter between them. "You will survive, I know it. That is all that matters. Take this, it is from your father."

You are never in any real danger.

Rowan shoved his hand away as gruffly as he had hers before. She reached for her fallen sword and stabbed it into the earth, using it to help her stand, with her teeth clenched tight across her tongue to hold back a shout of pain. She reached down, and with his help, pulled Colum up beside her.

Rowan looked around the field. It looked so much smaller than she'd taken it for. And it was so...far from where she thought she'd been when she entered. She could see a wide rushing river up ahead, but didn't see the dark forest she'd been riding through anywhere.

"Fairy," Rowan shouted. "Show yourselves. I am Rowan, of the house of Meave, practitioner of the flame of eternity, and your future queen. You will show yourselves, now."

Around the field a tiny group of maybe seven fairy appeared, some with militant stares, some with amusement coating their features and some just seemed curious and cautious.

"Heal these men," Rowan ordered.

One of the fairy laughed, looking Rowan up and down. "You are no one's queen here."

Colum was growing weak, he leaned heavily into Rowan, the heat coming off of him almost as strong as it had been off her flames. That lovely fantasy of the future flashed before Rowan's eyes. She saw everyone she loved gathered around a fire, Colum had his arm around Maureen, he was laughing quietly at a story Ferdy was telling and had Petal's head on his shoulder with Keagan next to his mother rolling his eyes. It was bright and warm and beautiful. Then Colum groaned his face twitched in pain, and he...faded away, and the light dimmed.

Rowan felt her tears burning to get out, but she wouldn't let them. She dragged them back inside and fed them to her rage. She might not be able to touch her fairy magic, but she could scorch these fairy with fire, and they all knew it too. She made sure they knew it. Her eyes burning with power and plums of steam rising off her.

"I will be. And I will remember you all." Rowan threatened. "Heal them."

"None of us are healers," another fairy said, a bit nervously.

"Then bring me healers!"

A tiny flame flickered before Rowan. It flared and the fairy who'd tried to stop her entering the field fell to the ground. He pushed unsteadily to his feet and rushed over, shoving his arm under Colum's free arm.

"Help me get them to Liadan," the fairy boy said.

"Liadan," Rowan gasped. The river before her was the Liadan? She was at the edge of the Fairy Realm when she'd been near Mt. Kieran this morning, impossible. She released the sword and lurched forward with the boys help.

"Tyce," Colum said with a little laugh. "Rowan, have you met my friend?" Colum coughed.

"Yes," Rowan said shortly. She needed to get him to the river. "Everyone get to the river." She shouted over her shoulder.

Colum looked around the field and for every man his eyes fell upon he grew heavier in Rowan's arms. "I brought us here," Colum choked out.

"You were tricked," Tyce argued. "You're a clever human. So they stopped trying to trick your head and just tricked your heart."

Colum gasped and his eyes tore across the fields. "Petal! She was never here was she?" Colum shuddered in their arms.

"Don't worry, she is safe." Rowan insisted. It was just a little bit further, she just needed to get him a little bit further, then the river could heal him enough for a healer to do the rest. "I'll bring her home, I promise."

Colum jerked suddenly in their arms, yanking them both to a stop. Rowan groaned at the sudden jarring motion.

"What is it?" she demanded, feeling a sweat breaking out across her brow.

"You have to bring *both* of my girls home," Colum said his voice burning and raw. "Ferdy sent me after his sister Rowan. To tell her where she belongs, where she has always belonged. With us."

Rowan gasped, and her eyes filled with tears.

"I am so sorry that I did not take your side, Rowan. It was a mistake, but I love you. You are the daughter of my heart. And you always will be." He broke off and his hand rose again to her cheek. "Out here, I see your fairy light—it is so beautiful. Every part of you is beautiful. Take this, please. Let your father apologize as well."

Rowan took the letter from his hands so he would stop fighting with her. His eyes kept drifting shut, and when they were open they were glazed and red and he kept whispering "it's alright" under his breath. Rowan's heart raced with terror. He couldn't die.

I don't want three new people. I want the ones I have!

"Come on," Rowan ignored his groan of pain and dragged him forward, nearly slipping on the blood the fell from his wounds onto the ground. She bit her tongue to keep from sobbing. He couldn't die. She couldn't do this without him. She couldn't do any of this without him in the world.

She kept seeing his eyes and wanting to tell him how much she'd always loved him, how she didn't blame him for anything. She remembered him lifting her high onto a fence post so she could help him *train* his knights when she was six. And his hand ruffling up her hair when Maureen said it was a wild mess. She remembered sly looks they would throw one another around the dinner table as they took turns stealing food off Maureen's plate before the triplets came along. She remembered like a glowing light inside of her the way the triplets would throw themselves into his arms when he came home. How her heart had ached from the sight of it, longing to be one of them.

And she felt the glow of that memory settling around her, felt it shifting, so when Ferdy was wrapped around his father's legs, and Petal clung onto his neck, and Keagan held his hand, Colum stretched out his last hand for Rowan to hold, and Maureen walked over to wrap her arms around them all. And they were all together, where they belonged.

But Rowan didn't dare speak. She just dragged them forward. He was going to live. He was going to live. He was going to live.

"Give people a chance to love you, Rowan," Colum was whispering, gasping for breath between words. Rowan ground her teeth across one another and dragged him forward. Tyce looked from Rowan to Colum sadly. Colum could not do this to her. He could not die.

"Give fairy a chance to love you. I know they will, and you will love them too. You will be such a marvelous queen." He kept on complimenting her and trying to teach her lessons. Rowan wore a scowl and her teeth burned from being ground down so hard. She did not breathe until she felt the water of the river against her feet.

She gasped for breath, pulling herself and Colum just a little further before throwing herself and him forward at the edge of the river.

It wasn't terribly deep along the bank. Probably no more than two feet, but Colum went under and wasn't coming up on his own. Rowan threw herself backwards into a seated position and yanked him onto his back with Tyce's help so his head was above the water. His eyes were shut, and though a few of his wounds were closing up, and his body was cooling, he still bled.

"Wake up!" Rowan shouted. "Colum!" Rowan screamed.

One of his eyes opened just a tiny crack. "It's alright, Rowan. I love you. This is how it should be. It's al—"

"NO." Rowan shouted right in his face. "No. You are going to live! You're going to be fine. You're going to go home and I will bring Petal home and you will be a family again."

"My girl," Colum choked on a laugh. "We're a family now, all of us. All of us." He gasped and both his eyes shut.

"Noooooo!" Rowan shouted. She yanked Colum closer to her and scooted out further into the water. Her eyes searching the banks behind her. There were a number of fairy around now, helping the men to the river, helping them heal. Nearly all of them but Colum.

"Heal him."

"My lady..." Tyce said hesitantly from her side. "I do not think he can be healed. Sometimes one is simply too far gone."

"No. He is alive!" Rowan argued. "I feel his heart beating. Heal him. Please," Rowan gasped. Beneath her hand she felt his heartbeats growing fainter, and his lungs barely raised as his breath thinned slowly from his chest. Rowan leaned forward, laying her lips against his forehead. "Colum, please don't leave me. *Please.*"

Rowan sobbed.

The water around them began to slosh wildly. Men who'd been wading into the water for healing were yanked forward. Colum's body gave a great jerk, as someone tried to drag him away. Rowan pulled him tighter against her chest and looked up at...half of a woman, made out of water, only her torso and head were visible as though she was standing beneath the water.

"Please let him go," the woman said gruffly, her voice broken. "We are here to help."

"Can you heal him?" Rowan demanded.

She looked down at Colum then back to Rowan shaking. "If the river cannot, nothing can. But he should be with his family. They should have a chance to say goodbye."

"I am his family."

The water woman nodded. "The rest of them deserve the goodbye you just had. Let me take him to Maureen."

Rowan supposed she was meant to feel comforted that this fairy, whoever she was, knew Maureen. But she wasn't comforted. She was...enraged like she'd never been before. Her whole life it seemed she'd fought to save her sister. *I will take from you what you love most*, Sorcha had said, and Rowan had fought against it so hard. She'd thrown all her energy into saving Roisin, determined not to let Sorcha win. But Sorcha...she wasn't just after Roisin.

Rowan had all but given her Petal. Sent her knights out to be nearly killed. Risked Gavin's life and his entire nation and now...Rowan yanked Colum closer and fought down a sob with the force of her rage. Sorcha couldn't have Colum. She couldn't have him.

"*HEAL HIM!*" Rowan bellowed at the top of her lungs. No, *louder*.

Her voice shook the ground. Shook the river. Shook the mountain. Even the air shuddered with her cry. Birds took off into the sky, fish leapt out of the river, and the fairy along the banks jumped back in terror. Even the woman of water cowered back.

When the shaking stopped the woman bowed; "Fairy queen." She yanked Colum away from Rowan as fast as she could, not giving her a chance to protest. She disappeared into the water with Colum dragged along, only his head bobbing above water.

Rowan gasped bereft as she watched Colum dragged away. She fell back onto her hands chest deep in the river and cried.

After the Scream

etal was growing impatient. She knew Braden was here, but Sorcha was confining Petal to the suite of rooms they'd been given, and the garden terrace that connected to it. There were no humans of any kind to be seen. Petal saw the same fairies as she had seen in the Fairy Realm. She began to suspect she'd been brought here, not to see Braden, but to keep her away from something in the Fairy Realm while Sorcha was away. The wolves most likely. Or Rowan.

Perhaps Sorcha had sensed her coming and brought Petal here so Rowan couldn't reach her. She'd certainly done something to her. The roses had stopped growing down the palace halls. They weren't dying or retreating, but nor were they spreading. Petal was a bit worried by that, it had given her such a boost in confidence. In truth she was worried by many things.

She didn't feel quite herself since she'd seen Rowan. She felt...at a crossroad. Something was waiting to change, and Petal didn't know if it was bad or good yet. She'd been so cold with Rowan, and it had come so easily. It had never been easy to be unkind before, even with Sorcha. But now she had been, and with someone she loved. It must mean the badness inside of her was growing. But it had been the only way to protect herself.

Why didn't that make her feel better?

"Was it always easy to hide yourself as you do now? Was it always easy to kill for her, and to feel nothing?"

"I have never said I feel nothing when I kill," Dervla answered. Petal could feel the rage in her, and the pain. But as usual her face gave nothing away.

Petal looked away. "I think one day...it will not break my heart to lie, or to destroy. I think one day I will be as ugly on the inside as Fairy Cache is on the outside, but I will have nowhere to hide from my insides. I keep dreaming of all the terrible things I can do. And at first they scared me, and made me sick, but now...I dream them and I think...yes, that will solve things."

Dervla was shaking, she looked around and around the garden, searching for threats, for hidden ears and eyes. After a moment her eyes found Petal again, and such light...a bubble of it so bright one could not bear to look at it surrounded them, and every effort Dervla put into hiding her expression drained away.

Her face was covered in tears, her shoulders were slumped. She looked heavy and distraught and much older than she'd appeared before. She grabbed tight hold of Petal's hands and squeezed with all of her might.

"There is more goodness in you than even you know. Do not give that up for anything. You are growing numb now, not because the evil no longer hurts you, but because you are afraid of that hurt...please...feel the pain. You will be better for facing it, than the rest of us ev—"

"HEAL HIM."

The shout burst their bubble of light knocking Dervla and Petal apart. Petal fell to the ground as her heart grew thorns and her eyes wept before she knew what she was feeling.

"Pa," Petal whispered, heartbroken. She could feel the love and the pain and the rage of Rowan's scream. She could feel Papa in it. Something had happened to him. "No. *Pa.*"

The talisman at Petal's throat pulsed soft and warm enfolding her with love, but it did nothing to stop the pain. Nothing to stop the tears. Pa was gone.

Sorcha sat on the queen's terrace overlooking the channel between Great Island and Reethurn as she took her tea. The sea was wild today sloshing and knocking about a little fishing boat. Sorcha loved the drama of splashing waves, and the dark clouds filling the sky, the light pattering of rain that brushed them every so often. But she could tell her company was not nearly as receptive to the more violent side of nature.

Queen Faylinn kept shivering and shrinking her shoulders in on themselves. Sorcha ground her teeth every time she saw it. It annoyed Sorcha endlessly, this woman's existence. She'd been briefly pleased to see her growing a spine in Braden's absence, but she was back to the cowering mess that she was never meant to be. She wasn't meant to be Alistair's bride. She was meant to be an unremarkable, but fairly contented servant in the other princesses household. But Tyrone did love his tricks. Tiny alterations to eternity that made gigantic lasting consequences.

It wouldn't bother him at all that this woman was forced into a marriage she didn't want. Forced into a new name, a new self, a new role, and none of it was she prepared for. She was a cowering mess of a woman, when she could have been a competent one, and all so Tyrone could keep Alistair from fathering the son Sorcha had foreseen— a sprite born to humans.

It had been such a wildly exciting, magnificent expansion of eternity, the idea that humans—of no fairy heritage—could be born with fairy magic. Sorcha had been vibrantly excited to meet such a creature. But she shouldn't have told Tyrone. She'd thought at the time that he would be as excited as she. He had as much passionate interest in the interworking of eternity, and the plight of sprites always overlooked or ostracized by the larger fairy community. But his interest was different. He wanted control. He wanted revenge. He wasn't a scholar. And he was never affected by the pain he caused on his way to achieving those ends.

Not to his brother. Or Sorcha, or Nessa, and certainly not to the woman before her.

Sorcha should be well past it herself. After all she had not killed the real Faylinn. Nor told Alistair to force her maid to be his bride. But every time she looked on the woman she wanted to shout and shake and force her to have more spine, to fight back, or to just hold her own. This woman enraged her like no other mistake she had ever made. Because every time she looked on her, Sorcha saw the woman she had forced herself into seeking Tyrone's love, or friendship. She looked on this Faylinn and saw the woman Tyrone had forced Sorcha into with that battle for the throne. She hated this woman for failing to do anything about it.

"Didn't you used to travel with a falcon?" Braden asked uncomfortably. His voice broke into Sorcha's thoughts and only then did she notice Braden and Prince fighting over tea cakes.

Sorcha smiled. It seemed these two must play rivals whatever their forms.

"I did. And I still do. But he had a task to perform. And Prince is pleasant company," Sorcha replied, running a finger down the bird's head as she spoke.

Prince cawed and shook her off, pecking suddenly at Braden's hand as it approached an orange biscuit.

"What does a raven want with a biscuit anyway?" Braden muttered snidely.

Prince looked right at Braden as he pecked the biscuit right off the table.

Sorcha laughed. "Come come boys, no need to bicker. I love you both."

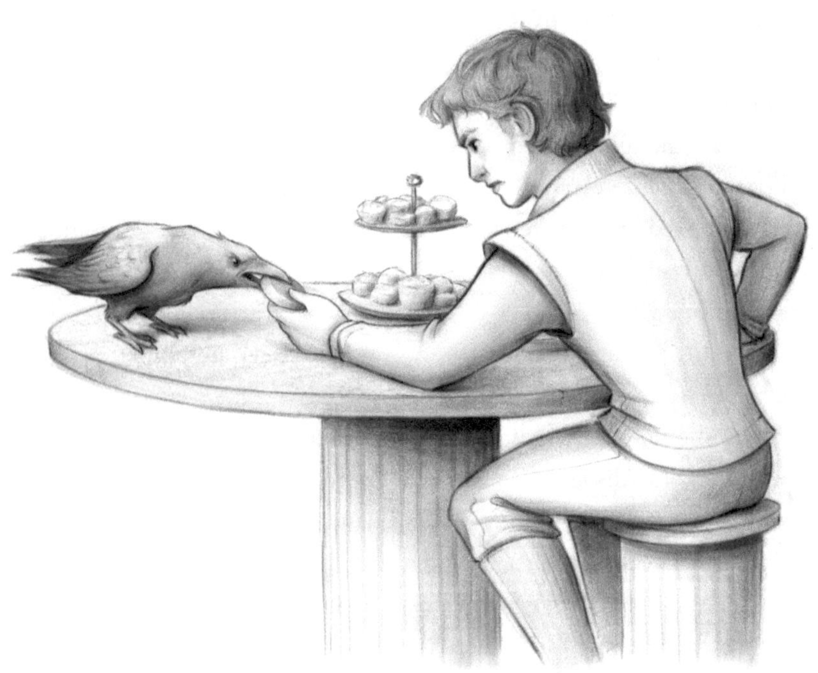

"Ravens are brilliant animals," Queen Faylinn said tilting her head to examine the bird. She held out a bit of fruit in her open palm. "And fiercely loyal."

Prince took the offered fruit, and gave Faylinn a little bow that both Braden and Sorcha observed with discomfort, but for entirely different reasons. Queen Faylinn giggled and pushed her cup of tea closer to the bird.

Prince approached the cup, dipping his beak inside and the table began to rattle. The air became electric.

Sorcha felt the pulse of it dancing along her spine, an urge to bow, and fiery, shuddering dance of power trying to dampen her own.

Prince began to shake and screech, falling over and writhing in pain. Then Sorcha heard it, the source of the tingle, the source of his pain.

"HEAL HIM"

Sorcha nearly smiled at the girl's suffering. But she couldn't—The mountain was rumbling, fairy were bowing to her, animals were fleeing her rage. That girl might be suffering as Sorcha intended, but somehow she was pulling more fairy to her in the process.

The air quieted. Prince lay still under the pain too large for his new form to contain. But what Sorcha noticed most was the sea. It quieted completely and a soft mist brushed up towards her in the form of a face Sorcha was well familiar with.

"I did warn you," Meave's misty spirit said without sympathy. "You forget what you owe to the Fairy at the cost of my support. Try defeating her when the heart of Fairy is torn."

Sunlight broke through the clouds, and the mist of Meave dissipated. None of her human companions had heard the Fairy Mother's threats, she spoke only to fairy. And the humans were all too consumed worrying over the bird. But Sorcha was enraged.

She stood with such force her chair toppled over.

"Sor...my queen," Braden corrected himself, cowering before her regard. "Are you quite alright?"

Sorcha glared at Braden with fiery eyes and fisted hands. She hadn't even lifted her scepter from its place leaning against the table, so great was her rage. Braden was turned, fairies were turning, now Meave was threatening to support that... poisonous human!

"Quite," Sorcha snarled. "Prince, now."

At once the raven, though he still shuddered and sunk under the weight of his screaming heart, leapt into the air and flew over to rest on Sorcha's shoulder. Sorcha yanked up her scepter.

"I have something to see to."

Enraged, Sorcha swept back into the palace with Prince on her shoulder, shuddering every few seconds. Sorcha vanished with the bird to the gardens where she felt Petal. Petal didn't sense her at once, she was curled up in a ball under a tree hugging herself as a bright pink light pulsed around her.

"Dervla," Sorcha shouted. At once the fairy appeared before her queen. It was on the tip of Sorcha's tongue to demand Dervla to round up all the fairy who were helping that, soon to be failed, usurper escape Sorcha's traps, and bring them here so she could watch them executed. But her eyes wouldn't be pulled from Petal, sobbing. "Leave us," Sorcha whispered and crossed the distance to where Petal sat.

Petal was rocking back and forth. Whenever the pink light of Petal's magic touched her Sorcha shuddered with pain. Sorcha wasn't who Petal wanted. Petal wanted to be far away from Sorcha with the people she truly loved.

It hurt so much Sorcha nearly bellowed. But instead she nudged the raven into a nearby tree because she knew he made Petal uncomfortable. Sorcha settled on the ground beside Petal and wrapped an arm around her shoulders.

"It's alright, my love. You are safe, Mama has you."

Petal gasped and cried even harder— but she did not push Sorcha away, or even seem to want to. So Sorcha held on tighter, offering Petal any comfort she could.

"Mama." Keagan appeared in the great hall, not sparing anyone in the room so much as a glance. "Something's wrong with Ferdy." He grabbed hold of her and threw out more of his power than he ever had before carrying them both to the hot springs in only one jump.

They appeared in the middle of the pool, and Keagan went under, the water deeper than he was tall. Mama dragged him out of the water with one hand and shoved them both towards the edge of the pool where Ferdy was struggling to stand. Keagan noticed several things in the same instant: Mama's feet weren't touching the bottom of the pool but she hadn't gone under, there was blood on his brother's face, but he didn't seem to be bleeding, there was an air of urgency and fear around him, and he could feel his brother's blood in the water, and he could feel the water offering a clearer glimpse of the future.

Almost as soon as his mind turned to the water, Mama, though she shouldn't have the strength, lifted Keagan entirely out of the water and shoved him up onto the rim of the pool beside Ferdy.

"Le...led me go," Ferdy fought against the fairy holding him, his words slurred slightly.

"What's happened?" Mama demanded.

"He...created a geyser that threw us both. He'll be okay, he just needs some rest. But Maureen..." The fairy was about to say more but Mama shushed him, shaking a hand in his face and looking off into the distance.

"Petal," Keagan said, trying to confirm what he thought Mama was sensing, even as he lay a hand on Ferdy and tried to settle him. Keagan couldn't get into his brother's thoughts, it was as if they were too jumbled to make out. And Ferdy was actively fighting him.

Before he could figure it out Mama shook her head again and her eyes filled with tears.

"We need to get to the river," she gasped. She lay a hand on each of her sons and water sprayed around them like a crashing wave; when it cleared they were ankle deep in startlingly cold water.

Keagan glanced around, Ferdy stumbled a bit, but Mama latched onto him, dragging him to her chest. Ferdy leaned back against her and gasped, burying his face in her shoulder to cry.

They were at the river, but it was so low Keagan didn't properly think it could be called a river. All around the banks of the river slowly filled with fairy, all of them looking upriver. Slowly the water built, the air filled with magic. Keagan could feel the fairy around him pulling at the water, dragging more and more of it near. Then he felt what had his brother crying and his mother still and silent. Not Petal. Pa. He was so...weak, nearly dead. So small Keagan hadn't even felt him.

The water sloshed growing higher and higher, it was at his thighs now, and Keagan leant his power to the tide of sprite magic, pulling Pa closer.

When the water reached their hips body's began appearing. Soldiers of Stonedragon, men who'd left with Pa to find Rowan, all of them dragged along by fairy made entirely of water. They washed up along the banks, some deeply injured, others just looked weak. They crawled up onto the banks coughing and gasping and...looking up river with heavy, grieved eyes.

Pa was almost here, but so close to death he might not even make it to them. He had to make it. Mama was here, she could heal anyone. He had to reach them.

Keagan began to feel something else in the water. A scream that reached inside of him, latching onto his will and overpowering it with a single command, and he was certain Mama and Ferdy, and all the fairy in the water were feeling—

Pa. He saw his head above the water, he was nearly upon them, the water rushing over him, carrying him home.

A woman formed out of the water, splashing up over the banks and pulling Pa gently up before Mama.

"Maureen, I—"

But Mama didn't listen, she cast Ferdy away and dove at Pa, answering the command of the water.

HEAL HIM.

Fairy closed in all around them. Ferdy moved to stand beside Keagan, his body shaking and his eyes looking so hopeless Keagan barely recognized his brother.

Mama lay her hands on Pa and the air filled with mist.

"My love," she sobbed. "Please, you cannot go yet."

She shook and she sobbed, and the air grew brighter and brighter, but Pa's life force didn't seem to be growing any stronger. Clump after clump of Mama's hair leeched color and turned grey before them and the fairy around them were gasping and talking in hushed tones.

"Maureen, you have to stop!" the woman who'd brought Pa said, stepping forward, but Keagan jumped into her path. No one could be allowed to stop her. How dare they? She was going to save—

"Leave me alone," Mama cried out.

Keagan spun to fight off another fairy only to see his brother grab Mama by her shoulders even as she slapped at him. Ferdy shoved her off of Pa.

Ferdy was crying as he shoved Mama away, he fell to his knees between them, shaking his head. Keagan felt his brother in his mind, he was still garbled and weak, but Keagan felt Ferdy begging for help, begging Keagan to—restrain Mama.

"You can't do it, Mama" Ferdy gasped. "You'll die too."

Keagan knelt on the ground slowly. His arms reaching out to hold his mother back, but she barely put up a fight. She couldn't. She slumped forward in his arms sobbing, too weak to do more.

"Colum." Mama stretched out her arm, but it fell to her side, she was too weak even to hold it up.

Keagan gasped. And his heart shuddered. He saw the blood at his brother's temple, his mother was shaking and weak, and his father wasn't even alive enough to be roused as Ferdy dragged Pa further from Mama. They were broken. All of them. Keagan could have lost them all in a matter of minutes. He heard a sob and barely registered that it had come from himself. He couldn't lose them. He couldn't. They were right here. Pa had promised that they were strongest together, but they were together now and they were falling apart.

Keagan sobbed in earnest his body shook with Mama's as his father faded slowly away.

"I'm sorry," Ferdy sobbed, rocking Pa's head back and forth. He lay his own head against it, his tears running over Pa's face. "I'm so sorry. I didn't mean it. I love you. I want be just like you. I'm sorry. I'm so sorry. It wasn't your fault. You take care of all of us. You make us strong. We need you. We need you."

The air began to fizz with moisture like the spray of a wave, and a soft greenish blue light colored the mist. *So bright.* Ferdy was glowing so bright. The mist wound around Pa and Ferdy, again and again, all but blocking them from sight. The water sprites grew anxious. The woman who'd brought Pa rushing forward again. But before she could reach anyone the cloud of mist and light popped pushing everyone back with a soft spray.

"Ferdy," Pa croaked.

Kegan gasped, wonderstruck. Ferdy was glowing so bright. And Pa...Pa was alive again. Ferdy had done that.

Ferdy lifted his head from Pa's just a sliver, and a smile of absolute joy slid across his lips.

"Pa." Ferdy fell forward as the word stole the last of his strength and the wound at his head opened once more, oozing blood. All of that startling light rushed off of Ferdy and fell onto Pa.

"Ferdy!" Mama shouted. Everyone rushed forward, and Pa fought gently against his son's body Trying to shove him away.

It was chaos, Keagan fell forward, unable to hold himself up. He felt Mama, he felt Petal, he felt Pa. Ferdy had saved Pa. But all Keagan could see was the blood at his brother's head, and his wide empty eyes, just like in the sketch he'd tried to shake off his foot.

Pa was alive. And Ferdy had taken his place.

Petal was wrapped in Sorcha's arms awash with pain and worry for her father, and utterly confused by the bits of comfort she felt from Sorcha, and the certainty these were not the arms she wanted wrapped around her. She wanted Pa's arms. Or Mama's arms. She wanted to be home, and safe.

Suddenly everything went quiet inside Petal. She felt a wave of love from her brothers, felt Keagan's shocked joy as their father woke. Everything was going to be fine. Her excitement sent out a pulse of love and magic. Flowers blossomed on the belt at her waist. Everything was—

"Aaaaa!" Petal sobbed in shock. She shoved a fist into her mouth as the pain grew stronger. Tears were ripped from her eyes and the flowers at her waist shriveled up turning brittle and clenching around her gut.

Sorcha pulled back. Her hand reached up and lay against Petal's cheek. "My darling, what is it?"

But Petal couldn't speak. Her heart was dying. She wasn't whole any longer.

All this time she'd been away from home she'd felt like she wasn't quite whole, like she wasn't herself. But it was nothing compared to now.

Something truly terrible had happened.

Ferdy was gone.

Petal pushed out of Sorcha's arms and stood backing away. She didn't want to be touched by another being. Nothing would ever be right again.

Inevitable

R owan sat in the river for a good long while, until the water was no longer spotted with blood, and most of the fairy on shore had vanished. Tyce sat beside her the whole while, not saying a word, as the sun sunk lower and lower in the sky.

Rowan didn't know what she was waiting for. For the water woman to come back and tell her all was well, that Colum was home with his family and recovering. Rowan laughed, and it became a sob, tears rushing out of her eyes.

"I used to imagine my mother coming back to life," Rowan said. "She would come and sit beside me in my imagination and say, 'You are such a beautiful wonderful girl I simply had to meet you.' I never told anyone." Rowan muttered, shaking the tears off her face. "I'd sound mad. And they already looked at me like…But he never did," Rowan gasped and more tears slid out of her eyes. "He was never afraid of me. He was just there, being my friend, loving me, no matter what. And she took him." The words vibrated quietly across the air.

Rowan stood up and walked back up the shore.

"Wait," Tyce called out. "Your shoulder is still bleeding."

Rowan ignored him. She didn't care. All along the shore, the fairy who'd remained jumped back, bowing to her, their eyes afraid to touch her. But Rowan didn't care about that either.

As she crossed the field something bright flashed in the distance, drawing her eye. She saw the jagged fluted spires of Fairy Cache rising off of Mt. Kieran. Another taunt. Rowan barely spared it a glance. What was the point?

Sorcha wanted to lead Rowan around and around in circles killing everyone she loved and ripping Rowan into smaller and smaller pieces. Rowan marched to where her sword stood upright in the ground and yanked it out, shoving it into her scabbard with a loud angry groan.

Freezing water splashed over her shoulder and Rowan jerked away in shock, and pulled back her arm to strike the fairy trying to help her. Tyce didn't back away. His eyes were full of sympathy as he stood before her fist.

"He wanted you healed," the fairy said after a long silent stretch.

"Where is Yseult?" Rowan demanded, slowly lowering her arm, she ducked to retrieve her bloody thorn.

"The horse?" Tyce asked.

There was something squishy and wet at Rowan's feet, and it could well be the water Type threw over her shoulder, but she didn't look. Couldn't bear to. She could recall a time when she'd wanted a battle. Wanted to test her skills in real combat, with real stakes, not just lessons. But the air still smelled bitter with bloodshed and sweat and her heart must be beating but it was so heavy in her chest who could tell?

Nothing was ever the way she imagined it.

"Likely ran away, ma'am. It has been days and we're many miles from where we entered."

"Days?"

The fairy nodded. "The spell, slowed time so it could draw out as much of your magic as possible, before releasing you to the field to...die."

"No." Rowan shook her head.

You are never in any real danger. Braden's voice accused.

"Not to die." Rowan shook her head. "To be injured. To be broken. And to kill—yes. But not to die. Your queen doesn't want me dead, not until she has ripped away every love I have ever cherished and ground every fantasy to dust."

The fantasy flickered before her eyes again. Without Colum. Rowan jerked.

She looked at the fairy before her. "Do you know who Petal is?"

He bowed his head and gave a little nod. "The daughter of Colum of Keen. The Fairy queen's chosen successor."

"Do you know *where* she is?" Rowan heard the question come out in a threatening growl and knew she should check it. This was the one fairy who had helped her. He had tried to save Colum, tried to prevent Rowan entering the valley at all.

Would Colum be alive if she'd heeded him?

Would she have been able to come to him with healers as Fairy queen and rescue him, alive?

Rowan jerked from her heart outward. She couldn't think like that. And she couldn't alter her tone. And she couldn't...she just had to find something to do. Anything. Because if she stood still much longer she might melt into a puddle of mourning and never move again.

"She was taken with the Fairy queen," a voice called out from behind Rowan. "To Anwyn."

Rowan looked at her new assistant. She had a vaguely familiar look but Rowan did not know why. She was somewhat shorter than Rowan, with stiff black hair and bathed in a pale yellow light.

"You are right to doubt the appearance of the keep on the hill," she said in a rush, her eyes scanning the field for attack. "That is not Fairy Cache. It is another trap."

Rowan nodded. "Why do you care?"

The fairy's eyes grew warm and sympathetic, she looked as though she wanted to rush forward and close Rowan in her arms, but she did not.

"I am Whisper, Your Majesty. I was one of Petal's teachers, until the Fairy queen sensed we were too close. You loved Petal's father, you tried to save him. And...Petal loves you. That is why I care." She bowed.

Rowan stared at the fairy before her, unable to come up with a thing to do. She could head to Anwyn, but Sorcha knew her movements, she might just leave and return here to torture Rowan further with her failure. Rowan could try again to make the way to Fairy Cache, but here before her were all the Fairy realm had to offer of fairy who wanted to help her. Or so it seemed. Right now, it took every bit of numb she had inside wrapping around her again and again, to keep from breathing out a fire so powerful it destroyed the entire nation in its rage.

Stay here forever? Lead the beings who'd allowed men to slice and pound and stab each other to death unknowing? Why?

Why would anyone?

They deserved Sorcha.

But she couldn't go home without Petal.

Rowan saw that fantasy before her eyes again. Colum was gone. Petal looked up from the spot where she'd been with her head laying against nothing. Her eyes burned across Rowan.

I haven't missed you, she hissed and stood up, walking out of Rowan's fantasy of her own volition.

Keagan stared at Rowan full of rage. Ferdy wouldn't even look at her, and Maureen fell forward, covering her face as she sobbed.

Rowan jerked as a hand slipped before her face. He didn't try to touch this time, but Tyce held out his palm open. The letter lay in the flat of his palm dotted with blood, and atop it were the two slivers of honeysuckle Rowan had cut from her wrist.

She saw the flowers and the fairy before her as if from far, far away.

For every one of you who dies another three pop up.

Rowan yanked the flowers out of his hand and threw them into the air spitting out a long burning stream of agony transformed to flames. She was screaming still, long after the flower ash hit the ground and the flame dissipated. Both of the fairies stayed. Petal's teacher panted in time with Rowan's breaths, but Tyce didn't appear to be breathing at all.

Rowan's side ached again. She lay a hand against it and felt blood oozing out. She'd reopened the wound from where Colum had stabbed her. Apparently the river hadn't healed her entirely. Rowan stared at the blood and felt tears fighting to get out again. When the air was twirling with smoke but the flames and the scream had died away Tyce's voice emerged low and choked.

"It is not your fault that he died."

Rowan laughed. "It is always my fault. If I was never born she would have no reason to torture them. Colum would be alive. Petal would be—"

"Petal would not *be* at all." Whisper reached out. "Maureen went to Stonedragon for your mother. Had you not been born, she would not have married the human. She likely would not even have met him. And it doesn't matter what might have been. All that matters is what is, and what can be. Go somewhere and heal, Fairy queen who will be. Fight again tomorrow."

Rowan took the oil cloth wrapped letter from Tyce's outstretched hand. She shoved it into her bodice and turned, trudging slowly back towards the river.

"Where are you going?" Tyce asked, trailing her.

"I don't know where I'm going," Rowan muttered. It wasn't the truth. But there was noting in her that cared much whether she was speaking the truth or not.

She was going to Turrlough. She didn't want three new people, three new friends, three new anythings. She was going to fight for the ones who were still alive, whatever condition they were in.

"Turrlough surely holds a trap as well," Tyce said, guessing or sensing the truth Rowan had not shared.

"Do you know any path that does not?" Rowan asked as she waded into the water. Entirely uncaring what horrors awaited her.

"No. But...perhaps you should not go alone. I will accompany you, if you wish."

"So you can die in my arms next? No," Rowan snarled.

"You do not seem to have any magic," the boy persisted. "And no mere human can stand against all the magic and armies at the disposal of the Fairy queen."

"I'll think of something." Rowan said no more. She was nearly shoulder deep in the water, Liadan stretched out wide before her. She'd never swam so far, and in armor no less. But she would today. She would do anything and everything she must today and every day until she'd succeeded.

She would save Gavin and his nation. She would bring Petal home. And then —She would *kill* Sorcha.

The fairy were right that Rowan wasn't ready to take Sorcha on yet. But she would be.

If it took picking apart the woman's spells one at a time, and hardening her own heart further and further. If it took murder or magic, fire or poison. Rowan would find the way. She would do anything now. No part of Rowan was scared of the burden, or of disappointing her long dead mother.

One day, not long from now, Rowan would stand over Sorcha and watch her cower. Hear her beg. She would watch the blood drain out of her and the light crumble slowly from her eyes.

Some things— were inevitable.

*D*alila Caryn is the author of fantasy novels *The Forgotten Sister, Future Queen,* and *Dust House and the West Wind.* Her love of poetry and epic fantasies influenced her unique writing style. Family provides her with constant inspiration for creating genuine stories of love and redemption. In her free time, she can be found in corners reading about magical worlds or creating them, always with far more coffee than mere mortals can stand.

Yenthe Joline is a freelance character designer and illustrator living in the Netherlands. She is passionate about telling stories with her art and uses flowing, energetic lines to make her pirates, superheroes, and fairies seem to leap right off the page. She is home- schooled and comes from a big happy family where she is the oldest of seven siblings. When she is not creating worlds and characters with her art, she loves to read, watch movies, and spend time with her family.

www.ingramcontent.com/pod-product-compliance
Lightning Source LLC
Chambersburg PA
CBHW051547100726
47898CB00001B/7